ISTEN KARDJA:
The Withering

Frank Nemeth

Isten Kardja: The Withering

by Frank Nemeth

Cover Art by Troy Little

www.isten-kardja.com

DEDICATION

For my Ginny, without whom I am nothing.
And for Sarah, Meghan, and Kaitlyn, who are my everything.

ACKNOWLEDGEMENTS

Thank you to:
Mike W, Brad, Mike S, Rod, Fred, Willie, Andrew, Ken,
…and others who sat around the table teaching me the power of imagination, sarcasm, and a
healthy sense of humour = Everything a person needs to get the most out of life.

Map – Vengriya

PART I

*****Of Princes*****

Prince Svato's eyes were cold and distant as he steered his horse through the debris-strewn fields outside the crumbling stone walls, calmly surveying the wreckage of the abandoned siege forts that surrounded his great city of Ascanium. Imperium troops had left in such haste that there was a small fortune to be scavenged the small fortifications that had stood for so long around the outer walls of the city.

It had taken very little time for the most ambitious of the local foragers to climb the palisades and raid the storehouses and armories, taking whatever they could carry and setting fire to the rest. Days had passed and some of the fires still burned, though Svato was pleased to see that the flames offered no threat of spreading to the city. No fire brigades rushed to save the forts from their fiery fate, and as much as Svato might have relished absorbing the fortifications into the city's defenses, he could not begrudge the people their desire to see all traces of the hated Imperium swept away, purged from the land by the vengeful flames.

He was content that his city, his principality, had endured their occupation, and he was now free to reclaim his title as sovereign of the land.

'*And who knows,*' he pondered to himself, '*...perhaps the time is right for a new Grand Prince of the Seven Tribes to be anointed once again?*'

He could imagine, even now, that the princes of nearby Mezoseg, Temeskoz and Sarkozy, would be surveying their newly liberated lands and thinking the same thing as he – Prince Ond Kedves of Temeskoz was probably the most ambitious of them all, but he was Onogur, not a pure-blooded Avar, and was unlikely to be the one the people would want to lead them back to greatness again. The other four princes were more subdued than Ond or Elod, or even Almos Farkas – these were the true warrior princes that would likely stand in the way of his ambition. He needed to move quickly to fill the void that the

Imperium had left behind, so he could minimize the chaos and be ready to act decisively.

His thoughts were wandering into the future when he realized that he had slowed his ride through the field, allowing someone to approach unnoticed through the smoke. He hadn't rallied his personal guard back into action yet, but he did not feel worried or threatened – not here, in his own land – as the cloaked rider slowly closed on him.

"You should not be out here, riding around the countryside alone!" the rider called as she neared, her dirty-blonde hair just visible from beneath the hood of the cloak. She wore a dull brass tiara across her brow, fashioned to resemble a woven cord of rope, that held the hair back from her face, but the wild curls fought against it, framing her slender face and deep green eyes that shared the same untamed look as her hair.

"Nor is this any place for a lady to be found unescorted," he responded with familiarity, opting not to rebuke the rider for failing to acknowledge his royal titles.

"I am not one of your courtly ladies, despite whatever bawdry fantasies you may entertain in your sleep…Your Grace," she bantered, adding the royal title almost sarcastically. "You asked me once to advise you, and so I do. You should not be riding about alone, without any protection."

"Lady Darellan, I asked you once – once – for your opinion…how long ago was that? And now it seems I cannot take it back!" he decried playfully.

"You make games, but I am serious." No longer straining over a distance, her voice flowed more softly, like a gentle wind over sand as she continued. "The people have their blood up with the Imperium leaving, and they have been quick to vent wrath on any collaborators. You, yourself, walk a fine line between 'Prince' and 'collaborator', and there are many who would be happy to see a change in the head that fits beneath your crown, despite all of Your Grace's other redeeming qualities!"

She looked around carefully as she spoke, pushing back the hood of her cloak to permit herself a more unrestricted view of the area around them. The Prince also paused at this, for it was not the first time he had felt himself in awe of her striking beauty. He was not a handsome man himself – he knew this and had long ago come to accept that he would never stir such feelings in any of the ladies of the court – and so he had committed himself long ago to seeking power rather than love as his life's ambition. He did enjoy dabbling in affairs with the ladies of the court, who were always willing to look past his less comely features in exchange for everything else a man of his position could offer. This was no secret – he knew their hearts were not true – and so he honed his skills at remaining distant and aloof in all such matters.

But somehow, despite his best intentions, he always took pause when Dar was present. She offered her service to his crown and never asked anything in return – other than that he heed her counsel when she saw fit to give it, as she was doing this day.

"And is this what you have followed me out, all this way, for? To chastise me for my recklessness?" his initial calm became more serious as he came full circle with his thoughts.

"No. not at all," she replied carefully, delicate with his sensitivities, "...but knowing you as I do, I would guess that you are out here making plans – regretting the loss of the perimeter forts for the city's defense perhaps – while planning your next steps to secure your crown, and perhaps more..." she guessed aloud, earning a nod from the Prince as she finished.

"But I would implore you not to forget my warnings..." she continued, to which he rolled his eyes and began to pull on the reins of his horse to turn. "You have more to worry about than just your crown!" she implored him, "The Imperium may have gone for now, but that doesn't mean that you aren't free from peril! The Imperium did not cause the rains to stop for a year, or the crops to fail last harvest!"

"No, they did not," Svato answered, "but neither did you warn us, either. In fact, in your one true role as my advisor, you had predicted both rain and an abundant harvest across the great plains – making you wrong on both counts! Truly, you have undermined my faith in your advice!" he finished, though the admonishment in his words did not carry through to his tone.

"You ask – I answer. If I am wrong, it is because something is tampering with the natural order of things. These are unnatural events, Your Grace, and they continue to spread, to grow!" Lady Darellan's voice was soft but stern. "There is word reaching us this very day of new plagues afflicting the people of the far plains – plagues that rot the mind as much as the flesh – there is a force behind this, and if we are not prepared, we will be swept away with it!"

The Prince appeared to relent.

"So, what would you have me do? I do not have magic to fight a plague or make the skies rain down on barren fields. Those who could wield that kind of magic departed these lands long ago – they either followed the Angyalok into the west or went mad and destroyed themselves – thankfully so! There is scarcely a court magician who can do more than change the colour of the banners to yellow for the harvest festival!" He sounded exasperated. "...And when they do, I still expect it's because they staged the whole thing and dyed the banners the night before. I mean, really, sometimes it's so pathetic I swear they are doing everything they can to make us believe that all magic is fake!"

"Be that as it may…" Lady Darellan seemed to ignore his protests, "You ask my advice and this is it: seek out the source of the troubles and put an end to them before they destroy all of Nyirseg and the other principalities, or you will become Grand Prince in time to rule over nothing but ashes."

"How?" came the question back from the Prince, simple and somber, "We are a kingdom of the defeated, waking from a long sleep, to find our heroes are dead and our gods are all gone."

Dar paused – not because she didn't know what she was going to ask of him, but because she knew he was going to hate it.

"The lands are in chaos, so we need to harness chaos to our will – in truth, some tasks are more suited to mercenaries than heroes. But… you must agree to reward them for their efforts…?" she both offered and asked.

"Mercenaries? Rogues?" Svato asked her, "You would trust our fate to scoundrels?" The disgust in his tone was more than he usually displayed when talking of things he normally felt were below him.

"What choice do we have?" she countered, "Our best warriors were lost resisting the Imperium. We have but ourselves to blame for the losing the wisdom of the ancients, and every day the temples cry blasphemy whenever anyone shows the slightest affinity for the tribal mystics…"

"The church calls it 'dark magic'…" he tried to interject, but she ignored him.

"I am afraid" she stated softly yet boldly, "if there is some power – something or someone – that has defied nature to alter the seasons, to stop the rains across all of Vengriya, then it is a great power. And great powers do not play at games! They have a purpose. I fear a dark purpose. And if we are not prepared for whatever that is, then we shall not endure whatever is yet to come…"

The prince was silent as she finished, turning his about the charred grounds as he considered her words before he replied.

"Do what you must. Find what, or whom, you can." He spoke over the soft thud of hooves as he wheeled his mount, "You go with my support, but I will pray to the gods that you are wrong yet again…" he finished, spurring his horse back to the city gate, leaving Dar to stare after him, silently wishing to herself that she would be wrong as well.

*****Omar*****

The pale shades of evening were giving way to pure darkness of night, and the stars were beginning to filter through the haze of the warm summer sky. The hum of the street vendors and people closing their stalls at the end of a long day of hustling their wares was slowly giving way to the softer buzz of insects that were beginning to descend on the discarded scraps that would not be sold this day, and no more swatting hands would try to dislodge them from their meals. Crickets were beginning to chirp from their hiding places between the shop stalls, under boxes and in the damp corners of the city that offered them shelter from the oppressive heat of the day. It had been a long, hot summer, and, for the second year in a row, the rains had not come as promised. People now spoke openly about "drought" instead of just noting the heat. It was already crowded in the market quarter, now the heat was producing all manner of new smells with which to entice the wildlife that hid inside the many cracks, crevices and tiny spaces behind the walls. The insects loved the heat, the garbage, and, combined with the easy access to water from the nearby river, it was a perfect environment for all manner of pestilence to thrive.

The market quarter had grown like a scar over an old wound, with new buildings attached to older buildings like lumps of tissue building up on a useless limb. Little by little, as people were drawn to the city when their crops turned to dust or their livestock withered in the heat, those who could afford to enter the city proper crossed the river and traded in their plowshares for trade-crafts: smithies fed the ever-growing need for metal-works coming from the manor houses; craftsmen, woodworkers, innkeepers, seamstresses – all plied their trades as they were able. But many crofters did not own their land, and with no other craft to offer when their crops failed, they were left on the lower side of the river, in the common market quarter, to fend for themselves and carve out any livable space they could: between, around, above, and even below the existing buildings that surrounded the central market square. It was a maze of streets, alleys, footpaths, stairways, ladders, and dead-ends – pathways only truly known by the folk who lived in the market.

Most who came to the market for trade came across the bridge from the city center directly to the square, where the great warehouses, near the river's edge, housed enormous stacks of goods unloaded from the riverboats each day. Towering three or four spans above the rest of the buildings in the quarter, these old stone structures were probably the oldest buildings in the entire city – and they looked it. With their missing roof tiles, rotting timbers, and cracked mortar, it almost seemed as though they were long-dead giants, and every home, shack and tavern that had been built alongside their walls was nothing but a scar, sore, or scab that had grown out of their seeping wounds.

Omar was lying on the roof of his aunt's small home, trying to distract his mind from everything going on in the tiny room below as the sun finished setting on his left and darkness crept across the sky from his right. A falcon was soaring on the wind almost directly overhead, not even flapping its wings as it caught the westerly breeze and floated motionless in the air. He had heard that some of the royal families were starting to train falcons to hunt and carry messages for them – he scarcely believed these stories, as he ignored many of the rumours that spread among the street people. Still, he looked up at the bird, seeming to fly without any effort, and wished their places were reversed.

How he longed to rise above the noise and smell of the city streets, where it was growing more crowded by the day, and one couldn't escape the press of bodies and petty disputes. The closeness made it easy to lift a purse here or there and slip away unnoticed, but even the purses were getting lighter it seemed, as the people became more and more desperate with drought and the poor harvest. Yes, he thought, it would be good to fly above all this, and be a royal falcon. And then the thought slipped away as the bird itself banked and flapped its wings, disappearing down to the earth, perhaps even landing in the belfry of the Ispan's manor.

With that moment passing, he quickly moved to the next distraction, and began to count the faintly flickering lights of the stars as they started to appear, one by one, only to be interrupted as he heard someone calling his name from the house below.

Taking one last look from his perch, Omar could see out across the shambled, haphazard landscape of uneven roof tops and tarps, and only dream about being one of the lucky ones who lived across the river, where the homes lay in neat, fenced, rows, up and down the winding streets of the city center. A gentle rise in the land would always draw the eye to the very center of town, where the manor keep sat atop a hill, like the jewel in a crown, catching the last rays of the setting sun while the lights of the night watch began to flicker and flit in the darkening streets. The keep was not as old as the warehouses in the market – while the hill had dominated the city for just as long, the manor keep had been razed to the ground more than once over the course of time, and the most recent rebuilding had only recently been completed by the current lord's father.

It was many years in the making, and Omar could not recall much of the previous keep, but this new one was quite lavish in its details, with only the finest stonemasons from the region taking charge of the finishing touches. Many people in the town had earned a living from the manual labour of carving and hauling stones for many years for the local Ispan – a sort of 'lord mayor' – a living which many of them now found themselves without as the major work had been finished. Some still worked on the walls that surround the inner city along the river, but the outlying quarters had no such protection, and it clearly was not something the Ispan felt was important enough to spend money on.

Rolling off the hard clay tiles, he swung gently from the rooftop to the trellis that ran up the side of the wall. Their home was little more than a shack attached to the side of a neighbouring building – just like every one of the homes on this side of the river – but at least it was one of the larger ones that had been built a little further back from the center of the square. It offered a little more peace and quiet than those nearer to the central market, although there wasn't anyone in this quarter that wouldn't try to sell you something as you walked the narrow, crowded lanes. He was grateful that it was well placed for him to have easy access to the rooftops, where he could escape from time to time.

What it didn't offer was an escape from the stench of the rendering pots next door – day and night they boiled they rotting animal remains cast-off by the butchers, extracting whatever they could from the steaming pots: oils to be sold again in the market, medicinal powders extracted from the crushed bones. He carefully climbed across the oil pots stacked against the wall as he found his way to the trellis by their door, wrinkling his nose against the foul aroma – just one more thing to hate in the world, and the price one paid when one couldn't afford any of the nicer homes in the city.

It had always been just him and his mother, and everything he needed to learn to survive had come from her first, then from the people he lived with on the streets of the market quarter. Every day was a struggle – not just for him, but for many in the city – and so he learned to survive. He had learned how to traverse the rooftops when he needed to avoid the streets. He knew where the best shadows fell during the full moon, and had mastered how to move without being seen, as there were many petty thieves who were willing to teach him how to do these things, in exchange for his services in helping them with their schemes. He counted himself fortunate to never have been caught, not that the city guards were much to worry about. They cared little for petty thieves; he had more to worry about from the private mercenaries hired by the merchants.

As he reached the bottom of the trellis, he stood hesitantly at the doorway, despite the apparent urgency of their calls. They had chased him out of the house when 'Baba Louhi' – the witch woman – had arrived. Not yet fourteen seasons old, he was too young in their minds to be involved in such things and would only have gotten in the way.

Strange, he thought, as it was his mother that was sick, yet they did not think he should be involved? After all, wasn't it he who had been at her side all these days, washing her face and placing the cloths on her forehead as the fever dreams gripped her? She hadn't eaten for days and had been sick for a fortnight, but his aunt had resisted sending for help – healers required coin for their services, or at least something in trade – and they had very little to offer. Only when she had run out of her home remedies and finally given up in frustration did she agree to send for help, such as she could afford.

There were choices one could make in these instances: The town had its share of apothecaries, mysterious chemists who spent their time concocting all variety of serums and elixirs; then there were the Javasember – healers from the temple – drawing on the strength of Ukko's faithful to remove spirits and contagions; the lay people of the church could bandage and treat wounds; and more and more these days, there were Shamans from the outer fields coming into town, following the tenant farmers and rural communities that were flocking to the city. There was even word of those who could – for a price – lead you to someone who knew someone who could connect you with one of the woodland folk – the ancient Taltos – who could use their power to commune with nature and restore one's health.

Of course, most of this last category were schemers and scam artists, looking to make money off the dimmer folk who still believed in the old ways – no one had seen a true Taltos in his lifetime, and though many remained afraid of the possibility that they might run into one if they strayed too far from the trail in the forest he could not name a soul who had any direct knowledge of a Taltos outside of the bedtime stories that his aunt used to scare him with to stay in his bed at night. It was said that the Taltos had six fingers on their hands, or sometimes even a third arm, which they used to cast hexes on unwary travelers. While Shamans might be taught by their elders, you had to be born a Taltos in order to be a Taltos.

So, the Taltos were clearly not an option, nor were the more expensive healers, so it was the Shamans they had turned to. There were a few, and they were more than happy to ply their trade in exchange for food or shelter. What he could not understand was why his aunt had asked for old Baba Louhi over all the others. Her reputation for scaring the bejeezus out of him was more than enough to make him prefer anyone else – even when skulking around the market's many alleys and hidden laneways, he would avoid her shack at all costs. Others would steer clear because of the smell, but he always felt a dark chill run down his spine if he looked at the hut too closely and could never bring himself to try to look directly at her face on the odd occasion when he would see her ragged, hunched figure shuffling down the street.

When they finally sent for her, the Baba could not come right away, as many in the market quarter had been falling sick these days, and her services were in high demand. It had taken her two days to arrive at their door, and when she did, Omar was glad in some ways that they did send him out of the house while she worked. Being the first to hear the knock at the door he had jumped to answer, only to have his breath catch in his throat as he found himself face to face with one of the most disturbing appearances he had ever seen.

Her wind-worn skin was leathery, wrinkled, and tired, and the milky-white clouds in her eyes contrasted sharply with the deep brown of her complexion, making him believe she was truly blind. She had come on her own, so she must have some sight, he thought, to have made her way through the maze of the market to their door. Her clothes were threadbare, tattered, and smeared with the still-moist stains of fluids that he could not begin to guess. Néni Marta brushed him aside as she ushered the old woman into the house.

It was very small – little more than three rooms for all of them together; one that he shared with his mother, one where his Néni Marta slept, and the main room, crowded with all their worldly possessions – which wasn't much – in one small space. While his mother was abed in her room off to the side, Marta brought the witch woman over and sat her at the head of the tiny wooden table in the center of the room. Balint, an apprentice smithy and friend of Marta's, was with them – it was he who had convinced her to finally send for the witch woman's help, including offering some of his own coppers to help pay her fee. Omar has been very curious to hear what the old woman would have to say about his mother, and he made no effort to hide his objections when Balint ushered him out so the grown-ups could talk. When it was clear that they were deaf to his protests, he had relented and took to the rooftop to bide his time, where his resentment of being excluded was tempered by his relief to keep his distance from the old hag, who smelled almost as bad as she appeared.

"OMAR!" his aunt shouted again out the small window, trying to get his attention from the roof. Turning back to the doorway, she was startled when she saw him step forward from the shadows.

"Omar, get in here," she chastised. "'Tis no time to be playing strange. This is serious."

Stepping forward into the light of the room, he wiped his hair from across his face and quickly glanced to his left, into the bedroom, where he could see his mother lying in her bed, the blankets soaked from her fevered sweat, her head rocking slowly from side to side.

"We don't have much time," said the witch woman, her voice barely a whisper escaping those yellowed teeth. "Not much time, and much to do."

"What is it?" Omar asked, looking at Marta and Balint as much as possible, trying as much as he could to avoid looking at the old crone at the table.

"Louhi has done what she can, but we need you to go on an errand, quickly now," said Balint. "We need you to run to the Tower and fetch the old man. He has magic that can help your mother. This sickness is spreading and has grown beyond Louhi's skills." Balint spoke of the tower with the definitive tone that made it clear there was only one tower that he might possibly be referring to, and only one man within it.

"What?" said Omar, "Another healer? We can't afford that! And how long will he take to come?"

"Enough!" hissed Louhi, with spittle flying from her old, cracked lips. "Take these…" she said, tossing a small bag across the table to him, "and bring them to the tower. He will come if he knows I have called on him – you can give him this, so he knows it is I who calls him." She slipped her hand into a small pouch at her side and tossed him a larger coin-shaped token covered in strange markings.

Dropping his eyes in the face of the scowls directed at him from everyone in the room, Omar gripped the small coin sack in his hands, counting the coins through the thin cloth. Nodding respectfully, he turned and made his way to the door and out into the night, to dutifully run the errand. After all, this was for his mother's sake…

Stepping out into the darkened street, he looked both ways nervously. A hundred thoughts and worries ran through his head, not the least of which was that this small pouch held the most money he had ever seen in his entire life, yet alone carried, and without thinking, he hadn't even tucked it away before leaving the house. He hurriedly slipped the pouch into his tunic and hoped no one was watching from the shadows – the market was not the safest place in the daytime, and it was even worse after dark. With shops closed and the merchants at home, the night watch did little more than ensure the lamps were lit and offered no real protection to anyone who ventured out of their own accord. He would have to make sure he made it across the market quarter on his own wits, and without attracting any attention.

Not that a slight figure like Omar ever attracted much attention – still young, small in build, and clearly no one of importance by his clothing, he was not someone the locals would ever consider to be a target of opportunity… unless, of course, they happened to see him tuck something mysterious into his shirt before quickly running off into the night. Curiosity would always be enough motivation to cause him unwanted problems. Without thinking of it, he dropped his left hand to his belt, and fingered the grip of the small blade he wore at his hip. His friends mocked him for the small size of the weapon – almost more of a long dagger than a sword, but it looked larger on him, oddly shaped with its wavy curves in the blade – but he found it useful for persuading those who felt too much affinity to their possessions. It likely would not be of much help in a serious sword fight, but nonetheless, it gave him comfort.

His next steps carried him into the lane where he abruptly collided with a taller man, wrapped in a dark cloak, walking purposely down the otherwise empty street.

"Watch where you're going!" the man yelled back over his shoulder as he almost knocked Omar from his feet, continuing on his way in haste. Omar caught himself mid-stumble and mumbled an apology without actually looking at the man as he carried on his way. He tugged at his shirt and adjusted his belt as he continued on his path toward the alley across the lane, checking that Louhi's pouch was still in its' place before pausing to examine the purse he had so deftly lifted from the man in the street. He was in a hurry so made a mental note to count it later and tucked it away from sight.

Omar knew exactly where they wanted him to go – the tower was probably the most recognizable building in the market quarter after the warehouse. And it was the one structure in the quarter that all the locals gave a wide berth to. Situated directly behind the main warehouse, it sat apart from all other buildings – a definite oddity in a town where everything was built upon whatever was beside it! Surrounded by a tall stone fence, a full head high, for privacy, the tower was the only building in the market quarter – or the entire city even – that rose higher than the warehouse buildings, stretching more than six spans above the rest of the town. Looking across the river, it almost rivalled the height of the manor keep itself, something most folks believed was a regular point of consternation for the Ispan, looking over from the city proper.

Within the wall, the tower formed the top of the triangle of the property, with the walls stretching back along the edge of the two lanes that split off from the street running across the back of the warehouse. There was an open courtyard within the walls, no more than a hundred paces long, to which a few small buildings – stables and storage – formed the base of the triangle. Vines grew along & over the wall with wild abandon and were the only things that seemed to be able to attach themselves to the main stonework.

Folk in the market told tales about how every now and then some new squatter would arrive, and seeing the opportunity, try to lean themselves against the outer wall of the tower where the property fence blended into the base. Such solid stone was appealing as a foundation for anyone seeking to make a new home in the market, and with no one ever seeming to be around inside the tower, it seemed there was little to fear. Yet invariably, within a matter of days, anything that anyone could build attached to that tower would meet a sad demise: it was either by fire, collapse, rot, or sinking into the mud of the street. Nothing would ever take hold, and the townsfolk would shake their heads at the newcomers' frustrations and carry on their way. The only exception was along the back of the property, where the city seemed to spring to life out of the outer buildings, leaning and stacking upon one another, to curl back around and surround the tower grounds, as if the city itself were trying to ensnare the tower within its grasp, even if it defied being touched.

Omar was within sight of the tower and could see a faint flickering of torchlight coming from within the tower courtyard. That was when he heard the steps behind him. He had moved quickly from lamp to lamp as he made his way through the narrow streets, and then did his best to slink unseen through the last stretch in the shadows, trying to keep out of sight and hopefully to make the final dash across the open square before anyone could spot him. Hearing the steps, he worried that he was being followed, and became more than a little nervous about the quality of his plan.

He slipped around the last corner and out of sight, stopping to hold his breath and listen, to see if the footsteps were getting closer. He was slowly edging his head around the corner to look back the way he came when he heard the creaking of wood, and a light flashed out into the darkness from the direction of the tower.

With his back to the corner of the wall, he could make out the silhouette of a person on horse emerging from gate by the tower courtyard. A fire blazed in the background, spoiling his night vision and making it hard for him to make out anything more from inside the gate. At that moment, he suddenly realized: he had never seen anyone come or go from the tower, and all of the stories that he had heard as a child, and to this day, none of them ever said anything nice about who lived in the tower, or what they would do to trespassers. And this was the person he had just been sent to find.

In an instant, a thousand terrible thoughts churned through his mind, all of them providing graphic detail of the reasons why he should not move another inch forward. And it was only when he heard again the sound of what he imagined a hard leather boot would make, scraping on the cobblestone of the lane behind him, did he gather his wits, remember that he was here to save his mother from sickness, and ran forward from the wall into the street and up to the horseman.

He stepped in front of the large, black stallion just as the door was closing, and the light from the fire in the courtyard was again blocked from his view. With the light from the open doorway, he looked back quickly over his shoulder, and while he couldn't be sure, he thought he glimpsed a shadow moving quickly back down the lane from which he had come. Then the darkness swallowed up everything again.

Sighing, he felt relieved about one problem being solved, only to be snapped back to the rider as the horse snorted and stomped in front of him. He quickly jumped back, looked past the muzzle of the horse into the darkened hood of the rider.

For a moment, his voice failed him, and the first sounds he could make came out as a squeak.

"Make way, boy, or you'll get hurt," said the rider, clearly and as a matter of fact.

Clearing his throat, Omar backed away only slightly and raised his hands to calm the horse, not wanting to get stomped by one of the massive hooves. He could barely see past the mouth of the beast and was definitely not tall enough to look it level in the eye, but he stood his ground.

"Forgive me, m'lord! The old woman bade me fetch you, that we seek your help!" said Omar, his voice growing in confidence as he focused on his mission.

"My help?" the rider asked, "Do you know who I am?"

'Garaboncid' he said to himself – *'wizard'* – thankfully holding his tongue before he spoke more properly. "You are the Master of the Tower, m'lord," said Omar, realizing even as he said it just how awkward and childish he sounded – he had never thought to ask just what the man's proper title was, and he had quite likely just given him insult enough to not come to their aid! Fearing he would be brushed aside for the lack of manners, he quickly blurted out the rest of his message.

"The witch woman has sent me for help for my mother, sick with plague."

"And how do you know who I am?" the rider repeated his question, glancing sideways up at the building beside him. "Perhaps I am just a simple merchant, out for a night's ride." His horse stepped noisily on cobblestones, snorting again, as if impatient to get going, as the rider tugged the reins and turned sideways to get a better look at the boy. Omar couldn't see much of the man's face in the darkness of the street, and the nearest lamp was a few yards away, but when he glimpsed a feature – an eye, a cheek, a chin, he could see that the figure was clearly not as old as he and his friends had imagined in their stories.

It then occurred to him: he did not know who lived in the tower, or what they looked like. He had simply expected to knock on the door and talk to whomever answered. Of all the thoughts and plans that had rattled through his mind on the way here, this situation had not occurred to him at all.

Desperate, Omar slowly lowered his hands and reached into his tunic for the coin purse. He saw the rider tense up slightly as he withdrew his hand, and then relaxed when he saw the purse. Omar held forth the token, raising it up so the rider could see it in the faint light of the streetlamp.

"You know this?" he asked the man on the horse.

"Yes," said the rider, squinting in the late evening shade to make out the token. "So, it is Baba Louhi that has sent you?"

Omar nodded.

"Very well then, why didn't you say so?" The rider slid his hood back slightly, and Omar could make out his face a little better. While the light from the lamp was faint, it cast odd shadows across the rider's face, and while he thought the rider was smiling, the actual effect was much grimmer.

"Go on ahead – I will be on my way in a moment – I must fetch my medicines," the man on the horse commanded. "You can tell Baba Louhi that I have just come from a council with the Ispan, and he has asked me to do what I can to cleanse the city of the plague. She should wait there, and I will do what I have promised to do."

"Now go, get back to your mother's side!"

"I will show you the way…" Omar began to say.

"Do as I say! When I am ready, I will follow the stench!"

Omar felt both relief and insult as he turned to run before he suddenly remembered the coins. He stopped and turned back, and held out the coin purse, in part to make sure anyone watching would be sure to see that he had given it away, which would make his trip back to the house a bit less stressful for him…

"Here – from the witch wo– … from Baba Louhi," he said, as he tossed the purse up to the rider. The horseman snatched the purse and deftly tucked it into his belt.

"Of course. Not necessary, but still appreciated." He replied.

With that, Omar turned and began his way back, much more relieved than when he set out and very pleased to be bringing some welcome good news to the house.

It was fully dark now, and Omar allowed himself a quick glance at the stars as he hurried back along his route. To his surprise, clouds had drifted in and made for an eerie glow around the moon. He had not seen any on the horizon just a few hours earlier, nor were any expected in the middle of a drought.... he slowed his pace for a moment as he pondered the problem, so distracted was he by this unexpected change in the night sky, that when the lightning flashed, he jumped as if it had hit him directly and he felt his heart skip a beat, nearly causing him to trip. The light was so bright his eyes were still adjusting to the darkness again when he realized that he had failed to hear any thunder following the flash.

Gathering himself quickly, he double-timed his way home, not caring if anyone had seen him jump in fright or running in such haste, without any care for stealth or disguise – he cared little for his reputation among the street folk, not this evening, not when his mother needed him most...

*****The Tower*****

Earlier that afternoon, Torick found himself venturing forth from his tower for the first time that day, though not of his own accord. In a rare show of desperation, he had been summoned by the Ispan to appear before the council and had barely restrained himself from roasting the two peacocks the Ispan had sent to deliver his message – the brief ride to the Ispan's keep in the center of the city did little to temper his ire.

The Ispan's keep was not exceptionally large, as Mercurum was a modest city-state, but the rooms were lavish, the result of a desperate attempt to outshine the glory of the cathedral across the square. The main hall was used for greeting visitors and grand banquets, but the council chamber was the place where the Ispan did his utmost to make a grand impression. The mosaic tile floor mapped the original city plan, and the large windows, braced by columns on each side, streamed light into the room that focused on the small, narrow oaken table that was in the center of the chamber.

Elegant chairs for each council member – seven in total – were arranged around the room, set back against the walls so they could observe all discussions from their perch. Narrow banners, woven of course, heavy cloth, hung between each of the council seats, insulating the room against the inherent cold of the massive stonework, with what were originally brightly coloured depictions of heroic scenes woven into each banner, reflecting back the heat given off by the fire set within the massive hearth. Smoke and soot had been absorbed by the banners, darkening the images depicted in the tapestries. At the head of the chamber, directly across from the doors, was the Ispan's chair.

While not a throne – this was just a city-state after all – it was ornately carved and inlaid with mother of pearl and fine tracings of gold and silver, with a large, cushioned seat of plush velvet. It was centered in front of a large open hearth that spanned the fullness of the wall. Whole trees might be felled and dragged directly into the hearth for kindling, without sawing a single piece to make it fit.

Torick ignored all of this as he strode into the chamber, his cloak and long black hair gliding in his wake as his pace belied his impatience. He marched purposely across the chamber to his chair against the wall to the right of the Ispan's seat, turning with a flourish to face those gathered in there already, and snapped himself down into his seat with all the haughtiness of a child who had been called late to dinner.

"Ah, Torick, you are here... finally..." the Ispan observed, rousing himself up from his low slouch, "I was worried you had ignored my summons and dispatched my poor messengers to some miserable, undeserved fate."

Torick's expression was stern and unamused – he hated being summoned, almost as much as he hated being compelled to be part of this council.

"I had given serious thought to roasting those fool peacocks you sent to deliver your message. Insufferable fools who serve no purpose but to...to..." he stammered to find the appropriate insult.

"Ha!" the Ispan laughed, "true, they are that, but you shouldn't go ruffling their feathers all the time – it's all the poor lads have!" He seemed to be quite at ease with Torick's theatrics.

"The Imperium has withdrawn," he continued, "their troops are almost to the western border, and when the spring rains are done, we will have seen the last of them in these lands. The people were not happy under them, and no one was sad to see them go. Why do you let these preening fools go on pretending like the Imperium is still here?"

The Ispan straightened up in his chair, pulled his tunic to straighten it out, and sighed. "Not everything the Imperium put in place was bad," he said, "and there are a few who will miss them... not to mention there are few who have chosen to stay behind, to live with us, instead of leaving with them."

Torick did his best not to roll his eyes, but the effort only seemed to exaggerate the effect. "As you say. But that is not the assigned time for a council – I have other things to do and did not agree to be at anyone's beck and call! What do you want of me?"

"There is a sickness in the countryside," the Ispan stated.

"I have heard," came the matter-of-fact reply.

"It's a nasty thing, from the tales we have heard," the Ispan expressed, as if he had just stepped on a frog and stopped to look at the result. He stood up and walked to the map of town inlaid in the floor. "The farmers have said the land is withering away, and now they are withering, too."

"And this concerns me how?" said Torick. He paused before continuing and heard the distinct sound of someone clearing their throat, getting ready to speak.

Torick had been looking only at the Ispan during the exchange, and it was only now that the others in the room seemed to come to life. There were several servants milling about, and he paid these no mind. In the flickering shadows of the light cast by the great hearth, he could make out several figures attending beside or behind several of the vacant council chairs, clearly subordinates sent to observe and relay events to those absent. There was one other who remained standing back by the doors of the chamber, not aligned with any absent council seat, though she — he was guessing — remained still and silent throughout what transpired. Of the seven council chairs, only one had an occupant, and he was now slowly rising to stand.

With a quick tap of his crozier, the figure seated against the wall to the right motioned for his assistant to help him to his feet. He was not too old or feeble, so Torick judged it was a wound or injury that required him to be helped from the chair, and not the frailty of age.

There was no mistaking the man for his faith — his finely woven linen robes, the brightest white and deep purple edging, with gold embroidering through the cloth, marked him as a man of importance before he even spoke a word. Long blonde hair, pulled tightly back, held by a golden braid and a fine golden circlet around his brow. His beard was full, but neatly trimmed, framing a face that, though worn by a lifetime of action, could not have been more than thirty years of age – not ancient, but quite young for someone to lead a community of faithful the size of which one would find in a state like Mercurum.

At his side, and just a step back, he was followed closely by his servant, who seemed much older and gave an impression of having served his faith for much longer than his master had been alive. Wearing simple robes, akin to those worn by monks in the abbey just a few leagues down the river, he held the Bishop steady as he rose, made sure he was steady, and then stepped back to his own seat, and watched, waiting for the next cue. Torick could not make out much else for the shadows in the room cast by the fire in the hearth, and so turned his attention more fully to the Bishop as he began to speak.

"It concerns us all," the Bishop said sternly, with the deep tone of someone accustomed to giving sermons to large crowds, "It is not a natural sickness that we are seeing this time – it is a dark plague that is coming, and it is spreading evil to everything it touches!" He rapped the golden metal mitre staff on the floor to add emphasis to his statement.

"Plagues are not good or evil, Your Grace," said Torick, "they take the wicked and the contrite."

"So you say," the Bishop retorted, "but just because you do not believe, does not mean it is not so."

"So many 'nots' – it's hard to untie your words, Your Grace. We have rains, we have droughts. We have good harvests, we have bad. We have health, and we have sickness. It is the natural way of things. A ripe apple is not good just because it is ripe. An apple left to fall and rot on the ground is not evil – is it the apple's fault it did not get picked at the right time?" Torick replied as he slowly walked along the face of the hearth, warming one hand against the flames.

Turning to warm his backside, he paused for a moment to glance at the figure who remained at the back of the chamber – hooded and cloaked in shadows, and they seemed to turn away as his gaze lingered, denying him a better look.

The Bishop stood by his chair and bristled at the wit of this upstart. He held the posts of the chair in front of him, gripping the knobs of the backrest so hard his knuckles paled with the effort. He raised his voice, to carry his point across the room: "An unpicked apple is a symbol of our excess, and we should not be surprised to be punished by Ukko for our greed – we have sinned in growing beyond our needs, sowing more than we can reap, and succumbing to avarice, gluttony – the sins of excess! The gods send plague to restore balance, and remind us to be humble in our nature, and we–"

"Enough, enough…" the Ispan interjected softly, politely interrupting the Bishop. "With respect, Your Grace, we are not here to debate theology. I asked you both here to find a way to stop the spread of whatever this sickness is, before the entire city is lost and we have nothing: no apples, no congregation, and no people to pay taxes or tithes! We have bent ourselves to the will of the gods, made the sacrifices, held the high mass for penitence, and you yourself have led prayer services every evening for a fortnight… and yet the tales continue to grow, and the fear in the people grows with them."

The rising exasperation in his voice almost seemed to exhaust him as he spoke, and the Ispan slumped back into his chair at the head of the room. "I need a solution, from anyone who can offer one."

Torick and the Bishop locked eyes, and both respectfully turned to the Ispan and nodded in silent deference.

"So, what do we do?" the Ispan asked, with only the slightest hint of desperation noticeable in his voice.

"The sickness is not natural," said the Bishop, drawing a sharp glance from Torick before he continued, "It seems to corrupt men's souls as much as it weakens their bodies. I have seen good men do terrible things in the countryside; people who worshipped and tithed faithfully have committed horrendous crimes against their own neighbours, friends, and even families, once they have been touched by this illness. It consumes them, and the healers have not been able to do anything. It breeds violence and death where we have seen it." The Bishop's tone had authority, but also a hint of fear. Torick sensed there was even more that he knew that he was not saying.

Turning to Torick, the Ispan added, "This is what the Bishop was telling me earlier, and it is why I asked you here this afternoon."

"Your knowledge is…" he paused, "…*different* from the doctrines of the faithful, and I thought you might have some insight into the nature of the situation – perhaps even a cure? We have word that there are many falling sick within the Market Quarter – merchants, farmers and travellers have been coming into town all season, and they are bringing this plague with them. If it has shown up in the Market Quarter, I am worried it will spread. Crofters – the faithful and the heretic – have called for their monks, healers, and shamans, all to no avail. Many now are trying to cross the river to seek Ukko's blessing directly from the Archbishop at the cathedral, and if they try, we will have no choice but to close the gates to everyone."

Torick stood up and walked to the tiles indicating the Market Quarter on the floor, looking at the markings for the great warehouses displayed in the mosaic tile, tracing the path of the blue tiles that mark the path of the river as it enters, then splits around the city proper, and marking in silver tiles the four bridges that created the four quarters of the town: the Market Quarter, the Crofters Quarter, the Tannery, and the Mills. He scraped with his toe at a little black tile in the Market Quarter that would be his tower, behind the grand warehouse.

"If we close the gates," the Ispan continued, moving back to his chair, slumping into his seat, "that will be the end for all of us. With this drought, we have had no harvest for two seasons – the granaries are empty. We would be safe from the plague, but we would all starve inside these walls within a fortnight.

"I need you to fix it for me" he continued with a sense of resignation, "for me, for us here in this room, for everyone inside these walls."

"And what does the rest of the Council think about this?" asked Torick, looking around at the seven empty chairs in the chamber.

"I have not invited the others, as they do not have the same faith in your abilities as I do," said the Ispan, rising again from his chair, standing at the table with the hearth to his back. "In fact, some of them even believe you and your experiments are to blame for the plague, and it is *you* that should be removed to save us."

"Well, it just so happens I was getting ready to leave anyway, so perhaps that will make them happy. After tonight, you can feel free to take credit for my leaving, if that would help," Torick said with a wry smile.

"So, you'll help us?" The Ispan's tone had the blended sound of relief and a query.

"Why should I?" Torick asked. "I'm not part of this council, nor am I indebted to anyone here. It would not be easy, and there is a good chance a lot of people will die, regardless, so why would I get involved? There's no upside for me, only blame."

"You always were a mercenary... I will pay you for your troubles," the Ispan said, resignedly.

"Now we're making progress," said Torick. "Pour the wine and let's talk more about just how many troubles it will make for me to fix this, and how much that will cost you..."

Torick and the Ispan moved over to the table, where the flagon of wine and goblets were waiting. Slowly, the Bishop turned and nodded to the deacon behind him, who promptly stepped forward to take his free arm in support.

"M'lord," said the Bishop, "I will take my leave, and leave the two of you to your negotiations. The afternoon is slipping away, and I need to set the altar for the evening prayers – the Archbishop himself has decided to lead the mass, and we must make our preparations. By your leave." He nodded, and the Ispan waived in his direction, more concerned with the wine than the departing cleric.

"Come, Brother Ralof, we must hurry," the Bishop called, turning to the door, "we have much to do before the sun sets."

Neither Torick nor the Ispan had paid much attention to the older man who now jumped forward to hand the Bishop his mitre, adjust his cloak, and then follow him to the door. His brown robes were simple and well worn, tied with the characteristic rope belt. He looked exactly like one would imagine, if someone said to imagine, a monk – except for the uncharacteristic look of disdain that he threw over his shoulder to the two men as they poured their drinks.

It wasn't as much a scowl of dissatisfaction with their drinking habit, but the Ispan almost seemed to feel that the old cleric had no respect for them at all and that this business was a complete waste of their time. It was an odd look, he felt, for someone in such a low position to feel they had permission to give, especially to someone of his rank. He made a brief mental note to speak to the Bishop later about ensuring the monastic orders understood their place a little better, and to mind their manners.

Thinking now about how many people may have been in the room, his mind turned back to the robed man – or woman? – he had seen standing by the doors. Clearly not a servant, he looked around the chamber now and could not find them anywhere. His curiosity made him think for a moment to ask the Ispan about who it was, than he quickly decided it wasn't worth the bother, and resumed his planning with the Ispan for the cleansing of the market quarter…

*****Path of the Righteous*****

The assassination of the Archbishop weighed heavy on Shagron's mind as he reined in his horse on the small hill overlooking the town. He had been travelling for days and did not expect he would be able to stop again anytime soon – the head of his order had told him it was urgent that he act with all due haste, and so he rode hard to get here as quickly as he could.

Mercurum was a crossroads town. In addition to the Duna river being a major thoroughfare for traffic and trade by boat and barge, four roads led away from the town – north, south, east and west – each roughly corresponding to the outlying town quarters. Not too far to the north, perhaps a half days' walk from the outside edge of town, there was another smaller intersection in the road, as it split along the natural contours of the land. Before Mercurum had started to grow, to spread beyond the island, and when it had fewer local accommodations, it had only seemed natural that this second crossroads would have made a reasonable spot for a someone – perhaps the second son of a farmer who didn't stand to inherit the farm – to seek their own fortune and build an inn, to offer rest to weary travelers.

The small, two-story timber inn had long ago seen the days of its prime come and go. Since Mercurum had grown and stretched even just a little closer, the inn had become less convenient and as a result, most travelers would now simply push on and find their way to the city before deciding to stop and rest. And so the inn, with no real name other than a simple carving above the door displaying a two-pronged fork – roughly resembling the road – above the shape of a bowl, soon found itself falling into disrepair, as fewer and fewer customers frequented its rooms. Its' near abandoned state made it perfect for Shagron's needs.

Hearing the rider come up and stop, the owner quickly stepped out to greet the unexpected traveler. His hospitality quickly outshone the humble accommodations, and as there were no other guests in the tavern room, he was equally quick to fetch his guest a quick meal before retiring for the night.

"It's been a quiet summer…" the innkeeper was saying as he showed him to his room. He was still talking about the lack of paying clients when his large guest interrupted…

"Hot water" he stated flatly as much as asked.

"Oh. Yes, hot water, of course, I will send some up directly…" the innkeeper answered emphatically and hurried off to his duties.

Shagron was pleased to see that it was still quite hot when it arrived, though he was worried that it would chill before he could use it, as the innkeeper was very talkative about everything – the current state of the inn, the weather, the latest news from town – clearly, he had not had anyone to talk with for some time.

"Thank you" he finally interrupted, "for your most gracious attentions," holding out a coin that was enough to make the innkeeper pause and take in a deep breath, although rather than ending the conversation, this led to even more waiting as the old man now professed his sincerest thanks and offered his services for anything else he might require through the night!

After his grateful host had left, the man closed the door, sighed deeply, and began to strip off his road-weary clothes and clean up before bed. Tall – at least two heads taller than the innkeeper – with broad shoulders, he was not the largest man one had ever seen, but he carried himself in a way that made him seem taller than he actually was. By his height, he might have been mistaken for one of noble birth, but one look at the long, oily hair, reaching just below his shoulders, and the knotted length of his beard would quickly dissuade an observer from that conclusion. Removing his shirt first, then his leggings, an unmistakable crosshatch of scars and wounds made it clear that he was not just a warrior, but a survivor.

Moving across the small room to the table where the innkeeper had left the water, he poured some into the basin, adjusted the small, round scrap of polished metal that served as the only mirror in the room, and set about washing off the dirt from his travels. When he had finished washing, and needed to do some more detailed touches, he opted to draw back the curtains, and, pulling the candle closer, used the reflection in the window to get a better view of his face than the dented and burnished metal mirror had provided.

He paused for a moment to stare at the face looking back at him in the reflection – he was no longer the young adventurer he used be, ready to take on every crusade and quest that came his way; he had fought his way out of more tight spots than most people might ever hear tell of from even the most talkative of bards, and yet here he was, still on the road, still chasing down ghosts from his past.

He couldn't help but notice how tired the eyes of the face in the reflection looked, staring back at him dully; his nose had been broken several times – on the field of battle and the occasional bar room brawl – and no longer had the slender elegance that spoke of his noble birth. Not that it really mattered since he had foresworn his inheritance when he had first joined the holy orders. The lines on his face made him appear older than his forty-some-odd years – he had to admit, he couldn't really remember how old he was anymore – might it be fifty already? That's what the solitude if his recent lifestyle had left him with: days blurring into weeks, into months, fighting when he found the right cause, and enjoying the peace that came in the moments in between.

Drawing a small, curved dagger from his pouch, he briefly checked the edge and then began to shave – first removing the patchy, itchy beard that he had grown over many months, and then moving carefully over his head, shaving all of his hair until the face looking back at him in the window was smooth, clean, and bald. Cleaning the blade before returning it to its sheath, he carried the candle over to the bedside table, tested the straw of the mattress – grateful to find it fresh – and made his final preparations.

Sliding the small bed into the corner of the room, he drew his great sword and laid the blade out on the floor beside the frame of the bed. A second, shorter blade was removed from his pack and placed between the straw mattress and the wall. And lastly, he took his dagger again from its' sheath and stuck it in the wooden frame of the small window at the head of the bed – all three blades within easy reach. Satisfied, he blew out the candle and retired for what he hoped would be the first good night's sleep in a long while.

Waking with the sunrise, he spoke briefly with the owner about the arrangements for his horse and belongings, paying a few extra coin in advance in case his business kept him longer than expected. He then set out only to walk the rest of the way to Mercurum, leaving the innkeeper waving happily from the gate until he disappeared out of sight down the road.

With long, quick strides, he moved quickly the last few miles from the inn to Mercurum – he carried himself with a confidence and purpose that added to his presence. He knew this, and it had helped him avoid problems on more than one occasion during his travels. The more experienced highwaymen along the way knew an easy mark when they saw one, and they also knew when to let the ones go by that were more trouble than they were worth. The less experienced robbers, who saw everyone passing by as a chance to make some easy coin, did not usually live to learn from their experience if they came across his path.

Still, he kept a wary eye on his surroundings as he made his way into town, feeling somewhat exposed after having left everything useful – including his blades – back at the inn.

The road to town was open, except for some slow-moving wagons, pulled by near-skeletal oxen, as a few farmers made their way from their homesteads to the city, hoping to find some solace from the famine and drought of the past year. He would look into the covered opening of the wagons as he passed them by, striding faster than the burdened beasts pulling the carts, and see only hollow, empty eyes in the faces staring back at him. They did not travel with hope, just desperation. Some, he could sense, travelled with even greater burdens, and he kept an even wider berth of those.

He reached the north side of the city by early afternoon. He was greeted by a sparse dotting of houses across the fields, which gradually grew denser and closer together as he walked on – they had no natural enemies, he gathered, as it was not a walled city. There were guards scattered along the road, but he took these to be in the employ of the merchant houses, as they paid little attention to who came and went on the road in front of them and seemed only to care if someone gazed a little too long at whatever building they were posted in front of.

It was a hot day, and so he found a tavern to quench his thirst and fill his stomach one last time. There were more than a few establishments to choose from, though none seemed different than the others, so he chose one with a good view of the street.

The entire trip was unusually quiet for him – the people on the streets were somber, and he only drew a few sideways glances from the early patrons at the tavern. It seemed like everyone was either tired, desperate, or fearful, as if waiting for something bad to happen, but they did not know what, or from where it would come. From where he sat, he wondered what they could be expecting that could possibly be worse than how things currently appeared to be.

Passing the hottest hours of the day at the tavern, he stepped out again into the main thoroughfare as the afternoon was ending and the sun was fading to the horizon, and, drawing the hood of his robe over his head, made his way across the bridge and into the city proper. This part of the town was walled, and on the far side of the bridge, a wide gatehouse stood across the road. The gates were open now, and people streamed in & out, busier here than in the outlying parts of town. They would draw the gate when night fell, once the evening mass was finished, and folks would settle in for the night in their respective neighbourhoods or be forced to seek some temporary accommodation until dawn the next morning, when the morning crows would herald the rising of the sun and the city would breathe back to life again.

Little more than a small island in a wide river, the heart of Mercurum was surrounded by water on all sides, and from the riverbank arose a solid stone wall, at least two heads high in most places, broken only by four gatehouses – north, south, east and west. This is where the four bridges, one to each of the town quarters, arched across the river, a marvel of stonework and engineering, allowing access to and from the heart of the city. Within the shadow of his hood, he nodded to the guards as he passed, who gave him little regard as he passed as just one more of the congregation heading to mass.

Weaving through the midday crowds, he only stopped briefly inside the gates to gaze up at the whitewashed stucco and brick construction that now loomed close around him. The buildings here were grander, more sturdy, and while they felt close and larger than the outer part of town, each was a distinct property, with many having walled yards, fences, and space between each building, the sort of space that could only be afforded by the most affluent citizens. Gazing between the structures, it only took a moment for him to spot the bell towers of the church before he dropped his head again and resumed his steady walking pace.

The island city had a slight rise to all the streets, ultimately leading travelers from any direction toward the keep that occupied the center of the island. Within another wall, the keep housed the Ispan's manor, a barracks, stables, granaries, several larger homes for members of the Council, and the Cathedral that drew the faithful to their prayers. Here the streets were entirely cobbled, with much less mud and effluence in the gutters. Every so often in the road, he could spot a small iron grate covering an opening, often no bigger than his hand – drainage holes, where the steady stream of sewage from the street flowed down beneath the road.

He had been blending with the earliest members of the congregation as they processed through the streets to the Cathedral, but he broke away from the crowd as they neared the final turn that would have brought them to the main entrance. Moving hurriedly, but trying not to attract attention, he worked his way around some of the side streets to the rear of the small basilica. He checked behind him to make sure he was not being followed and tried his best to stay to the darkest part of the laneway.

Reaching a series of doors that he guessed would be the rear entrance of the rectory, he slowed his steps and began looking at things more carefully.

Finally, he stopped at the third door and knocked.

"Si vindictam…" called a voice from behind the door, speaking the language of the Imperium. Imposed by the conquerors when they brought their religion to the Avar temples, the foreign tongue was but one more way in which they sought to sink their claws into the culture of the lands they conquered. But Shagron had always been a servant of Ukko, and he knew well the words to speak.

"…fodere duo sepulchra," he replied, his low voice scraping out the words like logs being dragged across a gravel road.

"Meridionalis gallerie," said the voice behind the door – two quick words then nothing more.

He nodded at the reply, turned, and began walking back towards the gathering crowd of worshippers lining up to enter the grand temple through the three arched portals that had been flung open wide to admit the faithful. Heavy timbered doors flanked each opening, with only the ornate carvings of saints & legends between the broad iron bands detracting from the fact that they would have seemed more at home on a fortress than a place of prayer and worship.

In truth, it was called a cathedral by the local faithful, but to the more travelled eye, it did not quite measure up to the size one would expect of the name. It had the same layout as he had seen in other, larger city-states, and certainly was the largest house of worship in Mercurum, but the scale and grandeur reflected the limits of the wealth of the local congregation. Rejoining the flow of people in the square in front of the church, he circled out wide, choosing not to enter by the West Entrance.

From this vantage, he could see the entire façade – the main doors, the scaled down lancets, framing the finely sculpted figures of… well, he didn't know who they were, but they were finely sculpted. A small rose-window was centered between two towers – in all barely two spans high – from which the bell spires rose just another span higher. They might have been taller in a wealthier town, and the towers had an unfinished look to them that made it seem like the architect had grander visions than the Archbishop's coffers, and so construction had been halted prematurely when the funding dried up. The other tale entertained by the faithful pitted the willfulness of the previous Ispan against the piety of the Archbishop, as the additions to the old temple structure threatened to overshadow the Ispan's keep.

There were other rumours, and so it would be safe to say that no one knew precisely what had put an end to that rivalry, but the work on the cathedral towers slowed and then halted shortly after the last Ispan's keep had mysteriously burned to the ground. The rebuilt keep now rose where its predecessor had stood, and like some kind of stalemate, its highest turrets matched the cathedral towers in height, except for the belfry.

The bells had been ringing the call to worship, and the echoes of the last rings were just beginning to fade out over the city. He continued to circle the square to his right, and, proceeding down the length of the building, worked his way over to the South Entrance doors, where it seemed the monks and other clergy were entering. Lowering his cowl, his cleanly shaved head blended with the other monks, to whom he nodded in silence, and dropped his eyes to the ground to avoid encouraging any other contact. Stepping up the few stairs to the entrance, he was relieved to find the doorway unguarded, as he had hoped – while guards at the West Entrance watched people closely for any who sought to enter carrying weapons, this was not a concern among the clergy.

As he entered from the last light of the day into the dark interior, it took a moment for his eyes to adjust to the light, and he stepped to his left to move out of the flow and paused to get his bearings.

A low hum of chanting reverberated around the interior, emanating from a small group of monks occupying the choir. It was time for evening prayers, and so the large stained-glass windows shed no light into the interior of the building. Instead, a series of round chandeliers hoisted below the vaulted ceilings shed candlelight throughout the interior, lending a soft, warm yellow tint to all of the stonework. Here it became much more apparent that the interior of the structure was something older and much more ancient than the sculpted exterior. It was lost to the lore of the region as to just how old the church truly was, and whether there was even a town in the location before the church was built here.

It was said to be a place of ancient power, with foundations that ran deep into the earth. Some said it had been a druid temple, but most did not believe that – the druids did not care for such man-made displays of arrogance over nature, preferring instead to carry out their ceremonies in more natural settings. A hundred years before was the earliest record any had of its use, and the gods that were honoured within – those gods were gone now, replaced by the idols of the Imperium and the worshipful practices they had brought with them as conquerors.

Through all the changes, the church itself grew in power as the population grew – as people returned to the cities once order was restored and they became comfortable with life under the Imperium, the city flourished again, and so did the coffers of the church reflect the new wealth of the new merchant classes. And so the ancient temple received a facelift, and the new Archbishop discovered the strength to build to new heights – which is where the dispute with the Ispan began.

There were no pews within the church, for it had been deemed beneficial for worshippers to stand during the service – with the longer sermons, this helped reduce the tendency for the less entertained to drift off during prayers. Two rows of columns flanked the west doors, and ran the length of the nave, past the transepts where he had entered, and through the choir, right up to the grand altar. Directly in front of him, where the nave intersected with the transept, he could see the Common Altar, where the cleric would conduct the evening prayers.

Today's service was not a high mass, so the Grand Altar would not be in use, and there would be few nobles attending in the choir. The people would congregate in the nave, and much of the church would be empty forward of the transepts. Looking back to his left, against the wall, just beside the door where he had entered, he could see a guard standing by the stairway leading up to the south gallery. Again, as many of the richer citizens and nobility could afford to pay their tithes, they often did not feel the need to attend every prayer service, and so the galleries on the second level, on both the north and south sides of the nave, were often closed for most events except the high masses.

The guard inside the door looked bored with his routine, and if he had ever hoped to see action, he was about to get his wish. Looking fully the part of a monk or clergyman, he walked directly up to the guard, and speaking with surety, commanded him:

"Brother, the guards at the West Entrance have asked for your help. It seems some of the peasants may have some sort of plague or disease, and they need help dispersing the crowd. Go, please, and help them."

The guard, collecting himself after being shocked out of his reverie, did not look very closely at who he was speaking with – in truth, one bald monk looks much like another, and he didn't know them all – but he did hear that he was needed, that there was work to be done, and he quickly hurried off to do as he was told. He was trained to follow orders, and sometimes it was hard to really know who was in charge…

As the guard sped away down the nave, he glanced to see if anyone was watching, and quickly darted up the winding stone staircase to the gallery. Out of view after just a few steps, even if anyone had seen him, he doubted anyone would have any reason to question a monk going up the stairs. Reaching the top, he paused and took another moment to survey the surroundings.

The south gallery ran the length of the church from the west entrance to the transept, with a small break, before continuing along the length of the choir, stopping near the grand altar. A similar gallery ran along the north side. There were two rows of pews, the second slightly higher than the first, to allow the best view of the proceedings during the mass. The view was obstructed only in a few spots by the columns he had seen from the ground, which supported the entire ceiling.

He quietly moved a short distance down the gallery, to where he could have a good view of the common altar – he could see the ornately carved chairs that the clerics would be seated in during the service and observe most of the crowd that would be gathered in the nave. He crouched low to avoid being seen and moved closer to the nearest column. Shifting to a position on one knee, he felt something when he extended his foot back under the pew. Reaching back, he felt around briefly, and smiled as he found what he was looking for, and gently pulled it out and placed it beside him on the floor.

It was a small package, wrapped in a lightly oiled burlap cloth and tied with string. Pulling the string to open it, he pulled back the wrapping to reveal a delicate, finely crafted crossbow, and a single metal quarrel. It was not the largest crossbow he had ever seen, nor was it the smallest, and the length of the wooden stock was decorated with runes and carvings that gave off an aura of power – runes that gave it a name in an ancient language. He could not read it, but he knew what it was – it must have cost someone a great deal to have obtained this weapon and would have been hidden here at great risk. It was a weapon that would kill, and he handled it carefully as he pulled back the wire, bending the metal bow into a tight arc, and locking it in place. He placed the quarrel gently in the groove, nocked against the string, again noting that the small metal shaft had similar rune markings running its length.

The echoing chants had now stopped, and the clerics had finished their procession to the small altar. Kneeling below the low wall of the gallery, he closed his eyes and waited. The silence drifted over him like a wave and unwelcome memories pulled him back into the darkness – he had spent a long time wandering in darkness, and it had eventually set him on his current path. A path which sometimes gave him cause to wonder: was this, now, his true calling? Or had his soul been tainted by the darkness he had spent so many years fighting? Was he any better than the prey he hunted anymore? He had come out of the darkness alive, unlike most of those who had gone in with him. Now it followed him. He did not seek it out, but he could see it all around him, and he could never find it in his heart to turn away when he saw a shadow taint the world.

Then he heard the first drumbeat.

Slowly at first, then followed by a second drum, the heavy, pounding rhythm echoed off the high walls and arched ceiling, an entrancing pulse that even the flames of the candles throughout the cathedral seemed to flicker in harmony. The entrance procession had begun.

Focusing his thoughts again, he put away the past and reminded himself of where he was in the present. He concentrated on the layout of the building, the flow of the people into the nave, the transept, the common altar, the choir. He pictured the faces, heights, hair colours, clothes – merchants and wealthy citizens to the front, then common townsfolk, farmers and peasants; the clerics seated at the left side of the altar – the grand chair, empty, flanked by the two smaller ones occupied by the priests, and behind them, the lay people and acolytes; the young servers standing motionless to each side of the altar, holding large painted candles – all swaying to the beating of the drums. With his eyes still closed, he moved his head, back and forth behind the low wall of the gallery, as if he could see through it all.

Concentrating, the picture in his mind shifted from the life-like picture of his memory to a colour-shift of light blue hues, which adorned and flowed around each figure. With so many assembled together, the entire image in his mind became awash in an ocean of calming blue light – all but one.

One figure out of the crowd in his mind was surrounded by a swirling cloud of the deepest black – an oily smoke that seemed to pulse and breathe as it hovered over its source. A single figure, standing apart.

This he held central in his focus. He followed the shape as it moved from the back of the cathedral, marching slowly forward to the beating of the drums, the crowd parting to make way, as it continued directly up to the altar, pausing briefly before turning left and proceeding to the grand chair between the clerics.

There was a small murmur from the assembled crowd as the figure slowly sat in the center chair. The cleric to his left rose and moved to the altar to commence the evening prayers.

Focusing now on nothing other than the swirling black smoke, he began to see glimpses – shapes and forms, in obscene positions; tears of pain; a sadistic smile – glimpses of evil. Unseen behind the rail of the gallery, his mouth twisted into a grimace as he felt the pain, yet also the satisfaction of knowing with certainty that his purpose now was true. He took a deep breath and held it, and whispered to no one but himself:

"Ukko, sed tantum dic verbo, et sanabitur anima mea."

In that moment, the beating drums went silent, the chanting ceased, and in one smooth motion he rose and swung his arm up to rest the small crossbow on the rail of the low wall – not once opening his eyes – taking aim at the center of the blackness in his mind and pulled the trigger.

In the quiet of the cathedral, with the chants and drumming still echoing faintly in the highest corners of the vaulted ceilings, the click of the trigger releasing was heard by all, followed by the rush of the taut bow line scraping rapidly across the neck of the stock as the energy of the metal bow flung the metal bolt into the air with a vibrato hum.

The bolt lodged itself deep in the neck of the victim, penetrating through and into the heavy wood of the chair, pinning his head upright in the seat. His jaw slowly opened, and blood ran out and down his chin, staining his robes, as his eyes darted briefly back & forth, not comprehending what had happened, even as his life flowed out of him. He never saw the shadowy figure peering down from the gallery as darkness crept in and his vision faded, his eyelids slowly drooped, and the shadows claimed him forever.

There was a moment of disbelief in the church before the horrified screams of the clerics and parishioners rent the air. Some stood in shock as others ran for the doors, while a few scoured the surroundings for the origin of the deadly bolt. Some pointed correctly to the gallery, while others followed the imagined arc to other parts of the cathedral – it would take a few moments before anyone could get their bearings on where to search for the assassin.

Still hidden by the shadows in the gallery, the marksman opened his eyes slowly as the first screams began to echo in the halls, and he could see the lifeless body of the Archbishop of Mercurum pinned upright in his chair, surrounded by a crowd of confused lay people and clergy, scrambling about aimlessly in panic. Watching the scene for a moment before he had to leave his perch, he locked eyes for a moment with the now lifeless corpse, and he swore he could hear the voice of patriarch echoing off the vaulted ceilings, crying out his name in rage!

He did not pause long to survey his handiwork, nor did he seem terribly surprised by the target. He had learned to trust his aim, and his sense of right and wrong.

He slipped the crossbow around his back, tightening the short strap to secure it in place, and then moved to exit the gallery. Turning back towards the stairs, he could see guards below moving in the same direction through the transept. Moving up to the second row of pews, he looked directly down the row and broke into a run. When he reached the end of the gallery, he stepped up on the end-rail with his last stride and launched himself into the air.

He carried the ten-foot span of the transept that split the gallery at the second floor, catching the far rail and pulling himself up into the choir gallery. The pounding footsteps on the wooden stairs signaled the approach of guards to his rear – they would have to either risk the same jump or go back down the stairs and follow along on the floor to the back of the cathedral, where the second stairway led down from the choir to the rectory.

He was glad in some ways that this was a smaller cathedral than typical, or his options would have been a lot more limited.

He slid through a doorway and ran down the stairs as he heard the clamour of swords and armor as more guards were closing in. Running into the rectory, he darted down a hallway that curved to the left around the rear of the cathedral, taking him out of sight as he raced to escape.

*****Caspar*****

Until just a moment ago, Caspar was having a good day.

As Guard Captain, his days were usually quite uneventful, and he very much enjoyed the comfort and security his role brought him. And he truly felt bad that some of the first thoughts running through his head the instant he saw the first blood spray from the archbishop's neck, included a great realization that he would likely be out of work tomorrow – unemployed at best, presuming he was not tied to a post and burned alive for failure in his duties!

Years of training helped him to assess and take charge of the situation – after all, he had a great career in the military before he moved to the temple guard – enough of that – focus, he told himself.

He directed the guards to lock the doors, and secure the people inside the cathedral, to keep the assassin penned in. This was followed by ordering more guards to each of the gallery staircases, to secure the high ground, as the most likely vantage point the shot could have come from. The time would come later to see how anyone had slipped past the guards he had stationed there earlier in the evening, to keep the gallery empty of any potential threats.

He must admit, even he hadn't really taken many of these precautions seriously… it was inconceivable that anyone would have sought to harm the Archbishop, let alone hire an assassin – they were prepared for scared mobs, crowds eager to touch the hem of his robe, and maybe the occasionally over-aggressive relic seeker. Several of his men were on the brink of tears at the shock of this, and he had to snap them out of it, and get them to their duties. He shouted orders for the bells to be rung, to raise the alarm, and two of them snapped to attention, nodded curtly and ran off to carry out his instructions.

Under his breath he mumbled a curse about the poor lighting that inherently came with the evening masses – the candles hung from the ceiling did little more than cast long shadows from the stone columns among the pews of the gallery, and the wall sconces in the nave flickered and flitted with every passing guard and citizen, making it hard to see any motion in the shadows.

Someone alerted him to a shape moving across the gap between the galleries, across the transept from the nave to the choir – an incredible leap, he thought to himself – but he quickly moved to chase his quarry. He ordered men to the stairs at the far end of the gallery, near the small chapels, to block any escape.

Reaching the stairs, a moment behind his men, he found them poised and ready at the base of the stairs, waiting for the assassin to come to them, and it was only by chance when he arrived that he caught a glimpse over their shoulders of something down the hallway to his left moving towards the rectory.

He led the charge himself from there, following the bend in the corridor, past several doors and into the meal hall, and then... nothing.

The hall was empty. The kitchens were quiet, having finished cleaning up from the earlier dinner, and the floors were still wet from the mops of the cleaners who had finished and retreated to their chambers.

Their quarry did not have much of a lead on them and could not have crossed the hall before they broke into the room. Nevertheless, he sent two guards on ahead to check, and then turned the rest of his men to double back and start checking doors.

The first two were locked, but the third was answered with a muffled response, followed by turning of the lock and lifting of the latch. He was greeted by the calm and composed visage of the Bishop of Ukko.

"Your Grace!" he blurted in surprise.

"Yes, my son," replied the older man who opened the door, "what do you need of me?" he asked.

"Your Grace?" Caspar was caught off guard, not realizing that in all the commotion, the second-in-command of the church probably had not heard what had just happened.

"Oh..." he gasped, catching his breath after their brief run, "Your Grace, something terrible has happened! The Archbishop is d-dead – assassinated!"

"What?" exclaimed the elder churchman. "How did this happen?" he asked incredulously.

"It was an assas–" Caspar started to say, when he was cut off by the older man.

"This is terrible," said the Bishop, "I must convene the Council of Elders immediately. We need to ensure succession, and..."

"Your Grace!" Caspar interrupted politely but forcefully, "we are hunting the murderer, and lost him between the gallery, the rectory and the feast hall. We are searching every chamber for the fiend, and..."

"...and what?" the Bishop asked, "He's not in here! Obviously! Go on, get on with your duties, and see if you can salvage anything from this tragedy. I must convene the council. Be gone, I need to dress and be on my way as quickly as possible..."

He closed the door abruptly, and Caspar felt his shoulders drop as his tension eased for a moment. He turned to his remaining men and sent them off to continue the search, and, turning neatly on his heel, he headed back to the cathedral to prepare for a reckoning that he was sure he would not look forward to...

The Bishop closed the door and reset the lock, turning again to his modest chamber – one of the few perks of his position was that he was entitled to forgo the modesty of his order and require a chamber that was more suited to his station. This afforded him a more comfortable bed, a writing desk, and a few comfortable chairs for greeting guests. There was no window, but he was provided with a small ante room, fitted with a wash basin, wardrobe, and lavatory, for his personal grooming. His back to the door, he waited as the tall figure emerged from the side room, drying his face with the small towel, then wiping dry the smooth sheen of his bald head.

"Well, Shagron," said the Bishop, "it seems you have proven effective yet again at accomplishing any task set before you."

Shagron said nothing and his expression remained blank.

"Did you have any problems getting in," asked the Bishop, "or finding the weapon?"

Shagron shook his head from side to side. "The lines were long – I suspect more than a few of the townsfolk may have the plague, so I kept clear of the West Entrance and entered with the holy orders. You may want to be careful about shaking hands with the faithful for the next little while."

"Ah, yes, I had heard about the sickness reaching the town earlier – I think we have taken steps to take care of that even as we speak," the Bishop noted. "You may want to leave the bow behind – it has certain blessings upon it that, well, made it very effective for the task at hand today, but would make it quite useless to you otherwise..."

"Not to worry," said Shagron, turning to the fireplace, where a healthy fire was burning. "It's already taken care of." He was looking at the glowing embers that still held the shape of the stock of the small crossbow sitting in the center of the flames. As if it knew they were talking about it, the metal bow rolled, crushing the ashen shape of the handle and sending sparks up the flue. "You would be wise to remove the metal of the bow and dispose of it before your chambermaid discovers it. We wouldn't want any traces leading back to you..."

"You look quite unconcerned about all the commotion," the Bishop noted. "I had hoped this could all have been done more discreetly, but I suppose you were right in your assessment – the people will need to see what happened, to truly believe that this wasn't something political within the church…"

Nodding, Shagron spoke, "You didn't summon me to this task for your personal gain, so we shouldn't let anyone think you had any reason to be involved. I will bear the honour and the blame…"

"…if they catch you," added the Bishop. "As we agreed, this needed to be done, for the sake of everyone he had harmed, and would harm, and I am ashamed that I could not do it myself. And you know that I will never be able to repay you for your sacrifice, should you be caught."

He moved over to his wardrobe and began to pull out his ceremonial robe and stole. "But as we planned, if you make your escape, none will truly know who did the act anyway, and you will be free to carry on with your business and your travels."

Shagron nodded again. "I could sense the truth of everything you told me and have no doubt that we acted for the greater good in this. I will carry this to my grave – whether that come tonight, tomorrow, next week or next year – knowing the righteousness of the truth in my heart. That is enough for me."

Finishing with dressing in his vestments, the Bishop poured two small glasses of wine, and handed one to Shagron.

Raising the glass, he said, "He will harm no one again. The blessing of the temple be upon you, Shagron, Holy Warrior of Ukko." They both drank and set the glasses aside.

"Wait until I have left, and when the way is clear, I will send Brother Ralof to guide you out of the city – he knows the backstreets that will lead you to the main road north, to get you out of town quickly and unseen. I will draw most of the temple guards with me as escort to the Ispan's keep when I go to meet with the church elders, which should keep things clear for your departure."

He held up his right hand as he finished speaking, emphasizing the bright ruby ring that adorned the knuckle of his thumb, capping the closed fist of his hand. Recognizing the gesture, Shagron slowly rose and moved to kiss the ring of the Bishop before he turned around to leave.

Moving to the door, he hesitated and asked: "Where will you go now? It will not take long for word to spread – if they have any description at all, it will be hard for someone of your stature to blend in on the road. The faithful, not knowing the true service you have done for Ukko today, will always be suspicious…"

Shagron simply shrugged and looked to the fire.

"I have been pursued my whole life. I will abide as I always do, and it would be best if you did not know where."

Sensing the question on the Bishop's tongue, he added, "If you have need of me again, trust that Ukko will share your prayers with me, and I will come wherever I am needed."

Shagron watched as the Bishop – soon to be the new Archbishop – nodded slowly, turned, and left the room. He locked the door behind him and sat down to wait, stirring the fire with the poker as he stared into the flames.

*****Cleansing*****

Torick watched as Omar disappeared into the darkness, and slowly wheeled his horse around to face the door to the courtyard. He took a final look up at the tower, rolled his head and loosened his shoulders.

Holding the reins in his right hand, he held out his left hand, palm up, lifted it to his mouth, and blew softly. A small golden light flared to life in his palm, glowing like a spark from a campfire, and slowly floated up, catching the breeze. The wind grew, and carried the ember over the stone wall, where it drifted over the open courtyard, swirling, rising, then dropping, down to the stables.

Pausing briefly, the wind seemed to stop entirely, and the spark dropped like a stone, into the center of a neatly arranged pile of hay. Then the wind picked up again, this time stronger, fanning the ember and sparking it to flame. Harder yet the wind grew, and the torches in the courtyard fluttered and flared, sending more embers upwards into the night as the heat from the now blazing stable made the smoke and flames swirl in a vortex of heat.

Turning once more, Torick touched his heels gently to the horse's flank and started to move at a casual walking pace. When he reached the main street, where Omar turned right, he turned left. The streets were mostly empty, and aside from a few tavern goers, and one or two unsavoury sorts, his path to the edge of town was unimpeded. The southerly wind billowed his cloak, and flared in the nostrils of his horse, striking an altogether unwelcome image, framed in the night by the growing orange glow coming from the area of the tower.

Just then, a flash of lightning arced across the sky, startling both Torick and his horse, and he felt a tightening in his chest that made him wince unexpectedly. He clutched at his jerkin and drew in a sharp breath – he wasn't sure what pain this was, but he swallowed hard and focused on controlling his horse, which had reared now, almost throwing him.

He grabbed the reins with both hands and yelled loudly for her to settle –

undoubtedly it only added to the dreadful image he cast to anyone who dared to peek out their windows, but he had to admit that it surprised him – coming up suddenly in the darkness, he hadn't noticed the recent change in the weather – certainly nothing so severe as to bring lightning. After the drought, he doubted any sudden storm would truly bring enough rain to alter his plans, and then he also realized: he was running through all these thoughts in his head as he knew he was waiting for the crash of thunder that would almost certainly follow such a brilliant flash, yet nothing came. He arched his eyebrow at the realization, then let the question go.

He had put a plan into motion, and the weather would not change it. Still, he thought to himself, as he spurred his horse forward along his route, he hated surprises.

Behind him, in the night sky, the flames grew, and the embers rose, flared by the growing winds, and soon the flames were fanned into an inferno. After a long hot summer with no rain, drought, and farms turning to dust, the market quarter was little more than a tinderbox of kindling. It quickly began to spread, and as each house, home, hovel, and shack in the market quarter were like one continuous chain, so they all began to burn.

As he rode through the street, he could hear the bells of the church from the city center ringing, calling the faithful to evening prayer. Echoing on the wind, the bells mingled with the first cries of alarm, slowing any chance the townsfolk might have had of waking in time to get ahead of the blaze and keeping it from spreading. Instead, fed by the dry winds, the tinderbox caught, and the fate of the market quarter was sealed.

Some would awaken in time to run, some would choke on the smoke as they slept, their last moments lost in fitful dreams of choking horror. Others would be too ill to do anything but watch the world around them descend into flame and agony. Some who were quick enough to flee would recount how the flames seemed to always be ahead of them, spreading fastest around the outer ring of the quarter, narrowing their chances of escape before turning inward to consume the ripe kindling that made up the many homes and shops. A few might manage to save themselves, but that was always the way of the world, he believed – the strong survived; the weak… well, they were weak.

He looked to the side of the road just then and saw a young girl, no more than twelve, wearing a plain sack-cloth dress, her blonde hair hanging in matted strands down around her shoulders, watching him pass by on horseback. Pulling back on the reins, he paused as she held his gaze, staring at him almost expressionless.

"You had best make for the river, little one, it's going to get very dangerous here very quickly." She did not seem to alter her gaze at all, but he immediately felt better for having given her a fair warning. *'After all,'* he thought to himself, *'I'm not a monster...'* as he spurred his horse and continued on his way.

By the time he had reached the small rise about half a mile outside of the city, Torick stopped to look back on the brightly burning cityscape that lit the horizon. The fire would likely not jump the river, but it had already touched the entire quarter. The alarm was raised across the city, but there would be nothing they could do but let the blaze consume the quarter. Consume and cleanse.

He turned again to the road, double checked the large pouch of coins at his belt, and wondered if the Ispan would ever agree to 'payment-in-advance' for anything ever again...

******Shagron*****

Several hours had passed, time Shagron had spent in prayer while waiting for Brother Ralof to return. He saw it as something of a courtesy, to respect the Bishop's offer to help him exit the city unnoticed – he was fairly confident he could have found his own way out, yet at the same time, the extra help might help him avoid any unwanted encounters on the way, which also meant avoiding unnecessary blood being shed.

He had no grudge against any of the temple guards or the Ispan's personal retainers; he had been invited here to handle a specific task – meting out justice to a pretender, and as a sworn defender of the faith, he was honoured to do his duty – but now that was done, and while it was important that he find a way to leave and continue his good works, he would rather not have to kill soldiers merely doing *their* duty.

When the knock at the door finally came, he finished his prayers and stood. Moving slowly to the door, he waited and listened.

"M'lord, it is I, Brother Ralof," he announced from the hallway, trying to keep his voice to a low whisper. "It is time to depart."

Shagron unlocked the door and opened it a crack, checking to see that Ralof had come alone. Seeing that he had, he opened to door wider and ushered him in.

"Ah, m'lord, you are here... good!" Brother Ralof expressed with relief as he entered the room and Shagron closed the door behind him quickly, locking it. "I had knocked several times and was beginning to worry!" Drawing a cloth from his belt, he dabbed the sweat from his brow, clearly seeming a bit nervous.

Brother Ralof was older than either Shagron or the Bishop – correction, Archbishop now – but was of slighter build. He definitely gave the appearance of being very fit for his age, particularly when lending his aid to the Archbishop, who seemed much frailer by comparison and always kept Ralof or one of the other members of his order close by for assistance.

Shagron did not know how long he had been a man of faith, but he guessed from his attention to fitness that he had pursued other interests before taking up the holy orders. Now in his later years, he still stood straight and tall, although was also very adept at standing back humbly and letting others take the spotlight. He wore his age in the lines on his face and the fading wisps of hair on the top of his head – the remaining hair around the sides and down his well-groomed beard were stark white as well, giving the casual observer the impression that he would be too old to be worth a second look – but his eyes were another matter. One look in his eyes, and it was unmistakable that he had seem and done much in his years and was as sharp with his wits today as he ever was.

Right now, though, he looked concerned, as if uncertain about something.

"My apologies, good brother, if I did not hear your knocking at first," Shagron answered, "I was deep in prayer, seeking affirmation of the path we are following."

Ralof's eyes darted to the door at the mention of the path they were to follow, and he seemed to want to hurry even more.

"We definitely must be on our way quickly. There has been a great deal of commotion after this evening's... 'events'... and we have a very limited window to get you to safety unnoticed."

Shagron nodded and started to move back to the door.

"No, no," Ralof interrupted, "we will go this way." Waving Shagron back to the other side of the room, Ralof began to fumble with the books on the small wall shelf, and with a click of some hidden trigger, he pushed against the bookcase and slid it back, revealing a hidden passage behind the wall. He moved through the small, low doorway first, ushering Shagron to follow. Shagron made to follow but stopped at the doorway. He looked back at the room, struck by a strange feeling that he was forgetting something.

His eyes settled on the hearth, where the earlier fire had long since burned out. To Ralof's dismay Shagron stepped back into the room and moved to the fireplace, where he poked about the cold ashes for a moment before lifting out a strange metal shape which he quickly tucked into a cloth and slipped into his tunic. He then turned and rejoined the aged cleric in the dark passage and closed the door behind them.

There was a small brazier on the wall with a few coals still smoldering in a faint orange glow. Ralof picked up an oily torch from a small canister on the floor and, breathing some life into the coals, lit the torch to light their way down the small, cramped passage. After a few turns, they took a ladder down, following a slightly larger tunnel that curved in a wide circle, which Shagron was certain was continuing to descend. By his guess, they were well below the height of the small hill that was the perch for the central core of the city.

Following the curve of the path, he did not feel that they had made much distance away from the base of the cathedral – a feeling which was confirmed when he saw that they were passing several side passages that led to rows of catacombs containing the solemnly interred remains of numerous members of the nobility and clergy. They reached another set of stairs and Shagron could now see an increasing amount of moisture and mossy growth on the walls of the tunnels – they must be close to the river now. Surprisingly, their path began to widen out into a larger passage.

When Ralof stopped to exchange his waning brand for a fresh torch, Shagron grabbed one for himself as well, and now, with the improved lighting, he could make out more detail of his surroundings. It was man-made, but old – older than any style he had seen – and covered with markings and mouldy murals that depicted a time beyond his recollection. The plaster was cracked and peeling, the colours were fading and battling against the black mould that was creeping ever further into the designs, making the depictions difficult to see completely.

Nevertheless, Shagron could see now that the tales he had heard over the years were true: Mercurum was a city built upon a city, built upon a city – no one was really sure how many times the city had risen, then fallen, but it had been told that it was a city of miracles, surviving floods, fires, earthquakes, storms and almost every natural disaster ever known to have been visited upon these lands by the gods. Each time, it was rebuilt, on the ruins of what had come before. Each generation of labourers and designers decided how much they would keep or bury of what had come before – although some of these cataclysms made that choice for them.

In this particular case, it seemed clear that these structures had somehow been sunk into the earth – perhaps an earthquake, or sinkhole, he would never know – and now it was being inhabited again by citizens of Mercurum.

He was surprised the first time he saw a pair of eyes reflecting back at him in the darkness, the flickering flame of the torches shining back at him as twin flames of red. After the first retreated, he began to see others, less shy and more curious.

"They are some of the less desirable citizens of Mercurum," Ralof explained, seeing the unasked question in Shagron's eyes. "They have sought out relief from their condition in the dark places that the city-watch and temple guards no longer take the time to patrol, and where no one else simply cares to go. Relatives no longer even venture into the crypts to pay their respects to their forefathers — they find it much easier to just pay the church for a mass than to risk getting their feet wet in these tunnels."

They were beginning to see more people now as they continued on their way. Most were dressed in the rags and cast-offs that they could beg, borrow, or steal from the city above, although Shagron was careful to note that there were several unsavoury types who seemed rather well equipped compared to their peers. Well-oiled leather, dark cloaks – good for blending in with the shadows – and carrying an assortment of knives and other weapons that all seemed to be in rather good condition, as if well used and cared for. The military training learned in his order made it easy for him to spot these men – and women – who hung back from those who were now closing in to greet brother Ralof.

Ralof had stopped now and was handing out some small packets – which he presumed were food, or some other necessity – and the people were thanking him by name. Clearly, he was not a stranger to this part of the city, which Shagron made a mental note to inquire about further – once they were safely away from the city.

When he was finished, Ralof resumed their march, leaving the open area and taking another tunnel, which Shagron could tell used to be a much broader passageway. Openings that once were windows were now filled with damp earth and roots, spilling into their path and frequently requiring them to reduce their posture almost to crawl on their hands & knees in order to continue on their path.

Shagron did not consider himself to be claustrophobic, having spent a great deal of his early youth adventuring in other underground settings, but he was not expecting this route out of the city, and the shifting nature of the earth and stone here was making him increasingly uncertain of whether or not Brother Ralof was truly leading him out of the city, or perhaps instead he had some other motive.

Almost as if reading his mind, Brother Ralof stopped at the next opening in the passage, where they were again able to stand upright, and spoke to him.

"Let's stop here for a moment and rest," he suggested. "We have been walking for a few hours now, and I'm guessing you have been trying to follow our progress against the path you might have taken through the city above. You might even be thinking that we have been going in circles at times, and that we could have been well away from the city by now, rather than stuck deep beneath it, with you having no idea where you are or what direction to go in next…"

"Well…" Shagron began, before Ralof continued…

"I need to tell you something and I know you may not believe me, but right now, I am saving your life."

"I beg your pardon?"

Ralof was very soothing with his tone, as if he were teaching a class of young schoolchildren.

"I am saving your life."

"Yes," said Shagron, "I heard what you said, I just don't know why you believe this to be the case. I could have chosen any road I liked out of the city; you were just supposed to show me some of the quieter lanes…"

"Every road was being guarded, and the Temple Guards had been doubled around the inner city. The Bishop did not draw them off to protect the council, as he suggested to you. In fact, rather the opposite – he could not tell the council he knew you, but he made plans to ensure you were going to be caught – and not alive."

Ralof paused to look at Shagron, to see if he was keeping up with what he was saying before continuing.

"You came to Mercurum in response to a summons from the Bishop to address an injustice – to remove an infection from the church before it could spread. It was embarrassing that something like this could have happened under the watchful eyes of the council, the clergy, the brotherhood, and the parents, and although many suspected, nothing could be done directly, as it would have appeared very selfish and political for the Bishop to have acted on his own."

"While the Bishop was sincere in appreciating your work, you are a loose end, which he needed to be tied off before he could begin his work in earnest. He did not want to live the rest of his life knowing that someone was out there who knew the truth of how he gained his rank in the church – nor did he want you roaming around, knowing that you were the type of person who would always be willing to kill the Archbishop of your own church if you thought it was the right thing to do." He paused to take a sip of water from his flask and looked over at Shagron again. "You're very intimidating that way, you know?"

Shagron sat silently, listening to everything Ralof was telling him, no longer sure who or what to believe.

"And why are you telling me this, now? Why are you helping me escape your Bishop – damn, Archbishop now, thanks to me. What is your interest in all of this?"

"My interest? My interest is simple: I believe the Bishop is a good man. He may have erred in his judgement on how to handle your role in this matter, but

I believe he did what he needed to do, for the good of the church, as did you."

He shifted his seat on the cold stone, and looked at his hands while he spoke, rubbing the grime from his palms.

"I believe he will do good things as the new Archbishop, and will hopefully help the people find their way again now that the Imperium troops have gone, but I also believe that even good people may do bad things, and so, to help keep everyone on the right path, I think it is good to have people like you in world – people who do not compromise on the difference between right & wrong, good & bad – to help ensure that those who seek to do what is for the good of the people do not start doing wrong things for the right reasons. I admire your courage, to keep to your convictions no matter the cost – I often wish I had your strength…" his voice trailed off for moment, as if considering some other affair in his head, before he returned his attention back to the matter at hand.

"And so, I have broken faith with my master, and decided for myself to lead you out of the city by this route, a much safer route than what the Bishop had in mind for you. I have faith that he will do good things for the people, but I know he will now think twice before considering anything less, knowing you are still out there, watching…"

Ralof smiled as he finished talking and took another long drink from his flask. He offered the flask to Shagron, who leaned forward to take it. It was not a sudden movement, but it was enough to cause the dagger to miss—flying out of the darkness, the deadly missile flew through the open space where his head had been just a moment ago and careened loudly off the rock wall behind them.

Acting on instinct, Shagron continued his forward movement and rolled to the ground from his seat on the rock, narrowing avoiding a second dagger that would have found his chest. Ralof dropped his flask in shock and was just starting to rise to his feet when Shagron, now on the ground, pushed forward and tackled Ralof at the ankles. He dropped suddenly, and again two blades flew out from the darkness and clattered off the rocks, both narrowly missing their target.

Scrambling to find cover, Shagron could hear curses coming from down the tunnel, back the way they had come. He glanced about and saw that the passage offered only one choice.

"Run!" he shouted to Ralof, pushing him to his feet again and urging him down the tunnel. Ralof made to reach for one of the torches.

"Leave it!" Shagron shouted, as he pushed Ralof into a run. Moving forward into the darkness, away from the voices behind them, he himself only paused a moment to grab one of the daggers off the ground before disappearing into the darkness.

Shagron was very much regretting now that he had left his equipment with his horse. He was without his armor, his sword, and pretty much anything else that would be useful in a fight. It was taking a moment for his eyes to adjust to the darkness, after having grown accustomed to the light of the torches – still flickering on the ground behind them, the discarded brands cast a faint glow down the passage that was just enough to save them from crashing headlong into a wall, but then even that faint light went out as their pursuers reached the spot where they had stopped to rest and extinguished the light completely.

As the light went out, Shagron had only a moment to glimpse a small recess to one side of the passage.

He gently pushed Ralof on the shoulder to continue, whispering "Make haste and draw their attention!" Stepping into the alcove, he pressed his back against the cold, wet stone, and waited.

He heard Ralof's leather-soled boots shuffling off down the hallway in the darkness, clearly afraid of tripping, and the good brother began making the oddest noises of pain and confusion as he kept moving away. These faded slowly as he moved further away, and it wasn't long before he could hear footsteps coming up from the direction they had just come. He couldn't tell how many, but they were moving quickly in the darkness, and didn't seem as concerned with masking their noise as with making up ground on their targets.

Waiting until he felt they were right upon him, Shagron crouched and swung his left arm as he spun out of the alcove, guessing his knife to be at stomach-level for anyone passing by. He was close.

He missed with the dagger, but his arm caught the man trotting down the passage directly in the mid-section, knocking the wind out of him. Temporarily stopped in his tracks, the figure bent over gasping for breath. Wrapping his right arm around the man's backside, he repositioned his left arm and plunged the dagger down into his neck above the shoulder. He was rewarded with a clean spray of blood, a groan from the winded man, and a slumping to the ground that made it clear he was no longer a concern.

There was a second man in the passage, but Shagron could not pinpoint where he was in the darkness, having lost track of the sounds in the scuffle. Still with his right arm around the first man's mid-section, he lifted his slumping form up to his side, and carried his body like a shield, pivoting around and stepping backwards until he could feel the cold of the wall to his back.

He felt more than heard the next attack, as the strike of the blade came down on the lifeless body in his arms, missing his head by only inches. He was thankful that the attack was by hand, as he followed it up with a bull-rush in the direction the swing had come from – he caught his attacker in the charge, pushing him back up against the far wall. Relying entirely on brute strength, Shagron pushed against the body of the first dead assassin to pin the second one against the wall as hard as he could, repeatedly thrusting his shoulder into both bodies, before pausing only slightly to let the first body fall to the ground, and then grappling with the second, live attacker – alive but gasping for breath now – opening his stance and wrapping his outstretched arms around whatever was in front of him.

It was a good strategy for finding his opponent in the dark, but it did leave him vulnerable to someone whose eyes were better adjusted to the local environment and able to see that his guard was down as he lunged forward to grapple. It was close quarters, and so there was not much room to pick targets carefully, but his assailant took the opportunity when it was presented and put his dagger to good use as Shagron closed again.

Shagron felt the knife in his side as his arms closed around the mid-section of his opponent. The wound flared like a... well, like a knife in the side – and he clenched his teeth to fight the piercing pain. He also clenched his arms more tightly around his opponent, feeling the warm air on his face as he squeezed the breath from his chest. Pinning his arms at his sides, his attacker could not strike again with the blade, and could only writhe in his arms as he tried to escape Shagron's grip.

But Shagron was a veteran of many wars and had fought many men before. His arms had grown strong from carrying the weight of his sword and shield, and his shoulders were broad and strong, having carried the heavy weight of plate armor into combat for years – his grip was not going to break. Rather the opposite. He continued his clench until the soft leather jerkin his opponent was wearing for protection gave way, and the soft popping of ribs could be heard in the tunnel.

Gasps for breath from the small figure in his arms now became wheezing noises, as broken ribs were pushed deeper, tearing holes into his lungs. When Shagron did release his grip, the body slumped to the ground beside his companion. The wheezing noises became shorter and less frequent until they gradually stopped altogether.

Shagron moved backwards to the far wall, and leaned against the stone to rest, trying to quiet his heavy breathing and listen for any sounds that might indicate more friends were coming to visit. He pressed his hand to his side to feel the shallow wound from the knife and applied pressure. He could hear nothing in the tunnel, but he did start to see a slow brightening of the passage, as a soft light emerged from the other direction, where Ralof had run.

As it got closer, he could make out Brother Ralof returning, holding in has hand a small token of some sort – he could not make out what it was for it was glowing brightly, flooding the passageway with a soft light. Shagron sighed, not sure if he should be relieved or concerned to see the cleric. He watched him closely as he approached, examining the scene. Ralof looked to the bodies, which Shagron could now see for the first time – he recognized one of the men from earlier in the cave.

"Are you here to help them finish the job?" Shagron asked. He was still leaning against the stone, but every muscle was tensed with readiness…

"Help them?" asked Ralof, "I have no idea who they are, or how they knew we would be here." He turned to Shagron, "I have no wish to see you harmed. As I said before – you are our insurance policy against corruption. I would prefer you live a long life, brother!"

Shagron felt a jolt of pain, like lightning shooting through him, and his body convulsed for a moment then relaxed. Still conscious, he slumped to the ground and Ralof rushed forward to look at his wound.

"Easy now," he said. "Let's take care of that cut and get us moving again!"

It took only a few moments for Ralof to quickly clean and bandage the small wound in Shagron's side, warning him that if the bleeding didn't stop quickly, it would mean there was more serious damage inside, and he wouldn't be able to fix it without the benefit of time – which they did not have.

They were just getting ready to restart down the tunnel as the glowing token began to fade, and Ralof lit another torch.

"Nice trick…" said Shagron, nodding towards the now dulled token, which looked like a simple copper coin. "Could've used that earlier, eh?"

"Hmm, what?" Ralof responded absentmindedly, striking a piece of flint against steel to spark the oily torch to life. "Oh, that – that's just for emergencies, and it doesn't last long enough to be of any practical use." He stood up with the fresh torch and turned to carry on down the tunnel. "Handy though, eh?" Shagron grunted as he stood up and followed Ralof down the tunnel, checking over his shoulder more than a few times as they carried on their way.

It was only a few more minutes before they began to hear what sounded like water flowing, and soon stepped out into a small cave that contained a rough stone pier leading to a slowly swirling pool. There was a slow current from under the rocky pier that pulled the water out and towards the far end of the cave, where light was streaming in from outside, and Shagron could hear the murmur of water as it merged with the river. There were two small rowboats tied to the pier, and Ralof moved forward to the closest one and began to step aboard. He quickly fitted the oars to the rings and reached for the rope to cast off. "Quickly now, step aboard," he called over the noise of the water, "we can take the river to put some distance between us and the city, and then choose a road once we are safely away."

Shagron stepped across the gap as the rowboat began to drift away on the current. Ralof steered them out of the cave and past a rusted, twisted gate that once covered the opening to the river – a bygone precaution from one of the city's previous incarnations, hanging off one remaining hinge, creaking in the current as they passed by and out into the river. It was well into the night when they emerged out underneath one of the bridges, and quietly slipped out into the main current. Clear of the tunnel, Ralof slipped the oars into the water and began to steer them along with the stronger current of the river.

Shagron and Ralof looked at the river ahead of them and exchanged curious looks – their forward progress was carrying them out from under the bridge and into a slowly falling rain of glowing embers.

The market quarter was fully engulfed in flames now as the fire that had started a few hours earlier was now completely out of control and was ravenously consuming everything in its path. Ash and embers from the conflagration were being thrown into the air by the wind & heat of the flames, and slowly drifting back across the rest of the city. People had gathered on the bridge and along the city walls to watch the fire consume their city, helpless to stop the blaze which had reached the natural barrier of the river and was looking for any way across. Small brigades of volunteers, armed with buckets and blankets, scurried around the inner city in a panic, chasing every glowing ember that drifted down to earth, attempting to smother and squelch each offspring of the Inferno before it could take on a life of its own and raze the rest of the town.

Witnessing the fire to one side and the city walls to the other – lined with the desperate faces of the recently homeless – all they could do was follow the flow of the river, drifting past the unbelievable panorama of fire and destruction, unable to render comfort or aid even if they could have avoided being arrested immediately. No one noticed them passing by in the night, their silhouettes – low & close to the waterline – cast only the smallest shadows that flickered and danced across the fast-moving waters. Everyone's attention was on the blaze and – remarkably – the resilience of the oldest & largest of the warehouse buildings, which seemed to resist the best efforts of the flames to catch on their ancient beams.

In short order, Ralof & Shagron were clear of the city, and they began to row until they had reached what they thought was a safe enough distance to disembark and continue their trek on foot. Grabbing a pack and a long staff out of the boat, Ralof pushed the empty craft back out into the river, letting the swift current continue to carry it further downriver. Shagron waded ashore and climbed up the mossy embankment to get his bearings.

"So, where to now?" he asked Shagron, settling the pack over his shoulder and leaning on his staff.

Shagron pulled his cloak around his shoulders in the darkness and looked back at Ralof. The glow of the burning city was far off in the distance now, and the only other light came from the near-full moon which cast a pale glow across the countryside and reflected off the bald and slightly oily forehead of Brother Ralof.

"Now…" said Shagron, "now we go get my horse!"

******Jason******

Jason dismounted from his horse and stepped onto the rocks at the edge of the river, dipping his helmet in the cool running water to retrieve a drink. Taking a long mouthful, he wiped his face with some of what remained in the helmet, waking himself up with the coldness of it, and then wiping back a splash of water over his jet-black braided hair. His horse, a chestnut brown mare, pushed forward alongside side him to take a drink as well, nearly pushing him off his perch and into the water.

Moving over to keep his balance and straightening up, he laughed and patted his horse on the neck and ruffled her mane as he steadied himself against the side of the saddle. Although it was sunny and technically still summer, it felt like fall was coming early – the morning air was chill, and the water even colder, and the last thing he wanted to do right now was soak his furs and armor in the cold water of the river.

He was thankful that the oiled leather of his boots kept his feet dry enough as he stepped onto a rock that wasn't quite as mossy and gave him better footing in the shallow water. He had a change of clothes at the camp, but it still wouldn't look good for his men to see their captain slip in the river like a fool child at play. No, he was here on military business, and needed to make sure everything over the few days went precisely to plan. After all, he was a member of the Imperial Legion, and the legion never did anything without a plan. And his plan for this very moment was to take in the view of the plateau before him this morning.

It was called the Lakhani Plain, and it was a sight to see.

A breathtaking view: mountains lay to the east, with their icy peaks reaching up into a clear, blue, cloudless sky; the tallest trees he had ever seen, lush with the bright green foliage and leaves getting ready to turn colour with the changing of the season, surrounded the clearing that emerged from the foothills of the mountains – the trees hugged the sides of the mountains almost as high up as the white snow caps that had been slowly retreating throughout the long, hot summer, but now that summer was coming to an end, the air at the higher altitudes was getting colder, and those who watched such things could see the icecaps starting to slowly creep down again as the air chilled.

The river that he was standing in snaked down from deep within the mountain range, carrying fresh, cool ice water downstream, running off from the melting snowpack. Flowing on its winding route between the various peaks and valleys of the range, it exited the mountains here, where the sharp rise of the rocks gave way to rolling foothills, before eventually settling into the plains. The water had cut its path into the hard rock of the hillside on Jason's side of the river, but across from him, where the trail re-emerged from the water on the far bank, the view opened up onto a wide plain, surrounded by forest, which – under other circumstances – would have been coloured a bright green with the late summer rebirth of fresh grasses and shrubs that grew in the open spaces that had been abandoned by the trees.

There had been a long drought for much of the early part of the year, but rains had come in the mountains in recent weeks, and though summer was almost done, the dry brown colours were yielding again to a livelier shade of green, if only for a short while before winter came again.

Today, the plain was not empty. It was full of all manner of activity as a small town of almost twenty thousand men – elite soldiers of the Imperium and their followers, companions, and herd animals – lay camped across the plain, turning the dry yellow grasses into a muddy morass, as steel-shod boots and animal hooves crushed back into the muddy soil any signs of life that might have been trying for a fresh awakening. Jason was a Captain of a company of Imperial Scout Cavalry – Rangers they were called – and he had been trained until it was second nature for him to pay attention to every little detail in the panorama of activity that sprawled before him.

Pennant flags flew above the tents across the plain, identifying legions, centuries, their commanders and ranks. By his training he knew all of them, and by friendship he knew many of the men in each camp. The flags fluttered in the chill wind, like the sound of a thousand gloved hands clapping. It was early in the morning yet, with the sun just finishing its slow rise clear of the trees on the far horizon. He could hear the echoing noise of the cooks from each company and brigade beginning to prepare breakfast. The horses penned at one edge of the clearing were anxious and snorting, as someone had placed them too close to the herd animals – many of which were now being culled and slaughtered to feed the assembled host. It was one of the dirty secrets of an army on the march – they had to be fed, and it needed far more than the simple rations they issued to the footmen to last a few days before and after a battle.

The simple act of gathering a force this size meant that preparations had to be made for them to sit in one place until their strength was assembled, which meant there was no plunder to be had, and the local wildlife was quickly depleted by opportunistic hunters looking for some variety in their stew. So, they had to bring with them the livestock they needed to keep everyone fed, even if some ate better than others.

The army camped here as it awaited its full complement to gather. They had been here for almost a month, which had not been the most pleasant experience for the first to arrive, as they experienced the full brunt of the hot summer drought, but things were starting to improve as the weather turned with the season. With the units from the furthest outposts slowly drifting into the camp over the next few days, they would soon be ready to break camp and continue their march west.

It was a sombre camp to observe. It did not have the energy or youthful exuberance of an army marching to conquest. Quite the opposite. It was an army pulling back, going home – not retreating, they had been told sharply by their commanders, as they had never been defeated in battle. No, this was a decision to return home to the Imperium, and to leave the frontiers to their own devices from here on.

They had only rumours to guess the why of things. Some talked about political turmoil in the capital; some whispered of fleeing the incurable frontier plagues; others said that there was a new threat from the West, and the army would soon be fighting again instead of just marching. Too many tales being told to truly count, some being just slight variants on others. Everyone seemed to know someone who knew someone who was sitting beside the Praetor at dinner some night, so of course, all of it was true!

None of this truly concerned Jason. He had his own plans to consider.

Just past his nineteenth name-day, he was young for an officer, and proud to oversee one of the best cavalry scout units in the army. It was only a few years earlier that his parents' wealth had secured him a commission in the legion, expecting him to honour the family name and perhaps make an easy transition from the military to politics – as his father had done – when the time came to truly achieve the greatness, they had planned for him. They had always planned great things for him since he was born, so he could only imagine their disappointment when he decided to choose the rangers as his unit for his service.

The rangers did not fight with the main body of the army – they scouted ahead, surveyed the enemy, disrupted supplies, and were basically the eyes & ears of the army when it was on the march. It was not a command that bred leaders and politicians, but it had never been Jason's ambition to become a politician. That was his first act of rebellion against his parents – and it wouldn't be his last. Like any other highborn citizen, his parents had surely thought he would return from his military service and marry into another noble family, ideally one well-suited to his parents' ambitions for him. But those weren't his plans.

He hadn't intended to fall in love during his time in the service, but he didn't shy away from it either.

Her name was Katerina, and she was the daughter of a merchant in Mercurum. He met her on official business, seeking supplies for his troops that he ended up purchasing from her father. Soon after that meeting, the trips for supplies became more & more frequent, and there was always something on the list that required a visit to her fathers' shop. It was not a typical courtship, but a successful one – at least he saw it that way.

He was an outsider, an occupier, and Katerina was soon disowned by her friends when they discovered that she was engaged to an Imperium soldier. They cared not for his rank, or the merit he displayed for this achievement at such a young age – these were impressive accomplishments in his mind, that made him a worthy suitor, but they did not care. As long as the Imperium was here as a conquering force, ruling the land as overlords, her love for him would be frowned upon by her people.

For himself, he sometimes worried that perhaps this was just another way of rebelling against his parents – it would take some time for word to get to them in the capital about his situation, and he was sure they would be apoplectic – but he would tell himself again and again that he really did not care what they thought. True, this might have added to his enthusiasm for the situation, but he loved her all the same, regardless.

Then the Imperium decided to withdraw from the East, and he saw his world begin to fall apart, as if someone was pulling on a loose thread in a poorly woven scarf.

The news had come as a surprise to everyone. Two months earlier, they had been resting at their barracks, just outside the west gate of a town called Mercurum. A few of the men were on patrol, but the majority had been riding drills all morning, and had just finished stabling the horses and pulling some water from the well. There were a few trees on the ground that they could use for shade, and they were gathered here when the two Imperial messengers rode into the camp.

There were other units stationed at the Mercurum barracks, but the scouts were the only ones visible to the new arrivals, so they rode directly up to the small copse of trees, and spotting Jason as the captain by the plume on his helmet, the two brightly feathered pompadours saluted smartly and addressed him.

"Greetings, Captain," the first messenger announced, saluting smartly at Jason. "We have a message for the commanding officer of the Mercurum Legion Barracks."

Jason leaned forward but did not rise from his seat on the grass – he never did care much for the messenger corps, even though they performed a useful service for the army. He was not sure if it was the decorative armor, which served no purpose in a real battle, the colourful plumage that made them stand out from everyone else on the field of battle, or if it was they was that most of them just seemed to wear that plumage with a certain amount of arrogance, as if it gave them some sort of status above everyone else. Maybe all of the above, he thought.

"The Commandant is away for the day. You can leave the message with me," he responded disinterestedly.

"Of course, sir," said the second messenger, reaching into his pouch and withdrawing a sealed scroll, which he offered forth to Jason.

Still sitting, Jason nodded to one of his men, who slowly got up from their seat on the grass to reach for the scroll. The messenger reacted with surprise, and started to withdraw his hand, as if it were some breach to hand the message to anyone other than an officer.

"Hold!" called out the first rider suddenly. "We have orders to deliver this message to the Commandant of the barracks. You will have to forgive the enthusiasm of my associate, but he is new and eager, and forgets that we have rules to ensure communications from the Praetor are delivered properly."

Ferenc stood beside the messenger's horse and turned back to look as Jason with a quizzical look on his face – as if to ask if he should pull the man off the horse and take the message – and waited for Jason to respond.

Jason sighed and waved at the rider. "Please, give the message to Ferenc, he will ensure that it gets delivered immediately – you can even watch if you like. And as Captain of the Imperial Rangers, I will deliver the message to the Commandant immediately upon his return." His tone was flat and tired, as if explaining something to an irritating child.

"Unless, of course, you want to wait around for the Commandant to return. You can sit with us and exchange tales of battle!" Jason offered.

The messenger seemed entirely disgusted with this total lack of proper protocol for delivering and accepting messages, and even more by the thought of having to wait around with this motley crew of soldiers, just to deliver a message. Jason suddenly wondered to himself how these arrogant trolls ever managed to survive dealing with any of the uncivilized tribes they had conquered in the history of the Imperium!

Exchanging looks, the first rider nodded to the second — an act that Jason thought would cause his helmet to topple forwards off his head from the weight of the plumage — and somewhat reluctantly the second messenger handed the scroll tube over to Ferenc.

No sooner had he let go of the slender ivory tube than he wheeled his horse and gave the flank a switch of his reins, taking off in a cloud of dust, with his companion close behind.

Ferenc waved at the cloud of dust in the air and walked over to where Jason was sitting.

"Pleasant fellows," he said, handing the scroll tube to Jason, who could now make out the ornately carved figures in the polished ivory. Removing the cap from one end, he did get the sense that this was more than just the usual message — most messages were delivered in a simple roll, sealed with the waxen seal of the sender. Few could afford to spare the expense of such ornate scroll tubes, usually reserved for messages that were of high importance and the sender could not afford the risk of damage from wear & tear, or even the carelessness of the messengers — had the couriers not ridden off so impetuously, they would have fallen off their horses in shock to see Jason reading the message for the Commandant.

Jason slowly read the message once, then a second time.

His company had gathered around while he was reading, watching his expression as he read, eager to get some hint of what the message contained. When he was done reading, he knew it would not matter to share all of it with his men — the parchment was filled with reasons and details that mattered little to him at the moment, beyond the basic fact of…

"We're going home," he said in a quiet voice.

"Who's 'we'? asked Ferenc. "We 'Rangers'? Or just you & I?"

"All of us," Jason replied softly, as the implications began to race through his head. "The Imperium is withdrawing from the Carpathian basin. All troops, all commands, all legates, governors — everyone. By order of the Emperor, all commands are recalled from the frontiers. We're leaving and returning to the Capital."

He looked around at the stunned faces of his men. Many were as young as him, or younger, but a few were older and more experienced. They had the most dumbfounded looks of all on their faces — the Imperium had never before retreated or surrendered. It seemed unbelievable to now hear that they were willingly withdrawing from a land that they had conquered.

And at that moment, all Jason could think of was Katerina...

That message had been almost two months ago now. They had scrambled to pack their gear and get their affairs in order before they shipped out. After logging their larger gear with the quartermaster, to follow on the baggage trains, they departed early on the third morning after receiving the orders. As scouts, they had to take the lead and make sure the route ahead was clear of obstruction or serious hazard.

It was a funny thing about the frontier – not just the frontier, but any of the lands claimed by the Imperium – the fighting never really seemed to stop, even after peace was declared by the victors. As much as the locals might have been happy to hear the news of their leaving, none of the legions expected that they would have a simple march west. They had paid in blood for every step on the way east, and now they knew that the locals would be sure to do everything they could to hasten them on their way back out.

Of course, this was not helped by the fact that, in the short time they had to prepare for their departure, each legion, from across the north, had raided every farm and market that they could find, to gather livestock, grains, water, and everything else needed to feed an army on the move. They may not be marching to war, but an army only moved as far as a full stomach would take them. And their orders did not leave them any room to be concerned about how the locals were to feed themselves after they left.

Jason was interrupted from his reverie by the arrival of his lieutenant at the river's edge. The second horse stomped in the mud, reaching for a drink as Ferenc reined him in.

"Captain, the company is back, and are making breakfast. They should be ready to break camp when they are finished – they'll be tired, but ready. And we – you – have been ordered to the Praetor's tent for noon to discuss plans for the march south. What are your orders?" he asked.

Jason noted that Ferenc referred to his command as a 'company' instead of what it was properly named by the Imperial Legions: he commanded a full Century; eight squads, each made up of eight men, plus their horses, dogs, and a few servants and orderlies for the officers. Including the officers, this was almost eighty fighting men, all under his command. Ferenc was not truly a citizen of the imperium, having been born in one of the conquered lands to the west and hadn't travelled to the capital until he was older, so he didn't always grasp the importance of the finer details of the mother tongue and often fond himself using the more slang translations in his speech.

Looking at the clear liquid still pooled in his helm, Jason reached his arm out and slowly poured the remaining water back into the river, watching as the breeze caught the cascade and scattered the droplets downwind. In the bright morning light, he could see the light refracting to form a rainbow in the mist – a good omen, he thought to himself.

He hadn't had a lot of time to make plans before they had set out, and though they could have arrived earlier – this small plain was only a few days ride from Mercurum for a mounted ranger; a week for a marching legion; through the hill-pass between the high ranges – they had purposely circled the site to scout the location. Though they were not the furthest outpost from the rendezvous point, they had waited on their departure for many of the outlying units to pass through Mercurum on their way west, before they abandoned the barracks for the last time, and formed the rear guard for the march.

This had been Jason's suggestion to the Commandant, and it had been well received. The Commandant especially liked the part about how the rear guard was likely to be seen as the critical link in defending the march against any hostilities that might break out. It was hard to say if it was his desire for combat or a true belief in the honour they would have for being the last units to step foot in the Eastern frontier. Either way, this suited Jason just fine – it gave him a few more nights with Katerina before he had to leave, and he couldn't put a price on that.

He placed his helmet back on his head and fastened the strap. Mounting his horse again, he looked at Ferenc. It looked like there was something else on his mind.

"What is it?" he asked. "You look bothered by something…"

"Sir," he said uncertainly, "it's nothing."

"Ferenc, we have been together since basic training, I know when you have something on your mind – and I can tell when it's serious, and not just whether or not you can remember the name of the girl you were with last night!" he answered back with a smile.

Ferenc flashed back a half-smile, but the tone of his response was more concerned.

"The men have been at work in the woods for a few nights now, and they persist in believing that they were being watched." He looked around as he talked, as if to make sure no one was watching now. "They were afraid the whole time that we had angered some forest spirit. We checked as best we could and could find no trace of anyone, but the feeling remained."

"Well, if we could find no trace, then there was surely no one there." He turned his horse toward the trail and continued. "Look, the men are tired, and we are expecting a lot of all of them. Don't break camp. Let them rest until noon, then make sure everything is packed and ready. They should be back at their posts directly and await my orders. I will go to meet with the Praetor, and we'll see how things go from there…"

Ferenc nodded and pulled his horse alongside Jason's as he put his heels gently to her flanks and started a slow walk back to where the unit had made camp for the night. He would not need to pack his bedroll, as one of the few perks of command was having an orderly to see to his kit when travelling. They continued to talk as they walked the horses back along the trail.

"While I am meeting with the Praetor, I want you and one or two men to come along. You can talk with the quartermaster about the personal effects for the company. You can return with them directly, and I will be along as soon as they are done with me.

"You don't think he suspects anything, do you?" Ferenc asked quietly. There was no one else on the trail on this side of the river, but he kept his voice low, nonetheless.

"No," said Jason. "Everything is going according to plan. Steel your nerves and see it through!" He spurred his horse onto the trail, and they swung through the scout camp to grab a couple men to join them before heading across the river and into the main encampment.

They forded the river where the trail led into the water, emerging at a guard post on the far side. The water barely reached their knees at the deepest point in the crossing. The guards who greeted them stood up lazily from the fishing rods they had resting against the bank, with the lines flowing out into the running water below the crossing.

"Any luck this morning?" Ferenc called as they passed. The guards finished their salute to Jason before responding.

"Nothing biting yet. The river is lower than usual this season – the fish must not be coming upstream as far this spring." The guard sounded truly disappointed – if they didn't catch anything before their watch was over, they would have to eat the basic gruel that was the standard breakfast for the common soldiers.

Ferenc glanced over at Jason, but nothing more was said, and they simply moved on. About a hundred yards into the camp, they split up, with Ferenc heading toward the supply wagons with the two other riders in tow. Jason watched them for a moment before dismounting and walking his horse the last bit towards the command tents. Here there were larger, more lavish accommodations for the senior commanders of the occupying army. Not just the Praetor, but two or three Generals for an army this size, senior lieutenants, advisors, and, judging by the strange hut that stood out from the others, they had at least one shaman with them.

While the other tents observed the legion standard for plain canvas tarps, posted entranceways, carpeted interiors with standard military furnishings, the third hut in the circle of six tents that occupied the command post of the camp was squat, dark, and seemed made of bits and pieces of animal hides, tied together with bits of rope, hemp and grass. Smoky torches made the entrance to the hut nearly impassable, not that Jason felt any urge to want to go into that dwelling. Shamans were usually locals – witch doctors, seers, or fortune tellers – and would almost never be found working with the occupying legions.

He gave the shaman's hut a wide berth as he tied his horse and stepped towards the Praetor's pavilion. The two legionnaires at the entrance nodded and waved him in as he approached.

It took a moment for his eyes to adjust to the lower light of the interior. Squinting and looking down to regain his focus, the first thing he noticed was the number of carpets covering the ground. Layered over one another to provide suitable insulation from the chill of the night, he found himself wondering if it took a full wagon by itself to transport just the carpets when they were on the move. Several tapestries were hung on either side of the narrow entryway, as well as the more open room that he stepped into, hanging from wooden frames & posts that were either part of the baggage train or recently cut from the surrounding woods. He wasn't sure what purpose the tapestries served aside from decoration, but they did well to mask the fact that this was still just a tent in a field. There were no windows or openings that he could see – even the smoke from the fire, contained in a large metal brazier in the center of the tent, was channeled outside through a makeshift metal chimney hung a few feet above the fire. Lanterns were hung around the tent, hanging from each of the five tent posts that formed the perimeter. There was a large table to the left of the fire, strewn with maps, markers representing various legions, centuries, and cohorts. There was no one at the table – all attention seemed to be focused on something to the right of the brazier.

Four figures were huddled together in the dim light of one of the lanterns, leaning over to stare at something on the ground. He approached slowly, as there was no one to announce his arrival, and he didn't want to startle anyone, as they seemed very focused. After a few steps, he could see another figure squatting on the carpet at their feet – he felt a small churning in his gut as he beheld the wrinkled form of the shaman.

He had never met this shaman before, but it was hard to guess otherwise. The worn, ragged figure fit every description, rumour and bedtime story he had ever heard about what a witch should look like – the long, dirty fingernails tracing patterns on the carpet; the bracelets of bones and small stones adorning the frail wrists, where the knobs of her joints stuck out from beneath the loose, leathery skin; the dark woolen fabric of her robes was smeared and stained, and had an odour of incense and ash; from beneath her cowl, he see wisps of grey hair escaping in knotted strands. And more than anything, the sound of her frail voice, muttering and chanting as she dropped, collected, and dropped again, a collection of small bones – some bearing a resemblance to small bird parts, and others that he could only pray weren't human – each time she would pause, consider what she saw, and then let out a small hiss of laughter.

The figures around her were silent, waiting, anticipating some grand pronouncement from her at any moment. He immediately recognized Praetor Corvus, easily identifiable by the heavy gold chain of rank that hung low around his neck, not to mention the bright polish of his armor – clearly not armor that had seen the field of battle in a long time, if ever.

The other three were the Commandants of the other three legions that filled the valley – General Markov of the Fifth Legion, General Vassilya of the Sixth Legion, and General Sukhov of the infamous Seventh Legion. The three represented the bulk of the Army of the Imperium, but it was the Seventh that the tribes of the frontier feared or hated the most. The first to arrive in these lands, years ago, they had been unrelenting in the terror they spread among the tribes they encountered. It wasn't until the arrival of the Fifth & Sixth Legions that any of the natives felt they had any chance of surviving their encounter with the Imperium. The Seventh brought only death where they went and when this was the only other option, it made the terms of surrender – however harsh – seem much more appealing. Jason knew them all by reputation, and certainly did not aspire to their levels of loyalty to the Imperium.

Right now, their posture seemed very much at odds with their rank and elaborate uniforms, hunched over and straining to see or hear what portents might be offered by the shaman.

They noticed his approach and offered only the slightest acknowledgment of his presence by glancing his way briefly before returning their attention to the proceedings. They parted slightly so he could see the bones being cast, and the Praetor also made eye contact with him from the circle – no words were said, and it was clear that they wanted him to be silent as well.

Only as he joined the circle could he see that there was one more person in the tent, standing directly behind the shaman – a dark figure, not very tall, covered completely in a worn, purple robe, holding an incense burner in his left hand, which swung slowly back & forth over the shaman's head as she cast the bones. Jason could not see the face under the cowl of the robe, as the shadows from the lantern light masked any details from his sight. What he could see, though, were the burn scars on the hand holding the incense burner.

He turned his gaze back down to the shaman and was startled to see her staring directly back at him. The bones lay untouched on the carpet – the casting had stopped, as had the mad chattering sounds she had been making.

When she spoke, it was clear, and with a sense of inevitability:

Regna nati sunt
Regna cremo
Regna resurgere
Fire and flood
Eagles in the rising tide
Love burn brightly
Brightest fires consumed fastest
Coldness abides

Spittle dripped down her chin as she spoke, as her face emerged from the shadows of her robes, her hood falling back on her frail shoulders, revealing to everyone the wrinkled, yellowed skin of her aged face. It was impossible for several of the assembled generals to withhold a gasp of surprise as they also looked on to see the horrid scars, where the flesh on the left side of her face and scalp drooped in small, crimson & yellow rivulets down the side of her head, looking like melted candle wax, reforming as it cooled. Some parts of the tissue were still seeping and moist, marking the freshness of the burns – the bone of her skull near the top of her head was exposed, as the burned flesh had yet to re-heal and fully close the wound. Jason had seen grown men writhe in agony from such wounds on the battlefield – he could not imagine how she was not doing the same as she spoke – perhaps her visions came from the delirium of such maddening pain.

She began to slowly rise from the floor of the tent, still rambling, and the assembled generals all took a collective step backwards.

Corvus repeated her words: "Regna nati sunt, regna cremo, regna resurgere." He looked towards his generals and continued: "It is from the old tongue of the tribes that lived where the capital of the empire stands today… hundreds of years old, and rarely spoken – let alone by a witch from the wilds!"

"And what does it mean?" asked Vassilya, the only other woman in the room besides the witch. Her sharp features marked her of high birth from the Imperium and were it not for the armor and the red scar running from her left eye down to the base of her neck, she might have been mistaken for a noble woman rather than a general. It was clear by her demeanor that anyone who might suggest that she bought her commission rather than earned it would find themselves on the wrong end of her blade.

"Kingdoms born, kingdoms burn, kingdoms rise again," answered Sukhov, "or something close to that." He scowled and Jason could see that he did not care much for portents or omens. He was educated enough in the old ways that he respected the knowledge but did not fear it.

"Why do we need to hear such prattling nonsense?" he asked in a loud voice, startling a few of the assembled men from there focus on the witch… or shaman, or whatever she was – it mattered not to him. She had joined the camp only a week before, offering vague portents and predictions – one, in particular, about Corvus's favourite horse, and when it happened to be true, he kept her in his company from that time onwards.

He was not sure what other thoughts she had placed in his head, but as paranoid as Corvus was about being betrayed, he was quick to seek anyway he could outwit and stay one step ahead of his enemies. The Praetor had mainly feared what the people of Nyirseg would do to harry them on their journey west, and so he had consulted with her every morning while they had waited encamped on this plain, and even had her hut set up along with the officers' quarters. That frustrated Sukhov more than anything and was almost more than he could tolerate.

Corvus did not pay Sukhov's dismissive words any attention, and helped the old woman to her feet, and on her way to the door of the pavilion. Her attendant followed behind them with the incense burner, which Jason was sure now was primarily needed to mask the smell of the old woman and her festering wounds! She seemed to be whispering something to Corvus as he helped her out, although her attendant interfered with anyone having a chance to hear what she was saying.

As Corvus held back the embroidered cloth that served as a door for the tent, the witch looked back over her shoulder at Jason, and he couldn't suppress the chill that ran down his spine – he wasn't sure if it was a smile or a snarl that crossed her lips, but it gave him no comfort to think that she would have reason to single him out for her attention.

When she had left, he turned to face his assembled commanders – and Jason, who still did not know why he was there.

"Generals," he said, "it is time to go. We will march tomorrow at sunrise. The

Imperium has need of us, and we shall not fail in our duty!" He had snapped himself up to his full height now that it was just his officers in the room, and he looked around at his men.

"Captain," he called, looking now at Jason, "have all remaining troops crossed the river?"

"Sir, yes sir," Jason replied, also snapping to attention, as the gathering now seemed to regain the more formal tone of military business, "all units have checked in and reported crossing to the main encampment. Scouts continue to report no local activity in the neighbouring woods, and the road south is clear."

"And the river?" Corvus inquired.

"Sir?"

"The river – our guards at the river's edge have been reporting that the water levels have been dropping significantly over the past few weeks that we have been encamped here – have your scouts discovered any evidence of why this might be?"

"Sir, no sir. No unusual activity has been spotted. It has been a very dry summer, sir, and perhaps this has taken a toll on the river levels," Jason posited.

"Hmmm. Yes, perhaps." Corvus paused, seeming to consider that possibility. "Well enough, we are leaving on the morrow anyway, so it matters not. Generals, please dine with me tonight, after you have passed along word to prepare to break camp. You are dismissed." He waved his hands at the men, after which each quickly grabbed their gloves and helms from a nearby table, and then proceeded to the doorway, reaching it at the same time as the guards from outside the tent entered and held open the cloth door covering for them. As they reached the doorway, and Vassilya was just ducking her head to exit, Corvus spoke again,

"Oh, one more thing, as we go out – I have something I should like you all to see." They paused in their exit, and then deferred to Corvus to lead them out of the pavilion.

Stepping once more into the bright daylight of the clear spring day, they all had to shield their eyes after being in the dimmer light of the tent for so long. They could tell that they were not alone in the central encampment, but it took a moment for them to make out just who was there, and then only a moment thereafter to understand why.

Assembled in the open space in the center of the officers' camp were perhaps thirty Imperial soldiers. They were assembled in various states of dress, some fully armored, some still in their bed-shirts, none of them armed, all of them tied by rope. The guards that surrounded the motley collection of men had spears levelled at the group, and it was clear that they were being detained for some unfortunate reason.

After pausing just for a moment to watch the surprised looks on the Generals' faces, Praetor Corvus began to address the assembled men and their generals.

"These men have been arrested and found guilty of treason, for deserting their posts, disobeying direct orders, and disloyalty to the Imperium. They, and one hundred others like them, being held just beyond the gate here, have been sentenced to death for their crimes, said sentence to be carried out immediately." He strode in front of the assembled men as he spoke. "Do you have anything to say for yourselves?"

He turned to the three generals as he spoke, and they seemed a bit baffled by a question that they had presumed was either rhetorical or, at the very least, more intended for the men before them. Corvus continued, this time clearly speaking to his generals…

"You are their commanders, their leaders, the ones responsible for inspiring them to believe in the glory of service to the Imperium. And yet they still felt it better to flee than to serve. At the very least, they do not seem to have been very afraid of defying your orders and had no respect for abandoning their brothers at arms."

The generals were clearly speechless now and could not hold eye contact with the Praetor.

"Very well. I will leave it to each of you to carry out the punishment for these men, as there are some from each legion present here." There was anger in Corvus' voice, but also disappointment. "We have until we reach the Capital to fix this, or we will be of no use to the Imperium when we get there."

"Commander Sukhov," the Field Marshall added, "you and the Captain shall walk with me." Corvus was striding out of the officers' encampment and both Sukhov and Jason had to hurry to accompany him.

They walked along past more groups of men, tied hand & foot, some of whom had heard his proclamation and looked quite distressed, even begging for forgiveness from the Praetor as he passed, while others appeared to have been too far away to have heard their fate, looking very confused by the behaviour of their compatriots.

Once they were once more among the rank & file of the main camp, and not watched as closely by those that were curious about the goings on at the center of the encampment, Corvus began to speak again.

"I am disappointed, Captain." He began, which drew a concerned look from Jason.

He knows.

"Your men have not crossed the river yet," he continued.

He definitely knows, Jason thought.

"We truly value the scout cohorts across the legion, and you men are among the best we have." Corvus spoke as he walked through the main pathway through the camp, nodding to men as they worked, whether they were sharpening blades or digging latrine ditches. "But I cannot help but wonder if you are certain of your allegiance."

He stopped walking and looked at the young Captain. "We have had reports of activity in the woods both north and south of the camp for the past week or so, yet you tell me there is nothing happening."

Shit, Jason thought to himself, as he looked the Praetor in the eye. Sukhov merely stood back a few steps and listened.

"They tell me you were engaged to marry one of these local girls – is that true?"

Jason did his best to hide his surprise – the Praetor was incredibly well informed, especially for someone of his lowly rank.

"You are well informed, sir," responded Jason, "but it was ended when we were ordered to withdraw."

"Good, Captain. Good." He nodded and looked to Sukhov as he continued speaking. "I have always heard about your qualities as a ranger, soldier, and leader of your troops, so I would hate to see others question your loyalty. It is so hard to find men of good talent these days, and we are needed in our mission. And I trust our little display back there at my tent was enough to make it clear to you about my feelings on such matters. Those men – though legionnaires – are worth more by the example of their death than they ever were as footmen, and I would be saddened to see any of our truly worthy warriors put down in such a manner…"

He stepped towards General Sukhov and turned back to issue his orders.

"I have asked General Sukhov and his guards to accompany you back to the ranger camp this afternoon and assist you with moving your encampment across the river before nightfall."

Jason was not one to ever be surprised, so he cursed to himself when he only now saw the six men step forward from the small ring of men that had slowly formed around them as they spoke. Blending in with the rank & file soldiers who were happy to see the Praetor up close, he hadn't noticed their approach – and one of them was leading his horse!

Praetor Corvus pulled his cloak around him in the early afternoon breeze, which seemed a little chillier to Jason in the moment. "We will leave the matter regarding the activity in the woods for now – we are moving out tomorrow, so I trust there will be no problems. We will talk about it later, though."

"Yes, sir," Jason snapped smartly, saluting the Praetor as he began the walk back to his pavilion, and he was left standing with the curiously smiling General Sukhov and the six guards who would be escorting him back across the river. A small consolation, he thought to himself, at least they were bringing his horse…

A light rain had started to fall as they finished talking, but Sukhov seemed oblivious to the rain as he moved closer to the young captain, staring him down, nose-to-nose.

"I do hope you're not planning any nonsense, as the Praetor suspects," Sukhov snarled.

"I agree it would be a shame to lose good men; and for the sake of your men, I hope you weren't planning something foolish just for yourself and thinking of leaving your men behind to pay the price for you wanting to dip your pen in the local ink." The words slid off his tongue dryly, though he was so close that Jason could smell the cheap wine and military rations on his breath. Sukhov was loyal to the core, and despite the Praetor's weakness for parlour tricks, he would obey every order with enthusiasm, especially if he had to punish a traitor.

Jason did not respond directly, but snapped to attention, neatly side-stepped in a crisp military fashion, and motioned for Sukhov to proceed with him toward the river and the ranger camp.

"Good!" noted Sukhov, "…but just a moment."

Waving to one of the six guards, he called the man over.

"Return to our camp and alert the officers. I want everyone ready with mounts, armor, and two days' battle rations by the time I get back. Go!"

The guard gave a quick salute and ran off. Sukhov's Seventh Legion was camped on the far side of the plain, furthest from the river's edge, and it would take a good ten or fifteen minutes for the guard to make his way through the encampment to deliver his orders. Sukhov expected they would have a few hours to make preparations – for what he wasn't sure. Rubbing his hand over his shaven head, he looked at Jason, who, in his opinion, seemed to be much too calm under the circumstances…

"You can never be too prepared," he said, and smiling, motioned for Jason to lead on towards his camp.

*****Sukhov*****

General Sukhov was a soldier's general. He started his military career as a simple legionnaire and earned his rank for valour and courage in the field of battle. He had been born to a family of humble fortunes, so he had to earn his commissions with his sword – a veteran of many campaigns, the natural mortality rate on the battlefield advanced his career quickly. This also raised his credit with the rank & file troops, and that loyalty meant they would follow any order he gave. Field commissions soon brought his name to the attention of the high command and there, too, he would prove that his wits were as sharp as his sword. Navigating the politics of the capital, he positioned himself well over the course of a few more campaigns, so that it was practically impossible for them to deny him his own legion to command. He had certainly earned himself a few enemies over the years – men who resented his lack of social status or family name – but he didn't mind. Legions acted independently in the field, and he was saved from having to meet directly with the other generals except on rare occasions.

This withdrawal had been one of those rare occasions and he was not enjoying the experience all that much. This made him all the more pleased to have a task such as this assigned to him by the Praetor. He had heard someone talk about Jason's skills as a scout and a commander, but he discounted this as nonsense – in his opinion, the young captain was wet-behind-the-ears and seemed quite likely to have done exactly as the Praetor suspected: given up his loyalty to the Legion and the Imperium in exchange for a warm bed and a pair of smooth thighs.

He walked with Jason along the path through the camp and back down to the river. They paused for a moment to look across to the trail as it started up the hill on the far side of the crossing. Jason pointed to the top.

"We are camped up there. Ferenc has been coordinating the scouting parties, so some of the men may be on patrol to the east and west," he said, pointing his arm up and down the river as he spoke. Sukhov's gaze followed the gestures, though there was nothing of note visible in either direction.

"Let's get going then," said Sukhov, "it's a long walk and I want to get back before dark."

They stepped into the river, and the water barely reached their knees at the deepest point. They had just finished crossing when Sukhov pulled Jason's arm to stop.

"What's that?" he asked, cocking his head to one side, listening.

"What's what?" Jason replied "I don't hear anything, except perhaps the wind in the trees…"

"Shhh!" Sukhov hushed him. "I heard something, a cracking noise, like a rock fall or… I don't know… something."

"Maybe. We hear those all the time, echoing down the hills from somewhere higher in the mountains. You can hear a lot more when you are away from the noise of the camp – that's why we prefer the scout units to camp a little further away from all the commotion. You'd be amazed what you can hear – a tree falling in the forest even!" Jason smiled and started walking along the path again.

The general hesitated, trying again to see if he could hear the sound, then gave up and turned to follow the path up the hill.

Jason was leading at this point, with two centurions guarding him from behind – spears at the ready – then the general, followed by the remaining three guards. They split off the main road and followed a game trail that wound its way up to the top of the hill, and eventually reached a small clearing that looked out over the main legion encampment.

Sukhov was a little winded by the climb – generals were more used to riding than long walks in the hills – and so he was grateful to take a break and take in the view of the assembled armies. The guards did likewise, as it was truly an awe-inspiring view of such a host gathered in one place. The collective might of an empire, and a full third of their ability to wage war.

"Is there a waterfall nearby?" Sukhov asked, "Your men are truly spoiled to be able to enjoy the perks of these camp locations you have chosen. Even in spring, a nice cold shower would do well to refresh the men..."

"True, we do have the benefit of scouting out the best locations for making camp," Jason answered, sitting on a small rock beside the general, taking in the view. "It's an advantage one should never underestimate."

"Take the plain below, for example," he continued. "We found this spot shortly after the order was given to find a safe route home and reconnoitered the area almost a month before the first legions arrived – that would be yours, the Seventh. You had the privilege of choosing whatever part of the plain you wanted, as it would essentially be divided up into four quarters once everyone arrived, and you chose the far southern side of the plain – a little far for carrying drinking water from the river, but less trafficked, which meant a little less muddy, a little more room to breathe when things started getting crowded."

"There, on the left, the Fifth Legion chose the eastern edge of the plain, nearest to the hills, and just a little bit higher ground than everywhere else, as the land slopes down from the mountains, through the hills. The plain is on the western edge of the hill country, and General Markov knew that if it rained, everything from his camp would flow down and away – you can tell this by where he placed his latrine ditches!"

"Vassilya staked out the river side of the camp to avoid most of this flow, as she did not have much to choose from by the time the bulk of her men arrived, and this left the cowherds, canteen orderlies and quartermaster to slog it out on the west side of the plain, with most of the mud, detritus, and run-off to deal with. All in all, not a bad placement of units in such a small space. But we make do with what we have."

Sukhov was listening to all of this, nodding in approval, but only half-interested in what Jason was saying. When the pause came in the conversation, he interjected with the question that was bothering him...

"Was it so easy to give up this girl, like you told Corvus?" he asked, "I mean, the Praetor is generally well informed, and if this girl meant enough that it would be reported to him as a path to treason, I am surprised that you did not have so much to say about it. So, tell me truthfully – and I will know if you are lying – what is your plan? Did you sneak her into your camp? Did you entice her away with promises of seeing the soaring towers of the Capital? I don't really believe you would want to stay here, but I still sense something is up... what is it?" He was beginning to feel relaxed during their rest and was getting his second wind after the long hike. With a tone that was a little friendlier, perhaps so that the young captain might also feel relaxed enough to trust him to share his plans openly and save him any further troubles. Looking at Jason sitting on the rock beside him, he could see something stirring in the lad's mind, as if trying to find the right words to respond.

As he waited, his naturally observant nature kept telling him that something was not right, although he couldn't put his finger on it yet. He could hear the birds, although they seemed fainter now, as if they were more distant. The wind was blowing through the branches of the trees, but there was something odd about the noise being made by the branches as they swayed in the cool breeze. It was almost as if the background noise of the forest hillside was cluttering up his senses, until he realized precisely what he was hearing...

*****Jason*****

Jason was sitting silently on the rock outcrop, facing out over the camp, and as the General finished his question, he could see the awareness of the situation slowly creep into his expression.

"We make do with what we have, General. And in this case, it means that we have a situation where we wanted to have the freedom to go our own way and live our own lives.

"What the Praetor just made very clear to me – to all of us – was that even if we had breached the subject in a civilized way, we would never be allowed to leave the Legion, and so we had to take steps to ensure that we would be left alone after today and that the Imperium would not try to seek us out."

The sound, which had at first sounded like a distant waterfall, or the rush of wind in the trees, was now growing louder in volume.

"Unfortunately," Jason continued, "as we just saw, this is a life and death choice for us, and so we have made our choice."

The noise became a roar, and Sukhov rose to his feet to look out at the encampment on the plain below, completely unprepared for what was unfolding before his eyes. The wind began to blow down the valley between the hills, along the path of the river, heralding the arrival of something terrible.

At the foot of the plain, where the river entered the clearing from between the hills, the first to notice that something was amiss were the perimeter guards. Looking north, in the direction of the wind that was now billowing out their cloaks, and tugging their shields from their arms, the guards heard the roar of the river grow and build, not realizing what it was until they could see the wave bursting out of the valley and onto the plain. Realization hit them at the same time as the water did, and that was the last thing they ever saw.

Even if they could have raised an alarm, it would not have mattered at the speed the fast-moving water was now travelling.

Exploding down the riverbed, the wall of water was nearly five spans high when it reached the clearing. Following the path of the river, it had built in speed and height as it followed the narrow canyon that the river had cut through the hills, until the force was released and free to spread in every direction. Some of the water immediately washed onto the plain to the right, while the main force of the wave drove straight on until it hit a hard outcropping of rock that jutted out from the hillside halfway down the plain.

The old river had worn away the rock where it was softest, yielding its path to the harder rocks that it could not erode so easily, creating curves and bends in the river. Now, the wave that had been released from upstream crashed into this outcropping and deflected at almost a right-angle – directly out onto the open plain, where it had little in the way of true resistance to hinder its path of destruction.

Sukhov realized he had been holding his breath, watching the scene below unfold as if in slow motion. Forcing himself to exhale and take in a deep breath, he watched as the wall of water crashed and roared into the assembled legions below. The water carried a mass of dirt, debris and rocks from upriver, which he could see was pummeling and wreaking havoc among the soldiers, wagons, tents and animals in the field, washing the first lines of the encampment away as if they were fleas on a dog.

"What sorcery have you wrought!?" he exclaimed, his eyes never leaving the scene unfolding below them, "You are in league with the old witch!"

"Hardly. This was simple geography. We scouted the plain and found that there were at least three pinch-points in the hills above that camp that we could dam by felling trees and sliding a few loose rocks down from the hills above. With little more than one or two larger logs acting as linchpins, which we could pull out and let the weight of the water push down the dams, we knew we could back up enough water over the last three weeks to do exactly what we needed. Even though much of the army marched down through the same mountain passes to get here, few bothered to note the rainfall in the higher ranges, or the seasonal warming that was melting the snow and ice from the higher peaks."

"To know the land and have that advantage, it was child's play to make a few small changes that would tip the balance in our favour and let us secure the freedom to return home as we wished. Our home – not your home, but ours. Where we want to be; where we want to stay."

Jason's voice faded in and out of the General's ears as he watched the death and destruction that had been unleashed below on a scale he had never seen before. He was a veteran of too many battles to count, from every major campaign in recent memory, and while he was familiar with death, he couldn't imagine how one captain, with fewer than a hundred men, had managed to betray them all, and cause so much pain and death – it truly broke his heart as he saw the men being washed away in the flood, who did not even have a foe to fight back against in defense.

This grew only worse for him as the water reached the far side of the camp, and the remains of the initial wave, now a rolling mass of mud, debris, and bodies, crept over the tents of the Seventh – his own men. The wave had lost much of its speed and ferocity, but the quagmire it had transformed into, dragging the camp materials with it across the plain, made it almost certain that anyone in its path would not be able to stand their ground against it, and any that tired would be pummeled and crushed.

He didn't hear Jason detail all the preparations, but if he had, he would not have been entirely surprised to hear that the Rangers had been thorough enough in their preparations to even ensure that trees were felled downstream of the plain – another makeshift dam – to keep the pooling water on the plain instead letting it drain easily down the path of the river.

The Legion was nothing if not effective at executing a well-laid plan. This added measure served to make the already muddy plain into an instant swamp, where those who survived the initial crash soon realized they were not to have any relief as the wave passed. The water remained, and those who found themselves trapped, pinned, or otherwise unable to regain their feet, were not to be spared, and instead of the swift death granted by the crashing wave, they soon suffered a slow drowning.

The roar of the wave subsided and changed to the desperate cries of the wounded and dying, mixed with the panicked screams of horses and herd animals that thrashed about madly in distress, some charging wildly about the remains of the encampment, adding to the chaos and carnage.

When the shock of what he had just witnessed begin to subside, Sukhov slowly regained his awareness of where he was, who he was with, and what his predicament now was.

Jason was no longer beside him on the outcropping, and as he turned to look for him, he found his ability to be surprised was now completely lost, in a perpetual state of shock. He looked about at his five centurions, all now lying face down on the ground behind where he was standing, each with at least two finely made arrows lodged deeply into their backs, depriving them of their ability to breathe, permanently.

Twenty or so paces further back, he could see at least ten Imperial Rangers – scouts under Jason's command – emerging from the trees, and the scout camp just beyond. Distracted by the events unfolding below, he had never even heard the arrows fly, nor the bodies falling to the ground. Jason was standing back with his men now, arms resting calmly at his side.

Sukhov knew that he was no threat to him – not anymore – and he would be shot down by several bows before he could take two steps. He slowly turned his hands out, palms up, and moved his arms up slightly. Jason spoke softly and slowly now…

"You are free to leave, back the way you came, to go and see if any of your men survived. We have no quarrel with you directly, and trust that you will have the sense to know that it would be folly to seek us out after today." He shifted his stance slightly, as the rangers nearest the trail moved back, clearing a path for him to leave.

"You are free to go…," said Sukhov, slowly choosing his words, as he knew he had little choice, but also knew he was still a general in the Imperial Legion – or whatever was left of it in the valley below – and he would not bow before anyone. "You are free to go do whatever it is that traitors do, but I do promise you this – the Legions may be leaving these lands, but I will remember this. I will remember you. And I will come back. I will…"

He was cut off as Jason waved his hand and turned away, clearly not interested in anything further he had to say, and he knew it – he was nothing now, his legion was gone, swept away in a flash, and he would need to consider his next steps carefully.

The Ranger Captain clearly felt it would have been dishonourable to kill him in cold blood here, respecting his rank and position for the moment, but also didn't feel at all threatened by him, without his legions to back him up.

He would have to find a way to make him regret that…

******Omar******

Omar winced as he followed the old woman on her way out of the Praetor's tent and across the small square patch of ground between the officers' tents. The burns were still fresh across his body, as were Louhi's, and it was all he could do to keep from crying out while carrying the incense burner. The witch had given him something for the pain that morning, but it was wearing off and he needed more if he was going to ignore the millions of needles of fire that seemed to prick his every nerve, a constant reminder of the flames from that night. A single tear rolled down his cheek – the moisture was cooling, while the salt stung the wound.

He held back the leather animal hide that served as the door flap to her small hut and followed her through the opening. The interior was small and cramped, much as it looked from the outside, and packed with all manner of animal skins, bones, totems – incense burners hung from the small ceiling struts, helping to cover the odour of burned flesh that seemed to persist in their presence. A small fire burned in a metal brazier in the center of the hut, giving off a small swirl of smoke that floated up through an opening at the center of the arched roof.

Omar bent over to set down the incense burner he had been carrying, being extra-careful that it not accidentally tip over onto the many furs and cloths that covered the ground – he hated being near even the small sensation of heat that the burner radiated, and was glad to move away from it, but the small size of the hut meant he couldn't go far before he was almost on top of the brazier, or one of the other burners. He did his best to make himself as small as he could in the tiny space and tried to push down the strange feeling in the back of his mind that wondered how he ever ended up in a situation where this was what he called home.

He turned to Louhi and helped her remove her cloak after she had set down the small bag of bones she had used in the casting earlier. It had been almost two weeks since she had saved him from the fire, and he was still unsure if he wouldn't be better off having died. They faced each other for a moment, a mirror image of melted and scarred flesh, before he had to turn away, clenching to fight the pain.

"Ahhh, my young friend, you are hurting. It is time for some medicine, is it?" she asked rhetorically, as she turned to a small table at the side of the hut and picked up a vial of a bluish-green liquid and offered it to him. He took it from her cracked, weathered hands and quickly drank the contents. He closed his eyes as the liquid burned down his throat as he swallowed it quickly and then fought the urge to throw it right back up again.

Thankfully, by the time he had suppressed his gag reflex, he was already starting to feel the creeping warm feeling of numbness that the small concoction brought to him. Slowly the burning sensation subsided, and he could feel his muscles start to unclench – even muscles he didn't know he was clenching – which was followed quickly by an overwhelming sense of fatigue, and he wanted nothing more than to lie down and sleep.

Closing his eyes as he swayed on his feet, he drifted on the wave of calm, and his mind cast itself back to the night of the fire, when his whole world turned upside down.

He had been rushing back to his aunt's house and had been almost there before he thought to stop and listen for the footsteps of the horse that he expected would be following along any moment. Not hearing anything, he slowly resumed his course, casting glances back over his shoulder and nervously wondering where the dark rider from the tower was – he said he was going to help, and even if he needed a moment to gather his things, he was on horse and should have caught up to him by now.

Reaching the house, he was just about to let himself in when he took one last look back, and that was when he saw the orange glow rising over the dark silhouette of the buildings behind him. He quickly reached over to the lattice on the nearby wall and climbed up the wall to the rooftop to get a better look.

From his perch, he could not believe his eyes: where once he was able to look up and see stars, he could now only see a pall of smoke, eerily reflecting the orange glow of the fire. He could not believe how it had started and grown so quickly, yet alone spread along the edge of the market quarter, encircling the town and its inhabitants before starting to move inwards and consume everything in its path.

Omar scrambled back down and burst in through the doorway, startling everyone in the room.

"Fire!" he cried, "Fire! The town is on fire!"

He looked around at the open-mouthed expressions of surprise from Néni Marta and Balint – he could not have read Louhi's expressions if he tried – and there was a moment of silence around the room, broken only by the echoing of bells.

They had sent him for help, and this was so far from what anyone was expecting, that it truly took a moment for Marta and Balint to move from surprise, shock, and then disbelief. Unfortunately for them, they settled in on the disbelief stage for their reactions.

"What the devil!?" cried Néni Marta, "what are you doing, bursting in here yelling and screaming, while your mother is sick and trying to rest right there not ten feet from your crazy mouth!?!" She rose from where she had been sitting by the fire, and quickly looked about for something she could grab to hit him with.

Finding a ladle hanging from a pot near the fire, she gripped it firmly in her hand and turned to move across the room towards Omar. Balint was still closing his mouth and focused his attention on Marta's reaction, stepping forward to intercept her path to Omar, trying to quiet her yells for the same reason she was chastising her nephew. It was very close quarters, and so it all happened very quickly and in a very small space, causing Omar to jump back and almost fall out the door he had just come in.

Fortunately for him, the door had not closed, and he tumbled back into the open doorway, allowing everyone inside the house to see the same glow outside that had caught his attention earlier. Omar scrambled to his feet to avoid being stepped on as Marta and Balint rushed to the door and saw for themselves what was happening outside.

There were people in the streets now, running in all directions as each sought a path away from the rising flames. Turning in a circle, it was clear that the glow of the blaze was reflecting in the sky from all directions now, having completely encircled the market quarter. What had been their advantage for solitude – being set further back from the main warehouse buildings and the bustle of the main market square – now put them closer to harm as their nearness to the edge of the quarter meant they were going to be caught in the path of the inferno sooner rather than later!

Smoke was hanging low over the town and embers of ash were floating in the breeze, hastening the spread of the flames. He could feel the heat on the same breeze, making the air feel thick and heavy. Omar looked up and could see the embers dropping on the roof of the building above them, and he knew they would not have much time.

He rushed back into the house and saw Louhi still sitting at the table; ignoring her, he rushed to his mother's side and took her by the shoulders, trying to shake her awake; calling her name to no avail, she remained in her fever-dream state, barely stirring enough to mumble a few unintelligible words before drifting away again. Turning to Louhi, Omar cried to her for help.

"You have to do something!" he sobbed, "She needs to wake up! We need to run!"

Louhi rose slowly but did not respond to him. She moved to the far side of the room and picked up her bag and her cloak. Omar rounded on the door as Louhi tied her cloak, looking to his aunt or Balint for help – but they were gone, having run out into the night to save themselves.

Looking back at the old witch, he stepped in front of the door to block her from leaving, his desperation to save his mother making him forget about all of his earlier fears about her appearance or demeanor.

"We brought you here to help my mother, and we paid you! You sent me to the tower for more help, and we paid him! Now you must help her – you can't leave until you help her!"

He tried to solidify his stance in the doorway, spreading his feet, straightening his back to be as tall as he could, and holding his arms out – fists clenched – to be as imposing as he could look, despite his slender build. The witch looked him up and down, with a crooked smile on her lips.

"You have some fire in you," she said, "but there is nothing I can do for your mother."

"Liar!" he shouted, realizing that he could now hear the roaring of the flames coming from outside as the fire swarmed closer.

"There are things I can do for you, boy," she hissed in a low voice, which he had to struggle to hear, "…to help you find closure in all of this, but your mother is past my help." She gave a nod to the door as she continued. "Judging by the fires outside, it would seem that the Lord of the Tower agrees with me and has taken a more dramatic approach to ridding the city of plague – cutting off the sickly limb to save the patient."

Omar stood silently, drawing deeper breaths as the air grew hotter, and he started to notice small bits of burning embers dropping from the ceiling – glancing up, he could see that the structure above their house was already aflame, and they were out of time.

"You have a choice to make," Louhi told him, "stay here and die with your family, or come with me, and live to get your revenge. I am willing to help with the things within my power – and you will find that my power is great – but even the greatest power has limits, and we all need to know our limits."

She adjusted her cloak, but otherwise did not seem very concerned about their predicament, as the creaking and groaning of burning wooden beams and collapsing buildings grew louder from outside. "You need to choose what you will do next."

Omar choked back tears, and looked over at his mother, still lying motionless on the straw mattress on the floor, hoping that something would cause her to stir, to rise, or even just to turn her head and look at him – to give him some indication of what he should do.

And so his heart soared when he saw her eyes flutter open, looking up at the ceiling above, and then roll her head to the side so she could see him.

Their eyes locked, and he saw the briefest hint of a smile across her dried lips, before everything flashed away in blaze of falling timbers and beams as the ceiling in the bedroom collapsed and the blazing flames surged in brightness, consuming everything in the room.

The rush of air from the collapse blew across Omar's face, causing the tears in his eyes to dry almost immediately, and the cry in his throat was muffled before it could come out. He closed his eyes, and he felt his body go limp as he relaxed his rigid posture from blocking the doorway.

"And so, the decision has been made…" said the witch, moving forward and edging past him out the door. "Come with me," she said, "only by saving yourself can you make anything good come from this." She touched his arm, surprisingly gentle given her earlier tone, and he turned to follow her.

Things were not much better on the street than they were in the house. People were running back and forth in a full panic now, as many were finding no avenue of escape from the surging flames. Omar stumbled in a daze as Louhi kept a firm grip on his arm, leading him into the street.

He was still coming to grips with what had just happened – his mother was gone – and nothing else really seemed to matter anymore. Louhi, though not panicking, was trying to hurry him along into the street, seeking an escape from the flames, and paused only as they heard a strange hissing noise coming from behind them – burning embers were landing on the stacked oil pots lined up against the wall of the rendering shop, and the seals were quickly melting.

A blinding flash of light was the only warning they had before the force of the exploding oil pots leveled the buildings around them and hurled everyone standing in the street into darkness.

That was the last memory Omar had of that night before he woke up for the first time in the old witch woman's miserable hut. The days that passed were a blurred cycle of alternating pain and sleep – sometimes both at the same time –

as the old woman ministered to his burns.

Someone was calling his name – he could hear the voice, calling as if from a great distance, gradually getting closer and closer, until he finally felt the world snap back into focus. His mind had wandered, grateful to be anywhere but here, awake, back in the old woman's miserable old hut.

Awake was pain, and the old witch woman's elixirs made the pain go away, but it made his mind go away as well. Not that he minded that very much. Anywhere was better than here, he told himself, awake. And so he fought the urge to follow the voice, willing his mind back to his dreams.

It didn't work.

"Omar!" She said his name again, forcing his eyes to focus on her gnarled hand. "You need to sit down. The bones have told me that we need to leave this place, so you need to sit."

"Sorry – what?" he asked, still disoriented, "If we need to leave, shouldn't we be packing?"

The old woman waved her hand at him dismissively. "Suit yourself," she snarled, stirring the coals in the brazier at the center of the hut. For no apparent reason he could see, Omar suddenly felt incredibly dizzy for a moment, and then found himself sitting on the carpet anyway. There was a roaring noise coming from outside the hut, with muffled screams of men and animals, and Omar found himself quickly panicking back to attention, rushing to the door of the hut to see what was going on outside.

Throwing open the bearskin flap, he found himself looking out from the top of a hill on the southern side of the Lakhani Plain; they were no longer in the camp, but somehow, they were high above it, looking down on a horrible scene of death & destruction, watching as the wave of water swept towards them through the Legion camp, and flowed out and down into the surrounding woods. It was a disturbing scene, and as much as he wondered how they were here when they used to be there, he was nevertheless incredibly grateful that they were no longer there.

The old woman emerged from the tent to stand beside him, watching the scene below unfold. After several minutes, as the water crested and eventually began to subside, Omar turned to the old witch woman.

"You have to teach me how to do this!" he said, with a desperate, insistent tone that summed up all his rage, frustration, desire, vengeance and more.

The old woman looked back at him and smiled. He felt the look was condescending and turned away, looking back at the mayhem on the plains below them.

"You saved me for a reason," he said, trying to calm the tremor in his voice. "You can find a servant boy anywhere, certainly one who is whole and not a mangled mess like me."

He was trying his best to act the role of the man of the family, the one who would be charged with seeking recompense for the dishonour and injury inflicted on him and his mother, but try as he might, he was still just a boy, who could not stop his jaw from quivering. His fourteenth birthday would be coming up in a few weeks, and the thoughts rushed in about how his mother would not be there to wake him and tell him how proud she was of how big he had grown; to tell him how he was such a great provider even if she didn't always agree with his mischievous ways; not that he would ever be able to lift a purse or a piece of fruit from a market vendor again – he looked down again at the melted flesh of his arm; the emotions hit him just as if he had been hit by the wave in the valley, and he began to sob uncontrollably.

Louhi furrowed her brow and did her best motherly voice. "There, there," came the sandpapery rasp, "everything will be alright." She gently put her hand on his shoulder and led him back into the hut, sitting him down on a bed of blankets and furs. She poured him a drink of some liquid, which he drank, and it soothed his nerves. He took deep breaths and slowly regained his composure.

"What sort of man am I," he asked himself aloud, "crying all the time?" The thought almost brought another wave, but she diverted his attention with a quick "Tut, tut now, Master Omar, you have been through much, and I have promised you that I will help, and so I will." He wiped his nose with a long swipe of his good arm across his face and looked up at her with reddened eyes.

"I want to know how to make a flood like that, to wipe out my enemies – I want to crush that stupid man from the Tower…"

"Torick" she interrupted, "His name is Torick, and he is a mage."

"Torick" he repeated, burning the name into his memory. "I want to find him and make him p…"

"Shush!" she interjected again, "Did you not hear what I just said? He is a 'mage' – do you even know what a mage is? Not some simple shaman, taltos, or even a garaboncid – you do not want him for an enemy. He is an angyalok – one of the ancient ones, the first ones to learn the art of channeling! If it truly was he who set Mercurum afire, you can be certain that you will need more than your tears to defeat him…"

"Teach me what you know! You have powers, too! I saw the wave coming – you moved the hut; show me what you know!"

"You think these things come easily?" she asked him. "The magi will spend their entire lives – and more – studying ancient secrets – secrets that will turn your hair white and curl your toes, and you think I can teach you a few tricks in a matter of days and set you loose? Ha!"

Omar sunk back into his spot on the carpets at the rebuke and pondered his next words. Louhi moved past him and threw back the flap to exit the hut again – this time she emerged into a cave, somewhere deep underground, lit with an assortment of candles, torches and braziers spread out around the walls. Omar leaned over to see that their hut had moved yet again, and quickly stood to follow her out, taking in their new surroundings with a sense of awe that quieted their discussion for the moment.

The cave was at least ten times larger than his home, with ledges, nooks, and crannies, all stuffed with books, scrolls, and bottles containing dark liquids and strange animal parts. Several tables in the room held artifacts and relics in various states of preparation or experimentation, with books containing rituals and recipes spread out for easy reference for the various tasks at hand.

It was almost a cliché from every bedtime tale his mother had told him, but he could see old, melted candles – too many to count – flickering and flitting in every space that didn't already have something in it. To one side there was a bed, to another there was a fire pit, looking cold and unused in some time. There were pots and plates scattered about between the papers, and in a few places, he could spot more than a few rats dining on the leftovers of previous meals.

Apparently, for all her mystical powers, Louhi had not yet learned a spell to clean her dishes.

"Come here," she beckoned, as she rummaged through the mess on one of the larger tables around the cave. "Let me see your burns – it's been a while since we've had a chance to look things over, and I think we can tidy up your wounds a bit better."

He cast his eyes back to the scattered mess around the cave that clearly was her true home and felt the irony sting as much as his burns. He truly hoped she was better at healing than housekeeping. He moved over to the table, sat in the chair, and removed his shirt.

"Don't judge!" she chastened, as if reading his thoughts. "I don't get back here very often, and when I do, I'm often in a hurry to leave again, so pay no mind to the mess!" She began poking and prodding at his wounds, and he winced with every touch.

In minute detail, she examined every inch of his burns, paying special attention to any areas that had not yet scabbed over, or were still seeping pus. When she finished her examination, she began grinding various ingredients in a large clay bowl, occasionally adding a drop or two from a vial of some unknown extract – he physically twitched when she spit in the bowl and continued mixing.

He was caught off guard when she resumed their earlier conversation…

"So, you want to learn my magic, do you?" she muttered from the other side of the table.

"Yes!" he replied quickly. He carefully drew his shirt back over his head, as it was quite cool in the cave.

"You will never be able to match him in skill or power – you are well behind already, and he will keep learning himself you know…"

"I know, but I need to try," he answered, trying to keep his voice from sounding desperate. He didn't think she would appreciate desperation as a good motivation to help him.

"Who knows if you'll even be good at it? He might die of old age before you've learned how to light a candle!" She came around the table from the other direction and gave him a light whack on his good shoulder to get his attention, motioning for him to take his shirt off again.

When he had done so, she began applying a cold, grey poultice to his wounds, completely covering the burned and scarred tissue. He shivered when she applied the first of it and winced more than a bit as she spread the strange paste over his wounds generously, then finally she wrapped it all with some cloth bandages. Finishing, she placed the bowl on the table and turned again to face him.

"And what is in it for me, to help you find this power within you? I have better things to do than tutor an apprentice. Who says I want to be spending my time teaching you ancient secrets and holding your hand as you screw up the simplest tasks and melt your own mind into pudding?"

He knew she wasn't seriously concerned about his well-being, and it was more of a question about what he could offer in return. And he couldn't think of a good answer.

The silence hung in the air like a thing, he could almost see it. She was giving him all the time he needed to come up with an answer. She was no longer moving about the cave, and in the silence of his thoughts, he could hear noises that he hadn't noticed before – the dripping of water, landing on a small flat rock somewhere to his right; the flutter of leathery wings up near the ceiling as bats jostled for position; and something that sounded like a cross between a purr and a growl, coming from the darkness beyond the well-lit center of the cave.

There was much more going on in this small cave than he could have ever imagined, and there was so much more that he wanted to see and do in life; first he would have his revenge, then he would find his place in the world, and have everything he ever wanted.

He just needed the power to do it. And in that he found his answer.

"I will do anything you ask of me…"

******Jason*****

The Rangers' ride back to Mercurum went much faster now that they were no longer encumbered by an army. Their horses were rested, and their hearts were anxious, brimming with hope and expectations of a simpler way of life in the north, free of the Imperium. It was all they could do to take their time on the treacherous mountain trails that crossed the barrier peaks, before giving the horses full rein to gallop home once they reached the more level terrain of the plains. Still, it was a long distance and took two days before they reached populated lands again.

When the first farmhouses had come into sight, they avoided contact, as many of their group still bore their Imperium uniforms and garb. They had dropped much of the insignia and badges of rank along the way, but the military cloaks and quilted red jerkins were too indispensable in the chill of the mountain air for them to cast aside too hastily. They agreed that they would seek to barter for better, nondescript clothing once they found some locals who were perhaps more sympathetic to their situation.

As a conquering army, soldiers of the Imperium were not always welcome everywhere they went, and though they maintained order in the cities, the rural areas were more prone to open acts of reprisal against their new overlords. Now that the Imperium had withdrawn, they were not foolish enough to believe that they would simply be welcomed back by everyone with open arms, even though they had deserted the Legion and were expressing their allegiance to their adopted homeland. Jason doubted many would take the time to engage in any real conversations before seeking to extract retribution for the harsh conditions the occupation had imposed on them – just one more thing he had to thank General Sukhov for!

They passed several farms once they cleared the mountains, and after camping one night in a copse of woods, and not seeing any lights or evening fires from one such farm, they decided to approach and see if they could find anything to address their wardrobe issues, and perhaps scrounge something extra for breakfast for the men.

It was just after dawn, and Jason had Ferenc select five men to join them in their little scouting party. They carefully approached the property, keeping a watchful eye for any signs of activity. Approaching unnoticed, they could see livestock in the field, grazing, and smaller farm animals scattered in smaller pens. Further away from any towns, this was clearly not a tenant farmer, working crops for a local lord, and so they could see that there was a great deal of variety in the livestock and crops they might expect to find here – this would do well for resupplying their troop.

As experienced rangers, they were cautious of any signs that were out of the ordinary, and they exchanged a great deal of information with subtle gestures and expressions. This was how Jason learned that the cows did not appear to have been milked in several days; a fox appeared to have raided the chickens several days ago; and despite the cock crowing all morning, there was no one moving about tending to any of the usual chores that a farmer would have been awake and taking care of by now.

The main farmhouse stood apart from a barn-like structure from which the animal pens emerged. The house had a central form that was built of sod – sturdy, but low and squat in size. Newer additions had been made, extending the house into a lightly larger wooden frame that had larger windows – compared to the sod foundation – and a little extra living space for the farmer & his family.

Jason signaled Ferenc to set one man as lookout, take the remainder to search the barn, and he would scout the house.

He moved cautiously up the door of the sod structure and knocked on the door. It moved inwards slightly at his knock, which he took as an invitation to enter. There were no lights or candles lit, leaving just the minute amounts of light streaming in through the narrow slits that passed for windows on a sod house. He could make out a table, a chair, and a stove at the far end of the small room. There were scraps of food on the table, as if dinner had started – several days ago – and rats had helped themselves to the leftovers. He could see no one, and after glancing behind the door, he slowly moved into the room and crossed the floor to the door opening that led to the rest of the house.

The ceiling was higher in the next room, and he could see a ladder leading to a loft which he presumed had beds for the family. In front of him was a bed for the parents, and a few other pieces of furniture, but what attracted his attention was the strange panorama of bodies that were sprawled across the room. The two smaller bodies, curled up in the near corner, were clearly the children, who appeared to have tried to crawl away from the terror before it killed them; a third body was on the bed, but the mess of the remains made it hard for Jason to identify this as the mother. The only clue for this conclusion was the form of a man standing motionless in the far corner, facing the corner, and holding a small hand axe in his right hand, hanging at his side.

The figure remained unmoving as Jason paused in the doorway. The morning light streamed in through the larger windows in this part of the house, and he could see the blood splatter covering the unmoving figure. Wearing simple farm clothes, it didn't take much for Jason to piece together what had happened, although the 'why' eluded him... until the figure turned around to face him...

Jason was rarely surprised, but he took a breath when the man moved, and he saw for the first time the bluish green colouring around the eyes, nose and mouth of the near skeletal face staring at him from across the room. The whites of the eyes had coloured red with blood, and he wondered if they could truly see anymore. Then the figure lunged at him, and he had no more time for wondering.

He stepped backwards through the doorway into the sod room, easily dodging the first swing of the axe. He felt behind him for the edge of the table, and moved sideways and around it, keeping his eyes on the man in front of him. He quickly found his way back to the door, sidestepping another clumsy swing before he could step outside into the open.

By the light of the early morning sun, he could see more clearly the person who lumbered out of the doorway, still following him, and it did not help the feeling in the pit of his stomach – his skin hung from his frame, dark and mottled, the colour of ash; he moved slowly but with purpose, and by the weapon in his hand, Jason could not mistake the murderous intent.

He drew his sword and prepared to defend himself, although he had to admit, he was feeling less threatened and more curious about what had affected this man, to make him turn on his family – and now him – in such a mindless, ferocious manner. He had heard of men who flew into berserker rages in battle, but this wasn't some frantic, wild man coming at him. This was something different – although he didn't have a great deal of time to consider it further.

His curiosity was abruptly cut short as an arrow flew in from his right and pierced the neck of the man in front of him. He stumbled to his knees, making slow gurgling noises as he choked on his own blood and eventually fell over and died a few steps from Jason's feet.

He looked to his right and saw Kiara shouldering her bow.

"What did you do that for?" he asked.

"What, save you?" she replied with a smile, "You're welcome."

"I didn't need saving," he protested, "I was trying to see what it was capable of–"

"Oh, right." She cut him off, with a bigger smile on her face now, "you were just playing with him, sure," she teased.

Ferenc and the others had trotted up now to join them, as they stared at the body on the ground.

"What happened to him? "Ferenc asked.

"I don't know, but whatever happened, his mind had died long before Kiara's arrow took him." Jason was puzzled and poked the body with his sword. "Look at the face – the eyes, the skin – is this the plague we were hearing about?"

Before anyone could answer, Kiara stepped forward, knelt beside the body and pulled on the shaft of her arrow, to remove it from the corpse.

It was to become a subject of much discussion around later campfires, debating if the man had stirred at that moment and raised his lifeless arm to strike at her, or if it was simply the force of her yanking that caused the body to move, but two swords swung – Jason and Ferenc, moving as one – quickly and cleanly removing the arm and head of the body, ensuring there was no longer any doubt about its demise.

There was little conversation after that, and they carried on their way.

It was the day after that encounter that they began to come across refugees coming towards them from the direction of Mercurum. The first few were stragglers, then it became a steady flow of people: clearly fleeing for their lives, many of the women bore the signs of having their hair forcibly cut or shaved; the men looked battered and abused; their clothing torn and dirty, some wearing just their sleeping gowns, as if roused in the middle of the night and ousted from their homes.

Some of the women carried babes in their arms and held out their free hand to beg for food from the passing rangers. All bore some form of the same wound: freshly cut into their flesh or burned by makeshift brands – it was a mark in the common Avar tongue, which Jason was not immediately familiar with. Ferenc soon provided him with a rough translation, which explained what they were seeing – collaborators.

When the Imperium withdrew, it seemed that the local population had turned on their own, punishing anyone who had been suspected of aiding the invaders.

At this point, Jason halted their ride, gathered his men, and gave them his final orders as their captain.

"Go your own way from here, as quick as you are able," he told them. "I release you from any obligation or service to either the Imperium or to me as your captain. We will always be brothers, but you each need to go and care for your loved ones. God speed!"

They had joined with him in his plan because they each had someone they cared about, in various towns, hamlets, and homes across the province, and they would reach them all fastest if they were free to go their own way – and Jason wanted no part of trying to keep the band together and say which loved one they would seek out first, and which would wait.

His troop dispersed, spurring their horses in various directions along the road or across the plain. He clasped arms with Ferenc and Kiara – they each had to suppress the urge to salute – nodded to some of the others and saw them on their way before he put the spurs to his horse as well. He, of course, was going to race to Katerina, and he could not help but feel the knot in the pit of his stomach turn tighter and tighter with fear for her safety with every passing moment…

Jason had only been in Nyirseg for a month when he first met Katerina. He was accompanying the quartermaster on a supply run into town, and they were near the end of a long day of haggling with the last of several crafters. In fact, it was her father that he had met first.

While the quartermaster was berating an apprentice smithy, Jason had stood back from the market stall, watching the discussions unfold. Observing, he could see another, older man doing the same behind the smithy – tall and broad shouldered, with a greying beard and thinning hair, he also watched the negotiating going on between this metalsmith and the Imperium quartermaster, casually scanning the crowd at the same time until they both locked eyes for a moment, and they exchanged a smile. Stepping forward, the man placed his hand on the smith, who, up to that point, had been very heated in his defense of the quality of the products they offered. Calming instantly with the touch, he looked back at the older man, nodded, and stepped back from the table.

"Shall we take a break from this haggling, for a moment?" he asked, "perhaps we can have a drink of something cool, to help soothe such a heated discussion… the day is too hot for such things, and we often forget ourselves in the moment…" He waved a hand and a young girl stepped forward from the tent behind the market stall, carrying a small jug, dripping with condensation. Pulling several cups from a small box, she deftly poured the cold water for everyone, sparing a quick glance at the young captain before stepping back again into the tent.

Jason raised his cup and nodded to the proprietor and took a drink of the refreshingly cool water. "Perhaps we could arrange to continue our talks somewhere more civilized?"

"Over dinner perhaps?" the owner responded with another smile, "perhaps, Captain, you and your retainer could join me at my villa for dinner this evening, and we can discuss the finer details of your needs. I'm sure we can resolve everything before we finish dessert!"

Jason nodded and returned the smile, placing his cup back on the tray. "Certainly…"

"Jozsef. Kalmar Jozsef." Said the older man, completing the introduction.

It was during dinner that evening that he saw Katerina for the second time. Jason's attentions were not lost on her father as he made the reluctant introduction.

"This is my daughter, Katerina," he stated, following Jason's gaze. "She has seen seventeen summers, but she is not for you!" he declared unambiguously, which drew as much of a reaction from the young girl as from the Jason, as they both looked at her father in surprise, and then at each other – instantly set on defiance of his wishes without scarcely having said a word to one another.

It took Jason nearly a month and several more trips back to the market – using every excuse he could come up with to visit the smithy – before he could say that they had struck up any kind of relationship. It would have been hard enough to expect her father would grant him – an Imperium Legionnaire – permission to court his daughter, and everything that would carry with it, but he knew it wasn't as simple as that. Katerina made it very clear from the beginning that she had a mind of her own, and he shouldn't expect that he could simply barter or trade with her father for her hand in marriage.

And this made Jason's spirit soar – he would come only when she was working at the market table, and ask for the most unusual crafts, argue the price, or demand refunds for work that was perfectly fine, just for the chance to speak with her. Her father was stubborn, yet also wise, and a true judge of character, so he conveniently found his own excuses to be away from the market stall whenever Jason came by, allowing Katerina to manage their affairs without his disapproving gaze.

And so it did not take long before their rebellion against her father became something more sincere. It was perhaps another month before he worked up the courage to ask Jozsef for his permission and blessing on their engagement – something he would not have ever contemplated doing without having asked Katerina first, of course – out of respect for her father more than anything else he supposed.

Then the Imperial messengers arrived.

Then everything changed, and it was no longer just a wedding that they had to plan. They had choices to decide, and new plans to make.

And up to this point, everything had gone according to that plan. Now all that was left was for Jason to return and they would have their chance to live happily ever after.

Jason arrived outside of Mercurum alone. Plumes of smoke were still rising from several parts of town, though the market quarter had long since burned itself out. He hadn't been there to see it, but the panic at the burning of the market more than a week ago had set off a powder keg of fear and rage – the simmering resentment the people bore for the now-departed Imperium troops boiled over the entire city and they had lashed out, venting their anger at anyone – Imperium sympathizers, city guards, old feuds and new grudges.

About a mile outside of the town, down the road from the south gate, hastily erected gallows made it clear that those who suffered the hot irons of the branding were the lucky ones.

It took nearly an hour to go through the forest of bodies swaying on their ropes before he could be sure that she was not among them.

A small glimmer of hope sparked for him as he ignored the harsh looks of the grave diggers who had assembled to complete their tasks, and he spurred his horse and raced down the south road into town. A warm hope that turned as cold as ash again when he reached what remained of Jozsef's villa amidst the smoking ruins of the merchant neighbourhood.

He dismounted and began to search through the rubble of the burned-out building, looking for any sign of Katerina or her father. Shifting half-burned beams to see the ashes below, he was not so distracted that he couldn't tell he was being watched. He knew that there were people passing by and some had stopped in the street to see who might be looting in the rubble. Most were simply curious, and he hoped the rage of the mob had subsided over the few days since the fires had been set. But there was someone else watching, too.

Gently resting a piece of half-burned lumber on one of the remaining bricks, he spun quickly, drawing his dagger from the sheath on his left leg, and poised himself to deliver a quick blow to the figure looking out at him from around the corner of one of the few stone walls that remained standing.

He was greeted by a squeak of surprise from the young girl that stood before him. Dressed in a dull white gown that looked more grey than white from all the ash, her blonde hair hung in a tangle down below her shoulders. Perhaps twelve or thirteen years old by his guess, she seemed more startled by his movement than threatened by his weapon. She never even looked at the dagger, but kept her eyes on his, and quickly turned her surprise into a grin of delight.

Jason had never seen her here before, and so she was certainly not any relation to Katerina that he knew of. She cocked her head slightly as she watched him process his thoughts, looking at him curiously. Jason straightened up and, realizing that he was still holding his blade on the young girl, he quickly blushed and sheathed his weapon.

"Sneaking up on someone is an easy way to get hurt," he admonished her, although she did not seem to be offended by it. "What are you doing here?"

"I live here," she answered in a spritely manner.

"What?"

"I live here," she repeated.

"Hmm, I don't recall Katerina mentioning anything about you..." Jason wondered aloud.

"Who is Katerina?" the young girl asked.

"This was her house – or rather, her father's – and I had been here often before this..." he gestured to the ruins around him "...and I have never seen you before. Were you a servant? Or a relative?"

"Everyone's a relative, silly," she responded with a giggle. "But I don't know Katerina."

"I thought you said you lived here." Jason was confused.

"Everyone lives here..." she said, "...in Nyirseg."

Jason rolled his eyes. "I meant here in this house, not the whole damn province!"

"Then why didn't you say so?"

"Ugh," was the only response Jason could muster at this point, and he turned back to his search through the rubble.

"Are you looking for something?" she asked curiously "I can help! I'm good at finding things, especially lost things!"

"I'm looking for Katerina," Jason answered, not really interested in keeping the conversation going.

"Is she short?" the young girl asked, squatting low in the rubble of the house, lifting the occasional brick or tile at her feet.

"Short? No, she was about my height–" he started to say, before she cut him off.

"Then why do you keep looking under such small pieces of wood for her?" There was a childish bewilderment in her voice, especially odd even for someone of her age, and Jason paused, not sure that he wanted to be the one to have to explain death to this young girl. He turned again to look at her, and she looked him directly in the eye.

"She's not here," the girl said softly.

"What?"

"She's gone, and she's not coming back. You can stop looking and go home – you won't find her." Her voice was less childlike now – flat and even toned. Jason didn't reply right away, so she continued:

"You should go now and prepare for the Withering. If you endure, you will eventually find what you are looking for." She paused for a moment, and then moved back around the corner of the wall from where she had emerged. Jason lunged forward, eager now to ask her more questions, but he knew what he would find around the corner: she was gone.

Jason finished his search of the rubble, but found nothing – no evidence that Katerina, her father, or any of their servants had been caught in the blaze. Perhaps she had left and escaped the mob before things got out of hand. But where had she gone, and why had this little girl delivered this strange message – who was it from? How did they know? It couldn't have been the girl herself, could it?

Who was she? And what the heck was a "Withering? He was certain that this was just a strange encounter with an escaped lunatic child and nothing more – he would find Katerina. Her father had probably fled to one of the other city-states – Ascanium perhaps – he would have to see.

He was still wrapped up in his musings as he began to walk out of the ruined villa when he stumbled over a piece of fallen ceiling timber. Dropping to one knee, he caught himself with his hands before he fell on his face completely – and he felt something through the covering of ash on the floor. Grasping it and pulling his hand out, he quickly blew off the ash & soot and found himself staring at a necklace – a simple metal chain, not gold or precious metals that might have melted more easily in the fire; crude in substance but finely woven, with a single small pendant, holding a single small gem.

His heart sank, as he knew she never took it off – she wore it night & day, because he had given it to her – there was no way it would be on the ground here unless she was on the ground as well. At the same moment, the young blonde girl's voice seemed to drift through his head again on the wind:

"She's gone and she's not coming back."

Jason wrapped the necklace in a piece of cloth and put it in his pocket. A noise behind him made him turn, hoping to see the young girl once more, that she might tell him where Kat was.

He never saw the blow that struck him across the jaw and had only the briefest of moments to feel his teeth shatter and mix with the salty taste of blood in his mouth before he was enveloped by darkness.

"Gyorgi, he's waking up…"

Drums pounded inside his skull as he could feel his pulse throbbing in his ears, as if his heart would burst from the effort of simply raising his head from his chest. His shoulders stung from the strain of supporting his weight with his arms bound behind his back, wrapped around one of the burnt wooden beams of the ruined manor house. A crust of dried blood covered his forehead and much of his face – it seemed more than one blow had landed after the first blind-sided attack had knocked him unconscious. And as if on cue, the sensation of raw, exposed nerves from his shattered teeth threatened to submerge him in a fresh wave of agony, with blackness beckoning rapidly.

From somewhere behind him, a hand reached out from the darkness and yanked his head up before he blacked out again, whispering angrily in his ear, "Now, now, don't go falling asleep again, legionnaire, we've got some business to discuss."

"Oh yeah," another voice echoed, "some long overdue business to take care of, eh!"

Three voices. Three blurred grey figures, shadows dancing in the firelight. Townsfolk by the sound of them. Maybe even the ones who had burned the house and done… lord knows what to Kat and her father!

"Fuhgh…"

He tried to talk but he choked on the blood in his mouth as his lips failed to move and make the right sounds. The fresh sting of cuts re-opening made his eyes water – at least he hoped it was water – as dried blood cracked open and flowed anew. There was very little sensation in anything below his eyes, but from what he could feel, he guessed that a large portion of his cheek was hanging well below where it should have been, and the large pool of blood around his knees in the dirt made it clear he had been bleeding…a lot.

"Oh, look, Piotr, I think he's trying to say something" one of the group observed, waddling over to stare him in the face, his eyes flitting over the various injuries. "Well, points for effort!" he laughed, stepping back and almost falling into the fire, the laughter quickly turning to shouts and curses as he stumbled about in search if his wine cup.

Jason's head would have dropped again if not for the grimy fist that clenched his dreadlocks firmly. Fighting through the haze of the pain, he rallied his senses to assess just how desperate his situation was.

He was outnumbered, at least three-to-one. Dressed like townsfolk, they were poorly armed but full of anger, resentment, and wine, with the need to lash out at anyone who might be responsible for their woes.

Bound by rope, his hands were numb but not entirely lost to him – he was already feeling his way around the large but basic farmers' knots which worked well to hold loads in place but were rather simple for nimble fingers to unwind. The post at his back was good timber, but had been weakened by the earlier fire, and though it was still embedded firmly in the earth below, experience told him the exposed ashen wood would snap quick enough if he threw his full weight against it.

The hand which had gripped his hair let go and the bulky frame of its owner shuffled around to his front. Larger than the other two, this one was clearly a smithy or dock worker, and brandished a small, curved knife that would have served well for slicing open packages or pieces of meat at a butcher's shop. Tonight though, it was being used to exact a personal toll.

"You shouldn't have come back" the one called Gyorgi snarled, holding the knife out between him and Jason, "you Imperials had the run of the land for too long, and we were less than dirt to you! Well, I don't know why you thought you could just come back, all by yourself, and expect us to just cower and shit our pants just cuz' you were part of some great army – well guess what, there's no great army here anymore! They've all gone, and now it's my turn!"

He lunged forward angrily, threatening with the knife, but clearly not ready to use it just yet.

"You thought you would just drop your coat and fancy cloaks and be able to ride right back in and fool us… but we ain't that dumb!"

"No sir!" piped Piotr, "We seen that pretty horse, and that shiny sword and we knew… only Imperium types likes their swords so much they polish them day in and day out!" They all laughed at their cleverness in spying him out.

The fire crackled and shot a flurry of sparks in the air.

With everyone looking at the fire for a moment, Jason decided now was the time.

Pressing backwards with all his strength, the wooden beam snapped, and he rolled his knees up to his chest, carrying his weight over to free his legs from beneath him. He dropped the now loosened ropes and rolled again to his side, reaching for the broken timber, ready to spring to his feet and come up swinging at whomever was closest.

At least, that was the plan.

His arms, more numb than he had realized, came up short of reaching the broken post and instead pawed the empty air. With neither the post nor his arms to support himself, his roll carried his face down in the hardened dirt, which triggered a howl of agony as an excruciating pain shot through his battered head.

Purely on reflex, his hands grasped his face, and he was alarmed to discover just how much of his cheek was hanging away from where it should have been. Now he was scrambling just to hold everything in place as fresh rivulets of blood began to seep between his fingers.

From his knees, he could see that his efforts had done little to improve his situation. All three were in front of him now, framed by the fire in the evening light, and all three laughed at his desperation.

Piotr and the other man were still laughing as a shaft of blackness whistled out of the dark and pierced Gyorgi's neck, cutting short his laughter into a whistling, wheeze of air through his perforated throat. The burly man dropped his knife to clutch vainly at the arrow protruding from both sides of his neck as he slowly melted to the ground.

Piotr was caught in mid-breath, looking down in surprise to see his hand secured firmly to his belly by shaft of another arrow from the dark. As he too dropped to his knees and fell over, the third man – Jason never did get his name – was spinning in circles by the fire, waving a metal rod that had been his weapon of choice earlier, searching frantically for their attackers. In his panic, he never saw the long, slender blade that slid through his ribs from behind, his eyes widening to stare at the strange steel protruding from his chest, as his blood began to bead and drip from the cold metal, before darkness quickly took him to meet his friends.

Jason was still trying to understand what had just happened, untrusting of his blurred vision to be sure, when he heard Ferenc's voice gently at his side.

"Easy now, we've got you!" he whispered, as the 'we' emerged from the darkness opposite the fire. Kiara was still holding her bow with an arrow knocked and ready, surveying the ruins of the manor house as she moved closer to Jason and Ferenc.

"I think that was all of them" she declared, no longer feeling the need for stealth or whispering.

"How is he?"

"He's alive, but…" Ferenc shot her a concerned glance as he cradled Jason to the ground and scrambled in his pack for a cloth to hold against his wounds.

"We'd best find someone where else to camp tonight" Kiara suggested, "in case any friends come looking for them. Can he ride?"

Ferenc shook his head as he tied off the cloth and put Jason's hand on it to apply pressure. Jason was trying to speak but he hushed him. "Tsk tsk, we leave you alone for a few minutes and look at the shit you get into!"

"I saw a cart a little ways back down the road" Kiara offered. She didn't wait to see Ferenc nod in agreement – they had ridden together for long enough that they knew what each other were thinking whenever they were in a tight spot. In short order she was back with cart and Jason's horse as Ferenc finished bandaging Jason's face – which seemed to be his only serious wounds – and they quickly got him to his feet. He was unconscious again as soon as they laid him out in the cart.

*****Voros*****

The fire was cold, and the ashes swirled when the polished black boot nudged the burnt logs. Stepping around the stiff, dead bodies of the three townsfolk, the tall, slender figure examined the scene with great interest, reimagining the previous night's events from the evidence on the ground.

"They took you by surprise, outnumbered, and had everything they needed to get the job done" he spoke aloud. "But still they lie here, failed."

"Did they?" he answered himself, alone in the night.

"Do you see another body?" he waved his arm across the scene.

"He might have crawled away to die... surely they struck a mortal blow – look at the blood!"

"I told you they were useless – we should have used professionals!"

"We should look around more..."

He turned quickly. "No, no, you are both wrong – there's no body, there are no assumptions. It either is or it isn't. No maybes!" he snapped.

"He had help then..." came the calm observation.

"But who?"

"Her?" he said curiously, bending over only slightly to examine the footprints in the dust and rubble of the ruined house, placing his large black boot beside a smaller print in the ash.

"Probably."

"She knows better than to interfere..."

"...and yet she does, time and time again..."

Anger crept into his voice as the singular debate continued.

"If she is going to break the rules, then we should break them too!"

"Yes. We must do what needs to be done."

"But which rule to break – that is the question... there are so many rules. So many things that could go wrong..." he noted quietly to himself.

"We will break them all if we have to" he answered, his teeth clenching. "This isn't the first time they have sought to interfere with our plans."

"We have played by their rules for too long. Now, we will make our own."

As he finished, another figure emerged from the darkness coming down the road. The echoes of hooves on the pavestones of the roadway were swallowed by the night as the oddly humanoid shape approached the dark robed stranger and awkwardly bowed, like a newborn fawn learning to walk. The fur covered figure held the bow until he could see the polished black leather of the boots tap the stone where his scarred snout almost touched the ground. Rising, he spoke in a hoarse voice.

"The trail is more than a day old – a cart and three horses – it leads to an old manor house atop the hill, about a league outside out of the town."

It paused, waiting for an answer that did not come.

"…Others have arrived to join them." Sniffing the ash-laden air, it suppressed a sneeze. "Master Voros, they are still disorganized and unsettled. We can muster a gang and route them before they…"

"No!" the answer came sharply, "We will leave them be for now. If they are being helped, then we must see to our own if we wish to have the numbers to succeed… I have another task for you now, Kemeny, one I trust you will enjoy. Come, now, we must prepare for a journey of our own."

The tall man turned on his heel and quickly strode away onto the night, leaving the creature to relax his awkward stance and settle back onto all fours as he trotted along after him.

A gust of wind swirled the dust and ash before it resettled again on the floor of the vacant manor home, and the night was silent once again.

*****Omar*****

Omar woke after a deep sleep – the best sleep he could remember in recent weeks. Not once had he been woken by the pain of his burns, or the nightmares of that awful night. This morning he felt refreshed, alive. Sitting up from the low straw bed, he stretched and began to hunt for his shoes. It was cold in the cave, and he could feel the chill in his bones. Then the strangeness of it all began to dawn on him – he could move without pain!

Slowly, he repeated his stretch – bending his arms up around his head and outwards – and was amazed to feel any pain or stiffness from his burns. Quickly unwinding the bandages around his arms, head and torso, he felt up and down along the side of his body, and could feel his skin, warm and fully healed, no scabs, no open sores, no nothing. He could see the rippled texture of the scarring from the burns, where the flame had melted the flesh and reshaped it like the melted wax of a candle left to burn too long, changing the patterns of his skin in places – and where he would never grow any hair again – but it had otherwise healed completely overnight. He felt some strength even to be able to move and bend as he had before he was injured.

He looked around and saw the old woman across the cavern, bending over the cooking fire and adjusting the coals, cooking something that smelled delicious, as the aromas drifted across the chamber to where he sat. Quickly putting on his shirt & shoes, he hurriedly walked up behind her, ready to tell her how amazing her poultice had worked overnight, all the while feeling a rumbling in his stomach that drove him to distraction as he was even more entranced by the smell of whatever she was cooking.

Without turning, she spoke before he could get a word out:

"Ahhhh, I see you are feeling better, yes? My medicines did their trick?" He could feel her smiling behind the words, as she paused to take a taste of the breakfast she was preparing.

"Yes, I feel much better this morning. Thank you." he said, doing his best to remember his manners while his mouth was watering. "It's amazing what that mixture and a good night's sleep could do." He stretched his arms again, swinging them back & forth like a newfound toy.

"A good night's sleep, eh? Well, I imagine if one good night's rest did such wonders, then you should be feeling incredible after sleeping for thirteen nights! Haha haha ha!" she cackled loudly, as if sharing a joke.

"Thirteen nights?" he repeated, his voice drifting off as he couldn't think of what else to say to that.

"Come, you must be hungry." She waved him over to the table and began serving the food. He sat down and took a plate, filling up on a variety of foods that he recognized, and some he didn't. He was hungry and thought better of asking what the stranger items were – everything he tried was tasting delicious, and he thought it better not to disrupt his appetite by asking questions he didn't want to know the answer to – she was a witch after all, and the stories about witches never seemed to include normal things.

Eating until he was full, it was only afterwards that he dared to imagine if any of his breakfast might have included an "eye of newt" or a "liver of cat." He was almost ready to drift off again at the table when he was interrupted.

The witch had been going through her books and scrolls, and finding what she was looking for, she brought it over to the table and put it down with a heavy thud. It was a small, heavily bound book, no larger than his hand spread wide, with a blackened leather cover, worn animal skin pages that almost seemed as thick as tablets, tied together with multiple loops of fine gold chain, so thin as to even be thread – he couldn't be sure. The chain shone brightly in the cave, while the rest of the book looked dusty and worn. So dusty that he had to choke back a cough when she dropped it on the table.

"What's that?" he asked.

"This…" she replied, gently patting the cover of the book like a pet, "this is your path to greatness – immortality even – if you dare to take it!" Omar sat up straight, attentive to whatever came next.

"I have your attention, then? Good, because you need to pay *very* close attention to what I am about to say." She was across from him, leaning forward on the table, staring intently at his eyes, as if looking for any hints or clues about whether or not he was understanding her.

"There are no shortcuts to wisdom," she continued, "but there are ways – old ways – that we can use to access powers beyond your imagination. All one needs to do is be strong in both heart and mind – especially in mind."

"I have healed your body and given you the strength to withstand what comes next, but you need to be sure that you are ready in here…" she said, pointing her bent finger towards his forehead, just above his eyes. This was the moment when Omar realized that her burns still had not completely healed, and her bandages were still showing signs of blood and pus seeping from her wounds.

"Wait," he said, as he reached for her hand. She withdrew quickly, before he could catch her hand. "Why did you heal me and not yourself? Why didn't you use the poultice on your own wounds?" he asked with a mix of curiosity and anxiousness.

"All power has limits," she replied quietly. "Mine do not always work so well on myself as they do on others. It can be both a blessing and a curse, such as now." Her voice was softer when she answered. He had asked about healing the burns, but she had a lifetime of other examples that now crept into her mind, where she could clearly remember times when she wished she could have done things for herself that might have changed her path of life a hundred different times. She shook off the reverie almost as quickly as it had come upon her and focused on the boy.

"If we do this, you will learn the secret of magic in the old worlds, though you will not have the benefit of all the years of study that other, learned mages have earned through a lifetime of practice and devotion to these arts. There will be powers revealed to you, but also dangers, and you will need to be careful of both if you wish to survive the experience."

Her tone was completely serious now and even a bit threatening, which frightened Omar just a little.

"You made a vow to me, and I will hold you to it. You will gain what you desire, and I will give you the time to master what you are given, but I will come to you when you are ready, and I will demand payment from you."

"I thought I said I didn't have anything to pay…" He trailed off as he spoke, trying to remember what he had said before he had fallen asleep.

"You said you '*would do anything*' for me," she whispered, moving around the table to stand beside him. Her eyes were only slightly higher than his, despite him being seated, and she was pressing close to him now. "…and I will ask you when I think you are ready." She brushed her finger along the side of his face, tracing the scars to his jawline, then out to his chin, where she gave him a little tap. "But don't worry, if you don't measure up or fail to master this power, I might never even call upon you for this favour at all. You might never see me again and live the rest of your life in peace."

Omar exhaled as she moved away, and he felt the tension release from his body – he hadn't even realized he was holding his breath – she was really quite creepy when she wanted to be, he thought to himself. He recalled what he had said, and though he felt some concern now in the back of his mind, not knowing what she might ask of him, he was still certain that he wanted power more than anything. And sensing that she could actually do it, that it could be his, he wanted it even more. So what if he owed her a favour?

"What happens next?" he asked, with all the cockiness of an impervious teenager.

Turning with a grin, she said, "Now we have to stitch you back together!"

"Huh?" was the best Omar could come up with at this point, being completely confused.

"Pay attention," Louhi snapped, "you need to know what is happening, so you can master it when we are finished. This is especially important!" She shuffled around the table again, and opened the small book to the middle, without seeming to pay much regard to which page it opened upon.

"All mages draw power from other planes. They bend it, shape it, harness it to their will. They do this after years of study and training. Anyone can do it, all it takes it access to the right knowledge, and a little talent – the more creative you are, the better! Some do it better than others – one might devote a lifetime to study and barely be able to light a match, while others will move mountains with barely a thought. The Avar peoples – you & I – were first taught how to do this by the Angyalok, who were here long before the Avar, the Torpek or the Alakvalto…"

"The alak-what?" he asked.

"The 'who', not the 'what', and stop interrupting – this is the short version, as we don't have years to teach you the full history of the Avar people in Nyirseg, let alone the whole world! So, shush! Where was I? Oh yes. The Angyalok taught the first Avar how to channel interplanar forces – or magic – as they had long before mastered it themselves. Being incredibly long-lived, they could learn a great deal in a single lifetime and could do wondrous things with their knowledge."

"Over time, the Avar realized that they would never live long enough to learn enough to be able to match the abilities of the Angyalok, so they turned their studies in a different direction. Soon enough, they discovered a way to reconnect a spirit with its past lives, and by doing so, the person would gain the benefit of the wisdom and knowledge of their forebears, vastly expanding their knowledge and abilities to channel magic. Soon they were able to match the Angyalok in their ability to do great things with this power and were proud to show off their newly enhanced abilities to their mentors."

"The Angyalok, however, were horrified by this method of connecting with spirits of the departed and found the practice abhorrent to their nature. Well, most of them did. Anyway, they slowly began to distance themselves from the Avar mages, and the Avars took this as a sign that the Angyalok were threatened by the power. There was still much the Angyalok could do that the Avar could not, and by withdrawing, the Avars thought the Angyalok were trying to keep their powers secret from them, to maintain some advantage over their 'students'.

"This created a great sense of animosity, which made the Avars begin to turn on their Angyalok allies, as well as the Torpek, the Alakvalto, and even the giant Oriasok – all of whom, until that point, had stayed largely uninvolved in teaching anything to the Avar."

"There were some Avar who were so hungry for power that they willingly stitched themselves to many of their past selves, greatly enhancing their knowledge, and they used this to hunt and defeat many of the other elder races, establishing the dominance of the Avar people in this world. The Angyalok, Torpek and Alakvalto are now scarcely seen, having retreated to their last remaining territories, though there are a few still around, here and there."

"Don't the Avar mages hunt them down now?" Omar asked.

"Good question, but you should know that much of this story happened many hundreds of years ago, and the Avar mages who did most of the destruction soon learned the curse of stitching – that is the most important lesson I need you to now learn: when we connect someone with one of their past selves, they will gain access to all of that person's lifetime's worth of knowledge and experience; they will know magic that they had learned, or how to farm a plot of land – we do not know for certain what any of us did – or who we were – in a past life, so we must take what we get once the die is cast."

"We may conduct the ritual with you tonight and discover that your ancestor was a very good poet, and you will have to decide how to use these skills to seek your revenge!"

"What?" Omar cried in astonishment, "What do you mean? You said I would have power to..."

"Yes, yes, yes! I know what I said! I also told you to stop interrupting me!!" she snapped back at him. It was during this break in listening to the story that Omar noticed that she was not reading anything within the book but had been working with her hands while she talked, slowly unbraiding and removing the golden laces that were holding the pages of the book together. He found this quite odd but decided it was best that he just keep quiet as she continued the lesson.

"The first Avars who learned how to stitch spirits for power found this to be a concern as well, and so they did their own research into the matter, and eventually found a way to detect the potential in an adept or apprentice that would identify where the strength of their spirit lay, and so they could have a good idea of when someone would have a high potential of having a connection that would help them in their current life. This was not a perfect predictor of results, but it greatly enhanced their likelihood of success. They could see the potential, but in some cases they could not see how many lifetimes ago that potential may have existed."

"They might make one connection, but find they needed to do the ritual a second or third time to connect with the spirit that had the potential they were looking for – it is all sequential you see, you can't skip along the line; you have to take what comes, in the order it comes. This is where things got to be problematic, and still are, to this day."

"The early mages found that they could stitch spirit, but in addition to the learnings and experience, they also connected with some of the intelligence – the memories, the personality, and very often, even the voice of the person they were connecting with. This essentially created two minds within one body. One person with the wisdom and abilities of someone who has lived two lifetimes, but also now a competition for which of the spirits would be in charge of the one host."

"In most cases the past spirit would be quiet, submissive, and silent. But as some Avars sought to challenge the Angyalok, they began to connect with multiple past selves, and in doing so, the risk became greater with each ritual that the past spirits would not sit idly by and let the host control them all. This risk was doubly dangerous as the early mages would often be repeating the stitching ritual many times over, as they might as easily have found themselves to have been a carpenter in a past life instead of a mage, and so they would have to return again and again until they achieved what they desired." The old woman paused and took a drink, tired from the telling.

"This is the reason now why we have such powerful schools of magic, run by families and not royalty. Once it has been found that the ability to channel magic is strong in a particular family, you can be sure that the schools will ensure that any progeny from those families will study magic, as their mothers and fathers would have done before them. Since there is a greater likelihood of a past life having been in the same family tree, this also increases the chances of connecting with mage abilities on the first or second try."

"These days, the risk of madness is so great among the Avar people that few will agree to stitch an adept more than one or two generations back, for fear that they will lose control and wreak havoc on the world as they go insane."

"What about the Angyalok," Omar asked, taking advantage of a timely pause in her story to interject with a question. "Did they ever learn how to 'stitch' their powers?"

"Some did. As I said earlier, most Angyalok felt it was obscene to consider connecting to a past spirit, that it somehow chained that spirit to the material world, which they could never consider inflicting upon one of their honoured ancestors. But like all races, there were those among the Angyalok who did not share these same compunctions. After the majority of the Angyalok had retreated from these lands, a few remained and sought out the secrets that the Avar had learned, including how to connect with spirit."

"Some of them took to it naturally and were beneficial; a few sought their revenge for what the Avar had inflicted on the Angyalok, seeing the Avar people as an upstart race of apes, lacking in the grace or character they deemed required to be worthy of their power and place in the world. Some say these Angyalok mages had connected too many times and had gone mad. Needless to say, they created some of the greatest periods of destruction and terror that had ever cursed the history of the Avar lands, and we are glad they are long gone into the past.

"But enough talk. You know what you need to know. Tonight, we will do what we need to do, and we will see what the morning brings."

She stood and held an arm up, dangling the long golden wire, woven into a single thread from the bindings of the book, and now threaded through a large, hooked needle, shining silver in the dim light of the cave.

Omar took a deep breath and swallowed involuntarily...

*****Plague Upon Plague*****

The darkness was quiet, but for the gentle gurgle of the water as it slowly swirled in the pool at the center of the cavern. The tall, solemn figure standing at the water's edge moved slowly to light the many candles that ringed the pool, reflecting their light in the dark water. The pool might have been considered large – it was nearly twenty feet across – were it not for the small island of rock that rose from the center, half as large as the pool itself. The constant swirl was created by the many rivulets of water that flowed in from the surrounding floor of the cavern, themselves fed by the dripping from the stalactites that hung from the ceiling – a never-ending stream of mineral-rich waters that flowed through the unnatural channels marked in the lava-rock cavern, merging and growing, winding their way to the center, emptying into a bowl-like crater that was now completely illuminated by the flickering yellow glow of the almost torch-like candles.

Master Voros appeared older in years – perhaps forty or fifty judging by the wisps of grey in his short beard – he was garbed in the plain dress of a simple peasant or farmer, though clearly, he was not. His hands did not bear the marks of such labour, nor did his face show the lines of worry and fear that the simple folk earned over the hard years of a short life.

No, his face showed little sign of enduring hardship, and he was almost fair in his complexion. Long hair hung over his shoulders as he peered down into the water, as if reminding him that he ought to pause for a moment to tie it back in a knot before he continued his work. His cotton shirt was stained with sweat and dirt – splattered with something reddish, rust-like, that might have been blood, but was dried now. His leather vest was covered with pockets, each buttoned firmly shut, except for the one or two from which he withdrew small pinches of powder and sprinkled it over the water of the pool.

The water bubbled and steamed, turning a murky brown as it continued to flow in circles – it hissed as a larger bubble popped and spit droplets across the stone lip of the cauldron, causing him to quickly step back to avoid the drops falling on his polished leather boots. The excited water subsided as the flow mixed in the current and moved around the far side of the island. He lost sight of the hissing water as it passed behind the black monolith that stood in the center of the island.

Four-sided and made of a single piece of dark obsidian, it did not reflect the light of the candles – rather, it seemed to absorb it, making itself visible more by the depth of its blackness than by anything the light revealed about it. It was adorned on all four sides by the engraved shape of a sword, long, narrow, and wreathed in flames. In one of the images, it was grasped by a gauntleted hand, in another, the gauntlet was still there but the flames were gone; in the last, the gauntlet and the flames were gone, replaced by a snake, coiled around the hilt and poised as if to strike at any hand that might reach for it.

"How different a story it would be if you were here with us…" he whispered, staring at the obelisk, before quickly snapping back to the task at hand, and stirring the muddied water along with a broad wooden paddle. Somewhere below the pool, through an unseen crack or crevice, the water emptied – slowly – into an abyss of darkness, and he knew he had only a short while to complete his work before the mixture he had made in the pool flowed out as quickly as the new, fresh water flowed in.

He reached down to grasp the earthenware pot lying on its side by his feet, looking like a discarded piece of trash. It was dirty, covered with clumps of soil as if it had recently been unearthed, and smelled musty and dank. He hefted it deftly in his hands, as if it were empty, them held it closer to his ear, listening for the quiet sounds of something shifting inside as he moved it about. The narrow neck of the jug flared into a wider opening, which was sealed with a stopper covered in hardened clay and a net of hemp-like string – clearly not something that was intended to be opened casually or regularly. Satisfied with whatever he had been listening for, he lifted the pot above his head and brought it down hard on the rocky lip of the cauldron, causing it to shatter and crumble to pieces around him. There, encased in the jug and now exposed to his sight, was a scroll, carefully rolled around a knobbed wooden core, balancing on the edge of the pool, much more precariously than he had intended.

He cursed under his breath, regretting his flare for the dramatic and quickly snatched the precious vellum from the rock before it might tip into the water. He fingered the smooth material as he turned it over in his hands, feeling for the waxy seal that held the maker's mark – a reptilian face, with narrow-slitted eyes, a snout and forked tongue, the mouth curled in a snarl revealing rows of daggers for teeth, encircled by an interlocking chain that began and ended where the neck should have been.

He held the scroll closer to the nearest candles – careful not to get too close, as the vellum had been softened and preserved with oils that not only made it quite enduring, but also considerably flammable. On the backside of the skin, faded markings in green ink could be seen depicting figures that resembled insects, one on top of another. Yes, he nodded to himself, this was what he had been hoping for.

The grave diggers who had died unearthing the nondescript pot had known nothing of what they had been tasked with retrieving, nor had the riders who had carried the jug back from the furthest borders of Uzhgorod to the trading post in Dej, where it had been sold to his antiquities buyer in Ascanium, then transported innocuously across the great plains as part of a refugee caravan. It traded hands several more times – all people in his service, whether they knew it or not – before it had arrived here as an offering for the cult.

He did not mourn that the grave robbers had to die – theirs after all, was a heinous offense – but they were the easiest links in the chain to replace, and the most obvious place to start if anyone were looking for links back to him.

He held the scroll gently in his hands, as if holding a precious child, and turned back towards the swirling pool, all the while mumbling words that were not the common tongue of man. These were ancient words, spoken for centuries before the Avar had ever come to these lands, by the faerie folk who were the first creatures to walk upon the land as both guardians and conquerors. Ancient and powerful creatures – ancient and powerful words.

His voice grew louder until it reached a crescendo, his arms raised high, and he pressed his thumbs into the hardened wax of the seal with force, cracking it open, and letting the pieces fall into the water, where it hissed and boiled at the intrusion. The aged vellum, released from its bondage, uncurled ever so slightly from its tightly wound composure, and the hissing noise changed instantly to a thrumming hum – a buzzing that grew and echoed in the darkness of the cavern, rebounding off the walls and ceiling in a cacophony of noise, then slowly aligning into a single rhythm, drumming – pounding – seeking a release from its captivity. Its power released, the ancient vellum crumbled to dust in his fingers and fell like sand into the waters of the pool, causing it to boil and hiss angrily.

The earth began to shake and tremor, and for a moment, it seemed that the entire cavern might collapse. Then, in a sudden burst of sound, the drumming ceased, and all was silent. The tremors stopped and the earth was still. The muddy water swirled and drained from the pool and was quickly replaced by the fresh streams of clear water running off from the tiny streams in the cave floor.

All was still again, as if nothing had happened.

He smiled to himself, dusted his hands against his shirt, and turned away from the pool and began to make his way out of the cavern. He was almost out when he heard a noise that made him pause to look back.

Rocks tumbled on the far side of the cavern, and a crack appeared in the floor, following the curved flow of the lava channel as it made its way from the edge of the chamber towards the center. It was soon followed by the hiss and cloud of escaping steam. He looked around the darkened chamber, and though there was no light by which to see, his eyes moved as if following the escaping heat – he counted four such steam vents now in the floor of the cavern and nodded to himself with a small smile.

Three more to go…

*****Jason & Kiara*****

Jason stood on the balcony of what passed for a tower in the manor house. The manor itself was only two stories tall but sprawling in size, with a sharply angled roof, covered in wooden shingles. This small turret extended from the west side of the structure, rising a full twenty feet above the roof, providing an unobstructed view of the surrounding area. There were balconies extending in three directions from the room at the top of the tower, and Jason stood looking out to the West, watching the sun begin to dip lower in the late afternoon sky.

His beard had grown over the past few months, making him look a little older, and perhaps a little wiser than his years would have suggested. His hair was longer as well, no longer being pressured to keep the short cut preferred by Legion officers. He stroked the hair on his chin absentmindedly as he surveyed the property – the growth covered many of the scars that now adorned his face like a broken spiderweb.

He had healed well since the ambush – at least, those wounds which could heal. He was still bereft of a good number of his front teeth, and aside from having to learn how to speak and chew all over again, his new aversion to smiling only reinforced his already grim demeanor.

Their ranks had swelled since they first sought refuge here, and a few nights shelter turned into weeks, then months. They were not the only disheartened legionnaires found on the roads – several members of his own scout unit stopped on their way – many returning with equally heartbreaking tales of their own lost loved ones, the victims of a vengeful peasantry, although a few returned with loved ones in tow, safe but outcast by the locals.

A scattered few soon turned into a solid company of well-armed, well-trained defenders, able to protect the manor from the roaming packs of plague-born – that is what they had taken to calling those poor souls that had succumbed to the mind-numbing sickness, rendering otherwise upright citizens into packs of wild savages. He had heard many names for the illness, and while this one didn't sit well with his meager learning, he wasn't one to argue logic with a mob, and it was the word that seemed to roll-off the tongue easiest in any conversation.

As evening now approached, he looked across the fields at the long shadows being cast by the wooden palisade that had been hastily erected around the perimeter, expanding from the iron gates across the laneway entrance and protecting the small farming plots that had been cultivated inside their protective ring.

Jason sighed as he turned back into the chamber and descended the winding stairs. He was tired after the long patrol earlier today, but he somehow felt obliged to do a quick walk-about of the property, just to see how everything was going. Ferenc and Kiara had pushed him to do the patrols, though he suspected it was just a ploy on their part to keep him busy – he knew they could see the sadness that had set upon him, and he also knew they were determined to see him through it. For his own part, he went along with their prodding if for no other reason that get away from his own thoughts – a distraction from his own self-pity.

Kiara was at the door as he exited the manor, and he knew she would want to hear his report from the patrol, so he waved for her to join him.

"Welcome back, sir," Kiara chimed, stepping up to his right. The track was muddy from rain the day before, so there was some occasional skipping to avoid the deeper puddles as she tried to keep up with Jason's pace. "How was the patrol?" she asked.

"It was good," he replied, his voice thick and weary, "nothing too exciting."

"That's not what I heard," she countered, "I heard you encountered some plague-born just a few leagues from here."

"It was just a few mindless ones, hardly worth mention" Jason noted calmly, as he walked out past the smaller homestead building that had been erected in the spring to help house the growing number of guests at the estate. He waved at the smith, shaping metal at the anvil, and the smith raised his hammer in salute in return.

There were several work sheds on this part of the property, where the crafters plied their trades. In addition to the smith, they had several carpenters, who doubled as cartwrights, coopers; a butcher who was also their furrier; a cobbler had set up shop as well, though they did not have a cordwainer, so they would have to rely on the cobbler for repairs, since new shoes would be scarce for some time.

He was grateful that they had found some folk with talent in the kitchens, to cook and bake for the growing community – many came as families, and cooked for themselves in the new homesteads, but many of those who served as men-at-arms or household staff relied on his kitchens for producing their daily meals.

"Do you want to know how the harvest is looking?" she offered, to which Jason slowly nodded absently without actually answering.

"Good, very good..." she replied, "...we should be well stocked for the winter, but it will be tight to try to build a storehouse inside the palisade – we're running out of room." Jason paused, looking around at the fields below them and then back up to the houses and craft buildings which almost obscured their view of the manor house from this angle.

"Any luck finding a new fletcher?" Jason asked, "...we had to count our shots today and engaged the plague-born hand-to-hand – a needless risk for our tiny band."

Kiara looked away at the mention of needless risks – she and Ferenc had been worrying for weeks as they watched their former commander take on increasingly dangerous patrols, often engaging in hand-to-hand melee without any apparent regard for his own safety, and he seemed numb to their concerns. They were quickly coming to doubt the wisdom of their plan to get him out of his stupor by getting him into a proper regimen of activity – Jason had been reluctant at first, but now seemed to be using it as an excuse to risk his life.

"Sorry sir," Kiara replied in a crisp, military tone, "we haven't found anyone in the camp with the skills, although we have been training a few who showed some rudimentary knowledge." Not much was not about how the plague spread, but his instinct was to stay as far away from an infected as possible – they still did not know how the fletcher had contracted the disease, but when the fury took him, it took several rangers to subdue him before they ultimately had to put him to the sword.

Kiara sighed. For the moment, it seemed they didn't have much of a choice in the matter. The fletcher had been a master – stitched at least once, perhaps twice – and had been invaluable to them, yet reluctant to take on an apprentice. They had suggested it to him many times, but he rejected every candidate they had sent him. Now, they lacked a shaman who was skilled in the old ways to even consider stitching one of the younger apprentices – not that they had any interest in delving into the ancient magicks that the local people had practiced since before the Legion had ever arrived – they were distrustful of such things and preferred to see people learn things in their own time rather than relying on shortcuts.

"Jason!" shouted Ferenc, interrupting his pondering, "Jason, you look like you could use some good news..." he said, walking towards them up the muddy trail with his arms on the shoulders of an average-looking fellow, clearly new to the homestead and looking quite lost.

"This is Kiraly, Boros Kiraly..." patting the man on the back heartily. "Kiraly is a vintner!" Ferenc was clearly quite excited by this news, although Kiara seemed rather unconcerned.

"A 'vintner'?" repeated Jason, quizzically – they used the local common tongue as much as they could these days, though not all the words translated well for him… "Do vintners make arrows?"

"He makes wine!" Ferenc explained cheerily, "and by his telling of it, he is quite good at what he does."

"He's not from Mercurum, is he?" has asked of Ferenc, ignoring the man presence for the question.

"No! No, he has been on the road for days now, lucky to have made it this far…" Ferenc replied, jumping in as the man was about to answer for himself.

Jason nodded in approval and smiled "Well then, welcome, Kiraly. I'm sure you will have your work cut out for you here. Has Ferenc shown you our vineyards yet? I'm afraid it's not much to look at, but perhaps with the right touch you can help us out."

Jason, still stuck in his own head, paused for a moment to wonder whether the vintner had come into his knowledge through his own experience, or if he had been stitched to one of his predecessors, stealing the knowledge of his forefathers. He looked back on the small craftworks he had just passed through and wondered how many of them may have done the same. Then he slowly shook his head and realized that he did not truly want to know.

Things were good as they were, and that was enough for him. He noticed Ferenc still seemed to be waiting there with the new vintner, and so he politely nodded to excuse them. Ferenc nodded back and pulled the new man along to show him the grounds, as Jason turned with Kiara to start walking back to the main house.

They walked back to the manor hardly saying a word – his mind was clearly elsewhere, and she was always a little too nervous around him to want to interrupt him when he was thinking. He was – still – her commanding officer, and she just assumed anything he was worried about was surely something important. Until she couldn't bear the silence any longer.

"I have been loyal to you, have I not?" she asked.

"Pardon?" he seemed surprised at the question, breaking his reverie.

"I have been with you since I first joined the Legion" she blurted, "assigned to the Scout Company when we were first deployed from the Capital to come… here. I earned that assignment. Of all the recruits in my cohort, I mastered the bow, the sword, riding, tracking, foraging – I worked harder than everyone else to earn a chance to join the Scouts."

"Yes." he answered, as she paused to take a breath, though clearly wasn't finished making her point…

"I have travelled with you, patrolled with you, fought at your side, and now committed high treason with you!"

He did not speak when she paused again, watching, and waiting for her to continue.

"You truly care about those under your command, we can all see it. I know – knew – many in the Legion of who would have given their left arm to serve under your command and there isn't a man or woman here who wouldn't lay down their life if you ordered it. When the orders were dull, you made them matter; when it was dangerous, you gave us courage; and when things seemed impossible, you inspired…"

She paused again, as she searched for the words she wanted to say but was having trouble finding them. They had been walking along a path, looking forward as they spoke, and as she began to speak again, she glanced towards him and could see he was looking at her, waiting, and the words vanished from her tongue once again.

When the pause became unbearable, Jason spoke.

"I'm not sure where you're going with this Kiara…" he began, "but I'm sorry to have dragged so many into this exile…"

"Don't be sorry!" she replied quickly, "This has been the greatest adventure that any of us could have imagined, and we are free to decide about it for ourselves!"

"But the drought, the plague-born… this land is cursed, and I have ensured that none of us can ever escape it!"

"We are with you" she answered, "I just wanted you to know that is all."

I am with you, she thought to herself.

"Thank you" he replied with a smile.

Kiara warmed as he smiled at her, and she had to look away before he could see the flush in her cheeks. She had wanted to say more, but she knew it was not her place to say any more than she had. He is – was? – betrothed to Katerina, and though things had not played out the way she had hoped since she joined his company, all she could do now was wait, and let him find his own way.

He had been planning to set out to search for Katerina months ago, hoping that she might have escaped and gone to Ascanium, or perhaps was hiding in a smaller town somewhere between here and there – someplace where she was not known and might still be safe. He carried her necklace with him always now, as a reminder to himself that there was always hope – he hadn't found her body in ashes, and she always seemed too quick, too smart, too ready for anything, to not have seen it coming.

He didn't know what to believe, but he knew that he always felt better when he convinced himself that she was alive.

Breaking from his reverie, he looked over at Kiara just as she looked away – he hadn't even realized she had been staring at him as they walked.

"You know it was never supposed to be this way," he said aloud, as if speaking to no one in particular.

"What do you mean?" she answered after a moment, almost surprised that he was talking to her about something that wasn't about the estate.

"When the plague hit, everything changed, again, and I no longer felt that I could abandon the men, their families, or any of the others that had come here for refuge. If not for that, I would have left long ago to look for her." He didn't need to explain who – she knew.

"I didn't think the Avar people would follow me if they didn't have to..." he pondered out loud, "I didn't ask them to come out here; I didn't even tell the men where I was going to be – they just came."

Kiara considered that for a moment. "They came because they heard what others were saying – good things."

Everyone knew what had happened almost a year ago. People had abandoned the countryside in droves, unable to finish the fall harvest without fear of being attacked, or worse, catching the plague and becoming one of the berserkers themselves. Most initially fled to the cities; the small ones offered little protection, and the larger ones – like Mercurum – could provide some temporary refuge in the outlying quarters, but the Ispan was quick to seal the gates of the inner city as soon as things started to look bad. This meant that it wasn't long before the plague began to infect those in the unguarded sections of the town, where they had no walls or guards to prevent the spread from outside. By the first snows of winter, all but those in the inner city were either victims of the infection, or victims of the berserkers among them.

Aside from the knights and bannermen that served the Ispans and other nobles, the former Imperium troops were the only other able-bodied fighters that were organized enough to offer any kind of real protection to those who couldn't fight for themselves. Many of the former scouts had returned to his banner, but some had not, and he hoped they would survive, wherever they were. Then the locals began to arrive at his door.

They were very tentative at first – rumours had been rampant after things happened on the Lakhani Plains, and eventually they all seemed to lead back to one Ranger Captain who, in one day, had defeated and killed more of the invading legionnaires than all the battles fought by all the Avar Princes and all their armies over the last generation! The truth was devastating enough that there was little any bard could do to embellish the incident.

So instead, they invented an image for the young captain that was enough to make any man believe that he was not only a ferocious giant, but he could swing entire trees as a club! On more than one occasion he could see new arrivals to the manor sizing him up, as if believing he should be bigger. Disappointed with the reality of it, they still were glad when he accepted them in, believing if anyone could save them from the plague-born, he could. Which was also enough to make the local Avars overlook that he himself was once a soldier of their oppressors — in this storm, any port was welcome for those cast adrift.

Except for bards — he had no care for the lies of minstrels and storytellers.

"We hoped it would end with the winter," Jason said, causing Kiara to startle — there were such long pauses in his end of the conversation that she wasn't sure he was still talking to her.

"I know," she stammered, "I was on the patrols. We had hoped they would die from the cold, but they didn't — at least not all of them did." It was still a very vivid memory for her, seeing the frozen bodies in the forest — some were lying in the snow, while others were still standing, facing a tree or a broken wall, as if it had suddenly popped up in their way and they couldn't figure out a way around it, and then just froze in place. It was chilling to know they were battling such a mindless scourge — it would either infect them with the madness or have them killed by madmen. No good choices.

"We still don't know where they keep coming from" she finished, "I hadn't thought there were that many people in all of Nyirseg or any of the Avar lands."

"I know," Jason sighed, "I can't believe it's been months now, and just how screwed up our plans have turned out."

Kiara was not accustomed to seeing this self-doubt in his attitude, but kept quiet, knowing when to listen.

"I know I'm not the only one who lost something in all of this — a few of the lucky ones have been reunited with their loved ones, but I wonder if we might've been better off just leaving with the Legions." They had reached the manor now, and he continued walking along the wall as they talked, not wanting to go inside just yet.

"Summer is ending, we have a harvest to bring in, preparations for another winter, it all just keeps moving — one thing to the next — and soon enough it will be too cold to consider a long trip, let alone the freedom to leave all this behind and search for Katerina. Not to mention that even if there a trail to follow, it has all gone cold – as cold as the winter – and, and…" he paused, then just groaned, "…aghhh!"

Kiara looked around, checking to see if anyone was around, close enough to overhear. It just wouldn't do for people to hear the Lord of Greymantle Keep express his doubts and frustrations this way – it wasn't the sort of thing that inspired confidence in his leadership. The rangers would always be loyal, she knew, but there were a lot of northerners in the compound who she was afraid still resented relying upon an Imperial Legionnaire for protection and might just as soon seize any opportunity to see a change in leadership.

"Sir, perhaps we should go inside if you want to discuss this further," she suggested. There was no one close by, but that didn't mean that wouldn't change.

"Discuss what?" he retorted quickly, "Discuss how all of this is hanging by the barest of threads? Shit, you and Ferenc have been running things from almost day one – and doing an amazing job of it – but let's face it, things haven't quite gone according to plan, have they? Damn, we haven't even begun to talk about the rumours of Alakvalto in the woods yet either!!" Jason raised his voice, getting more excited as he spoke. "Shit! Like that's all we need now: people running around spreading tales about faerie-tale monsters running around trying to steal babies and eat sheep! It's insane that we are expected to have to deal with this!"

Kiara could feel herself shrinking with every word as his voice grew louder and louder during his rant, until she could no longer bear the thought of his drawing unwanted attention. She closed her eyes, not that he noticed as he was hardly looking at her as he spoke, and then when she couldn't bear any more, she did it.

She slapped him across the cheek, with a solid crack that echoed much farther than she had intended, snapping him out of his rant. She immediately regretted doing it, fearing that she had only ended up drawing more attention than his ranting.

"I'm sorry!" she whispered, stepping back.

He had stopped talking, and the silence now felt louder than anything. He was looking at her with a mix of shock, surprise, and embarrassment. His cheek was red from where she had hit him, but both of her cheeks were even redder as she blushed and apologized profusely for her insubordination…

"Thank you," he said, interrupting her apologies. "I guess I was getting a bit carried away there."

"A bit." She said, "You were…"

She was going to say more but he had become distracted by a light flittering noise to his left, like a small child's toy, and he turned to take a closer look.

He didn't see where it was coming from at first, finally resting his eyes on something small sitting on the fence rail. Hearing the sound again confirmed it, and a second insect landed on the fence beside the first. They were large for an insect, each one with a body the size of his finger, with long crooked legs, and wings folded in against their body. They only paused briefly on the railing, and as he reached to touch one, they took flight again, moving out into the evening sky, the strange buzzing noise breaking the quiet of the early evening.

Jason shook his head and yawned to pop his ears – the noise was getting louder even though the bugs were moving away. He slowly moved around the corner of the manor house; catching the last light of the afternoon as the sun was dropping towards the horizon, he felt his heart sink as looked to the sky in the distance and saw the leading edge of the swarm moving in their direction.

It was still quite a distance away, but there were so many that it looked like a massive grey cloud creeping forward across the ground, stretching as far as the eye could see. Moving as one, the fluttering buzz of their wings echoed in unison across the sky ahead of them.

"Shit!" Jason muttered.

Locusts.

*****Torick*****

Torick reined up his horse as he reached the peak of the narrow mountain trail. The wind was blowing hard, driving the light snow almost horizontally across his face, obscuring his view of the valley and surrounding mountains. His mare shuddered in the cold, despite the many blankets hanging across the sturdy mount like barding. He stroked her snow-crusted mane with a dark gloved hand and looked down the trail behind him, waiting for his guide to catch up.

He knew they were close to his objective, and he had raced on to the top of the trail, anxious to see if they had arrived. About fifty yards back, the older Gomorian Sherpa, Nirmal, followed slowly on his mule, guiding him carefully up the rocky trail, where Torick had been almost reckless to race ahead. Living in the mountains his whole life, the Nirmal had seen many visitors fall to their death after losing their grip on the loose rock of the steep trails – he was in no hurry and had made sure that his family had been paid for his services in advance.

As he waited for his guide to catch up, Torick pulled a small piece of parchment out from his tunic pocket and unfolded it to reveal a map of the Matras Mountains. He traced his finger along their path and stopped where he believed they ought to be right now, before folding it up again and tucking it away.

Reaching the top of the trail, Nirmal pulled up beside Torick, whose horse was at least twice the height of the mule, forcing him to look upwards at his employer for the entire trip. He smiled cheerily when Torick met his gaze. Torick tried his best to hide his disgust for his Gomorian guide.

"Where is it? Torick asked impatiently.

Still smiling, Nirmal nodded head, saying "There, there," pointing forward on their path and just a little to the left, where the terrain dropped off in a sheer cliff, to a canyon floor almost two hundred feet below. At least that was what he had been told – the blowing snow obscured their view of anything more than fifty feet out, making it impossible to see anything clearly. Torick followed the direction he was pointing in with his arm and stared intently into the snow. "Kekes. There…"

"Damn it!" Torick muttered under his breath, with the words moistening the scarves covering his face, then almost freezing before he could take another breath. It was getting colder, and he was running out of time to find what he was looking for, and it was incredibly frustrating to see this old man take his sweet time the entire way! And now the snow was going to make it impossible to see the waypoints he needed to follow – a mountain should have been easy to spot, if not for this damnable weather!

Continuing to mutter his frustration under his breath, he dismounted and took matters into his own hands.

Stepping forward from the animals, he bowed his head to focus and shut out the wind and snow. He had done this a thousand times before, so much so that it was almost second nature for him. Reaching within his mind, he pictured his desire, his need – visualizing what he wanted to see happen and projecting his will. Then he opened himself up – this was the trick that many struggled to master – power flowed from other dimensions, other realities, other worlds; the ability to open oneself up to this power was the first step to mastery, and the second was to control the flow.

He had spent many years studying and mastering the ability to channel the energy that many considered magic, and he could bend it to his will. Feeling the power flow through him, he stretched out his arm, and though he couldn't see it, he felt the flow of energy pass through him, out through his arm, and into the wind and snow blowing between the towering mountain peaks.

His head was still down and masked by his hood, and he stood for a moment with his arm raised. Then the wind went silent, and he could feel that it was no longer tugging at his cloak. In the steely quiet, all he could hear was his guide calling out, again and again, "Amott! Amott! *There it is! There!*"

Raising his head, he could see clearly now, across the entire mountain range; white-capped peaks for as far as the eye could see, contrasting against a bright, clear blue sky; the sunlight glistened off the snow, almost blinding him, as he gazed again in the direction the sherpa had pointed in earlier.

The bluish mountain looked very much like any of the others around it, except for the symmetry of the two towering twin peaks. One of the largest mountains in the range, that alone deemed that it was important enough to bear a name in the local dialect, and likewise a degree of reverence and respect, as deserved by all wonders of nature. The contour of the rock between the two peaks was curved and smooth, almost as if cut by a perfect circle. The sunlight reflected off the icy sides of the mountain, gleaming in the range of hills around it like a diamond in a ring of white gold.

Of course, on his map Mount Kekes did not have twin peaks – it was supposed to be the highest mountain in the entire Matras range, towering above its neighbours, but when he looked upon it now, it looked nothing like what was drawn on his map. It was, however, just as he expected.

It took them the rest of the day to travel the relatively short distance from where they had first seen the mountain, circling the canyon before they could reach the base of the gap between the two peaks, arriving at their destination shortly before nightfall. The sun was setting between the peaks when they reached the far side of the plateau and could look beyond to the valleys and hills that continued on for miles.

Only when the sun had drifted below the topmost line of the hills – setting, yet still providing enough pale light by which to see before true darkness fell – could they clearly see the path of destruction stretching out below them. The carnage cascaded across the terrain, arcing downwards and at every point where it would have hit a peak, hilltop, or even a tree that dared to be taller than the rest of the forest, something had carved a path into the landscape.

It was as if the gods had taken a hot brand and dragged it across the landscape, blasting and melting everything it touched in its path. Strewn along the same path were monstrous boulders and rocks the size of whole castles, as if the mountain had exploded westward and scattered itself across the landscape. The path narrowed as it progressed, tapering to a point in the distance marked by a still blackened crater. That was his destination.

As if on cue, Nirmal made a sign against evil while staring at the path of ruin before them.

Torick dismissed him with a wave, hurriedly barking instructions to go and make camp before the last of the light was gone. He would go the rest of the way alone and would return only if he found what he was looking for.

*****Fenndragon*****

Dar sat patiently in the cushioned armchair by the fireplace, examining something incredibly interesting at the end of her fingertips, as the young girl quickly slipped from the large bed in the center of the chamber and hastily dressed before shuffling quickly out of the room – pausing only in the slightest to make a quick bow of respect to both the sleeping Prince and the blonde-haired woman sitting by the fire.

The Prince woke slowly after the girl's departure, rising first to sit at the edge of the bed as he wiped the sleep from his eyes, before strolling across the room to gaze out the window at the city far below, not caring in the least for his nakedness in the chill of the early morning air.

"Good morning, your grace"

Svato nearly jumped out of skin at the words, spinning around to search for his unexpected guest, abandoning modesty as he grabbed a nearby iron-work candle stand as the nearest weapon.

He hadn't yet found words for his astonishment before Dar spoke again. "My apologies, m'lord, I did not mean to startle you so" she said in her sweetest tone, which Svato knew to be mocking.

"For the God's sake woman, have you no respect for my crown in the least?!" he finally blurted out, relaxing his grip on the candelabra, and returning it to the table beside the window. He was still completely naked but seemed completely lacking in modesty about the situation.

"Again, your grace, my apologies for the intrusion. I heard you were entertaining petitions from the townsfolk and thought I would join the queue, though it seems like I might be overdressed…"

He cut her off with a scowl as he crossed the room towards her, grabbing a gown from the end of the bed to cover himself as did.

"Aww" Dar feigned disappointment as he tied the robe sternly.

"Would you mock me for my privileges?" he challenged her, "Am I not entitled to enjoy the benefits of my rank and station?"

"Oh, by all means, you may do whatever you wish. I merely came because you summoned me. I did not mean to interrupt your fun." Dar smiled as she straightened in the chair, enjoying herself with the exchange. "Did you grant her petition? I mean, I trust she got something in exchange for her ministrations, unless, of course, that was what she had petitioned for?" she asked curiously.

"I do not know why I tolerate being treated like this…" he sighed, rubbing his disheveled hair as he sat in the chair opposite her. "Any other prince would have your head for such talk."

"I don't care for any other prince that way you know I care for you."

"Care for me?" he asked, "you have completely spoiled my morning…" his voice almost cracked as he complained.

"Like a brother" she finished, "and besides, any other prince doesn't know what we've done to get you here."

"Speaking of getting here, you took your sweet time – I summoned you nearly three weeks ago. Where have you been?"

"Busy."

"Too busy to ignore your 'liege lord'?" he said sarcastically, knowing she respected no titles. "I mean, I know you are free to do whatever you want, but when you offer to advise me, I do expect that you will honor your word, and actually give me advice."

"Don't I?"

"You promised to find the source of these plagues and put an end to them!" he stated flatly, a little more seriousness creeping onto his tone. "It's been almost a full season since we last spoke and things have only gotten worse, so, I want to know what your doing about it!"

"These things take time…" she started to say.

"Time we do not have!" he cut her off, "…we are surrounded by princes who desire nothing more than to raid our granaries, and I am hard pressed to feed our people, yet alone raise an army to defend ourselves. Say nothing of our ambitions…" he trailed off as he thought about the opportunity to unite the seven tribes slipping away from him. "We will all wither and die if nothing can be done…"

Dar waited for a moment before replying.

"It will take time, your grace. Even once those we have found to help us can gather, it is no easy thing to undo nature gone awry. Seasons will pass before the rains return and the crops grow back, and…"

"…and the madness?" he interjected.

"I cannot say."

"Well, at least you are honest. But how long must we wait? Have you found those you seek?"

"I have found them, but now they must find us."

Svato's expression made clear his confusion.

"They will come to us – soon – and we must make them see the need, to agree to terms." Dar explained.

"They will come to us?"

"They do not know it…" she told him, "…but they are on their way."

*****Shagron*****

Though but one horse, the pounding hooves shook the earth as the charge began, every step beating the ground like a roll of thunder moving across the plains. Building speed to a crescendo, shattered by the crash of steel, grating and scraping, metal against steel – thunder followed by lightning – slashing blades followed by piercing screams and cries of pain.

Shagron rose in his stirrups, adding even more momentum to his blade as he swung downwards, again and again, on the massed host of bodies that clawed and grabbed at him and his mount, trying vainly to blunt the force of the charge and drag them to the ground.

Surely, they would have, if he weren't doing everything in his considerable power to carve a path forward through their numbers, emerging from the swarm with a powerful stroke of his sword, spraying blood and body parts forward as his steed continued to crush and trample any that still stood in his path.

They continued to gallop after breaking free of the throng, slowly coming to a stop some distance away before wheeling around to survey the damage.

Taking deep breaths, Shagron adjusted his helm from where it had shifted during the last pass, obscuring his vision. This was his third charge through the gathered mass of plague-born berserks, and he had cut their numbers down by at least half he guessed, leaving perhaps twenty or so still capable of fighting – the rest lay on the ground either dead or scrambling to find purchase in the mud, trying to stand without the benefit of a leg or arm, mortally wounded but too mindless to stop.

He looked down at Gypsy and could see the sweat lathering up on her neck. A strong war horse, she stood taller than most horses, and had a barrel chest that was pure muscle – a powerful creature of war as much as she was a loyal friend. He didn't have time for words, but patted her neck with his gauntleted hand, letting her know they were in this together. With one more deep breath, he slid down the visor of his great helm and spurred Gypsy forward for one more pass through the swarm of shrieking bodies.

He needed to thin them out just a bit more before he felt he could risk dismounting and taking them on foot. The burning sensation in his right arm was growing, his muscles aching from lifting and swinging the heavy hand-and-a-half sword again and again as he made each run through their lines – it wasn't easy to lift such a sword with just one hand all the time, and he knew that even he had limits for these types of feats. Nevertheless, he had a plan for how to deal with these creatures, and he knew he would do well to stick to that plan.

Screams pierced the air as Gypsy's steel-shod hooves crashed once more into the center of the mob, and Shagron followed with a long downward swing on his right, deflecting through their attempts to claw and scratch him down from his high perch. He could feel more than see the strikes that were landing against his shield on the left, guarding his side and leg as he was surrounded for the moment by their numbers – his left arm had gone numb from the deflected blows after the second pass, and was starting to tingle back to life now as he felt tiny shards of pain run up his arm to his neck.

He took turns swinging from right to left to clear the boldest of the fiends away from his path as he and Gypsy carried forward once more and quickly burst through the mass of bodies and thundered away from their cries of rage and agony.

The earth and sod were torn and trampled, and each step Gypsy took sank into the mud as he led her forward a few extra strides this time – a few extra moments to catch his breath before one final charge. Gypsy was definitely getting tired now – it was a lot to expect from even the sturdiest war horse: to carry his weight, fully armored, back and forth across the field so many times – if this were a more conventional fight, he would surely have stopped and taken to fighting afoot by now, giving her a much-needed rest from all this work. He had to remember to give her full credit when they were done, as he had no doubt that there were perhaps as many dead on the field from her trampling as cuts from his sword.

"What do you say, old girl, one more time?" He slapped her neck, and she threw her head back, snorting proudly in reply, seeming to resent the implication that she would be tiring before Shagron.

Once more the thunder rolled over the grassy plain, chewing up the turf into muddy, blood-soaked clumps, and together they slammed again into the wall of human flesh that stood in front of them, throwing bodies to the ground without regard or remorse.

This time, once they broke through the thinning numbers, Shagron threw his leg over Gypsy and dismounted, leaping to the ground – a considerable distance, as Gypsy was large even by war-horse standards – steadying his landing between the heavy sword in his right hand and the shield in his left. He dropped the reins, confident that the horse wasn't going to go anywhere without him, and took a moment to adjust things, shaking out the tingles in his am that he had had felt earlier.

The remaining pack were trying to close the distance, some moving faster than others, and this suited Shagron just fine – it allowed him to take on the faster ones first, methodically parrying their blows and countering with brutal sweeps of his heavy blade to any exposed areas – limbs, mid-sections, heads – few had the strength to parry his blows.

One that tried to lift a rusty blade to block his blow was rewarded by having his own blade forced back into his own skull, crushing the bone and killing him instantly.

This was not Shagron's first encounter with the plague berserks, so he knew what to expect and didn't hesitate in the least when his blade cut down even the women and children – all who succumbed to the sickness turned mad, and there was no cure. Killing them swiftly was the only mercy he could offer.

The rest of the pack had reached him now, and he found himself surrounded by six battered figures, some with weapons, and a few trying to simply grab him and pull him down. He blocked with his shield, countered with a sweeping blow that took one more out of the fight, but left his back exposed as he could not possibly cover every direction at once. As one creature began to stab towards his open backside, his head exploded to the left as a studded black metal ball crashed through his skull from the right.

Ralof stepped up nimbly – for his age – and swung his mace in a wide circle, clearing an area around himself and guarding Shagron's flank.

"Well, it's about time!" was all Shagron had to say, seeing the results without acknowledging Ralof's timely arrival.

"Sorry – I just didn't want to get run over by that monster horse of yours!" Ralof replied, as he deftly heaved the mace over his head and brought it down on another skull.

Shagron drew up to survey the last three, and then quickly saw an opening and rushed forward, ducking under a blow he saw coming his way – he caught his attacker under the arm with his shoulder, pushing him back with his shield, and then, when the creature tripped and fell backwards, he placed a foot on its chest and plunged his sword downward into its heart and through into the ground. Without stopping, he pivoted around the planted weapon, using his momentum to bash a second foe with his shield, stunning him, and allowing him to pull his sword free of the body on the ground, and with a broad sweeping swing, cleaved the creature's head clean from its shoulders.

Instinctively, he looked over for the one last opponent that was still upright and caught a good look at Ralof pounding his mace repeatedly into the prone body at his feet, thoroughly ensuring that the stubborn creature would not rise up again.

Shagron lifted the visor of his helm, to look around and make sure he had accounted for everyone before he took his rest. He drew a long deep breath, held it for a moment to relax, and then exhaled slowly, calming his pounding heart, letting go of the adrenalin that sharpened his reflexes during combat.

He took a knee for a moment and nodded towards Brother Ralof, who hardly seemed winded after his brief exertions, which was surprising for a man of his apparent age – Shagron had never asked him how old he was, but he wore the years in every line on his face, so he assumed he, too, was long past his fighting prime – if a man of the cloth such as he had ever had a prime.

He looked up at the sky for a moment as he caught his breath, set his shield down on the grass and stood up – there was still unfinished business to attend to. Turning towards the center of the small field, where the bulk of the horde had been run down by his charges, he began to walk slowly towards the still-moving remains that lay scattered on the blood-soaked earth.

Ralof stayed back and said a prayer over the fallen where he stood and allowed Shagron to carry on with putting the survivors out of their misery – the plague did nothing but compel them to continue to struggle, to strike out at any who were not infected, and so Shagron still needed to be careful, but with their resistance to succumbing to even the most grievous wounds, he knew he couldn't allow even one of the survivors to move on from here and risk spreading the infection. It was a grim business, but he was obliged to do it.

They had been engaged by a local town council to eliminate a roving band of infected who had been threatening the village for several weeks. Fortunate enough to have arrived before the town was overrun, Shagron and Ralof had tracked the small horde of somewhere between thirty and forty infected after they had withdrawn the previous night. They had given their word to do whatever they could to seek them out and put them to the sword. Now, that also meant making sure they destroyed anything that might infect anyone else.

Shagron had no fear of touching the bodies – he had learned very early on in the outbreak that if he were going to be infected, he would have caught it by now – so now his plan was to finish off the stragglers, burn the bodies, and be on their way.

He was raising his sword to swing at the neck of the first survivor, when he felt the hair on the back of his neck stand on end, and a cold shiver ran down his spine. His instincts immediately told him something wasn't right as he turned and scanned his surroundings, searching for something – anything – unusual; well, more unusual than the thrashing of the limbless survivors still gripped by the madness, seething, and foaming at the mouth as they cried in a mix of pain and rage.

It took a moment before he realized that they were calling his name in their screams – impossible, of course, because they could not have known who he was

– but then he could hear it more clearly, again and again, and he could see their eyes begin to focus solely on him:

"*Shagron!*" they called, "*Shagron!*"

"*SHAGRON!*"

This was not the plague, he could tell – this was something far more sinister; and evil that pursued him in particular.

"Show yourself!" he called out, gripping his sword with both hands now, taking a defensive stance, ready for anything. A moment passed and he felt the arm of the creature at his feet reach out and grab his leg. With barely a glance, he swung down and removed the creature's head in a single stroke.

Focused again on the center of the field, he could see that the rest of the creatures had stopped moving and spoke with a single voice.

"*It's time to come with us.*"

Near the center of the mass of bodies, the chest of one of the dead began to heave suddenly as if breathing new life into the mangled body. Pulsing and throbbing, it began to expand and stretch, until the flesh could no longer contain whatever was within it, breaking free in an explosion of blood and tissue.

Shagron blinked to avoid the spray, and when he opened his eyes, he could see a figure emerging – growing – out of the corpse, splitting apart bones and sinew as it rose, fresh blood running down its oily hide as it stretched, flexed, and uncurled its muscled form to tower over Shagron.

Its skin was a deep amber hue, with a rough scaly texture that rippled when it flexed and moved. Man-like in form, but over ten feet tall in height, its body was covered with hard nodules, some just small nubs, while others protruded like horns, pointed and sharp – as sharp as the fanged teeth that filled a horrendously wide mouth, set low into the face, almost part of the chest. The head extended directly from its broad shoulders without a visible neck.

It was the closest thing that Shagron could see that might indicate a weakness – that it might not be able to look around quickly if there was any risk of an attack from the side or behind, but Shagron did not see much chance of that happening as he stood alone in front of the creature. Then he was reminded that he was not alone.

"Demon!!" cried Ralof in a mix of shack and alarm, looking up from his last rites to see the monster emerging before the knight. "Shagron, look out!" he shouted, instantly realizing how obvious the reflexive warning was.

Shagron sighed, mentally rolling his eyes. "Stay back!" he shouted, "I will handle this!" He lunged forward to the attack, and the demon swung first, having the greater reach advantage. He rolled under the first blow and thrust forward with his sword as he came up, plunging deep into… nothing! Striking air as the demon followed his swing with a spin, it brought its other arm around to backhand Shagron square across the chest, knocking him backwards into the air. Landing ten feet away with a thud, Shagron groaned, rolled to his feet and stood up in a low defensive stance.

"You got this?" Ralof asked, with just a little sarcasm in his tone.

"Yeah," Shagron replied, looking down at his feet. "I just needed to pick up my shield."

Deftly bending over to scoop up his shield from where he had left it on the field earlier, he adjusted his grip on the sword in his right hand while he settled his shield in front of him and strode forward again. This time, he could see Ralof limbering up his mace in his left peripheral and decided to circle right. Focused solely on him, the demon took a step forward and met Shagron's swing, blocking the blow with the hardened scales on its forearm, smashing the other arm down to land a blow on his shield that glanced off and landed its fist down in the mud.

This brought Shagron face-to-face with the overly large mouth, which gave a horrible stench as it exhaled hot, sulphur-smelling breath so close to him. He pressed forward with his shield, bashing the demon in the face as he continued to apply force with his sword against the forearm, holding his blade steady between two of the curved horns, ensuring he had the creature's full attention for the moment.

The demon was strong — stronger than he was if they were to simply arm-wrestle — but he was well trained and knew how to use leverage and momentum to his advantage. Despite that training, he was beginning to doubt he could hold the creature's attention for much longer when he finally saw Ralof's mace come crashing down on the demon's head from behind.

Denting the skull through the leathery skin, the demon's left eye burst from its' socket from the force of the blow, dangling over the top edge of Shagron's shield. Fire and smoke billowed from the recently vacated ocular orifice, enraging the beast as much as it seemed to have harmed it.

Pulling up from the ground and turning, the long arms swung around in a blind rage trying to retaliate against the monastic cleric for his attack. Thankfully, the demon was tall and Ralof was not, and the wild swings went over his head as he easily crouched and avoided the blows.

Shagron immediately leapt to the attack again, determined to win back the monster's attention before it could land a hit on the older man. Taking the opportunity to strike the creature's exposed backside, he thrust his blade forward with all his might, using the point to pierce through the thick, scaly hide, and drive his blade in through where he might have expected the vital organs to be on a normal man, angling his thrust upwards. He felt the tip of the blade scrape against the inside of the creature's ribcage as he forced it deeper, until the sword erupted from the top of the shoulder blade.

The demon lurched and roared as Shagron's blade ripped through it, falling forward as it died, wrenching the hilt from Shagron's hands lest it pull him over with it. Shagron stood as he looked over the body of the fallen creature to see Ralof, who also straightened up from his crouch, having dodged the demon's attack and subsequent fall.

"Got it!" Shagron stated calmly between heavy breaths, "Thanks."

"No problem!" Ralof replied. "If you don't mind, *What* the *Hell* was *That?*" he exclaimed. "That was no plague victim – or if it was, Ukko help me, I'm done! That, that… was a demon – a creature of the lower planes, a servant of evil…"

Shagron let Ralof expend his adrenaline-fueled tirade, waiting until he started to calm down off the excitement of the moment.

"…These discarnate spirits don't just 'appear' on the mortal plane without being summoned…" Ralof continued, staring blankly at the body of a creature he never imagined he would ever see, while trying to remember what he had learned in the seminary as part of his exegesis of the grimoire of demonology and the ecology of the interplanar realms.

"…Or unless consigned to execute a commission made personally by an archdemon of the lower planes…" he finished, quoting the grimoire, and trailing off as he considered the implications.

"Do not worry yourself, Brother. It came for me, and I appreciate your help with dispatching it so quickly. Ugh!" Shagron grunted as he replied, dispatching the last of the plague-born that they still need to finish off. He set about gathering some sticks and brush for a fire, to burn the remains.

"Why would something like that be after you? And who sent it?" Ralof asked. "Will more be coming??" He followed Shagron into the nearby woods as he asked his questions, and Shagron politely pulled him close, grasped his hands and turned his palms upwards. He then proceeded to place several pieces of wood in his arms and continued scrounging for more.

"It is how I live," Shagron began to explain, "every once in a while, maybe once every new moon, something will appear, often when I least expect it, and try to take me by surprise. It matters not where I am – for a while, I sought shelter within a temple of Ukko, but the holy ground mattered not, and only resulted in a priest and several choir boys being killed or hurt; I sheltered with the other knights of my order for three months, and that too resulted in more people getting hurt before they politely asked me to leave. The smaller the location, the more likely whatever appears will not be as close to me and can often go on a rampage before I find it – or it finds me. It happened once, a few years ago, in a small town – Bodrogkoz – on a market day; that was very unfortunate."

Shagron shook his head as he remembered the various scenes from his past. "And you didn't think I was popular after Mercurum! – Ha!"

"But I don't understand – why? Why do these things seek you out?" asked Ralof, adjusting the growing bundle of wood in his arms.

"I am actually quite surprised today," Shagron continued, "I have not had such an encounter since you joined with me in Mercurum, and I thought perhaps your presence was proving to be an effective ward against them."

"Yes, but '*why*'?" repeated Ralof, sounding impatient.

"What does it matter, '*why*'?" Shagron asked back, "All that matters is that now you know, and you are free to go your own way from here. You are not a protection against their finding me, and it will only bring harm to you – if not today, then someday – and you will have a better chance of living out the rest of your years in peace if you take your leave when we get back to town."

"For now, let's go and set a pyre to the gods, and pray to Ukko that he will cleanse this field with rain, and his riders will come and bear the souls of the recently departed to the hall of heroes!" With a broad smile intended to lighten the mood, Shagron clapped Brother Ralof on the shoulder, almost making him drop the load of wood he was carrying and headed back to the clearing.

In short order, they had covered the corpses with a substantial pile of wood – Ralof wanted to be sure the fire would be large enough to consume everything – and lit the pyre. It was only when they had finished this final task that Shagron felt the tension release completely, groaning slightly as the pain in his side began to break through his resolve and he began to sag and lower himself slowly to the ground.

Brother Ralof moved to his side and helped to carefully remove his armor and sit him down on the grass. By the light of the bonfire, they took some time to let Ralof attend to Shagron's wounds from the battle, some of which he hadn't even recalled receiving. No words were spoken as he poked and prodded at the large bruises and shallow cuts, applying salves and bandages to speed the healing process. They only paused for a moment when the flames changed from bright orange to a strange bluish-green hue, which they assumed was the moment when the last remains of the demon were consumed, and both seemed to breathe a sigh of relief.

By the time everything was finished, and the daylight was starting to fade, they took a moment to toast their fortune at being alive, saluted the souls of the departed, and began the short ride back to the village, warmed by the wine and feeling quite pleased with themselves.

****

"You say that they have all been vanquished – none have survived?" asked Istvan, the young mayor. When the first mayor had been infected and ran out into the wilderness, there had not been many volunteers for the job, and so it had been assigned to young Istvan, with barely nineteen years of wisdom and experience to guide them.

"With our deepest condolences, we are sad to say that this is the case," explained Brother Ralof to the young mayor, surrounded by the majority of the town folk in the one tavern/inn that they had, located in the center of town. They had barely arrived back when the word of their return spread, and everyone came to hear the news.

"It did not take us long to track the mindless creatures" Shagron began, "they sometimes appear to have retained some of their intellect, but they really are quite childlike when they get enraged. A few mounted charges softened them up enough, and they never really grasped what they ought to do to avoid being trampled to a pulp by Gypsy's steel-shod hooves…"

Ralof was watching the faces of the assembled crowd and could see the growing horror in their eyes.

These were their loved ones – husbands, wives, sons and daughters – who had succumbed to the madness of the plague and ran off into the wilderness, perhaps not that long ago. He gathered from the hopeful looks in their expressions when they came running that some still held out hope that their families might yet be saved – and Shagron's description of events was clearly not what they were hoping to hear. There was one woman, staring at them from the back of the crowd, with wild blonde hair and fiery eyes to match, who looked as if she wanted to strike Shagron in the midst of his tale!

He decided to step in before they caused any more unnecessary pain.

"I'm sorry, your honour," he interrupted Shagron and addressed the mayor, "I'm sure you don't need to be bored with all the details of our travails over these past few days. As Shagron has said, we located the missing townsfolk, and after we did our best to see if there was anyone who remained in possession of their faculties, we regrettably were forced to end their suffering as humanely as possible, under the circumstances."

"You say that they have all been vanquished – none have survived?"

"With our deepest condolences, we are sad to say that this is the case."

The crowd dispersed slowly after that point, leaving Shagron and Ralof to conclude their business with the mayor. Though there were many who bore tears at this point, they were not afraid to show their thanks to the two adventurers for saving the rest of the villagers from falling to the same fate as the others. Ralof felt relieved that the wild-haired woman had also disappeared, as he did not relish enduring her gaze again.

The town was small and certainly not rich with coin. Though Shagron and Ralof were not in the business of profiting from the suffering of others – for them, it was their holy mission to save the Avar people from all the dangers of the corporeal world – but they did need to eat, sleep, and clothe themselves, so they often bartered and traded with those who were not able to pay with coin. This night, they were treated to a hot, home-cooked meal, a clean bath, and a warm bed. This was how they had spent most of the past year, helping those who could not help themselves.

When they awoke in the morning, they ate a hearty breakfast, courtesy of the innkeeper's wife and two daughters – the two teenage girls were old enough to marry but bereft of options in the small town; sadly, they had been utterly disappointed the night before to learn that both Shagron and Ralof had sworn vows of celibacy when they joined their respective holy orders under the banner of Ukko.

Shagron and Ralof were also disappointed to learn that the promised reward of a 'warm bed' was premised on someone doing the warming for them, and so they had to settle for the somewhat cooler options provided by the late summer temperatures. It was all the same to them though – they were of an age that sometimes they were just satisfied to get a good night's sleep.

After they finished eating, they spread their map of the principalities on one of the larger tables in the tavern, which was still empty at this early hour, and took some time to consider where their path would lead them next.

Shagron was staring quietly at the map for some time before Ralof had to ask.

"What are you looking for?

Shagron glanced up, as if woken from a dream.

"Nothing, nothing…" he answered, "just trying to see how we came to this…"

"To what?" Ralof asked.

"These are Imperium maps" Shagron stated simply, "To them, we are Vengriya – the 'Imperial Frontier'. To me, these are the Mad'arsko – seven tribes of the Avar people. Seven tribes, that came to these lands from the East hundreds of years ago, and by fire and sword, drove out the monsters that plagued the lands settled the great plains for the Avar people."

"So who do these lands belong to before?"

Shagron glared at Ralof, then continued.

"Don't know. Don't care." He stated bluntly. "The Avar lived here peacefully, seven principalities – one for each of the seven tribes – until the Imperium invaded, but they have only done with swords what others have been doing with plows and coins for years. Outside of Nyirseg, the Avar are now outnumbered by the Imperium from the West, the Onogur from the South, and other tribes and mercenaries too numerous to name." His gazed shifted across the map as he spoke.

"Sopron and Sarkozy were the first to fall to the Imperium, then circled South of the mountains of Gomor and pushed straight up into the heart of Nyirseg. The Imperium spread over the rest of the Avar lands like an inevitable tide, flooding into Mezoseg in the Eastern corner of the realm, and Temeskoz in the South. Only Gomor and Uzhgorod were saved from their wrath, protected by walls of stone – the Matras and Maramosi Mountains – but while they were not conquered, they still paid tribute to their new overlords. Avar and Onogur suffered equally under the Imperium because the great Avar Princes are seven, not one, and they suffered for that failure to stand together..." Shagron started to drift off as he spoke.

Ralof watched and listened and Shagron gave his history lesson – he had always been fond of how much he could learn just by staying silent. But then, sometimes you needed to give things a poke to keep the story going...

"You believe we need a Grand Prince to rule all the Avar? ...the Mad'arsko?" Ralof asked aloud.

"Don't you?" Shagron replied. "As one kingdom, we could defy the Imperium, bring peace to the lands, and..."

"...and stop these plagues?" Ralof interrupted, "Is that what you were going to say?"

Shagron was quiet for a moment, still staring at the map.

"Just what powers would a Grand Prince have over famine and disease?" Ralof continued, "I have heard the stories of the last Grand Prince, and I don't recall any such miracles in those tales. One has to go all the way back to Matras Vadas and the slaying of Sarkany to find a Grand Prince with such powers! – Yes, I know the old tales just as well as you do" he interjected, seeing the look of surprise on Shagron's face. "you aren't the only one who's spent time in a library...or a seminary!"

"In fact,..." Ralof began to offer, "One might argue that things have been better under the Imperium these past few years than they ever might have been under the Seven Princes!" Shagron looked like he was going to choke.

"Under Imperial rules, there has been less fighting among the nobles, no border raids, fewer bandits on the main roads, and better trade in the markets..."

"You're leaving out the unbearable taxes, foreign laws, and random executions…" Shagron spit at him.

"Yes, you're absolutely right" Ralof acknowledged, only a little intimidated by the warriors' tone. "These things are unfortunate, true, but we all pay taxes to someone, does it really matter who?"

Ralof sensed the bile rising in Shagron and raised his hands as if in surrender, conceding the argument to the singularly patriotic holy warrior. Shagron accepted his silent surrender and turned his glare back to the map, still trying to plan their next move.

"I fought for many of those noble families – you know that don't you? – in all those terrible little border battles that you hate so much. I was there. And we fought bandits, too, lurking around every bend in the common roads."

Ralof was content to just listen now.

"That work is gone." Shagron continued, "Now it's these, these… cursed, hollow shells of people that we must fight…"

He quietly chastised himself for letting his mind wander again. He resumed his study of the maps, looking for something, anything, that would help them make their next move.

"Our supplies are getting low," he murmured, "and my armor needs repair – more than a simple farm-smith can manage."

"You have done noble work…" Ralof's tone was kinder now, "…more than any could have asked of you, guarding every town and hamlet in our path, when the Ispan's and nobles of all the great cities have barred their gates and hidden behind their walls."

"Aye, but with no charter, no contract," Shagron spoke as he scanned the map, "we have worked to save those whom the Ispans have abandoned, and still the number plague-born grows with each passing day. Those we help are those have nothing, and so we get nothing in return. Much of my wealth is now spent, and even with what we have left, there is no place to spend it – these hamlets can barely spare food for themselves, let alone sell any of it to us, nor do any have proper crafters with the skill to mend steel…"

"So, what are you saying?" Ralof asked, with a hint of worry in his voice.

"I'm saying, we need to visit one of the great cities to resupply…" Shagron stated resolutely.

"We can't risk it," Ralof said, "even if you grew your hair all the way down to your knees, people would still see the sword, the armor, and that giant of a horse of yours, put one and one together – assuming they can add – and figure out who you are. The ransom the Bishop…"

"*Arch*bishop" Shagron interjected, absent-mindedly rubbing the growing stubble on his once-bald head.

"...'Archbishop' put on your head..."

"...*our* heads..."

"Yes, whatever, 'our' heads," Ralof continued, "...is enough to tempt even the most open-minded of Ukko's blessed children to turn us over to the local constabulary, and that won't end well for us! Not to mention the other thing..." Ralof paused as he considered his next words carefully. "I know I've said this before, but what about Soprom, or Sarkozy? We could ride South, leave all the attention in Nyirseg behind and..."

"No!" Shagron cut him off sharply, without looking up from the map, as if the answer was hidden in the lines and pictograms on the table before him, like a riddle waiting to be solved. "There is a darkness afoot in these plagues, and creatures of the shadow are revelling in it... We have travelled to the borders before and, I don't know how, but I can sense that, whatever is it is... the heart of it is here, in Nyirseg, and so here I will stay."

There was a long silence before he continued, "What if we headed to one of the larger city-states, kept our heads down, did our business and got out?" Shagron proffered. "Most of the great cities are so crowded – over-crowded even – that we would blend in easily and never be noticed. People are too distracted with the plague, the harvest, begging for scraps, we would never be noticed..."

"Never be noticed where?" Ralof asked.

Shagron thrust his finger down at a large dot on the map where the word 'Ascanium' was written in bold letters.

"It's time to stop running away and start running towards something."

Ralof sighed and slumped back in his chair. "Is it too early to have a drink?" he asked quietly...

*****Omar*****

The echoes of thunder resounded off the rocks, crashing but fading with each reply, until the pounding in their ears gradually began to subside.

Omar stood in the center of the small, rocky canyon, sweating in the bright light of the late summer afternoon sun, focusing on the wall of rock in front of him. His scars were hardly noticeable now, but there were places on his head where his hair would never grow again, and so he had let the rest of his hair grow in length to cover it. The same scars did not sweat the same as the rest of his skin either, and so the sheen on his forehead and face reflected the heat and glare of the hot sun unevenly.

He broke his gaze only once to wipe the moisture from his brow before it could run into his eyes and continued what seemed to be a staring contest with the rocks.

After what seemed like an eternity, he raised both his arms in front of his chest, cupping his hands as if he were holding a secret, and then flung his arms forward, palms out, toward the wall of the canyon.

Nothing happened.

Holding his arms steady for a moment, he slowly lowered them to his sides as he listened for the quiet sigh of disappointment to come from behind him. Louhi sat under the shade of the awning of her small hut, which looked like it had landed on a slight angle on the uneven canyon floor. From her perch she watched him practicing his magic, and with his attempt she began to let out a characteristic sigh of disappointment.

Omar shot her a look, pointing his finger in defiance of the anticipated assessment of his efforts, and gave her pause – she was not intimidated by his anger, even though he had never directed it at her in such a way before.

He squinted at her from the canyon floor, as much from anger and frustration as from the brightness of the day, clenched his teeth and curled his closed lips into a tight, wincing grin. Spinning quickly, he flung his left arm forward toward the same rocks, and a rolling stream of flames erupted from his palm, gathering for a moment in front of his hands as it built into a growing sphere of incandescent fire, then hurtled forward in a flash, striking against the rock and erupting in an explosion of breathtaking heat.

Omar regretted doing this as soon as he had done it, as something in his head reminded him that flames were not much use against something as sturdy as granite. In the same instant he realized from past experience that this also created an immediate hazard as the power and explosive force that he had channeled, finding no way to vent itself against the immovable stone, would then reflect back from where it came.

He dove to the ground as this realization hit him a moment before the force of the flames did, saving him from a more ignominious result.

Dusting himself off, he looked back in time to see the last of the flames licking and curling around the old woman's hut, never seeming to actually touch it, as the rest of the canyon walls in front and behind him now bore the blackened charring of the flames' searing touch. None of the rocks seemed otherwise any worse for wear.

He wanted to say he was sorry, but he caught himself justifying his frustration with the situation, and, seeing that neither Louhi nor her hut had actually been bothered by the flames, he decided on the spot that he really had nothing to apologize for. Then she spoke and it was too late anyway…

"Well, we know again that you are good with channeling fire," she said dryly… you seem a natural for it – I can't imagine why – but you know that won't always be helpful for you." She remained seated in the shade of the awning, fumbling always with the small bag of bones in her left hand.

"Well, then, I guess I just have to hope I don't ever get attacked by a bunch of rocks!" he replied sarcastically. The old woman threw him a glare, which he ignored like any teenager would.

He was getting frustrated with the time it was taking to learn how to tap into the knowledge that he had gained from the stitching ritual. Just thinking about it made him want to scratch the back of his neck, where he could feel the small lump of tissue that was the only evidence of the ritual – a small, two-inch scar across the center of his neck, crisscrossed by six "stitch" marks.

"This would be easier if you told me how to channel!" he called out as he began walking back towards the hut. "You speak in riddles – that I must summon my strength; channel my anger; and cast… I don't know what you want me to cast, but this is most definitely not fishing!" he ranted to himself as much as to the old woman, "…and never a word to the 'how;' of such things!"

He stopped before her, looking up at the rocky perch she had landed the hut upon.

"You promised to teach me magic, but I seem to be doing it myself!" he finished, staring at her.

There was a long pause before she said anything, as she sat calmly in her chair, looking him up and down as if they had just been introduced. Her voice was quiet and measured when she finally spoke.

"It is the nature of stitching to give time to allow the mind to find its own way to the surface, to share what needs to be shared…" she began.

"But I don't have…" Omar interrupted, only to be cut-short by her stare.

"There are many paths to power in this world, but there is only one path to magic…" she continued in her measured pace, "…stitching is a short-cut to power, but we must work with the marriage of the minds, to follow the same path, if it is to be successful." She paused, almost as if tempting him to interrupt, and seemed satisfied that he was, at last, listening.

"The path is singular, but it has had many names. The Angyalok called it 'channeling,' and that is how they taught it to their young Avar guests. The ancient Weilbark to the north of us called it 'conjuring'; The Imperium despised magic in any form, and persecuted any 'summoners' they discovered, believing that it disturbed the peaceful rest of their ancestors, but summoning their spirits to labour in the world. Those who practiced under the Imperial eye did so cautiously! Then there's the Sintasha, the wild folk of the eastern steppes – they call it 'weaving', looking for power in the patterns…" she paused to shake her head, "…they really over-complicated things, and so their magic became scarcer with every passing season. Slow, but powerful, their magic! The Varangian named it 'storm-calling' and chanted their will out into the wind, using it to great effect for exploration and battle! The Mycenaeans and Babylonians believed the power came from words, and they worshipped the books in which they wrote their incantations, while there are those beyond the Western Mountains – the Celtiberians, who live out beyond the Imperium – they work their magic from recipes, as if they were cooking dinner! Can you imagine that?!"

She laughed aloud at herself. "They cook up some mighty steel to forge their weapons – all paid now as tribute to the Imperium."

"Ah, the irony – the Imperium abhors magic in any form, but they accept metal and swords in tribute from these tribes, knowing how they were made, but they take them anyway, because they know they are the finest weapons to be found anywhere, and they need that!"

"Oh," she exclaimed, "everyone has their own name for it, and there are many ways to bend it to your will. The agnostics believe the power comes from within themselves, while the faithful pray to their gods for blessings to be granted to them. All different paths to power, but the power is the same. And we must learn to use it in whichever way suits us best. Because the world needs those who can wield such power…"

She stopped and looked at Omar, as if afraid she may have said too much and lost his interest, but he stood there, listening.

"It will come to you…" she finished, "…if you truly have the need and the desire to wield it."

"I think I'm done for today," he sighed, turning past her, and slowly walking over to the covered entrance.

"Are you?"

Louhi spared him a sideways look from her seat.

"Giving up already?" she asked, quizzically, "you usually beg me to tell you more before you get this frustrated…"

"It's this heat!" He cut her off, sensing just a bit of sarcasm in her tone. "It's not right for so late in the summer; I get tired standing on these rocks all morning, and for what?" He slumped his shoulders in resignation. "I can work on my runes back in the cave – I saw more of them in my dreams last night and should practice writing them out."

"You don't need runes…or her…"

The voice came into his head as naturally as anything, and he felt immediate agreement with the statement, without ever questioning where it had come from – as if it had always been there.

"Very well, we can go back," she agreed, and slowly stood up with the help of her cane, still clutching the bag of bones.

"Maybe I can try getting us back?" he asked, holding open the fur skin doorway of the hut as she passed under and into the dark, musty little tent. He followed her in and let the flap drop closed behind him, standing between her and the exit.

"Do you think you can?" she said, without turning back from the brazier in the center of the room.

'Ha!'

"If you help me," he replied, with a very deferential tone. "I will even cook dinner for us tonight," he offered, hoping he didn't overplay his intentions.

"Really? And what would you make us?"

"The fish stew you like so much! I have learned that recipe well. And we have plenty of vegetables from the garden to make it just the way you like."

She turned from the brazier and smiled at him.

"You have to visualize where you want to be. Easier if you've been there before, harder if it's just from a map or a drawing. The more detailed the map the better; if the picture in your mind is not accurate, or has changed since you were last there, it will become random. It's always best if you have a map and have been there before, but all these things come with practice."

He nodded silently, listening to everything she was saying.

"Objects that have been enchanted with power always make it easier to channel; they focus the energy in a specific way – for a specific purpose – which makes it easier for you to manipulate. Most objects of power are small, as they are not easy to enchant, and require a certain level of durability to hold the energy of the enchantment, but some, like this hut, were made by some of the most powerful mages during the early mage wars, hundreds of years ago, and we are not likely to see a mage who can create anything on their scale ever again. They are to be treasured, protected, and used carefully. You may find other trinkets in your travels and see other showmen performing tricks with something as simple as a piece of string, but never forget – the size of the object has nothing to do with how it was enchanted!"

"Now, enough of my talking, I could go on for months talking about enchantments and you would still know less than an Angyalok child about the subject. Focus your mind, and think about the cave, how it looks when we come out of the hut every time we travel. That will place the hut in the same spot that we always use – this is important now – I don't want to have to be cleaning up because you landed us on my bed! We keep that spot clear just for this reason!"

She was looking directly into his eyes now and, while stern, she kept her voice low and calm, not wanting to disrupt his concentration.

"It helps when you are a beginner to close your eyes and visualize the place you want to go, so do that now – close your eyes, and concentrate."

"How will I know when we are there" he asked, drawing a picture in his mind, just as she had directed. He could see the cave, the furniture, the bed, the table, the glass vials with the strange liquids, the dark shadows and the dripping candles. He tried to imagine he was standing in the one spot where they always emerged, and held the image steady, waiting for some signal from her that they were ready to go. He strained to remember if he had ever heard her say a command to make the hut shift through space, or to make it disappear.

When he hadn't heard her say anything for a few moments, he slowly opened one eye, to see what she was doing, but she wasn't there anymore. He was still in the hut, facing the brazier, and everything looked the same, except she was gone. He heard the rustle of the door flap dropping shut behind him and spun around just in time to catch a glimpse of the movement. Carefully stepping forward to the door, he peeked out. When his eyes were closed, concentrating, she had slipped past him and he could see her now, moving into the cave, placing her casting bones on the dinner table and moving towards her bed in the far corner. They were home, and she seemed content that he had done well enough. Stepping out into the cave, he looked back at the base of the hut and could hardly see any difference in the imprint it had made on the dusty floor, aligning well with where it landed every other time they travelled. He smiled and felt very pleased with himself.

"I will clean up and start dinner right away!" he called out to her, and he could hear a faint grunt of acknowledgment come back from across the chamber.

Leaving his cloak over a chair near the entrance to the hut, he began to move around the kitchen, arranging and preparing the ingredients for the fish stew. After chopping the vegetables and the fish – plucked fresh from the small pool that passed for a well in the cave where it had been sitting for the past few days since he had caught it outside in a river – he combined all the ingredients in a medium-sized pot over the cooking fire. He added some spices for seasoning that soon had flavourful aromas drifting around the cave.

Moving back and forth between various shelves in the open space that passed for both the cooking area and the central sitting area, he cleared away everything that was on the large table in the center of the room, returning many of the alchemy appliances to their spot on the shelves, closing and returning several tomes to their place on the shelf in the small library, and swept the floor while the stew simmered. The old woman had moved over to the far side of the area set aside for her bed chamber and was doing something with her back turned to him for most of the afternoon.

Once in a while she would tilt her head up, take a long breath and sample the aromas of his cooking, and perhaps toss a casual comment over to him from across the chamber, drawing a brief, polite reply, but otherwise no real conversation between the two. This was not unusual for how they would spend much of their time together when he was not studying with her.

And so she did not find it strange when he did not reply directly to one of her comments about being careful not to burn their dinner.

"Do you need my help with anything?" she inquired curiously, "it's starting to smell like something is burning."

When he did not reply she turned and stood to see just what he was doing, only to see that he was no longer there, and neither was her hut – both seemed to have silently disappeared at some point in the afternoon.

Shuffling over to the cooking fire, she stirred the pot, seeing that the fish had stuck and was starting to burn, and set the pot aside, away from the flames to let it finish simmering. Glancing around the open area, she detected nothing else unusual – he had not packed any of his personal effects that she could tell, not that he had accumulated many things over the past year that had any real value. She turned to the alchemy appliances and saw that all had been put away neatly, and the texts she had on the table were placed in the correct spaces on the bookshelf.

All the tomes seemed in order except for one empty spot on the shelf: the grimoire of stitching – with its dusty pages and golden bindings – was gone.

Her eyes narrowed almost to slits as she frowned and contemplated this. Above all else, the thievery of her hut could not be tolerated. Raising her right arm, she closed her eyes and snapped her fingers.

Omar stepped out of the doorway of the hut and stood for a moment under the small canopy that shielded most of the late afternoon sunlight and allowed him to adjust his eyes. Coming from the darkness of the cavern, and the low candlelight of the hut, the brightness of the outdoors was blinding, and he had to take a moment to allow his eyes to dilate and get a clear view of just where he was.

The sounds hit him first, and he could discern the noise of animals – horses, several horses, and a few cattle or oxen – and the smells: hay, dung, wet fur; most importantly, he heard no people.

Widening his eyes, he could see that he had arrived in some sort of livery or stables, surrounded by a variety of mounts. Sunlight streamed in from the high windows that also served to circulate the stale air that stank of all the wonderful smells of a stable. Adjusting his cloak, he pulled his satchel up on his shoulder and prepared to walk out into the day, where he could now hear people moving around on the street outside. He paused briefly and looked back at the hut, wondering for a moment what he would do with it now, or what would happen if a stableboy discovered it.

As he pondered the matter, the hut itself began to grow pale and shimmer in the light and then faded away as if it were never there, disappearing without a sound. Returning to the witch, he figured – no doubt she would have prepared some enchantment to prevent anyone from taking it far – and so he moved out of the stable with one less question to ponder, and perhaps a little trepidation, as he hoped that the hut would have no way of telling the witch just where he had taken it – and if it could, then he wanted to get away from this spot as quickly as possible, before she came looking for her book.

As the thought crossed his mind, his hand instinctively moved to the satchel and felt for the outline of the small book through the cloth, making sure it was still there, safe & sound.

Breathing a small sigh of relief, he moved into the street and joined the flow of pedestrian traffic. It seemed he had arrived somewhere near the main gates, which were open, but only partially, allowing a small flow of traffic in and out. Being inside the gate already, he moved with the people walking toward the center of the city, and quickly started looking for landmarks that would confirm where he was.

He had studied pictures and drawing in many of Louhi's tomes, in preparation for this possibility, and had even studied the maps of the greater principalities, familiarizing himself with all the great cities, what they looked like in drawings, and where they were located on the continent. He hoped he had concentrated well enough and remembered the landmarks correctly to get him to the right place to start his searching.

After navigating narrow lanes and broad thoroughfares, weaving through crowds of people larger than he had ever seen in Mercurum, he found himself a vantage point from which he could view the entire town, making out all of the key landmarks and towers that he had seen in the books, and he enjoyed a moment of satisfaction with himself: he had reached Ascanium.

The first night he spent in Ascanium he was so full of wonder and amazement at the size and beauty of the city, he doubted he would have been able to sleep anyway, so it was no problem that he had no place to live. The city was much more crowded than he expected – no doubt a consequence of the plague – and it seemed that there were almost as many people in the streets at night as there were in Mercurum on a busy market day. He had an ample amount of street-smartness from his years growing up in the market district in Mercurum that gave him enough awareness of potential trouble that might be coming his way in the busy streets, and he managed to slip out of a few potential scrapes with an assortment of thugs and pickpockets that kept him on his toes despite beginning to tire as the night wore on.

By the time the sun rose in the morning, he decided it was time to take to the rooftops to try and get above the traffic on the streets that was almost impossible to navigate without being tagged by someone with light fingers looking for a score. By the look of the people in the crowds, he doubted there were many big scores to be had these days, as despite the numbers, to his practiced eye most looked to have noticeably light purses these days.

Not unlike Mercurum, there were parts of the city that had grown with a clear respect for spatial boundaries, which made it hard to traverse such a neighbourhood solely by rooftop, and there were other areas – the majority of the city in fact – where buildings, businesses, homes, and shelters were squeezed into every available inch of space, leaving few if any gaps from one building to the next, and making the rooftops into a virtual express route of their own. Upon reaching the top pf one of these areas, he was surprised to see the number of people moving about at this height and began to realize that he truly was in one of the greater city-states now.

Moving about carefully, with everything he had in one pack on his shoulder, he began to connect with some of the others he encountered on these rooftops, and soon had a line on several housing opportunities – they were not easy to come by with the city so crowded, so it became a race to secure a room as soon as one became vacant.

He went to visit one that morning, and though there was in fact a room available that he could have for a reasonable price, the woman renting it seemed quite taken with his young age, too young in her opinion to be running around such a dangerous city on his own, and he quickly decided that she would be too maternalistic for his tastes and would likely not respect his privacy the way he needed, so he continued to the next opportunity.

The fourth referral seemed like the best for his needs. As he knocked on the sturdy wooden door, he heard an elderly male voice reply. "Coming," it called, and in a short time the door opened on an older man, no taller than Omar, who beckoned him in off the street. As Omar stepped in, he quickly looked around and could tell directly that this was not the usual inn or boarding house situation. The entryway was decorated as a small family home would be, although much quieter than he expected.

"Greetings, I am Omar."

"Festus..." the old man replied guardedly, "What do you want?"

"I heard you have a room available?" Omar asked.

The man looked at him with mild surprise. "Ha!" he said, shaking his head slowly. Omar noticed that his eyes were red, and at first, he thought about the plague symptoms he had heard from others, but this looked more like he had been crying.

"His bed is hardly cold, and word is out already!" Festus spoke softly, as if in disbelief.

"Pardon me?" Omar asked.

"It has been only a day since my son died on a scavenging patrol, collecting timbers and sod to sell for hearth fires," the old man said softly. "My wife succumbed to the plague a year before, and he was the last of my name."

"I am sorry to hear that..." Omar said, "...perhaps I should leave – I didn't know. I don't want to intrude on your grief." He began to move for the door when the old man stopped him.

"No! Please. I have already had three merchants at my door this morning asking me to sell my house – saying that it's too big for me now and I ought to move. They want to kick me out and sell rooms to the wealthier of the refugees." Festus paused, looking around the room. "It's too soon to leave – there is still so much here for me yet. Besides, where would I go?"

"No, no" he continued, "I would be very grateful to have someone else here with me now, and perhaps I can convince the merchants to leave me alone for a little while longer."

Omar stood his ground and gave the man a sly look. "Perhaps I can offer you a deal," he said, "I don't have a great deal of coin, but perhaps in exchange for convincing these merchants to leave you alone, we can set a reasonable rent for one of your rooms?"

The old man nodded and agreed to let Omar answer the door the next time they came knocking.

They did not have to wait long, although the interruptions did not persist beyond the end of the day. Word spread quickly about the sudden proclivity for people's clothing to suddenly burst into flames when they knocked upon a certain door, and so any interest in disturbing the home's occupants quickly dissipated. In fact, as grateful as the old man was, even he, too, was happy to leave Omar alone in his room whenever the door was closed.

Inside his new accommodation, Omar made himself at home, unpacking his meager personal effects, putting his short stiletto sword under his mattress by his head, and placing the grimoire on the table beside the bed.

After lighting the candles around the room to ensure he had good light, he sat quietly on the edge of the bed and stared at the still dusty cover of the ancient tome, lost deep in thought about what he was about to do.

His resolve set, he reached over and lifted the tome onto his lap and opened the book to the center, and then, finding the locking clasp on the gold binding wire, he unhooked the fine chain and began to unbind the pages. He carefully removed the length of the gold wire – as he had watched the old witch do – and fastened the lead end to a small, curved sewing needle he produced from his pocket. There were verses on the page that he had to recite – verses that the old woman had memorized ages ago, but that were still new to him, and he had to be careful he followed the steps precisely.

He paused at one point, and was interrupted by a knock at the door, as the old man offered his well wishes for a good night. Omar responded politely and then proceeded with the stitching ceremony.

He was prepared for the sharp pain that came when he pushed the tip of the needle through the skin of his wrist – after the first time he knew what to expect – he was ready for the sensation of falling through time; the vertigo, the nausea, and the waves of familiar memories that would wash over him, as he felt the experiences of a lifetime open up to him like a book – a book where he could flip the pages, skipping over the forgotten days of childhood, the tortuous years of youthful schooling and chores, nervous teenage encounters, young love, old love. Being prepared, he could stop the pages flipping by, and see the things he wanted to know who he was; what he was; what he had spent a lifetime learning, mastering, and what had eventually killed him doing. He was ready, yet still passed out from the exertion of reliving the past life in a fraction of a moment.

The ritual took a little longer this time, as he had to wait until he awoke each time to make a new stitch, and though it was only one lifetime added to his knowledge, it still took the full six stiches to complete and seal the connection.

He would recover faster than the first time, but the ritual itself took almost three days to complete. When he cut the thread and let the stiches heal, he rebound the book with the remaining strand, finding it just a bit shorter than before.

Festus was pleased to see him when he emerged from his room and had a full dinner ready to set and serve when he was ready to eat. Omar kept up his end of a polite conversation throughout the meal but could hardly contain his desire to get out into the evening. He sat throughout the meal flexing and curling his fingers; the cutlery had a light, almost weightless feeling in his hands. Thanking Festus for the meal and his patience over the past few days, he excused himself to go for a walk.

"Are you sure?" the old man asked cautiously, "The streets are extremely dangerous these days, especially at night!" As he spoke, there was a flash of blue light in the window that caught their attention and they both paused, expecting thunder to follow any moment. "…Besides," said the old man, "it looks like it's going to rain now!"

"Oh, that's alright," Omar answered with a wry smile, "…I'll be just fine."

*****Jason*****

"You're not serious, are you?" Kiara shouted, following Jason up the stairs of the manor and into his room. "You're not seriously going to leave now, are you?" she asked incredulously.

Jason had shot up the stairs, along the hallway, and into his room in barely the time it took for her to ask these questions, and now he was moving about his room, looking for his pack. He moved past Kiara to grab something from a chest behind her, threw it on the bed, and began to remove the tunic he had been wearing at dinner.

Kiara paused a moment as he began undressing, then continued her protests.

"Don't think I'm going to leave just because you're deciding to get naked! I've been around too long to blush like one of the scullery maids you have running around here!"

"Excuse me?" Ferenc asked, appearing in the doorway, having heard the noise from his room next door. "Who's getting naked?!"

Jason paused, naked from the waist up, and looked at his two friends, and let out a deep breath, letting his shoulders sag just a little, which did nothing to distract Kiara from the chiseled physique he had worked hard to maintain throughout their isolation from the plague. He had a forlorn look, as if he knew something and that he doubted he could explain it to them.

"He's lost it!" Kiara exclaimed to Ferenc. "He was hosting dinner as he does every night, then right in front of everyone, he stands up, announces that he 'has to go to Ascanium' and then takes off up the stairs and starts getting changed."

"What!?" said Ferenc, looking at Jason. "Why?"

"I followed him up, but he hasn't said a word! There's panic in the great hall, as people are freaked out enough by the bloody bugs, and now they think he's abandoning them!" Kiara continued to explain to Ferenc while keeping her eyes on Jason, who was now bare down to his loin cloth – a simple woven cloth wrap in the style common to the Imperium, rather than the northern tradition of wearing nothing at all, to Kiara's subtle disappointment.

Ferenc addressed Jason now with a more imperative tone.

"Jason! Just where do you think you are going?"

Slipping into his travel trousers and tying them up, he quickly threw on a linen undershirt and turned to grab his worn gambeson from the bed. He had to stop when Ferenc grabbed the garment from the other end and held it for his attention. He didn't say a word but held Jason's eye in a stare until he finally relented and released the gambeson and stopped his frantic preparations.

"You didn't see her?" he asked, "What she said?"

"Uhhh, I wasn't…" Ferenc replied, looking over to Kiara, who had a confused look on her face.

"See who?" she asked.

"The little girl."

"What, the one serving the wine?" Kiara wondered aloud, "That was Kiraly's little girl. What about her? What did she say to you?"

"No! Not her. The blonde girl, with the tangled hair…" he paused, remembering what she had said…

It had been a week since the locusts had struck, and it seemed that they were everywhere. They raced against the farmers to consume the crops before they could harvest them: grain, corn, beans, even the grapes – much to Kiraly's dismay! It was only going to be a matter of time now before either the livestock or the people would begin to start to suffer the effects, food was going to be in short supply, and they would be facing a very, very, difficult winter. For that reason – well, that, in addition to the plague – dinner that night in the great hall was a somber affair.

They did not feast any better than anyone else in the compound just because they were in the manor and others had their own homesteads; Jason had always ensured there were no special privileges for rank or position, to help alleviate the threat of envy among the people – this was as much for his own peace of mind as anything else. The last thing he wanted was anyone feeling jealous enough to want to poison his wine!

Ah, his wine – if there was one consolation of being in charge that he had to admit he enjoyed, it was the privilege to enjoy the virtues of the vintages that Kiraly was now managing for them. While he had only been there for a week, and they hadn't had the chance to do anything from their current stock, he had brought a few casks of some of his own finer vintages with him when he had arrived, and he was quite happy to share these with Jason and his commanders in exchange for his residency.

Jason looked over the hall as dinner was brought out by the kitchen servers. There was quiet music being played on some strange harpsicord-like instrument that he didn't recognize. It wasn't a festive melody, and he could barely even hear it – something for which he was even more grateful – his distaste of bards also meant that they were somewhat lacking in talent when the need arose for entertainment.

Nearly sixty guests filled the long row tables, many of whom were rangers, their wives, crafters, hunters, and a smattering of apprentices. He could see Kovacs Josef, talking softly to the metalworking apprentices sitting around him and his wife, Ilonka, discussing something about how folding steel made a blade stronger, and just how many times it could be done.

Across the hall, Szabo Ildiko was showing off her latest work – her skill as a seamstress was unmatched, and the other ladies competed for her skills whenever she wasn't working on the more basic clothing needs of the compound. There were so many conversations going on at once, but none, he noticed, talked about the plague, the berserkers, or the locusts. There was a sense of impending doom hanging over the atmosphere of the nightly meal, and no one wanted to talk about it.

Almost as if to drive home the mood of the evening, the servers brought a light appetizer to his table at the same time as it went to the other tables as well. It seems the chef had heard of the healthy attributes of the current insect population and had incorporated various elements of the now plentiful food source into a new dish for tonight's meal. Despite being certain that the chef was correct about the qualities of the locusts, Jason had not the appetite to eat the thing that was responsible for so much misery. And judging by the silence in the room, others felt the same.

He leaned back in his chair and waved, raising his goblet for more wine. He recognized Kiraly's youngest daughter, Giselle, with her long black hair pulled back in a ribbon, looking quite confident as a server despite her youthful twelve years, coming forward with a small jug to refill his cup. She smiled politely as she poured the wine smoothly and without spilling a drop, for which he showed his appreciation.

"Well done – thank you, Gizi," he said, returning her smile.

She nodded politely and moved back to stand beside the door to the kitchen, where she would wait with her jug under the watchful eye of Erzsi-nani, the head lady of the servers, who had taken young Gizi under her wing for training. A few seats further down the head table, Jason could also see Kiraly watching her movements, with a proud smile on his face – it was good for his family that she could find a place working in the manor house, which would make for a more comfortable winter for her, instead of working somewhere outside in the elements.

There were not a lot of options to be had these days, and so he was as proud as he could be. Sipping the wine, he turned his attention back to his plate for a moment, contemplating the creative presentation of the insects and waiting to see if the wine made any of it look any more palatable. His mind had begun to wander for a moment when he heard a small woman's voice.

"What are you looking for?"

"Pardon me?" he asked, turning to Kiara on his right.

"For what?" she replied.

"You asked me a question…" he said.

"No, I didn't," she said, taking a drink of wine as she slowly crunched on a mouthful of wings and insect legs. He made a bit of a face as he couldn't stomach the crunching noises, and she returned to her conversation with the older ranger sitting to her other side.

He looked around and saw that Gizi was still back by the doorway, and the chair to his left was empty tonight, as Ferenc had taken dinner in his room.

"What are you looking for?" He heard the question again, and this time he stood up slightly to see the small girl sitting on the floor in front of the head table. Her long blonde hair was dirty, tangled and hung about her head in a teased mess. She was playing with pieces of locusts on the floor, trying to put the legs and wings back together like some sort of puzzle. Looking up at Jason as he leaned over the table, she repeated her question one more time.

"You know what I'm looking for," Jason replied quietly, as if afraid he would scare her aware if he spoke too loudly.

"I remember you," he added, looking into her clear ice-blue eyes. She wiped at the smudges of dirt on her cheek as she looked back at him.

"When the withering ends, you will find her." Her voice was almost a whisper. Jason glanced to his right and could see that Kiara hadn't noticed their conversation. "The withering will get worse until you end it."

"Where is she?" Jason asked, the urgency in his voice rising as if he could sense she was almost done talking. "Please don't leave yet! I need to know where she is!"

Looking down at the floor, she pulled back her hands from the dead insect pieces, now in a jumbled pile. She blew on it softly, and with hardly a blink of his eyes it jumped away and disappeared under the rows of tables.

"She will find you in Ascanium when the end comes."

As she finished, he felt someone push the chair behind him into the back of his knees, making him falter on his feet and grab the table for balance. Looking away for only an instant, he looked back, and she was gone.

"Damn it!" he cried, this time a little louder than he intended, and there was a moment of silence in the hall as people closest to him turned to look his way, wondering what was going on. Kiara even looked surprised to realize he was standing up, seemingly oblivious to the fact he had been talking to someone just across the table from her.

Ignoring their looks, he pushed his chair back further and stepped away from the table. Sensing something was wrong, Erszi-nani stepped forward and asked if everything was alright, to which Jason announced in a loud voice, looking at her but intending for everyone to hear...

"I need to go to Ascanium. Now." And then quickly marched out of the great hall toward his chambers.

"And that is why I need to go. Now," Jason finished, concluding his retelling of the events of the evening.

Kiara and Ferenc exchanged looks. It was a strange telling, which she had witnessed – in part – but she was completely oblivious to the presence of any blonde child in the hall earlier that evening. They were his friends – his closest friends – and so they knew his earlier tale about the young girl he saw when searching Katerina's home last year; and so they also believed what he was telling them now; what they lacked was an explanation.

"I know we had talked about this before, but now I am certain – this girl is a messenger!" he said to them.

"Okay," said Ferenc, "but from who? Who is trying to tell you about Katerina? And why?

"I don't know – I feel it in my gut. She told me that I needed to endure the withering, and we have. We've seen nothing but cycle after cycle of nothing but plague, infection, fighting, and now bugs, for almost a full year, and she said we needed to endure it. Now she says I need to end it!"

"But why Ascanium? Why now? – You'll be lucky to get there before the weather turns, and then what? What are you supposed to do there?" Ferenc asked.

"I don't know."

"And what are we supposed to do here?" Kiara added. "People are looking to you to get them through the winter now, you can't just leave them high-and-dry"

"Well, you're wrong there,' said Jason, standing up from where he had been sitting on the end of the bed. He pulled the quilted gambeson over his head and began to fasten the buckles. "I don't owe anything to anyone here. They came to me, and I welcomed them as guests, and they agreed to share in the effort. I never promised anyone that I would safeguard them against all the troubles of the world. Just because I am good at it doesn't mean I owe it to anyone."

Ferenc and Kiara stood there, awkwardly, while he spoke.

"I chose to stay in these lands for my own reasons, and every ranger who stayed with me had their own reasons too – I didn't promise anyone anything except that I would help make sure they could remain here in peace from the Imperium! Period. Now, I believe my reason for being here is in Ascanium, so that is where I am going. Everyone else is free to stay here and do as they can with what is here or continue to find their own way – they've stayed alive one year more by staying here than they likely would have done on their own, so they should consider that a grace, be thankful, and carry on."

He paused for a moment to catch his breath, then continued more slowly...

"Ever since we made our decision to stay, things have been happening 'to' us, rather than 'by' us. I need to feel like we have some say in our destiny, in what happens to us – whether we live in happiness or sorrow; caged or free; alive or dead – I know things are tough for everyone right now, and they're only getting tougher, but I have to go and do this, now, to have any sense of feeling like I have any purpose in all of this; that there's any reason to be alive for myself, and not just for duty or responsibility, or honour, or any of that crap! I need to start taking control of what happens to me – I need to turn the ship into the wind, and steer the course I need to go, and not just let the storm take me.

"So I'm going."

"Okay then," said Kiara, turning to leave as she spoke, "let me grab my things and I'll meet you at the stables." She was halfway out the room before Jason could get out another word...

"What?"

"I'm coming with you," she said, in a very matter-of-fact tone, as if they were going for an evening walk.

"What do you mean," Jason asked rhetorically in astonishment, "I'm not your captain, giving orders here anymore – you don't have to follow me wherever I go…"

"It's like you said," she threw over her shoulder from the doorway, "We all stayed behind for our own reasons…" and then she was out the door and down the hall to her chambers.

Jason barely had a moment to consider her words when Ferenc joined the chorus:

"Me too," he added, "Just let me grab a few things and we'll get going!" and then he turned and almost ran out the door back to his chambers.

Jason was stunned at how quickly they had simply shifted from inquisitors to accomplices, but they were both out his door before he could say another word. By the time he had finished pulling on his boots and packing what he wanted to bring, they were both in the hallway discussing how cold they thought it would be if they rode in the evenings, and whether or not they should stop in the kitchen for some rations. When Jason stepped into the hallway, they stopped talking and stared at him.

"Shall we visit the armory before we hit the stables?" he suggested, to which they both smiled and nodded in reply.

They spurred their horses through the gates of Greymantle Keep in the middle of the night. They wore their armor, as it was easier to wear than to pack, and it was a good precaution against the berserks. By a stroke of luck, it was a full moon, and the weather was clear, which gave them reasonably decent light to ride by when they were on the plains. The adrenalin of being on the road, with no plans to be home at the end of the day, kept them alert and awake through the night and the next day, as if a sense of freedom was restored that made their hearts pound again with thoughts of excitement and adventure. Jason almost believed that they would have ridden right straight to Ascanium if the horses could have survived the challenge, but that was not ever going to be the case.

Ascanium was at least five or six days away – four if they rode hard – which their light cavalry horses could probably have done, as they were bred for making fast runs behind enemy lines, spying on enemy positions, and fleeing before being spotted or captured, and to be away from a home camp for days or weeks at a time. That was under normal circumstances, though.

Since settling down more and dealing with the near constant clashes with berserks and wild beasts, Jason – as well as Ferenc – had taken to wearing heavier armor than they had used to wear as typical rangers. Their usual Legionnaire armor was practical for scouting but didn't offer enough protection for more prolonged combat encounters. As a matter of personal preference, Jason had taken to wearing some more pronounced shoulder pauldrons, with plates extending down his arms and legs, switching at times between a thigh-length chainmail shirt and a mid-weight breastplate. He had been presented with a breastplate, as a gift from Josef, which had some beautifully sculpted horses on the upper portion and was gilded subtly with a ribbon of braided steel to trim the edges. It was Josef's way of saying thank you for sheltering him and his family, and he had hardly had a chance to wear it since he gave it to him last month.

It was almost as much for personal reasons that he chose to bring it along with him now, as he would have hated to see it left behind and fall into anyone else's hands. He also favoured a full helm now, which gave him better all-around protection when he engaged in the larger melees, though he would only wear that when he knew a real fight was brewing. Most of the time it remained fastened to the side of his saddle, behind the scabbard for his bastard sword. He had a bow fastened to his saddle bags, but it was left unstrung and curled almost in a complete circle when it wasn't under tension. Also bouncing on the flank of the horse was a good-sized quiver with a large quantity of arrows, with a small cloth stuffed in among the shafts to keep them from rattling too loudly with every stride the horse took.

Of everything they were leaving behind, he felt the worst about taking the arrows – they were in short supply lately, having lost their best fletcher recently, but he knew most of the scouts would rely on their own foraging skills to make their own as best they could. His guilt was not severe though, as he needed these arrows as much as anyone, and who was to say that if he killed a berserk while on the road, he wasn't saving the compound from having to kill that same creature a week later with the same arrow?

Ferenc was garbed similarly to Jason, although forgoing the large helm – that was Jason's signature piece, and he didn't feel it suited his style, preferring to balance protection with the need for speed and agility. Kiara had a style all her own, preferring the hardened leather armor that allowed for much quieter movement, with a longsword balanced for her height and strength, while she kept her compound bow wrapped around her waist when it wasn't strung, within easy reach to grab & string if she needed it in a hurry.

They rode quickly, not stopping to scout or survey – they knew where they needed to go, and how to get there; their only concern was to avoid any unwanted encounters to make the best speed possible. The road was often the worst way to travel if you wanted to avoid others, so they often found their trail cutting across the wide-open plains and farmers' fields, paralleling the road as the faster course, but far enough away that anyone they saw on the road from a distance was too far away to give them any concerns.

There were some wooded areas along the early part of their travels, before they reached the great plain, and they had even considered taking a route through the trees, were it not for an encounter on the second night.

They had been riding single-file along a game trail that wandered in and out of the trees – enough trees to provide some cover from the glaring sun overhead but hardly enough to be considered a forest, and certainly not enough for any of the locals to have given the woods a name worth remembering. Winding into the trees at one point, Jason held up his arm, signaling for a halt. He dismounted to examine something on the trail, waving Ferenc and Kiara forward to join him.

"What is it?" Ferenc asked, as Kiara jogged up beside him.

"Tracks," said Jason, pointing down at the ground, "but not from anything I've ever seen before."

Kiara knelt and traced the large muddy imprint with her hand, feeling the depth in the semi-soft earth. "It's large..." she offered, "at least seven or eight feet in height, maybe four, five hundred pounds – moving on two legs, but not a man – something different." She began to look around to where the tracks disappeared off the trail, leading deeper into the trees. "This track is not old – the turned earth is still wet – not more than half an hour in this heat."

Jason drew his bow as the other two strung their bows and knocked an arrow each. They were on a mission to find Katerina for Jason, but there was something in their blood as rangers and they all instinctively knew that they would not let this mystery pass them by without at least investigating it a little...

Jason took point as they slipped into the woods, leaving the game trail and their horses hobbled behind. Ferenc and Kiara spaced themselves out behind him, at least ten paces apart, to give sufficient room for each to draw and shoot at anything that might jump out at them – it was not just caution, but the natural result of their years of training and experience – they had a reputation as being the best hunters in all the Legion. The woods were thin near the trail but thickened quickly the further they moved inwards.

Ferenc was the first to call this out. "I can hardly see ten paces through all this foliage," he complained.

"Well," replied Jason, "at least whatever we're following is large enough that it cleared us a good path to walk in..."

"Uh, I'm not sure that's really a good thing," Ferenc answered, adjusting his grip on his bow as he looked around nervously.

"Don't worry," Kiara interjected, ever the true huntress, "just think of how many days we'll be able to eat off the kill."

Jason had stopped to kneel again and survey the tracks. He didn't wave for the others to join, but cautioned them...

"It's circled back on itself," he warned. Their prey seemed to have an awareness of where it was going, and what to do if it was being followed. This was troubling, as there shouldn't be anything out here that could think like that. And as he considered this, it occurred to him that they might want to reconsider which of them was playing the role of the hunter, and which was the prey. He waved his friends forward as he continued to move forward, following the curious footprints, staying low and trying to be as silent as he could – Ferenc and Kiara mirrored his movements precisely, while Kiara paused for a moment to dry her hands on her leggings before resetting her grip on the bow.

About another hundred paces into the woods Jason stopped again, and Ferenc and Kiara stopped as well, still spaced well apart from one another. He seemed frozen, as if waiting for something, then almost imperceptibly, Ferenc saw the slightest movement of his left hand, flicking two fingers rapidly then stopping. This was enough for Ferenc, and he shared the gesture with Kiara. She nodded, even though Ferenc hadn't even looked back at her. Drawing her compound bow back in a smooth gesture, the strength of the pull given away by only the slightest tremor in her grip, she loosed an arrow into the brush on their left.

The arrow cut through the brush with a whoosh of air and slicing leaves, cutting a path that she couldn't see, but could easily hear, as it travelled straight and true, narrowly missing the unseen target, which, at the same moment had begun to crash headlong through the thick underbrush to close the gap on Jason. Still facing forward, Jason held his position in a low crouch, switching to a two-handed grip on his bastard sword, as he listened to the noise of snapping wood and crunching foliage growing louder on his left, as if waiting for something.

With the arrival of a second whistling arrow, this time from Ferenc's bow, he could tell that clearly this one had struck home on the beast, which let out a vicious howl that echoed under the canopy of the towering trees. With this signal, Jason spun on his left toe, with his right leg bent and braced behind him, and held his broadsword forward, directly in front of him, ready to be hit head-on by the charging creature, now just a few strides away and bearing down on him fast.

He didn't have time to really see what the creature was as he turned to face it and was fortunate to steer the bulk of the force of the charge aside as he parried the charge with the tip of his sword, piercing whatever it was in what he guessed was the shoulder, directing it off to his left. Of the creature itself, he glimpsed the dark fur that covered its backside as it rolled over his shoulder, and the black leathery skin of the underbelly, pulsing and soft, but rippling with dense muscles that gave the creature prodigious weight and size.

His sword penetrated the shoulder and forced Jason over onto his back as the force of the charge carried the beast over his left shoulder and onto the ground.

Jason pulled back hard on his blade as he rolled backwards and came to a stop on his knees on the ground, sword at the ready to defend. The creature rolled past him into the brush, clearing several bushes on its way, before it rolled back to its feet, resting on all fours like a giant wolf. Ferenc's shaft was buried in its right flank, with just the fletching visible, and it was bleeding visibly from the shoulder.

Pausing only for a moment as it shifted its hungry gaze between Jason crouching to one side, and Ferenc appearing on the other, having sprinted up the path to join the fight. Another arrow flew out of the leafy cover and buried itself in the wolf's neck, spraying bright red blood across the vibrant green of the leaves.

Howling in rage the creature sprang forward onto Jason as the nearest prey, threatening to shred him with either its razor-sharp fangs, or the long, curved claws that were already blackened with blood and dirt from earlier victims. Jason threw up his left arm with the bastard sword to parry the bite that descended towards his throat, while reaching with his right hand to pull the dagger from his right boot. The claws of the beast struck his left arm and the sword, bowling him over again, and this time he rolled with the creature, clinging tight to the massive chest, wrapping his right arm under its armpit, making sure he was too close for the claws or teeth to gain any purchase.

He could hear the whirring noise of two more arrows flying and striking home on their target, but the great creature continued to struggle. Using the close quarters to his advantage, he stabbed repeatedly with the dagger, doing as much damage as he could to the chest and neck areas while he continued to struggle to keep close to the creature to avoid the terrible snapping jaws. Eventually the giant wolf-like creature managed to get its hind paws up and under his hips, and with a single thrust, threw him back across the small open space they had cleared with their fighting. Landing on his side, he was getting ready to roll back to his feet when he saw the creature closing again from behind. He braced for the rake of the claws that he knew was coming, only to feel nothing. Instead, all he heard was a high-pitched wail from Ferenc.

Trying to block the attack, but only having his bow at hand – and not enough time to draw his sword – he swung the small bow like a staff to distract the creature from its attack. Successful in his attempt, he was rewarded with the full attention of the raking that Jason had been expecting. He flew backwards as the oversized claws rent deep slices into his chest plate and rolled to a hard landing almost twenty feet away.

Jason paused for a moment as he witnessed his friend lying still on the ground and, pulling himself to his feet, stood at the ready as the dark eyes of the wolf turned back to him – he could see the rage and fury of the wounded creature, and could feel it being matched by the fire burning hot within his own chest. He could feel every nerve alive with the same fire and fury, and in a moment he played out the exact move he would make, how the creature would respond, the place he would strike, and the wound it would cause; he could see his follow-up swing, spinning around and catching it from behind, even feel the hot blood splashing against his face and arm as his blade hit home, and severed the creature's head.

It seemed like the pause became forever in an instant, and the next thing he knew, he was standing over the limp body of a dead wolf-creature, everything having played out as he had seen it in his head. Then Kiara was there, looking for a moment at the creature and him, before they both rushed over to Ferenc's body, lying face down in the dirt a few feet away.

"Ferenc!" they both called out. Rolling him over to check his wounds, they were instantly relieved to hear a moan of pain emerge from his bloodied mouth.

"Thank the gods!" Kiara whispered, and then promptly began to scold him for being a fool! "What the hell were you thinking? You have a bow – use it like a bow! Not a piece of driftwood!"

Ferenc coughed, and they were grateful to see that he wasn't actually coughing up blood from any internal injury – just a cut in his mouth. Their relief was short-lived as they saw the depth of the gouges in his armor and the flow of blood coming from beneath. Jason wasted no time with buckles, using his knife to sever the leather straps and remove the chest plate. As brutal as the wounds were in his chest, he also knew that if he hadn't been wearing the sturdy plate, they would not need to worry about saving his life at this point, as he would already have been dead.

Grabbing a flask of water from Kiara, Jason flushed out the wounds and cut away what was left of Ferenc's tattered gambeson.

"Move aside," said Kiara, taking charge of the situation from this point. "He's going to need stitches to close the wounds, but it looks like nothing went deep enough to cut anything internal. His ribs will be sore, and he will need time to heal, but he should live." Jason sighed, again grateful for the plate armor.

"Here," said Kiara, tossing him a roll of cloth, "tear it lengthwise into long strips – we will need to wrap the bandages around him to keep the bleeding under control."

Jason pushed himself back a little, getting out of her way, but still sitting on the ground, and began to do as she had instructed. Though he was used to command, she had more practical experience in the field dressing wounds and various injuries, so he was happy to defer to her knowledge on such things. As he was doing so, he took a brief look over at the creature they had killed – hoping it was in fact dead – and he was astonished to see that it had changed!

No longer a wolf, and still not a man, it had somehow transformed while they were attending to Ferenc, and now it appeared like some sort of strange humanoid-like creature – two arms and two legs, instead of four legs; a face instead of a snout; hair instead of fur – still very muscled, but perhaps only half the height and weight of what it had been. The black skin of the wolf was now replaced with a strange greenish-yellow tinged skin, which had the look of a wrinkled old man, hanging loose on the well-muscled frame of the body.

Jason got up to inspect the corpse lying just a few feet away, giving it a couple of kicks first to make sure it was truly deceased before he got too close. Whatever it was, he had never seen one before – not in the Frontier lands nor anywhere in the Imperium – and he wanted to make sure he took a good look at what it was, just in case he should ever cross paths with another one. He was considering a souvenir tooth when Kiara called over at him to ask how he was doing with the bandages.

"Good!" he replied, "Good. Almost done…." And he turned back to focus on the task at hand.

The fastest route was a little slower now, as they slowed their pace to accommodate Ferenc's wounds. Still, it took them eastward along the course of the Duna River, past Mercurum, before the river turned south and they had to continue to the northeast, entering a vast region of flat, arable terrain populated largely by great herds of wild horses, with just the occasional farm or settlement. After a few days' ride, they would meet the Tisza River, which ran from the north to the south, neatly bisecting Nyirseg into two almost identical halves. Ascanium was just a little further to the northeast from there, lying in the heart of the Great Plains, about a week's ride, all in all.

Ascanium was the oldest and largest of any of the cities in the collection of principalities that had made up the Avar lands. While all the provinces had a long history, Ascanium was the one place where people seemed to have been gathering for longer than anyone could remember, and where all that history seemed to collide most often.

The city itself was built from a bluish stone that was quarried a few miles from the city itself. Rising like a mirage on the horizon, the towering walls and piercing towers of the grandest city in Vengriya dominated the landscape for as far as you could see with the naked eye. While the true scale of the outer walls was hidden by the sprawling city that continued to grow out across the level fields, the buildings of the inner city grew upwards from within their protective perimeter, with wide, sturdy bases stretching upwards into crenelated crowns, gilded with green terraces and lush gardens.

The highest spires rose like needles trying to pierce the sky, their blue-green hue blending with the clear autumn skies, making them almost seem to fade away into nothing. The inner city seemed almost to rest on a bed of dark, earthen colours, like an eagle resting in a nest, as the wooden and stone structures of the outer city used a richer mix of materials in their construction – the cast-off pieces of stone that were not suitable for the inner city because of impurities in the colour, or baser materials such as stone, clay or brick. The grandest architects used the grandest materials, leaving the baser products for those of lesser vision or prestige. Lacking the strength of the quarried stone, few buildings in the outer city rose to a height greater than the city walls, and none reached as high as any of the noble spires of the inner city.

As they approached, they could begin to see the hastily constructed outer wall of the city, maybe a year old now, stretching around the broad perimeter of the furthest homes and businesses. Not every home seemed to have been lucky enough to be considered within the architects' plan for the path the new wall should follow, and certainly there was a role for politics to play in this, as some sprawling estates on the edge of the city found themselves within the wood and stone palisade, and others found themselves on the outside looking in. Abandoned now, any observer could be sure that these outlying property owners would have had to choose – quickly – between suffering the scourge of the plague-born berserks or relocating their families to somewhere else within the walls, no doubt at a steep price.

Fields dotted the plains around the city, and day workers – surrounded by guards – attempted to finish the work of the harvest as best they could, looking for scraps left behind by the locusts while the guards kept an eye out for the plague-born.

"Look," said Ferenc, staring out across the empty fields, "the locust have done their work here as well..." he noted, as they passed field after field of unharvested wheat, barley, and other grains, stripped bare of their most essential fruit, as labourers frantically worked to reap the remaining hay for feed for the animals, while others followed behind, some on all fours, looking for the smallest grains that might have fallen and been left uneaten by the insects. It was the most desperate attempt any of them had ever seen to try to get the most they could out of a harvest, and they knew it would not bode well for the population seeking to survive the coming winter.

It took them the better part of the day to ride past the fields and orchards that had been planted and farmed around the great city, while also passing more than a few reminders of the Imperium's occupation. There had been a similar response here when the Imperium had withdrawn as they had seen happen in Mercurum, and Jason had to remind himself that they needed to be careful, to make sure they blended in as best they could and did not attract too much attention to themselves or their Imperial heritage.

"I have an idea." It was Kiara this time, watching a caravan of labourers pass by while they had stopped to rest and have a drink. "Let's roll in with the next caravan that comes by, and ride along as guards. I have been watching, and most of the ones carrying weapons seem to be mercenaries, not military, so we don't need any uniform or badge, we just need to look intimidating." She looked at Ferenc. "Do you think you could look mean, for once?" she asked jokingly.

"Ha ha. Very funny," Ferenc answered. "Still, it's not the worst idea," he added.

"The best plans are the simplest ones," Jason agreed. "We just have to make sure we don't spook the guards too much that they turn on us."

"Okay," Kiara said, "let's do it! There's another farming party coming up the road now. We wait till they pass, then mount up and follow along. When we get up to the gate, we close in with the rear guards and start asking them about the weather, and we should be through by the time we get the forecast!" She had a wide grin on her face, feeling quite pleased with the idea, and sure that they would slip into the city with no problems.

To Jason's amusement, she was right, and they had no problems entering the city at all. They stood by their horses at the side of the road as the work group passed them on the road, waving and nodding to the guards as they passed on their way – looking like mercenaries on their way to Ascanium to find work. Bored beyond description by hour after hour of nothing but plains, the rear guard of the caravan had been happy to engage in some conversation when the three riders fell in behind them, and Ferenc was even friendly enough to pass around a wineskin that they all were appreciative of. Between the wine and the talk, none of them noticed in the least that their newfound friends from the road had entered the city gates with them, nodding at the guards with friendly smiles, and even carrying on for a few more blocks before asking where the best taverns were located. When they finally broke away from the caravan, there were even a few empty promises of where they would meet for more drinks later that night.

Gaining entry to the outer city was far easier than it would be to enter the inner city, even more so here than it ever would have been in Mercurum. They were learning that the Avars liked to construct their cities in a very similar fashion – whether by plan or just custom – but the walls here were a much more formidable barrier, and the differences between the outer and inner cities were much more pronounced. Although in all fairness, Jason really had no idea if he even needed to reach the inner city – there were so many people in Ascanium – many more than he had ever imagined for a frontier city: he had thought that Mercurum was large for such a tribal group as the Avars, compared to the Imperium, and never thought he would see a city the size of Ascanium in these lands. Of course, he had heard from others in the legion about the other frontier cities, but the stories did not do the city justice in terms of its size, and certainly not now that they were flush with refugees and travelers seeking safe haven from the chaos going on in the world these days. In all if this, he needed to come up with a plan, or he would never find Katerina here.

"Okay," he said, "let's start by finding a place to stay, something to eat, and then we can get out of the crowds, rest, and come up with a plan for what to do next."

"Uh, Jason…" Ferenc started to say, as the sound of marching became noticeable over the noise of the rest of the traffic and talking in the city streets. "We should get out of the street and lay low a bit, don't you think?"

"Agreed," said Jason, beginning to move towards a small alcove in the row of buildings that lined this stretch of the road, to get out of the way of whatever was marching towards them. Kiara followed, all three of them pulling their hoods up to mask their faces, and pulling their horses along behind them, using them for cover, still uncertain about what sort of greeting three imperials would get from the local citizenry. They did not have to wait long.

Coming around the corner, a troop of city guards, clad in light plate armor, carrying small round shields emblazoned with the crest of the Arch-Duke, marched into view, filling the street three columns across, and perhaps ten rows deep. There was a guard sergeant at the head of the column, ensuring that people cleared the road ahead of them, who caught Jason's eye as they passed, holding it for a moment too long for Jason's comfort. Trusting in his instincts for sensing trouble, honed by his years as a ranger, he drew his sword from beneath his cloak, still covered by the large bodies of the two horses on either side of him, and waited… something was going to happen, and he was going to be ready. He could sense the same from Ferenc and Kiara as well, on the other sides of the horses.

As he stood at the ready, he heard the sergeant's column come to a sharp halt before they had passed halfway by. As if on cue, standing in the middle of the road, the entire troop did a right-face, looking directly at where they were standing with their horses. There were a few others on their side of the street, all of whom seemed to be feeling equally nervous at the moment, until to their great relief they saw the sergeant move back down the line of the troop, stopping directly in front of Jason, Ferenc and Kiara, and turning towards the trio, he addressed them.

A man of average height, his heavy-set build suggested that he might be enjoying the benefits of his rank a little more than he ought to. His long dark hair was combed straight back, and had an oily sheen to it, as did the full moustache on his upper lip which curled upwards at both ends in a complete circle, tapering the bushy growth to a fine, well-groomed twisted strand of hair on each side of his nose. His eyes squinted in the bright daylight, which gave him the appearance of smiling as he executed his duties.

"Greetings" he said, in a gruff, assertive, yet friendly tone. "By order of his highness, Arch-Duke of Ascanium, Prince of Nyirseg, and Rightful Ruler of the Seven Tribes, you are to follow me to the Audience Chamber in the Grand Palace."

*****Torick*****

The Sherpa guided Torick back as far as the border of Gomor and Nyirseg, leaving him to ride the rest of the way to Ascanium on his own. He was also gracious enough to sell Torick his mule – for an exorbitant price mind you – which Torick appreciated for helping him carry his prize back to the city. After a little more than a week of comfortable riding – he wasn't in any kind of a hurry – he reached a point on the Great Plain where he could begin to see the city in the distance as a distinct shape rather than just a blur on the horizon. The land was so flat that he could see incredible distances, although much of this was due to his heritage, by which he had been blessed with far better sight than the average Avar. And so, for him, being within sight of the city still meant he was quite a way away yet.

It was late in the day before Torick found himself inside the gates of Ascanium – getting past the guards as an outsider was a simple feat for someone of his means – and so he began to search for an old friend before darkness fell.

He followed some makeshift signs to the crafter's marketplace, and from there began to make inquiries which eventually led him to an older looking home rather than a shop in the market. It was evening when he finally knocked on the door of a small cottage, and after a short wait, an aged Avar man answered, opening the door just enough to see who had come calling at this hour.

"Kovacs Melles?" Torick asked through the narrow gap of the door.

"Aye," came the response, "but I am retired and have no interest in callers seeking trinkets for their sweethearts! Go back to the market square and find someone else for your commission!" he shouted as he tried to close the door again.

Pressing against the door, Torick persisted – "I have coin enough for a master crafter!" shaking a pouch in front of the old man that would have been enough to live off for a year if it were all coppers, yet alone the gold talons it actually contained. But this got little reaction from the man, for which Torick was grateful.

"If gold holds no interest, then perhaps you would open your door for an old friend?"

The pressure to close the door relented as the wizened face peered around to take another look at his visitor.

Torick continued, "You were but an apprentice when last we met, but you showed great promise to your master at the time, and I too saw that you had a gift for making the anvil sing…"

It took a moment, but a flicker of recognition became a flame as the old man's eyes widened and he relented on door entirely. His next reaction was something more akin to a bow than anything else, as he stepped back and welcomed Torick into his house.

"Ahh, please forgive an old man forgetting his manners! I have not forgotten my friends, not the friends of father!" he spoke, beckoning Torick to enter. "But I must admit, your coming is a surprise. It has been many years – a lifetime – since my father practiced his craft for you…"

"I know, and I apologize for the lateness of my calling" Torick answered, wiping his feet respectfully as he entered, showing much more deference than was his norm. "I have come seeking your special talents for a very special commission – one which I believe only you can complete."

The old man looked on curiously as Torick reached into the pack he had hauled from his mule, placing a burlap-wrapped bundle on the table, which set down with a light thud that seemed too faint – too light—for the size of the package. Unwrapping the cloth, he revealed the glittering contents of the bag: blackened and dark in colour yet shining with tiny flecks of light reflected from the fire in the hearth, it almost seemed like a piece of blackness reflecting the stars of the night sky back at them. The retired smith's eyes were so drawn to the strange metal that he seemed entranced.

"The stuff of legends…" was all Torick said, and the old man nodded, slowly reaching out his gnarled fingers to touch the warm lumps of mishappen metal.

"Fashion me six long throwing daggers and you may keep a seventh-share of the metal for yourself." He paused, to let the information sink in, then continued, "There is more than enough still for other works, but you will hold the metal for me until I say what to do with it. The price I have offered is more than enough to cover your costs for all of this, and you can make whatever you desire out of your share, but as you need to eat and drink, I will offer you again the coins…" and reaching into his pouch he pulled forth the coins again and placed them on the table. "This is to buy your discretion: you will tell no one about this, or where you got it. Do this for me, and I will consider bringing more your way, so that you will retire with all the splendour of a prince. Any mistakes will be deducted from your share."

The smith nodded, reaching for the coins, and Torick's delicate yet powerful hands slammed down on the table, pinning his hands over the coins. "Wrong me in any way in this transaction – let word slip to a friend, fail in the making of the daggers, or lose even a scrap of the remainder – and I will destroy you and your family with such fury that your ancestors will wake from their eternal slumber to beg forgiveness for your soul!"

The trembling in the smith's body convinced Torick that he had gotten his point across, and he slowly withdrew his hand, gently releasing his grip on the smith's calloused but strong hands.

"Excellent. I will return in short order for my daggers. I am looking forward to seeing if your reputation is so well deserved." After which, Torick turned and left the man's house, leaving his wife free to enter the room, and see just what the two men had been discussing so loudly that it had roused her from her sleep. Without saying a word to her, Melles left the room to go out back of the small cottage and lit the small forge he used for his personal projects. Alone in the room, his wife curiously lifted the cloth on the table, gasped, and stared at the strange, mesmerizing metal.

In no time at all, the neighbours were surprised to the hear the sound of metal being hammered coming from the quiet home next door – to their dismay, the hammering and roar of flames would continue without pause, day and night, for the next week. The smith's wife would bring his meals to him at the forge, as he worked continuously on his commission, coaxing the incredibly hard metal to yield to his will, and shape itself to his design. It was no easy task, but nothing worth it ever is.

Seven nights later, when he was done, he was convinced that he had completed his masterpiece – the crowning achievement of his life's work, and he was not ashamed to say as much when Torick returned to claim his commission.

He hadn't sent a message yet – he would not have even known where to send it – but Torick arrived when the work was done, as if he knew, despite the lateness of the hour. Nevertheless, Master Smith Melles was proud to hand over his handiwork to his customer.

"This… metal… is incredibly strong by nature," he explained, "requiring little work from me to remove imperfections, strengthen or harden it. My mastery is shown in the crafting," he continued, balancing the six fine, slender throwing knives in his hand, one by one, "perfecting the shape, the balance, and the edge – it is the sharpest edge I have ever crafted, and it will never blunt or dull; it will not rust, crack, shatter or break, no matter the age or the use."

Smiling at his work, the old man boasted, "You were right to bring this to me – I doubt anyone else could have found the right temperature for the forging, for although strong now, it can be incredibly difficult – delicate even – in the crafting…"

As he was talking, Torick continued to look at him, as if he knew everything the master smith was telling him already, yet he was silently enduring the redundant explanation with as much grace as he could muster – which is to say, hardly any grace at all…

"Thank you, sir, for your handiwork," he said with a pleased smile as he placed each dagger in its place on the leather bandolier the smith had made to hold his handiwork. "You have a talent worthy of the ancient Angyalok craftsmen!"

"Oh," the smithy interrupted, "I should let you know, I put a fine layer on the interior of the sheaths as well, to prevent them from destroying the scabbards. This will make the bandolier quite durable as well," he added, as if quite pleased with himself for the workmanship.

"Excellent," Torick replied, shouldering the bandolier, and turning for the door, as if in a hurry to leave. He truly didn't have anywhere he needed to be, but he was growing tired of the conversation, and so wanted to be on his way. "I will send you word when I have a commission for the remaining material. Until then, guard it closely!"

And with that Torick opened the door and left the house, stepping out into the street.

He hardly had a moment to look up after closing the door behind him before he was greeted by a voice in the night.

"Greetings," said the voice, in a gruff, assertive, yet friendly tone. "By order of his highness, Arch-Duke of Ascanium, Prince of Nyirseg, and Rightful Ruler of the Seven Tribes, you are to follow me to the Audience Chamber in the Grand Palace."

Torick could see perhaps thirty men assembled along the road, all wearing the heraldry of the Arch-Duke; front and center was the sergeant who had just spoken, and to whom Torick then addressed himself, as he looked up and down the rows of men assembled in the street.

"Did you bring enough men?" he asked in a light-hearted, almost fun tone of voice.

"Probably not, should you choose to decline the invitation," the sergeant noted calmly, "…although your choice to attend the audience is entirely up to you, the consequences for yourself would be most inconvenient… eventually…" drifting off as he finished.

Torick sighed as he surmised the situation and considered the one bright side – at least he wasn't being summoned by a peacock!

"Lead on, my friend!" He waved at the sergeant, still feeling pleased with his recent acquisition from the smith, and quite certain that whatever business the Arch-Duke wanted with him, it would work out the same – if not better – than the business back in Mercurum. He even whistled quietly as they walked off into the night.

*****Shagron*****

Shagron's torch flared as the flame caught a draft and flickered to life, brightening the otherwise dark and damp tunnel for a moment, before settling back into the dull soft light given off by the usual somber glow of the burning thresh and oil-soaked cloths. Looking ahead, he could see the same light coming from Ralof's torch, just fifteen paces ahead in the passage but almost invisible in the encompassing darkness.

"Are you sure you know where you are going?" he called ahead, asking Brother Ralof the same question he had already asked him about ten times in the past twenty minutes. Ralof was tempted to not even entertain the possibility of answering, but he also was wise enough to sense that his friend, the fearless warrior, enemy of all things evil, and defender of the faith, was feeling very uncomfortable whenever they were underground, and so he tolerated his questions and tried his best to keep him calm in these tight spaces.

"It's not too much farther now, my friend," he replied calmly. "Keep coming, this way." He motioned with his hand for Shagron to hurry and catch up with him. "The faster we move, the quicker we will be out of here," he offered as encouragement.

"Not soon enough!" Shagron retorted.

"You don't seem to care for being underground, my friend – why is that?" Ralof asked as they walked, following the winding tunnels, as they followed whatever unseen path he was guiding them along.

"Is that a serious question? Who in their right mind would enjoy being underground if they didn't have to be?"

Ralof paused and looked back, as if waiting for a better answer.

"Everything bad in my life has always happened when I was underground," Shagron began to explain.

"But as a knight, do you not find yourself at home in a castle, with so many chambers, hallways, cisterns, dungeons, etc.?" the holy man asked him curiously. "Surrounded by so much stone all the time, it's like living in a cave, is it not?"

"Once, maybe, I would have enjoyed such things; but for many years now, I have found my calling on the road," he assured him, "I prefer the outdoors, where there's plenty of room to see things coming at you. Down here, in the dark, you can never tell what's around the next corner – behind the next column, rock, cave, or door. Shit comes out of nowhere and it can really start to wear down your nerves. Give me a clear sky, open road, and even a few trees, and I'm happy." Shagron grinned despite his constant nervousness.

"You mean it's easier to see things like those we saw the other day in the field – with the plague-berserks?"

"Yeah," Shagron said, "That too!"

"But what about seeking out evil and destroying it – are you not compelled to search out their dark lairs and dispatch them as they plan their evil deeds?" Ralof continued with his questioning.

"No," Shagron sighed, taking a moment to move past the preaching tone of the priest's words, "Evil doesn't always hide in the dark of a dungeon or a deep cave in the earth; I have found evil living perfectly at home in the bright of the light, and this is sometimes the most dangerous evil of all, because everyone in the light cannot see the shadows that surround them." He was keeping up well with Ralof now, focused on explaining his experience and less concerned with what lurked in the shadows.

"This is also the hardest evil to destroy, as you may find yourself opposed by other servants of the light in your quest to destroy evil; and the question becomes harder: do you destroy light in order to destroy the dark? Do we strike down our friends in order to strike down the evil that stands behind them, even if they cannot see it? My blessing, to see evil in all its forms, is also a curse, as it shows me the evil that lurks in the hearts of good men, or men who profess to be good, and it is not easy to share this knowledge with those who cannot see it themselves." He paused to take a deep breath before continuing. "And I should add, we need to be very careful in how we judge others; not all darkness is evil; and not all light is good."

"Ah, I see your dilemma," said Ralof, "but without the light, there is only darkness, so we have to preserve the light."

"But the brighter the light, the darker the shadow; as long as there is light, there will be shadows, and the more we win, the greater the light in the world, the shadows that remain will only be darker & deeper. Is there ever an end to this?" Shagron began to show his frustration in his tone as they continued their discussion.

"Brother," said Ralof, with a great deal of concern in his voice, "you have been at this battle for a long time, I can see. I can see in your eyes that you are weary, and I can tell that you will never stop, because you would not be able to ever bear to see evil win back a single parcel of what you have helped to win for the side of light in the world." He stopped and looked at Shagron with all seriousness in his voice now.

"You need to give yourself permission to rest; to step back from the front line of this battle and let others continue the fight for you. Only by resting can you find the strength to carry on to the true end; if you do not, you will find yourself dead before your time, and Father Ukko will frown upon your face for coming to him early, leaving your ultimate work undone."

Shagron's eyes widened at the suggestion and his mouth opened just a bit, although the words of any reply escaped him. Ralof saw this yet carried on.

"This fight has been going on for millennia – light versus dark; good versus evil; it will still be going on long after you and I are gone from this world. We all have a part to play in Ukko's plan, and that is what we must focus on – win or lose, that is his plan, and we must fulfill our role in the plan before we leave this world. Like day and night, sometimes the darkness is complete, but then the light will have its turn. A day, a season, a millennium, it is all as nothing to the grand plan, and while we are guaranteed to be by Ukko's side in the final battle, we will be dust in this world before that war is finished. All we can strive for is to do our best to live our lives to the fullest extent possible, to complete our role in the plan. And for you, my friend, you need to rest before you can finish what Ukko has planned for you!"

Shagron continued to listen and finally nodded in agreement, then asked: "But what is Ukko's plan for me now, after all I have done, how will I know when I have fulfilled my role?"

"Good question," Ralof answered, "…for another time! For now, we are here…" Pushing on a small lever in the wall where they had stopped, he opened a small door that swung out into the passage, and light from the other side flooded into the small space. The opening was no more than four feet high, so they had to duck to pass through, emerging through the back of a large cold hearth into a reasonably sized bed chamber, decorated liberally with the unmistakable hallmarks of a priest of Ukko – the purple- and gold-coloured linens and curtains dominated the room, casting a purplish hue on everything else in the room that was reflected in the light of the candles and their torches.

Dropping their torches in the hearth, they had enough light from the many candles in the room to see the numerous pieces of artwork and sculpture that depicted all manner of heroic and angelic poses of the great father, including a small shrine, complete with icons, kneeler, incense burners and prayer book, situated prominently in the far corner of the room.

"And where is 'here' again?" Shagron asked, "Is this your room?"

"My room? No. No! Of course not!" Ralof almost seemed insulted by the suggestion. "We are in Ukko's temple in Ascanium, where we will be free to stay, unharried, unless of course, we decide to go for an excursion around the town. This room is set aside for guests, but is never used by the chapter, for obvious reasons…"

"Obvious?"

"The door, silly," Ralof chastised, "the access to the underground is essential for free travel to & from the temple, especially if… well, for people like us. I mean really, did I have to explain that??"

Shagron sighed. "Okay, Okay, it's obvious if you put it that way… I just don't like making assumptions. I thought you had more stories to tell…"

Ralof rolled his eyes and Shagron dropped his pack on the bed. "So where do we get to sleep? And how do we get the horses in? We're not going to leave them beyond the wall, are we?"

Ralof moved to the main door, knocked in an unusual fashion that clearly seemed to be a code for announcing an arrival, and in short order someone opened the door from the outside, looked around at the two new arrivals, and then stepped out, closing the door.

"The stable outside the walls will arrange to bring the horses to the temple – discreetly – tomorrow, and you will have everything you brought in your packs. The novice…" he said, waving back to the door, "will fetch our hosts, and they will show us to whatever rooms are available. Things may be a little crowded since the plague, so don't expect too much, but it will be enough to give us someplace to rest and recover before we start looking for supplies in the market.

Some of the novices can help us with getting some of the basics, and we can see about getting a farrier to visit the temple stables once the horses are here, but some of the things you need, we will need to visit the craft quarter ourselves to purchase."

"Good!" Shagron answered quietly. He began to relax, just a little, and took a seat to wait for their reception to arrive. He had hardly touched the cushion before the door opened and he jumped to his feet again, as the room was flooded with high-ranking members of the local clergy.

"Father Ralof!" was the chorus echoed by everyone entering the room, and there were a great many embraces shared with the older cleric, who smiled and embraced each of them in return, calling them by name, and exchanging personal greetings that indicated he had a much more involved relationship with this particular temple than he had let on to Shagron.

Shagron stood and watched, drinking in the scene as Ralof could only smile back at him across the room as he engaged with his flock. He waited and knew that there would be explanations coming in good order.

It was a few days later, after Shagron had introduced the farrier to Gypsy in the stables and seen to it that she had a fresh set of shoes and was well taken care of, that he decided it was time that he go out for a walk in the city – to 'stretch his legs' he explained to Brother Ralof, who was insisting that Shagron never call him 'Father' Ralof – and see some of the wonders of Ascanium.

"I still don't think that is a good idea," Ralof had protested, even as Shagron agreed to don the monks' robes for the occasion, to keep a low profile. Eventually Ralof relented and agreed to join him, if for no other reason than to hopefully help to keep him out of any trouble – it seemed to have a way of finding him, as it often does to a person of honour, especially in a city like Ascanium, where even under the best of circumstances the seedier elements of society often gravitate to the opportunities afforded by so many people being so close together in one space. And now, with the press of humanity seeking shelter from a series of plagues, he was doubtful they would get two steps out the door before something offended the good manners and righteousness of his travel companion. Since Shagron wouldn't relent, he consoled himself with the fact that at least their partnership had provided some of the best entertainment he had enjoyed in many years – so there was that to look forward to…

Stepping out of the seminary in their nondescript robes, they began to walk about the crowded midday streets with no real purpose or plan, just simply to explore. Ralof had a few suggestions for some of the grander buildings that

Shagron might want to see, and they considered those, but it wasn't long before the heat of the unusually long summer led them to reconsider their priorities, and instead began to seek a reputable establishment for a beverage.

This became more of a challenge once they realized that they were still clothed as cloistered monks, who were supposed to have made vows – vows that included swearing off corrupt libations.

"This is ridiculous," Shagron finally exclaimed, pulling at the hood and collar of his robe, loosening the shirt so much that is almost fell completely off his shoulders, revealing the loose linen undershirt, stained with sweat from the heat of wearing the heavy wool robe for the past several hours.

"If I don't get a drink soon, I'm going to expire – and I mean a real drink: ale, not water!" he said loudly. "No one's going to serve ale to me as long as I'm wearing this robe, so it's time we changed our plans a bit."

Around them, people were beginning to look at the two monks as they stopped in the street and debated their goals for the day. Ralof was still intent on avoiding attention and seemed all the more stressed when he saw the hilt of the longsword on Shagron's hip, now exposed as he shuffled the robe down to his waist.

"Fine," he said, "let's just go inside here," waving to an establishment that they had been debating for the last few minutes before Shagron had begun disrobing.

"Fine!" was Shagron's relieved reply, and they began to move toward the tavern door, as Shagron literally stepped out of the robe as it fell around his feet, leaving it for Ralof to pick it up from the street, dust it off and bundle it over his shoulder.

Shagron led them up the three steps to the door and was reaching for the handle as the door swung open. A man stood in the doorway, holding a large stein of ale in his hand. Average in height and heavy set, he looked somewhat small standing directly in front of Shagron. He had a cheery countenance – definitely helped by the stein of ale in his hand – with dark oily hair, combed straight back, and a curled moustache; Shagron could see that he wasn't moving in or out of the doorway, and so they stood facing one another for a long moment. Shagron opened his mouth to offer his pardon and look to move past him into the tavern, but the man side-stepped in front of him as he started to move, deliberately blocking his path, and spoke over him in a very military tone.

"Good day to you, sir" he proclaimed, to which Shagron offered the perfunctory "Good day" in return.

"I have been ordered to invite you to attend an audience in the Great Hall of the Royal Palace," he said.

"Ordered by whom?" Shagron asked, while at the same time he could hear footsteps behind him – armored, clanking, swishing of chainmail, along with the distinctive scent of oil, used to protect the armor and weapons of the assembled troops from wear and the elements – he had always said you could smell an army on the move before you would ever see them, and this was the case today. He could have guessed how many men had gathered behind him by the smell, without needing to even look.

"By order of his highness, Arch-Duke of Ascanium, Prince of Nyirseg, and Rightful Ruler of the Seven Tribes," the sergeant replied. "Will you come along peacefully?"

Calmly and slowly, Shagron reached forward with his right arm, grasping the tankard of ale the sergeant was holding. Locking eyes, he took the cup from him, brought it up to his mouth and took a long drink, emptying the tankard. Handing back the empty container, never shifting his gaze, he nodded to the sergeant.

"Peacefully."

*****Omar *****

The Great Hall of the Arch-Duke's Palace in Ascanium was a grand structure, constructed nearly a century ago by Prince Matyas Bela to be the primary entranceway to the main palace. It had taken half his lifetime to complete, as the soaring vaulted ceilings were higher even that the great cathedral, and every inch was covered with some manner of decoration, covering the otherwise magnificent blue-hued stone.

To either side of the large double doors of the main entrance, glittering tile mosaics depicted the epic battles of ancient Avar heroes: on the right, Matras Vadas, naked with only the smallest pieces of plate armor attached to his forearms and shins, wielding Isten Kardja – the legendary "Sword of God" – in his battle against the evil Sarkany, the equally legendary seven-headed dragon; on the left, Nemes Ilona – fully clothed – was depicted leading the exodus march of the ancient Avar people through the mountain passes of Uzhgorod and onto the Great Plains, ending with their elation at finding salvation through the bountiful harvest of the many fields and orchards of the new promised land.

The center of the floor was a vast open expanse of polished stone and inlaid tile, worn by the footsteps of royalty and commoners alike that visited the hall. There was room for hundreds of people to stand – maybe a thousand, even – with three rows of raised benches lining each wall to the east and west. Above the seats, a series of rectangular tapestries were hung – each longer than they were tall, depicting some great battle or other significant story that the current prince wished to be shared with everyone.

One could easily see which tapestries transcended a given ruler and had been hanging for longer than the other, more recent depictions of the heroic conquests of the current Prince of Ascanium – it was quite common for a new prince to honour his predecessor by retaining a few of the older depictions, and one could often tell just how strong the bonds of familial love held these relationships together by the length – or brevity – of time that the new prince would tolerate the prior art to remain on display.

Six towering columns reached from the floor to the ceiling, wide at the base and tapering towards the top before they spread open again like the petals of a giant flower, supporting the vaulted ceilings and their enameled paintings of all manner of mythical and magical beasts. The angelic Angyalok, tall and elegant, depicted in dance as they shared with the Avar their secret teachings; the stout and strong Torpek were depicted showing the Avar all the secrets of the earth – extracting rare metals from their dark caves beneath the mountains; sweet child-like Tunderek played games and fluttered about with the aid of beautiful butterfly wings emerging from their backs; and lastly, emerging from the corners, there were various depictions of the shape-changing Alakvalto and the large, lumbering Oriasok – giant creatures that emerged from the woods and the earth to terrorize the Avar. The last panels showed how the Avar people fought and chased the Alakvalto and Oriasok from the surface and banished them forever from the world.

The hall itself was legendary as much for how it was built as for the grandeur of the results. It was said that Prince Matyas had wanted to keep the finished chamber a secret as much as possible during its construction – not only did he have the workers live and sleep within the great hall, but in his desire to ensure that the acoustics were to his satisfaction, he sought out the blind from across the land, tasking them to listen to music and orations in the hall as it was constructed, that they might hear and offer feedback without any of them being able to see the work in progress and risk spoiling his grand reveal.

This story was later told – with some embellishments – as a tale of benevolence, of their Prince creating a school for the blind and otherwise destitute members of the population. It was also told that these same blind students also tested the shape of the hall – the domes and arches, the sweeping curves – and it was said that one might whisper in one corner of the hall and have it heard all the way across the hall in the opposite corner, even if there were a feast going on – if one knew what to listen for.

These, of course, were just rumours, though many also wondered why there were so many blind servants wandering about the halls of the palace even to this day.

Omar took in much of this as he was marched along the long walk from the large double doors, across the polished ceramic tiled floor, and towards the raised dais at the far end of the room. While the room could hold almost a thousand people, it held perhaps a hundred at the moment, all clustered towards the far end of the chamber. As they passed each pair of columns supporting the ceiling, they also passed the four large braziers that surrounded the base of each column, providing much of the heat for the chamber, while the flames helped the embattled candles that hung from the undersized chandeliers, struggling to provide enough light to the large hall. He had a lot of time to take in the view as he walked, mainly because he had been shackled hand and foot and could only shuffle along to keep up with his escort of guards.

As he passed each set of braziers, the flames would visibly flare up, growing in height and brightness, raising more than a few eyebrows amongst the assembled crowd at the end of the chamber.

Some of the guards had started to react as well by the time they passed the second set of columns & braziers, but a quick snap from the burly, heavy-set sergeant with the slicked back hair and curled moustache kept everything under control until they had reached the front of the room and presented their guest to the Prince.

Sitting upon the dais was a large stone chair, flanked by several viziers, clearly identifiable by the cloth stoles that each wore draped over their right shoulder, bearing the heraldry of their rank and station for all to see. Of course, this only worked if one knew the heraldry – which Omar didn't. More important to him was the look on the face of the man sitting in the stone chair.

The Prince was a tall man, between six and seven spans in height, with a tanned, weathered complexion, and a lean, muscled physique, that one might not have expected of someone who had languished for years as puppet leader under a conquering, occupying force. While others might have taken the opportunity to be grateful that the Imperium would let him hold his title – and benefits thereof – after being defeated, and simply gotten fat off the tithes of the people, this prince had maintained his edge, his strength, and his vision, to be ready should the opportunity ever arise that they could rid themselves of their new overlords – as it had a year ago.

Quickest of the seven principalities to reclaim his title and lands, he had mobilized his people and his bannermen to quickly ensure that he was ready to protect Nyirseg from any of the other princes that might have thought his lands to be easy prey. For a time even, he had contemplated expanding his reach into

Temeskoz or Sarkozy, but the onset of the plague quickly erased any plans for a summer of conquest.

Now, he was sitting askance in the throne, leaning on his right elbow, cradling his chin in his hand, staring directly at Omar, looking wholly unimpressed as the guards parted and Omar came to a stop at the foot of the dais, putting an end to the seemingly endless clanking of chains that had echoed throughout the room for the duration of his long walk.

As the herald announced his name and title – titles – to the assembled crowd of viziers and nobility, he made a mental note: next time, he would have the prisoners brought in from a side door, closer to the front, to cut down on the drama. He waited for a perfunctory pause after the introductions before he addressed the prisoner.

"So, this is the thief, 'Omar Stiletto'?" the Prince asked aloud.

"Mage," replied Omar, defiantly cocking his head.

"Adept," interjected one of the viziers.

"Pretender," said another.

"Whelp!" finished the Prince, with a singular tone that made it clear the rapid exchange was, indeed, finished.

Omar might have said more but decided to bite his tongue instead.

"You have entered my principality," the Prince continued, "usurped the local guild master, thrown your sparklers around like a court magician entertaining a crowd at a festival, then you refuse me the local custom…" he turned to a vizier to ask "… did I miss anything?"

"Uh, yes, your grace," mumbled a short, gangly man to his right, looking at a scroll in his hands. "There were the murders of two city guards, two civilians, one merchant, six cats, a dog, and a dozen chickens, plus the various charges of thievery, robbery, shoplifting, bribery, extortion, assault, and violating the decency of the ladies' baths in the harem district." Omar smiled as if remembering an old joke as the list of charges was completed.

"Well, what do you have to say for yourself, boy?" The Prince glared at him.

"It was a slow couple of weeks, I guess…" he answered, his voice trailing off as the Prince's eyes widened, and the guard to his left yanked hard on the chain attached to the manacles, pulling him downwards and almost making him fall.

In the moment it took him to regain his balance, Omar could see that the Prince had regained his composure after letting his temper slip through his quiet façade ever so briefly and was now reclining back in the oversized stone chair, contemplating his next words.

"Very well," he said, rising from the throne and walking forward to the edge of the dais, to tower over the young boy standing in front of him. He paused for a moment, looking into Omar's eyes, and waited. There was something he was looking for and did not find – something he should have seen aplenty in the mind of a young, inexperienced fourteen-year-old boy.

Fear.

There was no fear in Omar's eyes.

Grown men trembled before his power, yet not this child, who he would have thought probably still wet his bed!

He turned back towards his throne and nodded in the direction of the oldest of the six viziers. The heraldry on the blue stole he wore was nothing more than the outline of a simple eight-pointed star, which Omar could see more clearly as he moved forward, stepping down off the dais, and approached Omar to within a few inches of his face. Tolvaj Balasz, the Prince's High Vizier, looked to be the oldest person Omar had ever seen alive, and seemed as though he had stepped right out of the pages of a faerie-tale book, the way they described the ancient Angyalok – tall, frail, yet radiating power, though clearly not an Angyalok – the high vizier added his own air of arrogance to that image.

He had a wizened look, though he stood straight and tall despite the apparent years etched into his wrinkled features. His hair was white, cut short to his head but thinning on the top, although the colour was hard to distinguish through the black and red, dried, mud-like paste that painted much of his head. Applied by hand, the intertwining streaks of red and black swirled in a pattern that was too purposeful to be random, leaving his face exposed except for two small lines tracing down his forehead from his hairline to his eyes.

Omar watched him as he approached, and quietly wondered to himself why it seemed that anyone who dabbled in the arcane arts always seemed to get so weird with their appearances.

Without looking Omar in the eye, he moved slowly around the young boy, as if inspecting him for something, perhaps by sight or smell, but he never touched him. After a moment, he motioned to one of the guards, who stepped forward and roughly removed Omar's shirt, pulling it down to his waist, exposing his youthful features that spoke of energy, but lacked in actual physique. Which is to say, he was skinny.

It also exposed the patchwork web of scars that remained across his back from the flames that had threatened to consume him in Mercurum. The witch's salves had healed him, but the scars remained.

Omar could feel every one of the eyes from around the room that stared at his flawed, misshapen skin, feeling humiliated and embarrassed by the way they made such a casual display of him. There was even a brief moment when he could feel his anger burn through his veins, and he knew that his hands were beginning to glow red & orange as the flames built up inside him.

The moment subsided just as quickly as it rose, feeling the cold tip of the iron spear press into the soft space between his shoulder blades, as the guards reminded him that they were prepared for anything he might try. They still remembered how he hadn't wanted to come along as peacefully as they had hoped, and they clearly still had a grudge about the problems he had caused before they were able to subdue him.

The Vizier examined the boy's back, and turned to the Prince, pointing at the scar at the bottom of his neck.

The Prince looked at the Vizier, and then back towards Omar.

"So, this explains your courage, I think."

Omar continued to stand upright, straight-backed, and proud, as the silence echoed around the chamber, interrupted finally when someone cleared their throat.

Everyone looked over at the cloaked young woman who stood among the nobles on the floor. Blonde hair peeked out from the cowl covering her head and much of her face in shadow, leaving only a glimpse of a delicate nose and sharp cheekbones. She slowly raised her gloved hands from beneath her cloak and slowly tapped her right hand against the inside of her left wrist.

"But perhaps there is something more to you yet..." the Prince continued, nodding to the Vizier. The Vizier seemed to give a condescending sneer towards the girl – who made no reaction whatsoever – as he stepped back to Omar and removed the crumpled shirt from his arm, and holding up his wrist, revealed the second stitching scar, still red from the freshness of the recent healing.

"Ah, there it is," the Prince said softly, "this – these two stitchings – I think explain much about how someone so young could know so much about fire and thievery!"

"Very interesting," said the Vizier, releasing his grip as Omar shrugged and pulled his hand away. He slowly moved back across the dais and resumed his position standing behind the Prince, though his eyes remained focused on the young woman now, not Omar, nor any of the others assembled in the audience hall.

Omar put his shirt back on, now that the inspections seemed to be over, and everyone seemed satisfied.

"Do you hear the voices?" the Prince asked.

"No," Omar answered.

"Have you mastered your memories?"

"No," came the same answer again.

"And yet in just three short weeks since arriving in Ascanium, you have infiltrated the local guild, assumed control of a network of spies to feed you information – which they did willingly – and used this information to exact revenge for your imagined slights."

"You saw the scars," Omar replied, "Did they look 'imagined' to you?" The crowd buzzed amongst themselves at the audacity of the boy's tone with the Prince.

"So, this man and woman you burned in the market, in front of dozens of witnesses, they were the ones who did this to you?" This came from the other vizier, who had listed out the charges earlier. His stole was marked with the image of a balancing scale, with a sword running up through it – the chief justice.

"No" said Omar, "they didn't set the fire, but they abandoned me to it!"

Omar remembered the day last week when he had learned that his aunt and her lover were living in Ascanium. Marta and Balint had fled the fire in Mercurum, escaping to the river and then finding their way across the plains to Ascanium – after leaving Omar and his mother behind, they had nothing left in Mercurum but the reminders of their guilt, so they sought shelter as refugees from the plague.

While Omar could find out little about Torick's whereabouts, he was more than happy to learn that these two were still alive, which gave him a chance to show them his appreciation for all they had done for him. He had found them in the market, where it appeared they had resorted to feeble attempts at thievery to feed themselves. There was some initial shock when he first confronted them, alive, much to both their amazement, although they had no idea of what he was now capable of, in either his channeling abilities or his desire to ease his pain with revenge.

In what he considered a "just reward", he felt it was only appropriate that they should finally experience the agony they had sought to escape when they sacrificed him and his mother for their own selfishness – immolating them in flames, right there in the middle of the market. He had watched coldly as they stumbled about at first, shrieking as they tried to extinguish the flames, setting fire to several of the vendors' stalls before they finally stopped their pitiful wailing and collapsed to the ground, curling up in painful contortions as they choked on the smoke of their own burning flesh. No one had stood in his way as he walked away from the market that day, but he had to admit now, as he stood in shackles in the palace hall, it was perhaps a bit foolish to have done the deed in such a public place.

He sighed as he relived the memory, still feeling satisfied that he had done, and regretting only his lack of discretion. Oh, well, he thought – live & learn...

"So, you don't deny their murder then, either?" the justiciar vizier asked.

"No," was all he received in reply.

"Enough!" the Prince interrupted. "There is no doubt about the charges against you. I have asked you here to discuss your punishment."

"Asked?" Omar mouthed silently, as he finished tucking in his shirt and the guards refastened his shackles.

"In fact," the Prince continued, "I have asked all of you here to discuss how you can make reparations for past wrongs, by serving your prince to make some things 'right' again."

It was in this moment that Omar noticed there was something unusual about the crowd that was standing before the dais. Mentally chastising himself for assuming that he was the center of attention for the day's festivities, he looked around more closely, and could see that among those assembled in the great hall, there were actually some smaller divisions in the crowd, setting some apart from others.

While he happened to be in the middle, as the most recent guest to be brought in, he could see that there were others standing in front and apart from the noble lords, although none were subject to the same tools of incarceration that adorned his hands and feet. There were a scattered number of guards around the room and in the crowd, and what he thought before was a random mixing, now became more apparent as he could see who they were guarding.

He let his mind shift Into a neutral sort of calm, as he let the subconscious memories of the stitched intellect scan the room for him, and he could see the players around the stage.

There was the young ranger, standing with two companions – one was wounded and in need of rest.

There was a larger man, who stood with authority and command, and despite his garb as a monk, he took him to be a warrior. He was accompanied by a smaller man who looked the part of a monk much more sincerely.

The last one to catch his attention ought to have been obvious, and he silently cursed his pride for being too blind to have seen him when he first entered. Almost in line with him and down the row, on the far side of the rangers, Omar could clearly see the face of the man from Mercurum – the Lord of the Tower – Torick, the Mage – the man who murdered his mother!

Shagron watched the exchange between Prince Svato and the young boy, interested if not mildly confused as to why he – why any of them – had been summoned to observe this curious exchange. He and Ralof had been waiting for some time in one of the smaller rooms adjacent to the audience hall, and then once they had been ushered in, they waited again – with no explanations – while the young prisoner was then summoned and escorted into the chamber.

Not that he couldn't tolerate standing on his feet for a few hours, but the not knowing of any reason why he should be here was beginning to wear thin his patience. So much so that he decided to try to see if he could move things along somewhat.

"Pardon me," he announced, "but may I inquire as to what this has to with us – with the good Brother and myself even – we have only just recently arrived, and I am aware of no offense that we have caused your grace. I do not know this boy, and by what I have seen of his character in just these few moments, I would just as soon not know him any better than I already do. Which leads me to wonder just what sort of business you might be intending to engage in, and I would greatly appreciate if Your Grace could enlighten us as to your intentions."

"Oh, well said!" the Prince acknowledged, "you are ever the polite, learned one; so much more than one would ever expect from a simple man-at-arms!" he said with a sardonic tone. "How long has it been since you have bathed, yet alone stepped foot in the High Court of any of the Seven Princes? Years, I imagine – you have been branded an outlaw by the Archbishop of Mercurum for your assassination of his predecessor and have hardly been seen in any civilized setting for more than a year – and anytime you have, it always seems that fire and death soon follow – in fact, there are even rumours that the legendary 'Shagron, Holy Warrior of Ukko' set off this plague when you killed the Archbishop! I find those tales to be the most delightful! Don't you?"

"I can't say I have had the time lately to listen to tall tales around the campfire, Your Grace, but I wouldn't believe everything one hears from frightened milkmaids…"

"So, what I have said is not true?" he asked, wandering across the dais to stand closer to the edge.

"No, it's true…" Shagron noted, lifting his head and straightening his back, "I am now, and always shall be, a Holy Warrior of Ukko, Defender of the Faith, Guardian of the Weak, Champion of the Oppressed, Slayer of All Things Evil, and Sworn Enemy of the Dark." He paused to take a breath then continued, "You may have left out one or two things, but you were correct in who I am. The rest…" he trailed off and shrugged his shoulders "… I did have a bath last week, but I don't believe you would have been informed…"

Shagron honestly did not know where the sudden burst of attitude came from that would make him talk so forthrightly to one of the Seven Princes, and he silently attributed it to the contagious arrogance that he had been watching in the exchange the Prince had with the young boy just moments earlier. He instantly regretted the pompous tone he had used and shook his head, embarrassed with his own lack of humility.

"Forgive me, Your Grace, that was very impolite of me," he started, taking advantage of the pause that hung in the air after he had finished his first outburst. "You are correct that I have been away from such courtly manners for perhaps too long and should not have addressed you in such a fashion.

"I have been away – from everything – for a very long time, even before I was called to avenge the injustices enacted by the Archbishop that resulted in his death for his crimes; but if I am branded an outlaw, it is by the will of man alone, and not by the truth of my actions and not in the eyes of the All Father. If that is the crime for which you have brought me here, then I have no choice under the law but to submit myself to your secular verdict; I entrust the judgement of my soul to Ukko." He lowered his eyes to the ground as he finished.

"There you go…" the Prince smiled, "it's coming back to you now, isn't it? All the polish and forbearance that we are so accustomed to hearing every day at court." Moving around the front edge of the dais, the Prince continued speaking "I wish all my lords – and ladies – would remember such civility; you have been in the wilderness for many years, and yet it glides from your tongue with but the briefest reminder; many of my most loyal subjects would be at a loss to recall the last time they spoke with even a hint of the same humility. They are more akin to this young boy, here," he motioned to Omar, still standing silent but upright in his shackles, "arrogant, entitled, and full of fire."

"Hmm," he shrugged, continuing almost as if talking to himself, "it seems everyone is full of fire these days, but where was that fire when the Imperium arrived? Where was that fire to fight for their freedom? Their sovereignty? Their Prince? No, many of these very same people you see in this hall today were quick to sell their loyalty to the Imperium in exchange for the 'freedom' to keep their lands, their 'power,' their money, as soon as they thought the tide of battle was changing – some decided even before the battles, but most of these folk are no longer alive to bother us…"

He stopped his pacing in front of Jason, Ferenc and Kiara.

"Imperial Rangers, are you not?"

They nodded.

"And why are you still here?" the Prince asked, bending his knee to lower himself to look Jason directly in the eyes.

Jason was opening his mouth to respond, when a voice from behind the throne answered for him…

"He's here because he is a traitor to his own people!" the woman's voice said sharply. Stepping forward from the cluster of royal viziers, Jason and the rest of the assembled crowd could see a figure emerge that had been somewhat hidden by the angle of the raised dais and behind the numbers of the other bodies on the platform.

Wearing a gilded suit of field plate armor that was as much a uniform as it was protection, a woman strode forward to stand two steps behind the prince and to his left. While the stole draped over her shoulder clearly bore the symbol of crossed swords that marked her as a military vizier, Jason was fixated on the singular red scar that ran down her face, from her left eye to the base of her neck.

He locked eyes with General Vassilya for the first time in more than a year, and all he could see was her rage – she was finally face-to-face with the impetuous whelp that had wiped out her entire Legion in an instant, killing thousands, destroying her career, her reputation, her honour, and her entire life's ambitions in less time than it took him to wipe his ass!

"Good to see you again, Captain." She said through clenched teeth – the emphasis on his title seeming incredibly hostile, despite the otherwise pleasantness of her words.

"General Vassilya," Jason acknowledged. "Good to see you alive and well," he added, with just the faintest hint of a tremor in his otherwise steady voice.

"Ah, so you are acquainted," said the Prince happily. "I was afraid I would need introductions." This time the sarcasm was abundantly obvious in his tone. Pointing to his Justiciar Vizier, the Prince began to read aloud the crimes by memory…

"A mutinous officer and his cohorts, accused of ambushing and killing thousands of soldiers – even though they were the enemy – including superior officers, livestock, destruction of personal property, theft of a Nyirseg noble's manor house and properties, squatting on said properties, and… and I think that's it. Well, I'm really not sure if I should be holding you here as a criminal or if I should be giving you a medal! You have single-handedly done more for the freedom of the Avar people than our combined armies did over the past ten years. Although there are some who would consider these crimes…" he paused, his eyes darting over to Vassilya. "It is a long list – I expect there might be more we could add, but it sounds like enough, though, don't you think?" The Prince returned to sit on the throne as he finished speaking.

"No," said Vassilya, moving forward again, "Nowhere near enough! Each of those murdered soldiers should be a charge unto themselves, and each should bring a penalty of death!" She stood tall on the edge of the dais, looking down at Jason. The next words she whispered through her teeth were barely audible to anyone else in the chamber:

"I lost a great many friends and comrades by your treason! I will see that you pay for that, personally!"

"I gave the Praetor every chance to…" Jason began to protest, but she waved him silent.

"Just be glad that is I who found you, and not General Sukhov!" she gave a half smile. "Or should I say 'Praetor Sukhov' – many of his legionnaires survived and he has been seeking dispensation from the Imperium to return and hunt you down." She paused to let her words sink in. "You have many enemies for yourself – and your friends," she said as she looked toward Ferenc and Kiara.

"Will this one live?" she asked, gesturing to the bloody bandages on Ferenc's chest. "It would be much too easy for him to simply die and avoid what Sukhov has planned for you if he ever finds you again – and believe me, he has sworn a thousand oaths to do just that – though it would be a shame to rob us of entertainment like that." She looked back at Jason, "You, on the other hand, are mine to decide what to do with…"

"Ahem." Someone cleared their throat from the direction of the throne, and she glanced briefly with her eyes in a subtle display of irritation.

"Your time is up, little captain!" she finished and turned to walk back to her place behind the throne, this time making sure she remained visible to Jason and his companions, staring only at him throughout the rest of the audience.

"Let's start this all over again, shall we?" the Prince began to speak again. "Now that we have dispensed with all the animosity and 'who owes who' and 'who killed who', I need to make you all a proposition, that I believe you will find fair and reasonable for each of your situations.

"It will not be news to tell you that the Avar lands have been subject to a great deal of ill fortune over the past two years – you have all seen the same things we have: The Imperium, heatwaves, droughts, famine, disease, plague-born berserks, and now, swarms of locusts set loose to destroy what meager crops we have scraped out of these once-fertile lands. Nyirseg has suffered the worst of this, with the Great Plains becoming little more than a barren desert, with the largest herds moving to greener pastures. The outer principalities have managed to survive with what little trade they have with the territories beyond the mountains but even that exposes our weakness to new predators!"

"What you may find to be news," he continued, "is that we have discovered that all of these afflictions – aside from the invasion by the Imperium – all of these things have not occurred naturally."

He waited for a moment to let that statement sink in for everyone assembled in the hall. It took a few minutes before the whispers and hushed talk subsided enough for him to continue.

"These things have been wreaked upon us – conjured, summoned, channeled – whatever you want to call it, they have been created by other than the will of the gods. Created with only one purpose that we can see: to drive out or kill every Avar man, woman, and child."

"My god!" was the refrain echoed by many of the people listening to his words.

"Who would want to do such a thing?" one person asked aloud.

"Who do you think?" answered another, "the Angyalok have finally returned, seeking revenge!"

"Of course, it's a Garaboncid – a rogue warlock—they are all mad, and they are known to bring terrible storms!!" shouted another, and then it was only a moment before the first voices were lost in a babble of theories about who might be behind such a mad plan of destruction.

"What are we to do?" was the one cry from the assembled crowd that finally led the people to subside in the outbursts and look to the Prince, seated calmly above them on the unmovable, solid stone throne of Nyirseg.

Looking at the people waiting silently now for his words, the Prince gripped the arms of the throne with his strong, weathered hands, and lifting himself slowly to his feet, he spoke again with a voice that everyone in the crowd would all agree later was as imperious and regal a voice as any of them had ever heard.

"We are going to find and destroy whoever or whatever is attacking us with these plagues and show them that the Avar people will not be swept away from the face of the earth like so much chafe before the wind."

He raised his voice with each word, building into a crescendo of righteousness.

"We have been attacked and we will retaliate as befits our history as warriors! We have been wounded; our strength is depleted; and we have little with which to defend ourselves, so we have gathered those who have the strength we need to fight this battle for us!"

He had been addressing the crowd at first, and now turned to look at each of the adventurers standing closest to the dais, and the tone seemed to shift, from inspiring to admonishing.

"You were each brought here because you possess qualities that may be able to undo these harms that we have endured. You have shown abilities that warrant you a place in this company, but make no mistake, there are many who doubt your quality – your character – for being worthy of the challenges you must face, of the trust we must place in you."

The Prince held his gaze on each of them.

"You are all trying to escape your past, and for this, we can offer you the one thing that none of us have: a future."

He hoped it was a rousing enough speech for the assembled crowd of nobles – and enough to convince the usually self-interested adventurers to consider serving a purpose greater than their own well-being. He knew Shagron would take up the challenge for honour alone, and Ralof would follow him; but the others, he knew, would not be so easily swayed.

They took a moment to look at one another, considering the words of the Prince as they understood the reason for their gathering, now quickly beginning to estimate their chances, evaluating, and judging one another: gauging strengths and weaknesses from their appearances, coming up with instants odds on the likelihood of surviving of they had to depend on the others in the room. Omar looked only at Torick.

"Do this, and we will see to it that all of your crimes are erased, honour restored, debts repaid, and your actions rewarded." One more incentive, the Prince hoped...

The hall was silent, as people seemed to hold their breath, considering the consequences of the decisions being made.

"NEVER!" shouted Omar, breaking the silence to the shock of everyone. "I will never do anything with that murderer!" he exclaimed loudly, pointing his arm across at Torick. "I will have his head, and that of anyone who stands in my way, before or afterwards!"

Almost instinctively, the three Imperial Rangers standing between Omar and Torick took a small step backwards, giving the two a clearer line of sight. Behind them, the guards and crowd of nobility also moved backwards – several steps – clearly having no intention of getting between the two. The only exception was the young woman in the full-length cloak who had earlier directed the Vizier to inspect Omar's wrist for evidence of his stitching.

As the only person in the room who seemed unconcerned about the loud outburst from Omar – other than Torick, who remained incredibly nonplussed about the whole thing, with barely a glance in Omar's direction – she slowly began to walk around the outside of the undrawn circle that the group had formed around the dais, pulling back her hood to reveal her face and long blonde hair, falling in curls around her shoulders.

The Prince, still standing, directed his attention to Omar, and spoke loudly to get his attention.

"I have seen how you have been wronged, Omar Stiletto, and know that you seek revenge above all else. While I cannot reward you with the return of your loved one, I can offer you something that will give you peace now, and perhaps let you see past this rage. Lady Darellan, if you don't mind?" He nodded once as he finished speaking.

Omar looked at the Prince, wondering what he meant, splitting his focus for a moment between Torick on his right and the Prince to his front, which was enough for the young blonde woman now standing behind him to reach out her hand and touch his head gently, like a mother comforting her child. Her eyes closed — as did his — the moment her hand made contact.

There was a brief flash of light, and when it cleared, he found himself standing on the roof of his aunt's house, back in Mercurum, before the fire had destroyed everything. It was evening, just as it was that night more than a year ago, when he had last lain here looking at the stars. He slowly looked around — there were no people anywhere on the street or other rooftops — the city was empty and silent. He finished a complete circle and then saw her standing in front of him, as real as anything else, though she had not been there just a moment before.

"What is this place?" he asked. "This can't be real!"

"You're right" she said. "I brought you here to talk for a moment."

"Why?"

"Because there's something you need to know," she answered.

"Know what? Who *are* you?" he asked, as the questions kept coming faster than he could even think to ask them. "What are you doing this for? What could you possibly know about me that I don't already know? You weren't here — I was! I remember it all!"

"My name is Lady Darellan Fenndragon, and I am here to help you see." Dar was dressed here much the same as she had been in the audience hall — leather leggings with large sinew stitching, knee-high leather boots with a fur cuff, and a soft leather jerkin decorated with red-flowered embroidery. Her blonde hair fell about her head in loose natural curls, held back from her forehead by a headband of twisted cord, with small, beaded braids dangling off to one side. She wore a short cloak around her shoulders hanging to the back of her knees, with a cowl that resembled the sleeping form of a small wildcat curled around the back of her neck. She stared at Omar intently as she spoke.

"In order for anything I say to make sense, you have to accept one basic premise," she said quietly, "One that you may not want to believe."

"What's that?"

"That you've been played, Omar."

"What? By whom — Torick? Why?" he asked, still unsure of why she was doing this.

"Not Torick," she replied. "Louhi."

"Baba Louhi? Why should I believe you?"

"Listen first — decide for yourself later," she answered. "We know that Torick started the fire to cleanse the plague from the Market Quarter." As she spoke,

Omar could see the glow of flames rise in the distance, starting near the mage's tower, and spreading rapidly in two opposing arcs around the perimeter of the quarter. Their house was set back from the warehouses, away from the bustle and closer to the edge of the quarter. He could see the flames moving outwards, consuming everything in their path, and he struggled to hold back his tears as the memories of that night began to flood back.

"You were in the street when the fire started, and never saw the path Torick chose for the fire to follow," the woman explained. "You couldn't have seen how the fire encircled all of the quarter first but left this road open – your road – so that you and your family might escape. You had given him Louhi's token, and he made sure you were given enough time to escape."

Omar was silent, as the landscape blurred, and they were inside the small house. He could see shadows of everyone – Marta, Balint, the witch Louhi, and his mother, lying in the next room. He watched Marta and Balint run out to look at the flames, and then flee down the street.

"You see these things like they are shadows – memories – of what happened that night, but you could not have seen then that there were other magics at work that night – other than Torick's – magic that had a different purpose in mind." The scene had shifted to where the fire was starting to break through into the home, and Louhi was trying to convince him to come with her. As he looked at his sleeping mother again, the woman held out her arm, and suddenly he could see the thin blue smoky tendrils of power flowing through the flames.

"What is this?" he asked.

"This is Torick's magic, driving the flames forward across the town, following his will," she said, and then she turned her hand, closing her fingers, and he could see larger tendrils of green smoke filling the room. These tendrils seemed to emanate directly from the shadowy form of Baba Louhi as she stared at Omar.

He remembered the dilemma in that moment, of whether or not he could leave his mother to follow Louhi, and so he could feel himself scream silently within his mind as he saw the green fingers of smoke – something he could have never seen at the time – reach upward, around the beam of wood over her room, clutching it and pulling it crashing down on his sleeping mother.

He was still trying to scream when the scene shifted again, and they were out on the street. The same green tendrils of power filled the street – their escape route—with roaring flames, as the rest of the fire, fed by the blue energy, held itself back to either side of the route. He remembered how she had led him out of the fire, created the sense of gratitude for saving him, and how she had nurtured his desire for revenge and what he would need to do to gain the powers he needed to seek that revenge...

"Enough!" he called out, closing his eyes on the shadow world she was showing him.

He never actually felt her hand on his head, and so he never felt when she removed it, but he could tell that it was over, and he opened his eyes, finding himself in the same spot in the audience hall, wondering how much time had actually passed...

"...*barely an instant*..." was the answer he felt in his mind, her presence fading rapidly as she gave him this one last answer before she was gone.

"Well, that was interesting!" he said plainly, his voice hoarse, as he took a moment to adjust himself, feeling somewhat uncomfortable that this had happened in front of everyone, and he had no idea whether they had any idea of what he had seen. Despite the borrowed wisdom from the stitching, he felt the shame of his wrongness about Torick wash over him and could feel the anxiety building up as he anticipated being asked to apologize – which was just about the last thing he ever wanted to do!

He could not even bring himself to look at Torick from this point, as he struggled to make sense of what had been revealed to him. The woman behind him had stepped forward now, and he could look at her in the flesh rather than the shadow form: she was young, perhaps twenty, and really quite beautiful, he thought.

She had sharp but delicate features and a slender face, with soft skin and a bronzed complexion that reflected the warm light of the fires burning around the hall. Her brown eyes held a warmth and kindness that he had never seen before in his – albeit young – life. It was a feeling that seemed to be reflected in her smile, although he could sense that while she looked not too much older than him, she had a sadness about her that undermined any joy one might have seen in her expression.

"Why did she do it?" he asked her "Why did Louhi give me this, and then let me steal the ritual? She knew I would use it; I did it once, and I would do it again if I needed to!"

"Baba Louhi is not a witch woman or a shaman," she answered, "Come talk with me after this is done, before we leave, and I will explain further."

As they were speaking, the guards removed the last of the shackles from Omar and stepped back. The Prince, who was still standing where Omar had last seen him before he went into the dream-trance – or whatever it was – was looking at the group, still waiting for their answer – or at the very least, for Omar to retract his refusal.

"Are we good?" asked the Prince.

Darellan nodded, and Omar answered, "We're good."

"Good. Everyone's good." The Prince continued, "Is there anyone else who strongly objects to what we are asking of you?"

The room was silent again, and this time there were no surprise interruptions.

"Good. If I were a different man, this would be the part in our meeting where I would tell you about how we would deal with anyone who would seek to leave this room and go back on your word; how we would not tolerate to live anyone who would double-cross us and ensure that you would find no rest anywhere in the Avar lands for the rest of your very, very, short lives.

"But I am a trusting man, a man of honour, and let's not forget, a prince of the Avars."

As if on cue to highlight his words, there was a bright flash of lightning from outside, followed almost immediately by a rolling boom of thunder that seemed to shake the glass in the ornately painted windows near the entrance of the hall. Sudden and unexpected, most everyone in the hall flinched and startled at the sound.

"I expect those of you who aren't already acquainted will need some time to consider putting your lives into one another's hands but know this – each of you was selected for a purpose, and we expect that all your skills will be of value in this quest, at one point or another, never doubt that.

"You should expect to stay for dinner after the Grand Council has been dismissed; afterwards you can return to your homes or stay the night in the palace; whatever your choice, you should be prepared and ready to travel by the morning."

"Milord," Jason interjected as the Prince finished his piece. "Ferenc is not fit to travel – he is wounded and needs time to heal. We cannot go without him…"

"I leave it to you to decide if your friends should accompany you or not," the Prince answered politely, "it is your name ascribed to the crimes that have been committed, not theirs. You have until the morning to decide."

"Travel where, your grace?" Shagron asked "We have not been told the name of our foe, or where to look for them…"

The Prince paused, a tactic Shagron was quickly learning he loved to use to create an unnecessary feeling of drama for even the most mundane announcements. He clapped his hands, and the viziers behind the throne turned and began to filter out of the great hall through doors to either side of the dais. The rest of the nobility began to walk back to the main doors; it took several minutes for everyone to make the walk and exit out into the rain. As the last one stepped out, the guards closed and locked the doors, remaining at the far end of the hall to guard the doors.

With just the assembled group of adventurers remaining, and a few others, namely Lady Fenndragon, Military Vizier Vassilya, and High Vizier Tolvaj, who stepped down off the dais and joined the group on the floor of the hall. Only then did the Prince continue speaking.

"His name is Voros Vaszoly, and we believe he is an Angyalok Garaboncid – a rogue who can manipulate weather – as we have seen from the drought – and probably able to channel much more than that. He will be very dangerous, although we do not know why he is doing this. The Angyalok..." he glanced at Torick, "...or at least most of them – abandoned these lands to the Avar hundreds of years ago. I doubt there are enough left in all the lands to take it back, but..." he trailed off in thought.

"Why do you people always say that the Angyalok '*abandoned*' this land?" The dryly worded question came from Torick.

"Pardon me?" Dar responded on behalf of the Prince, who seemed distracted by the interruption.

"I always hear people speak of the Angyalok as if we *mysteriously* choose to leave this world – '*sailing away across the seas to the home of the alfar*' or '*abandoning this world for the sweet haven of Ascalon, or Alfheim*' or wherever it is you think we have gone! But we didn't leave – we were cast out! Killed. Betrayed. Forced from our lands when your wandering tribes, fleeing whatever had chased you out of the Great Eastern Plains...'

He waved his arm, gesturing to the great murals that decorated the hall, "...and taking this land as your new home, as if it were yours for the taking. Graceful hosts, we shared our wisdom and knowledge with the Avar, only to learn too late that you had no intention of honouring us in return."

"Instead, you repaid my people with fear and death – our very name is used for curses and sickness in your homes and temples – when one of you falls ill, you say they are 'alf-schot'; we are the villains in your poems; hell, the Avar even say '*ganga álfrek*' when they have a big shit – which is literally '*drive away the elves*'! So you tell me – why should I help you now? I have committed no crimes for which I must make penance, I owe no debt to your crown – if anything it should be the reverse. So, tell me now, or I will gladly take my leave."

There was a moment of silence in the hall when Torick finished, as the Prince slowly and deliberately moved towards him, sensing the gravity of his words and showing a willingness to respond with equal sincerity.

"I brought you here to answer for the burning of Mercurum, nothing more, nothing less," he began.

"I cleansed the market quarter as I promised the Ispan – nothing more, nothing less!" Torick replied, his voice almost a hiss.

"You killed a great many people–"

"Who were either infected or going to be infected and die anyway. I did them a mercy – an absolute ending before they became mindless zombies that would feed on their own children!" Torick answered, drawing another pause.

"I cannot answer for my forefathers–" the Prince began again, before Torick cut him off again.

"Why not?" he demanded, "You are the Prince, the rightful ruler of all the Avar lands. You are what you are if not only for the sins of your fathers."

The Prince straightened his back at this, and a worried look crossed Dar's face. "For all that, I am but one man among many. I cannot undo what the past has done, nor can I return what you feel was taken from you… not that I would even care to."

"No?" said Torick.

"No." The Prince answered defiantly. "It has always been our way to keep what we kill. Yes, we fled an invasion of our ancient lands. We were defeated and our enemy took from us because we could not stop them. And yes, we came here, saw the beauty and richness of the land and decided to stay. The Angyalok welcomed us, shared with us, and when we grew powerful again, yes, the Angyalok did choose to leave! We did not force anyone away!"

"Bah!" was all Torick could muster as an answer, spinning away with a sweep of his cloak. He took two steps and turned back, anger in his eyes. "Many of my brothers and sisters died on Avar blades; were enslaved in Avar prisons, forced to conjure magics to shape your cities and make your harvests overflow, while their children were held at the tip of a spear to force their obedience. So don't tell me we were not forced away. Many fled, went into hiding, or concealed themselves to avoid provoking hostilities. You are a crude race and deserve whatever it is that Voros is conjuring for you!"

"You see…" the Prince shouted at Dar in frustration, "I told you this would not work! He is more likely to help Vaszoly than to aid us!"

Like a referee trying to separate two fighters in the ring, Dar moved forward with her hands raised, seeking both sparring partners to back down for a moment. "Please!" she voiced softly yet firmly, looking at Prince Sato as one might look at a child who had done precisely the opposite of what his parents had just told him not to do. Her look to Torick was softer, apologizing for the tone of the Prince without speaking the words out loud.

"Though true, this may not be the time to right all the wrongs of the past. Perhaps we can find a way to look on this as we stand here, today, to see one another and know that we have a common purpose," she offered in a soothing voice, bringing down the intensity of the moment. "There are righteous men and angyalok, on both sides; and there is evil – evil that needs to be stopped regardless of where it comes from. What Vaszoly is doing to the lands is killing Avar and Angyalok alike, and as much as you might be afraid to admit it," she added, looking at Torick, "you would be loath to count yourself as one so vile as Voros Vaszoly. Am I wrong?"

"No," came the answer, "you are not wrong. But why should I be bargaining with you? Why is the great Prince of Nyirseg relying on a Sword Sister, a Taltos, and whatever else you may be, to make his deals for him? What is your interest here? Your order is dedicated to finding the great 'Isten Kardja'..." he said, waving towards the tile mosaic, "the great 'Sword of God'. Your treasure hunters told everyone that finding the sword would unite the seven tribes again, and when that didn't happen, it was supposed to free us from the shackles of the Imperium," he scoffed, "and what, now you're hoping to find the great blade to save us from bad weather and insects?!"

"This is not about me or my Order," Dar deflected calmly, not rising to the bait, "this is about you and your blood debt to the Prince...!"

"Blood debt? Is that what you call it? I stand by my word. I did nothing more than what I had been asked – paid to do – and it is not my fault the dim-witted Ispan failed to specify his terms! But this point is moot – I am here by my own will, and nothing more. I have no reason to fear you – any of you! You are demanding I commit myself to this service, but you have no ability to make me. I honoured my word to the Ispan – that alone is what I live by. You had best choose your next words more wisely than he if you wish my help."

"Agreed," Dar answered, "There is a price for everything, and if you would name yours, we can surely put this to rest and move on."

The Prince had retreated slightly from the conversation and was seated again on his throne, eyeing the wizard with suspicion. Torick looked back & forth between Dar and the Prince, still looking uncertain.

"Your treasury is vast" Torick began, watching for any indication that anyone was being anything less than fully sincere in their answers, "I would ask to choose but one thing, a trinket really, to have for myself. That is my price."

The Prince leaned forward on his throne, "What thing is it that you desire?"

Torick raised a finger, "I will make my selection when we return, victorious, as I have no doubt you would not be so foolish as to agree to payment in advance. Nor would I care to let you know what it is that I value of all your precious hoard, lest it somehow disappear between now and when we return. That is my price."

"And you will overlook all wrongs done to your people, for a trinket?" The Prince asked snidely.

"No, but we all have a price and I make no secret of my willingness to serve any master for the right price. You can buy my services for this quest, and this quest only, and you can rest peacefully in the knowledge that Voros will not be able to outbid you for my attentions, as what I want – what you have – is unique and singular in nature, and he cannot offer it to me. Only you can – if you agree to my terms." Torick offered his hand to Dar, who, after looking for at the Prince for approval, took the hand in agreement of the terms.

"That's settled then," Dar stated flatly and with relief. "We will talk more in the morning about where you are heading."

"Until then, it is better that the fewer that know, the better, as Voros has many eyes and ears across the lands, and it would not do well to have him know that we are looking for him. We have suspicions for where he may be, and how to find him, but make no mistake – this is not a simple errand we are asking of you. Time is short –we have but a few months before the seasons change; food will be rationed; and the closed cities will be sorely tested for survival."

The thunder and lightning flashed and boomed again, this time so close it felt like it was in the room with them, so loud and deep that many could feel the rumbling, deep into their bodies.

"Your grace, it seems the storm is right upon us," said Darellan. She looked concerned as she turned to the Prince. "There is nothing natural about this!" she cried out loudly over the sound of the wind and rain pelting the stained-glass windows, the worry in her voice clearly rising. It was then that she noticed everyone in the hall had doubled over, in apparent agony from some unseen source. *'The storm!'* she thought to herself… and then she began to feel the tightening in her own chest as well, and the sharp piercing pain in her abdomen as she fought the urge to cry out. The others had dropped to the floor and weren't moving as a flash of lightning struck and thunder echoed across the hall in a deafening boom!

"Shit!" was all she could say before the blackness took her as well.

PART II

"CLEAR!"

"Nothing!"

"Keep up the compressions!"

"Charging!"

"CLEAR!"

Every muscle in his body tensed and contracted in a moment of spasm, and every nerve seemed like it was on fire! In the next instant everything relaxed, and he could hear voices around him, talking loudly in urgent tones, as he could hear them rushing about.

"We have a pulse!"

"BP 140 over 90," called out another anxious voice.

"Give me sixty milligrams epinephrine in the IV – first six mils direct; hang the rest."

"Normal sinus rhythm."

There was a pause for a few moments as readings were checked.

"Okay, looks like we're in the clear. Hey, I think he's waking up…"

His eyes fluttered briefly as he strained against the bright lights to see what was going on, and who was speaking. But he couldn't see through the watery film that blurred his vision, and the effort just drained the energy from him, so he gave in again to the fatigue and slipped back to the warm embrace of a deep sleep.

When he woke again, the light was softer, and he could hear the footsteps of someone moving around the room opening the curtains. He raised his hands to his face, wiping away the moisture from his eyes before he tried to open them. This time, he focused on his hands first, adjusting to the light as a female voice from across the room greeted him.

"Good morning," she said softly, "Welcome back to the land of the living!" she joked in a playful tone. He could make out her blonde hair first, long and straight, held back in a tight ponytail. Wearing matching light blue pants and shirt, she smiled as she tapped away on a tablet in her hands, before checking something on the equipment beside the bed, and then making more notes.

The walls of the room were faded beige, and the bed he was lying in was large but not very comfortable, with white linen sheets and a thin blanket folded at his feet. There was a curtain halfway around the bed, deflecting the sunlight from the window so the room wasn't too bright for him.

He could not see any hearth or fireplace, yet the room seemed warm, without the damp chill that one was always accustomed to feeling inside any of the larger buildings in Ascanium.

"…."

He tried to say "hello" back to her, but all that he could make come out of his throat was a croaking noise, and he suddenly realized how dry his mouth felt.

"Oh dear," she said, moving closer and reaching for something on the bedside table. "You must be thirsty!" she said, holding a small cup towards him with some water and a straw. He took a short sip and felt the lump in his throat that made it hard to swallow at first. This gradually got better as he took a few more sips – he felt he had to try, as the taste in his mouth was absolutely horrible – but his confusion was only building, and he wanted – needed – answers, so he tried his best to speak again.

"*Where am I?*" he croaked out first, "*What is this place?*"

"You're okay," she answered with a smile, "You're in the ICU at BGH, and we're happy to see you awake – you gave us quite a scare yesterday, but everything's looking much better today. Your nose and throat may be a little sore for a while – we removed the NG tube yesterday when you first woke up, but it's not the most comfortable experience!"

"*Where is everyone? Who are you?!?*" he struggled to ask, becoming a little more agitated, as he was becoming increasingly confused by his surroundings. *"ICU? What the hell is 'BGH?"* he thought, giving up on trying to voice every question all at once!

"I'm supposed to call the doctor as soon as you wake up, so I'll be right back. Just try to relax and she'll be right with you!" And with that she stepped out of the room.

She was dressed strangely, which set off a sense of concern. Looking down and seeing the crisscross web of wires and tubes that were attached to his body brought this concern to the level of a panic from which he immediately began to try to escape! A painful sensation as he tried to move revealed even more tubes connected below the bed sheets.

He was beginning to try to pull at the things in his arms when a tall woman walked in, followed by the first girl. They were both dressed in the same manner – all in white, and… clean. The taller woman's hair was pulled back, and he could see that she was a little older than the first girl, and spoke with a more commanding voice, which made her seem to be less interested in befriending him than just doing her job.

"Good morning, Tibor, I'm Doctor Guray," she greeted him as she came to the bedside and calmly placed her hand on his arm, keeping him from attacking the tubes. "I know you must feel a little disoriented, but we're glad you're awake and talking! That's excellent progress for your recovery."

He relaxed almost involuntarily as she said his name.

Tibor.

The name sounded so familiar to him, and still totally foreign, all at the same time.

"We've called your sister, to let her know that you're awake – she should be here very soon."

Sister?

Tibor? No – that wasn't right. Who did they think he was?

This was wrong – he shouldn't be here!

"No," he croaked again, instantly wanting another drink. "*I need to go back!*"

"Go back?" the doctor looked at him as he made the effort to speak. "Go back where?"

She reached her hand to his forehead and held each eye open as she flashed a light in his eyes. She then began talking to the nurse.

"He seems a little disoriented but that might be the medication from yesterday. He doesn't know just how lucky he is – not many people run into the street, get hit by a car, fall into a coma, and then just wake up, good as new!" she said, with just a hint of sarcasm, "He seems fine otherwise… a perfectly healthy seventeen-year-old boy, who's gotten a lot of rest and probably just wants to get going!" she noted, looking at the electronic charts. "Let's keep an eye on things for the next few days to see how he handles solid food and go from there."

"*They need me – I…*" he tried to talk but stopped as he was overtaken by a fit of coughing.

"It's alright, just try to relax," said the doctor, reaching out to hold his shoulder and helping him to lie back after the coughing subsided. "Don't try to talk too much until you've had a chance to let the inflammation go down."

Moving towards the door with the doctor, the nurse asked: "He has seemed very disoriented and trying to move. If he doesn't settle down, would you recommend a mild sedative, to make sure he doesn't get too excitable?"

"Sure," the doctor agreed, making a note in the chart, "something mild. I think it's a bit early to consider restraints – it might only make things worse until he readjusts to where he is and what happened. Is his sister here yet?"

"She's on her way," answered the nurse, before she lowered her voice: "we thought it best to wait till she was here before we talk to him about what happened."

"Good. Hopefully she'll get here before the police – the have questions for him and it won't help matters any if they get here first…"

*****

"What the hell is going on?" the young woman demanded, her entrance startling the two uniformed officers who stood on either side of Tibor's bed, not to mention the young nurse who nearly jumped out of her skin as she announced her presence to the entire floor. Appearing scarcely a year or two older than Tibor, her red hair telegraphed her demeanor to everyone in the room and even Tibor straightened up at her arrival.

"Uh, we're here to ask some questions about the accident?" the first officer replied,

"Who might you be?" the second queried, turning slightly to stand between the woman and Tibor.

She frowned and shouldered her way around the officer, taking Tibor's hand as she sat herself on the side of the bed.

"He's finally awake and the first thing you want to do is interrogate him?" she asked incredulously, her voice rising with every word. She turned her head slightly and gave Tibor a sympathetic glance.

"Ma'am, you're interfering…" the first officer began to say, before she cut him off.

"You're interrogating a minor without the presence of a parent or guardian" she said without looking back. The two officers exchanged uncertain looks.

"Look, we were called that he was awake, and we are trying to get some sort of explanation for what happened. If you're not his mother, then I'm going to have ask you to leave…"

"His mother is dead." She stated the fact flatly, "I'm his guardian, and I think you are the ones who should be leaving now." There was a tone of finality to her voice that made it clear that the discussion was over. She could see that tears were beginning to well up in Tibor's eyes, though she didn't know why.

Exchanging confused looks again, the first officer nodded his head towards the door, and they began to make their way out of the room.

"We will be back tomorrow to get a full statement."

"You do that." She replied, barely acknowledging their departure, her gaze fixed on Tibor and the puzzled expression on his face. "You look pretty tired for someone who's been asleep for three months!"

The tears that had been building up in Tibor's eyes now broke free and began to run down his face unabated.

Everything had changed – his world was gone - and his only comfort was that this woman's face at least seemed vaguely familiar…

*****Dreamland*****

"Well, one thing's for sure, the cops weren't too impressed with your answers."

His sister was talking as she drove Tibor home from the hospital. It was raining, and he had begun to lose himself in the drumming rhythms of the heavy drops on the soft-top of her jeep. She kept talking when he didn't reply right away.

"…but I mean, what did they expect? The guy at the comic shop was sure you hadn't stolen anything, the place was busy, he had no clue why you ran out into the street… and, well the guy driving the truck was more surprised than anything, so they just assumed that you had taken something and run… but, I mean, what the fuck, they had three months to confirm that you didn't steal anything, so I don't know why they had grill you so hard! Jeez!"

Tibor just stared out the window as she drove.

"This looking familiar to you?" she asked, looking over at him as she turned onto a narrow street, slowing things down a little. The window had started to fog up as they drove, and Tibor did not bother to wipe it away, staring out at a world that looked alien and strange. Something wasn't right – he could feel it in his gut – but the feeling of being lost was overwhelming to the point of helplessness.

He wanted nothing more right now than to open the door and run – he had no idea of which direction he would go but running was what his gut was telling him to do.

It had been a week since he woke up in the hospital, and despite the police interrogation and a few talks with the staff psychologist, he still felt like a stranger in a strange land. The doctors worried that he had a form of amnesia, and his memories were a little slow to return – memories of here, he told himself – and the only thing he had learned definitively was that the less he said about Vengriya, the more likely people were to think he was okay and leave him alone – and that was something he craved most dearly of all.

Beyond that, each day was a struggle, as he clung to a vision of Vengriya that was growing increasingly vague, while what he could only describe as 'new' memories of this world flashed into his head randomly - like a video that had been recorded over top of another recording, where glimpses of the original program interrupted his thoughts without warning. It was incredibly disorienting and was starting to give him headaches.

Thankfully, the hospital had given him a prescription before they released him, to help him manage.

Now, as he felt his sister's eyes examining him for any trace of recognition, he winced his eyes shut as he tried to stave off the most incredible headache. He wanted nothing more than to go home, but he seriously had no idea where that was.

Still staring out of the Jeep, trying not to focus on anything but the raindrops as they trickled down the window, he could feel her gaze return to the road, and he felt a wave of relief pass over him, no longer needing to answer her questions.

"I don't know if this matters much right now either, but you got your acceptance letter from Queen's in the mail yesterday" his sister seemed to this that talking was better for him than silence, so she filled the quiet pauses as much as she could. "That makes it a yes from all three – Waterloo, Carlton and Queen's – which is great! I know we already sent your acceptance to Waterloo for you – we wanted to make sure that if things got better – if you woke up – which you did! – that you wouldn't have lost the chance to go to university while you were in the hospital…" She paused in her stream-of-consciousness talking to see if he would acknowledge anything of what she said.

"Thanks" was his only reply. She thought he might've said more but they were interrupted by a flash of lightning that seemed like it was striking almost on top of them, followed immediately by a deafening boom of thunder, and she swore Tibor almost jumped out of the car in fright.

They drove in silence for the remaining few blocks back to her house, where she soon had him settled into a spare room, saying goodnight cautiously, and leaving him to try to relax and get some sleep.

Finally alone, Tibor fumbled in his pocket for the small orange bottle he had been given at the hospital, eager for some relief from the constant aching in his head. Twisting the cap off and pouring two of the plain white pills into his hand, he stared at them, then at the multitude of pills that remained in the bottle. He couldn't recall how long he sat on the edge of the bed staring at the pills, pondering a single question:

Some, None, or All?

He slowly lifted his hand holding the pills, and gently tipped them back into the bottle, resealed the lid, and placed it on the side-table. He sat for a long while, staring into the shadows, listening only to the sound of his own breathing, until at some point his mind settled enough to let him fall asleep.

*****Into the Void*****

Wanting something and knowing how to get it are two vastly different things.

It had taken him some time to work it out, but eventually he saw his struggle for what it was: two competing realities, at war with each other for his sanity, and the only way to find peace would be to commit to one or the other. It seemed a very existential dilemma – he was sure his therapist would have thought so, more so than one might have expected even for a typically morose teenager. He didn't understand the 'how' behind any of this, but he knew what was going on in his head – it was still his head after all.

He was certain of one thing though: he was miserable and would rather be somewhere else – anywhere else - than here.

He had a life somewhere else – somewhere other than here. An adventurous life. One with purpose. One as real as everything he could see and touch right in front of him, here, but it was somewhere else. He could remember some of it, as much – sometimes more so – than he could remember his life here. Here. There. Some days, here was there, and some days there felt more like here. These were the days when his headaches felt the worst.

Both felt as real as the other as far as he could tell. There was nothing that his memories of either lacked for in detail, accuracy, vividness, or any other measure he could consider – aside from what felt like enormous gaps where he could remember nothing. In the end, he felt like it was just a question of choosing which world he wanted to live in, and then finding a way to make it happen.

He wished fervently that there was someone – anyone – that could help him this, that he could talk to, but he was sure that anyone he told would have thought him crazy, and he was having enough trouble convincing his family and his therapist that he wasn't. And so he took to wandering about the city, keeping his thought to himself, taking long walks and letting his feet remember what his mind had forgotten.

Tibor had spent his life growing up in a small town, nestled in what should have been an ideal spot – a hub in the center of a booming economy, a bedroom community in search of its' own destiny. It was big enough to have once had a bustling downtown, and just modern enough that everyone had abandoned the core to the first wave of urban sprawl.

These days, though, downtown was just a bunch of boarded-up storefronts – dirty windows showcasing signs for "final sales" and "everything-must-go" discounts, all hallmarks of the desperate attempts to lure people back to the dying heart of a boring town. The only real character that the sleepy city may have once – it's one shot at truly having a soul - was the eclectic collection of outdoor vendors that used to gather downtown every Saturday morning for the farmer's market.

In the heart of the city, a thriving circle of small businesses ringed the open parking lot that would be transformed into weekend into potpourri of a vendors – local farmers, self-employed crafters, hobbyists, traders, and entertainers – all selling fresh food, hand-crafted wares, and entertainment to a regular crowd of families.

Then the city council gambled on their future by building a shiny new mall in place of the market square – gambled and lost.

In one fell stroke, the city had surgically removed its' own heart, replacing it with a cold, brown-brick artificial heart and then promptly failed to plug it in. There was no CPR, no trauma cart, that could breathe life again into the dying downtown core. Death was inevitable.

Tibor had been there to watch the patient fade. Although the death was slow, the symptoms appeared almost immediately: the small shops that hadn't been displaced by the construction began to atrophy as no one came to shop. Then the smaller, niche business, that counted on the pedestrian traffic on the street to trickle into their doors, they too began to feel it all slipping away, slowly shrivelling up and dying, as no one was interested in walking along the backside of the new mall, and fewer still were interested in going inside – the trendy, clean aesthetic lacked anything that could even remotely be considered character or charm. Within a few months, sales of plywood skyrocketed, as businesses up and down the main streets closed, and windows were boarded up. From the front window of the comic shop on George Street, he had met with his friends while the town around them slowly, bit-by-bit, began to shut down.

It was here, in what used to be the heart of the city, that Tibor now found himself, sitting on top of the empty three-story parking garage, looking out at the rusting fire escapes and rotting structures that formed the backside of the stores and shops that faced the main street through the old core. Facing the street, these buildings had wonderful stonework façades, with signs and glass windows, painted brick and stucco from top to bottom. Butted up, one against the other, these buildings formed an impervious wall along the street, opening rarely to allow pedestrians to cross.

From the parking garage though, you could see what they looked like from behind, and it wasn't pretty. Like watching an aging burlesque star taking off her make-up after a show, there were no fancy façades, or fresh coats of paint on the backside. The wartime structures were nearly a century old, crumbling, rusting and broken, on the verge of tumbling backwards into the old canal that ran along behind them – another legacy of more bygone days of the shipping trade off the nearby Grand River.

'*Damn!*' he thought "*I really do hate this friggin' place!*"

From his perch he could look down in the alley behind the structure, and he wasn't terribly shocked to see someone having fun tagging a building – a recently whitewashed garage door across the alley was the unfortunate victim. He was actually more surprised that anyone still cared enough to try to whitewash over the previous crap – as if they thought this would somehow dissuade anyone from tagging it again – but they did, and the taggers enjoyed the fresh canvas.

He wasn't sure how long he was watching for, but he admired their daring. He had always been a good kid and would never have dared to do something even remotely delinquent like graffiti. Defacing public property was a misdemeanor, and he would hardly jaywalk! He could see the guy was working quickly – it was late morning, and even though the market had been pushed aside to a terrible location a block away, there were still going to be people coming & going, and some of them might not have the same appreciation for artwork – he gave pretty even odds the guy would be spotted sooner rather than later.

Just as he was thinking this, there was the blare of a car horn from elsewhere in the parking garage, and the tagger stopped for a moment. Looking around to see if the coast was still clear, the artist/petty criminal finished their recon with an upward glance, and they locked eyes for the briefest of moments. It was quick, but the tagger looked spooked, dropped the spray can and took off running, leaving behind a plastic grocery bag with what he assumed was variety of other paints inside.

Tibor watched as they ran off down the alley alongside the canal – he really shouldn't say "canal" anymore, as it was barely a damp trail sunk below the ground level these days, with only the heaviest rains giving it any sort of water, not since they cut off the mouth of the canal from the river years ago. Now it was full of tall weeds, saplings and large bushes that took advantage of the pooling water to try to grow in the otherwise concrete downtown core. He lost sight of the tagger as they ducked underneath the cover of the garage some ways up the trail and didn't pay them much mind after that.

Looking at the unfinished mural, he could see that there was an image taking shape that he could almost recognize. The tagger was pretty good - in his limited opinion - although he didn't know much about street art. From his angle, it looked something like a flaming sword, pointing upwards, held by a gauntleted hand, with the tip of the sword piercing a red sun. It also looked like there was a vine or a snake entwined around the base of the sword and the guard, with the head of the snake biting down on the metal of the gauntlet at the wrist, piercing the steel and a small amount of blood – or poison – running down the metal. It was very nicely done, and the colour choices looked great on the whitewashed background. He couldn't make it out from so far away, but it looked like there was even more detail on the blade and hilt of the sword – unusual for such rushed work, but interesting.

He was still staring at the mural when he heard a shoe twisting on gravel behind him. He spun around quickly, surprised to see the artist standing right there.

Her auburn hair was pulled back in a tight, neat, ponytail, and covered with a dirty black toque; a dark 'Iron Maiden' concert tee was mostly covered by a small leather jacket, with several dirty rags tied to the sleeves and shoulders, in places where it seemed she could easily reach one to wipe her hands while working. She wore a longer shirt, unbuttoned under the jacket, that extended down past her slender waist, and her faded denim jeans were torn in a few places and stained with paint, old and new.

"Admiring my work?" she asked, her voice soft yet deep. Her eyes were bright blue, and she wore a fair bit of dark eyeliner; her pale complexion contrasted with the darkness of her hair and eyes; her mouth was small and held in a tight smirk as she examined him just as thoroughly. She was not at all as unkempt or dirty as he might have expected of a street kid, which made him wonder if perhaps she was just a rebellious bougie kid who had a real home to return to at night. He thought she looked maybe about the same age as he was, but he was terrible at guessing that sort of stuff.

"Shit!" he the best he could muster on short notice.

"What, you don't like it?" she replied in a raised voice, moving over to the wall of the garage to look down on her work.

"No! No, you just surprised the shit out of me!" he said back to her, almost squeaking the last part. "I thought you had taken off, and, I don't know, I guess I just wasn't expecting you to just show up here…"

"Ahh," she said, leaning over the wall thoughtfully. "But you didn't answer my question then – do you like it?"

"Uh, yeah…" he paused, "it's pretty cool."

"Hmph." She seemed disappointed by the lack of awe and amazement in his voice. "It wasn't finished. I was rushing - I guess I still get spooked pretty easily with these things." The top level of the parking garage was surrounded by a guardrail; she stepped up onto the first rail, leaning against the second rail with her thighs, still looking down at the ground, three stories below. "I call it "Isten Kardja" – it means 'Sword of God'," she announced without him asking, "I saw it in a book once, and it spoke to me…"

She stepped back off the railing and turned to him. "So, what are you doing here? Taking in the sights? Or stalking your next victim?"

He could feel himself blushing – he had never been very good at talking to girls, and this was starting to count as one of the longest conversations he had ever had with one aside from his sisters. She was very confident of herself, and direct, and he was neither.

"I was just looking for somewhere quiet, to think…" he said eventually, looking more at the ground than at her. She didn't say anything right away and he was just about to start walking away to leave when she spoke.

"I know somewhere good for that – you can just watch the water go by and let your mind go…" she offered, "C'mon!"

She quickly turned and ran across the open parking lot, towards the stairwell at the far end. She turned back when she realized he wasn't following and waved for him to join her. He thought about it for a minute and then just decided to take a chance and follow this strange person he had just met. And besides, she was a girl, and she was talking to him… he wasn't going to waste a moment like that!

He ran after her, but she had a good head start and had widened her lead by the time he got to the bottom of the stairwell. Looking around, he could see her running up the hill towards the armories building. Still following – and still trying hard to close the gap - he watched as she crossed the street and started down the other side of the embankment, which led them under a bridge.

The Lorne Bridge was a couple hundred yards long and rose high over the Grand River below. After dodging a couple cars, he came to the top of the embankment – he was catching up, but he still had to find a path down the hill that wouldn't kill him. By the time he finished zigzagging down the steep grade, he could see that she had moved downriver a little ways and was walking out along the old concrete dam that slowed the flow of water as the river passed through the city.

He slowly followed her out along the dam to where she was sitting – low dams like this were designed to slow the flow of water, not completely stop it, and across most of the length of the concrete wall the river water dutifully backed up until it was high enough to flow over the top of the dam in a nice, steady, even flow, making the river deeper where it flowed under the bridge. Except for this end of the dam, near the shore.

On this side of the river, there was a small break in the dam and a few stones had fallen in and the river was quick to flow into the gap. He supposed the dam must not have been perfectly level because not a lot of water came toward the gap, with most of it still preferring to overflow near the center of the span. This meant that for the small stretch of concrete nearest the shore it was clear and dry, and you could sit and let your feet dangle in the slowly swirling water on the deep side of the dam. The adventurous young girl already had her shoes off by the time he reached the spot and was dipping her toe in the river to see how cold the water was. He quickly joined her, removing his shoes slowly as he surveyed the water, as if it were dangerous.

"You're not from around here," she both stated and asked, "else I expect you would have come here first if you were looking for somewhere quiet."

"Naw, I'm from here..." he answered quickly, "I was just always told to stay away from the river when I was a kid. I just guess my parents were kind of protective when we were young."

"And you are the kid who always does what he's told."

"No!" he lied, then, "...yes."

"So, what's on your mind that's so important you need to think about it so hard that you need to be all by yourself?" she prodded, smiling at him slyly.

"Nothing," was the first reflexive answer he gave.

"Right." She nodded. "That's okay, you don't need to tell me," for which he must have looked relieved before she continued, "I mean 'cuz, if you had something incredibly important to consider, and you were having so much trouble trying to figure it yourself that you needed time alone from any distractions to focus on it, then who better to talk about it to than a complete stranger? Just think about it: you can tell me the whole thing, judgement-free, and I can help you run through your options, even if it's embarrassing, and then you never have to see me again!" She waved her arms about as she spoke and splashed her feet in the water for effect.

He sighed, watching the water go by. Maybe she was right. Maybe it would be better to talk about it out loud, even to a complete stranger – he might hear himself and either come up with a good idea or realize just how crazy he really sounded.

He looked at her, sitting silently on the dam waiting, as she could see him thinking it over.

"Have you ever had the feeling that you don't belong?" he started, to which she gave him a look that seemed to say "duh?" as she held out her arms for him to look at her.

"No, not like that. I mean…" He stopped himself, still certain she would laugh at him if he was too honest about it all. But she waited silently for him to continue.

"I don't feel like I belong here – in this world."

"Brantford?"

"No, here – everywhere, now… ughh!" he threw back his head in frustration at not being able to explain.

"Do you ever feel like you're living in a dream?" he asked, restarting. She nodded.

"That is what this feels like to me," he said, gesturing to their surroundings. She resisted the urge to interject with something witty, and it showed on her face, but he ignored it as he continued.

"…It's as if this is the dream, and reality is the thing that I remember as somewhere else… and I need to find my way back to it."

"Why?" she asked curiously, "Is it so much better than being here?"

The "yes" that came out of his mouth so quickly in response to her question carried all the venom of contempt for this world and his passion for wanting to be back where he had been.

"So why are you here?" she queried again with curiosity.

She was still sitting on the dam, listening, but she stopped swinging her feet in the water, and the smile was a little smaller than before. He continued.

"I woke from a coma recently. I had…" he stopped himself – if he told her that he hit his head, she would immediately see that as the cause for his craziness and dismiss everything he was saying, if she hadn't already – "…while I was in the coma, I think I was living another life – it felt like I was there my whole life; in that world, I could see lightning - lighting that flashed, stronger and stronger - until finally it came so close that I could feel it in my chest. The last time it happened, I woke up and they were hitting me with the paddles from the crash cart stuff in the hospital." He paused, checking to see if she was still paying attention.

"They said I had a heart attack - it was a blood clot, and my heart stopped, but… I don't know. It just seemed weird that they would shock me, and… and the timing, it…" he trailed off a bit as he watched her for a reaction. She seemed to be listening to what he said, and he couldn't read the expression on her face.

He began to panic and started explaining himself. "I know it sounds crazy, and you're probably thinking I must have hit my head or something to put me in the coma in the first place. I don't know, you're probably right. I–"

"You want to go back into the dream-world you were in before?" she interrupted him to state.

"NO! That's the thing," he almost shouted as he sat beside her, "I don't think it was a dream! Everything about it was so real, and I remember so many of the details that it couldn't possibly have been just a dream – I feel like I lived it."

She squinted as she stared at him. "Okay, so it was real, but you were still connected to your body, here?"

"Yeah, that has a better sound to it…" he followed.

"Okay… and so your mind," she continued, "somehow 'left' your body here and went to a 'different' body in this other world?" He nodded, following along as she spoke. "But how did you live a whole life in this other body but not age here? It can't be that you were only experiencing this while you were in a coma for… how long were you asleep?"

"I was in a coma for three months, they said - which is different than sleeping!"

"Okay, okay." She backed off a little, seeing his sensitivity about the definition of the terms. "So how do we account for the difference in time you spent in each world?"

"I don't know…" he answered sullenly. He felt was well versed in time travel theory – almost every major comic, movie, or TV show had used it as a vehicle for storytelling at some point or other, and he knew all of them. Yet he struggled to understand how time would flow at different speeds in these different worlds – he could feel the headache begin to start as he thought about it, clenching his eyes, and putting his head in his hands.

"My head is starting to hurt," he finally said.

"Okay, that's cool," she said, "look, I've got some other things to do," as she pulled her feet out of the water and began to put her shoes back on, prompting Tibor to do the same. "I'll be here tomorrow afternoon if you want to talk more," she offered, and before he could even say "bye" she was heading up the side of the embankment and was through into the trees and gone.

Tibor finished tying one shoe before he raced up the embankment after her, but she had left – he couldn't even see which direction she had gone. He realized at that moment that he hadn't even gotten her name!

Tibor was excited when he woke up the next morning. Having someone to talk to about this was great – even if she thought he was crazy – and he had found some things on the internet last night that he wanted to add into the mix.

He raced to the river, finding his way down to the dam again a little faster now that he knew the way, only to find that he had arrived first. He checked the time on his phone and decided he would wait – it was still early in the afternoon, and she hadn't really said when she would be there, precisely.

He threw rocks in the water and even dangled his feet in water to cool off as the afternoon warmed up. All in all, he waited nearly two and a half hours before he decided to walk around a little and see if he couldn't find her back at the parking garage – maybe that's where she figured he would come, and was waiting for him there? He cursed himself for being an idiot to not check there first and he jogged up the embankment, down the road and into the parking structure. He ran up the ramp and scanned each level until he reached the top.

She wasn't there either. He looked down from the top of the garage and could see the canal and alleyway he had looked across the other day – everything was the same, except it looked like the owner of the building she had tagged was whitewashing the garage door again, obscuring her artwork.

There was no sign she had ever been there.

He sighed and sat down, leaning back against the railing – his head was starting to hurt again already…

*****Revelations*****

A year later, Tibor couldn't help but relate to the depressing, sucking noise of the hydraulics as he stepped off the bus — that inexorable pull that the town seemed to have, sucking the hope out of everyone who lived there, slowly draining them and leaving behind nothing more than sad, empty husks, all milling about but going nowhere. The door of the bus closed behind him with the air of finality usually reserved for things like prison cell doors, and the Greyhound pulled away from the curb, leaving him to his fate as it continued purposely on its route.

He had been away at school for a year, and even now, as he shouldered his pack and moved towards the terminal building, he could feel himself regretting the decision to return. But the semester was over, his lease in residence was done, and like it or not, he had nowhere else to go but home. At least it wouldn't be for long.

A short walk later, he stood on Lorne Bridge, his pack at his feet, looking out at the water of the Grand River below. It flowed down the shallow riverbed and around a bend just a few hundred yards downstream. Closer, before the bend, he could see the line of concrete that was the dam, which made the water at the foot of the bridge just a little bit deeper than everywhere else along its path.

He stood with his toes on the base of the railing, leaning out to watch the water swirl as it passed between the concrete footings of the bridge, flickering between light and dark as the sunlight pierced the water and gave brief glimpses of what lay hidden in the murky riverbed. It was hard to guess if someone might survive a fall from the bridge, as the depth seemed to change with every rainfall, despite the presence of the dam.

He held his arms out, leaning against the top of the railing with his thighs to feel the wind in his face as he continued to stare at the water below - the thin film of water that crested the dam, and the same water that sought to escape the damn through an ever-widening crack near the embankment — the same spot where he had sat with the mesmerizing young girl a year ago.

He had tried to forget about her but found it impossible. Instead, he fixated on every word she had said that day, searching for clues and answers in the simplest of phrases. He could never forget her, though he had most certainly convinced himself that he was never going to see her again.

So, when he looked down from the guard rail and saw a tiny figure sitting on the small dry section of the dam near the shoreline, his heart skipped a beat.

It wasn't her, he told himself – probably just someone else who had found the same ideal spot to idle away the day.

That's what he told himself as he suddenly found himself moving as quickly as he could to the side of the bridge where the worn footpath cut a trail down to the embankment and ran along the shoreline to where the dam met the bank of the river. He slowed his pace as he reached a line of bushes before the small clearing, not wanting to alarm whoever it was.

Taking a deep breath and wiping the sweat from his brow, he emerged from the cover of the bushes to see a familiar young girl with auburn hair sitting on the concrete dam, dangling her feet in the water just as she had more than a year before.

She looked up and smiled at him as he approached – dressed almost identical to when they first met, with even her hair pulled back in the same ponytail.

"It's about time," she said as he dropped his knapsack and walked out a few steps onto the dam, "I thought you were going to stand up there all day!"

"Me?" he answered, "ME? What about you? Where have you been? You know I came back and waited for you – where were you?"

"I'm right here," she replied plainly, "so are you going to sit down or what? You're sweating all over the place – you'd probably be better off just jumping in!"

He looked at the slowly swirling water, and almost as if she could read his mind she continued, "Don't worry, you won't get swept over the dam or through the gap!" He frowned at her.

"That's not what I was thinking," he said, his tone still angry that she hadn't answered his question. But he was sweating after his sprint and the water did look welcoming, so he slipped off his shoes and sat down on the dam a comfortable distance away from her – something in the back of his head made him think she just might be the type of person to push him in if he looked too afraid.

"So what have you been up to?" she asked.

He hesitated, swallowing his initial anger as she seemed too polite to hold anything against her, grateful just to see her again. He pondered her question more seriously than he should have, wondering if it was simply a greeting for polite conversation, or if she really wanted to know his whole story, in detail.

"Not much," he eventually answered, deciding she must have meant the former, at the same time biting his tongue to keep from venting about just how casual she sounded despite having left him twisting in the wind for all this time!

"Really?" she asked with a clear tone of disbelief, "You've gone from having an existential crisis to 'not much' just like that?"

"No, not just like that," he replied with a little more defiance than he intended, at the same time realizing that he should have gone with the latter choice just a moment earlier... "It's been pretty shitty since we talked, so yeah, things have changed for me!"

"Whoa, whoa, chill there, dude!" she said, raising her hands in surrender while still swirling her feet in the water. "I was just asking a question..."

"Yeah, well, I don't owe you any explanations!" he threw back quickly – more quickly than he intended, letting his temper get the better of him for the moment. "I don't know what I was thinking coming down here again – you don't even know me..." he trailed off as he was talking but stood up on the dam and began taking a few steps back towards the riverbank.

"Sorry dude, I wasn't trying to give you grief – I was just... look, forget it! I was just trying to talk – I'm sorry it took so long to find you again." She seemed sincere with her words, and she had a way of using her voice that made him just want her to keep talking so he could hear her voice, as it soothed him.

"You sounded like you had a lot going on last time we were here, and I guess I'm glad you've straightened things out – you look like you're a lot more in control now–"

"That's just it," he stopped her, "I haven't straightened anything out – I've just pushed it aside and started to forget about it, just to survive everything else that's been going on."

"Like what?" she asked softly.

Tibor sat quiet for a moment, wondering just how much to share about the last year and a half. Everyone he knew or had turned to was going through their own shit, and that always seemed to leave him on the outside looking in. Not that he thought anyone really believed him when he tried talking about things.

They were still sitting on the dam, and the day was getting warmer. She took off her jacket, laying it on the dry part of the concrete, revealing a tight-fitting black tank top that flattered her figure nicely. He was feeling the heat as well after sitting and talking in one spot for so long and decided to take off his jacket and shirt as well – it was really too warm for a jacket, but it had been cooler in the morning when he had first gotten up to get the bus. Taking off his T-shirt, he flung it to the riverbank and leaned over the edge of the dam, looking down into the water.

He considered himself to be skinny for his height, but in truth he had a lean physique and while he didn't quite have "washboard abs", he was fit enough, more like a runner than a bodybuilder. He looked over and caught her staring not at his physique but at the scars on his wrists – two small lines, one on each wrist, maybe an inch and a half long, going straight across. That was the real call for help, he had learned; if he had been serious about wanting to leave, he was told, he would have made the cuts along the length of his arms, so the wounds would have been harder for the paramedics to deal with.

She looked away when she realized he was looking at her.

"Was that your first try?" she asked quietly.

"No," he answered, waiting before he continued, unsure if she wanted the whole story. Not that he wanted to tell it either.

"After I woke up, it took me weeks to talk about anything, and even months later, when it was clear no one believed me, you could be sure as hell I wasn't going to talk to them about this…" he said, holding up his arm.

"They thought I was crazy when I started all the daredevil stuff – thought I was trying to kill myself – but they didn't know. If they didn't believe my story the first time, then how would they understand me trying to get back?"

"That's what it was at first, trying to do anything that might get me back to Vengriya – the more dangerous the better." He paused.

"None of it worked, and so I started thinking, hey, maybe it's all the safety shit – the helmets, ropes, whatever, made my mind feel too safe that nothing bad was going to happen…" He looked over at her, as if to make sure she understood. "I didn't want to… but I knew I had to come close…" he sighed as he recalled, "…at least at first anyway…"

"What do you mean?" she asked, holding her knees as she sat on the dam.

"I would try pretty much anything that had a good chance of giving me a solid knock on the head – like what had happened in my accident – to get back into a coma," he continued, in a very matter-of-fact tone. "I was going to tell you when I came back the next day that I had done some searches on the internet, and at the time, I was pretty sure that whatever had happened to me might be somehow connected to what goes on when someone has a 'near death experience'– so anyway, I tried a few different things, not the least embarrassing of which was me trying to run headlong into a low-hanging tree branch at a full run, which just ended up giving me one hell of a goose-egg and a headache for a week!" He almost smiled remembering that stunt.

"Over the past year I've blown my tuition money on every stunt imaginable – and went from daredevil stunts to trying to hurt myself intentionally, which I discovered is frowned upon by the law and several welfare agencies – always with the same end-goal. Stunts seemed to be more socially acceptable, but they weren't as effective - I might pass out, hurt myself, or end up unconscious, but I haven't yet found that same result and so after blowing my chances with school, I even began to doubt my own memories…" he paused, gathering his thought, and she let the silence last as long as he needed before he continued.

"It's funny…" he continued after several deep breaths, "…You will do the craziest shit when you believe in what you're trying to achieve, but once you lose that faith, when you start to doubt your own sanity, the wheels fall off pretty fast. That's what led to this…" he said, holding his wrist up again for her to see more clearly, "…me giving up and running away for good."

"It sounds like you've been busy," she said, when he seemed to have finished his story.

Tibor looked at her squarely as she seemed to blow right through everything he was sharing and sum it up so plainly.

"Yeah, I guess I have" he answered. "You know, it's been so long, I'd really given up on trying to figure out whatever it was that happened to me. It could've been an NDE; it could have been the drugs in the hospital…" He took a deep breath, "in the end it was all just a dream… who knows what made it all seem so real, but it was still just my mind playing tricks on me…"

"Is that what your therapist told you?"

"Yeah."

"And how much did you tell her?"

"Everything."

"Everything?"

"Yeah, everything. Not that she believed me. Why?"

"Did you tell her about me?" she asked, pulling her feet up out of the water, folding her legs together in front of her, and clasping her knees with her arms.

"Tell her about you?" he repeated back to her, "What would I tell her about you? …I don't even know your name!"

She was standing up as he was talking and began to lift her tank top up over her head, revealing a small black bra that contrasted sharply with her pale skin, which he couldn't help but stare at. He had finished talking and was sitting beside her mutely as she began to unbutton her jeans now, wiggling her hips slightly to make them drop down her slender legs into a bundle at her feet.

"What are you doing?" he asked, hesitantly, as she stepped out of the pile of clothes at her feet and pulled her hair out of the neat ponytail, letting it fall down around her neck and shoulders. He was staring, following the flow of her hair as it stopped just below her shoulder blades, and couldn't help but continue to stare at the soft curve of her back, down to the line of her underwear and the athletic lines of her legs.

"It's hot…" she answered, "I'm going to cool off," and she stepped off the dam on the deep side, into the cool, slowly swirling waters of the river.

She stayed submerged for nearly a minute, and he could see the pale colour of her skin reflecting the sunlight through the water, like a silver mermaid swimming just below the surface. She surfaced for a moment to take a breath, flinging the water from her hair in a motion that any Instagram influencer would have given their right arm to capture, before diving under again. He couldn't help but feel a curious twinge when she flipped in the water, and he caught the briefest glimpse of her dark underwear and the smooth curve of her buttocks flashing at the surface before she was gone again under the water.

This time he watched as her pale form swam in a circle below the surface before moving towards where he was sitting – he was not expecting her to suddenly surface between his legs, making him almost fall backwards as she splashed up from the water. She rested herself on her elbows on the edge of the dam, the rest of her dangling in the water below, perched between his widespread knees – he tried to lean back to give her more room than she probably wanted, at the same time trying not to reach back too far and fall off the backside of the dam. Her wet hair was slicked back over her head, revealing a slender, delicate neck, which gave him his first opportunity to see the small tattoo that ran up the side of her neck, stopping just below the right ear.

It seemed familiar but he couldn't place it – a slender dagger – no, not a dagger, a sword – flaming, thrusting upwards, gripped by a gauntleted hand entwined with a snake biting the hand. The water dripping down her neck seemed to run like blood – or poison – from the snake bite; he had seen it before somewhere, but where? Then the images began to flash into his head – the graffiti!

"*No!*", he thought – well, yes, but he seemed to remember it from somewhere else, too, somewhere larger, more prestigious… thoughts raced through his mind like a child's flip-it book, and hitting the last page felt like being hit by a lightning bolt -

There it was: Isten Kardja

The Sword of God – Matras Vadas, wielding the blade; slaying Sarkany, the great seven-headed dragon; the epic mosaic in the Great Hall of Prince Svato; the Palace of Ascanium! Shagron! Torick! Omar! Jason!

Tibor's eyes were saucers, wide and unblinking as he stared at the girl in the water as if she were a ghost, his mind churning through thoughts at a pace he could barely keep up with!

For her part, watched him quietly at first, her face remaining calm and restrained before she began to allow herself a mischievous grin as she could see the dawning realization of the truth play itself out in his expressions.

She waited until it seemed he had grasped enough before she spoke plainly and directly, keeping it simple so he would understand.

"Hi Tibor, I'm Darellan – Lady Darellan Fenndragon – but you can call me 'Dar'."

"Welcome back…" she smiled, "…I've been waiting for you."

*****Going Home*****

Tibor was still lying down on the grass on the bank of the river as she finished drying off. Dar casually slipped into her jeans, then walked along the top of the dam as she dried her hair with her shirt before slipping it over her head, leaving it hanging loose over her jeans. She carried her shoes in her hand as she walked up the embankment to sit beside him. Waiting a while as he seemed to be staring at clouds, she finally spoke:

"Trying to get a handle on the moment?"

Tibor didn't reply right away, but eventually he turned his head towards her with a very perplexed expression.

"Are you seriously quoting *Men in Black*?" he asked, "'cuz that would be a really cheesy way to screw-up everything I've been trying to sort out for the past half hour that might explain what is happening right now!"

She had to laugh out loud. "It's probably just easier if you ask your questions, and I will answer as best I can, and we'll see how close your guesses are…" she said, smiling back at him.

He lay his head back and tried to decide what to ask first.

"Okay. So first, just to be clear, I wasn't dreaming about Vengriya, Ascanium, any of it – it was real!? I was there!" he said. Anxious, he sat up to watch as she answered, crossing his legs to sit in the grass across from her.

"Hmmm. I don't know for sure about the dreaming part, but if it were a dream, would that make it any less real?" Dar replied.

"Uh, yeah!" he answered, "…wouldn't it?"

"Interesting. So, if you have a dream that you're running, and your heart rate starts climbing in your sleep, and you wake up sweating, does that mean the dream wasn't real?" she offered for him to consider.

"Well, I guess, but you don't die from an arrow or a fireball in a dream."

"Really? You don't think that people who die in their sleep maybe were having a bad dream, that triggered a heart attack or whatever?"

"In dreams, people usually wake up before they hit the ground" Tibor pointed out.

"Not the ones who don't wake up!" she retorted quickly, "How do you know the fall didn't kill them?"

"Maybe some dreams are deeper than others," Dar continued, "but more than that, you haven't considered that there are many worlds and planes of consciousness out there, some we can touch while we are alive, some afterwards, and some when we are in that place between alive and dead – sleep is when most people are closest to that in-between place, but it's deeper than that."

"What do you mean, 'deeper' than that?"

"I think you know…" she offered, watching him pause to consider the meaning.

"The coma?" he asked.

She nodded. "That's what I – and a few others – believe, but it's not ever been something that we've had to explore until recently."

"What do you mean?"

"Ascanium, Vengriya, the whole world, is very real, but not everyone who lives there stays forever. Some people come and go. Some create their legend and then depart, never to return; others stay and live a long, happy life for themselves; then there are those who seem to come and go, leaving and returning, and we simply took it to be a part of life. We never looked for answers beyond the veil – we never needed to. Until someone started tampering with the pattern."

"Tampering? Tampering how?" Tibor asked, listening intently.

Dar shifted her legs, looking as if one leg had fallen asleep as they were talking. "Let's walk," she said, as she got to her feet. There was a loud splash out in the water, somewhere further up the river, and Tibor turned to look. Dar put her hand on his shoulder and brought his attention back to her. "There is a lot to explain, much of which won't make sense if you aren't well versed in the mechanics of just how the world works – I'm not going to be able to tell you everything, as we would need days – months – just to get the basics covered." She began walking up the hill towards the road and the bridge, and so he followed.

"The easiest way to say it right now is this: you were woken too early."

"Too early? I was in a coma! I should be glad to be awake at all!" Tibor exclaimed excitedly. "I still don't understand how I got to Ascanium, or how you got here! All I know is that I want to go back, and I want to know how!" he said as he threw his arms wide in frustration.

"I can tell you how to get back, if you truly want to, but it will mean sacrifice in this world." She had a concerned tone to her voice now.

"I don't–" he started to say, when she cut him off.

"I can tell you, but I won't. Not until we finish some things here that need to be taken care of," she said dryly.

Tibor sighed as they walked. "Okay, I need a break – I need something to eat – I can't think well on an empty stomach. Do you like subs?" he asked.

"Sure," she replied, and he led them down the street towards the sub shop. Tibor didn't ask any more questions until they had ordered their food and sat down on a bench outside. They ate quietly for a few minutes, and Dar watched him, waiting patiently for him to be ready to start again. She knew it was a lot to consider, and he must still have a hundred and one questions in his head but needed to figure out which ones to ask first. She allowed the silence to continue as they finished eating and he got up to throw out the wrappers & napkins. He paused at the sidewalk garbage can before asking aloud…

"Have you been here before?" he said.

"Where? This world? The city? The dam?"

"Yes – any of it."

"Not specifically here, but I have visited this world several times before. There have been others…" she continued, "who travelled to Ascanium for adventures, or for learning, or a variety of reasons, and I have sometimes travelled to visit, as the situation may require."

"If you haven't been to Brantford before, how did you know about the alley behind the parking garage, the dam by the river?" he asked curiously.

"I saw it all in your head." She could see from the look on his face that he was quite confused now.

"I am part of an order that tries to remain neutral in all things and observe the balance of nature in the universe. Beyond the simple aspects of nature, we have trained ourselves to harness certain abilities and energies that allow us to see beyond the veil that shades each world from another, allowing us to see the multitude of dimensions where people exist and travel from. To come here, I needed to look within your mind, and in doing so, I was able to draw from your memories to know where you live in this world, where you travel, and even what kind of girl would catch your eye…"

"Catch my eye? You mean you could've just shown up and said 'hi' anytime you wanted, but you played around for the last year or so until I figured out what was happening!?" He had raised his voice now, feeling anger that she had taken a very indirect approach to enlightening him!

"I wasn't playing with you," she replied calmly, "I needed to know if you could handle the truth, and simply showing up and surprising you could have damaged your psyche; I needed to see if you could piece things together yourself, and as it were, you were – are – still struggling with the reality of it, so yes, I feel my approach was justified! This isn't my first rodeo you know, although…" she trailed off.

"Although what?"

"Nothing" she said, "Not important. What is important is that we need to find out what happened to you, that made you wake up early."

They were standing in the center of the downtown core, near the mall entrance, and it was nearly noon.

"This way" Tibor said, as he started walking. Dar followed, "Where are we going?" she asked.

"BGH – the hospital where I woke up. They would have a medical file or chart for me," he guessed, "maybe that might tell us something – the name of the doctor, or one of the nurses – someone we could talk to…"

"Okay, sure," Dar agreed, "Is it far?"

"Just a quick bus ride," he announced, as they rounded the corner to the transit terminal. "I hope you have exact change!" he joked.

*****Paperchase*****

Twenty minutes later they stepped off the bus at the stop across the street from the hospital. Dar turned and stared at the vehicle as the doors closed and it pulled away from the curb. She wrung her hands as if trying to remove something dirty from them, frowning with a mix of contempt and disgust. Tibor ignored her and stared up at the modest, seven-story, red-brick building that sprawled before them. There was relatively little traffic through either the emergency or main entrances, so they decided to use the main entrance.

They were greeted just inside the large rotating door by a young lady in a pale blue uniform wearing a surgical mask and a plastic face-shield. She was smiling politely – at least that was what Tibor presumed from her eyes – as she handed out masks for all visitors to wear – which the two willingly donned – and then followed her directions over to the aptly named "Visitor Support Desk" a few steps to their left.

Following the posted instructions, they pumped a generous amount of hand sanitizer and were still wiping it into their hands when another lady, somewhat older and clearly less happy with her assigned duties than the first young girl, sitting behind a wide desk, asked them for their names, phone numbers, and who they were here to see. Dar and Tibor exchanged glances as they quickly calculated their next move.

"Do you take everyone's name when they visit?" Tibor asked, seeming surprised by the new and high levels of scrutiny and contamination protocols.

"Oh yes," the older lady replied, "We have been upgrading all of our visitor screening over the past few months, just as a precaution against some of the outbreaks we've been hearing about in Toronto and other cities – just to be safe!" She nodded her head as she spoke, though it was hard to see her true expression because of the mask.

Dar nodded along with her, wringing her hands below the counter of the visitor desk before swinging her arm out in a wide, sweeping gesture. Tibor could see the puzzled look in the screener's eyes, as it took a moment for whatever Dar had done to take effect. Those same eyes began to droop ever so slightly at the same time as Tibor heard several crashes in the area surrounding them, as people – including the greeter and the screener – slowly dropped wherever they were standing, in mid-step, mid-sentence, or mid-thought.

"What did you do?!" he cried out, louder than he had intended.

"Don't worry, they're just sleeping!" she replied curtly. "Quick now, they have a log of every visitor, so get behind the desk there and look up your name – we should be able to see everyone who came to see you!" Tibor paused, then, with one last quick look of astonishment at her, he ran around the desk and gently pushed the rolling chair aside, making some room at the keyboard so he could type.

It took a few moments, but he shouted when he had done it: "I found it!" he cried, and then quickly checked the sleeping form in the chair beside him.

"Don't worry so much," Dar assured him, "they won't wake until the spell has run its course! What did you find?"

"Let's just go!" he said with alarm, "they may not wake up, but someone will come through any one of these doors any second now, see everyone passed out but us, and then we're screwed!"

He grabbed a printout from under the table and grabbed Dar's hand as he ran around the desk and then out the large rotating door, staring curiously as they passed the sleeping form of a pleasant-looking older lady sitting in her wheelchair, riding in circles as the door continued to slowly spin.

Walking as casually as they could, they were down the street and out of sight when he began to explain what he had found. The list was short – mainly his sister's name over and over again, but there was one name he didn't know: Arcady Sorkin.

"Who's that?" Dar asked.

"I don't know…" he answered, "but it seems like a good start if you're looking for something out of the ordinary…

"What do you suppose the odds are that the name isn't even a real name?" he said out loud, not really expecting an answer.

Dar smiled, "Never underestimate the arrogance of powerful people..." she said, "you can only create fear among the townsfolk if they know who it is they're supposed to fear!" as she took the list from Tibor and scanned the names. Shrugging, Tibor pulled out his phone and did a quick search on the name, reading the results intently as she walked along beside him.

"Anything?" she finally asked.

"Yup," he answered, "if it's really the same guy, we have an address – and you'll love this – it's only a short bus ride away, maybe thirty minutes, tops."

"Ugh," she sighed, "...another bus..."

"Don't worry, this one will have nicer seats!" he assured her.

*****Vaszoly*****

Vaszoly walked down the hallway gently cradling the young girl in his arms, carrying her as one might carry their most precious possession, fearful that it might break at any moment. The air was cold, and he could see his breath in front of him as he moved through the heavy timber door at the end of the passage, being careful not to let the delicate form in his arms brush any part of the opening as he passed through, that she not be disturbed in any way. There were several lanterns lit in the room he entered, but none appeared to improve the temperature.

The girl in his arms stirred and gave a tiny cough, expelling only the slightest puff of warmth into the cold air. He paused and looked at her, moving again only when he was sure her eyes were not open, and that she was still adrift in whatever dreams she may be having.

The room was long and wide, with rows of beds lined up against each wall, perhaps twenty to each side. The small metal frame beds were reminiscent of a hospital from the 1930s, with a simple mattress on a rounded metal frame, sturdy and durable, but with no sharp corners or edges to trouble the more vigorous patients. Several of the nearest beds he passed were filled with sleeping occupants, each connected to tubes running up to bags of liquid hung at their bedside on aluminum poles. Some even had tubes to help with their breathing, though not all. He stopped when he came to the first empty cot.

He laid her gently on the mattress, and adjusted the covers for warmth, lifting her arms and crossing them on her chest. She looked to be thirteen, perhaps more, perhaps less – it was getting so hard for him to tell these days. It seemed the older he got, the harder it was for him to place an age on the young; they always seemed to act more and more mature, and with far more insolence than he would have ever considered showing when he was their age. But then, he conceded to himself, that was such a long time ago…

Vaszoly found himself staring at the young girl far longer than he expected and was almost surprised when the nurse arrived at his side to request his instructions. Broken from his reverie, he waved casually, and the young man proceeded to set the usual IVs for sedatives and nutrients. As a new patient there would be time before the feeding tubes would need to be prepared, and the priority for now would be to ensure the sedatives remained effective.

"Use the pentobarbital – it's not as effective, but I need to obtain more thiopental," he said to the orderly, who nodded and noted his instructions before responding.

"We lost two guests last night, m'lord – respiratory failure," he stated cautiously, without lifting his eyes from his notepad. "As I mentioned to you before, we lack the proper equipment to care for those who go too deep, too quickly, and can't maintain themselves without assistance. I expect some of the older guests are at risk of an embolism due to clotting–" He stopped midsentence as Vaszoly raised his hand.

"I am not concerned with our losses – we will find other volunteers to take their place!" he said abruptly, dismissing the cowering man to continue his duties.

"Ah, yes," the nurse answered slowly, "…it would be so much easier if we had those who truly volunteer – there are those who would gladly serve you in this cause, if we but–"

"I do not need believers! I know what works best, and what works best for me is finding those who would rather be somewhere else – anywhere else – but here!" came the quick reply, cutting him off.

The nurse moved quickly to carry out his tasks although he remained hunched in his posture throughout, as if suffering from an ailment that contorted his spine unnaturally. If one paid incredibly close attention to his hands, one would see the tufts of fur extending from beyond the long sleeves of the pale blue scrubs, down the back of his hands. His fingers were short and somewhat clubbed, with unusually long nails, but despite the appearance of clumsiness, he deftly managed to set the needle for the intravenous injection on their newest guest and hung the bag without piercing the thin plastic shell. Finished with the initial tasks, the nurse shuffled off with a gait that made it seem he would have preferred to have been on all fours rather than upright on two feet.

Vaszoly gave it no notice whatsoever. He had slowly walked to the entrance of the room, scanning the beds as he rubbed his stubbled beard – traces of grey on his otherwise black-haired chin and head were beginning to show the first traces of age on an otherwise youthful looking face – youthful but weathered, and creased with smile-lines and crows' feet from the intensity of his lifetime of studies. His pale complexion was tempered by the sun-kissed tan that spoke of years of outdoor living, not being restricted just to the libraries and archives of a hundred different schools. Pale blue eyes – almost more grey than blue in the dim light of the room – contributed to his youthful appearance despite his age, being open and bright, looking amused by whatever he was thinking. This belied his true nature in most things and was perhaps the single most effective reason for why he was misjudged by so many with whom he found himself in opposition.

Looking around the room, he felt at ease – none opposed his efforts here. He passed bed after bed, his sleeping guests representing those who would be least missed by the world they came from. As insignificant as they were here, he felt almost proud to be giving them a chance to be something greater – heroes even – giving their lives a greater purpose, even if only in the service of his ambitions.

True, not all of them possessed the vision or imagination to make themselves truly invaluable as warriors to his cause. He paused to note the chart at the foot of the nearest bed. The occupant had been homeless, alone on the streets and hungry. Now he was sleeping peacefully, living a dream-like existence where he had everything his heart desired, free to drink to his hearts' content while he waited for his master's call.

And call he would, for he had need of pawns such as this.

Many, many, pawns.

He turned to leave, stopping at the end of the room to look back and survey the long rows of beds. There were still too many empty beds for his liking. He checked his pocket watch, noting the time, and turned to leave.

Time enough yet to fill them, he told himself…

*****Preston Springs*****

Tibor and Dar stepped off the Greyhound bus in Preston, near the base of King and Fountain Street. It was a short bus ride from Brantford – less than an hour, despite a few stops along the way to pick up and drop off passengers – and Dar did appreciate that the seats on the Greyhound were more comfortable than the local transit buses. But as it was, it was approaching dusk when they arrived in Preston, and both were happy to take advantage of the cover of night for their next activity.

"Well, there it is – the old 'Preston Springs' hotel…" Tibor noted as he pointed at the five-story, stucco building at the end of the road. It stood at the base of a large hill, with trees rising up the hillside behind it like an ominous backdrop. The front of the hotel was maybe a hundred yards across, with a large, two-story olive-green veranda over the main entrance and several of the adjacent rooms. They could see where later additions had been made to add additional floors, and more rooms to the west side of the building, not covered by the green veranda. The rest of the façade was a tan-coloured stucco, contrasting sharply with a recently added red metal roof.

The hotel had been long abandoned, and the new roof – the elegant remains of a recent investors' attempt to breathe new life into the building – was the only thing that kept the rest of the century-old building from falling into an even greater state of disrepair.

"It was built in the 1890s as a luxury hotel, with a beautiful countryside estate that the rich elite could enjoy. It fell on hard times in the 1920s, closed, then reopened as a sanatorium – a health spa, not the place they put crazy people – taking advantage of the sulphur springs coming up from the limestone of the hill into the basement. They offered x-ray treatments and even had an operating room – god knows why a spa would need an operating room though! When that ended, it had another chance at life as a retirement home, until that went bankrupt, and the owners just walked away – leaving thirty elderly residents to fend for themselves! There are stories now that it's haunted, and every once in a while someone pries open a window and sneaks inside to do a YouTube tour."

"Wow. What are you, the local 'tour guide'?" Dar asked, only half sarcastic.

"Google," Tibor replied, holding up his phone, still glowing with the information on the screen. "They even used it for training nurses in WWII before it was a nursing home. It's been empty since around 1990 – so nearly thirty years – being sold and resold while people try to figure what to do with it; it's been boarded up, but homeless and street kids like to hang out there a lot."

"And our guy, Arcady, he lives here?" she asked.

"Nope. His address is off Fountain Street, at the top of the hill, right behind the hotel – you can see it peeking out over the top of the peak of the hotel roof there…" he said, pointing to a spot on the hill behind the hotel.

Dar could see the outline of an older-style home, looking almost as old as the hotel, but set higher up on the hillside. She couldn't have described the house as Victorian style, as she didn't really know about such things, but it was. It had covered balconies on two of the three floors facing towards them, out across the river; a pointed roof topped the three-story tower on the right side of the structure. It was getting harder to see the details of the building in the failing light of the evening, but the front-gabled and decoratively corniced house displayed an architectural elegance that seemed at odds with the neglect and disrepair evident in the faded and peeling paint.

There were no lights on in either structure, which they took to be a good sign – hopefully they could sneak in and see what they could find without being detected, and that always worked best if no one was home.

"I'm gonna suggest we go around the back of the hotel, find a way up the hill and get into the house through the basement," Tibor offered as a plan.

Dar shrugged – it seemed like a good enough idea to her. They worked their way across the busy street to walk along the front of the abandoned hotel, close enough to scan the boarded-up first-floor windows along the covered front porch, seeing no signs of a way in. This wasn't too much of a surprise to Tibor – they were facing the traffic from the street, and it wouldn't make sense for anyone to pry open a window in front of so many passing cars. They would have to be more careful around the back of the building though – the last thing he wanted was to have any problems with any squatters who decided they didn't like uninvited guests nosing about!

It was dark as they turned the corner and moved behind the rotting structure. A sour smell, like a blend of rotting wood and sulphur, drifted across the lot, almost enough to make them want to hold their breath rather than breathe in the noxious odour. Clearly a regular haunt for those who came and went from the property surreptitiously, they headed towards a hole in the fence where the footpath seemed to lead in the most direct path towards the house further up the steep hill.

Tibor held back a folded-over piece of chain-link to let Dar pass through, before slinking under himself and letting it drop down behind him. He took a brief look backwards – in part to make sure they weren't being followed, and partly to make sure he remembered which way they had entered the path from. It was a slow climb up the barely visible trail, which zig-zagged back & forth up the hillside, using exposed tree roots and rocks for steps in the steeper sections. He quietly hoped they would not have to make the return trip in any kind of a hurry, as he was sure they would break their necks trying to race the course in the dark!

Tibor struggled in the near-total darkness to keep up with Dar, who seemed to step lightly up the hill with very little effort. There was no fence surrounding the house as they approached, and Dar found herself waiting near a basement window for more than a few moments as Tibor hurried to catch up without hurting himself. He bent over to catch his breath as she selected the most likely point of entry – one of the lower windows was broken, just above the ground level where the foundation of the house disappeared into the slope of the hill, and she began to pick away the larger pieces of glass to clear an opening that they could enter through. Tibor heard a slight scraping noise as Dar slid through the window opening, dropping down to the floor on the inside. He followed her through with notably less grace, making his lack of burglary skills immediately obvious to any who was close enough to hear.

Dar frowned at him as he stood up from the floor and began dusting himself off noisily. The room they had dropped into was not empty but had clearly not been used much. Dar held up a small light and scanned around the room – stacks of cardboard moving boxes were scattered around the room in a random arrangement, and a thick layer of dust made it apparent that while some had clearly been sitting untouched for some time, others looked to have been opened quite recently. Moving slowly, they crossed to an open doorway that led to a stairway up to the main floor. There were other doorways along the short hallway to the stairs, but these rooms looked empty as they glanced in on their way to the stairs. Creeping up cautiously, they were both incredibly aware of every creak and groan that echoed from the aging wooden stairs, waiting for that moment they were sure would come, when the lights would flash on with a blinding brilliance, and someone would angrily confront their trespassing!

But it never happened.

They reached the main floor and began to search in earnest for any sign of the owner, occupants, or any other clues about who lived here. Emboldened by the lack of any immediate reaction to the small amount of noise they were making, the darkened and dusty state of the house, and the heavy covering of dust on most of the furnishings, they felt quite confident that they were alone in the dwelling, and so they searched with greater enthusiasm.

The house itself was decorated as one might have expected based on the exterior: antique furniture, ornaments and décor were staged about the home in abundance, giving the appearance that it was a house out-of-time. Tibor might have expected a butler or a servant, dressed in an old-fashioned maid's outfit to step out of the kitchen doors any moment, in what he imagined would have to be a very British accent, and ask if he wanted some tea! No one appeared and offered any tea though, much to the disappointment of his imagination. Nor did he find anything that would suggest that anyone lived here who might have come to see him in the hospital.

Dar moved up to the second floor, and Tibor followed closely – not that he had anything to fear, but because she had the only decent source of light, he assured himself. A long, curved stairway brought them to the second floor, and he was immensely relieved that the hardwood steps, replete with a fine carpeted runner, did not creak or groan nearly as much as the basement stairs, making him much more confident that they would not be alerting any sleeping residents to their presence.

After glancing into the first few doorways and seeing empty beds within the resplendent rooms, Dar made her way directly to the corner of the house that was dominated by the turret they had seen from outside. Tibor agreed with her instincts on this: if there was going to be anything suspicious going on in an abandoned house, he would look in the turret first, too, if there was one!

The door to the first level of the turret room was closed but not locked. Dar lifted the heavy metal latch, which seemed out of place among the more ornate glass knobs that adorned every other door in the house. The heavy wooden door was braced with two strips of decorative wrought iron, which added to the sense of strength and weight that the door seemed to radiate menacingly. Tibor winced at what seemed to be an incredibly loud and piercing squeal made by the hinges that just screamed for oil as Dar pushed inwards and opened the door. He suddenly wished they had just rushed through the door and entered the room, rather than endure the slow, piercing wail that seemed to go on forever as Dar opened the door slowly and cautiously, which just seemed to make the agonizing noise go on forever!

They waited for what seemed like an eternity, holding their breath as they listened for any sound in response that might tell them that someone was alerted to their presence.

"Well," Tibor said aloud, "if anyone's home they certainly know we're here now!"

"Come on!" replied Dar, ignoring his sarcasm, and exploring the room. The door opened into a chamber that resembled the library of a well-read nobleman, with rich, dark wooden shelves, filled to overflowing with books – many stacked in piles upon the floor, on either side of a large reading chair. An oil lamp sat atop the piles of books beside the chair – unlit – along with an empty teacup and saucer, balanced on the edge of one of the hardcover texts, as though waiting for the librarian to return. A Persian rug dominated the center of the hardwood floor, with a small coffee table in the center, also holding numerous texts and tomes that did not reveal their titles or contents on the spine as one would have expected in a modern library.

There was a bright flash and Tibor flinched reflexively. Dar's light had swept over the metallic sheen of a suit of medieval armor that stood guard over a small wrought iron staircase that wound its way up the far wall to the top of the turret. His momentary shock was relieved when he saw the cobwebs and dust that made it almost certain that the suit had been inanimate for quite some time and offered them no threat.

"Let's work our way down from the top, shall we?" said Dar, as she moved to the stairs. As ever, Tibor didn't really feel like she was one to invite debate on her plans, so he followed along behind her, again, he assured himself, because she was the one with the light.

The second floor of the turret was the high point of the house, and, as they soon discovered, was also the only room in the house that appeared to have been lived in recently. Almost devoid of any of the dust or cobwebs that adorned the rest of the mansion, this room was clean – not uncluttered, but certainly clean – and the small makeshift bed of blankets and sleeping bags in the corner made it undeniable that the house was still occupied, though to Tibor's immediate relief, the resident was not currently at home.

Scattered around the circular chamber were more books and papers, many of which seemed to have been hand-written quite recently, giving Tibor the impression that a mad author had been furiously labouring to write their masterpiece on every scrap of paper, cardboard, wrapper, or napkin that could be found. Even some of the art on the walls had been covered in scribbled notes. Dar moved too quickly with the light to let him get a chance to read any of the writings, not that he felt he would have been able to make much sense of the little bits he did glimpse.

When Dar finally stopped moving about and began to scan some of the papers herself, she quickly called him over.

"What is it?" he asked.

"Here," she said, "hold this," handing him the light. He took it from her, and only then realized that she wasn't actually holding a flashlight as he had thought, but a small leather pouch, about the size of his thumb, that covered most of a small stone, about the size of a marble. A small leather cord was attached to the stone and threaded through the back of the pouch. The stone itself glowed with a brilliant white light, given direction by the opening of the pouch. Tibor wondered at the nature of the stone, and how it could give off such a bright light, while also trying not to blind himself by looking at it directly for too long. While he fiddled with the mysterious stone, the leather pouch slipped further back, uncovering the entire stone and flooding the small room with enough light to see everything by.

"Oh, that's much better, thank you," said Dar, without noticing his fascination with the source. At the same time as he was being amazed by the light emitting from the stone, Tibor could now see the entire room, and paused to slowly turn around in a circle to take in the whole scene. Unlit candles were scattered among the books and papers on every available ledge or shelf. Scraps of food and empty take-out containers littered one corner of the room, right beside a small fireplace that he guessed was being used as both a heat source and an easy method of recycling most of the garbage in the room back to ashes. Clearly the past few weeks had been quite warm, as the fireplace looked cold, and the garbage seemed to be piling up.

"Do you know these names?" Dar asked, holding out a piece of paper towards him. He took it and scanned it.

The names on the list were typewritten, and beside each there were handwritten comments. Of the hundred or so names on the page, he knew almost none of them – except for perhaps six names in the middle. They weren't uncommon names – there were millions of people in the world with the same names, he told himself; but of the hundred names, how likely would it be that he would see a cluster of names that matched his five closest friends?

Dar looked over as she waited for him to reply, and seeing him pausing, asked "Well, any of these sound familiar to you?" The question jogged him out of his thoughts...

"Yeah," he answered, "some of them could be familiar – or just a coincidence. There are some strange notes on the list though, and I'm kinda concerned about what they mean."

"How so?"

"Well, a lot of the list are already crossed out, and it looks like he has been grouping them by location. Some show dates – probably when he was in the area, or maybe he's still planning to travel. He held the paper out for her to look at it as he talked, trying to decide if he believed those really were the names of his friends – after all, that would just be wild speculation – what would they have to do with any of this?

Dar noted his comments, but soon turned back to her rummaging around the room, looking for anything more that would help them understand just who this person was. So far, all they had was a name on a visitor log, which they presumed was false, and the mess in this room.

"There's got to be something more here" Tibor expressed excitedly now, "something that explains this list!"

"I wouldn't count on that," Dar interjected, "This isn't a play, where the villain details his devious plan to the audience in a grand speech!" She sounded somewhat frustrated with her search efforts this far as well, though Tibor could see her pocketing curious items and parchments several times as they pored over the room. "Aha!" she nearly shouted, "Come see this!"

Tibor was looking at table covered with a variety of small green figurines, looking remarkably like ornately carved medieval chess pieces - scarcely a few inches tall but incredibly sculpted and almost lifelike in detail - which he almost dropped when she shouted her alarm; resettling his grip, he quickly pocked one of the figures and moved across the room to see what she had discovered. "What did you find?" he asked, holding the glowing stone out as he looked at the papers in her hands.

"Not these – there!" she said, pointing directly in front of her. Two disordered piles of books neatly framed a small door set into the wall, about four feet in height, and only two feet wide. Some recently moved papers revealed a small foot latch, which Dar proceeded to flick with her toe.

Before Tibor could raise any concerns about the possibility of a trap, the small door popped open and swung inwards, revealing a small, concealed chamber, nestled behind the walls. The ceiling was sloped and low – barely five feet in height – so that neither would have been able to stand up straight inside. Just beyond the door was a round opening in the floor, and on the wall opposite they could see the metal rungs of a ladder, each step bolted into the wall, descending into the darkness below.

"Where do you suppose that goes?" Dar asked, hunching over slightly as she moved into the closet-sized room. Tibor squeezed in beside her, and held out the leather pouch over the hole, shining light down the shaft.

"It seems to go at least as far down as the basement," he guessed out loud. Dar shifted past him to reach the ladder, and as he tried to make room for her to pass without rubbing against her backside more than would be proper, he fumbled with his grip on the small leather pouch, squeezing the brilliant stone out of its protective sheath and setting it free – free to fall down the length of the shaft, occasionally bouncing off the sides as it made its way down into the hillside.

After watching the light slowly shrink and finally disappear into the darkness, Tibor could feel Dar's stare at him – he only felt it, because he was having trouble seeing anything now in the near-pitch black of the room – "I guess it goes down a little further than the basement, eh?" he offered weakly.

"That was my favourite," she said with an uncomfortable level of calm and quietness in her voice, which made him flinch in the darkness even more; "it better not be broken when you get down there!"

Tibor sighed. "Right. I guess I'm going first then…" stating the obvious from her tone. He reached out and was grateful that the room was small enough that he didn't have to step forward too far to find the metal handles – the last thing he wanted to do now was follow the stone down the shaft the fast way. Once he had a firm grip with both hands on the metal rung, he stepped over to the lower rung with his right foot and began his descent down the shaft with his left.

In the darkness, he relied only on the regular spacing of the bars as he moved steadily down the ladder, pretending that he was on a simple stepladder with his eyes closed, and trusting the next rung to be there when he moved his feet down with each step. He could hear Dar moving above him, and trusted she was having no issues with the lack of light – she hadn't said anything, so he could only assume everything was fine.

He noticed a faint glow emanating from below as he progressed, which gave a faint shadowy outline to an opening to his left as he continued downwards – it looked like the basement hallway they had first encountered on their way in, and the light below was still a good distance below. By the time he could see well enough to see the bottom approaching below him, he figured they had descended at least as far as the bottom of the hillside, perhaps lower.

He wrung the stiffness out of his fingers as he looked around and waited for Dar to climb down the last few rungs. She moved directly to where the stone was lying, just outside of the small landing area at the bottom of the ladder, where a narrow passage extended in front of them. It was damp and cold in the tunnel, and an abundance of moss and roots coming through the low, arched stone ceiling, hanging down in places like matted hair on a wet buffalo, made it awkward to walk without any of the slimy substance touching him at one point or another.

Dar did not seem troubled by the growths or the damp or the cold and proceeded to lead them the rest of the way forward. After perhaps fifty yards the tunnel ended at a door, which had been left open, from which they emerged into a larger chamber that they both guessed was part of the basement of the neighbouring hotel. The room stretched to their left for fifty feet and was thirty feet across.

Along the near wall, which they presumed to be the hillside – although both had been turned around so much, they were not terribly certain of their direction underground – the wall was actually exposed rock, where the foundation of the hotel cut into the limestone rock of the hill. Water trickled in a steady stream from several points along the exposed rock and ran down worn channels in the stone to gather in a trough set below the level of the floor, which then directed the flow of water along the base of the wall and into the next room.

The rest of the room was filled with derelict equipment that seemed to be responsible for heating, plumbing, and electrical supply for the rest of the hotel, although all of it seemed to have come from another era: turn-of-the-century boilers, scarred and scored with the years of durable use; coal furnaces sitting cold, with their gates hanging open like hungry dragons, waiting to be fed before breathing fire one last time; and archaic electrical panels with ceramic insulators and frayed cables, like the head of a monstrous mind flayer, its tentacles reaching throughout the nervous system of the building, asleep, waiting to be awakened. The entire place had a terrible smell – sulphur from the springs which combined with what was surely black mould from years of moist negligence plus an assortment of animal droppings, creating a putrid smell that neither cared to enjoy for very long.

Moving to their left, Dar followed the flow of the spring water, coming to a door at the end of the room. It was unlocked, and led into a larger open area, whose function was impossible to tell, having been cleared of everything except piles of broken bricks that had been carelessly tossed into piles around the base of the supporting columns. At the far end, there were two openings, and Dar led them across the room to explore.

The first opening led to a short hallway that ended with an open doorway on the left. As they approached, it seemed likely that this was once the elevator shaft for the hotel, although the mechanism and doors had been removed long ago. There was a smell coming from the end of the hall, distinctly different than the smell of rot and sulphur they had encountered earlier, but definitely getting stronger as they got closer. This was something equally foul but harder to identify – until Dar reached the opening to the elevator shaft and peered down on the decomposing flesh that was now only barely recognizable as human.

Tibor fought back a gag reaction as he reached the doorway, as it was apparent that many bodies had been dropped here over a period of time and were each in varying states of decay. Rodents had made a decent attempt to feed off the remains, but enough of the bones remained that the use of the shaft as an unmarked grave for these poor souls was undeniable.

"I really don't think this is a good idea anymore" Tibor whispered, to which Dar only stared at the bones in response. Quickening their pace, they followed the other door to an equally short hallway leading to a metal stairway which emerged from a maintenance closet into what must have once been a grand reception lobby for the original hotel. It was dark, but the white light of the glow-stone illuminated most of the large room, casting long shadows in every direction over the few remaining pieces of dusty furniture.

Despite the use of the room as a reception area during the nursing home period, the long wooden hotel reception desk remained in place, affixed at one end to the base of the central staircase that led to the upper floors. In front of the desk, the room opened up into what must have been a large sitting area, though nothing remained that would have shown it. Peeling paint, broken plaster and an abundance of graffiti were apparent everywhere the light shone.

A faint light from the outdoor streetlights bled through the front windows, long ago broken and boarded up with plywood. Moving out around the counter, they stared across the room, past the main doors, over the broken tiles and scraps of broken plaster & lathe that littered the floor, and they were struck by the large stone fireplace that dominated the far wall – a blank space above the mantle marked where a stag's head had once overlooked wealthy merchants and political elite having afternoon tea or telling tales over brandy and cigars long into the night.

They had just stepped around the desk when they heard the distinctive sound of a door closing coming from somewhere above, followed by the steady rhythm of footsteps and then another door opening and closing.

Freezing in place at the sound, they looked up instinctively, though they could see nothing but the crackling paint on the ceiling fifteen feet above them.

They exchanged looks that made it clear they were silently debating whether this was something they should run towards or away from. With the sight of the unfortunate remains in the elevator shaft still fresh in his mind, Tibor's first instinct was the latter, though he was sure Dar was going to choose the former.

And so he wasn't surprised when she took the lead and moved towards the stairs, sheathing the glow-stone back within its leather pouch, leaving Tibor to follow by the faint light that streamed through the cracks in the plywood-covered windows.

The wide staircase was of sturdy construction, with square oaken balusters still standing firmly, rising from classic craftsman newel posts at the base of the staircase, with broad railings running the length. Remarkably for their age, the steps creaked very little as Dar took the first few hesitant steps on the worn stairs, testing each step to ensure she would not fall through, not fully trusting the aged wooden structure. Halfway up she paused again, motioning for Tibor to stop as well, listening for any noises that would give them a hint of who else was in the building.

Tibor wanted to protest, feeling incredibly unprepared for any sort of confrontation – if this was the person who had come to see him in the hospital, then wasn't he also the one who had done something to wake him up, which meant that he knew about Vengriya, that Tibor was there, and that he wanted to eliminate him from whatever was happening? And just what did 'eliminate' mean? He thought again of the elevator shaft – of course, that's what 'eliminated' meant! They had no weapons of any kind and were just exploring a theory – they didn't have any sort of plan for what to do if they actually found someone! But then Dar was on the move again – and the last thing he wanted to do was give away their presence by calling out after her! – So he followed, hoping that she had a better plan in mind than he did…

Dar moved quickly but cautiously up the stairs, wishing she had really thought more about a plan for what to do if they found what they were looking for.

She pushed the concern from her mind for the moment as she reached the second floor, where the stairs turned back to the left and continued up to the third floor. She was sure the noise had come from further up and was hoping that whoever it was hadn't seen the light, to alert them. She quickly ran through their last few actions in her head, confirming that they had been fairly quiet as they had moved about, so she was confident that they were as yet undetected!

The second-floor landing had an open area that would have been used for a small lounge or concession but was now occupied by a couple of old refrigerators, lying open and broken. She quickly glanced right and left down the long corridors, ignoring the large letters on the wall spelling the word "DON'T" above an arrow pointing to the hallway to their right. She felt a chill down her spine at the sight of the scrawled letters. The sound of stones scraping on broken plaster behind her betrayed Tibor's best efforts at a stealthy approach.

Unable to see as well in the darkness. he bumped into her after she had stopped on the top step, apologizing quietly. She looked back at him and could see the frustration in his eyes. Quietly moving forward again, she followed the stairs up to the third floor, with Tibor following an arm's length behind.

Dar cautiously exposed her light source, revealing a third floor that looked as distressed as the rest of the building. They could see signs of recent attempts at renovations: newer drywall clung to metal studs which had replaced some of the rotting wooden timbers along the corridor, but it was all punctuated with holes and graffiti, in varying states of disrepair. A wide hallway circled the main stairs, with four openings – two to the right, and two to the left - revealing hallways leading off towards what once would have been the guestrooms for this floor of the old hotel.

"Someone's been here recently," she whispered, "there are steps in the dust leading to that door," she indicated. Moving forward into the open area that mirrored the same space they had seen on the second floor they approached a metal door set into the brick wall that almost certainly was an exit to the outside. Without opening it, Dar turned and led them back in the direction the footprints had come from, taking them down the corridor to the left. The hallway went only a short distance before they reached a doorway, and a relatively newer door.

Sheathing the light again, they could see a faint glow emerging from the crack under the door and could hear the faint hum of machinery on the other side. Dar looked at Tibor and made a sign that seemed to indicate she was going to open the door, and that she wanted him – he was guessing – to follow her and move to the right once they were in the room.

"Whoa!" Tibor whispered, putting a hand on her arm as she was getting ready to turn back to the door, "Don't go all 'Leroy…'"

"Stop!" she quickly cut him off before he could finish. "That is so… old! You can't seriously still be using it!?"

Tibor looked slightly hurt at the comment.

"What am I supposed to do here?" he asked in an anxious whisper, "I don't have any weapon or anything useful here! Just what do you expect me to do?"

Dar looked at him for a moment, with an expression that he felt was something akin to either pity or disappointment, then she handed him the leather pouch. "Hold this! Make sure we can see when we get in there! Leave the rest to me."

Turning back to the door, she turned the handle and pushed it open quickly, stepping forward enough to allow Tibor to follow her in, pausing in a crouch as she surveyed the room. Tibor moved to her right and held out the glow-stone in his hand.

They saw the rows of beds, lined up evenly on either side of the room casting eerie shadows down the entire floor of the old hotel. The new drywall and framing stopped where they entered, leaving exposed brick and cracked plaster along the walls running the length of the room. The floorboards were worn and dirty, covered with bits of fallen ceiling tiles and broken pieces of lathe and other scraps, piled in the spaces between the beds that made the makeshift hospital ward resemble a scene from a war zone.

Most of the beds were filled with sleeping occupants, all connected to IV drips.

A small diesel generator at the far end of the ward whined away in the shadows, adding a layer of oily blue haze to the dim lighting, as it supplied power to the few pieces of equipment that required power, the least of which was a turntable that was softly playing a eerily haunting cello concerto that flowed down the length of the room, barely audible past the doorway. There was little else in the room that might draw attention from the outside – even the faint lanterns scattered around the ward were hooded, and spare blankets covered the plywood over the windows, giving an extra layer of blackout protection from any curious outside eyes.

The scene was a lot to take in a single glance, but that was all they were permitted, as the clang of a metal tray dropping to the floor at the far end of the ward made them jump to attention!

Unsure if it had been dropped in surprise or discarded intentionally, something was alerted to their presence.

The dim light faded in the distant corners of the room, and they found themselves straining their eyes to see if they could discern any movement from the shadows in the direction of the noise.

Their efforts were not in vain, as a slow-moving figure began to emerge into the faint light, shuffling slowly in their direction. Tibor's first impression was that the figure seemed to walk a little funny, but this soon turned to realization that the figure was in fact loping, eventually even dropping down to run on all fours like a large dog, looking less-and-less like a man with each stride.

Panicking, Tibor stepped backwards and turned to run out of the room, quickly darting back out into the hallway and towards the opposite hallway. He fought with the small leather pouch, trying to keep his grip on the small glowing orb which lit his way into the hall, stumbling through another door on his right, almost falling into what might have once been a guest room for the hotel.

His foot caught on a broken floorboard as he crossed the threshold of the room, and he completed his stumbling approach with a noisy fall to the floor, trying and failing to muffle a cry as he landed. He did manage to finally close the leather pouch around the lightstone, which plunged the room into darkness again. With scarcely a pause he scurried across the floor, feeling his way towards a hole in the far wall that he had only glimpsed as he entered, clambering across the debris littered floor in the darkness to get through the small opening and hide in the adjoining room.

Only when he had stopped, crouching with his back to the wall, did he realize to his horror that he had taken their only light source when he ran and had left Dar in the ward-room to face the beast alone!

He winced in a grimace of both panic and shame, trying to calm his breathing enough to listen for any account of what was happening behind him.

Dar was still squinting in the dim light of the wardroom to make out the shape in the distance when she realized that the light had dimmed and turned to see Tibor running out of the room.

With a quick glance over her shoulder at the figure that was now loping towards them – her – with increasingly rapid strides, she decided quite prudently to follow Tibor's out the door. She stepped lightly to the right as she cleared the doorway and followed the wall down the hallway until she felt an opening – a doorway- and stepped into whatever room the darkness was hiding for her. Her movement was more graceful and silent than Tibor's exit, and she could hear his muffled groans as he stumbled about in the darkness, having followed the other hallway across the main staircase they had ascended. She closed her eyes to help her focus on her hearing as she wished Tibor would stop moving about so much, to avoid drawing any unwanted attention.

As she was listening, she could hear the padded footsteps of their unseen adversary reach the doorway to the hall and pause, looking into the darkness for any sign of its recently announced guests. She could hear the creature's breath as it inhaled deeply, searching for the scent of its' prey.

Dar sighed with disappointment as she heard the footsteps resume, heading away from her and towards the hallway Tibor had fled down. She was disappointed that Tibor had turned and run so quickly – not just because he had her lightstone, but because she had hoped for more from him. She always saw the best people, and Tibor had the potential to be great – if only he stopped running long enough to see it for himself. With a sigh, she opened her eyes, better adjusted now to the near darkness that she could see well enough to get around unaided and prepared to go save him.

Tibor was doing his best to slow his breathing as he sat on the floor, incredibly aware of just how much noise the wind through his nostrils was making in the dusty hiding spot. Aside from his breath, it was silent enough that he could hear the soft footsteps approaching from the hallway – the heavy thump of each step conveyed a sense of massive weight, followed by the scratching rasp of claws that dug into the aging hardwood floor. Whatever it was that was following him, it was large, and it was hunting him.

He was a little relieved that he hadn't heard any screams or sounds of fighting – he hoped that meant that Dar had escaped as well, and hopefully she was hiding, though that didn't offer him much hope of how he would get away. And he had no illusions – no weapons, no nothing. This was all about getting away in his mind, not fighting!

He finally calmed his breathing back to a semblance of normal as he heard the creature pause outside the door of the first room, sniffing the air for the unseen trail it was following. If he moved now, the grist on the floor would make any chance of quietly sneaking away virtually impossible, so he sat motionless as the sound of the heavy breathing and lumbering footsteps drew closer into the room behind him. He fought the urge to even peek through the hole in the wall to get a glimpse of what was stalking them, not wanting to do anything that would give away his hiding place. The sound of his heart thumping in his chest was like thunder in his ears, blinding his senses to how close the creature must have been now; his nerves tensed every fiber of his being, his muscles coiled and clenched, ready to explode as he held his breath, waiting.

The wall above his head shattered and exploded, scattering debris across the ruined bedroom as the creature's clawed hand sliced through the rotted construction as if it were paper. A deafening roar echoed off the bare walls of the structure, adding to the chaos of the attack.

Tibor sprang away from the wall, diving headfirst across the floor of the room, trying to duck below whatever was coming next, still unable to see in the dusty darkness. He landed on his side against the far wall and looked up to see a silhouette of the creature framed against the faint light from the wardroom – it was tall, unable to stand up straight beneath the crumbling ceiling, with massive arms that swung like timbers of a giant oak tree as it smashed through what remained of the wall between the two rooms; it had a massive chest for a trunk, and squatted on dog-like haunches that could have made it seem even taller if the low ceilings allowed.

Tibor scrambled to his right and out the door of the room and into another hallway, turning to run back in the direction of the main stairwell, which was the only way out that he knew of.

He made it to the main hallway as the creature burst out of the room behind him, running on sheer adrenalin to keep himself but a few claw-lengths ahead of the beast. Watching behind him as the lupine form scraped and clawed at the wooden floors to get traction for the pursuit, he turned the corner again to get to the stairs and nearly tripped trying to stop as he found himself face-to-face with Dar, standing dead center in the hallway at the top of the staircase.

He tried to stop his sprint when he saw her but failed to keep his footing as he slid on the dusty floors, landing in a pile at her feet.

He could see things better now as he realized that she was glowing, radiating energy in the darkness as she prepared to face the creature as only she could.

From his spot on the floor, Tibor looked back as he heard the heavy footsteps and scratching claws bear down around the corner behind him, and he did his best to scramble around Dar and move towards the metal door they had thought – now hoped - led to the outside.

The creature had ripped and discarded the blue medical scrubs it had been wearing when they first entered, and was now covered in the long, mangy fur that best resembled a wild wolf; its arms and legs were now clearly paws and haunches of a wild animal, ready to slash at the steadfast figure of Dar, poised and ready to meet its attack.

Weaving her fingers at her side as the creature approached, unfazed by the morphing features and snapping jaws that raced towards her, Dar readied herself.

She had to admit that she hadn't expected to encounter an Alakvalto here! She cursed herself for not being more prepared for such an encounter as she decided her first move, opting for defense over offense. Damn! She swore again – she had none of her usual wards or protections at hand in this world and hadn't even brought a bloody dagger!

She put her hands up to block as the shape-changing wolf slammed into her at a charge, knocking her backwards to the floor. A faint blue glow pulsed from her forearms as she took the full force of the blow, then the same flash of colour flared from her back as she struck the floor, snapping her head back in what Tibor thought was a concussion blow as she hit against the floor!

She wasn't moving as the creature continued to attack. Sparks flared as it struck at her exposed mid-section, but her protections held. Frustrated by the deflection of his assault, the creature stood and roared, turning instead towards Tibor, snarling with a feral rage.

Tibor was frozen in disbelief.

This couldn't be real! Not here!

It had been a crazy day – his head hurt with everything that he could remember, yet alone the things he couldn't. But this – this, he could remember! The Alakvalto were creatures of legend – even in Vengriya – one of the most feared beasts of Uzhgorod. But... this wasn't their world, and this sort of shit just didn't happen here! It shouldn't! It couldn't – could it?

He looked over at Dar, lying motionless on the floor, and then back at the Alakvalto as it moved towards him.

He clenched his hand, flexing his fingers around the shitty little stone that glowed, wishing for an axe instead!!

Tibor started to back away from the wolf creature and found himself moving back down the short hallway and into the wardroom. He didn't know why it wasn't charging straight away; maybe it suspected he was playing lame and trying to lure him in, or perhaps it was cautious of disturbing the patients lying still in the beds. Nevertheless, he only stopped backing up when he felt the bricks of the wall behind him, leaving him nowhere else to run.

He was cornered, and the creature knew if had him.

Desperate, Tibor looked for anything at hand he could use, his gaze at last settling on one of the lanterns on the bedside table of the nearest cot – without a moment to think, he sidestepped as the creature leapt and reached for the lantern, swinging it down to the floor where he had been standing, spilling the fuel oil and bursting into flame. The wolf struck the wall and scurried out of the fire with a howl, although it did not look to be truly bothered by the fire – it seemed more frustrated at having missed its first try!

Tibor jumped over the low cot and moved toward the center of the room. He could see Dar beginning to move out in the hallway, but the wolf now seemed entirely focused on him. He had no idea what to do, and the thought of those claws ripping into him was making his heart race with a new level of fear and panic that he had never felt before. He desperately hoped that Dar would recover and do something as he turned to face the wolf as it mounted the cot and glared down at him, but he could not see past the flames of the burning lantern. Everything seemed to be on fire around him as he stared numbly into the teeth of the creature as it poised to strike. The creature attacked and Tibor again was left with no time to think about what to do next.

He raised his arms to defend himself, knowing it would do little to stop the massive jaws that lunged towards him! He closed his eyes - hoping like a child that it might just be a dream, and it would all go away – giving up hope even that Dar might yet intercede and save him.

And so he deprived himself of the rare moment of looking into the Alakvalto's eyes as it made its kill - a moment that few have ever lived to tell about – the jet black eyes of an apex predator, a creature out of legend that lived only to devour prey. Even more rare, he did not see the moment that those same eyes changed from rage to fear, when the hunter realized that something had changed, and it was now about to be the prey!

Tibor did not see the searing blast of flame that erupted around him, but he certainly felt it! The hairs on the back of his hands curled and melted, and he could feel the wave of heat flash over him.

In an instant the wolf-like creature was gone, turned to ash by a furious blast of energy - almost as if someone had opened a doorway to the sun in the middle of the room – and then it, too, was gone as quickly as it had appeared.

The flash was outlived by the echoes of the fearful cry still coming from Tibor as he crouched by the cot in the center of the room, still expecting to feel the teeth of the creature come plunging down at any moment! By the time he realized the threat had passed, and opened his eyes again, Dar was on her feet and walking towards him.

"What happened?" he asked, still working to catch his breath.

"You don't know?"

Tibor tried to focus his thoughts. "No. I mean, I saw the werewolf…"

"Alakvalto…" she corrected him.

"Right. Alakvalto. I saw it knock you out…"

"Hey!"

"Well, it did! Anyway, it turned on me, I reacted – just reflex, y'know – I thought I was toast!"

"You should have been!" Dar told him calmly, "Do you know what you did?"

"What I did?" he wondered, "I closed my eyes – I thought you killed it."

Dar pointed to the hole across the ceiling and out of the far side of the building, "Does that look like it came from where I was standing?" she asked.

Tibor stared at the burned edges of the hole, at least a yard in diameter, and through to the stars visible in the exposed night sky.

"We have to get out of here," Dar said, "a lot of people probably saw that, and we should not be here when they come looking."

"What about this?" Tibor said, waving his arm to the rows of beds and the sleeping occupants, none of which had responded in the slightest to any commotion.

"The fire department will call the police and paramedics – they'll wake them or get whatever help they need. Either way, they'll be out of the equation in short order. Now let's go!" She turned, leading them back out of the room, to the exit door they saw in the hallway earlier, and made their way out down the fire escape. They didn't stop running until they heard the sirens of the fire engines responding, at which point Dar slowed them to a walk, looking like any other casual pedestrian on the night streets.

*****Tibor*****

After they were well away from the hotel, they slipped into a coffee shop to settle down and get their heads on straight.

"So, that was pretty intense," Dar said, as they took their coffees over to a table near the windows, where they could see the silhouette of the hotel building illuminated by the flashing red lights of the fire trucks that had responded first to the reports of a fire on the roof.

The coffee shop was divided into two seating areas, divided evenly by the entrance. The place was nearly empty, with just a couple of other customers seated on the opposite side, also showing some casual interest in the emergency vehicles. Dar had overheard them as she waited in line to be served, as they wagered on whether or not the old building would burn to the ground or if it was a false alarm. She was relieved that neither seemed to be talking about any flashes of light or fire, which improved her hopes that the magic may have gone unnoticed by the public on the streets.

Moving to the seats furthest from any unwelcome listeners, she felt she needed to address what had happened with Tibor as soon as possible.

"Wow," Tibor replied, "I know you said you saw it, but I just can't believe I was shooting fire out of my hands!"

"You think I would make something like that up?" she asked him, pretending to sound defensive.

"No, but this sort of thing just doesn't happen here!" he remarked, "That's some next level shit – I mean 'stuff' – even for Ascanium!"

"Well, you're righter than you think..." she said, as she sipped her coffee, blowing through the small hole in the lid to cool it off. "What you did tonight was incredible, not just for channeling magic in this world, but also for the amount you channeled!"

"What do you mean?"

"I mean, you have had no training here that could have helped you do what you did, and because of that, you also had no control over how much energy you channeled into the casting – it could have destroyed the whole building – me, you, and anyone else within half a mile!" Tibor looked wide-eyed with shock as she explained the situation to him.

"A lot of people can channel magic..." she continued, "but those who lack control are usually weeded out by the College and shut off from the source early on, or they end up being consumed by the energy they draw forth and destroy themselves before they learn enough to become a danger to others. Tell me," she asked, "what were you thinking when you summoned the fire?"

"I… I don't know," Tibor stammered slowly, trying to recall, "I was scared, mainly."

"Geez," Dar whispered to herself, "I should have started with this: do you actually know how to channel fire? Have you done this before?"

"No!" Tibor answered, a little too loudly for Dar's liking. She glanced over at the clerk behind the counter and was glad to see they were still being left to themselves.

"Never," he told her again, a little quieter, "I had no idea I could do that!"

"Okay, then, whatever the case may be, you seem to be able to do it, so I have to tell you: don't ever do it again!"

"What?"

"You need to keep your fear in check, and don't try to summon anything – especially fire – again!" she insisted, "…not until you get some training."

Tibor had a very disappointed look on his face, having felt like the hero of the story up to now, saving them both from the creature in the hotel, only to be told that he couldn't use his super-powers any more…

"You summoned a great deal of energy from the elemental planes of fire, without really trying; if you were to try that again, knowing what you could do, but without any training on how to throttle it down a notch – or seven – you could open a channel that would consume you, and if it did, there would be nothing left to shut the channel again. It would incinerate everything."

She paused to let the thought sink in. "Do you get it? It would be like leaving the house with the taps running, and the sinks would all overflow… You have a gift – that much is clear – but we have to either get you some training or get you back to Vengriya, where there is a more natural balance to harness these things!"

"I would very much like that," Tibor said quietly, "…to go back, not to flood the house!"

"Well, I think we can do something about that," Dar said with a smile. Tibor was relieved to finally hear something good out of all of this. He was going to ask how when Dar held out her hand to hush him, as the bells on the door to the coffee shop jingled, signaling the entrance of a customer, and he decided to hold off on the conversation until it was more private.

Tibor had his back to the door, so he didn't see who had entered, but Dar, sitting across from him with a good view of the doors, was watching the customer intently as he "hmmed" and "haahed" over the selection of honey crullers and chocolate dip donuts. Tibor slid around in his seat to get a better look himself.

The older gentleman looked to be about sixty, with wispy white hair curling out from under a grey tweed flat hat. He wore a blue plaid cardigan that would have seemed cliché if it hadn't also seemed as worn and weathered as the man wearing it. He might have been taller than six feet if he could have stood up straight, but it seemed that his age and other infirmities had shrunk him to something closer to five feet in height, leaning heavily on a carved wooden cane.

Dar watched him as he completed his order, slowly turned while carrying a coffee and a small bag of donuts in one hand while his other hand managed the cane for support. He pushed the door open with his back and stepped out without saying a word, and as soon as he was gone, Dar was up from her seat, looking at Tibor to follow.

"What?" he asked.

"Didn't you see that?" she quizzed him, "He looked everywhere except right at us – he scanned the room, looked at the other customers, the cashier and even the baker in the back, but he never once looked at us!"

"So?" Tibor was confused.

"He was intentionally ignoring us – look around..." she waved her arm, "we're dirty, sweaty, disheveled, and look like we've run a marathon through a garbage dump – we should have attracted his attention like a flashing neon sign, and he deliberately avoided looking at us. He was checking us out and was trying not to draw attention. We have to leave, now!"

"Maybe he was just afraid of us?" Tibor offered weakly.

"We're a mess, but – no offense – you're not that intimidating!"

"Thanks!" he replied, taking a last drink of his double-double as he got up and followed her to the door.

Leaving the coffee shop, Dar looked both ways to see if she could see where the old man had gone but saw no trace of him. Before they could take another step, a car at the side of the parking lot started up, its headlights flooding them in a bright white light. Raising their arms to shield their eyes initially, Dar grabbed Tibor by the strap of his backpack and pulled him in the opposite direction of the car, around the corner of the shop and onto King Street.

The street was well lit and there were still a few cars on the road despite the hour. They walked briskly up the road, glancing back to see if the car from the coffee shop was following.

The lights changed at the intersection, and they could soon see the headlights of a car turning the corner and heading in their direction. They both turned away and walked a little faster, looking up the road for oncoming traffic. Fortunately, they were on a good pace to reach the next corner by the time the car would be passing them.

"Keep calm," Dar said, as they moved towards the next intersection, "as the car gets close, we're gonna turn left and run down the next side street. If we wait till he is right beside us, he won't be able to make the turn, and will have to circle back to follow us. If he does try to follow, then I'm right about that guy, and we're probably in more shit than I had planned on, but whatever. Are you ready?"

Tibor nodded, fighting the urge to look back again as he heard the noise of the car engine pulling closer from behind them – approaching but slower than most of the other street traffic.

"Wait for it…" she said slowly, as they judged the car was just about to pass them, then, "Now!" she yelled, pushing him along ahead of her to the left and down the side street. They had gone only a few yards when Tibor was sure he heard the car gun its engine as it went by the intersection, too late to make the turn.

"Hurry!" Dar instructed, "This way — we have to get out of sight!" She darted to the end of the building and ran into the parking lot, following the inner wall back to the main entrance – it was a church, and Dar was counting on it being open!

To their relief, they were able to slip inside the doors, quickly moving to the far wall and slinking to the ground – the doors were glass, and they would be visible if the car came through the parking lot looking for them!

Breathing heavy and not yet talking about what to do next, they were startled by the middle-aged lady who approached from the doors of the sanctuary. Moving slow as she tried to assess the situation, she was dressed modestly and held her hands clasped in front of her, clearly uncertain of what her guests' intentions might be.

"Can I help you?" she asked softly. They looked at her for a moment, looking at the empty parking lot before getting to their feet.

"Sorry for the intrusion…" Tibor started.

"…but we were just looking for a washroom," Dar finished. "I needed to go really bad, and so we thought we would try the door!" She bent over slightly; her knees clenched tightly together as if trying to hold something in.

The matronly lady did not look entirely convinced, but her charitable nature shone through as she pointed to a door on the far side of the small lobby. Dar nodded her thanks and disappeared into the small room and closed the door behind her, leaving Tibor to smile sheepishly at the woman. He pulled out his phone and proceeded to tap away as they waited for Dar, trying to casually remain out of the line of sight of anyone passing the parking lot.

"Good news," he said, as she emerged a few minutes later, "I called for a ride – should be here in a couple minutes, and we can be on our way." He looked over to the church custodian. "If it's alright with you, we would appreciate waiting here for just a few more minutes." She nodded, with a polite smile, and, sensing that the two were not a threat, turned to go back into the sanctuary, to finish whatever it was she had been doing.

A few moments later a taxi drove into the parking lot and pulled up to the doors.

"A taxi?" Dar asked as they were getting into the car, "I thought everyone was using Uber these days…"

"Yeah, well, my credit ain't that good, so a taxi will do just fine," Tibor answered as he closed the door. "You take cash still, right?" he said to the driver, then looked over at Dar. "Where to?" he asked, not having given it much thought himself.

Dar looked at the driver, "Trinity Anglican Church, Galt," and sat back in the seat.

"Why there?" Tibor asked, and was silenced quickly by a look from Dar, switching her eyes back & forth quickly between him and the driver. Tibor sat back and was silent, not entirely patient, but willing to wait for his answer.

*****Absalom Shade*****

It was a short ride from Preston to Galt, and Tibor went through a great many questions in his head during the silent drive. They pulled up in front of the old church, paid the driver and stood for a moment looking up at the old stonework façade and three-story bell tower. It wasn't the grandest church he had ever seen, or even the largest in the city, but it certainly looked old.

"Will you tell me now why we're here?" he asked, checking the street for any other traffic. It was late now, and even though they were in downtown Cambridge, they were far enough from the main drag to have much in the way of traffic of casual observers. The church itself was dark, except for the decorative security lights that illuminated the exterior of the church, but there was no other visible sign of any security system. As Tibor had noted, Trinity was not the grandest church in the city, and so did not attract a lot of attention from anyone interested in any valuables inside.

Though old, it lacked much of the character and flare that the two nearby Presbyterian churches offered in their architecture. Aside from the squat, square, three-story bell tower that barely emerged above the roofline of the chapel, it was a rather unremarkable edifice. The main doors were painted a deep shade of red and were flanked by two other sets of doors – one under the bell tower, and the other set leading to the connected rectory – both recently painted grey. The doors were heavy oaken portals, with wrought iron straps binding them together, and looked as strong as the day they were built. To the left of the building, there was a large open green space, surrounded by a low stone wall, with a neatly manicured lawn and a single tree adorning the center. Further back beyond this was the rectory building where the pastor lived.

Dar was moving towards the bell tower doors, still not answering Tibor's questions. As she reached the base, Dar suddenly veered to her left and vaulted a low wooden gate, landing on a small stone path that ran up the side of the church. The path led towards another door, at the far end of the building that connected the rectory to the church itself, but that was not her destination. Tibor had barely turned the corner after her before he saw her disappear off the path to the right, into a small clump of growth behind the bell tower.

Between two bushes that were flowering with very ornate, globe-shaped white blossoms, he found her crouched down, fumbling around in the dark under the upright branches of a fir tree. He was just about to give her a piece of his mind about being ignored, when he noticed her clearing away the dirt and mulch from a patch of earth, sliding aside a metal grate that revealed a small circular opening into the ground. Smaller than a manhole, she struggled with the weight of the covering – Tibor considered helping, but stopped, feeling like perhaps she should consider including him in her plans first, if she wanted his help with anything.

He was feeling quite pleased with his stance on the matter, and almost missed watching her drop down into the hole. Startled at the speed with which she was racing into such a dark – and undoubtedly dangerous – environment, he hesitated at the top of the hole, taking a moment to peer down and see where she had disappeared. As he did so, he noticed a marker above the opening, set into the foundation wall of the church – it was an aged stone, worn by the elements, but he could distinctly make out the carving of the sword of Isten Kardja – the same sword he had last seen in the mosaic in Ascanium, and tattooed on Dar's neck.

Without being able to see where he was going, he swung his feet into the hole, feeling the steps cut into the side of the stone, and followed Dar down.

She was waiting for him at the bottom and had finally pulled out the glow-stone to help him see where they were.

"Trinity Church is the oldest church in the city…" she started, "it was built in 1844, and the construction was funded and overseen by Absalom Shade, on behalf of his patron, William Dickson." She was speaking quickly, and only paused at brief intervals as she tried to decide just which information was useful at the moment, and what wasn't. "Dickson was a wealthy landowner and businessman, and Absalom, who oversaw several of his properties and investments, was a pioneer, businessman, and visionary. He was someone who was open to new ideas, and clever enough to recognize opportunities and seize change as a chance to innovate. He was a man of faith and conviction, and as a visionary, he was also a gifted dreamer – which is what brought him to us."

"I know you want answers…" she continued, as Tibor looked around the room, surrounded by strange stone carvings and images that were at least as old as the building above them, "…but there is so much to explain, and we have very little time." She continued talking as they moved into the next chamber. "Absalom – who we knew as the 'Peacemaker" – travelled with us for a time, and when he could no longer travel, he committed himself to a new calling, as a guardian of the Order."

"Wait!" Tibor interrupted, "You *knew* Absalom – not just knew *of* him, but you *knew* him? Traveled with him? That would have been almost two centuries ago!"

"What, you got something against older women? Stop interrupting!" she instructed curtly, "Our Order is sworn to observe and protect, and while we understand the nature of how to extend one's consciousness to other realms, we typically refrain from actively facilitating the experience. We would prefer to let the natural order of the world determine the ebb and flow of how magic is channeled in the world; to let those who possess the gift to see beyond the veil discover new worlds on their own – we do not try to force such awareness on the unwilling or the uninitiated, lest it corrupt or distort the true value of such gifts.

"What you saw earlier tonight was someone trying to manipulate the balance of power in all Vengriya, recruiting and subjecting people to the conditions that make the transition possible. But as you saw for yourself in the elevator shaft, it doesn't always work out well for the unwilling or untrained participant."

"I believe this, this…" She dug in her pocket for the list of names they had obtained earlier that night from the hospital, "….'Arcady Sorkin' is working for

Voros Vazul – or maybe he *is* Voros Vazul – and in addition to harvesting an army of heroes, he is also deliberately and methodically trying to eliminate those who might stand against him – in any world."

They stopped talking for a moment and surveyed the shadowy chamber – they had landed in what appeared to be an old storeroom for the church, filled with folded tables and old chairs, unused and collecting dust. Dar held the light high as she scanned the walls of the small room, pausing to push aside a stack of chairs once she appeared to have found what she was looking for. Tracing her fingers across small markings on the natural stone, Tibor could hear the whir and click of a mechanism buried somewhere within the walls, as lines appeared in the seamless stone and a door opened at Dar's command. She moved through without even a glance back at Tibor, knowing that he would follow.

They entered a chamber that looked to be carved out of stone rather than constructed of brick and mortar. The octagon walls were at least ten feet across, and the ceiling was low, with barely enough room for Tibor to stand up straight. Along the walls on either side were an assortment of arms and weapons, ranging from musket rifles that seemed to have last been used when the church was built in 1844, to more medieval "sword-and-shield" fare; all of them were covered with a layer of dust that made them seem much older than they appeared. In the faint light, Tobor could see another opening in the far wall, pausing only long enough for Dar to close the hidden door behind them.

"Absalom was not the first guardian for the Order in this world," she continued, "…there have been many over the centuries, but he was one of the latest – he saw that there might be a need for those who shared this understanding of the nature of the world to be able to meet and share their knowledge in a practical yet safe fashion, and so he ensured that several of his construction projects included consideration for uses that were not necessarily part of the original plans. It is only by chance that this church is the only construct to have survived over the passage of time."

"I wouldn't be so sure to say that this place has 'survived' the passage of time," Tibor interjected, swiping at the cobwebs and dust that layered every surface from years of disuse. "When was the last time anyone was down here?" he wondered aloud. Dar ignored his comments and kept moving.

Moving quickly through this chamber, they turned to their left and the short passage opened into a large underground hall, which Tibor guessed must be directly underneath the main building of the church above. Moving down several steps as they entered, the floor continued downwards on a gentle incline, mirrored by a similar upwards angle in the ceiling; the walls opened more broadly in a circular shape, and Tibor soon felt it all resembled a very large egg. This suited him quite well as the smaller spaces had been starting to make him feel a bit claustrophobic. There were several columns throughout the chamber that appeared to be carved out of the same stone, as if the chamber had been hollowed out around them, supporting the arching ceiling. A colourful but dust-covered tiled pathway led directly to what appeared to be an altar at the center of the room.

There, on a raised dais, was a low stone table, looking very much like the warrior tombs found in the oldest cathedrals, where crusaders and kings were laid to rest. The markings around the stone table were written in a strange language that somehow seemed familiar to Tibor, but he could not read it. He remained completely lost to the moment and followed Dar's every instruction as if he were a child again.

Looking out from the center of the room, Tibor could see that against the curved outer wall, lining up with the spaces between the columns, seven stone effigies of knights seemed to stand guard over the chamber. Sculpted from a white stone that was clearly different from the rock of the cavern, they had an amazing element of realism to their face and form that made it seem that each was ready to spring into action at any moment. Posed in a state of permanent readiness for battle, these stone warriors were uniquely crafted with no two alike, yet all held one common element – the gauntleted left hand of each clutched a long sword, pointed toward the apex of the arched ceiling. On the ceiling itself was a faded painting, distorted by the shadows and streaking light, yet the image was discernible enough – a monstrous seven-headed beast writhed and roared as its' serpentine form spread across the expanse of the ceiling, unravelling upon itself within the circle, yet held in check by the seven blades that appeared to pierce the scaled-hide of the beast whenever it drew near one of the golems' upraised stone blades.

While the craftsmanship of everything else was unique, the swords were identical in shape, size and styling, and engraved with runes of the same language that adorned the stone table - foreign yet familiar, the same words repeated over and over throughout the chamber:

Isten Kardja.

Tibor felt himself physically wince as an unseen voice inside his head violently screamed in the silence, as if desperate to tell him the secret of the blade, yet he could not hear it. To his eyes, it was clearly the sword from the legends of Vengriya, yet he had no recollection of any order – no knights, wizards, nor pilgrims - sworn to these words, to this sword, though now he was all but immersed in it!

And then there was Dar – he still couldn't figure out just what her role was, but she definitely acted as if she had a plan for everything that was happening!

"Come here!" Dar called with authority, motioning for him to join her at the stone table. She had placed the glow stone into a lantern hanging from the ceiling and, fully exposed, it shone with its full brightness, illuminating the length and breadth of the chamber. The room was large enough to hold the entire congregation from the church above, seated in a circle around the circumference of the altar-like table.

"I can return you to Vengriya right now," she said directly.

"I thought you just said your order was sworn not to interfere with people travelling between worlds or whatever..." Tibor challenged her.

"I said we '*prefer*' to let the natural order take its course – now do you want to go back, or would you rather quibble over grammar?" She raised one eyebrow as she finished, clearly not amused with his hesitation.

"Yes!" he answered excitedly. "What do I need to do?"

"Hop up on the table and lie down," she instructed, as she set his backpack on the ground for him and began to fiddle with a needle and a small vial.

"What's that?" he asked, with just the slightest hint of anxiety at the sight of the needle.

"Arcady – or Vazul – whoever he is, he was using thiopental and pentobarbital to put his victims into a medically induced coma. I grabbed a vial of thiopental when we were there, and it should work to help restore you to a state where your mind can free itself and return. Thiopental will work quickly – especially since I will be giving it by injection instead of a drip, so you should feel the effects pretty quick."

Tibor was nodding in agreement, as he liked any plan that allowed him to get back to Ascanium, but he suddenly frowned as he processed things a bit further...

"Wait," he said, "what happens to me, here, once you give me that? I mean, this isn't a hospital or anything, how will my body stay alive here?"

Dar smiled at him gently – despite her youthful appearance, the look she gave him resembled that of a mother gazing politely at a child before explaining something simple to them...

"I will watch over you here," she reassured him. "I and others of my order maintain chambers like these whenever we have a guest. This isn't the usual way we might try this, but the thiopental was handy, and will do just fine in a pinch. Normally it doesn't work for very long, and you might wake up if unattended and not given regular doses, but we have some tricks for that. And as for food, you can rest assured that there are enchantments on the table you're lying on that will slow and preserve your bodily functions here."

"You mean like 'suspended animation'?" he asked, lying back on the table, but still propped up on his elbows, curious about what was happening.

"Think of it more like *'sleeping beauty'*, never aging until her prince finds her," she answered with a clever smile. "Give me your arm," she instructed, pushing up his sleeve to expose his inner elbow. She tied a rubber strap around his bicep, tightening it enough to make the veins more visible, and positioned the needle. "You might want to look the other way," she suggested, which Tibor decided might be prudent given the size of the needle she was holding up to the light, inspecting the dosage.

Lying back on the stone, he turned his head and found himself looking back towards the doorway where they had entered. There was a figure standing there, tall enough to fill the doorway, with a long black overcoat that billowed like a cloak on an unseen draft of air that moved through the chamber.

His first thought was that it might be the caretaker for the Order that Dar had mentioned earlier, but he quickly dismissed this thought when he saw the dark expression on his face. It wasn't the old man from the coffee shop either, that they had worried was following them – in fact, he couldn't recall ever seeing the person before. Before he could say anything to Dar, he felt the needle being inserted into his arm and the hot burn of the injection entering his bloodstream, moving up through his arm. In the end, all he could get out about the stranger in the doorway was a single word:

"Shit!"

"Oh c'mon, it didn't hurt that mu–" Dar started, but cut off in mid-sentence as Tibor pulled her arm and pointed to the man.

"Shit!" she whispered as well, dropping the needle and releasing the rubber band from around Tibor's arm.

Vazul stood for a moment in the doorway, quickly surveying the scene. He had abandoned all disguise now, with no need of pretense or imagery to mask his presence from the common folk on the street. Catching a breeze from an unseen corner of the chamber, his long coat billowed out behind him and revealed the hardened leather doublet, dyed a deep red and enameled to glisten like fresh blood in the flickering light of the chamber.

His loose leggings were tucked into high, hard leather boots, held up by a wide belt that was adorned with silver buckles and the hilts of several daggers. His face was smooth and ageless, youthful despite his years, bronzed by millennia of exposure to the rise and fall of a thousand sunrises, with not a single wrinkle to crease his face. Moving forward, down the steps into the chamber, he held his arms outwards, and an ambient green glow began to emanate from his body – first from his hands, then crawling across his arms to cover his entire body – bathing the stone columns and walls in a haunting, eerie hue.

"You should not have meddled in my affairs," he spoke, his deep voice echoing around the hall, amplified, and reflected back by the vaulted arches of the ceiling. "You have done much more than just observe, my dear."

Tibor tried to rise from the table, but the room swirled and blurred, and it was all he could do to not crack his head on the cold stone of the table as he fell back and lay still, trying to control his nausea. Dar – who had been holding his hand – released him and stepped down from the dais and backed away from the dark figure continuing to close the distance with her.

"You have violated the oath of your order," Vazul continued, "which I believe frees me from any constraints that would prevent me from killing you!"

"You don't get to lecture me on broken oaths," Dar countered. "You have corrupted everything sacred about our world!" Her hands were glowing now, as she began to channel her power, but the subtle blue hue from her hands was hardly noticeable as the hall continued to be flooded with the ambient green light.

There may have been more they wanted to say to one another, but a crackle of energy drowned out any further words as Vazul thrust one arm forward and a bolt of green lightning arced across the room towards Dar.

The forking bolt raced towards her then stopped suddenly, exploding like fireworks as she deflected the energy with her own. At the same time, the rock at Vazul's feet began to flow upwards, entrapping his legs and holding him immobile. He paused, and, looking down at the fluid rock as it hardened once again, he raised his right arm – glowing brightly now with energy—and smashed it down, shattering the stone and freeing himself to move again.

While his attention was diverted, Dar channeled more energy, pushing herself to her limits, and then extended her willpower to fill the room. Blue tendrils snaked out and touched each of the statues set against the wall, arcing from tip to tip of each upraised sword, and then flashing bright for a brief instant, followed almost immediately by a deafening boom of thunder within the chamber.

Vazul cringed as the thunder and lightning display blinded him for a moment, and when he opened his eyes again, he was distinctly aware of the seven stone warriors walking forward from the perimeter of the hall and closing in towards him.

He glared angrily at Dar as the golems approached and took a moment before they reached him to flick his wrist while his arm was still down at his side, catching her off guard as he sent a small dagger of energy flying towards her faster than she could follow with her eyes. Trying to react, but exhausted from summoning the golems, she was not able to twist out of the way as quickly as she might have under better circumstances, and the missile struck her in the chest, knocking her from her feet.

Tibor could hear and see things happening around him, but he could not find the strength or ability to move even the slightest inch to do a thing to help – not that he felt he would truly be of any use to Dar against Vazul!

His head was turned to a slight angle, which permitted only a partial view of the events unfolding around him in the chamber, and he struggled in vain to strain to see more than that which was directly in front of his eyes! The was a great deal of magical energy flying about the room, which he knew he had no defense against, but somewhere, somehow, he knew he had channeled something back at the abandoned hotel to save them from the shape-changer, and perhaps there was something he could do here, now, when they needed it most!

He clenched as tight as he could to try to fight the drugs that Dar had just given him, only to find that the darkness was creeping into his vision even more now after he relaxed. He felt as if he was falling down into a pit of blackness, with the chamber and all the flashes of magic disappearing into the ever-shrinking opening of light in the distance above him.

He tried to scream, to yell, anything to try to wake himself up and fight the darkness enveloped him, to no avail. Then there was nothing – no light, no sound. Just darkness.

It was surprisingly soothing, to be wrapped in nothingness – warmer than he might have expected- which only served to lull him even further into a sleep-like trance, enjoying the sensation of weightlessness as he fell deeper and deeper into the void.

It may have been mere moments, or hours – time had begun to blur – when he realized that there was a light in the void, and things seemed to be getting brighter. At some point he became aware that the blackness was now a greyness, and he could tell that there was something beneath him, something approaching, that was bringing light with it – growing brighter with each passing moment.

It was more than light, though.

There was a sensation of energy – power. Yes, he could sense that there was a power here.

A gentle thrumming, like the purring of a cat, emanated through the light and into his body, and he was glad to know that he could still feel such sensations.

The vibrations began to tingle, and the light became warmer, as he felt that he was getting closer to the source, which was still below and behind him as he fell backwards into the void. Calmly now, embracing the warmth and comfortable with the fact that he was not likely to ever stop falling, he summoned a thought – a desire – to roll himself over in his mind, and change his perspective to see where he was falling to, rather than where he was falling from. He was rewarded with a view of a brightening light, though he could not make out any detail of its source.

Strangely, he no longer had he sensation that he was falling towards the source, but that it was now moving towards him.

The sleepy purring had changed, as if the cat had been awakened by his presence and was now coming to explore whatever had disturbed its slumber.

He could sense that it was moving back & forth as it approached, weaving as if searching for him, and he could feel the warmth now becoming an uncomfortable heat. There was definitely power here. Power that had potential and direction, but no one to channel it – no purpose.

No one to give it life. No one to bring it out of the darkness and into the light of the world.

Tibor reached out towards the burning core of the light that floated before him, extending his arm as a gesture even though it was his mind that was doing the work.

It seemed to almost be alive – that it wanted to be found, to be used. It was asking him for help.

He turned his mind back towards the surface – back the way he had fallen – and pointed the way to the world beyond.

Then he felt the sensation of wind in his face as he flew forward, riding a wave of pure light and energy as it rose, gaining speed as it went.

Dar lay on the ground for a moment, twitching and convulsing as the piercing sensation of the electrical charge slowly dispersed. On her back, gazing up at the chiseled stonework of the ceiling, she felt weak and tired as the last of the spasms faded and her muscles burned as if they were covered in molten steel. Groaning like the day after the hardest workout she had ever done, she fought the urge to just lie on the floor and sleep, instead, pulling herself up to a sitting position and taking a moment to survey the scene. The stone golems were part of the security system for the channeling chamber, and though she had never actually tried to use them before, she was glad to see that they were proving effective.

The energy to activate the golems had taken a lot out of her, on top of the pain from the dart of electrical energy that Vazul had shot her with, but she could see from the activity on the far side of the hall that she might be able to savour a few minutes to catch her breath as the golems carried out their orders.

Vazul had stood his ground as the golems nearest the doorway reached him first and began to pummel at him with their stone fists – even though each held a stone sword, these were not truly weapons appropriate for a golem. Their method was pure brute force, and when they were created, they were imbued with simple commands to carry out. While their attacks then were not elaborate or highly skilled, they were nonetheless very effective.

It was only with great skill that she could see that Vazul was able to dodge many of their blows, and using his channeling skills, he was crafting a slow but stable defense. Possessing some skill at his craft, he dodged and deflected blows, and used his relatively smaller size to take advantage of their inability to get close enough for them all to attack him at once.

She had bought them some time by animating the guardians, but she knew the golems would not be able to defeat him. Looking over at Tibor, lying still on the stone altar – she would not be able to protect him either. As she knew his mind would be sent afar, his body could no longer be left here in safety. Somehow this wizard had compromised their secrecy and followed them here; she was going to have to find somewhere else to hide.

She collected her thoughts and gathered her wits, slowly rising to her feet and making her way back to the altar table.

She checked Tibor's pulse, making sure he had survived the unorthodox dosing for the medication, and hoped that he was in fact reaching the intended state of deep unconsciousness that would bring him home. This was where he wanted to be, she was certain, but yet, there was still no way to cut the metaphorical cord that would free him – or anyone, for that matter – from the bonds of the home world from whence their journeys began. She glanced over at the battling golems, and she could see that several of the stone giants were now broken – in part or in whole – and that it was only a matter of time before she would have to fight – or flee.

Flee, she decided.

She searched around the table for what she needed, and was soon on her knees, working her way around the edge of the dais, marking a chalk circle on the stone that surrounded the altar table.

Another golem exploded into a thousand pieces, sending a thunderous boom echoing back & forth through the chamber, raining a cloud of dust and pebbles on her and Tibor as she worked.

She traced another circle around the top of the table, moving faster now, but being careful to trace the runes properly or the casting would fail.

She could hear the distinct sound of glass shattering but did not dare break her concentration to look. If she had, she would have certainly appreciated the craft that it took to transform one of the stone golems into pure glass, then striking it with a hammer-fisted blow of channeled energy that shattered the construct into a million fragments!

Her focus now was on her own channeling. She could feel her arms and legs burning with fatigue as she opened herself up to the ethereal planes, looking to bend and warp the fabric of space around them. It was going to take a tremendous amount of energy to do what she was hoping to do, and such things normally took time to build up to; now, she was trying her best to rush – to open the gates that she has had just recently told Tibor he needed to be careful about keeping closed, lest he lose control and destroy rather than channel.

And then she had no more time – the last golem fell to Vazul's fury, blasted across the chamber with a force that left nothing but crushed stone rubble in its wake.

He straightened from his battle stance and looked towards the center of the room. In the midst of his fighting, he had not noticed how the light in the room had shifted from green to blue; he, too, was tired now, and his aura had faded as Dar's had grown.

He could see the intensity of her effort as a small sphere of blue energy was beginning to take shape in the center of the chamber, crackling, arcing, and jumping about like a will-o'-wisp on the wind. He didn't know exactly what she was doing, but he could sense that she was channeling a great deal of power to do it – power that she was not directing at him!

He sensed that he had an opportunity now to strike.

Dar sensed it as well, and she quickly ducked down behind the table as he began to march towards her.

Hiding was a reflex on Dar's part, hoping to gain a few extra moments of time to gather her strength, and perhaps she could cast her spell before Vazul destroyed them both.

Crouched behind the stone altar, her hands planted firmly on the cold stone floor, she felt something completely different than what she had experienced when they had first entered the room – something made her feel much more connected to the energy of the chamber. It took only a moment for her to realize what was happening – long enough to curse herself for being such a fool!

She was older than most, and considered wise among her peers in the Order, but this was not her home, and so she could hardly be blamed for failing to recognize that this was a sanctuary chamber built by one of the Guardians of her Order, and even though there were no longer in Vengriya, this was still a place of power. The Guardians of the Order only built their sanctuaries on sacred ground, where the lines of energy between the worlds intersected, making them sites of great potential for miraculous works. This one was newer than many of those found in other, older parts of the world, but Absalom had discovered it nonetheless, and chosen it as a location to be protected for a reason. A reason she was just now beginning to appreciate, to her great relief!

Pressing her hands against the stone with confidence, she felt the energy of her channeling surge through the natural rock below her, flowing into her as she embraced the natural power of the earth within her – cool, refreshing, re-energizing energy that surpassed anything she had ever experienced. Empowered, she closed her eyes and began to visualize her will.

Without the distraction of the events happening around her, she *felt* more than *saw* the casting take place: she felt a slight wave of nausea as a wave swept over her like a ocean storm lifting a small boat; she saw the walls of the room fall away, then the floor; she focused her mind on her home: the colour of the sky, the trees, the plains, the birds, the flowers; then it was more than just her world but a specific place in her world – a city, a building, a room; and then the walls reappeared, followed by the floor, a ceiling, candles, banners – everything as she remembered it. As it was.

As it is.

Dar opened her eyes and looked around the small square room, smaller than the chamber she had just been in, with four stone walls set close in upon a space barely the size of the dais from the sanctuary. The stone table was there as well, but it lay empty - Tibor was missing.

She swallowed her momentary panic as she surveyed the scene. The sanctuary was gone – Vazul was gone – all replaced by the small stone chamber.

Banners on each wall were still fluttering in the unseen wind as the power of the channeled energy subsided - the same wind that was making the many candles around the room flicker and dance, making the room seem to shift and waver as her eyes adjusted to the new environment. There was a wooden door to her right, and she hurried to open it, still unsure of what she would find.

The hallway was empty but for a single guard, who stood staring out towards another door across the hallway, which led to a balcony. To her great relief she could see Tibor on the balcony, leaning against the stone railing, surveying the night sky.

"Please be so kind as to summon the Prince," she instructed the befuddled guard, ignoring his unsettled and curious expression as she gave her orders, "and let him know that I have returned."

After ensuring that the guard had departed to carry out her instructions, Dar followed Tibor out to the balcony, approaching slowly as she watched him taking in the night scene. The city below was aglow with fires, and the night sky was tinted orange with the glow of fires burning even farther away across the horizon.

Watching Tibor, trying gauge his reaction to what he was seeing, Dar stepped up to his side, still not saying a word.

After a moment, he realized she was there and turned to her, his eyes betraying his most heartfelt appreciation for everything she had just done and where they now were. His mouth opened and he fumbled to find the right thing to say, but, not finding the words to express everything he was feeling at the moment, he settled on just one thing…

"Thank you…" he started to say, before she cut him off.

"Shhhh!" she hushed him softly. "There is much we need to do…" she said in a quiet voice, watching as his eyes began to drift out of focus.

The world was spinning, and she knew what was happening – that feeling of watching oneself as if outside your body – she knew he was looking at himself standing on the balcony, at her, at the city from above, and at his own bewildered face. She could see his knees begin to weaken and buckle.

"…but first you need to sleep!" she finished saying, reaching out and tapping her finger softly on his temple. His eyes fluttered, closed, and he slumped quietly to the ground at her feet.

Part III

"…while the Plutonium, below a small brow of the mountainous country that lies above it, is an opening of only moderate size, large enough to admit a man, but it reaches a considerable depth… …and this space is full of a vapour so misty and dense that one can scarcely see the ground. Now to those who approach the handrail anywhere round the enclosure the air is harmless, since the outside is free from that vapor in calm weather, for the vapor then stays inside the enclosure, but any animal that passes inside meets instant death. At any rate, bulls that are led into it fall and are dragged out dead; and I threw in sparrows, and they immediately breathed their last and fell. But the Galli, who are eunuchs, pass inside with such impunity that they even approach the opening, bend over it, and descend into it to a certain depth…"

Strabo.

Geographica

*****Cybille*****

It felt like dusk when Erzsébet and the Daughters of Cybille arrived at the sanctuary, for though the sun had not yet set, the high walls of the narrow canyon had covered the small grotto in shadow long before the sun had begun its late day descent. Shielded from the mountain winds, there was still enough of a breeze to swirl the air and disperse the mists rising from the ground. Torches fluttered, casting shadows that flittered and flicked around them on the stone walls of the sanctuary. Erzsébet fiddled with her cloak, trying to keep it close to her as she suppressed a shiver that had little to do with the chill in the air. She had come this time not because she was afraid, but because she was afraid not to.

Just fourteen years old, a great many things still gave her reason to fear the world, though she had not yet seen enough to know her place in it. Her parents had talked of arranging her betrothal to the blacksmith's son, which would be an ideal match – they thought – as the smithy was a good and respected trade, valued greatly by the nobles and their men-at-arms, and much preferred over the back-breaking life of a peasant farmer. Erzsébet did not know the smith's boy, though she had seen him at the market and was quite certain that she wanted nothing to do with him in the least.

Then her Néni Anna came for a visit.

Néni Anna had decided long ago that she would not be a farmer's wife, running away from the same homestead before she was to be betrothed. She disappeared into the city, emerging again some years later as a much sought-after merchant, travelling from town to town, creating and selling the sweet scents that the women – and a surprising number of the men – from the noble houses craved so dearly.

Wildly intoxicating, most sought her mixtures for anointing their lace handkerchiefs to mask the smell of the streets when they were out and about the town, more so than to please their husbands on the occasions when they were home for the night. Néni Anna had been on one of her rare visits home when Erzsébet's betrothal was announced, and her aunt could plainly see Erzsébet's reaction was not one of joyful obedience.

Taking to her chores the following morning, they walked together in the sparse, dusty fields that her parents had toiled over for years. It was still early in the day, but Erzsébet was already sweating through the coarsely woven clothes that she wore when she was working. Her aunt, on the other hand, wore a fine dress, quite unsuitable for the fields, with her long blonde hair falling down around her shoulders in a loose braid, tied with a net of fine silver chain that sparkled in the sunlight. A thin sheen of moisture across her brow was the only evidence that the morning freshness was warming into a hot afternoon, which could be detected as she stood tall and straight beside Erzsébet, who was bending over to pull weeds from the soil around the plants.

It was here, away from any curious ears that might betray her confidence, that Anna told her about another way to live – a way to find her own destiny. Filled with the fear and anxiety of the recent proclamation, Erzsébet grasped at the chance to avoid the proposed marriage, and they quickly made their plans.

Two nights later they left by horse and rode – they rode for days, barely stopping until they reached the latest town that her aunt was calling home. Situated in the foothills of the mountains, they were far away from the trade routes that crisscrossed the great plains, and more than that, no one would guess to look for her here.

The first few weeks were a complete joy for Erzsébet – Néni Anna immersed the sheltered young girl in all the wonders of the modern world: Néni Anna was a liberated woman, not beholden to any man for food, shelter or possessions, and was respected by all of the townsfolk, especially the noble ladies of the court. Just above the town, as the hilly land rose into the mountain ranges, the squat, square castle of Diosgyor, with its four sturdy, square towers, stood watch over the mountain passes – the solemn duty of young Baron Rakoczi Gabor, inherited when the Legions of the Imperium had slain his father, Baron Rakoczi Laszlo.

The court was not as large as the capital, but Baron Rakoczi took great pride in presenting his house as a place of culture and etiquette, despite their remote and inhospitable location. He frequently threw lavish feasts, with music and dancing to celebrate all the high holidays, and routinely invited the lords of neighbouring duchies to partake in his renowned hospitality. Of course, this also drove the local noble women to do their utmost to ensure they were supplied with all the latest trends and fashions from across the rest of Vengriya, and this fueled Anna's fortunes.

Though unmarried and sometimes scorned for it by the townsfolk, Anna had parlayed her instinct and expertise into becoming an invaluable resource for those who had the wealth to afford her wares – valuable enough that they were willing to overlook her untraditional status to secure her latest offerings. Not only did she have access to the rare delicacies they craved, but Néni Anna's lifestyle also gave her license to traffic in other, less traditional – often taboo – activities. She profited greatly from sharing exotic tales and techniques with the noble ladies of the court, guaranteed to satisfy their lovers – and their husbands – for weeks, or at least until the next time she visited town again!

This was the world she introduced Erzsébet to – this and more. For Néni Anna had another life as well – a life that she told Erzsébet was the source of her strength and independence; a wellspring that gave her the strength to stand on her own and do what others said could not be done. She was joined with others like her – free women, who gathered in secret to share their lore for mutual gain.

Erzsébet had only attended two gatherings so far – this night was her third – and it was only the second time that she had been permitted to join them in their full ceremony, which is what her aunt told her was the secret to their strength – where they showed their true commitment to one another. It was a mysterious gathering, but she loved the mystery and rituals of it all, and though she had felt nervous the first time, it also seemed very natural to her, like she finally belonged to something truly special.

Standing barefoot on the cold stone of the small rocky basin nestled deep in the foothills of the mountains, the light blue silk of their scarves fluttered in the evening breeze. Stealing out of the city discreetly, they had followed the narrow cart path from the city into the hills, not lighting their torches until they were far enough away from prying eyes to ensure that their gathering would be private. Once out of sight, they gathered into a more formal procession, leaving the path and winding over the broken stones until they reached their destination. The cave entrance was low – even the shortest of the sisters would have to bend her head to enter the narrow opening – and was barely as wide as their shoulders.

The entrance appeared more as a slice of stone missing from the rough wall of exposed rock – a crack that ran up from the ground as if the earth itself was struggling to contain something within and had reluctantly yielded ever so slightly to the pressure. A white cloud of vapour was steadily drifting out of the opening, and on clear days it would be caught by the wind and dispersed as it escaped the cave. At night, however, as the air chilled, the strange vapours sank close to the ground and hung about the small, paved courtyard that had been constructed a millennium ago by worshippers of various ancient gods who all believed the cave to be a gateway to the underworld. The damp fog clinging to the ground was the only visible sign that there was something different about this cave from all the others – something that would explain the dozens of tiny bodies scattered around the opening and into the mouth of the cave.

Birds, drawn by the warmth, their tiny brains blissfully unaware of the poisons that flowed out on the drafts, killing before being dispersed by the mountain winds. More than just animals, there always seemed to be a steady stream of adventurers, explorers and men of faith who were always attempting to disprove the might of the old gods by daring to cross through the passage, only to succumb to the mysterious forces that protected the cave from the uninitiated.

Tonight, however, was different.

Tonight, Erzsébet was among the initiated – she was one of the Daughters of Cybille now. And if Cybille was their 'mother under the mountain', then these women here tonight had become her new sisters!

Each of her sisters wore the blue silk robe of their order, but underneath they remained barkeeps, milkmaids, bakers, and more than a few of the noble wives among them. The light silk of their hoods might have blown off, revealing their faces were it not for the scarves wrapped over their mouth and nose – nothing that would prevent them from breathing the poison, but enough to shroud their identity from the casual observer. It was clear that while they knew one another, they were here in secret – to do what they knew would not be accepted by their husbands, brothers, and uncles – and yet here they were.

When the last of the procession had entered the clearing, they formed a semi-circle around the entrance, facing inwards at each other, holding their torches low out in front. In a brief lull in the wind, one of her sisters struck a chime. By the second ring Erzsébet reminded herself that she was supposed to be breathing, matching her rhythm to the tone of the chime as it rang out ever so lightly in the wind. All the sisters were doing the same, and the torchlight almost seemed to be alive as they moved up and down ever so slightly with their focused breathing. The chimes grew further and further apart, and she could feel her lungs filling up with air, stretching her chest with each breath, and she could feel that she was able to hold her breath a little bit longer each time. She was starting to feel just a little bit light-headed when she could see that they were finally starting to process into the cave, and she remembered the reason for the chimes.

At the next strike of the triangle, the sister nearest the cave moved forward to the entrance, bowing her head, low enough to enter, but also trying to stay above the creeping mist, and then walked rapidly into the passageway, the darkness of the cave quickly swallowing the meager light of her torch. She was gone for a matter of only a few heartbeats before the chime rang again, and the next sister moved forward to follow the first.

The line of sisters on each side of the semi-circle moved forward, and Erzsébet could see that she would likely be one of the last to enter – which meant she should take it easy on the deep breaths for a few moments or she would risk passing out before her turn came!

She patiently followed the line, watching as her aunt took her turn a few places ahead of her, sharing a quick wink, and surely a smile before she went in, although only the wink was visible above the scarf. In short order it was her turn, and she found herself taking one more practice breath, holding, releasing, before she heard the chime that marked her turn. Moving forward to the entrance, she bowed her head, but kept her shoulders straight, staring as the swirling fog as it danced around her waist. As all of her sisters had done before her, she took one last, deep, breath and held it as she strode forward into the cave.

Straightening her head as soon as she could, when the ceiling of the cave rose just within the entrance, she couldn't help but look at the desperately sad bodies of birds on the cave floor, in various stages of rot and decay, which, under other circumstances, might have smelled repulsive. Here, just above the cloud of gas that clung to the floor around her, the scent of sulphur was almost overpowering, and she silently gave thanks to her aunt for providing the perfume which she had generously doused on her scarf before they had departed for the procession, or else she was certain that she would have been retching by now.

Focusing on holding her breath and holding her small torch out straight in front of her, ever careful not to let the shifting breeze in the passage blow her silks on the exposed flame, she traced the steps of her sisters on the sand of the cave floor, noting with relief that the number of corpses dwindled rapidly as she progressed. There were several short twists and turns, and though she had been through the passage once before, it had seemed like an eternity had passed that first time before she emerged into open air.

This time seemed no different until she began to feel the pulse in her head as her breath was beginning to fade and she was starting to feel the floor rush up to meet her. Her footing slipped on the sand, jerking her mind awake as her heart skipped a beat and the floor vibrated and rocked — it wasn't just her feeling light-headed, the earth was actually shaking!

Dust and stones began to fall from cracks in the ceiling, and her vision quickly became obscured as she lurched from side to side. The trembling earth rumbled and echoed through the stone with deafening loudness, making her feel as if the walls were collapsing upon her. She could hear cries in the dark coming from ahead and behind her, and she reached out her hands to steady herself from falling as the quaking continued.

Unable to move forward, she gasped as she felt her hand slide down on the smooth stone and fought to keep her balance, quickly losing her leverage as the walls widened towards the bottom of the passage.

And that was all it took.

In an instant she realized what had happened — she had fallen to her knees as the earth shook and she was now engulfed in the mist. Her instinctive gasp of alarm had exchanged her last breath of good air for one quick breath of the poison vapours.

Even though it was but the tiniest gasp, and she caught her mistake instantly, she could already feel the burning sensation beginning in the back of her throat as she rose and tried to stand above the fog again. But it didn't help. Fear began to mount as her heart began to pound and her eyes widened, panic rising in her chest! The poisons mixed with the moisture in her mouth and throat, following a burning path down into her lungs that spread like wildfire.

Hoping to hold the last gasp of breath, praying that it hadn't been enough to harm her, her eyes began to well with tears as she could feel the burning sensation building in her chest. It blossomed and burned so quickly that she could not contain it for a moment longer as her senses were overwhelmed by the need to scream out in agony. Finally opening her mouth to cry out, all that she could muster was a weak, wailing rasp, as there was little left in her lungs with which to signal her desperate situation. S

he was on her knees again now, as she inhaled deeply, clutching at her throat with both hands, having dropped her torch – useless to her now – trying in vain to squelch the fire that now burned within her. Her next attempt to scream was cut short as another acolyte, running blindly up the tunnel from behind her, tripped over her prone form in the darkness as she panicked, desperately trying to escape the narrow passageway before she, too, fell prey to the poisonous vapours.

Anna stood in the cave on the far side of the passage, watching the sisters emerge as the shaking subsided, looking at their faces and trying to remember the order they had been in the procession. The ceiling was higher on the interior of the cave, opening into a large chamber carved smoothly from the rock by lava from some long dormant volcano. It was warmer inside the entrance, and so the vapours that rose from several pits throughout the cave quickly reached up to the ceiling and escaped through small cracks and vents in the stone above.

There was one such pit near the entrance passage, from which the vapours were caught in a cool draft – these were the vapours that flowed out of the cave and into the cold night air, creating the poisonous gauntlet that all of the sisters had to navigate. Though the quake had now ceased, the sisters were shocked and disheveled, gathering near Anna as they quickly realized several of their numbers were missing, and all were trying to ascertain who.

From the safety of the interior chamber, several sisters stepped forward and moved a wooden cover over the stone vent from which the vapours emerged near the gate – it was not perfect, but it blocked enough of the gasses to make the passage safe to traverse. As the mists dispersed, two more sisters then went back into the darkness and brought out the bodies, gently laying them side-by-side – Néni Anna looked down sadly at the beautiful, unmoving, features of her young niece. Her face had blessedly relaxed from the contorted screams of pain that had been her final moments – she imagined it was the barest hint of a smile that she could see on her pale, dry lips. After a moment of compassion, Néni Anna straightened to her full height and fidgeted with her robe.

"Gather them gently, sisters. We will pay Vaszoly his price but be quick about it – Cybille awaits."

*****New Beginnings*****

There was a small crowd at the door to the room when the Prince finally arrived. It had been the middle of the night when he had been roused by word that Lady Darellan had returned and brought a guest. He was not terribly surprised by her return - he'd dreamt about it a few nights earlier and had set a guard to watch the chamber he had seen in his dream, to await this very moment. That she had brought someone with her was surprising, though, as she had said nothing of this in his dream. As a result, he took the extra time to ensure he had dressed properly to receive guests before he made his way to the tower with his entourage.

He arrived at the chamber to see the guard now standing on the edge of a small crowd in the hallway, all peering into the room.

As the Prince of Nyirseg, he had always favoured a hunting spear over a royal scepter, and so he was in the habit of walking with a heavy metal spear whenever he was about, either indoors or walking the palace grounds. Adorned with gold, silver, and an assortment of precious stones, it was a fancy yet practical weapon, heavy enough to command attention when he wanted to do so, and this was precisely one of those times.

Striking the butt of his spear on the stone tiles of the hallway, the ten or so assembled viewers in the hallway immediately stopped what they were doing, turned, bowed, and made way to either side for him to pass. He recognized the young lady ranger Kiara in the crowd, and her fellow ranger, Ferenc, which gave him some idea of who to expect to see within the room. Reaching the door, he looked into the room, and saw that it too was filled with people. From the doorway, he immediately sought and found Lady Darellan, standing at the far side of the room, overlooking a strange stone table, with an unusually dressed man lying, asleep, on the flat stone surface.

Around the room, also looking at the figure on the table, were the assembled adventurers that he had summoned to investigate the Withering: the wizard adept, Omar Stiletto stood uncharacteristically quiet beside Lady Darellan, herself dressed quite unusually for the occasion; to Omar's right, the young ranger lord, Jason Greymantle stood staring at the person on the table as if assessing a threat for weaknesses; high priest Ralof was next to him, closest to the Prince by the door; on the other side of the table, Shagron, holy warrior of Ukko, stood as if in prayer, with his eyes closed, holding out his hand towards the young man as he slept; the mage, Torick – he had no other title that the

Prince was aware of – stood beside Shagron and completed the circle back to Dar.

Dar was just in the process of completing a channeling spell of some kind and looked up to see the Prince's arrival at the door. She smiled and greeted him with a small bow – as much as could be permitted in the crowded confines of the room.

"My Lord," she said, "we have returned, as promised."

"We are very pleased to see you return to us," he said, nodding in approval, "And who is this guest you have brought? I presume he is not our enemy – he seems far too small and frail…"

"This is one who may have the power to aid us in our cause," she answered, to which the Prince smiled and looked again at the sleeping figure.

"It seems I am the last the know this news" the Prince observed, "or at least the slowest to attend."

"They are the reason he is here, so it is fitting that they should be present on his arrival" Dar answered. "But for now, he must rest, and I have completed casting the tempus-stasis spells to keep him whole as he sleeps. We…" she said, looking to everyone in the room, including the Prince, and waving her hands, "…should leave now and let him rest here while we continue with our task at hand."

The assembled group turned to leave, pausing only because the Prince occupied the doorway.

"Very well," the Prince said, "I am looking forward to hearing everything you have to tell me about your travels."

Dar nodded from across the room, then began shepherding the others out of the room, pausing briefly as they left to give the sleeping Tibor one last look before she closed the door, leaving a very nervous-looking Caspar alone again in the hallway to guard the door.

*****Dar*****

The fourth tower in the North Wing of the palace was one of the highest towers in the palace, and the broadest – so much so that it held two chambers at its peak, rather than the more conservative single room that was easier for most tower architects to fashion at such heights. With the palace itself having three main wings – West, North, and East – and the North Wing belonging solely to the Prince and his consort, the prominence of the North Wing demanded that it have the greatest towers of all the palace, and the fourth tower on the North Wing was the greatest tower of them all. Reaching a hundred feet into the air above the highest battlements of the palace, the smooth facing of the circular walls, with barely distinguishable seams of mortar between the polished stones, gave the structure the appearance of a needle stretching skywards, reflecting most brightly the light of the dawn and dusk – resembling the polished steel of a sword in the morning, and a pillar of shimmering flame in the evening.

The tower housed the Prince's most prized possessions and was his favourite place to sit and contemplate the most serious problems that arose within his domain. For this reason, the small chamber nearest to the top of the tower where Dar had chosen to reappear with Tibor was perhaps the most secure location in all of Nyirseg, and set across the hall from another small chamber, which opened onto a large balcony. It was to this room that the Prince retired as the others departed, and to which Dar followed him.

It was late but the night sky had the feel of sunset, as the clouds which blocked the stars – although yielding no rains – reflected the light of the fires burning below, casting an eerie reddish-orange glow across the countryside.

"You have been gone for nearly a month," the Prince said angrily as Dar moved to the balcony railing beside him – close, but not so close as to appear improper for someone to stand next to their liege lord – "... much has changed since you left – none of it for the better."

Dar looked out at the panoramic view that the wide balcony offered, taking in much of the city below the palace, as well as a great deal of the surrounding countryside. Across the entire scene, flickering orange flames were everywhere – houses across the city burned through the night as townsfolk tried in vain to toss buckets of water on the burning buildings, either residents hoping to save their only shelter within the city walls, or neighbours desperate to prevent the flames from spreading to their homes. Beyond the walls of the city, patches of light in the distance told Dar that the nearby forests and plains were aflame – this broke her heart the most – and would spread out of control like wildfire on the wind. Without her even asking the Prince explained:

"After the drought, the plague of berserks, and the locusts, we have been beset in a quickening scale with curse upon curse: famine has weakened the population, pestilence and disease have sickened the weak, and rainless storms have struck the land with lightning – lightning that ignites the parched land like kindling for a bonfire! Even the smallest strikes are fanned by the winds and grow to consume everything in their path.

"In the city, we do what we can, but the wells will run dry before this is over. In the countryside, the fires spread unchecked, and we are showered daily with the ash from so many fires that it chokes out the sun."

"I will see what I can do to help with the fires, but what about the other Principalities, Your Grace?" Dar asked, "Are any of the others faring better, that we might ask for assistance? Surely Mezoseg or Sarkozy could send help?"

The Prince continued to stare forward, his dark-toned features cutting a sharp profile in the glow of the firelight – Dar could agree that he was not the most handsome man in the kingdom, but his features were strong and imposing. When he spoke again, he was solemn, for this is what he had come to contemplate this night:

"We can ask for help, but I would not expect any – the Withering is everywhere."

"…'W*ithering'*, Your Grace?" Dar asked, hearing the expression for the first time.

"We are alone, Dar. You can call me Svato here…" he said quietly, pausing only briefly before he continued, "the 'Withering' – that's what all the seers have been calling it – a type of 'judgement day' or 'reckoning' that has been set upon the land. The people are putting their faith more and more into the visions of the old seers, but they only spread tales about what they hear is happening across all Vengriya – some have even turned to ancient prophecies and lunatic writings that foretell the end of the world, and the rebirth of Sarkany – they see the hands of the gods in this…" he said, waving his arm across the eerily glowing night scene of fire, smoke and destruction, "…they do not see how Voros Vazul has returned and is manipulating all of this! A person – an ancient, apparently undying, Angyalok! – not gods or demons!"

"Nor should they, Svato," echoed Dar, "…it is far better for now that people believe this is something mysterious and supernatural – that we can do nothing about!"

"How is that better?!" he cried.

"People turn to their faith to defend them from the unknown," Dar explained, "…better that they should crowd the temples – and pay their indulgences – rather than to know that there is truly an enemy out there; an enemy who despises their very presence on their sacred lands; one that our ancestors failed to defeat the last time he rose up, and one that – at the moment – we have no idea how to stop! The people trust the gods to deal with the unknown; if they know who the true enemy is, they will turn to you for satisfaction – are you prepared for that?"

Prince Svato sighed as he leaned against the railing of the balcony. "I have missed your blunt counsel," he conceded, "the others defer to me too quickly to be of any real use… Time has passed, I know, but when last you were here, you told me you believed he was working his magic from somewhere within Vengriya - you mentioned Scarbantia…"

"Yes, to the west…" she nodded as she answered, "… there were tales of Torpek spilling out of the caves in the foothills near Lake Balaton, on the border of Sopron and Sarkozy. More stories too of Oriasok – giant folk – hunting the Torpek by night – killing anyone they found, Torpek or otherwise, just to be safe! The ancient Angyalok always liked to use the Oriasok to hunt for them."

"It's been more than a hundred years since the Torpek have been seen above ground…" said Svato, "and never has anyone ever accused them of running from anything – certainly not a fight, and definitely not from a fight with an Oriasok!"

A servant had arrived, bringing a goblet of wine for the Prince, and seeing Dar with him, quickly set about pouring a cup for her as they continued their conversation. Neither gave the servant a second glance as they spoke.

"…It does not prove anything, but if I were hunting for an interloper, that is where I would start. The Angyalok mages were always a source of chaos wherever they went, and that has been the most interesting word I have received in many months." Dar sipped her wine as she finished talking.

"It is good enough for me," said Svato. "I will ask High Vizier Tolvaj to speak with Ispan Bako tonight, and he will ensure that you and your friends are equipped with everything you need for your journey."

"Now…" Svato continued, "before the night is over and the sun dawns on what is sure to be another horrible day, please do tell me about your latest adventures!"

Dar gave him a small half-smile, and slowly took a sip of her wine as she considered just how much she would tell the Prince about her travels…

*****Introductions*****

As they were to depart the next morning, those who chose to stay at the palace were given space in an empty barracks house near the courtyard to spend the remainder of the night. Initially some turned up their noses at the accommodations, especially given other options that the palace could have afforded them, but in the end they all chose to remain together. Shagron made himself at home on the nearest straw-filled cot – a luxury compared to the many nights he had been sleeping on the ground – and was undressed and ready for sleep by the time Ralof had finished making the necessary arrangements to have someone retrieve their remaining gear from the cloister by morning.

Jason, Kiara, and Ferenc took three cots close together, and as they prepared to bed down for the night, it was clear that despite the passing of a month, Ferenc was still feeling the effects of earlier wounds. Seeing this, Ralof, joined them to offer his services to inspect the injuries and see if he could help with the healing process.

"I would highly recommend his ministries," volunteered Shagron, rubbing the scar on his side from where the assassin's dagger had done its damage back in the tunnels of Mercurum. Jason nodded and Ferenc opened his shirt to reveal the still-healing scars from the Alakvalto attack in the forest. The striped gashes of the claws had closed, but the surrounding flesh remained red and inflamed with infection.

Ralof examined the wounds with a few well-timed "hmms" and "ahhhs" and then took a few minutes to crush some herbs and ingredients to prepare a poultice, which he then spread across the original injuries, like a greenish butter on a piece of burned toast. He was covering the poultice with a bandage when Omar came over as well to see what they were doing.

"It's not the most appetizing odour," he remarked casually, "though I find the aroma very familiar to one I was given some time ago for a wound. It was effective for me – presuming it's the same salve..."

Jason looked up as he was speaking, and it took only a moment before the awareness registered on his face.

"I've seen you before!" he exclaimed. "You were in the Praetor's camp, on the Lakhani Plain, assisting an old witch woman with portents! You are not of the Imperium, but you were there – I am glad to see you survived!" The last part came out almost as an apology.

Looking equally surprised, Omar regarded Jason, narrowing his eyes as he searched his memories – resisting the urge to search the combined memories of his alter egos, knowing that this was something he had experienced for himself – and then he recalled the assembled Imperial Generals, and the young Scout Captain.

"Yes," he confirmed quietly, "My injuries were still quite fresh at that time – as were the old hag's – but as you can see..." pointing to his face and neck, "...the witch did her work well – I indeed survived..." he remarked about his injuries, thinking less about the flood. His mind began to drift as he recalled the fire where he got his scars and considered the things that Dar had revealed to him, realizing that he had yet to speak with Torick about any of that.

"I can give you the ingredients if you like," said Ralof, not realizing that Omar's mind had moved on to a new topic already, and so he was only mildly offended as Omar turned away as he finished speaking, without formally excusing himself from the conversation. Ralof chalked it up to the poor manners of youth as he finished tying the bandage around Ferenc's chest. "You'll be moving around like normal by morning," he assured the ranger.

Omar was looking across the barracks to the bed where Torick had placed his cloak and was now in the process of moving another mattress from a neighbouring cot to double up for comfort.

"I owe you an apology" he said, standing at the foot of the bed as Torick made his final adjustments to the heightened mattress.

"Apology? For what?" Torick answered, looking up from the bed as he sat on it, testing the firmness.

"I swore I would destroy you for burning the market in Mercurum; for killing my mother; for leaving me there to die…" Omar's voice was flat and monotone, as he struggled to keep down the feelings of rage that he had felt for so long, knowing now that they were entirely misplaced, but yet, he had been living with that anger – fanning it like a flame – using it to drive his studies of magic.

"Oh my…" Torick replied, lifting a single, thin eyebrow, seeming otherwise unconcerned by the news.

"I just wanted to let you know that I forgive you now – Lady Fenndragon has shown me the truth, that you are not to blame for everything that happened that night…"

Torick, still looking more interested in his sleeping accommodations than anything Omar was saying, answered with what could only be considered a sarcastic tone: "Well, I suppose I shall sleep all the more soundly tonight, knowing that I have nothing more to fear from this terrible blood feud!"

"Don't mock me!" Omar said, feeling that it would be quite easy to dislike this wizard in front of him.

Torick sighed. "I am not 'mocking' you – ugh, what a word: *'mock', 'mocking', 'mock'*…" he repeated the word over and over, "…who comes up with this stuff? just the feeling as it rolls out of one's mouth: *'mock, mock, mock, mock'*; what does that even mean? It has absolutely no sense to it! – Sorry, I digress! Look, I am absolutely certain you meant every word you said, and I'm equally certain that you are sorry for wanting to try to destroy me. *Anyone* who has ever wanted to 'destroy' me has ultimately gone away feeling sorry – you've simply saved yourself a great deal of embarrassment by realizing this before anything more came of it! You are indeed wiser than you appear and will go far in whatever it is you choose to do with your life."

Torick rose from the bed as he continued his reply, "If I might offer you a bit of advice, though – if you have a grudge against someone, you should never actually tell them – it severely impairs your chances of succeeding when you eventually decide to act out your revenge. I might also suggest that if you should decide – as in this case – to bury the hatchet, unless it's in their skull, there's no real need to tell the person you are no longer going to kill, as it comes across quite confusingly if the person never knew they were the target of your revenge in the first place…" he shrugged and scrunched his face in a uncertain grimace, "…it just makes things… *awkward*…"

"Now if you don't mind, I need to get some rest before we depart on the morrow. I might suggest you do the same as well." And with that, he signaled the end of their conversation by turning away to address the situation of the flat and uncomfortable pillow at the head of the bed, leaving Omar to glare at him from where he stood, eventually deciding that it was better to walk away than to try to argue like a child trying to get attention.

If Omar had learned one thing in his relatively short years, it was to never let people see how you really felt – feelings were a sign of weakness on the streets of Mercurum, and even though he had not yet perfected his ability to stop the flow of tears when they rose, he did try his best to hide his anger now. He turned and slowly walked back to the cot he had chosen for the night, thoughts spinning in his head, so jumbled that he was not entirely sure they were his own.

He didn't object to the ideas he was seeing, but he felt the strangeness and familiarity at the same time that he recognized from the stitching. True, he was only fourteen, and others may not be intimidated by a youth such as he, but he had wisdom beyond his years; wisdom that told him that Torick was always going to be his rival – always – and he would indeed surpass his power in time – somehow, he swore to himself he would find a way! The voice in his head told him this would be so. It was a comforting voice, clearer now than it had ever been before, and he was glad to listen to what it had to say to him…

*****Vaszoly*****

The cave was cold when Vazul woke, and he was immediately grateful for the heavy fur blankets of the crude bed carved into a nook in the wall. He could feel this rather than see it, as there was no light, and the pitch darkness was absolute – even to his angyalok eyes. He lay shivering for some time, trying to rub some warmth back into his fingertips, which were numb and clumsy, much like his mind felt after such a long journey.

We should find some light, he thought to himself, reaching out with his mind, raising his right arm and feeling the heat flow from his core, out through his arm, and into the darkness, seeking out the flammable wick of the nearest candles and sparking them to life. Sitting up on the edge of the nook, he rubbed his eyes and scanned the room; spotting the fire pit in the center and waving his arm once again, he brought it to life with a flare of light and flame. He wrapped the bearskin blanket around his shoulders and walked over to the fire, quick stepping with his bare feet on the cold stone floor, in a display that he was sure would be entirely unbefitting someone with his reputation. Still, the floor was indeed cold, and he was glad to get quickly onto the small carpet near the fire pit, taking a seat on a small stool from which he could warm himself. As he did, he took some time to gaze around at the strangely furnished chamber that he had found himself in, trying to assess just where he had arrived.

"I was not expecting you so soon!" came a wizened, old voice from the darkness at the edge of the room. Vazul turned to his right and stared harder into the dark, although despite his turning away from the fire, the image of the flickering flames still danced in his eyes, obscuring his vision beyond the perimeter of the lighted area.

"And we were not expecting to arrive here at all!" he responded. "Tell us, what is your name, and where is this place?"

"So many questions, so many demands; what a rude guest we have welcomed into our house!" the voice replied. "How strange it is that the great and wonderful Voros Vaszoly, greatest and most powerful of all the Angyalok, should enter under our roof and yet still be so lost," the female voice continued, this time coming from his left.

He turned to follow the voice, and this time was able to see the shambling, hunched form of an old crone moving forward out of the shadows, leaning on a small wooden cane, her face covered by an old shawl of torn grey cloth. More candles began to flicker to life around the cave, which seemed to expand as the light grew, illuminating a vast chamber, filled with an eclectic mix of magical relics and basic home furnishings. Vazul ignored much of the scene as he focused on the old crone, narrowing his eyes into a thoughtful squint as he considered her form and her movements as she circled the outer edge of the chamber, moving slowly around until she was directly in front, but still many yards away from him.

"We are happy to see that you still remember us – blood of your blood. You have nothing to fear from us, old woman," Vazul cautioned, "We have no interest in your trinkets and would just as soon be on our way."

"Oh, I'm sure you would," she replied, "You are very busy – yes, indeed – which is why I imagine you have forgotten about your barátok…" she paused,

"…your family…"

"…and even your brethren!"

She had stopped moving around the room and was slowly approaching him now, staring at him across the flames of the fire pit.

"My dear Louhi," he said apologetically, "How could we ever forget about you? You are our patron; our muse; our 'ihlet' – inspiration!"

He spread his arms as if to welcome an embrace, to which the old woman scowled.

"You have been up to dark things, Vaszoly – and you have been very secretive about it!" she scolded him, "Scurrying around in the dark, you've made your plans and cast your magicks at the land… but you are not the only one who lives in the dark here…" She had closed the distance to the fire pit, and stood across from Voros Vazul, staring at him with her glazed white eyes, as if looking through him.

"We have never made a secret of our ambitions," he answered her accusations, "We have simply had no one to share them with!"

Louhi was silent for a moment, so he continued.

"Where was our 'family' when we were banished for wanting nothing more than to reclaim our lands from the Avar?! They said they came in peace, and we shared our glories with them – our wisdom, our magicks – where were our brethren when we were stabbed in the back by our new 'friends'? Usurped by our own teachings, chased from our homes – the elders retreated to their hidden refuges in the mountains and whispered that *'they were tired of this world'*… Liars! These are the lies that the defeated tell themselves when they are forced to flee the field! They let themselves be driven out by invaders that should have been our slaves – not our betters!"

"The Avar channeled dark secrets that your brethren did not want to corrupt themselves with," she interrupted, "they chose to leave rather than lose more than just their lives – their very souls – in a battle over what? A piece of ground. Look around you – there are many pieces of ground in this world, enough for all to share!"

"Like a herd of sheep *'choose to leave'* when the farkas are at the door? Bah!" He scowled back at her. "They fled when they should have fought! We stayed; we fought; and they left us to the wolves!"

"And yet here you are…"

"Yes, here we are – freed by our own hand, and free to do what we must! Whether our so-called brethren thank us for it or not, we will ensure that our race is not confined to the realm of myth and legend! We will cleanse this land of the vermin that infect it like a disease!"

"Yes, we have seen your workings – like the plagues of old you did smite the land with all manner of afflictions – and yet the Avar persist… they are more stubborn than you thought, perhaps?"

"This, this is nothing!" he gloated, "…this is but the appetizer; let them have their day of rain to cleanse their pallet; we will serve the main course soon, and it will cleanse the world of their presence once and for all!"

"You would destroy everything just for the sake of your revenge?" Louhi asked calmly, as if curious but unconcerned…

"We would. You know us better than anyone… We were once so much more than we are today, filled with a glorious legacy and driven to a destiny of greatness. The Angyalok were the guardians of a rich history – musicians, scribes, poets, hunters, crafters, dancers, philosophers, builders – and we, we were the ones they trusted to keep them safe. We were guardians, protectors, keepers of the faith – but they broke faith with us. They told us to 'stand down' and bid the younger folk to enter our lands, to grant them our peace, our protection. We warned them, we warned them all…" He was staring into the fire as he remembered…

"We had seen them before they came to our lands – we knew they were barbarians, and cruel—but still we were told to stand down. So much now has changed – so many have been lost… there is so little now that remains for us to protect… so little that keeps us from failing at out charge completely! But you know this – you know us – we will do whatever we must to achieve our ends." His voice was rising as he spoke, "We will warn you only once – do not interfere in our plans again! There are things yet to be done – they have brought an interloper into the game that we must now deal with, and we have wasted enough time here explaining ourselves to you."

He turned as he finished speaking, dropping the fur blanket, and stepping up to the edge of the fire.

"Stay out of our way, Louhi, and we will stay out of yours. We have both been at this longer than any of these wretched Avar, and we will be at it long after they are gone – don't forget that when you consider whether or not you can resist the urge to meddle in things!"

His tone was more relaxed now, and she could sense that he was preparing to leave, but remained silent, letting him continue to enjoy the sound of his own voice.

"You are wise, Louhi, and have seen much. We hope we can talk more when the world has returned to as it once was, and we are at peace again with our nature. Perhaps then even you can put aside your disguises and walk the earth as you did when we first met?"

"Keep your silver tongue to yourself, my dear Vazul," she demurred, "I am no damsel to be swayed by soft words – there are too many voices inside your head for even you to keep straight, but I know them all, and I will take my own counsel on what is best for the world."

"Have it your way!" he answered curtly, and with a small wave of his hand, almost is if he were saying goodbye, he stepped forward into the fire, which flared up into the air and then settled back into the pit in an instant. Even Louhi's eyes needed a moment to adjust to the sudden brightness, but she knew without needing to see that he was gone.

She had learned much from this dangerous intervention.

Intercepting his journey home was not an easy task, nor was tempting his wrath, but even though their conversation was brief, she had learned a great deal about his plans – much that was troubling and needed to be considered, studied. There was something else – something coming that she could not yet see. Indeed, she was giving this a great deal of consideration as she shuffled across the cave to lie down in her bed. She was tired from the effort of the channeling, so much so that her head had barely touched the straw pillow before the sounds of her snoring echoed around the cave, and one might believe she didn't have a care in the world…

*****The Searchers*****

The following morning, they found the Prince was true to his word – their horses and belongings were ready and waiting for them in the palace courtyard, along with three additional pack animals carrying food and supplies provided by Ispan Bako, who stood in the courtyard himself, holding the reins of the lead horse of the supply. Though the presence of the princely palace made Ascanium the capital of Nyirseg, the Ispan was not always involved in palace affairs, and so any opportunity to be present in the service of the prince was always an opportunity to win favour with the court. Unfortunately for Ispan Bako, the prince was not present this morning to see them off.

Dar joined them shortly after breakfast, looking like she had slept very little through the night, but prepared nonetheless to ride with the assembled company. Dressed and fed, there was little for the adventurers to do but mount up and depart, without any fanfare or acknowledgment of the grandeur of their quest. Omar was perhaps the most disappointed of the group at this development and said as much.

"I would have thought the prince would have come to see us off on our journey at least – after all, we're doing this to save his kingdom…" he said aloud as they began to ride out the palace gates, moving from the solid stone tiles of the palace to the cobblestone pavers of the city streets.

"Bah!" Shagron retorted, "Who needs to waste time with all the ceremony, pomp, and circumstance that you have to follow whenever someone with a crown on their heads shows up! And by the way, this is a *'principality'* that we're saving, not a *'kingdom'* – speaking of which, can someone tell me if he is actually a *'Prince'*, or an *'Arch-Duke'*, and just what the difference is these days?"

"Does it really matter?" added Jason, "all royals are the same – they wear crowns to keep their heads from getting too large!" He laughed, as did Kiara and Ferenc, who rode along behind Jason in single file.

"How is your chest feeling?" Ralof asked quietly as Ferenc rode up beside him.

"Incredible!" he replied, "I feel as good as new this morning, and could hardly see the scars when we removed the bandages. You have done fine work, brother Ralof!" to which Ralof nodded and smiled as Ferenc rode ahead to help clear the road on their way to the main gates.

There were few people about this early in the morning, except for those who had nowhere else to sleep. It had rained overnight while they were sleeping – a long-needed and heavy rain, that helped to douse the many fires across the city and replenish some of the wells. Even those caught out in the open seemed to be cheered by this event, evident in the smiles and greetings they received as they rode briskly though the winding streets of the city.

There was more of an armed presence when they arrived at the city gates, including two rather large ballista, positioned to fire directly at anything that put itself in the way of the main gate. After exchanging a few puzzled glances, the Ispan spoke up to explain.

"The days are mostly peaceful, but at night, after the gates are closed, the plague-born grow bolder and will gather to try to find a way in. We normally wait till later in the day before opening, but in this case, we will clear a path for you across the ditch, and hopefully speed you on your way without incident."

Jason looked around at the ballista crews winding back the screws to prepare to fire, and then surveyed the assembled foot soldiers who were on duty in case anything went wrong. His gaze was drawn upwards to the battlements of the low stone gatehouse that arched over the large wooden gate, beyond which an iron portcullis held back a throng of groaning, shambling plague-born, growing more active with the increased activity coming from within.

This sound was mixed with the grunting and groaning that came as the soldiers hefted large stones up to the battlements and let them fall to the ground on the other side of the iron bars, crushing and discouraging more than a few of the disease-ridden mob, giving them some room to open the gates and lift the portcullis before any might try to rush through. His eyes stopped wandering when he locked with a familiar face atop the gatehouse walls, recognizing the hate-filled stare of General Vassilya – now Vizier Vassilya – glaring back down at him, her personal guard arranged around her, echoing the sentiment. Jason looked away, though he remained nervous enough to never quite let her out of his sight.

The guard captain barked a command, and the two sides of the wooden gate were pulled open quickly, as the portcullis was ordered raised at the same time. This seemed to surprise some of the plague-born, who had retreated a few steps and were now looking up and preparing to surge forward. Before they could, another bark from the captain sent two large iron missiles hurling forward from the ballista, plunging straight into the assembled mass of diseased flesh that crowded the roadway before the gate. Several were skewered outright and sent flying backwards as the bolts flew straight and true, leaving none standing in their path. Those that were not struck directly were knocked into the low ditch on either side of the road, into which soldiers on the wall dropped more stones.

The screams of the wounded were almost drowned out by the creaking noise of the windlass turning as the ballista crew began the slow process of reloading the giant weapon. The guard captain waved the riders forward to the now cleared roadway, taking advantage of the momentary carnage so they could ride out without any obstruction before the disoriented creatures could regain their feet.

Jason wasted no time in spurring his horse forward, followed by Kiara, Ferenc, and the others, making sure to watch his head as he passed under the gatehouse, should Vassilya seem poised to drop a rock on him as he rode by – she didn't, to his relief. They rode past the two spent ballista bolts after a no more than a few strides and couldn't help but stare at the impaled bodies held firm by the cold iron, some of them still squirming like worms on a hook – it was a disturbing sight for most of them, and not one they would likely soon forget. Neither that nor the sound of the heavy gates scraping closed behind them, and the portcullis as it locked them out with a crash of finality.

As much as it had rained overnight within the city, the landscape beyond the walls was entirely unchanged from the night before. Smoke from the burning forests in the distance loomed high in the sky, blocking the morning sunrise and casting an unnatural orange glow over the land with the pale light that filtered through the clouds. The dry grass nearest the city had already burned when the embers had first drifted in this direction on the wind, leaving a charred, blackened landscape on both sides of the road. Houses and villages abandoned by farmers and townsfolk as they fled to Ascanium to avoid the plagues had burned uncontrollably, leaving skeletal frames sticking up from the otherwise barren plains.

Dar looked at Torick, and as if reading her mind, he nodded, focused, and summoned a warm breeze from behind them, blowing gently, yet strong enough to allow them to travel in a channel of air along the roadway, now free from smoke and embers. This was a simple casting yet would require Torick to maintain some of his focus on the summoning for as long as they needed it. This was a simple task for him – one which Omar observed as closely as he could.

It was going to take them at least a week – if the weather held – to reach Scarbantia, in the furthest western reaches of the realm. They would have to head due west, across two rivers, and their path would take them through a small trading town on the Duna River called Aquincum by the end of the third day. From there it would be another two days to the mountain pass near the Lakhani Plain, skirting the border with Sarkozy, past Lake Balaton, and crossing into Sopron. Once across the mountains, they would turn south for another two- or three-days' ride.

They had just finished the first day of riding, stopping on the eastern banks of the Tisza – the first of the two rivers they needed to cross – and Dar was reviewing the proposed course on a crude map that she was carrying with her. She was waiting now for questions as she watched the faces of the assembled company, doing her best to read their reactions.

"Do we need to cross the Lakhani Plain?" asked Jason. "Perhaps we could follow the plains south, into Sarkozy and go around Lake Balaton to the south, and approach Scarbantia from there – the terrain will be flatter, easier on the horses," he suggested.

"True, but we have been hearing rumblings out of Sarkozy recently that do not bode well for anyone from Nyirseg caught travelling in their lands. They have been hard pressed by the plagues and are desperate. It is best to avoid the region entirely" Dar answered.

"I would be just as happy to steer clear of Mercurum to the south as well" offered Shagron, adding, "Although I understand why you might want to avoid the Lakhani Plain – I have heard that it is haunted now by the ghosts of the Three Legions, and I don't imagine they hold you in very high regard!" he finished with a laugh, looking at Jason.

"No, I don't suppose they do – good thing I don't believe in ghosts! Or goblins, or boogey-men under my bed!" Jason responded with a friendly smile. Ferenc shifted uncomfortably at this, looking over Jason's shoulder.

"A lot of time has passed since you were last there," Dar said, directing her comments at the three former legionnaires, "I'm sure there is nothing to worry about – it will be the fastest route, and we need to move quickly."

"Right, you heard the lady." Shagron concluded things; "Let's get a good night's rest – we have a lot of hard riding ahead of us. I'll take first watch."

"Wake me for second," offered Jason.

"Third!" called Kiara, jumping in before Ferenc, as if it were a competition, and drawing a scowl from Ferenc for her efforts.

It was late on Kiara's watch when she heard the howls.

Morning was not far off, but everyone was still sound asleep as the sky was beginning to show the hints of brightness that signaled the coming dawn. She was stoking the embers of the fire – it had burned down through the evening, though she had been careful to ensure the embers still had enough spark to re-ignite the fire for preparing breakfast in the morning. It had been silent all night on the plains, with very little wildlife remaining after the plagues, drought, and locusts destroying the once plentiful grazing that supported the great herds of auroch and bison that the region was legendary for, which made it all the more disturbing when Kiara heard the first howls. If they were used to hunting the large herds, and the herds had left for greener pastures, then whatever was howling would be looking for food, and they were the only things alive on the plains that she had seen.

The second time she heard the howls, she could tell they were definitely closer. The horses began to get skittish at their pickets, also sensing that something was approaching, and she decided to start waking people.

Grabbing Jason by the shoulder, she shook him awake then moved on to Ferenc. There were the usual protests and questions from the rudely roused team, to which she quickly responded to get their attention: "We've got company!" she announced to those who were awake enough to hear, as Shagron woke Ralof and the snoring wizards.

They all heard the howling this time.

"Farkas," she told them, "a pack by the sound of it, and they're getting closer."

They quickly set about packing their gear and saddling the horses, eager to be on their way. The plains were just that – flat and clear, and the rising sun was quick to cast long shadows on the gathering shapes coming their way from across the dried landscape.

"We scouted the river before we camped…" Ferenc advised everyone as they were grabbing their gear, "we have to go south maybe another mile to the nearest ford. Don't put on anything heavy in case you fall in the river – the river won't be very deep, but it will drag you down…" he warned. Shagron sighed when he heard this, putting down the heavier pieces of his field plate and chainmail, placing them back in his pack. Grudgingly he finished buckling his gambeson, threw his pack on the trail horse and mounted Gypsy with only his leather leggings and boots instead of even the mail shirt that he would have preferred – no point in drowning just because of a few wild dogs, he supposed, but he still felt naked without wearing something sturdier than the quilted padding of the gambeson!

Despite being up last, Torick, Omar and Dar were the first to be mounted and ready to go, having less heavy gear to worry about than the others. Ralof attended to the pack horses as the others mounted up and they began to ride south along the riverbank. There was some light brush and tree cover along the bank, and so they found themselves weaving to and from the water's edge as the path permitted, always staring down a pack of farkas that matched pace with them from perhaps a hundred yards out.

It was hard to get a count as they dropped in and out of view with the terrain, which was a little more interesting this close to the river, with ruts and ridges carved out of the banks by years of seasonal flooding and erosion. Nevertheless, they counted at least twenty animals to be in the pack, which was a number they might have considered dealing with, under normal circumstances.

These, however, were not normal circumstances.

The farkas had gathered in numbers as they broke camp, and in the new light of the morning, it was easier to see that these were not ordinary creatures.

"I have not seen the berserk plague infect animals, just people…" Jason remarked, "…until now."

"Berserk or not, let's hope they can still die!" replied Kiara, loosing an arrow from her composite bow as they rode, narrowly missing one of the pack. "Damn!"

"I don't know…" said Ferenc, guiding his horse with his knees to the left side of the party to get himself a clear shot, "I think you may be losing your killer instincts," he remarked to Kiara, pulling back his own composite bow – pausing only briefly to feel the stretch in his mostly-healed chest wound – and letting loose a shot that struck home on the hind quarters of a farkas. With a yelp, the injured animal dropped back in the pack, but continued to follow their pace. Ferenc spared Kiara a smile, taking pride in his marksmanship.

"Nice," she acknowledged, "but not a kill; barely even a flesh wound by the look of it, so don't hurt your arm patting yourself on the back!"

"Come along, ladies!" barked Jason, spurring the two rangers to hurry up as the rest of the group was pulling ahead, "We don't need to waste time killing wild dogs just to risk an injury to one of us that would slow us down!"

"Well then why don't one of these great wizards we have with us just blow them up or something impressive like that?" Kiara retorted smartly, to which Jason didn't really have a reply. She did see Dar look back at her from the head of the column, but nothing more was said as Dar returned her attention forward and spurred her horse on harder to make for the ford.

The farkas shadowed them for the full ride to the shallows of the ford, keeping their distance from the rangers' bows, but still clearly interested in their prey. After a short way, the river widened at a small bend, doubling in width to more than two hundred spans, which also lowered the water level and reduced the current significantly, permitting them the opportunity to cross. The farkas, still frothing at the mouth, followed them down to the embankment as the horses plowed into the slow-moving waters to make their crossing.

The water level came up to their saddles at the deepest point, almost sweeping Omar from his mount at one point, as the horses balanced between walking and swimming, but they all made it across safely. Looking back from the far side, they could see the hungry pack milling about on the opposite bank and howling, frustrated by their escape and unwilling to swim for a meal, at which point it only took a few moments for the hungriest of the pack to turn on the wounded member of the pack, limping from Ferenc's arrow, and quickly making a meal of the injured animal, to the delight of the rest of the pack.

Kiara was still watching the savagery of the feeding in the distance when she sensed Dar's horse come up beside her and Ferenc.

"The magicians here do have great power," she told them, "but we also possess enough wisdom to know when to use it, and when we can perhaps spare the lives of some innocent, hungry animals just by riding out of their territory." She then turned her horse and walked back to the head of the small column, and led them off at a slow walk, allowing the horses to catch their breath after their early morning pursuit.

Kiara looked at Ferenc, who, feeling suitably admonished, lifted his eyebrows, pulled on the reins and spurred his horse to follow the group as they continued on the trail.

"Hmmph," was all Kiara could say, turning her horse and falling in as rear guard behind the pack horses.

*****Caspar*****

It was still early in the morning as Caspar walked across the palace courtyard, fresh from the barracks where he was pleased to have had a peaceful night's rest. He nodded politely to some of the palace servant girls as he made his way to his post, guarding their newly arrived guest in the fourth tower of the North Wing. What had been a very mundane and almost punishing assignment was now the most highly regarded post in the palace, and rumours abounded about the identity of the man who had returned with Dar from her travels.

Overnight, he was almost a celebrity in his own right, and found himself to be the object of a great deal of attention, from his peers in the guard company as well as from a number of courtly ladies who frequented the taverns – he had gone from the loneliness of drinking alone to never having to buy another drink with his own coin ever again, so long as he had some new tale or interesting tidbit of information to share about their new visitor – and he was happy to make the most of this opportunity.

The palace servants often enjoyed relaxing in each other's company in the tavern directly beside the main gate of the palace – so much so that they had a separate entrance through the palace wall, specifically for palace servants, so they could come and go with discretion. It wasn't officially part of the plan for the palace, as it completely violated the security of the palace walls and guards, but it was well known to the locals, and the palace governors seemed okay with the idea that the servants be discreet in their pleasures.

He was trying to be discreet himself, but with the importance of his posting, well, let's just say: two different young ladies in the span of two nights – and one of them was even an underservant to one of the royal consorts' personal handmaidens! Indeed, he was in a good mood as he strode through the palace to reach the North Wing and ascended the stairs of the fourth tower.

His mind this morning was on a red-haired lass he had just passed in the courtyard, who had smiled at him. He hadn't seen her before – she must be new – but he was certainly hoping she would be at the tavern tonight!

Reaching the chamber where Dar had arrived two nights earlier, he approached the night shift guard, saluted him with a smile, and was greeted with one in return – his newly enjoyed popularity also seemed to extend to Laszlo as well, as the only other guard who shared the privilege of this assignment, and he, like Caspar, had been taking full advantage of it!

With the changing of the guard complete, Caspar settled into his routine – opening the door before Laszlo left to ensure their guest was still present, asleep, and undisturbed – and releasing his friend from his charge. Though it was early, and Laszlo was sure to be tired after taking the night shift, he didn't doubt for a moment that the old guardsman wouldn't be heading straight for the Queen's Cup, as there would no doubt be other servants finishing their shift that would be eager for the latest updates, and Laszlo was quite likely to parlay his tales – true or otherwise – into an intimate encounter at least once before he returned to the barracks for breakfast!

Sometime later Caspar was still lost in his daydreams when he heard footsteps approaching from around the corner. Snapping alert, he was very pleasantly surprised to see the young red-haired maid that he had seen that morning in the courtyard. He was not able to contain his smile, which she returned with apparent enthusiasm as she approached. She was carrying a small wash basin, with a pitcher of warm water resting inside, and an assortment of small cloths draped over her arm.

"Good day, sir," she greeted him, still smiling.

"And to you, m'lady," he replied politely.

She blushed and demurred, "Oh, you know I am not a 'lady'! You are either too kind or too cruel, good sir, I don't know the which!"

She was perhaps eighteen, certainly no more than twenty – at least ten years his junior – with pale skin and flush lips that almost matched the bright red of her hair. She flashed her dovish eyes at Caspar in a way that he had seen often in the tavern of late, and he could suddenly feel his interest stirring in a way that was most unprofessional for a guard while on duty, and yet, he could only feel that this was just one more perk of the job these days!

"And what can I do for a beautiful lass this day?" he asked, relaxing to lean on his spear.

"Oh, I'm sure we can get to that after I'm done with bathing our guest," she replied.

"Bathing?" Caspar asked curiously.

"Of course! The Prince left specific instructions with the housemaster for us to properly care for his guest, including washing and a new shirt," she stated as if from memory, "apparently the Prince felt there was a bit of an 'aroma' in the chamber when he was present the other night, and thought we should do our best to freshen things up before his next visit. I don't think our guest will mind – being under a spell and all…" She winked at Caspar, "…then we can get on to other business."

"Right…" he paused, waiting.

"…Milly," she answered.

"Right then, Milly," Caspar said as he looked down at her, being at least a foot taller in height, and decided there was no threat here, and besides, it was ordered by the Prince and housemaster, so he nodded and turned to open the door for her. She paused as he did so, looking into the room at the large stone table that dominated the center of the small chamber. Tibor's sleeping form lay still upon the table, with his feet to the door.

Both Caspar and Milly took a moment to stare at the faint glistening of the protective aura that glowed around his form, forming a small protective dome over the table, arcing around his unmoving form, looking like nothing more than faint, silvery dust-motes hanging in the air. This was the nourishing spell that Dar had cast to preserve and protect Tibor during his deep sleep, ensuring he would need neither food nor drink while she persisted in channeling power to the aura.

Milly finally collected herself and apologized to Caspar, feeling silly for being awestruck by the magic on display, and stepped into the room to carry out her duties. She glanced once more as Caspar, giving him a quick smile as he closed the door.

Alone with Tibor, Milly turned to a small alcove on the right and set the basin down. Draping the cloths over the edge of the basin, she poured half the contents of the pitcher into the basin and set the pitcher on the floor. Taking two of the cloths, she wet one thoroughly, keeping the other for drying, and turned to the Prince's guest. She began by wiping his face, neck, and hands, applying the wet cloth, then drying afterwards. She glanced once to the door as she thought she heard voices passing by outside but continued with her work. Removing his shirt, she wiped his chest, dried it, then, after a quick glance at the door, she bent her head into his left armpit, placing his arm around the back of her head, and straightened herself up, raising Tibor's limp form upwards. She paused for a moment as she could see the tiny flecks of silver that made up the protective bubble swirl in the air as she moved him upright, although the bubble itself remained intact, as if bound to the table and not to Tibor. She proceeded to wipe his back, taking time to examine his back, especially the back of his neck, as if searching for something, noticing the paleness of his skin now that it was upright and outside of the tinted hue of the magic shell, and she could see him in the natural light of the lanterns in the chamber.

Drying him off, she replaced his shirt with a warmer undershirt and a leather tunic, and then gently lowered him back onto the stone table exactly as she had found him. She finished quickly with his feet, placing new leather boots on his feet, and neatly stowed his shirt and shoes in the alcove with the basin, leaving his jeans in place as she was unsure how to remove them. Cleaning up quickly, she emptied the remaining water into the drain on the floor, stacked it in the basin with the cloths, and made her way to the door, knocking softly for Caspar to open it for her.

She smiled again as she left, promising to see him later that evening when he was finished his watch, and he grinned from ear to ear, still holding the open door as he watched her leave down the hallway, waiting until she was out of sight around the corner before he broke his gaze. He took a quick glance inside the room to make sure everything was as it should be before he closed the door, when he paused.

He quickly observed the new shirt and boots – he felt they looked more appropriate now than what he had first been wearing; his leggings were still unusual but that was not what caught his attention. Looking at Tibor from the door, he could see his head was now turned to his right side, looking towards the wall, instead of up at the ceiling. Curious, he noted, but then, Milly had just been washing him, and was likely to have moved him in the process, so this was not something to report. He waited a moment, staring for any sign of movement, and not even seeing his chest rise or fall from breathing, he slowly stepped back out of the door and closed it behind him. Smiling to himself, he went back to his daydreaming, looking forward to his visit to the Queen's Cup this evening!

Milly looked back at Caspar as she went around the corner, throwing one final smile his way before she disappeared from his sight. Moving down the hall a little further, she stopped at the next door, and looking both ways to make sure the coast was clear, she opened the door and stepped into the chamber, closing the door quickly and quietly behind her.

The door had barely closed when she let the facsimile spell drop, and she leaned with her back against the door and faced the animal-skin entrance of the small, squalid hut that was jammed into the chamber. There was barely enough room for the chamber door to open, but thankfully Louhi was small, and her frail hunched figure shuffled the short two steps she needed to move from the door of the chamber into the entrance of her travelling hut, pulling back the skins and making herself comfortable for the trip home.

She had seen all that she needed to see, and even had a little giggle as she wondered how long the handsome guard would wait for her at the tavern that night! She was still laughing when she emerged again from the hut, into the cave she called home…

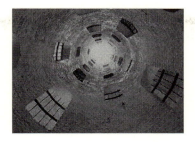

*****Aquincum*****

Shagron was on his back, looking into the jaws of the angriest farkas he had ever encountered, pinned to the ground by one massive forepaw as he stretched his chain mailed arm deep into the creature's mouth, trying to keep it from tearing into his face. He struggled to pull his blade from the dead farkas on the ground to his right and was grateful for the heavy chain links that kept the creature's razor-like teeth from ripping into the flesh of his arm – which wasn't to say it didn't hurt like hell when the damn thing chomped down each time, but at least his arm was still attached!

The attack had come at dawn, just as they were preparing to break camp – Ralof had insisted on a hot breakfast for once, being tired of so many days of cold rations and fortunate to have come across enough kindling for a fire on the barren plains.

The pack had been stalking them since the river – they must have been starving to have dared swimming the river to keep pace with the party of adventurers, and even more likely incited to action by the intense aromas of the fried meats prepared by the reverend brother – and their attack was a stealthy one. Ferenc and Kiara had barely enough time to raise the alarm before the attackers had burst out of the tall grass and swept into their camp. If they had attacked any sooner, they would have caught everyone completely unprepared, which would have made their predicament even direr.

As it was, Shagron had been able to stop one farkas with a stab of his sword before a second one had borne him down to the ground, and he could see that Jason, Ferenc and Kiara were back-to-back-to-back, surrounded by three more of the creatures, while Ralof was swinging his mace at two more, seemingly standing guard over the frying pan that still held their breakfast, sizzling by the fire.

He could not see any of the wizards and feared that they had been victims of the same razor-sharp fangs, bereft of the protection of any real armor.

Giving up on pulling his sword free, he released his grip on the hilt and moved his free hand to his waist, pulling a small dagger from his belt. Then, being careful of his fist and arm still being halfway down the creature's throat, jammed the small blade up, through the neck of the beast and into the base of its skull. Shagron closed his eyes as the hot lifeblood of the crazed animal sprayed across his face and shoulders – with barely a whine, the farkas immediately relaxed its efforts to bite his arm and dropped its full dead weight onto his chest, forcing out an uncharacteristic groan from Shagron, as he then struggled to lift the large corpse off of himself and regain his footing. Dropping the dagger and pulling his sword from the chest of the first farkas, he surveyed the scene to see where he was needed most: the horses were panicked but unharmed; Jason and Kiara had dispatched two of their opponents and seemed ready to finish the last two with Ferenc, so he moved forward to help Ralof. Although he was defending himself capably from two farkas, he was not making any progress with dispatching either one of them – a stand-off, of a sort – until Shagron stepped in. Two swings made short work of one, while Ralof was able to brain the other with a focused swing of his mace.

"Thank you," wheezed the aged cleric, as he took a moment to catch his breath, looking around for the next wave to come. "Where are the wizards?" he called out to Shagron's back, as he had already turned again to look for a new target, only to see Kiara already finishing off the last farkas that had been circling Ferenc and Jason.

"There," said Shagron, pointing out to the far edge of their camp, where Omar, Torick, and Dar were visible about fifty yards out, facing away from the camp.

Moving carefully in their direction, watching the tall grass for any movement, Shagron and Jason called out to the wizards as they approached…

"Sorry to have woken you all so early, but I don't suppose you could have lent us a hand over here?" Shagron shouted sarcastically.

Only Dar bothered to spare him a glance over her shoulder, offering no reply until he closed the distance and joined them.

Though the land was flat, and generally referred to as "The Great Plains", as they were nearing the second river crossing the land was becoming a little more undulating, although the dips could sometimes be hidden by the unbroken expanses of tall grass. This was something that became more apparent to Shagron – and the three rangers coming up behind him – as he reached the spot where the wizards were standing.

Beyond them, the ground sloped down and away in a gentle slope, dropping only a few feet, not rising again for almost a mile. It wasn't much of a dip, but it was enough to hide a person walking upright from view. It was from this direction that the farkas had come, approaching without being seen until they were almost on top of the travellers, as they could see from the trails in the grass leading back toward the campfire.

Looking out beyond, into the lowland area, the tall grasses were trampled and flattened, broken by the steps of nearly a hundred farkas, which had all been tracking towards their campfire.

Shagron tensed up for a moment, ready to draw his sword again, until he realized that they were all lying in various states of death or dying – most had been grabbed and entwined in long grass, which seemed to shimmer and flow like a million snakes, entrapping their victims and squeezing the life for them A few had been consumed by flames, leaving ashen scars on the fields, and others had been impaled by some unseen object and left to bleed out scarlet on the brown grass.

Shagron was almost speechless as he looked out over the field of bodies, summing up his thoughts with a single word.

"Damn!" he said softly.

"I have seen wizards work their magic before," added Jason, "but never outdoors, on a scale such as this..." his voice trailing off. Torick turned to head back to the camp, followed by Omar, and Dar paused to look at the others.

"It was a shame that we had to do this," she explained, "I would have preferred to let well enough alone, but they were plague-ridden and starving, and it was either us or them." She sounded truly heart-broken, looking back at the closest farkas, seeming more like a large dog now, lying prone and lifeless on the grass.

"This was but the simplest of the magicks we could have used – very effective outdoors and with large groups of enemies – not every spell is as effective, but these were simple creatures..."

She also turned and followed Torick and Omar back to the campfire, leaving Jason and Shagron to take in the scale and numbers of dead animals on the field. Shaking their heads, they rejoined their companions at the fire, where Ralof was happily portioning out the breakfast he had prepared into separate bowls for everyone to enjoy, very pleased to have saved his cooking from being spoiled!

They were packed and mounted shortly after breakfast.

"Where's Dar?" Jason asked the assembled riders, who each looked about, as if she were hiding nearby.

"I saw her sitting in the grass by the farkas while we were eating," Kiara recalled, "It looked like she was praying or meditating or some such thing..."

Jason spurred his horse gently over to the field where the animals had fallen to the wizards. He had a better vantage point from atop the horse and could see that something was different as he approached: the field was still spotted where the bodies had lain, but nearly two thirds were now small mounds of earth and vines – vines that, from a distance, almost seemed to be moving, as if reclaiming the fallen animals.

"There were too many bodies in one place," Dar said, standing beside his horse. Jason almost fell out of his saddle when he heard her voice unexpectedly appear beside him like that. He and his scouts were legendary for getting the drop on others and took it as a personal badge of honour to never allow themselves to be taken by surprise, and yet he had no idea she was there until she spoke.

"Dammit, woman!" he exclaimed, more upset with himself than with her, "I going to have to give up calling myself a Scout if you keep doing that to me! What were you saying?"

"The farkas – there were too many dead in one place – it was not natural – and it would have attracted too many scavengers to the area. We are getting close to the city, and it would not be well to leave the bodies out in the open. Once the scavengers came, they would turn to the city for their next kill, and that wouldn't be right."

Jason was about to respond when he was interrupted by a large rain droplet on his face – he wiped it away and looked at the rapidly gathering clouds, changing what had appeared to be a nice ride on a clear, sunny morning into a long day ahead of slogging it out on a muddy road.

"Great," he muttered to himself, as he pulled on the reins of his mount and prepared to move out.

Aquincum was a day or two's ride north of Mercurum, and much the same as her larger sister to the south, the city's fortunes were closely tied to the river, except that where Mercurum dominated the river from a small island and spread to both shores, Aquincum was restricted to just the West bank. Much wider here, the water flowed with a strong current and enough depth to make fording impossible, and, until recently, too broad a span to make a bridge practical, so the original settlers from Sopron had simply decided to make their side the place where they would build their homes and trade crofts and left it for others to decide how best to span the mighty river.

The West bank of the river was of a higher elevation and provided a much better view of the plains to the east and gave some natural protection where the flow of the river had eroded a steep cut into the shoreline – convenient enough to dock river traders, but small enough to prevent any sizeable force from landing without coming under terrible fire from archers above. The East side of the river was deemed too far away and too difficult to cross to make for any sort of permanent settlement, so the citizens cared little for what happened there, leaving it for a few entrepreneurial sailors to try their hand at establishing various methods of crossing the river. It was too broad for barges pulled by ropes; the current too strong to push against with poles; too deep and wide for horses to swim; all in all, it was a natural defense and an engineering challenge that few had managed to solve.

The party had arrived on the East bank of the Duna around midday, though it was hard to tell for certain as the sun had been obscured the whole day by the rain clouds. A mixed blessing, the rain had soaked everyone, causing some – especially Shagron – to complain about how their chainmail was starting to rust, which drew little sympathy from the rest of the group that were wearing more appropriate loose garb and oiled leather cloaks, better suited to the change in the weather. No one complained about how the rain had settled the ash and dust from the burned, barren landscape, removing the need for everyone to wear the smothering masks across their faces, to avoid choking on the air they breathed.

Approaching the eastern shoreline, they were greeted by the plume of smoke that rose from the still-warm ashes and embers of the fires that had consumed much of the trading hub that been Aquincum. Large stone buildings, sculpted and carved, could be seen rising from the top of the far bank, presenting an elegant façade for a city that had such high aspirations, but the smoke rising from behind these structures told the real story.

Along the riverbank, there were several boats and barges tied to the shore, some in various states of decay, indicating the success or failure of their ingenuity at attempting to provide a reliable means of crossing the span of water. Several small craft were out on the water, most of which were quite small and moving under sail, like some sort of personal shuttle service – not at all suited to moving eight people and a dozen horses. There seemed to be only one option for them to consider when it came to judging just which of the larger barge services was still operating, and they had a chance to observe it in action as they approached.

The sign near the wooden shack said "Bartok's Ferry" in simple black painted lettering, and the operators could be seen out on the river. They had just finished loading and launching a large-sized barge, carrying a rather small load of something in bales on the center of the craft. Two burly-looking sailors poled the barge away from the small wooden dock that extended only a few feet out from the bank, pushing them out into the current of the river. From there, another man at the tiller steered the barge out, fighting the flow of the river to carry them out into the water. They could see one of the men notice their approach and try to alert his comrade about the arrival of new customers, but his mate brushed him off, pointing across to the far shore, and motioned for the first sailor to get back to his pole.

"Looks like we just missed the ferry" Kiara noted, as the barge began to drift out into the river current.

"Maybe not…" Jason observed, "they left a mooring line attached" he said, pointing to a rope in the water.

Kiara giggled, "Silly, that's the anchor line. Look over there…" she pointed across the river, where they could see another barge departing from the opposite bank. "Not at the barge…" she explained while pointing "further down the shore – there – the mooring stone. And here, on this side as well…" Tracing the mooring line back to the shore, they could see that it was attached much further down the bank to a large marker stone, set along a path that ran down the bank.

"That is the line they use to meet in the middle" she said, as they continued to watch.

Both barges, now caught in the flow of the current, steered themselves out as far as the rope would allow, pulling tight on the large shoreline anchor, which then brought the barges on a wide sweeping curve out into the center of the river. Using the current to power their barges to the limit of the length of rope, it was clear that each cord had been carefully measured to exactly half the span of the river, so that each barge, when extended out to its maximum range, would flow downstream with the current, and if the tillerman was skilled enough, their arc would sweep out and they would meet in the middle of the river.

It had taken a few minutes, but they could now see the barges nearing one another. The crews hurried into action, throwing ropes to pull the barges together, and then, in the middle of the river, linking the barges with a heavy chain and a massive hook. There was a moment of uncertainty for those observing when they could see the heavy mooring ropes from each shore snap taut and rise up out of the water as the current now pulled both barges down, though they were held fast in place by their mooring lines and held together in the middle of the river by the anchor chains.

On board the barges, crews from both sides signaled for their respective passengers and cargo to cross between the mated craft as quickly as possible, as both barges creaked and groaned with the strain of fighting the current. Omar looked doubtfully at the weathered logs and rusted bolts, amazed that they were holding together at all, and silently hoping they would continue to hold for just a little longer…

The transfer completed, each crew gave a sign and a man from each barge swung a large hammer at a pin on each of their craft that simultaneously released the chains holding the two barges together. Free of their connection, each began to swing downriver, still anchored by the mooring lines from shore, which brought them each back to their respective shorelines in a large, graceful arc, albeit a fair distance down that bank that was half as far as the river was wide. A small stone dock had been built on each side of the river to accommodate landings, and within a few minutes, each barge was docked and unloaded of their cargo by a waiting crew on the shore and carted into a small warehouse building nearby.

"Ingenious," exclaimed Ralof, marveling at the operations, and spurring his horse down to the river to explore. As he rode by, an older man emerged from a small shack to greet the riders, pulling a broad brimmed hat onto his head to shield himself from the rain.

"Are you 'Bartok'?" asked Ferenc, remaining on his horse.

"Indeed, I am," came the reply.

"We would like to cross to Aquincum," said Ferenc, "and yours seems to be the only barge running."

"Aye, indeed it is," the old man replied with a smile.

"What is the toll?" asked Ferenc, to which the old man looked around him to scan the size of the group, and his smile widened. "What is the toll..." he repeated back to Ferenc, counting in his head.

"Come inside and have a drink while we discuss the price," he offered, bowing slightly, and gesturing to the small shack, "It will take several hours for the barges to be pulled back to their loading docks, so we have much time to discuss!" Business must have been slow, because the old man just couldn't seem to stop smiling about his potential windfall from such a large party of travelers. Ferenc dismounted and joined him – his last look back at Jason and the others gave the appearance of a man going to the gallows, as he anticipated how the one-sided negotiations were going to be, before he ducked under the low frame of the door and disappeared inside.

Crossing the river did not take long once the teams of horses on each side of the river had dragged the barges – not an easy task on the best of days, let alone with the horse struggling to find their footing in the mud being churned up by the recent rains – back upstream to their departure points once again, and everyone was able to lead their horses aboard for the trip.

It was a quiet ride – with more than a few nerves showing at the point when the barges joined in the middle of the river – as most tried to enjoy a moment to themselves looking out at the water; that is, everyone but Ferenc, who cursed to anyone he could find to listen about the extortion they had to acquiesce to from the little ferryman just to get across the river. He was not happy about the price and didn't mind letting everyone in earshot know until they had landed downriver and began the short ride back up the small trail that traced the edge of the river, back to the mid-point between the two barge piers.

Here, the city gates were cut into the rock of the steep embankment, which, now that they were closer, was clearly more of a sheer cliff of rock than a muddy embankment like the eastern side of the river, rising from the river's edge at least a hundred feet, towering over them. They had picked up an escort of city guards when they had landed, who now brought them to a pair of double-wide, heavy wooden gates, at least thirty feet wide, reinforced with iron bands, inset with metal rings that attached to chains that were used to pull the doors open and closed.

They were able to ride through the gate with still enough room for Shagron to have carried a lance at full upright and not touched the arched center of the frame. Looking up, they could see the lower spikes of a large iron portcullis, ready to be dropped at a moment's notice if there were an emergency. They went only a few paces through a tunnel equal in size to the gate, before they entered a large open area, round and at least thirty paces in diameter, where they looked up and saw the sky a hundred feet above them.

Kiara involuntarily let out a small gasp of wonder as she gazed upward at the sky, then observed the winding pathways cut into the stone that wound around the circumference of the courtyard, almost hidden behind stone railings and balustrades. Their escort seemed accustomed to waiting a few moments to let guests observe the spectacle of the gatehouse, before they ushered them to one of the two entry ramps leading upwards and around, past small storerooms of supplies, crates and barrels that dotted the cobblestone pathway, around and around; they watched as several times they could see wooden pallets being lowered from above by cranes and winches casting long ropes down the large open-air shaft, being immensely easier than trying to control rolling barrels going down the winding path.

"Going down seems easy enough," Shagron muttered to no one in particular, then adding, "I'd hate to be the poor bastard that has to roll up a barrel full of ale on a hot day!" laughing aloud as he finished.

When they reached the top, the city guards gave them a perfunctory salute, with a brief warning about some town by-laws about keeping their weapons sheathed and not intimidating the local citizenry, and they were free to go about their business. They found themselves standing at the edge of a large market square, with space to their left for animals and feed, food and supplies for human consumption to their right, and a wide path into the heart of the city leading directly ahead. Behind and above them were the large palatial buildings of the

Ispan of Aquincum and several other major nobles, plus their administration, barracks and guards. The more favourable views over the river were saved for the nobility, while the guards and administrators had the view over the city itself, though it was not much of a view these days. Every third building seemed to be burned, abandoned or otherwise uninhabitable. Of those remaining, most had seen better times, as the toll of the plague, famine, pestilence and disease had wreaked their toll here as it had everywhere else.

As they walked forward through the market, there seemed to be an abundance of foodstuffs made from every imaginable method of preparing insects – locusts in particular – as a delicacy, dessert, or something ground up to act either as a flour or breadcrumb substitute in the local diet. Jason inquired and received directions to the nearest suitable stable that could accommodate their mounts and pack animals, and then proceeded to get directions to some suitable accommodations. It was getting late in the day – waiting for the barges had eaten up most of the afternoon – and all were eager to get a hot meal and a bed, so no one really called Jason out when he led them to a tavern near the stables that boasted a faded sign, dripping water in a steady stream onto any who approached the door. The aptly named "Red Onion" was the source of many bad jokes throughout their dinner – thinly veiled sarcasm, sharp humour and layers of spicy metaphors did not leave room at the table for anyone with thin skin that night! All were groaning and ready to retire as soon as the last plate was cleared.

Everyone, it seemed, except Omar. Pulling up his hood and heading towards the door instead of the stair, he stopped when Dar called out to him.

"You're not going to get some rest?" she asked innocently.

"No," he answered quietly, "I just thought I would go for a walk."

"Would you like some company?"

"No," he said, quicker with the reply now, "I have some family in Aquincum, and thought perhaps I would seek them out before we get busy tomorrow with resupplying. I won't be long, but I would prefer to be alone. You understand... don't you?"

He didn't wait to see Dar nod before he went out the door and into the night.

*****Omar*****

Stepping out of the tavern, the street was dark, and it took a few moments for Omar's eyes to adjust after the light of the tavern. He took a deep breath – aside from the intense smell of smoke and burned timbers, it felt a lot like home, and for the first time in a long while, Omar suddenly felt homesick. He didn't tolerate the feeling for long. He wandered a short way down the street, looking for signs of activity from some of the other establishments that offered entertainment for travelers at this hour of the night, and was rewarded with seeing a few lights around the corner.

Waiting outside, his patience was rewarded when he observed a small mob of kids – none that appeared to be older than he – rush across the path of a few of the exiting patrons, clearly lightening their pockets of whatever coin they may have had left after their night of festivities. He followed the youngsters as they ran off into an alley, and then through several twists and turns in the back alleys of the town, often through rubble and across recently burned-out timbers that had been squelched by the rain earlier in the day.

They watched to be sure they weren't being followed, but Omar knew these tricks himself, and avoided detection until they had arrived at their hideout. He carefully approached until he was close enough to overhear them talking to someone about their plunders for the evening and turning over their spoils to their leader. This was the one that Omar wanted to talk to, and so he made his presence known.

There is nothing more fun – for him, at least – than scaring a bunch of people who are accustomed to being the ones doing 'the scaring'. Reactions were always unpredictable, and might vary from fear, to panic, or even bravado.

Omar was delighted to see the small crowd choose fear, racing for the closest exits as soon as he stepped out of the shadows and said "hello" – be it a door, window, or hole in the wall, the youngsters fled with a practiced panic that left the middle-aged man on the stool in the center of the room all by himself to face Omar.

Being a little more practiced in his trade, the man on the stool did not react quite the same, as he could clearly tell that Omar was not with the city guard, nor any of the personal militia of the local nobility, and so he was a little cockier in his response.

"I hope you know just what you're doing," he said in a threatening tone, "because you just disrupted several transactions that are now going to go to my competition! That's not something I take lightly to, and will need to be compensated for…"

"Fear not, brother, I am here on family business," Omar replied, sauntering up to the still-seated man in the center of the room. He followed the man's eyes as he made a slight gesture with his left hand as he approached, noting that the man saw and recognized the sign, and the expression on his face changed immediately.

"Well, you're a damn sight younger than I had expected!" he said, standing up from his stool, and looking around out of an abundance of caution, and once confirming that everything seemed clear, he added, "Right this way, m'lord" and moving to the only closed door in the room, he opened it, and led Omar down the stairway and into the darkness below.

"Good morning," Kiara called out to Omar as she came down the stairs in the morning. Kiara and Ferenc were the first ones down for breakfast and were pleasantly surprised to see Omar already at the long table in the tavern waiting for them. The tavern owner and his son – also known as the serving boy and the cook – were busy making noise in the kitchen getting the cooking fires started, after having prepared kettles for warming the wash-water for their guests. None of the other visitors – including their friends – were awake yet, so the rest of the tavern was empty, with just a few streams of light peeking into the windows between the wooden shutters that were still closed from the night before. Kiara took the liberty of opening the shutters to let in more light as Ferenc sat down across from Omar.

"I didn't hear you come in last night," Ferenc noted playfully, "Must've found yourself a good time somewhere," he teased.

Omar smiled with just one corner of his mouth. "Oh, I found something really good last night!" he answered. "Just wait till the others get down to hear it!"

They didn't have to wait long as the others soon filtered down, one or two at a time, some more awake than others, and sat down to their breakfast.

"I ha–" Omar started quietly when Ferenc talked over him.

"Omar found something last night that he wants to share with us," Ferenc announced to everyone, drawing a frustrated glare from Omar.

"Yes, as I was saying, I found something I think you will all find very interesting…" Omar began before stopping himself. He suddenly felt very odd, and it seemed that others around the table were feeling it as well. He glanced down at the breakfast they had been served, wondering if it had been spoiled, or worse, poisoned…

Shagron, Torick and Dar all let out a loud gasp, while the others could only close their eyes and put their hands to their heads, as if each were in the grip of a terrible migraine. Their vision blurred, and, seeming to feel the worst of it more so than the others, Shagron, Torick and Dar fell out of their chairs as the room spun violently – then stopped, just as quickly as it had begun. Several of the group were only just opening their eyes as Kiara saw Dar pull herself to her feet.

"This can't be happening!" Dar cried, "This shouldn't be…" as she turned from the table and stumbled to the door, past the young serving boy, who had come running when he heard their collective cries, wondering what was going on! Kiara called after Dar to wait, as she followed her to the door, confused by her reaction as much as she was by what they had all just experienced.

Bursting through the door before it had even closed, Kiara looked up & down the street, but could not see Dar anywhere. Stepping out into the street, it was only by chance that she glanced up, and for a moment, caught a glimpse of a falcon rising up, disappearing into the distance, heading east. Looking up and down the road one last time, then into the sky, Kiara went back inside. The others were getting back in their chairs and rubbing their heads like a bunch of drunkards coming home from a late-night binge – nothing that would kill you, but a damn shame to experience without at least having enjoyed the night of drinking beforehand!

"What the hell was that?" Shagron bellowed, reaching for a cup of water.

"It wasn't fun, whatever it was," muttered Ferenc into his cup.

"If it was an attack, it wasn't like anything I have ever experienced," Torick stated, then looked at Kiara, "Where's Dar?" he asked her.

"I… I don't know" Kiara answered slowly, feeling bewildered.

"You followed her out the door," Torick pressed her, "she couldn't have just disappeared…" he finished, half statement, half question.

"The street was empty, no one, just…"

"Just what?" Ferenc joined in, a little more friendly in his tone than Torick had been.

"All I saw was a bird. A falcon – I think – flying east."

"Turul!" whispered Ralof softly. The others looked at him, but he said nothing further and drank from his cup.

"So Dar is gone," Shagron concluded.

"What does this mean?" Jason asked, "Was this some kind of spell? A curse?"

"It was no spell…" answered Torick,

"…Nor was it a curse," replied Ralof with authority, as he finished off his breakfast, wiping the plate with a piece of bread before eating the last crust.

"Wait a minute…" This time it was Ferenc, looking confused, "…maybe we all drank something rotten at the same time, but does no one seem to care that our 'guide' on this journey might be an Alakvalto? – A shape-changer? – We have encountered them in the wild before and they are notoriously dangerous and not overly fond of the local population – believe me, I know!" he exclaimed emphatically, to which Jason and Kiara had to nod in agreement.

"She is not an Alakvalto" Torick replied quietly.

"How do you know? Ferenc objected.

"Because I know what she is – and definitely what she isn't…" Torick kept his tone level as he rubbed his temples, still recovering from whatever had affected them, "…She is a mage – a powerful one. But more than that, she is a Taltos…"

"A Taltos?" Omar asked, "She doesn't look like any of the druids who visited Mercurum…?"

"That's because those were not true Taltos – fakirs and herbalists, many people hawk their wares and potions as being druidic in nature, to play on the trust of the people for the old ways, but there are few of the forest lords remaining, and even fewer that live in the open after years of persecution under the Imperium. I don't know what her reasons are for working with Prince Svato, but she is definitely not Alakvalto, so you have nothing to fear on that front. What we should fear is that she may know more about what just happened and has left us in the dark…"

Torick stopped there, not wanting to speculate more about what had happened without having more information. His explanation seemed to satisfy the others, who had all returned to their seats, and sat silently for a moment, pondering what had happened, and what Dar's sudden disappearance meant for their quest. The silence was interrupted at last by a quiet word from Omar.

"So…" he started slowly, "…if we are inclined to wait for Dar to return, we might want to look around the area a bit while we are here." Shagron and Jason turned to look at him as he continued. "I had some news from a friend last night that Voros Vazul has some henchmen working out of a cave just a couple miles west of the city, disrupting caravans, looting traders, and just overall being a pain in the ass for the town when they're trying to get supplies to help weather the plagues. There's no official bounty or reward from the Ispan, but my friend tells me that we would be welcomed as heroes if we were to take care of these bandits ourselves, and the Ispan would be sure to reward us for our assistance!"

The group exchanged looks across the table, and Ralof frowned at the young boy from the other end of the table.

"I don't think we are in any rush to be 'heroes' these days – heroes die gloriously, which sounds great, but doesn't make them any less dead!" Ralof volunteered to Omar in a fatherly tone. "Nor should one seek to do any sort of good because you anticipate being rewarded for it afterwards – our faith tells us that we must do these things for the rightness of it, not for the reward!"

"So, you'll do it, even without a reward?" Omar asked excitedly, which Ralof was clearly not prepared for.

Shagron looked at Ralof, "You should have quit while you were ahead, padre!" he told him with a smile, which was met with an admonishing frown. "I suppose we can leave word with the innkeeper in case Dar returns," Shagron added, "I mean, it sounds like it won't take more than a day of our time anyway… although I need to visit the forge first – I need a few dents knocked out of my armor before we head out for Scarbantia again!"

"So just where do we find these bandits?" Jason asked Omar, who smiled and began to share the rest of what he had learned the night before…

*****Taltos*****

The peregrine falcon is the fastest bird in the world, flying at speeds up to sixty miles per hour in normal flight – almost three times that when diving for a kill – and with a good tailwind this can increase even further, making it capable of travelling distances in a span of a few hours that would take days or even weeks to cover on horseback. So it was that a certain red & black feathered falcon landed on the parapet of the fourth tower of the North Wing of the royal palace in Ascanium, just under two hours after it had taken off from Aquincum. If there had been anyone else on the roof of the tower at that moment, they would have then observed a startling – and undeniably magical – transformation as the very air around the large falcon shimmered and flowed like a mirage on a hot summer's day, and in a matter of seconds, the outspread wings became arms; the crown of feathers became hair; and the falcon was replaced by the upright form of the Taltos Priestess Lady Darellan Fenndragon, dressed and equipped as she had been the moment she stepped out of the door of the tavern in Aquincum.

Rolling her shoulders slightly as she resumed her normal form, she quickly stepped to the wooden door that led down into the tower proper (unlocked, of course, because why would anyone think there would be a need to lock a door at the top of an unscalable tower?) and let herself in. She moved with a sense of urgency – just as she had in flight, the entire time sensing that something had changed – after the flash of pain in the tavern had subsided, she felt like her senses were more alive than ever. On fire for a moment, but then, once the initial disorientation had passed, she struggled to find a way to describe the increased sense of awareness that she had of the world around her. Not a totally foreign experience to her, as her druidic talents gave her an increased sensitivity to all things natural in the world, but this was also different — it was as if she could sense what was going on in the tower, in the tavern, and in the air during her flight, all at the same time, as if she were in three places at once. And what she could sense in the tower of the palace was an awareness of the surroundings that was awake when it should have been sleeping, and that was the most troubling aspect for her!

Though no longer a bird, she practically flew down the flight of stairs until she reached the floor where the guest chamber had been prepared, emerging with such haste that she almost impaled herself on the spear that Caspar had levelled at the stairwell upon his hearing the rush of footsteps coming in his direction!

Collecting herself, and her breath, she held out her hand hoping Caspar would hesitate for a brief moment as well, allowing her to introduce herself properly, at which point he raised his spear and relaxed his guard.

"Has anyone been in the room since we departed?" she questioned him sternly.

"No m'lady, just the household staff that were sent to clean and change his clothes," Caspar responded dutifully.

"What do you mean 'household staff'? — I gave no such instructions!?"

"Um…" Caspar stammered a bit, "one of the housemaids — 'Milly' was her name — she said she was ordered by the Prince to make our guest presentable…" trailing off as the obvious question hung in the air — household staff were never given written orders; how was he to have known if the Prince truly ordered this or not? One does not trouble the Prince to verify such mundane instructions, else nothing would ever be done…

Dar paused for a moment to consider this herself before she continued. "Step aside," she ordered, even as she felt the truth of the matter already in her mind. She moved forward, taking the latch handle in her hand and opening the door carefully, knowing what she would see when she entered.

Tibor was sitting upright on the stone table, staring into his hands as they rested on his lap. He looked up slowly as he saw Dar enter the room, and a small smile crept across his face.

"You're here." he said quietly, sounding relieved but not surprised.

"You shouldn't be up," Dar said, moving into the room, splitting her attention between Tibor and the table, wondering what had happened to her enchantment. "Do you remember who woke you?"

"No, I remember you giving me a shot, then everything got blurry. I do recall someone bathing me with a warm cloth, but I thought that was a dream, and then I woke up here," he answered, gesturing to the stained-glass window as he continued, "I don't seem to have much of a view, but the room, the walls, this feels like… Am I really where I think I am?"

"Yes."

"Wow," he said quietly to himself. Despite everything, he somehow had always felt like perhaps he was mad, and that Dar had simply been feeding into his delusion – something he didn't mind playing along with, because it had seemed like an adventure – but now he was here, and it was taking a moment to sink in.

"Can you walk?" she asked, "We should leave – people know you are here, and someone has interfered with my enchantments, so it may not be safe anymore." She looked nervously at the door, still slightly ajar, and could see Caspar's back as he looked down the hallway. As she was looking around, Tibor slid off the table and got to his feet.

"Caspar," she called, getting his attention as they opened the door, "we're going to the library. I need you to go to the stables and arrange a carriage, then go find a long cloak and meet us in the library."

Caspar nodded and moved to carry out her orders.

"…and do not speak to anyone about why you need these things, other than that it is by my authority! Understood?" she added, and he nodded again before leaving at a jog.

*****Tibor*****

Tibor and Dar moved quickly through the halls of the palace, making their way from the North Wing over to the central building, and then into the royal library, which was just a few doors down from the main audience chamber and the palace gates.

"Why are we rushing?" Tibor asked her quietly, bothered that he couldn't stop to take in all of the magnificence of the palace as they moved through so quickly.

"Shhh!" was the only reply he got from Dar, as she ushered him past wonderful works of art and heraldry, statues, and sculptures. At one point, Dar looked back to see that he was gone, and had to backtrack to find him standing inside the door of the main audience chamber, staring at the great mosaics. Pulling him along by the arm, she could only glare at him without drawing any more attention to his presence than she feared he might have already. That is, until they were in the library and the door was shut behind them. Only then did she pause to look at him and explain.

"I'm sorry for this, but it's for your own good!" she explained, "No one was supposed to know that you were here, and yet somehow, someone not only found out about you, found out where you were hidden, and managed to sneak past the guards into your chamber, but they also knew enough about my enchantments to move you out of the protective shield long enough to ensure that the spell would fail and that you would awaken. These are not common things to know!" she concluded, sounding quite unsettled by the failure of their security.

Tibor went with the vibe she was giving off and held back his questions – for the moment – as it clearly seemed she had more to say, but just needed time to catch her breath as well.

"I'm going to move you – get you out of the palace and over to my tower. It's smaller, but much easier to defend, and with much less traffic wandering about inside, so we'll know exactly who's supposed to be there and who isn't!" She walked Tibor over to a large oak table, adorned with carvings of fantastic creatures, and motioned for him to sit. "I am going to find Caspar – he should have been here by now, but he must have run into a problem with our ride – when we get back, we'll have a cloak to disguise you better, so no one will be able to report seeing you leave. Until then, just sit and wait. I won't be long!"

Tibor nodded across the table, and watched her turn to leave, closing the heavy wooden door quietly behind her. They were in her world now, and she seemed determined to make sure he was safe, even though he wasn't so sure he needed it.

The door had barely clicked shut before he was up from the table and exploring the library. Apparently, Prince Svato was not an avid reader, as it was not a grand hall with soaring ceilings, large windows and books lining every inch of the walls – '*Belle would not be impressed,*' he thought to himself. Instead, he found himself at the head of a crowded, low-ceilinged chamber that was much longer than it was wide, with two long rows leading away from the audience hall; each corridor was lined with bookcases and nooks for scrolls and tomes of various sizes, and aside from the gilded chairs at the head of the room where he was standing, it did not appear that the rest of the chamber had seen any real use in quite a long time.

He peered down the long book-rows but could not see much past the range of the candles at the front – wisely, they did not light the further reaches of such an easily flammable room unnecessarily, so he resorted to grabbing a large candle from above the small fireplace that might have been used to heat the room when it was in use and used it to light his way as he began to stroll the rows of ancient and undoubtedly valuable manuscripts that were piled haphazardly on the shelves.

He doubted he would have been able to find a specific book if he were looking for one, but he still found it interesting to browse the strange and unusual titles that lay gathering dust.

The cobwebs and dust grew heavier as he reached the far end of the chamber, and he was glad to see that there was an opening to allow him to cross to the other corridor for the walk back. He had to be quite careful on more than one occasion to avoid igniting some of the larger cobwebs, which burned like fuses, threatening to lead the tiny flames back to the brittle parchment, which would surely have been disastrous!

On a whim, he pulled a book from one of the shelves on his way back to the table, thinking he would crack one open out of curiosity – he even thought to make sure he grabbed one that was small enough to carry along with him, though he didn't know what would possess him to do this. He was eager for Dar to return so they could talk more, and perhaps he could see more of the palace first-hand, and so he settled half-heartedly into reading the opening chapter of what turned out to be a compilation of sorts, with a rather interesting story by someone named 'Strabo' about visiting the *'Gates of Hell'* …

He had only read a few pages when Dar returned, slipping in the door and checking behind her to make sure no one was watching. She had a large cloak over her arm and was in the middle of tossing it on the table towards Tibor when noticed that he appeared to be reading a book.

"What are you reading?" she asked, puzzled.

"Oh, just something I grabbed off the shelf – the title was catchy. You should read it…" he answered, casually closing the book to pick up the cloak, not seeming to have noticed how Dar was staring at him.

"That is an ancient book, written in the Avar tongue – how are you able to read it??"

"…uh, yeah…" Tibor hesitated, fastening the cloak around his shoulders as he glanced down at the book on the table. "I wasn't sure if you had any idea about this when you brought me here – physically – instead of just falling asleep…"

"… *'falling asleep'*?" Dar echoed.

"I'm just trying to explain this simply – anyway, instead of falling asleep and waking up as I'd done before, I woke up here as something different than I ever expected."

"Than you expected?" she asked incredulously, "Why would you have expected anything at all?

"I don't understand what you are talking about," she continued, "or how you can read ancient Avar writings." Dar was uncomfortable with uncertainty. "You can explain it to me later though – right now, we have to get out of the palace before anyone else knows you're awake, so we have to leave now."

She reached up and pulled the hood of his cloak over his head, and he could feel her, standing quite close in front of him as she looked him in the eye. "Keep your head down, do exactly what I tell you, and don't look at anyone. Caspar is waiting with the carriage just down the hallway and out the door," she instructed.

Tibor nodded silently, seeing her standing in front of him; within the darkness of the hood, and with distractions removed, he found he could also see more than just looking at her back – it was as if he could see through her, and see what she was seeing!

It was disorienting and he quickly threw back the hood to take in a breath of air, fighting back a bit of nausea.

Dar quickly turned back to him and pulled the cloak around his head again, chastising him to remain hidden, unaware of his condition. Taking another deep breath, he closed his eyes as she turned and moved to the door to avoid getting too disoriented. Still with his eyes closed, he followed her out into the hall, seeing the corridor through her eyes as they walked quickly to the carriage and exited the palace grounds as discreetly as possible.

They settled into the carriage for the ride to her personal residence, and Tibor opted to say as little as possible until he understood it better himself.

*****Kelevra*****

Kelevra waited until everyone had left the library before she stepped out from the shadows between the bookcases. The well-oiled black leather garment blended easily – and silently – into the shadows that flitted about the room, cast by the flickering candles on the table that seemed to dance with every opening and closing of the only door into the room.

She had not intended to spy on their conversation, but then, she was there first, and just decided it would have been bad manners on her part to interrupt.

She was still pondering what she had heard when she detected a familiar aroma – a scent that preceded its owner even before he opened the door of the library. It was the sickly, sweet scent of heavy oils – oils that he mixed with the clay-like paints that constantly adorned his face – were it not for the oils, his ritual make-up would dry, crack and crumble with every word and expression he made.

She felt herself tense up involuntarily at his approach and had to force herself to remain calm and master her emotions for his entrance.

"Welcome back," Balasz greeted her, waiting to speak until the door was completely shut and he was sure they wouldn't be overheard. "I trust everything went according to plan?"

*****Bad Girl*****

Kelevra was a bad girl.

She knew this, although she did not remember why. Only that it was what the Vizier had told her, again and again, over, and over, until she had no choice but to believe it.

This is what High Vizier Tolvaj told Eszes, the Vizier of Temeskoz, when he gave her to him. She was to be a gift for Prince Kedves. A surprise, Tolvaj said – a secret surprise.

'Of course!' she had answered. Her wide-eyed expression holding a half-smile that resembled a puppy waiting for its' master for attention – she wanted nothing more than to please the Vizier, hoping that he would tell her she was good – he so rarely did that, which only made the joy so much greater when he did!

She went with Vizier Eszes, but he did not present her to Prince Kedves – at least not directly. He treated her well – he had servants who gave her warm baths, brushing her hair with silver combs and scented oils; they rubbed the hard skin from her hands and feet, and taught her how to paint her face the way the nobles liked; Eszes gave her a beautiful silk dress to wear, a warm fur coat and boots to wear, then told her she was going on a journey. He told her she needed to do something for him, and if she did as he instructed, the rewards would be wonderful; but most of all, he told her that if she did this thing for him, she would be a good girl.

It was a long trip, and she enjoyed every moment of it: riding in a beautiful carriage, through beautiful countryside – it was much more regal than the secretive trip when she had first been brought to Eszes' estate; that trip was done in a small, windowless wagon, because Tolvaj said it was supposed to be a surprise, so she had to stay hidden. She felt like a princess, and she had the whole carriage to herself – the servants and guards rode alongside, envious of her accommodations.

They camped in the wilderness many times over the course of the journey before they arrived in a wonderful, yet cold, castle that was situated in a lush valley at the base of some rolling hills, overlooked by a towering range of mountains. It seemed they had gone North, as it was still late summer – far too early for such cold weather as what greeted her when she stepped down from the carriage to a most elegant reception at the gates of the castle. It was evening, and torches were lit all about the entrance and along the high walls.

She was still looking up at the flickering lights winding their way along the tops of the high walls and towers – the castle was lit for a celebration of some kind – when she heard the creak of wheels as the carriage pulled away, turning in the small circle of the courtyard, and proceeding to leave, returning to Temeskoz. This was not a surprise, but she still felt her heart sink a little as she saw her connection to anything familiar disappear outside the castle gate and into the dusk of the evening.

She was hurried inside by her hosts and led through hallways with many twists and turns, and stairways constantly leading upwards. Eventually they arrived at a beautiful bedroom that she was told was to be hers. New handmaidens awaited her here, who helped her out of her travel clothes, and prepared a warm bath for her, which she very much appreciated.

Throughout the bath and the dressing and hair brushing that followed, all of the handmaids giggled and chattered about how lucky she was to be presented to the young prince, how handsome he was, and strong, and a number of other much-embellished attributes that they all envied her for getting the chance to experience first-hand so very soon! She was trying her best to listen to everything they were saying, but their accent was different than hers, and it was hard to keep up with everyone talking all at once. One thing she could definitely make out was how strange and exotic they found her dark, bronzed-brown skin to be, as they applied beautifully scented oils and perfumes when she exited the bath. Apparently, this was very much a rarity in this part of the principality, and likely something the young prince would have never experienced before.

She was surprised when they said she would be meeting him very soon, as she had hoped to rest – the warm bath and the long trip had made her quite tired, and she was sorely afraid that she would not make a good impression if she were introduced right away!

Good heavens, she worried, *what if he was a talker, and she fell asleep listening to him talk*?! That would be horrible, and Eszes would be angry, and so would Tolvaj! She didn't want to be bad!

Sensing her tension as they chattered, the handmaidens mistook her apprehension for that worry that they all felt the first time they were intimate with someone, and they quickly sought to assuage her fears, telling her how sweet and gentle the young prince was, and that they were sure he would be gentle with her! He was a great fighter, and strong, they told her – again – but he was a gentle lover – or so they had heard – and so she had nothing to fear.

Kelevra tried to relax, and then pinched herself hoping the pain would snap her head clear and dispel the fatigue. The handmaidens giggled again as they saw her pinch herself, laughing out loud that 'oh yes, this was really happening' as they brought over her jewelry box, which had been among the items from the carriage that had eventually made their way up to her room. It was not a large selection to choose from, but simply a well-matched ensemble of a broach, necklace, two rings and a simple tiara – not royal, yet elegant – all selected and sent along with her by Eszes.

When they were finished, the young hand maidens all stepped back and pointed her towards the full-length mirror so she could examine herself fully. Her long black hair had been combed back into silver chain hairnet, framed with two simple braid on either side, resting level with her shoulders and revealing her swan-like neck, adorned with a silver choker necklace from which a single, large emerald glistened as it hung in the delicate crevice of her neck. The tiara was a simple silver band, also with a single emerald dangling from a single strand of looped silver above the center of her brow, matched again by the emerald stones in the two rings on her hands.

Her dark eyes had a sharpness that reflected the candlelight of the chamber, displaying an edge that belied the fear she seemed so consumed with. High cheekbones, ice-blue eyes, and lush mouth made her appear even younger than she thought she was – try as she might, she could not remember how old she was, frowning at the reflection in the mirror as she sought to recall something that should have come to her so easily! She could remember Tolvaj, but nothing before, or even how she came to be in his care?!

The handmaidens saw her frown and – again – immediately moved in to help lighten her mood with re-assuring words about how wonderful the evening was going to be, and they began to lead her across the room, pulling back a curtain that covered a door she had not seen earlier. They led her through into what she could only assume was the prince's bed chamber, as it was so much more elegantly adorned than the room she had just been in – a room which, until now, she had thought was the most luxurious chamber she had ever seen!

They guided her to a silk-sheeted bed that was large enough for all six of them to lay upon and still not have to touch one another. Panels of silk hung from the ceiling around the bed, offering a suggestion of privacy, which was ironic for a room that seemed so singularly focused on sensual self-indulgence of the kind that defied any sense of modesty.

The handmaidens quickly ensured her dress was splayed properly across the bed where she sat, facing a different doorway into the room, and made a few last-minute touch-ups to her hair to ensure that the first impression the prince would have when he opened the door was as perfect as could be. She was almost touched by the pride they seemed to take in their handiwork – almost, if it hadn't also felt like they were preparing a lamb for the slaughter!

It was late in the evening by the time her preparations were complete, which was very timely, as she had learned from the servant girls that the Prince was coming directly from the feast hall where he was celebrating his twenty-first name-day! The evenings' festivities were winding-down across the castle, though a few celebrants might stay for their last drinks after the Prince had departed the celebrations – the castellan would surely be wanting to secure the gates for the night, with all those who were staying within the keep to their rooms, and those who had to leave quickly helped on their way. The Prince himself would be making his way to his chambers, dismissing his counsellors, chief viziers, and even his royal guards as he walked, finishing the last business of the day as he entered the wing dedicated to his personal residence, and prepared to see what gifts awaited him in his chamber. He had been told that emissaries from Temeskoz had prepared a special gift for him, and his curiosity had been aroused all evening!

Kelevra didn't have to wait long after the servants had left before the door opened and a young, handsome man stepped into the room confidently, closing the door behind him and walking directly to a table near the entrance.

She only caught a glimpse of his face before he turned to fix himself a drink, leaving her to examine his backside – he was average in height but stood erect in a way that made him seem taller; thick, wavy, dirty-blonde strands fell about his head in a messy mop of hair, held in place by a silver circlet that resembled her own. His shoulders were broad, and his frame suggested the truth of his rumoured physique under his tight-fitting silk shirt and finely stitched leather breeches, finished off with polished black leather riding boots.

She tried not to focus on the way the leather breeches fit around his buttocks, trying to remember that she was there for a reason, and no matter how handsome her suitor was, he wasn't interested in her perceptions or opinions. She felt the earlier fatigue vanish as her heart began to beat faster – she recalled her purpose, and it was if a switch had been flipped.

She swallowed as he turned around and was not disappointed by the cut of his chin, or the pleasant smile, reflected equally in his eyes as his mouth as he walked slowly towards her, carrying two glasses of what she was sure was some expensive liqueur that she was sure was intended to help 'relax' her nerves… and perhaps her inhibitions as well.

She didn't mind this so much, taking the offered glass with a courteous nod, raising it in his direction as a salutation, after which she perfunctorily drank the whole glass in one gulp. With a smile he did the same, then took the empty glass from her hand and placed them both on the table beside the bed.

He moved to sit on the edge of the bed to her left, and without saying a word, slowly raised his hand – fingers slightly curled – to brush her hair back over her ear, allowing him to see her face more clearly. She continued to stare straight ahead, fiddling nervously with her rings as he stared at her with ice blue eyes that were both piercing and excited at the same time.

"You have nothing to fear" he whispered softly, his right hand still behind her head as he fumbled with the laces on the front of her dress with his left. He slowly reached inside her dress to caress her as he eased her back gently to lie on the bed.

"Nor do you…" she replied, reaching her hand out towards his face, her fingers curled but not closed, extending one finger to trace the line of his circlet from his forehead around to above his eye, gently flicking it off and running her fingers through his lush hair as he lay down beside her on the bed, locking eyes with her the entire time. He only winced a little - a reflex - when her hand caught on something in his hair.

"Ow!" he said quietly, still smiling, then pausing to put his hand to the back of his head for a moment.

"Sorry…" she whispered, "I didn't mean to hurt you."

He pulled his hand away from his head and saw a small dot of red smeared on his finger. Grabbing for her right arm, he clutched her wrist and held it out to see her hand.

"Wha-at…?" he asked, the smile replaced now by a look of confusion. The light was already fading from the ice blue eyes, and his grip on her wrist had loosened enough for her to pull free, being careful not to prick herself with the small pin that had been exposed beneath the large emerald stone.

She pulled her left arm from beneath his still form, looking at his eyes to see that he was still alive, but fading fast.

"Good night sweet prince. It just wasn't meant to be." She could see that he was trying to answer, but paralyzed and unable to breathe, he could not make a sound to call for help or move from his prone position. In a few moments, when the air from his last breath would be expended, he would suffocate, pass out and die quietly. With luck, his fine head of hair would keep anyone from ever seeing how the poison was delivered.

Rolling on her back, Kelevra used her left hand to carefully twist the emerald setting to retract the pin to its' hidden position in the ring. She calmly sat up on the bed, pulled her robes closed around herself, and walked over to the young prince's closet to find something warmer to wear.

A few moments later she finished tying up a pair of black leather breeches, feeling thankful to find ones that must have been a bit older, as they were smaller in size and fit her well enough to pass inspection by the casual eye. The best shirt she could find was loose and billowing, but she tucked it in snug and threw a dark cloak around her shoulders, pulling up the hood as she crossed the room to lock the door to the hand-maidens chambers.

Casually surveying the room, she paused once more to take a sip of the liqueur from the bottle he had poured from earlier, steadying her nerves - *'patience'* she told herself, *'hurrying causes mistakes, and we don't want to make any mistakes tonight'*. She took a deep breath before slipping out the door that the prince had entered through, closing it tight behind her and making her way quietly down the empty hallway.

There were a few drunken guests wandering the halls despite the late hour, but thankfully because of the night's festivities, few were cognizant enough of their surroundings to notice anything unusual about someone they must have thought was simply another random party guest moving about the corridors. Most of the staff and servants were already busy cleaning up the feast hall, and she steered clear of these areas as she worked her way to the exit.

She wasn't heading to the main doors though – she was working her way by trial and error to find her way to the stables, which would also lead to the courtyard and then out. She had to pause once to ask a young boy carrying some empty wine pitchers for directions – *'careful'* her inner voice told her, *'do not say too much – your accent will give you away'* - but otherwise found her way to the stables quite quickly. Time was of the essence, as she knew – she wasn't sure how, but she knew – that the gates of the castle would be closing for the night soon, and she had very little time to leave before she would be locked in for the night!

As many of the guests were already in the process of leaving, many of the stable hands were busy with getting their horse and gear prepared when she slipped in through the interior stable door. She could see out into the courtyard, and saw that just a few riders were left, talking to one another as the work horses were being harnessed to the last carriage.

Taking advantage of the tall shadows cast by the many torches, she slipped into one of the stalls and helped herself to one of the Prince's riding horses, grabbing a bit & bridle but nor bothering with a saddle. She took a quick step on the wooden fence of the stall and lifted herself onto the mare's back, quickly settling her cloak around her legs and over the hindquarters, to hide herself and the lack of proper riding gear.

With the door of the stall open, she slowly walked the horse forward, being careful to watch that no one was paying much attention to the stables and were still focused on the departing dignitaries. When the last carriage was harnessed, the guests loaded, and the final farewells made, she watched as the carriage followed the circle from the doorway of the keep and out towards the gate of the castle. The four remaining horsemen who had been casually talking amongst themselves - part of the entourage that preferred to ride mounted rather than in a coach - followed the carriage around the circle and out towards the gate. They had almost passed the stables completely – the carriage was out the gate, and the horsemen were right in front of her – when the voice in her head shouted '*Now!*' and she put her heels to the horse and quickly moved out of the stables and dropped neatly into line behind the departing riders, under the raised portcullis, through the banded wood & iron double doors, and across the small moat that she hadn't even noticed on their way in.

The carriage turned right to follow the road further into the town, and she slipped to the left, following the road South – away from the city and towards home.

It was dark, and she knew the road would be dangerous to travel at night – the risk of the horse tripping was enough to worry about, yet alone dealing with the potential for bandits, berserkers, or even wild beasts on the prowl! - but she had to ride and get as far away as she could before any alarm might be raised.

She hadn't gone very far outside of the city before she came across the smashed remains of a familiar carriage on the side of the road.

Even in the dim light of the moon she could recognize the remains of her transport for the past two weeks. She dismounted to inspect the wreckage: the wheels were smashed, the seats were torn, and clothing from the luggage was strewn about the road, looking like bandits had pilfered their prize. Looking around to be sure she was alone, she quickly ducked into the door of the carriage and pried up the passenger seat to retrieve a leather pack from its' hiding place.

She opened the bag and found everything was there, just as she had been told to expect, and then closed it up again and pulled her horse over to the front of the carriage to help her mount up again – she was not very tall and the large mare was bred for war, where size mattered - not that she had much chance to shop around when she stole it!

There were tracks continuing South down the road, and she set out again at a steady trot. Kelevra knew the 'bandit attack' was a ruse that her handlers had staged, to try to throw off any pursuit: Those who hadn't been riding their own horses had unharnessed the carriage horses to ride – the castle guards were too focused on the festivities and noble guests arriving to have noticed that the horses pulling the carriage were far too well bred to have been saddled with such a menial task - and now the whole group were moving much faster than they would have been if they had kept the carriage and all the luggage.

They had pretty much a full nights' head-start and she needed to catch up with them as quickly as she could – without the carriage they could compress a two week ambling journey into one week of fast riding, and even though she was sure somehow that she could manage the ride on her own, now that she had reclaimed her gear from where it had been hidden, it would be far easier if she could rejoin her escort and enjoy some safety in numbers. All she had to do was make sure she didn't get lost or injured riding hard into the night!

It was late on the afternoon of the following day that she found them, closing the gap as they were walking their horses to rest them for a bit. There was time now for her to change from her stolen outfit to her stashed riding clothes – it was a little thing, but it gave her a much greater sense of comfort, feeling more at home in her own skin. There was little talking or greetings among the company – the fact that she was there meant the job had been done, and they knew they had to make it back to Temeskoz territory before they could feel safe.

So they rode on.

After three more days of hard riding – on the last of which one of the horses had stumbled and died from exhaustion - they reached the border of Mezoseg and Temeskoz, and from there, they knew, they could relax their pace. They had ridden in fear of pursuit, but no one gave chase, and so, after passing the border, and several small stations of assembled Temeskoz militia and military camps, they stopped that night at an inn, to celebrate their success with a warm meal, a soft bed, and a full nights' sleep!

There were only a few other patrons at the tavern beneath the inn, which was good, because their party took up all of the available rooms, as well as most of what the cook had been keeping warm on the fire for the evenings' dinner. Some of the riders were a little more talkative now and clanked their tankards with enthusiasm, toasting a mission accomplished - as enlisted men were wont to do - but Kelevra preferred her own company, and sat alone by the hearth to savour her drink – a harsh whiskey that burned as she swallowed it, nothing at all like the sweet liqueur she remembered from the Prince's chamber.

She wished for a moment that she had taken the bottle with her - it had helped to fuel her courage, not to mention giving her something else to remember about that night other than the sad look on the young Prince's face as he struggled to comprehend what had gone so wrong on his day of celebration.

She took another swig of her drink to help wash away that memory and tossed the cup into the fire.

"Hey!" she heard the serving girl cry out, "those are not cheap, you know?" moving up to the hearth to see the flames beginning to lick at the alcohol-soaked wooden cup.

"Add it to my bill!" Kelevra told her, slowly rising to make her way to her room. The serving girl looked at Kelevra, still frowning, but saw something in her eyes that made her decide to just nod and let it go, wiping her hands on her towel as she walked back over to the bar to make sure the innkeeper noted the added expense.

She went up the old wooden stairs to the second floor, and followed the narrow hallway to the end, opening last door on the left. She had dropped her gear up hear before dinner and was familiar with the layout – the floor in the hallway creaked in front of the door, the latch was rusty, and the door creaked when opened, slow or fast; there was a window that looked out over the stable, which others found smelly and unpleasant, but it suited her just fine.

There was an armchair beside the window, between the wall and the small bed, and a small table. It was a simple bedroom, made small to afford the innkeeper as many rooms as possible. It was her inner voice that noted and listed all these things, not something Kelevra had ever paid much attention to herself. The same inner voice that had told her what to do with the prince, and when to move in the shadows of the keep, and how to ride hard in the night. Though she didn't recall much about life before High Vizier Tolvaj, she had the feeling that she had never listened to her inner voice as much as she had in the past week. It seems…

"It seems like you are getting used to listening to the voices in your head." came the voice from behind her, startling her enough to spin and crouch.

She had let her guard down in the tavern and had no weapons at hand with which to defend herself as she scanned the room for objects she could use; At the same time, she tried to make out details on the person emerging from the shadows behind the door – *'stupid girl!'* she chastised herself – *'always check behind the door when entering a strange room!'*

"You have nothing to fear."

'Now where have I heard that before?' she thought to herself, as the figure emerged further from behind the door, and the candlelight revealed the aged form of Vizier Eszes, dressed in robes that, while casual and informal, were still quality enough to befit his station, although without any of the hallmark stoles or badges of office that he usually wore around the palace in Temesvar.

"I was not expecting to see you here, m'lord" she replied to the High Vizier of Temeskoz, hiding the surprise in her voice as she rose from her crouch to stand at attention, bowing her head in the perfunctory salute that was expected of all who stood in his presence.

"I came to await news of your journey – it was expected that if all went well, you and your companions would likely stop to celebrate, and this is the nearest settlement to the borderlands, so I followed a hunch and, well, here you are…!" the old man moved slowly past her to the armchair and took a seat. "I hope you don't mind, I have been standing there for almost half-an-hour waiting for you to finish that drink and come to bed…" he said, as he settled into the seat and made a groaning noise as he adjusted his back against the cushions, "…and my back is not what it used to be."

Kelevra watched him closely – it was unlike him to appear so frail, though she had not been with him long before she had been sent on her mission – she did not want to be surprised again.

"I have done what you asked of me" she said quietly, pushing the door shut with her left arm to ensure their privacy.

"Ah, I am pleased to hear that" he replied, "I expect we will hear word from messengers confirming this in a matter of days, likely accompanied by threats and demands, possibly even a declaration of war – who knows!" he grinned mischievously, not unlike a schoolboy playing a prank on their headmistress.

"Have you brought the payment?" she asked him.

"Payment – oh, no, I don't think we'll talk about payment until we are sure that everything went as planned" he answered derisively, although Kelevra watched his right hand drop from the arm of the chair to the top of his right leg, reflexively gong to where the pouch of coins was likely hidden on his person.

"I was told I would be paid when the mission was completed, and it has been done; My being here should be proof enough – you had me delivered into their hands; the only way out alive would be to kill the Prince and escape while everyone believed he was bedding me for the night. You said nothing to Tolvaj about waiting for messengers or declarations of war!"

"Oh, so you were listening to our private conversations?" he exclaimed.

"Not so private actually – you both have loose tongues when you think those around you are too stupid to understand your little plots. Yes, I heard much of your plans, including the terms of payment. I do not have much time to be away from here and back to Nyirseg - once they realize what has happened, there will no doubt be a bounty on the head of a certain young girl, and I do not have armies and castles to hide behind on my way home. So, if you don't mind, I'd just as soon take payment now – since you have so conveniently come this far to meet us – and be on my way."

"Well," Eszes thought aloud, "I guess we can tell which voices you're listening to, can't we!"

"What do you mean," she retorted, "were you expecting to come in here and tell this little lady that she was a 'bad girl' and expect us to roll over and do what you say?" The look on Eszes' face was enough of an answer.

"You made her weak – you preyed on her fears, and tried to bend her to your will, to make us your puppet – but guess what? You brought me into the mix, and I'm nobody's puppet!" She snapped at him as her anger was rising but kept her voice quiet enough as to not carry outside of the room.

"You most certainly *are* a bad girl!" Eszes replied, trying to apply the techniques Tolvaj had told him to use, but he no longer had the certainty in his tone that made the words effective. "You need to remember who you are and who I am! I am the High Vizier, the right hand of the Prince of Temeskoz, rightful King of the Seven Tribes of the Avar, and you will do as I say!" He got to his feet as he finished, trying to assert his authority over the situation, though he was hardly as tall as she was, which was not very tall at all.

Kelevra sensed the tremor in his voice and slid to seat herself on the edge of the bed, moving closer to his chair and raising her head slightly to look up at him, replacing her defiance with a docile, pleading look on her face.

"You are right!" she sobbed in a quiet voice, "I don't know how I could have ever listened to that, that… thing, telling me to do those awful things!" She managed to make a tear well up in her eye, as she reached out to hold Eszes robes, as a child begging for forgiveness.

Eszes was caught off guard for a moment by the sudden change in demeanor, but he recalled that Balasz said that the personalities in her head would be drastically different, and it was essential that he use his authority to make sure the submissive child always remained under his control. He was pleased to see his approach had worked, and the doe-eyed face looking up at him seemed truly apologetic…

"You have been a very bad girl," he repeated, "talking back to your elders, forgetting your place, and, and…" he started to stammer as he felt her hand shift from clutching his robes to moving to the top of his thigh, gripping the inside of his leg firmly yet suggestively.

"I don't want to be bad!" she pleaded to him, "Please don't tell Tolvaj I was bad! I will do anything to be a good girl!" she continued, sounding desperate, and at the same time sliding her hand further up the inside of his thigh, brushing his groin with a light touch of the back of her hand, awakening a tingling sensation in his loins that he found himself ever so willing to satisfy with her.

He sat down on the bed beside her, almost stumbling as his knees began to tremble with anticipation of her attentions.

"I can show you how to be a good girl" he whispered.

"But what if I still want to be a little bad?" she whispered back, giving a wink as she cupped his privates in her hand, fondling them gently.

He closed his eyes and began to tilt his head back, anticipating the pleasure to come, when he suddenly felt a sharp prick of pain in his groin, followed by a flash of warmth that quickly spread up an into the rest of his body, sped on its way by his throbbing pulse and quickening heart – a throbbing pulse that was meant for other purposes, it now hurried the effects of the poison through his system. His head jerked up and his eyes opened wide to look at her.

"Oops, I'm sorry. I didn't mean to hurt you." she said softly, though her eyes made her intentions clear.

It was all Eszes could do to silently mouth the word '*no*" as he felt his body go numb and he lost all control of his muscles. He lay back on the bed, silently suffocating to death as Kelevra stood up and looked down on him. She held out her hands, twisting the emerald in the second ring to reset the needle, and gazed at his groin with a frown.

"At least the young prince didn't soil himself in his final moments" she said quietly, before gathering her things to leave. She stooped over the corpse to remove his valuables, including the pouch containing the coins of her payment – intended for High Vizier Tolvaj actually, from which he was supposed to give her a cut - then proceeded to open the window to the stables and letting herself down into the yard. It was a simple matter to find her horse – she may have stolen it a few days ago, but it was indeed hers now - and be on her way again.

She turned out onto the road, heading south initially, blending her trail with the many tracks on the road, before eventually finding a good spot to leave the path and begin heading home…

*****Rogue*****

"Welcome back," Balasz greeted her, waiting to speak until the door was completely shut and he was sure they wouldn't be overheard. "I trust everything went according to plan?"

Balasz paused for her reply, looking her up and down with equal measures of judgement and unfulfilled lust.

"It did." she answered quietly, placing a leather pouch on the table, then stepping back. She kept her eyes lowered, not looking directly at the High Vizier. He moved closer to the table, looking at the pouch but not picking it up.

"I must say…" he observed, "I was not expecting you back so soon…" he trailed off as he spoke, waiting for the unasked explanation. His arrangements with Vizier Eszes included him retaining her for future services – although not without ensuring his customary cut, from which he was expecting he would reap him some substantial profits. He had trained her well since he had purchased her on the black market, training which had cost him a great deal of time and money, which he was now eager to recoup from selling her services to the highest bidder.

She was younger then, and frail. The slaver who had brought her to his private residence – not daring to sell slaves in the palace proper – knew of Balasz's tastes, and when he had arrived in Ascanium, he had left his other stock on the market and brought her, in secret, to the Vizier's private estate, where he could do business discretely, and not as the 'High Vizier.' He was the second most powerful man in the city – in the Principality – and all the traders who came to town knew his tastes for the exotic and unusual, and that he would pay double what any other customer might have been able to afford.

The girl had been a prize from a caravan that had departed Mercurum during the Imperial Purge, on their way to Ascanium to seek refuge. Her father had died trying to protect her, as had most of the men in the caravan, and the raiders had brought their prizes to the black quarry just outside of Ascanium. There, the slavers had their pick of the haul, and he had immediately spied the girl as being something he knew Balasz would pay good coin for.

They had never asked her name – she could still remember it then – as no one here saw her as anything other than a prize, to be bought and sold. It was only when Balasz had purchased her from the slaver that he gave her a new name – 'Bad Girl.' Over and over, every day, he whittled her spirit down until he was ready to mold her back into the shape he desired.

It was well into her training that Balasz had called her anything other than 'bad,' and so she was happy to have a name again – he had done so much to beat down her will over the course of many months, and so when he called her 'Kelevra' she felt like she had been born again. Her new self was happy to serve, always looking to do whatever her master would ask of her, desperate for his approval. S

o desperate that she did not protest when he subjected her to the first stitching. His method was similar to Louhi's, but also different – the research of the ancient Avars had yielded new insights into the magic of linking consciousness, such that Balasz was able to step outside the boundaries of familial heritage, and bind his subjects to specific named individuals, regardless of their lineage. Where Louhi's method supported abilities inherited through bloodlines, Balasz could do more, but also required more = he had to spend years researching many candidates for the process, requiring more than just a name – which took more to confirm once you strayed from family lore – as well as requiring a physical relic of the person, to seal the connection.

This was often the trickiest part, as many relics were not as true to their purported lineage as their hosts proclaimed – something that he had learned with a great deal of trial and error, and for which those who procured such relics for him had learned the painful price of disappointing him.

Everything she could remember about the stitching ritual was cloudy in her memory, as if she were watching it happen to someone else through a pool of water – Balasz drugged her wine that night, because being submissive was not enough for him. Prone upon the table – the room was cold - she could feel his robes brushing against her as she lay naked and exposed for his inspection.

She could remember the feeling of not being able to move – surely the effect of whatever he put in her wine – though she could feel the touch of his rough hands upon her skin. The red and black paints on his face moved in and out of her view, blurring and transforming from a man into a demon – a demon that whispered dark secrets and vulgar desires in her ear as she struggled to scream but found her breath to be frozen in her chest.

He searched her over, looking for the most discrete places to place the stitching marks, while she could only watch, helplessly, as the golden thread seemed to float back and forth in front of her eyes. She could not recall how many times he had completed the ritual, but she was reminded every day that it had worked, at least once, and very well at that.

He had bound her to an assassin – a killer of legend – a master of their art, and a dominant will that struggled with her every day to control her destiny.

Every day she struggled to remember more of who she was, and every day Balasz reminded her of how small she was, which made it easier for her to give in to the voice in her head; the voice that plotted with Balasz, that carried out his plans, and sought every opportunity to keep her down, submissive enough to let him live again through her.

The assassin had spirit – and he didn't like working for Balasz any more than she did.

"Plans changed" she said to Balasz, still not looking up.

"You've been a bad girl, haven't you?" Balasz responded. "You were supposed to…"

"Eszes was a pig!" she cut him off. "I may appear soft, but I do not care for sucking dick any more than you do, especially not for that withered old fart."

Balasz looked flustered as Kelevra seemed to be resisting his voice. Slowly and carefully, he reached for the pouch on the table, at the same time, reaching into his robes to pull out the small riding crop he had used so many times before to good effect. Moving around the table as he hefted the pouch in his left hand, he kept his right – and the riding crop – concealed at his side as he moved closer.

"You haven't taken your cut?" he asked, feeling the weight of the pouch.

"I will before I leave" she answered, lifting her head just slightly enough to look at him through the top of one eye. She could see the anger rising in his eyes as he slowly walked towards her, and she could easily tell he was hiding something in his other hand.

"I think perhaps we should spend some time first learning some manners again" he started to snarl, raising his hand to let her see the riding crop - to let her remember how it felt when he whipped her with it – the memory of fear and pain was just as effective, if not more, than the actual pain itself sometimes.

…But not every time.

Kelevra turned to face Balasz, raising her head in a defiant stare, fixing her eyes on his. She didn't reach for a weapon, but she didn't back away from him either. She kept her arms loose at her sides as she stared him down, daring him to make the next move.

High Vizier Tolvaj Balasz stopped, holding his arm with the riding crop raised in the air, still threatening, but clearly re-evaluating his next move. He could see she wasn't afraid; it wasn't the young girl in charge anymore; he had underestimated the strength of the assassin, who was clearly in possession of all her faculties now; the High Vizier was no longer in control. He slowly lowered the riding crop and his arm, though his face was still curled in a snarl.

"Smart move" Kelevra said.

"I guess it goes without saying, but I'm going freelance from now on…" she continued, and then added, as she watched Balasz's face relax and then start to look a bit worried, "…but don't worry, I'm not going to kill you for my freedom – it wouldn't make sense to kill my best customer!"

"You can have the payment from Eszes – I don't need it" she told him, as she walked away from him and back around the table towards the door. "I have something I need to go look into, but you know how to reach me if you have another job – don't expect any discounts though!"

She gave him a small smile as she opened the door and slipped out of the room. Balasz stood motionless for a long while, considering what had happened and just where he had miscalculated in his plan. Taking a deep breath, he released it slowly and let his anger and frustration give way to calm. It wasn't the first time one of his plans hadn't gone precisely the way he expected, and besides, he did manage to have the Prince of Mezoseg assassinated, and with Eszes dead, there was no trail back to him, so that was something.

He would have to go back and rethink his methods for subjugating someone to make them more controllable, but that's the way these things go. All-in-all, it could have been much worse – he got off better than Eszes did! - and he still has access to a highly trained assassin if he needs one... he'll just have to pay a bit more than he was planning.

*****Tibor*****

Tibor said little during the short ride to Dar's compound, despite her intense examination of his face as the carriage rocked and rolled through the cobbled streets of the city, showing incredible patience on her part to wait for him to share his secrets.

They could see her home long before they arrived at the low doors of the gateway – the large oak tree that dominated the compound was the tallest tree in the city and could be seen by all from a great distance. Surrounded by a small stone wall covered with flowering vines, the carriage pulled through the narrow gate and into what might have easily been mistaken for a forest grove, were it not located in the heart of Ascanium. The path itself was green and barely marked by their wheels, and the entire grounds presented a perfectly balanced garden, reflecting wild growth and perfectly manicured shrubs, bushes and trees of various age and species, many not even native to the region. Dominating the center of the garden was a stone & wooden building, constructed around the trunk of the massive oak tree, and following it up for at least two or three floors before it was obscured by the foliage of the tree.

The carriage rolled away and exited the grounds as soon as they had stepped out, and Tibor could hear the gates closing as it left. The main door seemed to be carved entirely from a single piece of wood, the size of which Tibor had never seen before, and opened into a warm and lush foyer, but the trunk of the grand tree still dominated his view of the interior as much as it had the exterior.

Dar led him to a sitting area off to his right, decorated modestly yet containing more books, tomes, manuals, scrolls and maps than the entire royal library, all arrayed in a neat and orderly system reaching up the side of the tree itself. Dar waved Tibor to a seat, poured two glasses of wine, and quietly watched as Tibor took a sip and sat back in the chair. Tibor finished looking around and then finally broke the awkward silence.

"So, you need to know something…" he started, to which she raised an eyebrow as if he were stating something obvious.

"This is so weird," he continued, hesitating, trying to find the right words to describe what he was experiencing. "It feels like vertigo, and it's coming in waves, each one getting stronger than the one before…" He paused, avoiding her stare as she looked for answers in the lines on his face.

"I wanted to come back, but I didn't expect to come back as I am right now, in the flesh… I…" he fumbled for the words. "I feel like I am here, and somewhere else at the same time. I can see and hear things from different places all at once, and it sounds like a roar in my head!"

"You are not from here," she interjected when he paused again, looking for answers to her questions, "…you may have visited here before, but you, physically, should never have come, and you should never have awoken! I was desperate to save us and drew upon unfamiliar magics to save us from Vazul, and how you ended up here directly is beyond even me. But that doesn't explain how you have suddenly gained knowledge of our world – our language – to be able to read and speak…" she paused as she watched Tibor's expressions.

He hadn't realized that he had been speaking the Avar tongue this whole time, and as she said it to him now, she could see the realization dawning across his face, surprised and amazed. Then it became clear!

"You can tell me what you are feeling, seeing, but you have no more understanding of the *why* of it than I do!" she stated.

Tibor opened his mouth as if to answer, but he had nothing to say because she was right, and so he said as much.

"You're right," he replied calmly, "I have no idea what is going on, and this is not what I was hoping would happen when I said I wanted to come back here – this is all quite a lot more real than I was expecting."

He put his hands to his eyes, rubbing them as if to get something out.

"And what do you see now?" she asked.

"Now? Now I see fire!" Tibor said, with the flat, emotionless tone of an observer trying hard to make out what they were seeing. "…Burning trees, flames everywhere, smoke, destruction, and bodies – I can't tell whose, but they're fighting."

Dar looked concerned, leaning forward in her seat to hear every word.

"Did they survive? Are they alive? Who are they fighting – is it Vazul?" she asked nervously, worried that she had left the group on their own at the wrong time!

"I can't tell – it's not over yet…" Tibor answered, as he lowered his head and closed his eyes, trying to clear the scene from his mind.

Dar moved about the room, coming back over to Tibor after a moment, handing him a small silver chalice.

"Drink this," she told him, "it will keep the visions at bay."

He raised his head with a look that said he was both grateful and suspicious but took the cup without a word and drank. It tasted like nothing more than wine to him.

"You will likely still have some very potent dreams, but your waking hours will be quiet," she said, "You must tell me about your dreams, though," she continued, with an insistent tone, "...I will need to know what you see – it's important!"

He nodded, staring blankly into the empty cup...

*****Ralof*****

"Religion is not unlike politics in my opinion," said Omar, almost seeming to enjoy how this would provoke the old cleric.

"What?!" replied Ralof, shocked at hearing such a comparison, "Whatever do you mean?"

"It's simple really," Omar continued, "politics and religion are like siblings in the womb – separate, but alike enough as to be twins; two sides of the same coin. Both are comprised of nothing but people seeking other like-minded people to share in their beliefs, putting their faith in a leader – often people cannot agree on which would be best to lead them, as there are so many choices to choose from - which means you can always find one that suits you perfectly without having to change who you are! Someone they praise when things go well or blame when things go bad; it's nothing but a desire to feel validated, and a complete rejection of personal accountability for whatever happens in the world around them."

Ralof's jaw dropped as he listened to Omar, losing count of the blasphemies as he spoke. "I have never heard such rubbish in all my years!" he replied. "Faith is the truest expression of the heart, the imperviousness of the soul, and the fulfillment of the promise of the creator! I know less of politics – a creation of man, not the gods –but I can't believe you would lump the two together in such a comparison!"

"Enough!" hissed Shagron, "We're here..." ending the conversation abruptly, although not the stares the two gave one another. They had been walking their horses for the last mile, trying to stay low against the already flat terrain, and had arrived at a small copse of trees that hid a depression in the plain. As they closed the distance, the depression began to look more like a crater, curving down into the earth in a sharp slope.

"It's like something exploded or struck the earth with great force," Torick said quietly, "and it exposed a natural cave there, near the bottom." Torick pointed to a man-sized opening in the size of the crater, about a full span above the bottom, requiring those entering or exiting to navigate a narrow set of steps carved into the exposed stone that lined the slope of the lower half of the crater. Whatever had caused the explosion must have happened long ago, as soil deposits had flowed back in over time, levelling the base somewhat, and allowing water to pool and trees to grow in the damp soil, trees that now stood tall enough to clear the rim of the crater and give the improvised oasis that appearance of being just a few trees from the plains above, while it seemed more like a forest to those within. The occupants of the cave had also constructed a small wooden structure, a corral for their horses, and even a pen for a few pigs that must have been stolen and kept for food. A path leading almost the full circumference of the crater sloped upwards to give their riders an easy route in and out of their hidden lair, which Omar couldn't help but admire for its beauty and simplicity.

"Incredible," he muttered, as they lay down near the lip of the crater, "No one would ever suspect so many could be hiding so close by, trusting in the plains to expose anyone from great distances. I bet these riders could strike out at the city itself and not be found!"

"Oh, if they aren't careful and rouse too much interest, a large enough troop of guards will eventually stumble across them," replied Jason, lying next to him and squinting to try and count the number of men in the hideout through the trees. "They are smart to just content themselves with traffic on the roads – it's small risk, small reward, and they will never be pursued by caravan guards, so their lair will stay a secret for as long as they don't get too greedy."

Shagron and Ralof were silent as they peered into the crater – Shagron's eyes were closed, though he moved his head slowly back & forth, muttering as if in prayer. When he was finished, they both slid back from the crater's edge and sat in the grass, waiting for the others to rejoin them.

"So, what's the plan?" Ralof asked aloud to no one in particular.

Omar opened his mouth to begin to answer, only to have Jason talk over him before he could say a word…

"I can't be sure how many are inside, or even how large that cave might be, but I counted at least twenty horses, so that's about three each," Jason stated with authority, looking around the group. "Don't worry Ralof – Kiara, Ferenc and I will handle your three!" which drew a scowl from the priest. "At least five men outside at the moment – maybe we can surprise a couple of them, then the wizards can cause a distraction to draw the rest out and we can manage them as they come out – that entrance is pretty narrow, so they will only be able to come out single file…"

"Sounds like a plan to me," said Shagron, as Ferenc and Kiara pulled out their bows and checked the strings.

"And what if they don't rush out to meet us?" asked Ralof, to which Jason and Shagron exchanged looks and shrugged.

"We'll deal with that if it happens, otherwise, we stick to the plan," Jason reassured him as he un-limbered his composite bow and prepared to crawl over the lip of the crater and down into the underbrush, to find the best vantage point from which to snipe at his targets. Kiara and Ferenc were close behind him, while Shagron had moved further back from the edge, so he could stand, and began to jog around the edge of the crater to find his own way down.

Ralof sat with Torick, watching silently as the wizard flipped through the pages of a small notebook, making curious noises as he scanned the pages quickly. "Is this how you prepare?" he asked the wizard.

"Hmm? Oh, uh, yes," Torick answered, distracted from his task, "there are quite number of options one can consider for making a good distraction – and I can't be expected to remember them all off the top of my head – although I have to choose something that won't completely incinerate our friends in the crater…"

"Wait – you mean you could do something that would destroy everyone in these woods – all the bandits? – and you didn't say something?" Ralof was floored by this!

"Uh-huh," Torick muttered as he continued to flip pages, sitting relaxed in the grass.

"So why didn't you?"

"Well, they seemed so happy with their little plan, and no one seemed at all interested in asking me, so I thought it best to let them feel like they had it all under control," Torick answered. "Ah!" he exclaimed, "this one should do it!" as he settled on a single page, then snapped the notebook shut with a smile. "Omar, what are you…" he trailed off, wanting to compare notes with the young wizard but was suddenly surprised to see that he was not with them.

"Do you suppose he went off, sneaking down with the others?" Ralof offered.

"I hope not," Torick replied, "Wizards die when they rush forward – best to stay back and control things from where you can see everything that's going on… although to each his own."

Ralof gave the mage a sideways glance, a bit concerned about the display of nonchalance coming from one of their own, and then resumed scanning the woods for any sign of young Omar. He was young, and though he had to remind himself sometimes that the wizard had been stitched, he knew enough about such things to know that the host was always the strongest will, and unless he was beaten down by the weight of the others, Omar would likely be the one making most of the decisions. This meant that he would quite often be foolish enough to act like the fourteen – almost fifteen – year-old boy he was, rather than listen to the wisdom of his peers. And so Ralof worried for him…

He needn't have worried. Omar had taken a backseat as Jason usurped his role in the planning, watching how everyone so quickly forgot about him or what he could offer to their tactics. It was almost physically painful for him to watch them forget that this little mission was his idea, his discovery, only to ignore him like a child being forced to sit apart from the grown-ups at the dinner table. The grown-ups all seemed to have their role to play, leaving him nothing but the scraps – an afterthought. With this little foray he'd thought perhaps he had found something of value to the group that he could contribute, that only he could bring to the table.

But the others seemed to think otherwise, cutting him out of the final scene.

He was relegated to observer – not the lead role he had desired, but one that taught him much, nonetheless.

He watched Ralof, presumed the elder statesman of the group, rein in Shagron's bullish enthusiasm; a seasoned, battle-worn brawler, Shagron knew much about winning but precious little about subtlety; Jason, he still carried himself like an officer despite telling everyone he was done with leading, barking out orders the instant things got too chaotic for his liking; it was hard for him to stomach watching Kiara, fawning over Jason like a schoolgirl with a crush – it was laughable that no one else noticed it!

And then there was poor Ferenc, equally infatuated, but with the young Kiara, despite it being clearly unrequited. It was all sad to watch, but sadder still that they always seemed to leave him out of their circle – they clearly thought of him as nothing more than a child, not worthy of consulting, despite his 'borrowed' abilities. Well, if that was the way they wanted it, then he would either have to prove them otherwise, or make the situation work to his advantage…

Sparing little more thought on the matter, he quietly slipped away and into the bushes as his friends readied their plans. With a little practiced stealth, he made his way through the ground cover of the hollow, down to the edge of the clearing around the rocky opening. He paused for a moment to survey the surroundings, looking for a way in without being seen – he couldn't wait too long, knowing that the others would be following along shortly, and he wanted to get inside before the excitement began. Watching the few bandits that were outside the cave, he was grateful that they had been so successful in their raiding – it had made them confident – over-confident – about their hideout. Not being as careful as they ought to be, he was easily able to sneak through the flittering shadows cast by the towering trees.

'*Don't get cocky*' he told himself, making a conscious effort to slow his pace a little as he moved from the soft soil of the forest floor to the sandy stone surface of the cave opening – the gritty texture of the small pebbles would give him away to even the most distracted of ears if he lost his focus on the task at hand. He easily slipped unseen behind the lone man leaning against one wall of the opening and moved into the cave.

The walls were damp and covered in moss, but he could feel the warm draft of cooking fires coming from ahead of him. There was little smoke in the main entryway, which meant they must have another opening or exit somewhere for the smoke to escape – this would be a smart feature for any choice of hideout, else they risked being trapped by any who approached, with no way of escape. Rounding the corner, he saw the cave open into a larger chamber, in which there were several fires going cooking their meals for the day while also trying to dry some of their laundry. Inwardly he gave a disappointed sigh: the smoke was slowly wafting up to the ceiling of the cave, and through a small natural vent in the rocks above – he saw no back-door escape route and thought to himself, '*this is not going to end well for them in a few moments!*'

Ignoring that this was where they lived & slept, he quickly spied around for his true objective, finding it in the far corner. He moved along the left wall, keeping to the shadows as he spotted the small makeshift shelves and barrels that the bandits were using to organize their collected loot. Making sure no one was looking, he picked up a cloak and hat from among the clothes scattered around the hay mattresses that made up the sleeping area of the cave and stepped quietly between the pallets as he made his way to the loot.

It was not guarded – the cave, though poorly lit, was full of twenty or more bandits, all of whom held an equal stake in this bounty, and each would surely raise the alarm if a stranger were discovered in their midst, so it wasn't 'unguarded', but because there were so many of them around, they didn't bother to post a guard specifically around the booty, and so Omar was able to make his way into the assorted stacks of barrels and boxes undetected, to quietly begin to rummage about.

His pulse was pounding as he did so, as any mis-step or the smallest of noises on his part would surely give him away, and he would be incredibly outnumbered if he were discovered, but there was the confidence of that other voice in his head – one that had been so successful as a thief and night prowler that this little escapade was nothing more than a walk in the park for someone of his skill – and though long dead for reasons that he would not share with Omar, it was this skill that Omar now benefitted from the most!

As he began to move about the chests, looking for certain items of particular value that the local guild had brought to his attention the other night, he began to hear noises of battle coming from outside. Quickly the alarm went up within the cave, and men began to drop whatever they were doing, or rouse themselves from their sleep, grabbing whatever weapons they had close at hand and began rushing out to meet the attack.

Omar knew he had very little time left now – not that he didn't believe his new friends wouldn't soon win the fight; in fact, he knew they would, and they would then soon be within the cave as victors, and he would no longer have time to himself to pick out the choicest items!

They would leave him out of their plans, so he would leave them out of his, as well! All in all, a mutually beneficial arrangement that the prince had enforced upon them, he thought.

Outside, Ralof did not have long to worry about where Omar had gone, as they waited for Jason to get in to position and make the appointed signal. Jason, Kiara and Ferenc had each taken up positions from which they could target three of the bandits at a reasonable range for their bows, and Shagron had crawled halfway down the far side of the crater, not moving further for fear of giving away their presence with his armor and natural lack of stealth. From the ridge of the depression, Ralof could see Jason's back as he staked out his target. Squatting low in the brush, Jason pulled his bow from the small harness on his back and retrieved the bowstring from a pocket on his chest.

Smoothly and silently he slipped one knotted end into the notch at the top of the bow, then stretched it down to the lower end, ensuring the string lined up with the padded grooves carved onto the wood – padding where the string touched the bow helped reduce the noise when firing, along with the small tufts of beaver fur woven into the cord just a few inches short of the where the string met the wood of the bow to lessen the vibration of the string when he released it, all to make sure the hunter was as silent as possible when stalking their prey – he did all this without taking his eyes off his target. The bandit, sitting about forty yards away, had just finished dropping some hay for the horses in the corral, and was facing in Jason's direction, but couldn't see him through the brush.

With the string set, he nocked an arrow and smoothly drew back the bow and set his aim, feeling the tension in his right shoulder as his pulled with his back and shoulders, bending the curved bow as far as it would go – he was strong enough to have pulled even harder, but such strength did not always translate to accuracy or speed. His bow had been handmade for him by a master craftsman and suited his strength perfectly. Patiently, he held his hand just below his chin, feeling the string and the feathered fletching brush against his chin as he carefully lined up his target, knowing that Ferenc and Kiara would be doing the same for their targets.

Waiting just a brief moment to ensure that everyone would be ready, he let his fingers relax and released the pent-up energy of the bow as it snapped back to its natural form, its energy flowing through the string and into the shaft of the arrow as it sped past his fingers with their steady grip on the bow and flew silently through the air towards his target.

The tip of the arrow struck home with deadly effect – piercing the chest just above the nook of the collarbone, through the windpipe and penetrating the spine, burying the shaft up to the plumage of the fletching, with the bloodied arrowhead emerging out the back. A shocked gurgle of surprise bubbled through the bandit's throat, the sound muffled by the blood that quickly filled his throat and ran down his chin, halting any immediate alarm from being raised by the surprise attack.

His nearest companions had time enough to hear the faint whistle of Jason's arrow flying and striking home but could do nothing to react as they too were struck by bolts loosed by Ferenc and Kiara, with equally lethal consequences.

Seeing the first three targets drop, Shagron burst out of his prone position in the woods and began a headlong charge through the sloping brush to challenge the enemy nearest to him, though he took a moment to close the distance. As he did, the bandit raised the alarm with a loud cry, drawing a sword from a scabbard at his hip, and prepared to meet Shagron's charge. The clang of steel rang loudly in the woods but did not echo greatly – it was enough to cause the other two remaining bandits to turn towards Shagron.

It would not have been Jason's preference to shoot the men in the back, but he considered to himself as he notched and drew another arrow, it wasn't as if three-to-one were fair odds to start with anyway – drawing and releasing more quickly this time, he had to raise an eye in surprise as another arrow from his right flew in almost simultaneously with his, and the impact of both bolts drove the man face first to the ground, dead before he hit. Glancing to his right but unable to see through the brush, he almost laughed aloud as he heard Kiara's voice over the rising clamour…

"MINE!" she yelled, moving forward to get a better vantage point from which to snipe the cave entrance.

"Says you!" Jason chided her back playfully, moving forward himself to get in position.

Jason could not see Shagron's fight, but from the top of the ridge Ralof could – he watched intently as Shagron emerged into a small clearing, this time foregoing his shield to instead attack with both hands on the hilt of his bastard sword, raising it above his head in a high guard position. Though it was at a distance, Ralof could hear the clash of steel as Shagron struck first, only for his blow to be parried by the smaller, nimbler swordsman. The parry seemed to knock the lesser armored man back somewhat, and so Shagron closed again, this time bringing his blade down with enough force that it shattered the smaller longsword as the bandit attempted to block his blow again.

Ralof would have watched more, but he felt Torick's hand on his shoulder, gently pulling him back from the edge of the crater to stand slightly behind him. There was a reddish glow to his other hand, a clear sign that he was channeling something, and it was his turn to do his part – to create a commotion that would draw the remaining bandits out of their cave. He waved his right hand forward, then joined with his left, to which the crimson hue leapt and spread like a fire between two torches.

It took just a moment to prepare, then he spread his hands out towards the crater, palms down, fingers spread. Ralof watched as the glow brightened, and then seemed to combust into flame, building and burning until Torick's hands seemed to be consumed by the bright yellow and orange flame. Reaching just below the lip of the crater, the flame exploded from his hands like a wave, knocking Ralof back in surprise as a loud crackle and bang echoed above the plain, and the wave of fire sliced across the top of the crater like a scythe, burning and destroying everything in its path.

Disappearing almost as quickly as it had been summoned, all that remained was the burning treetops that had once towered over the oasis, and Ralof watched in awe as, one by one, the flaming foliage began to slowly tip over and fall down into the woods below, as if someone had cut the strings on a marionette.

In the woods below, the heavy cover of the branches and leaves made it almost impossible for Jason, Shagron or the others to see just what had happened other than hearing the thundering bang that had accompanied the pyrotechnics display. Looking up in response, it was Shagron who first cried out to Jason.

"Run back!" he yelled at the top of his lungs, hoping that Jason would hear and heed the warning, as he himself began to scramble back up the shallow incline, trying to avoid the largest of the falling timbers.

Jason heard the warning, and while he couldn't be sure that Ferenc and Kiara had as well, it seemed a pretty common-sense thing to do, looking up at the falling tree trunks, bringing smoke and ash down with them as they fell to earth with tremendous thudding impacts. Each trunk landed and shook loose their burning leaves, which then dropped to the floor of the small woods and began to consume the already drought-ridden bushes and detritus at a rapid rate.

Back at the top of the crater, Ralof was aghast at the devastation and fire that Torick's spell had caused and let him know it.

"Are you mad?!" he cried out, "Our friends are down there! They're going to burn with the rest of the woods!"

"Calm down..." Torick advised him calmly, "...I'm not finished yet."

Indeed, he had already begun to concentrate on a new casting, focusing, and drawing this time on elemental forces of wind. Even as he was speaking, Ralof's wispy white beard was beginning to blow up into his face in the rising wind – a wind that Torick seemed to be shaping with his mind as much as his hands – turning and twisting it, funneling and controlling it – until a small cloud began to appear above the trees, taking shape as it gathered in the smoke and flames from the fires below. The strength of the updraft seemed to suck the fire right out of the burning woods, robbing it of the fuel it needed to burn as it captured and funneled the heavy smoke up into a cyclone; it grew, as if taking a deep breath, before suddenly flinging itself down again, sweeping into the crater and dispensing its smoke and ash-laden contents directly into the mouth of the cave, before dispersing with a powerful gust of wind.

Several small fires flickered and burned around the suddenly quiet forest, where the unnatural silence was broken at first only by the crackling of those few small flames. Gradually sound returned to those left alive to hear it: Jason could hear the trees settling to the ground as burned branches cracked and snapped beneath the weight of the fallen timbers; Ferenc and Kiara called to one another to make sure everyone was okay, and Shagron could be heard cursing across the far side of the bandit encampment.

The next moment, the chorus of noise was joined by the distinct sound of men – cries and coughing began to echo out of the cave entrance, followed by shouts of confusion and anger. All eyes turned to the focus of their plan – the bandit lair – and the rangers began to nock new arrows to their bows where they stood.

At first it was like a carnival game, the archers easily picked off the first few figures that stepped out of the entrance, and the bodies pitched forward to fall off the small ledge to land on the floor of the crater below. By the fifth or sixth, it was clear the others were becoming aware that they were being targeted, and their strategy changed – some charged headlong out of the cave, diving straight off the ledge, hoping to land and roll to safety, while others tried to avoid an arrow by crawling low around the corner to the pathway leading down.

Neither plan worked for long. Jason and the rangers easily marked those trying to sneak to the path, and Shagron waited at the bottom of the ledge to welcome any who were unfortunate enough to land and still be able to get to their feet. In fact, Jason was pretty sure he even saw Shagron step back at one point, to allow one of the bandits a moment to regain their feet after rolling to a stop and draw their sword so it would be a fair fight. Shaking his head, he offered none of his targets a similar chance.

It took longer to let the smoke clear than it did for the assembled warriors to dispatch the twenty-five bandits who had been inhabiting the encampment. This gave Torick and Ralof ample time to gather their horses and walk them down the inclined trail than ran around the crater, and meet up with their comrades in the remains of the corral where the bandits had kept their mounts – all of these were gone now, having stampeded when the trees fell and the fires spooked them into a frenzy – which was of little concern to Torick, but seemed to matter quite a bit to Jason and Ferenc, who thought they could have sold the horses for quite a bit of profit.

Gathering, it was Shagron who was the first to share his opinion of just what he thought of Torick's 'distraction' to lure out the bandits…

"Are you out of your bloody mind?!" he exclaimed to Torick angrily.

"That's what I said!" echoed Ralof.

"You almost killed the lot of us with that shit!" Shagron continued, his red-faced anger contrasting sharply with Torick's pale-faced calm. "Whose side are you on?"

"You wanted them out of the cave – they all came out of the cave. You are all unhurt. What exactly are you unhappy with?" Torick reasoned in a soft voice, which bothered Shagron all the more.

"That was the sort of shit I'd expect from the kid, not from…" Shagron started, until Ralof interrupted, "Where is Omar anyway? He wasn't on the ridge with us. Has anyone seen him in all of this?"

"Did you check under a tree?" Shagron offered, staring at Torick, but clearly not angry enough to do more than that. Something else was bothering him that he hadn't figured out just yet, but now he had to find the boy…

As if on cue, they were greeted by a voice from above, on the ledge leading to the cave. "I'm right here," Omar said, drawing looks from everyone assembled.

"What are you doing up there?" Ralof asked.

"Well, the plan seemed simple enough," Omar explained, seated casually on the rock, wiping black smoke marks from his face with a damp cloth, "...but it didn't seem like we had a good idea of just how many people were in the cave, so I decided to scout it out while everyone was getting ready."

"You weren't seen?" Ferenc asked curiously.

"I can be pretty sneaky when I want to be," Omar answered. "I took care of a couple on the inside, just case anyone was wondering if I was carrying my own weight with this enterprise. I wasn't expecting all the smoke..." he said, looking sideways at Torick, "but I managed to stay low until everyone was out. We should be able to account for thirty bandits when we talk to the Ispan – that'll be a nice bounty!"

"We're not here to collect ears!" Ralof countered quickly, sounding disgusted by the practice of collecting bounties.

"Speak for yourself, Brother," Kiara replied just as quickly, "We've lost the horses as a prize, I'm not going to give up the outlaw bounties, too!"

"Ugh!" Ralof grunted, clearly wanting nothing to do with the practice. "Don't worry about a share for me! You can have all the ears you want!"

"We should probably check inside now that the smoke has cleared..." Omar suggested, "to see if there's anything of any value that we can claim..."

"...or return to their rightful owners." Shagron finished the sentence for him, ignoring Omar's frown.

"Alright, let's get on with it and get back to the city before nightfall," Jason urged them, "I'm not going to camp here and wait for any of their friends to return!"

*****Omar*****

Most of the others were still asleep the next morning when Jason made his way down for breakfast. They had worked quickly and ridden hard to get back to town before nightfall, and as it was, the innkeeper had already given away three of their rooms – despite their payment in advance – so he had to move quietly this morning as he slipped out of the room, to not awaken Ferenc or Kiara, while Shagron, Ralof and Torick had shared the other chamber.

Omar had waived his room entirely, saying he had family in the city that he would stay with instead, which was why Jason was somewhat surprised to see him back in the tavern so early this morning, already having a cup of wine and waiting for him as he came down.

He also noticed that Omar seemed to have acquired a change of gear, dressed now in a well-made, high-collared black leather jerkin, matching leggings, knee-high black boots, metal bracers – also dyed black, of course – and with fitted black leather gloves, sporting an elegant deep red stitching that was common across the entire outfit, even the mid-length travel cloak that he currently had flipped back over his shoulder as he hunched over his drink.

"You're up early!" Jason greeted him as he made his way between the tables over to the hearth where Omar was sitting on a long bench. "Not spending time with your family?"

"Oh, we did a lot of catching up last night, and I wanted to get up early to get our claim over to the Captain of the Guard before things started to smell too much." Omar replied, sipping his wine.

In truth, he had been up all night. After saying his goodbyes to his travelling companions, he had moved swiftly through the darkened streets to find his contact at the local guild, and only when they were sure they were safe from prying eyes did he reveal what he had found in the bandits' lair. Unwrapping the cloth for his fellow guild master, he displayed the green-hued dagger, carved from a single piece of bone from a creature that neither of them could identify. The exquisite carvings made the straight, thin, blade look more ceremonial than practical, but an experienced knifeman could tell the balance was perfect, and the blade itself razor sharp.

"This is it then?" Omar asked, seeking confirmation.

"Aye," came the answer, "as much as it has been told to me, this is one of the last remaining fae slayer-blades that the ancient Avar crafted. Not so much the sharpness of the blade that you are seeking…" he explained as he passed his hand over the weapon, never actually touching it, "…but imbued with the magic needed to sever an Angyalok from their light – to make any wound a mortal wound to one of the faerie-kind."

"Fair enough," Omar replied, covering the weapon with the cloth wrapping and sliding a small sack of coins across the table. "Deal is a deal."

The exchange had taken very little time; the rest of the night he spent awake, alone with his thoughts, unable to let his mind rest enough to get any sleep.

He casually slid a bag of coins across the table to Jason, "This is what we got for the bandits. Four hundred fifty silver pieces; fifteen for each bandit killed, plus another twenty silvers for each of the horses – I took the five we found wandering near the road on the way back over to the quartermaster this morning as well. He was happy to take them for the militia but didn't want to pay anything near a fair price – it was everything my brother and I could do to get twenty – but it still makes for a good split! Almost sixty-nine silvers for everyone – if we count Dar as well, which, y'know, I don't know what everyone else thinks, but, well, she wasn't there, but she is part of the group, I guess…"

"Just a moment…" Jason interrupted Omar's rambling as he scanned the contents of the pouch, "I thought the bounty on bandits across all of Nyirseg was thirty silvers?"

"Oh… yeah,… well, that's what I said to the Captain, but he said he didn't believe we could have possibly killed that many ourselves – just the seven of us – and we started to argue, and then he accused me – us – of cutting ears off caravan victims! Can you believe that? That the raiders had probably attacked a caravan, killed the traders, and then we took their ears to pad the count! Well, I was shocked, but at the same time, I didn't really have any proof of the truth of it, and there was no official bounty from the Ispan for this particular band of marauders, so he agreed not to arrest me, but since they couldn't verify the ears, they gave me half the going rate. I mean, what could I do?! They were going to arrest me and then come for everyone else…"

"Alright, alright, I get it." Jason waved him down, as Omar had been rising from his chair, getting more and more excited as he told the story. "We'll add it to the gold and silver we found in the cave – minus whatever personal effects Shagron thinks we can return to their rightful owners – and we still have a pretty good haul – enough to cover supplies to Scarbantia and back, and maybe a little extra!"

Omar had a sullen look when he was reminded that Shagron still wanted to turn over some of the more identifiable loot to the Ispan's administrators, to try to return them to their owners – but at the same time he had to admit, they didn't have a lot of time to sell the items themselves and get any real value – worse, if he took it to his 'family' at the guild, they would be sure to take advantage of his need to unload the items quickly and undercut the price terribly. So he took another long drink and resigned himself to the loss.

Slowly the others drifted down to breakfast, after sleeping in a fair bit later than usual, which was well earned by the action the day before. Aquincum was not a large trading center, which was helpful for many of them – like Shagron – who wanted to keep a low profile, yet they also had enough guilds in service that they could provide everything the group needed for the remainder of their trip.

"I do hope that Dar returns soon." Ralof voiced his concern, which everyone else seemed to be thinking. "She seems to know the most about this 'Vazul' fellow, and just what we're supposed to do when we get to Scarbantia, so I don't see how we can accomplish much without her…"

"Yet we are losing time just sitting here – the ride does not get any easier once we cross the mountains…" Shagron added, which also caused Jason to look down at his drink, thinking again about how they would have to cross through the Lakhani Plain again, which he was dreading.

"So we will get what we need this morning, regroup here at noon, and be on our way," Shagron said with authority, "We can make good time in half a day if the weather holds, and Dar will at least know where we are heading if she does return and needs to catch up!"

While almost everyone had seemed to defer to Dar's knowledge of their foe as enough justification to follow her on this quest, there hadn't been any discussion about any one person being in charge in her absence. Despite agreeing as a group to follow Omar's lead on dispatching some raiders, it was evident that everyone still saw him – despite his magicks or stitchings – to still be just a boy, and not someone they would take orders from. Torick always seemed too disinterested in what was going on to be depended on for making quick decisions, and with Ferenc and Kiara deferring to Jason, and Ralof deferring to Shagron, it seemed like it was between the two of them, the most deliberate minded of the group, to see which of them the collective group would permit to give them orders.

In this moment then, it was a rather mundane decision that Shagron seemed to be ruling on and there was no controversy in arguing the matter, so Jason was the first to nod in agreement, quickly followed by the majority of the others, and it seemed like the decision was made. Jason also shared the portions of the bounty that Omar had brought, and they were each quickly on their way to track down whatever they needed for the next week on the road.

****Tibor****

Dar returned to the palace in the morning, leaving Tibor alone with the many books in the library. As much as he wished he could see the rest of the city, there was a part of him that felt he already had, and so he was quite content to spend his time exploring her library. Dar was much more organized and cared for her books like treasures – like any true mage would do – and he was able to find several interesting tomes that he wanted to explore, piling them up on the floor by the most comfortable chair he could find in the room, where he quickly settled in for the day. Or at least that was the plan.

As interesting as some of the books were, it was his thirst that first led him to start to explore the interior of the compound further. Setting aside the third tome (though appearing large, the handwritten script did not put many words on a single page, so he was finding that he could move through the books much quicker than he originally expected), he stood, stretched, and began to wander in search of what would pass for a kitchen. He passed through the main foyer again and circled the trunk of the massive tree around which the entire building was centered. Across from the hall was another sitting chamber, connected to a room which looked like a formal dining area.

All these somewhat pie-shaped rooms were connected by a series of doors that followed one after another, and he reasoned that the next one ought to bring him to the kitchen or pantry, and he was correct. The room was not very large but contained a small coal fire against the outer wall, keeping a pot of something warm, along with tiny kettle that seemed ideal for tea. There was a table in the center of the kitchen, and a few cupboards around the side, and a well-stocked pantry near the tree.

As with the other rooms, at no point did any of the construction invade or damage the central tree in any way, always respecting its dominating presence in a way that made it seem like Dar had sought its permission to live here, like a landlord; rather different than if an architect had tried to incorporate the tree into the design; this was something more intentional, of a shared purpose, though he could not guess what the tree received in exchange for permitting her to reside here.

His curiosity at this thought led him to forget his thirst for a moment, as he walked closer to the smooth-barked trunk that was exposed here, cautiously touching it with his hand. He withdrew quickly in surprise, feeling what he at first believed to be a pulse, but then quickly dismissed the idea. He followed the curve of the tree into the next room, and found himself back in the library, having completed a full circle.

There were other chambers that spread out further away from the center of the building, like spokes on a carriage wheel – one of these led to his guest room – but he had his attention now on the stairway leading upwards – one he had not noticed the first time he was in the room. The railing and steps here seemed to grow out of the tree itself, flowing in a way that made it impossible to distinguish if the railings were carved or grown. Tibor almost started to run up the stairs but controlled the impulse and stepped carefully.

As he moved upwards, his head began to emerge into the room above, but he was unable to make out any details as he found his vision was suddenly beginning to blur. A wave of nausea followed, and he found himself gripping the stair rail tightly in his hand as he struggled with his balance, trying to keep himself from tumbling backwards down the stairs. The blurry room began to spin, for which he could only close his eyes, which made the sensation even worse! He felt one leg go numb at the knee, and then had the sensation of falling backwards and rolling down the stairs, which was the last thing he remembered before everything went black.

He awoke on the small chaise longue in the library, not knowing how he had been moved from the bottom of the stairs. He squinted then rubbed his eyes, trying to remember what had happened, and was surprised to see a young girl, perhaps thirteen, with tangled dirty-blonde hair, setting down a cup of wine on the table beside him.

Her face was small and round, scuffed with marks of dirt as if she had just come from playing in the woods, with little bits of leaves caught in the knots of her shoulder-length hair. She was close to him as she set down the cup, and he couldn't help but feel like he was in a forest, surrounded by the scent of damp moss and fresh pine needles after an autumn rain.

She gave him only the barest hint of a smile before she turned and walked away without saying a word, and didn't look back when he called after her, leaving him alone in the room again. The sense of disorientation lifted, coming back briefly as he sat up, but then disappearing entirely with a sip of wine. It was a blend he had never tasted before, with a heavy, oaken flavour and hints of vanilla... much like the forest tones of the young girl who had served it.

He presumed the girl was a servant of some kind, and thought about going after her, but when he approached the doorway she had exited through – the one near the stairs where he had last entered the library – he felt a twinge in his gut as he neared the base of the stairs, reliving the nausea he had felt earlier, and decided to give up on any further exploration of the house and returned to his reading chair. If he was lucky, perhaps the young girl had at least left the rest of the bottle for him to enjoy.

As he made his way back to the reading chair, scanning the floor and tables for any sign of a wine bottle, his eye caught the reflection of light off a piece of glass near the curtain of the only window in the room. Grinning with anticipated delight, he reached down and brushed the heavy fabric back with his hand as he grabbed for the bottle, only to find it empty.

Disappointed, he was placing it back on the floor when he noticed a small stack of books underneath the table beneath the window – unusual, he thought to himself, as everything else in the library was so immaculately shelved and organized, to see something stored so casually under a table stand. He slid the stack out into the light, and turned to see the spines, looking for the titles – an old habit from another world, which had yet to come into practice here – he saw nothing to indicate their topics, but recognized a familiar symbol on one of the books near the bottom: a flaming sword, pointing upright, held by a metal gauntlet. It was a little more stylized, with a circle of gold surrounding the blade, and some unusual runes above and below, but he could make out the legendary sword as clear as anything.

He pulled the book out from the stack, not caring about the ones above it that toppled to the floor, and scanned the cover, which had a larger depiction of the rune sword embossed on the cover. The cover had a velvety texture, like the fur of an animal – black in colour and soft to the touch, with a warm sheen – runes were painted on the hide, matting the short fur with a glossy red ink that was rich and deep. It looked so different from most of the other books in the library, he wondered why it had been relegated to such a lowly station, hidden beneath poorer tomes, out of sight beneath a table. He lifted the cover – it was heavier than it appeared – and revealed the cracked and worn vellum pages, supple and well crafted, with the distinctive veining apparent even in the dim lights of the candles. The script was a mix of Avar, Angyalok, and Torpek dialects, which made the reading a slower process, but Tibor was quickly absorbed by the strange text, forgetting even his quest for more wine as he settled into his reading.

Dar returned in the early afternoon and found Tibor still seated on the floor, near the small window where he had discovered his latest treasure. Rousing him from his reading, she cordially asked how his day had been before quickly proceeding to recount the events of her day in the palace – how she had explained to the Prince the situation with the discovery of Tibor's presence, his waking, and how he had accepted her assurances that she would safeguard Tibor in her compound, to maintain secrecy. The Prince, she explained, was distracted by other affairs of state, and seemed less concerned about this than she thought he ought to be.

"We are at war," she stated flatly, with a definite air of disappointment – not so much with the concept of war as being ridiculous in her mind, but in that it would distract resources – and the Prince – from the things she was more concerned with!

"The presumptuously named 'Kingdom' of Sarkozy has declared war with Nyirseg, believing us to have an inferior claim to the right of rulership, and accusing us of breaching our vows of trade by hoarding food while the Onogur people starve and die." Dar took a deep breath as she explained this to Tibor. "At the same time," she continued, "The newly christened 'Kingdom' of Temeskoz has declared war on the Principality of Mezoseg, for pretty much the same reasons."

"We – the Prince & I – believe that Prince Ond Farkas of Sarkozy and Prince

Almos Kedves of Temeskoz are in league, and while they may not yet agree on which of them has the greater claim to being the rightful king, they have both sought to isolate us from our closest ally by declaring war on Mezoseg at the same time, hoping to divide our attention and our forces."

"Their timing is not good!" Dar noted.

"We have made little progress on stopping Voros Vazul, the plagues, and whatever else he was planning, I can't believe any of these princes think they could field a decent fighting force. There are more plague-born than footmen who are strong enough to lift a blade!" Her overall tone was one of disgust for anyone who seemed to think that now was a good time to start a war!

She could almost picture the scene in her mind: battlefields with of rows of starved and diseased soldiers, lined up to face one another, barely strong enough to hold their weapons, waiting to see which side would fall over dead from exhaustion first, for the other to claim victory without striking a blow!

"The Prince has always had good relations with Mezoseg," she continued, not seeming concerned with whether or not Tibor was able to follow along with the politics, though he seemed to be listening intently "but Prince Elod himself – and many of his people – are Onogur, not Avar, and he will not resist their unification for long…" Dar poured herself a goblet of wine and took a seat, looking tired from the politics of the palace.

"If the Onogur are uniting, then it means there will be scant support for the realm to follow an Avar Prince – this will not bode well for Prince Svato's dream of unifying the seven tribes under his rule… Prince Svato has sent messengers to Prince Elod, but we have yet to receive any reply, so he is concerned and worried about our chances before even setting foot in the field!" It seemed to Tibor like she wasn't even talking to him now; she was just going over her own thoughts out loud, trying to stay ahead of whatever came next.

"We should rejoin our companions in the field," she stated to him at last, though she was referring to her companions more so than his – he hadn't even met them yet!

"Whatever happens with the politics, it will be a moot point if we don't stop Vazul. And maybe, if we are lucky, our success might be enough to swing favour back to Prince Svato. Either way, there is more we can do in Scarbantia than we can do here."

"Ah, about that!" Tibor practically jumped out of his seat when he realized the conversation had turned back to something relevant to him. "I found something I think you might be interested in…"

****Jason****

By noon they were all gathered again, mounted, and ready to ride, with Omar strangely seeming to be the most eager to lead them out the gate. They expected it would take them anywhere from seven to nine days to reach Scarbantia, depending on the roads, the weather, and the health of the horses, but there were more dangerous things than bandits about these days, and they watched the horizon carefully for danger as they rode. By the end of the first day, they could see the faint lights of Solva, a town on the north side of the Duna River – which had turned west somewhere north of Aquincum and paralleled their course.

The river was still too wide to cross easily, and so they camped outdoors instead of going out of their way to reach the town, which drew no complaints from anyone. The next day they entered the foothills of the southern branch of the Matras Mountains, following the beaten trail that the departing legionnaires had travelled not so terribly long ago. The foothills had been forested at one point, but the long-ranging wildfires had reduced much of the woods to ash, some of it still smoking as they passed by.

Eventually their path narrowed and blended into the river; slowing their horses to a walk they carefully worked their way over the slippery stones in the cold yet shallow waters in this stretch of the river. The river wove a winding path into the mountains, and when they once again emerged onto a dry trail, it was onto a scene unlike any they had ever seen before, and even Jason had to pause at the sight.

Jason and the other men of the scout unit had left the region directly after they had triggered their trap, not looking back or wasting time with remorse. Now, he, along with Ferenc and Kiara, who had been a party to the plan, looked out upon the enduring impact of what they had done to secure their freedom from the Imperium.

What was once a vast green plateau, ringed by lush woods and wildlife, was now a debris-filled swamp from which the water refused to retreat. Emerging at the level of the river was different than looking on it from above – here they encountered both the scattered remains of wagons, carts, tents and shields, and also the gouges that the charging water had carved into the soft soil that created new channels for the river to follow, submerging much of the plain in a marshy quagmire from which they could see broken trees stretching up from beneath the mud, like the hands of buried giants reaching up out of the earth.

Where the plain had been flat, it was now ridged and lumpy, where the mud piled up against obstructions to form small islands. And everywhere, the stench – despite the passage of time, the remains of so many human and animal carcasses, decaying in the mire, hung across the open plateau like a gruesome reminder that death had stained this land, and it would not wash clean.

Climbing one of the smaller mounds of debris, Jason could make out a pack of animals in the distance – probably wolves – digging in the dirt to uncover one more piece of buried flesh that would sustain the pack. The sky here was cloudy and overcast, with a feeling of moisture in the air, like a threatening rain that never seemed to come, giving the region a look of perpetual dusk. Birds circled above, close in because of the low clouds, drawn by the easy picking for carrion eaters that constantly scoured the shifting landscape for whatever the slow-moving water might uncover from the mud each morning.

Squinting for a moment, staring at something that caught his eye, he quickly dropped back to rejoin the group at the base of the mound.

"We're not alone," he announced, triggering some alarm. "Don't worry, they're not close – maybe half a mile into the plain – I counted maybe six or seven, well-armed, but other than that I couldn't tell…"

"Can we get through the plain and on our way without looking for trouble?" Ralof asked, suggesting discretion.

"Perhaps," Jason answered, shrugging his shoulders as if he hadn't really considered the option of trying to avoid an encounter.

"Who are they?" Omar asked. "I mean, are they even a threat to us? Maybe they're here for a good reason."

Jason exchanged a look with Ferenc and Shagron. "Maybe it's just me…" he started, "…but ever since the arrival of the plagues, I haven't bumped into too many people in the wilds that wanted to be my friend… and wouldn't expect good odds of that changing in a place like this!"

"They may be bandits or scavengers," Shagron offered, "pilfering the last resting place of these legionnaires."

He sounded disgusted by the thought, as if it were no better than grave robbing, his tone drawing a sympathetic nod from Ralof.

"I don't see them," called Torick, standing close to the top of the mound, peering across the swamp.

"Southwest corner," Jason replied.

"Nope. Did they see you?" Torick asked.

Jason scrambled up to a better vantage point, insulted by the insinuation from Torick, but bothered that he may have been right. Pulling up against a dead tree branch, he did his best to disguise his presence while he scanned the swamp for any sign of the people he had spotted earlier – he saw no sign of life, until a small flock of birds flew up from where they had been sitting to rejoin the rest of the flock in the air. He quickly dropped back down.

"They've dropped down below the debris and are moving in our direction. We still don't know their intentions, so it's probably best if we stick by the river and just try to follow it across the plateau – we don't need to turn south until we are out of the foothills, so we can avoid the swamp entirely – but we must get moving now if we want to avoid any surprises!"

They began walking their horses along the low bank of the river where it cut along its original course through the plateau, with Jason leading while Kiara and Ferenc took turns trying to see if they could spot movement on the plain. It would take them the better part of an hour to reach the point where the river exited the plain to the west, moving cautiously on the slippery river rocks, but Jason hoped that they might yet find the rising trail that would take them to where the rangers had camped, using the high ground to their advantage. But they would need time to reach the path...

"Are you sure you saw someone?" Ralof asked Jason, struggling to keep up the pace with his sandaled feet on the slippery river stones, "I mean, I can certainly understand why you would want to avoid our exploring the plains – it was not a pretty scene for you back then, nor has it improved any with time – but I'm not sure I see the need to move so quickly on such poor ground. Even the horses are having trouble with their footing in the water, and it's getting late in the day – we should be looking for a place to camp!"

Jason turned back to answer, looking at Ralof with a scowl, which quickly turned to something else, looking past Ralof as he yelled:

"Get down!"

Shocked but alert, Ralof ducked, and as he did, a crossbow bolt whirred past his head, and lodged solidly into the neck of his horse! Rearing up, crying out in pain, his horse fought free of Ralof's grip, trying madly to turn its head to bite at the wound. Ralof looked back at where the bolt had come from and could see what had caused Jason's alarm. Kneeling atop the upturned roots of large tree stump, two crossbowmen were firing upon the party. The second had released his shot towards Shagron, but the cry from Jason seemed to have caused enough movement to make him miss his target.

As if the crossbows were a signal, three more figures emerged to the left of the party, coming over the top of a low mud embankment, all three lowering spears as they descended rapidly to the water's edge, reaching the group nearest to Torick and Kiara.

Torick did not immediately see the threat, standing on the right side of the horse, blocking his view of the attackers; Kiara saw them come down the embankment and drew her sword to meet their charge. She swung to deflect the spear coming towards her, which she thought was successful until she realized that the man had not been targeting her with the rush at all.

Wearing light leather armor, reinforced with small straps of thin steel bands laced over the soft padded animal skin, each with different versions of a metal skullcap draped with light chain down the back of their necks, the attackers thrust their spears into the horses, quickly releasing after driving the shafts home, and drawing longswords. Two of the three spears pierced Torick's mount with deadly results, drawing a loud squeal of pain from the horse before it dropped dead, splashing into the water at the surprised wizard's feet. The single spear directed at Kiara's mount deflected slightly as a result of her attempted parry, preventing a killing blow but still sorely wounding the horse in the left flank, causing it to stumble and struggle to walk.

The second spearman was in the middle of drawing his longsword to continue his attack but was cut down by a massive stroke from the much larger blade wielded by Shagron, who brought the man down with a loud cry as he stepped into the fight. Kiara, her sword in her hand, looked around for the first spearman, stepping forward to insert herself between Torick and her opponent, positioning herself to protect the unarmored wizard. The clang of the swordplay echoed loudly over the water, rebounding off the steep embankment on the far side of the river and back out over the plain, mixing with the wild screams of injured horses and the cries of the combatants as the encounter escalated.

Ferenc had rushed forward to close the gap on the two arbalesters before they could reload their crossbows, and seeing his approach, they soon gave up on the cranking process and drew swords to engage him. Omar and Ralof had been surprised by the suddenness of the attack and the pandemonium of being somewhat surrounded by their attackers, while also trying to decide whether to try to calm their panicking horses or release them and focus on their opponents.

The decision was pretty much made for Omar as he saw a small figure looking over the party from behind the crossbowmen, still sitting high up on the overturned tree-stump. Though there was no glow or aura of a casting, he could sense the magic being channeled, and decided this was going to be his dance partner for the ball!

Passing the reins of his horse to Ralof, he started his own casting, trying not to draw attention to himself as he did so. Considering his choices for how to handle this target, he opted for something subtle, cupping his hands in front of him, then folding them together as if he were holding a small bird in his hands.

Almost immediately, the young girl in the tree stump began to grasp her face and throat, as if she were struggling to breathe. Impossibly, her hands seemed to stop in mid-air, just inches from her face, held back by an invisible force that was preventing the air from passing through as well. In less than a minute, her panicked breathing had consumed everything breathable, and she passed out, slumping against her perch.

For the moment, Jason felt a bit out of sorts, not having an immediate target for himself, but that quickly changed as four more figures descended from the embankment ahead of the party and began to close on him in the shallow water. Getting a better look at their opponents as they moved forward with their swords held low but pointed directly at him, he could see the ashen grey colour and rough texture of their skin; covered with an abundance of dark body hair that curled out around the collars of their chainmail shirts, Jason recognized all of the telltale signs that said these were Torpek – though he scarce believed he was seeing them in the flesh!

Torpek were faerie creatures – or so he had been told – that lived in caves beneath the earth and stole small children who didn't listen to their parents. Tales of their cold-hearted nature were as old as the hills themselves, though no one had ever claimed to have seen one alive since the Angyalok ruled these lands; every once in a while, a treasure hunter would come across a lost map of a Torpek hoard, usually in the depths of a cave somewhere, and a group of brave adventurers would set out on a quest, only to never be seen again. Now, Jason had to blink his eyes to believe what he was seeing and try to remember if the stories said anything special about how to kill them!

"Shagron!" he called out, knowing that four-to-one were long odds, even for someone as skilled as he thought he was, before he moved forward himself, to position himself between the party and the advancing Torpek, trying to choose a spot in the shallow water where he could steady his feet.

This also meant that he would wait for one of the four to attack him first – in which they seemed more than willing to oblige. As he had hoped, the slippery footing left the first attacker off balance as he dodged the first swing, and he was able to counter with a solid swing to his back, landing the Torpek face down in the water, still alive but struggling in the slippery rocks. It wasn't long before he heard Shagron's long strides splashing up behind him.

They paired off, each facing two of the Torpek as they moved to surround them. The next attacks came fast, as the remaining three attacked at once, allowing the fourth to crawl back a few steps and regain his footing. Most of these exchanges were a series of swings and parries, raising the volume of the clash dramatically, as the sound echoed off the hill to one side and out over the plains, where a light fog was starting to roll in from the woods.

Ferenc had closed with the two descending from the tree stump, and quickly dispatched the first with a thrust as the Torpek landed in the riverbed, removing his sword just in time to parry a blow from his companion. Kiara stood with her sword levelled at the two remaining spearmen on their flank, who yelled out in anger as Torick slowly cut the throat of the first spearman that Shagron had originally knocked to the ground, ensuring his demise.

Preston

The figure in the bed appeared to be sleeping peacefully, tucked in neatly beneath the plain white sheet, with one arm over the covers, allowing the IV feed to be unobstructed. Without warning, the young boy's whole body seized with tension, snapping his head off the pillow as he clenched his teeth in his sleep. Relaxing as suddenly as he had convulsed, his head fell back on the pillow, and a small drop of blood formed at his nose, slowing running down his cheek as his head rolled to the side and he quietly expired.

Kemeny stood at the foot of the bed, his hunched figure standing watch over the many guests in the abandoned hotel. He silently wrote on his chart, noting the time of death. A quiet sigh escaped the short fur of his muzzled face, as he thought about the work he would have to do now to dispose of the remains – always an unwelcome task, but one to which he was quickly becoming accustomed.

He was disturbed from his thoughts only a moment later as his ears perked up and turned towards sounds coming from another bed – first it was the change in breathing that he heard, then the spasms in the bed creaking the old springs in the mattress – across the dark room on another of the small cots. He shuffled across the room, looking at each of the beds he passed on his way, noting the sleeping occupants.

Arriving at the last bed, he again paused, and surveyed his guest. It was always the same – they would spasm, almost like they were having a bad dream, then they would simply stop – stop moving, stop breathing, stop everything. You couldn't tell the brain had hemorrhaged, unable to cope with the reality of what had happened elsewhere, and, cut off from their mind, the rest of the body simply stopped working. Kemeny raised his clipboard and noted the time of death.

He looked around the room, wondering – something must be happening, and whatever it was, the master would not be happy. He paused to lick the burned fur on his right forearm, one of several wounds that were still healing, only to look up again as he heard the telltale sound of creaking bedsprings as yet another patient seemed to be convulsing. He looked at the clock on the wall and began to shuffle over to the source of the noise, to record yet another time of death.

No, the master would not be pleased at all...

*****Kiara*****

Kiara did well to parry the blows coming at her, which gave Torick the opportunity he needed to concentrate – slowly, but with building intensity, small red globes of burning energy formed around his hands as he wove invisible sigils in the air.

Whirling around in circles of increasing speed, the orbs flashed out with a flick of his finger, weaving and swirling through the air until they reached their targets, penetrating then circling, again and again, burning their way through both of the Torpek facing off against Kiara. Their screams died in their throats as the glowing orbs perforated their lungs, leaving any remaining breath they contained with too many opportunities to escape. The orbs gradually faded away to nothing as the two bodies slumped to the ground, smoke drifting up slowly from the burns in the padded leather armor.

Kiara took in a deep breath of her own as she witnessed magic the likes of which she had never seen before in her young life, pausing briefly to glance back at Torick, nodding her thanks, before surveying the river for a new target. It was too late to consider stringing her bow, so she looked for where she could be of the most use with her sword. Seeking a better view, she climbed up the slope that the three spearmen had just descended, hoping a little height would reveal any new threats.

Looking upriver to where Jason and Shagron were engaging with four attackers, she considered herself lucky to have heard – over all the clamour of the battle – the unmistakable click of a crossbow trigger coming from the other side of the of the embankment. It was enough to allow her to begin to dodge. Not enough to allow her to escape the pain of the bolt plunging through her hardened leather jerkin and into her side, just below the ribcage, but enough to have saved her from having it plunge into her heart, where it had been aimed!

She tumbled back down the embankment, crying out in pain as she clutched at her side, rolling to a stop at Torick's feet, as he stood looking at her with a look of surprise on his face. Recovering, he wove his arms through the air, evoking a shimmering sphere of blue light that surrounded himself and Kiara as he knelt by her side. Seeing the depth of the bolt in her side, he held her down as she tried to rise.

"Stay here!" he ordered her, then called out, "RALOF!!"

The priest looked up from where he was crouched, still holding the reins of the horses in one hand, and his mace in the other. Torick waved him over with a flick of his head, and Ralof could see the prone form of the only female ranger lying on the ground beside the mage. Leaving the horses, he quickly ran to see what he could do about her wound.

"It's deep!" Torick told him, "Under her ribs…she's bleeding a great deal…" when he was interrupted by the clicking noise of a crossbow bolt deflecting off the blue sphere of energy that surrounded them. He looked at Ralof, "Do whatever you must – the shield will protect you while you work. I will handle the Torpek!"

He stood up, still within the protection of the blue sphere, and stepped in front of the priest and the ranger. He could have thought of several suitable spells that would have done quite well at dealing with the older-looking Torpek warrior that had stepped up to the top of the embankment to fire down upon them, but this time, he decided he wanted to do something more visceral, more satisfying. Setting his feet in the mud at the edge of the water, he flung back his cloak over his right shoulder, revealing the bandolier of throwing daggers that he was wearing slung over his left shoulder running down to his hip.

With an elegant grace, he reached out in a blur to draw two daggers – one with each hand – with a speed that reduced their motion to a blur. The movement ended with his arms flung forward, the blades having been released with deadly accuracy towards their target.

With only the top of his shoulders exposed, the Torpek expected he had good cover from attack as he had fired his crossbow. Now, he barely had time to see the daggers that had been thrown in his direction, which was a good thing in a way. Had he seen the projectiles fly, he would have been tortured by the sight of the sharpened tip of the first blade as it flew towards the edge of the cover, impossibly slicing through the stone at the top of the rise and continuing its way into his right shoulder, embedding itself to its hilt, severing an artery and spraying warm blood against his own face. The second blade was worse for him, travelling the distance cleanly & swiftly, piercing his left eye and driving into his skull, stopped again only by the carved hilt. He truly would have been tortured by the experience if he had lived for more than a fleeting moment after being struck.

To his right, Torick could see Jason and Shagron dispatching the last of the four Torpek that had charged them, and to his left, he could see Ferenc finish off the second of the arbalesters. Omar was climbing up to inspect the young magician still sleeping in the tree stump, and Ralof was attending to the injured Kiara behind him.

With a wave of his hand, the blue sphere of energy moved from Kiara & Ralof to himself, and he moved up the embankment to ensure that no more surprises waited for them. Seeing no new threats, he counted the eleven slain Torpek – no, he corrected himself; ten slain, one captured – against the wounded Kiara, four dead horses, and two wounded animals that likely would not survive the night, let alone be fit to carry a rider.

Presuming Ralof could save the young ranger, the loss of six mounts was a heavy price, so far from any trading post where they could replace them; the Torpek were earthers, choosing to march about through caves and tunnels beneath the surface, forgoing any form of traditional mounts, so they were unlikely to secure new rides from their opponents. Watching as Ferenc helped Omar move the body of the Torpek enchanter down to lower ground, Torick decided to join them, and see what information their prisoner would yield.

*****Preston*****

Kemeny looked across the room, with the cots lined up neatly against the walls in two rows. The crisp white sheets were pulled up to cover the heads of all of his guests but one. Whatever had happened, it had not turned out well for the master's guests. He felt sad standing there – it was his job to watch over the master's guests while they served the master's bidding, and though he could not say he had failed them, their demise left him with a feeling of emptiness. He hoped there would soon be more guests for him to care for. He liked working here.

With a long sigh that almost sounded like a whine, he turned and grabbed the foot of the nearest deceased guest, pulling on it as he turned and started walking away towards the door of the room. The still warm body slipped out of the bed and landed with a thud on the floor, leaving a trail in the dust as it was dragged unceremoniously out of the room and over to the open doorframe of the elevator shaft. Kemeny tossed the body through the doorway and listened for a moment to hear the soft thud as it landed in the base of the shaft several stories below.

The elevator itself had long been removed, and the open pit was the most effective method they had for discreetly disposing of guests. Landing in the pit below even the lowest level of the old hotel, Kemeny repeated this task until all of the beds but that of their one still living guest – which Kemeny double checked, just to make sure nothing had changed – had been emptied. He then rolled a large barrel over to the elevator shaft opening and dumped its contents – the liquid slopped out of the barrel in a massive pour, the corrosive acid turning from a single wave into a downpour of raindrops by the time it reached the bodies piled below. For good measure, he tossed an unused mattress down, to help disguise the decomposing remains.

It would be many years later, when the condemned hotel was being finally demolished, that the remains would be found, and several missing persons' cold cases would finally be closed.

****Jason****

Jason was at Kiara's side almost as quickly as Ralof once the fighting had finished. Ferenc joined them as well, forgetting about the unconscious Torpek and leaving him with Omar while they saw to Kiara's injury. Jason was holding her hand when Ferenc arrived, and he was doing his best to keep her focused on his face as Ralof removed her armor and examined the wound.

Her breathing was shallow, and her expression was pained with every breath, but she kept her eyes locked on Jason. Ralof offered no warning when he pulled the shaft from her side – preferring surprise over the anticipation of the pain – and Kiara did her best not to cry out too loudly when he did so, though Jason was sure he would see the scars on his hand from her grip for some time afterwards. The poultice that was Ralof's specialty came next, then bandages for the bleeding, and all the while he continued to mutter to himself as he worked – prayers of Ukko's faithful, seeking his guidance and intervention, to bless his hands and make his handiwork worthy enough to preserve life.

"I am sorry, Priest" Kiara managed to whisper as he worked, "but we do not share in the same beliefs – I'm afraid your god will not look kindly on me…"

"Don't be ridiculous," Ralof answered with a grin, though he was focused seriously on his work, tying the bandage, and making sure it was secure and would not come loose. "Ukko smiles on all his children, regardless of whether or not they smile back." Try as he might, Ralof could not stop the doubt from coming through in his voice – he recited the prayers that he had been taught, word-for-word, line-by-line, desperate for any sign that Ukko was listening to his pleas, and quietly despairing that his prayers were going unanswered, and Kiara would be the one to suffer for his heresy.

"Let her lie here for a while," Ralof said, this time to Jason and Ferenc, as well as the others who had also gathered around to see how Kiara would fare. "She can rest for a bit, and when we decide what we are doing next, I can give her something for the pain."

Ralof stood up and stepped back, turning to find his horse again, as did Ferenc. Kiara held Jason's eyes for a moment longer, offering a weak smile. "Sorry, boss," she said, "I got careless!"

"No worries. This seemed like a good place to camp anyway," Jason answered back, as she laughed at the irony.

"Rest," he told her, "That's an order!" before releasing her hand and rejoining the others.

Shagron, Torick and Ralof were talking about the horses when Jason arrived. "We should camp here for the night," Shagron suggested, "It will give everyone a chance to recover a little bit."

"I know just the spot," said Jason, looking back up the hill on the far side of the river, to the spot where he and Sukhov had stood so many months ago...

****Spy****

Jason had looked directly at him – at least it felt that way – but apparently even his keen eyes were not infallible, as he had not seen the figure crouching in the brush near the top of the hill. He had been watching the fight since he first heard the clang of steel echo out over the plains. Well hidden by the low brush cover surrounding his vantage point on the hill, he was able to make out much about the group of adventurers that had wandered onto the plain, and he could even watch as the Torpek had sought them out and closed the distance, moving carefully and purposefully between the many natural obstacles that now littered the field, to make their attack with as much surprise as possible.

It didn't take much to recognize the tactics and fighting style of the former legionnaires among them, and though he was too far away to make out what they were saying, he could tell who seemed to be giving the orders. There was a moment when he thought he might have been spotted, as they looked up in the direction of the overlook on the hill where he was perched, but he was confident that he had ducked behind cover quickly enough to avoid detection. No matter, he was already mounted and riding back to camp before they would even manage to cross the river and climb the hill path, and he did his best to make sure he left no tracks.

He rode hard and fast for nearly a full day. His armor was minimal, and the horse was bred for speed, so he was able to cover more ground than most casual riders, certain in the thought that his news would be considered urgent, even if it killed the horse.

It was noon of the following day when he spotted the encampment and raced the final stretch to reach the perimeter guards. He was waved on quickly as they recognized his patrol colours and he barely slowed until he reached the command tent. The entire camp was modest in size, with plain brown tents pitched in orderly rows that suggested perhaps fifty men encamped, and another fifty bivouacked around the tents. The command tent where he pulled up his horse and dismounted was indistinguishable from the others – unless you belonged to the company – and he paused only for a moment after setting foot on solid ground again to steady and prepare himself, drawing back his shoulders, straightening his tired back, and moving into the tent in a crisp march rather than a disorderly run.

He was greeted as he entered by a large man standing over a small table, reading the maps that were spread across its surface in an overlapping mess. He wore fitted boiled-leather armor, with bands of polished metal stitched in place for reinforcement. His breastplate was lacquered and embossed in gold with two golden stallions, rearing up, facing an upright sword in the center. His once shaven head was now covered with a bristling layer of grey hair that still looked military in nature, despite all other evidence to the contrary.

"General!" the scout addressed him, saluting crisply. "I have a report from the East, of activity on Lakhani Plain..."

Mention of the plains brought the General's head up with an almost audible snap, his eyes narrowed, and brows furrowed as he scanned the scout standing in front of him. Everyone around him knew that the Lakhani Plain was a sensitive subject and would not dare even mention the place unless there was good reason.

"Carry on," he replied, giving the young legionnaire permission to continue.

"Two days ago, I witnessed a skirmish on the plain..." the scout began, "...between a group of eleven Torpek scavengers and a small adventuring party, seven in number, plus horses. The seven were ambushed but bested the Torpek, losing several mounts, and possibly one of their number, at least severely wounded."

Sukhov nodded as he listened to the detailed report, but it was clear from his expression that he had yet to hear anything that would make this an urgent matter for his attention. "And?"

The scout cleared his throat before continuing. "The party, sir, was made up of two magi, a warrior that I believe was Shagron the Wanderer; he was accompanied by the priest Ralof, whom I heard them call by name; and there were three former Imperial Rangers – one fair, two dark – and one had long dark hair, braided, hanging to his shoulders..." The scout paused, watching the General for any reaction... "I believe it was him, sir..." He trailed off. Everyone knew who he meant by 'him' – there wasn't a soldier left alive from the Seventh Legion that didn't know the story about what had happened that day; how they were betrayed by one of their own; and how the General had sworn he would one day have his revenge on the young captain that had destroyed his legion, his career, his life! He could see now from the cold expression on the General's face that he knew whom he was talking about, though he remained silent, his mouth set tight in a grim clench as he battled with his emotions to decide how to respond to this news.

Sukhov was not expecting this news at this moment – a sighting so close; and at the scene of his crime! – and so he considered his options. He no longer commanded a legion, no longer served the Imperium even; unable to bear the shame of returning to the capital with the dishonour of having been bested, and his legions wiped out, he had instead gathered the survivors of the Seventh Legion – less than five hundred out of five thousand men – and led those who chose to remain loyal to him in the life of a mercenary company.

"Tell the men to break camp. We ride at once for the Lakhani Plain – you will lead us to where you saw him, and we will find his trail from there!" The scout saluted sharply, spun on his heel and sprinted out of the tent to carry out his orders. Sukhov looked down at his maps, ran his hand over his head, and did his best not to yell aloud in anger as he thought about what he would do when he was face-to-face again with the upstart ranger!

****Omar****

The lone surviving Torpek looked at Omar with suspicion as he slipped the knife between her hands and sliced the ropes from her wrists, releasing her as promised. It was evening, and darkness was coming quickly in the valley, allowing the ashen-skinned Torpek to quickly slip away into the shadows, obscured from their sight within a matter of moments of her being released. Shagron stood beside him, watching as she left. "I hope you know what you're doing," Omar said aloud, "…and that she isn't going to come back with reinforcements to kill us in our sleep!"

"We gave our word, and she gave us information," Shagron answered him. "What are we, if we can't make simple bargains like that and not keep our word?"

"I know what 'we' are – and if they are anything like me, I wouldn't expect to get much sleep tonight!"

Shagron sighed loudly. "Well let's just hope that there's only one of you in the world, because I don't think we would survive for very long if everyone were as distrustful as you! Besides, though they are very dangerous – and yes, mostly evil – every Torpek I have ever encountered has had an iron-clad commitment to their word. She gave her word she wouldn't return, and I have to believe her. So relax…" he said, clapping his large hand on Omar's shoulder, almost making his knees buckle, "…and let's get everyone moved up to the campsite. They won't know where we have made camp, and we can watch the path to make sure we are not surprised by any uninvited guests!"

It was very close to nightfall as Shagron and Omar finished climbing the winding path that led to the lookout point at the crest of the hill. They had made camp at the overlook, from which they could easily see any that might approach. To their rear, the terrain was wild and overgrown, making any route to their location either impassable or entirely too loud to cut a path through, thus alerting them to anyone who might choose to travel that route. They had brought the surviving horses up, taking extra time with two that had been injured – Ralof prepared some of his salve for the animals as he had for Kiara, hoping it might aid with their healing as well – though they all had a very good sense that they would be on foot for the rest of the trip, or until they found another trading post along the way.

Kiara came up on one of the remaining horses and was resting by the fire – Ralof's poultice worked to ease the pain, but her wound continued to bleed whenever he checked the bandages. The others joined her after they had set up the shelters and settled their gear, taking some time to go over everything that they had learned from the Torpek girl.

"I still don't think we should have just let her go like that..." Ralof muttered, as he stirred the pot containing their dinner as it warmed over the fire. "What if we have more questions?"

"We will always have more questions," Torick answered, "...are you suggesting we should have kept the girl as a slave and dragged her along with us on our travels? No, Shagron was right – we asked what we needed, and now we must move on."

Shagron was more than a little surprised to hear support from the usually distant and self-focused wizard, but he took it for what it was worth. "Look, we learned where he's *not*: we know that Vazul is not in Scarbantia – that's the most important thing!" he interjected, "Whatever reason Dar had for thinking he was there, the Torpek said he isn't there anymore – this will save us a lot of running around and backtracking! We also learned where he *is*..."

"Oh, yes..." this time it was Omar, "...he's in '*The Gates of Hell*' – wherever that is! It's a name, not a location – it doesn't really tell us anything, and on top of that, we don't actually '*know*' any of this – we believe it, because we believe her. We can't be sure the girl wasn't lying to us just to save herself!" He made no effort to hide the frustration in his voice – young and full of fire, his spirit was hard to dominate, and he was learning – on his own – how to let the voices in his head waste their energy competing with one another, letting him maintain control of their destiny. For now, at least.

"I can," Shagron answered, "I can believe her, and I can believe that she was telling the truth." The others were all looking at him now, all wondering the same thing but no one asking the question...

"Call it a gift," he continued, "call it whatever you want, but I have always been able to tell when someone is lying to me..." Ralof arched an eyebrow at this statement, which Shagron couldn't help but see, and he shook his head. "If I am not caught unawares or off guard – when seeking it, I can know if a truth is being told to me. This has proven to be very useful to me over the years, and though I am as fallible as any man among us, this Torpek had my full attention, and I sensed no deceit in her words. Fear, yes; evil, definitely yes; deceit… no. Not in what she told us – well, except maybe the part about leaving and never returning. She may have been lying about that, but I expect it will depend on whether or not she can convince enough friends to come with her to make it worth her while… She might have wanted to, but I doubt many will want to brave our blades in the night!"

Omar practically jumped to his feet, almost spilling the small bowl of stew that Ralof had been passing out to the group as Shagron spoke. "Wait a minute! That's not what you told me a few hours ago, when we released her to return to her friends! – You said she gave her word not to return and you trusted her!"

"I do trust her," Shagron replied quickly, "and even though I sensed she might be lying about that point, I try to give everyone the benefit of the doubt, to let them earn the trust I give them. We spared her life, and she may consider that to be worth something! Evil is not her true nature – it's rarely anyone's *true* nature – and I am giving her the opportunity to choose a better path, to make the right choice…"

"Oh, Shagron!" Ralof put his head in his left hand – the other hand still holding the ladle for the stew – "You choose the worst times to try to save lost souls!"

"Forgive me, Father, but I don't see that the 'right time' has ever waited for it to be convenient for us, and I wouldn't be who I am if I were one to choose convenience over rightness. Besides, we have moved to a secure location here: we can observe any approach, and we are prepared – not that I think anyone will come, because I have faith that she will make the right decision!"

There were several sighs around the fire as they turned their focus to their dinner, after which they made sure everyone knew their turn for taking watch – Shagron took the first and agreed to be up early for the last watch as well. He was comfortable in his confidence about the Torpek being people of their word, though he was sure to be diligent in his watch duties… just in case.

*****Diosgyor*****

The sky was red the next morning, casting an eerie glow over the landscape as the sun rose, and what might have otherwise been a warm, bright sunrise was instead filtered through the obscuring pall of smoke that hung not only in the valley, but across the entire region. Higher up, the westerly winds blew against the unyielding stone of the mountains, fanning the flames of forest fires that had been creeping through the pass from the hills of Sopron. What trees and vegetation there had been on the rugged hillsides, dry and starved of water from the years of drought, were quickly being consumed by the ferocious appetite of the flames. A shift in the winds overnight had now placed the maelstrom directly in their path. It would be hours, perhaps a day at most – if they were lucky – before the fires reached the plains, and the group were quickly packing their gear as they decided where to head.

"It would seem we were spoiled by the presence of our Taltos friend," Jason noted dryly, as he slung Kiara's gear onto one of the remaining horses, "She brought the rains wherever we went – enough to make one forget just how terrible things had become…"

He let out a reluctant sigh as he tightened the leather straps holding the pack in place, moving to run his hand through the horse's braided mane and patting her neck. It was quiet for a moment as he waited to see if anyone would reply, and when they didn't he looked around, wondering what else might be distracting them. He could see Ralof cleaning up the breakfast pots; Ferenc was seeing to Kiara, helping her get up, to stretch and walk; he couldn't spot Omar, but Torick and Shagron were huddled together, discussing something that clearly looked serious, judging by their expressions, although they were keeping their voices low. That seemed like a good enough reason for him, so he walked over to join the conversation.

"What's up?" he asked, not bothering to keep his voice low as he greeted the two. Shagron and Torick exchanged looks before answering. "Whatever it is, you both look quite intense about it…"

Shagron sighed. "You tell him," he directed to Torick, "…this sort of thing sounds better coming from your type…"

Torick frowned but explained, "We both had the same dream last night."

"Really?" Jason replied. "Amazing. I didn't think you had the same taste in women!"

Torick ignored the attempt at humour and continued. "Everything was the same – every detail, every word, every image – I believe it was a message, but Shagron isn't convinced."

"A message? From whom? And what was the message?" Jason asked aloud, drawing the attention of the others.

"I'm not sure it was even a message," Shagron interjected, "communing with divinity usually takes on a more surreal sensation than a dream, and I sensed nothing of Ukko in this – if it's not from the All Father, then I am suspicious of whatever placed these dreams in our sleep!"

"But it was so specific to us, to where we are and what we are trying to do!" Torick argued. "It had to be a message, and I suspect Dar had a hand in it, even if she wasn't in the dream – it had a familiarity to it that was unmistakable!" Shagron nodded slightly to concede this to him, though he still did not appear happy.

"*WHAT* was the *MESSAGE*?!" Jason asked in frustration. Ralof and the others were listening closely now, and Torick looked at all of them before Shagron nodded for him to proceed.

"I – we – had a vision in our sleep last night. It was almost entirely comprised of images – some we recognized, some we didn't – we have spent the morning trying of make sense of it, and I'm still not sure we have all of it, but we agree on the following: we saw a castle, not the largest, but it was a stout, square structure, dominated by four square towers; it had a view of the valley and the town below it; and there were mountains, and caves; we saw one cave, with a grand entrance, with smoke or steam billowing outwards, and every creature that tried to enter – man, beast and bird – lay dead on the ground only a few steps within the mouth of the cave. Inside – I think it was inside – there were lakes of water, orange and yellow in colour; giant teeth of stone descended from the roof of the cave; there were torches, incense – yes, I can remember the smell; even in the dream we could smell the heavy sweetness of the incense filling the air, covering the smell of sulphur and rot."

"There were people in the cave – witches. They were chanting, humming, an eerie sound that echoed off the walls and drifted throughout the passages – not carved passages, but something worn, by fire or water, and smooth." Torick spoke as if in a trance, recounting the imagery from the dream to the assembled group. Shagron listened and nodded along with his descriptions. "The witches surrounded one other, as if lending him their strength."

"This one looked to be a wizard…" Torick looked at Shagron, who kept nodding, although he had lowered his head, as if recalling the dream in his own mind as Torick spoke. "We think it was Voros Vazul. He was standing over a pool – a large bowl carved from the rock of the cave, but it was not water in the pool – it bubbled and burned, and the fumes it gave off flowed out of the cave and covered the land. It burned, choked the life out of the trees, and drove men mad." Torick's voice was quieter now, as he recounted the images of the plagues that Vazul had summoned across all Vengriya, speaking more solemnly as he continued.

"As each plague scarred the land, the earth shook; in the cave, with each tremor, one by one, the great stone teeth would fall from the ceiling, crashing into the rock below, and cracking the floor of the cave. When the last stone fell, the floor collapsed, and revealed a chamber below the cave. Fires burned, and the rocks themselves melted and flowed in rivers of fire, and deep from within the shadows of the pit, the sound of something stirring…" His voice trailed off, his eyes focused on something – not at anything that was in front of them, but as if he were still trying to see what lay within the pit.

Shagron finished the telling… "We heard only one word in the entire dream – just once, near the beginning – "*Diosgyor*" – it was the faintest of whispers, then nothing."

There was a long silence after they had finished, as each seemed intent on finding their own interpretation of the dream, and none seemed to have anything to offer right away. The silence was interrupted abruptly as Gypsy moved up behind Shagron and nuzzled the back of his neck, startling everyone as they realized how much they had been focusing on their own thoughts, to the exclusion of all else. Jason was the first to speak.

"I think I know this castle – maybe – I haven't seen it for myself, but I have heard tales among the Legions. There was a keep in the north of Nyirseg, on the border mountains with Gomor – it was old, built in the traditional style – square with four towers. It changed hands many times during the days of the Imperium, as the Legions tried, but never succeeded, to cross the mountains into Gomor. Raiders would sneak out of the mountains to attack the keep whenever the legions were away on patrol, forcing the Praetor to bring troops from elsewhere to retake the keep. Though troublesome, the commanders would often admire how effective the locals were at attacking then disappearing into the surrounding countryside to evade pursuit. There was talk as well about how the areas was riddled with caves – some that were old mines, and others that were created by nature."

"That sounds promising," Ralof noted, "if we agree that this dream truly is a message... Myself, I am of a like mind with Shagron – this does not sound like a vision from the All Father! Who is to say this is not some ploy by Vazul himself to lead us astray from our path – to keep us from reaching Scarbantia?"

For Ferenc, this had the feeling of a contest, as he watched and listened, looking back & forth from each as they spoke, every point seeming valid, and now looking back to Torick to see if there was a response to Ralof. He was watching Torick's face for a moment before he realized that he was holding his breath and had to force himself to relax.

Then it was Shagron's turn: "If nothing else, the scene we observed... if we believe the Torpek, that the 'Gates of Hell' are indeed our destination, then the scene we have described seems to suit the name better than anything I can imagine!"

"Your point is valid," Torick finally acknowledged, "were it not for one last detail, which I can only describe as this: the voice I heard..." at which point he paused and looked at Shagron, who returned his look, not moving his head in any way, neither affirming nor denying – if one were to guess by his expression, he had been discussing this very element with Torick when Jason joined them. ... "even though it was a whisper, giving just one word, I know it was definitely Lady Darellan Fenndragon. For me, this confirms the verity of the message, and that we need to change our destination!" He looked at the rest of the assembled group. "I believe she is trying to tell us that we need to change our plans – that Vazul is not in Scarbantia – and we need to head to Diosgyor instead."

Shagron did not move as Torick finished. He had heard the voice, he had heard what it said, but he had not been confident in identifying who was speaking. Nevertheless, Torick seemed confident in his assertion.

Jason had been listening quite intently and could only shrug at the end. "Very well, we go north to Diosgyor Castle."

"Huh?" was all that Ralof could muster in response. "That's enough for you? To simply abandon how we have travelled all this way and now just want to change direction? Reverse course, backtrack at least two days and now head north. What a bloody piszmog!?"

Jason smiled. "It's not like we have much choice – the fires are approaching from the West, the road to Scarbantia is ablaze and blocked, and we need to get back through the Duna Pass into Nyirseg before we are cut off from the Eastern Principalities entirely for who knows how long! And now, we'd best be on our way – we have enough horses for Kiara and the supplies, and perhaps one or two of the rest of us to ride – but regardless, we will not go faster than a walk for the rest of us, and we will need to keep moving to keep ahead of the fire!"

***** Tibor****

Tibor awoke and was startled to see Dar hovering over him. There was no sign of the young servant girl as Dar herself poured a glass of wine and handed it to him.

"Well?" she asked, not waiting for him to swallow his first sip, as he propped up on his elbows to hold the cup.

"Well, what?" Tibor answered, knowing full well what she meant, and seeing from her expression that she knew this as well. With a small sigh he gave up the fun and replied, "The message was delivered. Now it's just for them to realize the truth of it and act accordingly." He hesitated for a moment, drawing her in.

"What is it?" she asked, "What did you see?"

"They encountered some Torpek – they prevailed, but Kiara is badly hurt, and they lost several mounts. They will be travelling slowly and will not reach Diosgyor anytime soon – Kiara may not reach it at all." Tibor took another drink, sipping slowly as he was not yet accustomed to the practice of drinking wine all the time. "I don't suppose you have some water?" he asked quizzically, hoping to have something he could down more quickly to clear his mouth of the pasty-taste that still coated his tongue. In his short history of drinking alcohol, he had not yet discovered a real taste for beer, despite the prevalence of the drink during his first year of university, preferring instead the smoother flavour of a rum and coke – he had always recalled his dad drinking Seagram's 5-Star whiskey, and the one time he stole a sip when no one was looking, he found that drink to be too bitter on the tongue for his tastes. Wine was new for him. Being here, he was astounded to find that this was the drink of choice for breakfast, lunch and dinner, and it was taking some time to get used to.

Dar frowned. "We have some water warmed for you to wash up, but I wouldn't recommend drinking it – unless you don't mind having the shits for the next few days..." she smiled to herself as she got up from beside the bed where he was lying and moved to the door. "Take your time getting used to things here," she advised, "...but not too long!"

"I will see what I can do for Kiara, but I need you to get ready to travel – you need to get started on the road to Diosgyor, and I will catch up with you."

"Wait, what?" Tibor asked with alarm, his voice rising and almost cracking as he shot upright in the bed. "Why can't Ralof help Kiara? That's what he's there for, isn't it? And what do you mean you'll 'catch up with me'? Aren't you coming with me?? I can't ride out there on my own!"

Dar paused in the doorway, a worry line creasing her forehead as she looked down before turning back to look at Tibor.

"Ralof has some baggage of his own to deal with before he can be the priest he used to be. Until he resolves things for himself, he is of limited help to them – us – in finishing this quest. When they get to Diosgyor, he will likely be more of a liability to himself than be of any further help to the party – which is why I need to go."

"Okay, I get that…" Tibor persisted, "…but why do I have to be on the road on my own? I mean, I want to get out there – to explore, to see everything – but I wasn't expecting to have to do it on my own! Shit, it's dangerous out there!"

Dar couldn't help but let out a laugh despite Tibor's protestations. "That's funny!" she exclaimed, sounding for a moment more like the Dar he knew in Brantford than the quiet, reserved lady of the court that she carried herself as in Ascanium. This was strangely comforting, he felt, before frowning as he realized he had no idea what she was talking about.

"Why is that funny?" he asked.

"It's funny because you have the potential to be so much, and you don't even know it! But don't worry, I will see to it that you have an escort on the road, and no one – certainly not Voros Vaszoly – will ever know where you are!" Tibor relaxed into the bed slightly at her assurance, as she continued, "Be ready when the knock on the door comes and make haste to Diosgyor!" and with a quick spin, she was gone out the door.

Tibor relaxed back on the bed, his head spinning just a little from the strong wine. Forcing himself to get out of bed he set out to find the warm water that Dar had mentioned earlier, and made a mental note to grab a few books from the library for the trip…

*****Dar*****

Jason wiped the soot from his leather gloves before reaching up to remove the cowl from his face. Ash was drifting down like a winter snowfall, covering everything in sight with a layer of grey grit, creating a surreal landscape as the sun began to drop in the late afternoon sky, casting long shadows among the leafless trees.

The terrain on the north side of the river was fairly flat despite being on the edge of the foothills of the Matras mountains, and the wind that pushed the forest fires forward relentlessly also occasionally whipped up the ash and completely obscured their vision for long periods, forcing them to stare at the worn strips of the trail at their feet in order to keep moving forward in the right direction. They had emerged from the mountain pass carved by the river after taking most of the day to traverse the uneven terrain carefully, trying not to aggravate Kiara's wounds and stopping frequently to change her bandages.

Despite their apparent solitude on the trail over the past day, Jason insisted on burying or burning the discarded bandages each time they stopped, and had Ferenc watch their trail to ensure they did their best to cover their tracks. He was determined that they would not attract any unwanted attention from anyone – Torpek or otherwise – who might be looking to follow their trail, although most of the others felt that fires dogging their footsteps would do enough to erase any sign of their passage.

He looked up to the west at the mountains that ranged for miles along their path. Though it was still afternoon, the sun would soon be dropping below the highest of the peaks, darkening things much sooner than usual, which, combined with he heavy smoke and ash filling the air, would bring an early end to their travels for the day.

"We will not make Solva before dark." Torick had come up beside him as he had paused on the trail. He'd had some experience travelling around this area recently and had been helpful in choosing the best trail to follow to make sure they emerged on the north side of the river as they headed to Diosgyor.

"No," Jason agreed, "we'll be lucky to find a decent spot to shelter before the sun sets behind the mountains."

"What about moving towards the foothills a bit more? Perhaps we can find a cave or some large rock to break the wind…" Torick asked.

"No. I don't want to risk another encounter with any wandering Torpek – especially at night!" Jason answered emphatically. He stopped as Torick seemed to look away at something over his shoulder, and he turned to see what the wizard had seen. He squinted, searching for anything out of the ordinary in the orange sky, scanning until he, too, could see the approaching bird. It was flying directly towards them, not circling or gliding, ignoring the ground below it – clearly not hunting or otherwise behaving at all like a wild bird should. It grew larger in his sight and began descending, diving rapidly at them before pulling up sharply at the last moment.

The transformation that occurred was like a blur – neither Torick nor Jason would be able to say they saw precisely how it happened, but they could recall a blurring of images as the falcon grew in size and its outstretched wings were quickly replaced by the outstretched arms of the young druid priestess; the razor-sharp claws became leather boots; and the ruffled feathers fell down into a cape that hung about her shoulders. It was a magic unlike the channeling practiced by the mages, which mystified Torick somewhat – or at least as much as anything seemed to draw a reaction from him – as it was a power that flowed from the earth itself and did not need to be summoned here from elsewhere. He found that very intriguing, and thought that perhaps someday, he would learn this for himself. Some day.

They had hardly blinked twice before Dar was there – in the form they were accustomed to seeing her – walking towards them across the grass, striding forward with purpose.

"Where is she?" she addressed Jason, before quickly looking past him at the horses slowly coming up in the distance with the rest of the party, to which she them directed her attention and continued walking. Jason smiled at Torick and they both turned to follow her.

She was soon beside Kiara's horse as they pulled up, and she reached up to take her hand, looking at her pale complexion and tired expression. She shook her head and helped her down, Kiara wincing in pain as she slipped her leg over the saddle and dropped to the ground. Dar walked her over to a stone where she could sit, and began to examine the wound, pausing only briefly to throw a scowl towards Brother Ralof, who hovered behind her, a look of frustration on his face. Standing slowly, she pulled Kiara to her feet and looked directly at Ralof, her disappointment evident on her face; she opened her mouth as if to say something to him, but then thought better of it, considering the others that had gathered around them to watch.

"She needs specialized care," she announced, "I don't have the herbs I need here. She'll need to come with me to Diosgyor if she wants to live."

Standing in a small circle around her, no one had anything to say in response to her dictates, taking her at her word, having no better ideas or solutions to offer. Kiara was not getting better, and the ride to stay ahead of the flames was not helping. As if reading their concerns from their faces, Dar continued, "You will have a better chance to stay ahead of the fires if she comes with me and you have the horses to ride the rest of the way unencumbered. There is a road along the foothills on the other side of Solva, so you will make better time tomorrow. I can ease the winds for tonight – it should give you enough time to rest, but it won't be enough to stop the fires completely after I leave with Kiara."

"We'll make camp here then," said Jason.

"I brought some fresh food," Dar added, pulling some wrapped packages from her rucksack.

"How did you carry that…" Omar began to ask, to be answered with a wry smile from Dar, that told him enough – if one could master the ability to change into a bird, then the magic for carrying meager possessions would surely be a simple feat to master as well.

"Have a good meal – you've been riding hard; you should enjoy something before you have to ride hard again."

Ralof nodded and took the packages, avoiding her gaze as he turned away to start preparing a cooking fire.

As the others began to make camp, Dar asked Kiara to gather her things while she took a moment to focus on the trail behind them. Staring into the path of oncoming fire, she closed her eyes, summoning her strength, and let herself feel the wind blowing into her face; the heat of the fire on the wind, the smell of the burning embers, and the sound – the crackle and roar of the fires that consumed everything in their path, like a ravenous beast feasting on everything in its path.

She felt the elements expending their energy, their fury, across the landscape, and she embraced all of it. Hers was the ability to feel nature in all its majesty – the power, the beauty, the peacefulness, and the fury. This was hers, not to control – as it would ever be foolish to think that mortals could control such power – but she could connect her will with the elements, and, in a manner that can only be explained as a 'negotiation', she could persuade the forces of nature to cede to her will. She would empathize with their rage, and reason with their fury, and if she fulfilled her end of the bargain, she would often find that her will would be done.

Though there were many magical forces at work in the world, manipulating the natural order of things, it was not beyond her power to find some solace for her weary friends this day, harnessing the winds and flames – even if only for a single night – to hold them back and give them one night to rest before continuing their ride. It was only a matter of minutes before everyone felt the winds begin to rise, changing their natural easterly course and instead blowing back to the west. The winds built and grew, travelling faster than any rider or creature on the grasslands, blowing back into the mouth of the raging fires that were creeping over foothills that anchored the towering peaks of the Matras Mountains to the landscape. The prevailing winds, summoned to be as unnatural as the plagues that brought the catastrophic inferno to the Avar lands, slowly pushed against the advancing flames, sending them backwards to feed upon the scorched earth for just a little longer before they would race forward once more.

Like a breath expended, the breeze moved past the weary group of adventurers, and they could see Dar slump forward as she relaxed and released her strength into the effort. She rolled her head to stretch the tension out of her neck and returned to the camp, where Ralof had started a fire. She stood for a moment, staring into the small flames that he was preparing to cook over, and then looked around for Kiara. "We have to go."

Kiara nodded.

"This is going to feel a little strange," Dar started to explain, as she raised her hands to Kiara's head and held her gently, "...but I'm going to share a little trick with you. All you need to do is relax, and remember to fly wherever I fly..."

"...Wait, what?" were the last words Kiara said aloud, as she heard Dar's voice in her head... *'Trust me'*...

*****Tibor*****

Tibor fidgeted in the saddle, adjusting the small pieces of plate armor that seemed to constantly bounce and jostle with every step the horse took, trying to keep them in place. They had been on the road for less than an hour and he was already beginning to regret his earlier demand to be as well armored as his escorts.

They had arrived at Dar's compound around midday, and he was taken aback somewhat by the sight that had greeted him when he opened the gate to see who had knocked. As Dar had warned, he was expecting an escort to arrive, to bring him to Diosgyor, but he had to admit, he wasn't sure what he was expecting. The twenty heavily armed & armored guards that sat mounted in the street awaiting his exit from the compound were more than a bit intimidating, and he had doubted for a moment that they were meant for him.

They had assured him, most certainly, that Dar had ordered them into service for this purpose, and they were committed to carrying out her commands to the letter.

What he had perhaps expected to be a leisurely ride changed in his mind as he saw that these men and women were clearly expecting trouble along the way, and he decided on the spot that he needed to be equally prepared.

Despite their orders, he had managed to convince their captain that it would be in their interests – that being, in the interest of ensuring he was well protected – to stop by the royal armories to acquire similar protection for himself before they started their journey. Tibor didn't think anything of it when the captain offered a compromise and agreed to stop at a local armorer located on the edge of the market, near their route out of the city, and purchase him whatever he needed. It was a hurried transaction, and he could tell that the captain had some sway with the fellow running the smithy, as he was quickly able to overrule any concerns that arose about how this armor was intended for the army being raised to set out to defend the southern borders of the principality – of course, his influence over the reluctant smith may have had something to do with the size of the coin purse that he handed over in order to seal the deal.

Regardless, Tibor had initially felt quite better at having acquired for himself a suit of rather nice-looking field plate armor, which apparently had been intended for some other young lordling in the Prince's court. He was still relatively slight of build compared to the more common men-at-arms in the city, but the lord who had commissioned this suit was apparently somewhat younger, and with some minor adjustments, it seemed to fit him quite well. That is, until they began their journey.

They were riding at a steady trot from the moment they had left the city gates, clearly hoping to put some distance between them and Ascanium before nightfall. He presumed this was to continue to keep his location as discreet as possible from whomever had woken him from his slumber – Dar had given no indication before she left that she had learned anything more about the identity of this mystery person, although she had seemed fairly certain that the young servant girl who had attended him while he slept was a disguise, as none of the other servants in the Prince's household either matched the description, or knew of anyone named 'Milly' in the employ of the Prince.

Tibor wasn't truly certain what all the fuss was about, although he had to admit, he had been asleep when Dar fought with the mage – Arcady, or Vaszoly, whatever his name was – and so he had no real sense of what they were facing. From what he remembered of Vengriya though, it probably was something he should take seriously, and so he wanted the armor before they left.

As they camped on the first night, he gingerly unbuckled the leather straps that held each piece of finely polished steel in place and rubbed his sore muscles through the heavy underpadding that he had hastily grabbed to wear under the plates. He was certain that if he removed his gambeson, he would fine a good number of blisters and sores everywhere the metal plates had rubbed his skin raw, despite the heavy padding.

He wouldn't know for sure as he stopped removing his armor when he saw that most of the guards were not bothering to remove most of theirs for the evening. Born and raised as true sons and daughters of Nyirseg, they were used to these hardships when travelling in dangerous circumstances and did not have a problem getting their rest in the most uncomfortable of gear. Tibor on the other hand, despite his memories of life in Vengriya, was quickly realizing that there was a sharp difference between how his mind had travelled here before – that the forms he had inhabited were not his own – and the physical reality of standing here, in the flesh, with a body that, while he thought it had been in reasonably good shape, was simply not used to the hardships of the period.

He was slowly getting used to the preference for drinking wine over the questionable quality of the water, though he imagined it would be some time before he felt himself to be more tolerant of its effects. One thing that was definitely going to take him longer to adjust to was the lack of some of the more basic modern amenities that he had up to now taken for granted.

He ran through several of these thoughts in his head as adjusted his helmet on the ground where it was serving as his pillow for the night and tried to settle in for the night. He tried not to worry about toiletry habits, wine-induced stupors, or heaven-knows-what these guards were here to protect him from, and let his fatigue take him to sleep.

When he awoke in the morning, he would remember his dreams vividly as most do, as fleeting thoughts that were quick to disappear in the chaos of getting up and getting ready to travel again. He tried hard to retain as much as he could – not that he had anyone he would tell them to, but just to try to make sense of the visions for his own curiosity – but all he could remember was the feeling of flying through clouds, looking down on a nighttime landscape dotted with hundreds of small flickering fires, advancing like a long line across rolling hills. He could still recall the scent of the smoke, filling his nostrils as he flew rapidly, the landscape passing beneath him like water passing under a bridge. Then he could see the low, square towers of a castle becoming larger in his view and felt the sensation of descending as the morning sun rose over the plains and illuminated the mountains in the background in a warm red glow, which felt both beautiful and ominous. He woke before he landed in the dream, but he recalled the image from the books and from Dar's descriptions – this was Diosgyor, their destination.

Their small camp was bustling with activity as it took very little time for the men-at-arms to pack their meager gear and saddle the horses for another day of fast riding. One of the younger guards must have taken some pity on him, seeing him fumbling with the buckles of his breastplate, and came over to help him cinch the straps a tad bit tighter this morning, to help lessen the jostling on today's ride, and he was grateful for the assistance.

"Good to see you made it through the night," the young boy mentioned as he fiddled with the buckles.

"Huh? What do you mean?" Tibor asked him.

"The road is full of many dangers for unwary travelers, and we will do our best to protect you from bandits, but the most dangerous time is at night. The kisasszony – 'fair maids' they are called in the Bodrogkoz – have been known to lure many a man from their beds, leading them off into the wilderness of the great plains where they are never heard from again."

Tibor looked around at the area surrounding their campsite, as if expecting to see one hiding behind a rock or a stump as they spoke.

"Wouldn't it have been better to tell me about this *before* we bedded down for the night?" he asked, to which the young soldier just shrugged, and finished tightening the straps.

He took a deep breath as they gathered, mounted, and checked to ensure everyone was accounted for before heading out to the Northwest again. The captain said little as they all knew what they had to do and where they were going.

Tibor waited until half the troop had taken the road before he put the spurs to his horse, and the remaining men fell in behind. It would be at least another day or two before they reached the castle if everything went as planned. He absentmindedly tugged at his breastplate as it began to ride up with the trotting motion of the horse. Two more days, he told himself… *'Time enough'* answered a voice in his head…

*****Diosgyor*****

The clouds flew by at an incredible speed, and she felt the wind in her face, cold and sharp, stinging her eyes. The ground below was hidden by the wispy mist that carpeted the horizon in every direction. There were clouds above them as well, blocking her view of the sun, causing her to lose all sense of direction and motion, so that she could not tell from one moment to the next if it was the clouds that were moving, or if she was. From the moment Dar had reached out to touch her forehead, she had been completely lost in the sensation of flight, her transformed body working on a subconscious level to know how to fly, and to follow the larger bird that was Dar. Like a passenger, she flew the distance to Diosgyor in a few hours – a trip that would take days for the rest of the group to follow by land – marveling even at the incredible sense of being pain-free for as long as it lasted.

It was almost with a sense of regret that she noticed they were descending, approaching their destination in a gentle glide, taking the opportunity to survey the lands surrounding the keep and the small town in the valley below the castle, which was built on the top of one of the many hills that rolled out of the nearby mountains. The air was wet and heavy as they drew closer, and fog covered many of the low-lying hollows and depressions in the landscape. Fires lit on the four towers of the square keep guided their approach, and she marveled at the clarity and detail of all she could see through the eyes of a master predator. Small movements of people – and even rats – constantly pulled at her attention as she drank in the once-in-a-lifetime chance to see the world from so high above. But then it was over as they gently alit upon the stone walkway of the castle wall, and she felt solid earth beneath her feet once again.

The transformation back to human form was disorienting and she had to reach out to a parapet for support to keep herself from falling – Dar was much more accustomed to the temporary vertigo created by the shift in her vision, from being so far-sighted to suddenly being reduced to the limited sight of a normal person. As she reached out to hold herself up, Kiara was instantly reminded of her wound as pain ripped through her mid-section as punctured muscles tried to flex and failed. Despite having a hand on the wall, she doubled over and dropped to her knee as the pain returned in a flash. Dar was helping her to feet as a figure emerged from the tower to their left, moving forward, quickly at first, then slowing as he surveyed the surprising appearance of the newest arrivals.

Dressed in loose-fitting brown robes, with a tangled mop of thinning brown hair that betrayed the years he had dedicated to his particular craft and emitting the distinct aroma of bird droppings – evidenced by the ample stains that decorated his clothes – this was not the typical formal reception that most guests expected to receive, which was why Dar was not surprised by his first question…

"Um, hello…" he said hesitantly, "you didn't happen to see any falcons approaching, did you?" he continued almost absentmindedly, looking around at the sky more than at the two ladies who turned to face him: "I saw the messenger birds approaching but they did not land at the aerie as they were trai… Oh!" he stopped, realizing his mistake, aided by Dar's expression.

"Tell Baron Rakoczi we are here! She is hurt and needs help!" Dar barked sharply, bringing the attention of the falconer into focus and spurring him to run back the way he came to get the help she requested. Dar and the limping Kiara worked their way along the parapet and down the long stairway that led to the inner courtyard of the castle.

Normally a large open space, with room for craftsmen and traders, the courtyard was dominated now by strings of pennants and flags being hung from the parapets of the outer walls, creating a carnival-like scene within the castle. Holes were being dug for several large fire pits as preparations appeared to be underway for some sort of harvest or feast-day celebration. This was somewhat surprising at first glance, given that it was incredibly unlikely that the harvest in Diosgyor had escaped the ravages of the many plagues that were ravaging the rest of Vengriya, and Dar could only wonder at what they might have to be celebrating. She paused as they reached the bottom of the stairs and could see the Baron and his entourage approaching from across the courtyard. They were moving quickly towards her – or at least as quickly as his limp would allow.

A young, handsome baron, Rakoczi Gabor had been earning his honour as a knight for several years before his adventures were cut short by an unfortunate encounter with an Oriasok while hunting. Surviving – barely – he had lost much of the use of his left leg, cutting short his attempt to create a suitable legend for his name, and now had to settle for managing the family inheritance. While many sons of noble birth spent their time on such adventures, only returning to their familial duties after they had grown too old and slow to master the dangers of the wilds, Gabor was now one of the youngest Barons to come into his inheritance, being granted the oversight of his own keep after his injuries by a thankful Prince and receiving the lion's share of the fortune his parents had inherited from their parents a little earlier than most. This also made him one of the most eligible bachelors in the Principality, or most of Vengriya for that matter – a fact which he was happy to use to his personal benefit. His wavy red hair, green eyes, and lightly freckled face made him a unique candidate for many of the noble daughters who sought to better their chances in the world, though many also regretted that Diosgyor was one of the most remote locations in Vengriya.

Lying well to the north and west, and on the border with the mountainous Principality of Gomor, the castle and the small town below it were a long way from the more common trade routes and saw very little traffic coming through the mountain passes from the isolated state of Gomor, whose people preferred to keep to themselves as much as possible. As a result, they did their best to attract the best craftsmen and women, paying a premium to have all of the latest trends available here that were the talk of the capital, in order to attract attention to their little corner of the realm. This was also why Dar knew she would be able to get the help and supplies she needed to help Kiara here, not to mention to follow the trail that they hoped would lead them to Voros and an end to the plagues.

Judging by the number of young ladies following behind the young baron, their efforts had not been in vain. A result that the aging falconer was also now enjoying, as he walked along with the entourage, telling all who would listen about the strange appearance of the two strangers.

"Greetings, my lord," Dar began the introductions, knowing that she had clearly caught them off guard by their unorthodox arrival, although she also expected that by the falconers' description of things, they would no doubt be guessing wildly about the circumstances and character of their latest arrivals. "I am Lady Darellan Fenndragon, advisor to the court of His Grace, Arch-Duke Svatopluk, Prince of Nyirseg, and heir to the Crown of the Seven Tribes, and this is Lady Kiara, Royal Ranger and Defender of the Realm." She paused as required by custom to await the formal response.

"Greetings, my lady." She was answered by an older man standing just behind the Baron, who wore the chains of office as his chief council. "We bid you welcome to the court of Baron Rakoczi, loyal bannerman to Nyirseg. How can we be of service?"

Dar nodded at the Baron, ignoring the councillor who had spoken and acting as if the Baron had said the words himself – for this was the custom.

"We apologize for arriving so unexpectedly, but this Lady has need of medical care, and I need the proper supplies to help her. I would see to her aid as soon as possible, and then perhaps afterwards we can discuss some matters of import to the Baron?"

"Of course," the Baron answered this time, "we would be glad to be of assistance. Take her to the infirmary." Looking over his shoulder as he spoke, waving his hand, two servants stepped forward and took Kiara's arms to help her to the infirmary. "Let us know what you need, and you will have it. We can speak when you are finished tending to your friend." Another councilor stepped forward to ask Dar what supplies she needed, and they moved off to follow Kiara and the others to tend to her care.

Several hours later, Dar emerged from the infirmary. Kiara was sleeping peacefully; resting yet pulsing with the energy she needed to recover from her wounds - a process that was as draining for the patient as it was for the healer. Dar was met at the doorway by a servant boy who was instructed to show her to a chamber that had been prepared for her use, where she could clean up before meeting the baron. It was well past nightfall when she was ready and joined the baron in the main dining hall.

The evening meal had finished, but there were still many folk in the hall, drinking and talking when she entered. The volume in the hall quieted as she was announced to the assembled courtiers in a manner she would have only expected if she were in the royal court in Ascanium, and she was also pleased to note that they had remembered her formal names and titles correctly from the brief introductions earlier. Another servant brought her to the front of the room, where she was seated and presented with a plate of warm food and a goblet of wine.

The baron did not press her with questions right away, but instead raised his silver goblet in a silent toast to welcome her to the table and allowed her time to eat before they would commence any discussions. Several of those who had been finishing their drinks got up and left before she finished eating, taking their silent cue from the more senior counsellors who slowly changed seats and grouped themselves near the high table. Servants cleared the tables and began to clean the floors which ushered out the last few stragglers who were not members of the Baron's inner circle, allowing them to conduct their business in private. Only a single bard remained, plucking quietly on a lute that mingled nicely with the clinking of dishes and cutlery as the noise of the kitchen staff working in the next chamber did well to mask their conversation from any unwelcome ears.

"Your reputation precedes you in your journeys, m'lady Darellan..." the Baron began, breaking the silence that had settled over the assembled group.

"Please, 'Dar'..." she interrupted politely. "I have never cared much for all the other words, except for when doors need to be opened."

"Our doors are open to you this night," the Baron replied with a warm smile, "and you may call me 'Gabor'."

"Thank you, m'lord. I am grateful for your help with my friend. It was an unfortunate encounter with some Torpek, and I'm afraid she would not have lasted another night without the right attentions." Dar was careful to note the concerned looks that were exchanged when she mentioned the Torpek.

"May I ask where this unfortunate encounter took place?" Gabor inquired.

"Not in your lands," she answered, "it was several days' ride to the south, near the Eastern pass into Sopron along the Duna." Still watching their expressions, she continued, "You do not seem surprised to hear of the Torpek moving about on the surface...?"

"Sadly, no." came the response from the man sitting to the right of the Baron. "We have been hearing more and more of raids being carried out by the underfolk. For many years, our children believed they were only tales, to scare them to eat their dinner or do their chores, and many did not believe they had ever walked upon the surface of these lands. But we are mountain people here – as much as the Gomor are – and there are still those among us who remember what it is to have fought for our place here."

Another man to his right continued... "It was a sad day for all of us when the underfolk started foraging again on the surface. No one knows what stirred them from their sleep…"

"…if they were sleeping at all…" said another.

"…and woke them to the lands above being ripe for plunder, but we have been fighting them like ghosts for many seasons now," the second man finished.

"I had not heard this in Ascanium," Dar commented, "Was the Prince advised of the danger? Were troops sent?"

Gabor interjected now, "The reports never made it past the High Vizier – Tolvaj? Tolvaj Balasz, I believe – our reports were met with disdain and rejection as childish rumours, and not worthy to bother the Prince, who did not have the time for such fanciful stories." The Baron took a drink of his wine and stared in the cup as he spoke. "We were told to muster our courage and rid ourselves of these bandits by our own hand."

Dar listened in silence as she absorbed the news.

"So we have kept their menace at bay – or at least we thought we had." Gabor looked up at Dar, "until you tell us that it seems like they have shifted south a little." He let a small smile slip out, curling up his lip as he thought about it… "At least we did well enough to drive them away, to try their luck elsewhere…not bad for a small border keep!" he said proudly.

"Well met!" Dar agreed, raising her cup in salute.

"What other news do you have for us?" someone asked, as the Baron tried to hold Dar's gaze. She turned away slowly to answer the question, not having seen who had asked it.

"As you have likely heard by now, the Prince is preparing for war with Temeskoz and Sarkozy," she offered, happy to see the heads nodding around the table, to see that they were being kept informed. "You may not have heard that Prince Előd of Mezoseg fell to an assassin's mark. We suspect by someone supporting Temeskoz." There was some surprise around the table at this news.

"Svato was upset to hear this, as he thought he would have more time to prepare before fighting a war on two fronts, but he was not surprised: he knew Előd was Onogur and not true Avar, so he was likely to capitulate quickly. We just thought that there would be more time to allow us to deal with Sarkozy before facing Temeskoz. But if they are in league, then we must face them both," she finished dryly, looking around at the sullen faces.

"We had not heard the news of Előd…" Gabor said, "I agree, it would have given us more time, but I suppose – as you say – it was not unexpected that we should not count on our neighbours for help. We have lived on the border with Gomor for a long time, and I cannot recall them ever coming to our aid – when the Imperium arrived on our doorstep, we did our best and fled to the hills when hope of keeping the castle was lost – the Imperium was never able to penetrate the mountains of Gomor, but neither did Gomor ever seek to sally forth from the safety of their caves to lend us aid. They were content to be left alone, and even offered ransom to the Imperium to permit trade. No, if there is to be war again in the seven realms, and it is to be fought based on blood, then we are the last Principality of the Avar."

He was quiet as he finished, and the room echoed the mood. Glancing around at the somber faces, he was not about to let this spoil the evening.

"I think this is enough of such news for one night," Gabor announced, breaking the mood with his enthusiasm. "We have scraped a meager harvest this season, and we had the good fortune to find a herd of wild boars migrating across the hills, and so we are preparing for a celebration. We have another day of preparations to make, but we hope you will join us on the following day for a simple festival. After all, when things look grim, we need to celebrate even the smallest things that can bring a smile – and trust me, when these beasts emerge from the roasting pit, dripping with flavour, you will see why our kitchens are the envy of the capital! Until then, please be our guest and enjoy our hospitality!"

"Many thanks for your hospitality, m'lord," Dar answered, "Indeed I will have several friends joining me here within another day, who have travelled long – we can talk on the morrow of our quest – and I would be honoured to have them join your invitation to the feast, by your leave?"

"Yes, yes," Gabor replied excitedly, "they can tell us all the tales of their adventures – especially these Torpek that they encountered – I am sure the telling will be exciting for all to hear!"

Dar nodded and raised her cup one last time to toast to her host, before retiring for the evening.

*****Parting Ways*****

It was on the morning of the third day that Jason and the companions saw the silhouette of Diosgyor on a hill in the distance. They were in the small town beneath the keep by mid-morning and were working their way along the road that led up the hill to the castle, when Shagron noticed something amiss.

Looking around, he could see that Brother Ralof had stopped further back on the road and was simply sitting on his horse in the middle of the lane, watching blankly as the peasants moved around him. Shagron called for the others to wait for a moment as he turned back to see what was wrong. By the time Shagron reached him, Ralof had dismounted and was leading his horse to a quiet spot at the side of the busy avenue, looking concerned.

"What is it?" he asked, "What's wrong?" Shagron scanned the street, looking at the people; the low buildings; rooftops; street vendors; looking for anything out of the ordinary.

"Everything is fine, my friend," Ralof answered, his voice quiet and unusually somber. "I have come to a decision."

"Decision? What kind of decision?" Shagron replied, confused, dismounting to speak with his friend without shouting over the noise of the street.

"I cannot go any further on this journey" Ralof began, watching the expression on Shagron's face as he continued to explain. "I have been praying for guidance these past few days; seeking an answer to explain my failings…"

"Failings?" Shagron interrupted, "You have not failed at anything, my friend!"

Ralof raised his hand to ask for silence so he could continue. "I have failed you all for some time now, but you have been too generous to see it. I was not able to summon the strength of my faith to heal the girl, and she almost died – she yet may have, I don't know – but it was my place to do this and I couldn't!" He turned to a bale of hay that was stacked nearby and sat down, slumping his shoulders. "I have fought more with my mace than with my faith, and this had always seemed to be enough, but now it is clear to me that I am more of a hindrance than a help in this endeavour. I no longer hear the answers to my prayers…"

"Then let us pray to Ukko together! He will not–"

"Shh! Enough!" Ralof cut him off quickly, his tone a mix of anger and shame as he put his hands to his face, feeling the sense of anguish rising up inside him. "Ukko will not help me! Cannot help me!" he moaned angrily into his hands, adding to Shagron's confusion. He was sitting beside the priest now, looking back at the others, who were still waiting on the road, watching their conversation but too far away to hear.

"The all-father will always hear our prayers" he told the priest, putting his hand on the old man's shoulder in an act of comfort, "even if he does not choose to answer them…"

"No, you aren't understanding me!" Ralof replied angrily, looking up at Shagron, feeling frustrated by the knight's attempts to console him. "The all-father does not talk to me because he knows the truth of my heart! I have not been true to him – I am not worthy of his blessings.

"I have not been true with you either…" he continued, opening up the floodgates, "…I am not worthy of your comfort now! You come to me for absolution, but it is I who must confess now to you… I am not a servant of the all-father, a priest of Ukko!"

He waited a moment, watching Shagron's eyes to see the words sink in.

"What do you mean?" was the expected reply.

"I am not a Priest of Ukko. I am – or I was – the High Priest of Freyja in Ascanium. Not Ukko. Not Jove. Not anything else they have made me swear to save my miserable life!"

"For many years, in the same cloister where you and I hid when we entered Ascanium, I led Freyja's servants in worship of the goddess of fertility, beauty, and love. I was her most faithful servant and she blessed me with her many favours. I had found my true reason for being after travelling north to the winter lands, where the sea raiders worshipped their gods with the fiercest passion I had ever seen. I came back as a true believer in Freyja's graces and sought to spread her word everywhere I went."

"And I did it well – until the Imperium arrived. To my shame, I was weak in the face of my own peril, and I disavowed myself of her love to save my wretched existence; I swore fealty, first to Jove, then to Ukko – it got easier every time – whatever it took to keep them from tearing down my beautiful temple and taking away all the glories I had achieved for myself. Ukko never favoured me – he saw through my heart despite all the sacrifices and prayers. I still had all my learned knowledge of the healing arts, but my blessings could not bring a rich harvest, health to livestock, or even ensure a happy marriage; the only power I had in the church was the power the legate bestowed upon me to oversee the people and preach the will of the Imperium!"

"When I could take that no more, I took to the road, where I could release my frustrations through my mace, making people believe it was my faith that was powering my blows and not my sins; I created a name and reputation for myself for a time, but then my health began to fail me – I grew too old to carry on the adventurers' path and I took to being a pageboy for the Bishop in Mercurum, where you found me."

Shagron was silent as Ralof recounted his tale, listening intently while he also recounted the past in his own mind, to try to see how he had not noticed these things for himself – the monks in the cloister following them with their eyes – how many of them were followers of Freyja as well? He let Ralof's pause hang in the air as he traced his memories, and did not notice the others coming back to join them, dismounting as Ralof continued unloading his burdens on the sworn champion of the divine being he was breaking faith with…

"I truly tried to be sincere in my faith to the all-father, but it always seemed to be undone. Nagging thoughts that crept into my mind – self-loathing for my own weakness – always leading me back to my first promise, my first betrayal; I knew that despite what the princes would call me in their praise, I would never achieve the truth, the peace that my heart sought."

"Did any of my confessions to you ever reach the ear of the all-father?" Shagron interrupted him, a deep level of concern in his voice. For some time now they had been travelling together, and the holy warrior of Ukko had believed himself to be in good standing with his maker by virtue of his weekly rituals with the priest – but now the priest was confessing to him that he was not talking to his god any more…which meant what for him? The situation was rapidly becoming an existential crisis for them both, as the sting of the deceit became more than just a problem for Ralof, cutting the heart of Shagron's virtue… and he was getting angry about it!

Ralof did not have an answer for him other than a forlorn stare from his watery eyes.

"I must leave you now," he said again, this time to the whole company that had gathered in close to see what the problem was. "I wish you the best in your journeys, but I must go back to Mother Freyja and seek her forgiveness before I can do anything more for anyone…"

"…And with that, he stood, took the reins of his horse, walked away from his friends, and disappeared into the city, ostensibly in search of a temple of Freyja!" Ferenc finished telling the tale to Dar, wiping his mouth as he took a swig of ale from his cup.

"I did not see that coming!" he added, having taken on the responsibility of recounting the whereabouts of their cleric to the young druidess once they had arrived in Diosgyor Castle. Shagron himself was still far too angry at the turn of events to say anything, very much focusing inwards on his own concerns, and the rest of the group seemed reluctant to try to explain what had happened, having only come into the conversation partway through – this was not enough to stop Ferenc, though, from filling in the blanks with his own conjecture to make the telling complete, and Shagron did not bother to correct him.

"Hmmph," was Dar's first reaction, as she felt herself being watched by Torick and Omar, who both seemed quite intent on just what her reaction would be. "I did not see that coming either," she added, looking away as she thought about what would happen next.

"And what news of Kiara?" Jason asked, eager to hear word of his injured ranger.

"She is well, healing quickly – the spells have begun to do their work and she is relaxing in the healing springs as we speak," Dar told him, soothing his concerns. "With any luck, she won't even have a scar – though I expect she will be disappointed at that!"

"There is a feast to be held tonight, with much drink and dancing," she continued, "I'm sure Kiara will join us as soon as she is ready, and we can talk tomorrow about where we go from here." She paused, as if considering whether or not to go on, and then decided to do so...

"There is one other coming who I believe will be able to help us with this challenge. The traveler you met earlier in Ascanium – he was awoken by servants of the arch-mage, and so, in part to hide him and in part to put him to good use, I have arranged for him to be brought here tonight. We can plan our next steps when we are all together tomorrow."

There was an exchange of looks between several of the assembled group, which led next to several long draws on their drinks, each opting to keep their own counsel on just what this would mean, or what he could do for them.

"If that is all," Shagron said, "then I will be off to my chambers to prepare for tonight's feast."

"I need make myself presentable as well... and find some more wine!" Jason added, getting to his feet and following Shagron out of the chamber.

"Shagron..." he called to his companion as he stood outside in the hallway, but the knight was already walking quickly away, and only waved his hand as he turned a corner – clearly not interested in talking to anyone. Jason sighed quietly, hoping that the old man would be able to get over whatever it was he was feeling about the departure of the priest. They were going to need more than just wizards and schemes to get the job done when they finally managed to track Voros down, and he wanted to make sure that Shagron had his head in the game.

He decided that there would be time enough at the banquet tonight to make sure he drank his worries away and was set right for tomorrow. Pausing, he briefly considered wandering the halls of the keep seeing if he could find Kiara and check on her himself, but he quickly thought better of it, knowing it would be better to find his own chamber and wash off the dirt of the road before they would surely meet again at the banquet.

The others slowly filtered out of the room and likewise made their way back to their chambers to get ready. Omar seemed intent on asking Torick all manner of questions about his channeling experience, while Ferenc walked away quietly to his room, feeling quite alone without Kiara's banter. He nodded once to Dar before taking his leave, and she blew out the candles at the table as she left, pulling the heavy door shut behind her.

The smoke was still drifting up from the glowing wicks of the candles when a figure stepped forward from the shadows at the back of the room – a figure that had been watching Dar in Ascanium and was doing so again here. The room was dark now, but she moved about with casual ease, finding her way to a seat at the table – Jason's seat – to stare at the faint glow of the candlewick, puffing on it slightly to make the ember glow a bit brighter for a moment before it went out completely – enough to see the faintest hint of green in her eyes before darkness engulfed the room.

*****The Dance*****

The harvest festival was a strange mixture of solemnity and excess – the folk from the town who arrived to join in the festivities all smiled and acted polite, mingling with cups in their hands that never seemed to empty of wine. Yet the tell-tale signs of the creeping doom that was the plagues of Vaszoly were evident everywhere – the glow of the evening sky reflected the glow of distant fires; the low autumn clouds mingled with smoke to carry a distinct aroma that could be only partially masked by the fire pits in the castle courtyard where they were roasting the fattest hogs they could find to feed the nobles of the court – hogs that would have been considered anemic in any other year were a lean reminder of the meager season they were enduring.

There was music being played by a quartet of musicians on a small stage at one end of the courtyard – two high-pitched fiddles squealed out a melancholy tune that had men singing lowly into the cups around several tables, as the steady thumping of a bass kept the rhythm, accompanied by the trembling tones of a cimbalom.

The tune finished as Dar arrived in the courtyard, having taken some time to refresh after welcoming her friends to the keep, and the musicians began to play a more upbeat arrangement, drawing several of the locals to their feet to dance. It was a traditional tune, and one which challenged the local men, many dressed sharply with black vests and hard leather boots, encouraging them to show off their talent for intimidating one another with a vigorous display of quick footwork and slapping their boots in rhythm with the quick beat of the music. Then the women joined the dance, with a rousing display of spinning and twirling that mesmerized the crowd with their brightly coloured skirts and elegantly embroidered blouses creating a hypnotic display of colour. There were whoops and hollers as they danced, and it seemed to Dar like a new tone was set for the evening with just a single choice of tune.

The people seemed like they were ready for any reason to make them forget about the dismal prospects that lay just a few feet outside the castle door and immersed themselves in the illusionary excitement that emanated from the music, like the spell of an enchantress over her thralls.

Dar did not partake in the dancing. Though she wore a festival dress for the occasion, beautifully embroidered in the same fashion as the local ladies who spun about the floor in front of the musicians – a dress graciously provided to her by the Baron's stewards – such distractions were not her preference for participation, and so she choose to stand apart, to simply watch and enjoy. The same could not be said for Ferenc, though, who was more than receptive to being pulled up by one of the young village girls to join the dancing. Though foreign to him, he did his best to emulate the steps and enjoy the moment, taken in for the moment by the friendly smiles and the generous servants who were diligent at ensuring every cup was filled throughout the night.

A serving girl came up to Dar, offering a selection of appetizers – local fruits, cheeses, and breads – but Dar waved her away politely. The selections were varied, but all were undersized, unripe, or but a day away from being considered rotten. Dar could tell from the look of embarrassment in the young girl's eyes that the server herself knew this, yet she continued to move about the room, doing her best to present the meager offering to all. Seeing now her own rudeness, Dar rebuked herself for own reaction and made a quiet promise to be more considerate the next time a plate was offered to her.

She walked around the outside of the crowded courtyard, scanning the faces for any sign that Tibor had arrived with his escort – she trusted Caspar to do his job well, at the same time regretting that she had to rely on anyone else to do even the simplest of tasks, wishing she could have guided his travels herself. But as much as she might have wished otherwise, she was not yet powerful enough to be in two places at once, and so she had to endure the very human stress of relying on others for the time being.

She could not find Tibor in the crowd, nor had the Baron himself appeared, for which she was grateful, as it allowed her to focus more on the task at hand without being distracted by his attentions. As it was clear that she was a friend and advisor of Prince Satopluk, the young Baron was sure to occupy her with whatever scheme she was certain he was devising to entreat her to bring his humble holdings to the attention of the Prince – another good reason why she usually did her best to avoid such events as this.

This was the sort of politicking that she would rather have left to the other members of the high council – viziers who enjoyed playing games and trading favours. With everything else that was going on, all the moving pieces that she had to keep track of, the last thing she wanted to do right now was to have to deflect the advances of a social climber like the ambitious Baron Rakoczi.

As she continued to look about the courtyard, she noticed Jason and Shagron had joined the festivities – Shagron still looked quite somber, while Jason looked to be in better spirits, laughing at Ferenc's attempts to follow the intricate steps that the other village men were demonstrating for him. Ferenc had started to perspire profusely from his attempts, and seemed grateful for a break in the music, bowing graciously to the dancers as he darted to catch a serving girl passing by with several tankards of ale in her hands, more than happy to relieve her of a few!

In the moment of silence after the applause for the musicians had died down, Dar was about to close the distance between her and the two men, only to hesitate as she saw Jason freeze in his expression, as if he had been struck dumb by a thunderbolt. Shagron had been saying something to the young ranger lord when he too noticed his distraction. They both followed his gaze across the courtyard, to the double-wide oaken doors leading to the castle interior that had been swung wide for the festivities, and through which a small army of servers had been constantly flowing back & forth throughout the night. At this moment, however, all that traffic had come to a stop, as even the servers stood back to permit the entrance of the raven-haired beauty who had stepped through the doorway, pausing at the gateway to the courtyard.

Looking for all the world like a young princess on the eve of her coming out party, Kiara stood straight and tall in the doorway, her hair combed and tied in an elegant weave, wearing a dark red dress – the colour of a full-bodied merlot on a moonlit night, accented with the most elegant yet subtle jewelry that glistened in the torchlight like stars on a summer's night. Her bare shoulders revealed her raw strength as she moved forward gracefully, her ebony skin glowing from the lotions and oils applied by the castle handmaids. She nodded slightly at several guests as she walked, strangers whom she felt she had to acknowledge as they stared at her passing by with such obvious amazement that she was almost uncomfortable with the attention.

After spending much of the day relaxing in the natural springs, then spending hours bathing and preparing her hair with the help of several of the ladies-in-waiting attending to her, she had agreed to wear the dress they had obtained for her, although she had made some alterations to it herself, preferring to remove some of the more constraining elements of the gown that hindered her movement. The result was perhaps a fair bit more revealing than the local custom might have deemed acceptable, to which might be attributed some of the attention she was getting now, but she was not one to care that much about what anyone else thought, so long as she felt comfortable.

Moving through the crowd now, she was beginning to rethink her preparations, as the balance of feeling comfortable in her clothes for the evening was contrasting somewhat with the level of discomfort, she was feeling from all of the attention her entrance was drawing – if she had known the music was going to stop at just that moment, she would have stayed inside until they resumed playing! As it were, even the musicians now were on their feet craning their necks trying to get a look at just who had arrived that was drawing such a reaction from their audience.

In the mistaken belief that perhaps the Baron had joined them, they began to play a more ceremonial fanfare, which Kiara regretted even further, as it drew even more attention to what should have been a short walk into the courtyard. Now, every step seemed a mile amid the wondering gazes of the local nobles and merchants, and it seemed to her that an eternity had passed rather than just the brief minute it took for her to reach her friends.

Both Jason and Shagron were clothed in the local military dress uniform, graciously donated by the Castellan – tight-fitting black tunics with rows of gold braid fasteners across the chest; short capes – one royal blue and one a deep burgundy – were draped over their shoulders, and both wore the same tight-fitting black pants, tucked neatly into high, hard leather riding boots. Each also wore a ceremonial sabre, hung low across their hips, generously adorned with a variety of glistening gemstones and gold leaf.

Kiara was looking at them up and down as much as they were doing the same of her, with little notice for Dar's approach. Dar could immediately tell from their bemused expressions that none of them felt comfortable in the formal attire they had been provided, being quite different from their usual preference for far more practical garb. The two fighters bowed politely to Kiara as she joined, and she did her best ladylike curtsy in reply.

There was momentary pause as the group was reunited – Shagron and Jason were astounded not only to see no sign of any injury, but also taken aback by the unexpected beauty of their fellow woman-at-arms. Living and fighting side-by-side with someone every day had taught them respect for her abilities, and – rightly or wrongly – they found themselves oblivious to some of her other more feminine qualities, as they were not accustomed to looking for such things among the rank & file of the regiment. At the same time, Kiara had always prided herself on being recognized for her quality as an archer and ranger above all else, fighting hard for her rank and position, despite everything the Legions had professed about being warriors first and all else second.

Ferenc arrived at the small, gathered knot of adventurers at the same time as

Dar, nearly tripping over himself in his haste to greet his recently recovered compatriot.

"Kiara!" he exclaimed loudly, breaking the silence with his exuberance, still breathing heavily from his attempts at dancing. "You look… amazing!" he said, looking her up & down unabashedly as she deferred quietly to his inspection, not yet feeling comfortable in her dress. The music had paused in that moment and the band quickly began to start into an easily recognizable waltz, so Kiara decided to take advantage of the moment and change the terms of engagement.

"Would you like to dance?" she asked, staring directly at Jason. He was wide-eyed at the proposition but nodded in agreement and took her hand and led them to the dance floor, passing several approaching lords and nobles who had such looks of disappointment after having mustered their courage to make a similar proposition. Ferenc did his best to keep the same expression from his face in the moment and turned to watch the couple proceed to the floor, turn, take each other in their arms, nod, and begin to move about the center of the courtyard, spinning and turning.

"Thank you for saving me, m'lord Greymantle," Kiara whispered to Jason, interrupting his focus on keeping step with the music.

"Saving you?" he stammered back, "I did nothing of the sort – it was Da…"

"…from the gaggle of pretentious nobles who have been staring me down like they were hunting a prize twelve-point stag ever since I walked in." She finished her thought, after which Jason realized her meaning, and turned a wry smile.

"If only they knew how dangerous their prey actually was," he replied, "they would think twice about hunting anything ever again."

"So true!" she smiled back, "though they do not know I have already been snared…"

"Ha! Lucky is that huntsman, to have captured so elusive a target. I did not know you had time to give to such ambitions, nor that you would ever submit to the yoke of a relationship. I always thought you too spirited…"

He was interrupted as she leaned forward into his embrace and kissed him on the lips.

Kiara held the moment for more than a few turns as the music continued, before slowly drawing back. His reaction was given away by the manner in which he reciprocated her kiss – which is to say, he did not respond at all. His face was a look of mild confusion, apprehension, concern, and pity, the last of which she sensed was for her while the others he processed for himself.

"I'm sorry…" Jason began.

"You have nothing to be sorry for, m'lord" she replied, "I did not intend to overstep, but I…"

Jason stopped dancing and held her apart, pulling her hand down from his neck and holding her gently by the elbows, locking eyes, but not with a look that reciprocated her intentions; a feeling that was confirmed for her when he quietly spoke again.

"I am flattered by your gesture, but I must declare that my heart is sworn to one, and only one, and I will not stop until I have found her again. I am sorry if I ever gave any impression that my intentions were otherwise, for I would never mean to lead anyone astray in such matters…"

"Of course," she answered, marshalling her composure. She stepped back and curtsied to him, thanking him in a voice loud enough for all to hear. "Thank you for the pleasure of the dance, m'lord, but I am afraid that I simply cannot permit you to monopolize my attentions, for the evening is young, and there are many more dances to be danced." With which she turned with a flourish, spied the crowd and confidently moved towards one of the more handsome of the patrons moving about the courtyard. Taking the young noble by the hand, she took her new partner to resume the dance as the musicians were already beginning the next tune.

Shagron and Dar did their best to pretend they hadn't been watching as Jason walked towards them, turning to Ferenc, only to find that he had gone. They caught only the briefest glimpse of his tunic exiting the courtyard, heading in the direction of their chambers. There was only time for a brief exchange of looks before Jason rejoined them, having grabbed a tankard from one of the servers. Taking a long drink, he swallowed, took a deep breath and paused before stating probably the most obvious thought on everyone's mind.

"Well, I did not see that coming!" he said.

"Hmmph," was Dar's reaction, as Shagron shrugged, "There seems to be a lot of that going around lately."

"How many people do you suppose we would offend if we just skipped dinner?" Shagron asked Dar, who simply frowned and shook her head.

"This is going to be a wonderful evening," Jason replied. "Say, where did Ferenc go?"

*****The Feast*****

Kelevra gazed down from the window of the southwest tower, taking in the celebrations below. The music of the waltz lingered in the air as the fragrant aromas of the kitchens carried up to her on the warm breeze were enough to make one's mouth water with anticipation of the meal being prepared for the guests.

None of the colours or sounds of the nights' festivities interested her though – nothing but sight of the young couple dancing in the courtyard below. She watched, as did everyone else, as these guests of the baron stole the spotlight for the duration of the song, climaxing with a kiss that drew envious sighs from many of the ladies of the court. Though four spans above the scene, Kelevra could see and hear all of this, and it was more than enough for her.

She quickly brushed back a stray strand of red hair that fell across her eyes, and turned away from the scene, stepping back from the window, back into the darkness of the small chamber atop the tower. She was careful to step over the prone body of the guard, lying propped up against the wall by the inner window – he would wake later with a terrible headache, his price for paying more attention to the inner window than to his duties. There was a second guard in the room, but he stood motionless, facing the corner, mumbling something undiscernible under his breath, completely focused on something that clearly was not her, as she stepped silently to the stair and crept to the parapet.

She watched the guard carefully as she ascended and quietly said a prayer for those who remained in the keep, thinking they were safe from the worries of the outside world. From the parapet she descended the outer wall, her strong, slender fingers finding unseen handholds in the cracks between the stones – as she had first entered the keep.

Landing gently in the short grass, she glanced around to ensure she remained undetected, and then disappeared into the night.

*****Riding at Night*****

It was getting late into the evening as Tibor and his escort arrived at the small town that sat just below the castle of Diosgyor. With the smoke from the constantly burning fires drawing closer as they approached the foothills, it gave the appearance of darkness falling sooner than usual. The Captain had suggested a few hours earlier that they should stop and make camp and press on to the city – and the castle – in the morning, but Tibor had insisted that they try to get there tonight. It wasn't anything specific – certainly, nothing he had read from his connection with the others, whom he knew had already arrived to rejoin Dar by now – but he just felt like tomorrow might be too late. What convinced the young Captain in the end was his explanation that for a few more hours of riding, they might all sleep in a soft bed in the town tonight and let someone else tend to their mounts; that convinced them all that it was worth pushing on for a few more miles.

They had stopped at an inn near the center of a small, rural town, and the guards were dismounting and finding their way inside as they handed off their horses to a very young, and very panicked stableboy, who seemed quite unaccustomed to having to check in so many horses at such a late hour. The Captain approached Tibor, who remained mounted in the street, and he extended his hand, which Tibor shook vigorously in appreciation.

"Thank you, Captain…" he began to say, and then paused, as he realized with embarrassment that he had never called his escort by anything other than 'captain' then entire trip…

"…Caspar…" the Captain graciously added, to fill the silence, nodding and waving a slow salute as Tibor quietly spurred his horse to begin walking down the street towards where the road left the town and headed up the hill towards the keep. He looked back once but the street was empty, almost everyone having quickly gone into the tavern – most likely enticed more by the thought of a draft of ale more than a soft bed, but happy to be off the road all the same. The young soldier who had helped him with his armor days earlier remained in the street, waving with a sly smile. Tibor waved back and remembered to watch out for the kisasszony.

Tibor could not recall the name of the small town from any of the maps or books he had studied, but it was not very large, and the homes and scattered buildings quickly fell away as he rode towards the hill. Despite the usual agrarian odours that wafted to and fro on the night breeze, he was almost overcome by the powerful sulphur smell that dominated his senses almost from the very minute they had reached the town, and which seemed to grow stronger as he came closer to the rising hills. He did know that Diosgyor Castle was built over a natural hot spring that had been discovered bubbling up from the earth many years ago, and which the ancient Angyalok had told had healing and restorative powers to any who bathed in the water.

The Angyalok had seen the springs as a source of natural power in the region, and it was something that the druidic Avar healers almost seemed to worship for a time. That is, until an Avar noble sought to exercise greater control over the region and decided to build his castle directly over the springs, and monopolized access to the sacred site for hundreds of years since. The castle had been rebuilt several times since then, by different owners, each drawing on the wealth of the region to expand on the strength of the defenses, and all drawing revenue from those who now had to pay for access to their shrine. Not from the Angyalok though – with the arrogance of the Avar on clear display, they left the natural power of these springs to men, and quickly learned not to share their secrets with others.

Tibor pulled his scarf up higher around his nose and mouth, to try to mask the sulphur smell. He wondered how the people who lived here had learned to put up with it their whole lives. He supposed there were some things you just got used to…

His train of thought was interrupted as he began to make out figures walking on the road in front of him in the darkness – shadowy shapes in flowing, pale-coloured robes, walking side-by-side towards the castle. Hearing the footsteps of the horse approaching behind them, the figures stopped and turned to watch his approach.

He could see they were all women, perhaps eleven in number, following a single figure carrying a torch to light their way. Tibor dismounted before he reached them, rather than appear rude by riding through them. They parted in silence, bowing their heads slightly as he passed by, each face expressionless, masked behind thin silk veils that hid their features – not that he imagined he would recognize any of them.

Smiling and nodding to each as he led his horse forward, he arrived at the head of the column to be greeted by the blonde-haired torchbearer. She had let her veil drop to greet Tibor, and he could see her smile clearly by the flickering light of the torch in her hand. Not young, but not old either, she had a striking quality to her features that Tibor found to be quite mesmerizing.

"Good evening," he offered in greeting, bowing slightly to the lady, "…you are not kisasszony, are you? Fair maidens out in the night trying to lead me astray?"

"M'lord," she responded demurely. "Arriving late for the feast?" she asked, ignoring his comment while scanning him and his horse. Her question drew Tibor's attention over her shoulder to the castle, where he realized he could now hear the faint sound of music echoing over the walls, which he now noticed were well lit with torches around the entire perimeter. They had been approaching a small split in the path, where the trail turned towards the small gatehouse that guarded the entrance to the castle, which was illuminated even more brilliantly in the night by torches and braziers, with brightly coloured banners fluttering in the wind to welcome guests to the festival.

Tibor was unaware of the festivities, and it must have been apparent in his gaze. She turned her head and followed his gaze towards the castle, exposing for the briefest of moments the bare skin of her neck, giving Tibor a glimpse of a familiar tattoo – the upright sword of Isten Kardja. Turning back to Tibor, she could see the puzzlement on his face, and before he could bring himself to ask the question on the tip of his tongue, she let the torch in her hands swing down towards the ground.

The unexpected action drew his attention down towards the flame. He would only see in hindsight that this was a clever maneuver, and would appreciate the subtlety, even though it was to his detriment. He wouldn't recall feeling the blackjack striking the base of his skull, as one of the maidens took advantage of the narrow gap between his gorget and the base of his helmet, a weakness created by the movement of tilting his head downwards, even if just for a moment.

The guards at the gatehouse, their night vision blinded by the light of the flaring torches arrayed around at the gate, remained oblivious to what was happening just a stone's throw away from their post. Listening with envy to the music being played inside, imagining the feasting and dancing going on without them, they were happy to enjoy the surprising pleasure of a few cups of ale – even though they were on duty – graciously brought out to them by sympathetic servant girls – a saving grace for those who had drawn the short straw for guard duty that night. They would hardly notice the procession moving past on the other side of the simple moat, as the ghostly figures of the maidens moved past the trail to the gatehouse, taking the turn to the left instead, leading up the hill further and onwards into the rocky terrain of the mountains.

Omar was awoken early the next morning by the sounds of the castle coming to life, which was much to his dislike. Skipping much of the festivities planned by the baron, he and Torick had instead retreated to the small but quaint library of the keep and discussed a variety of techniques and methods for channeling magic.

It mattered little to Torick what Omar may have thought of him, and it seemed he didn't even recall that Omar might have had a grudge against him before they had undertaken this quest. This, of course, suited Omar just fine – he was not looking to make friends; he wanted to learn as much as he could, as fast as he could, and if Torick was blind to his ambitions, then all the better for him.

He would use the current circumstances to his benefit, and pry as much information from the ancient wizard as he could, while he had the chance.

And what a productive night it had been.

Most fascinating for Omar had been the revelation that there were an array of tokens, rare stones, and other assorted trinkets that could be used to focus one's channeling, depending on just what it was you wanted to channel, or how you wanted to channel it. This opened up for him a wholly new understanding of just what he could shape his conjurations to be.

Of the more rare and coveted items that one could possess were talismans from otherworldly creatures. And, as luck would have it, Torick let him know their new friend, Shagron, had quite an impressive collection of otherworldly souvenirs, earned from the creatures that he would encounter on a seemingly regular basis. He had heard tales that Shagron was plagued by many such burdens – demons, devils, and unholy beasts from the depths – the curse of an ancient demon deity, it was said, though he knew not the details that would convince Omar that any of these more fanciful tales were, in fact, true. Nevertheless, Omar did make a mental note to endear himself to the holy warrior at some point and inquire if he would permit him to purchase any of these valuable talismans at the very first available opportunity.

They had ended up talking very late into the night, and so he was quite unprepared to be roused so early and was more than willing to take out his dissatisfaction with the first person he encountered upon opening his door.

To his regret, he flung open his door only to see Dar standing before him, arm raised and ready to knock.

"Oh, you're up! Excellent!" she said quickly, "We are gathering in the small council chamber to confer with the Baron. Tibor – our visitor – has gone missing, and we need to find him. Please, come!" She turned and began to march away down the hallway before Omar could even think of a response, still only half-awake and desiring to be even less so.

With a sigh, he reached for his things and stepped out into the hallway, almost getting run over by a stableboy, who almost pirouetted to avoid him while apologizing profusely before bumping into two other maids before continuing his course down the corridor. Omar walked in the direction that Dar had gone, though she had long since disappeared from his sight (it didn't help that he was shorter than most everyone else in this misbegotten keep, he thought to himself!). '*If they only knew what I could do*', he thought to himself, '*they would clear my path and not step out again until I was out of the kingdom!*'

The thought gnawed at the edge of his mind as he continued to weave through the crowd of servants, groundskeepers, men-at-arms and other assorted rabble, until he finally found himself nearing the more formal section of the keep, and the volume of traffic seemed to die down significantly, which kept the noise to a minimum where the Baron conducted his affairs. It took his exploration of several chambers before he finally discovered what must have been the "small council chamber", as everyone seemed to be there already.

A modest room, it resembled more of a tavern common room, with a long row table dominating the center of the rather smallish room, surrounded by at least a dozen chairs pushed up neatly against the walls. Everyone in the room was standing around the table, discussing something that seemed quite interesting based on the attention they were all giving it, although a few familiar heads turned to greet him with a nod as he entered.

Aside from his companions Omar could identify the Baron, with two of his advisors (not grand enough to be considered 'viziers', since he was not a 'prince') along with a guard captain and a couple of his squad, who seemed to be giving a report of what they had been doing the night before.

"We escorted him to the city, where he insisted that he carry on the rest of the way to the Keep by himself..." Caspar was explaining again – not for the first and probably not for the last time – since Dar had summoned him to the keep before dawn to get his report on their journey and the whereabouts of his charge. "We had actually suggested stopping early to camp, but he insisted that we press on and reach the city after dark."

"...And you just let him ride away like that? Alone?" Dar was questioning him, with a great deal of concern in her tone, though little anger.

"He is a grown man, and it is hardly a third of a league from the city to the gatehouse – a simple walk for a man on a horse!" Caspar objected, trying to defend his decision from her withering criticism – something he immediately regretted as he caught the fire in her eyes, and quickly dropped his gaze to the table. There they had spread the Baron's best maps of the surrounding region, trying to decide if their charge had wandered astray, taken a wrong turn on the trail, or if something worse might have befallen him.

Omar settled into a chair along the wall and waved over one of the attending servants, hoping to get some breakfast brought to him, for he was quite hungry after missing the dinner the night before. The servant had barely stepped out the door when it was flung open again, signaling Ferenc's arrival. He marched quickly into the room and right up to Jason, where he saluted the Ranger Captain with an arm across his chest and proceeded to make a full military report.

"We found a fresh trail on the road outside the keep – several trails actually."

"Here…" said the Baron, pushing a map across the table, "Show us on the map."

Ferenc stepped closer to the table and pointed out the tracks he had discovered. "Many of your guests stayed within the keep for the entire night, so there was little traffic heading back into town to disturb the most recent tracks heading up the hill. We tracked a small group – women by the small size and style of their shoes – coming up the hill that turned away from the keep here."

He pointed to a spot where the trail parted just before the gatehouse. "They are joined by a horse before they reach the keep, and then their trails are mixed as they continue into the hills. There is also another set of footprints going to & from this tower, just south of the gatehouse house, but these again are not from our quarry. The trail for the group and the horse becomes trickier to follow as they cross onto the stone as the trail rises into the hills, and I needed to turn back to make a report before going any further."

"Do you think we could follow the trail into the hills?" Jason asked, knowing the skill he shared with Ferenc for tracking prey. "I believe it will be a challenge," Ferenc replied, "their shoes are soft, and the rock will give little sign, so unless we are fortunate enough to see some sign dropped, I…" he trailed off as he spoke, confirming his uncertainty.

It was Dar who noticed the looks exchanged between Baron Rakoczi and his advisors, as the others were focused on the map and Ferenc's report. "What is it?" she asked, "What are you thinking?" posing the question directly to the Baron, who looked at her with surprise, clearly believing he was more subtle than he actually was.

"I was thinking…" he started, "that there has been some trouble of late; trouble we thought was just a minor annoyance – a distraction for some of the ladies of the court, to go out and prance about in the dark while their husbands were out keeping the peace in the countryside. They were not causing any harm, so we didn't pay it much attention…"

The Baron stepped back to his chair and took a cup of wine from the tray held by a lone servant standing beside the chair. "Are you familiar with the tales of '*Cybille*'?" he asked, speaking to everyone in the room. Looks were exchanged, and heads were shaken – but one.

"I am…" said Dar, "…it is an ancient cult – they call her the 'Mountain

Mother' – brought to Avar lands by the Imperium, from their conquests beyond the southern reaches of the Avar lands. Cybille was a goddess – or perhaps just a demi-goddess – governing the domain of fertility, healing, and wild nature. Her ceremonies were said to be quite…" she paused, looking for the right word, "…*invigorating* for those who participated."

The Baron nodded, "You are well informed," he acknowledged. "We thought the presence of the cult in this region was something more local, but as you described, the Imperium forces seemed quite comfortable with tolerating their practices – preferring them, in fact, over the local Avar customs."

The Baron took another drink. "I believe several of the ladies from the local noble houses have participated in their rituals at some point or another, though the location of their temple has been kept a secret from the uninitiated."

"Then we need to close the gates of the castle immediately, and put them to the question, before everyone from the festival has departed!" Shagron placed his hand down on the table loudly as he announced his idea, though from the Baron's immediate reaction, it was clearly not a popular suggestion.

"I don't think it would bode well for my continued perch atop the barony were I suddenly to tell all of my bannermen that they are being held for questioning – after inviting them for a feast no less – or rather, their wives are being held for questioning – oh, that's so much the better for me!" The sarcasm dripped heavy in his tone.

"No," the Baron continued, "I think there is a better way." He paused, as if waiting for someone to ask…

"What? What would you suggest?" Jason gave in and asked the question.

"All of the ladies were at the banquet last night – or at least most of them were. We simply need to identify one or two who were conspicuous in their absence and make some discrete inquiries."

"And you can do that?" Dar asked.

"Well, not me personally, but my court is well attended, and there are many who keep count of such things for their gossip circles – I am sure that we can quickly make some inquiries and see who may have been in attendance, and who was not!"

"Very well," Dar agreed, as did the others, "Let's get to it…"

****Captive****

He couldn't be sure if it were the ringing in his ears that roused him to wakefulness, or the piercing pain behind his eyes that felt like a spike driven into his temple. Neither were particularly enjoyable, and Tibor soon wished he could return to the blackness of unconsciousness. That was not going to be permitted though.

He winced and let out a small gasp as he turned his head, feeling the lump and sting of where the blackjack had knocked him senseless the night before. Taking a deeper breath, he almost gagged on the heavy smell of sulphur as his other senses began to awaken. He could hear the gurgle of water all around him and feel the cold hardness of the rock beneath him – his first thought was that he was back in the basement of the Preston Springs Hotel – home, a world away, and the past few days were perhaps a dream?

...No, he stopped himself, it was a moment that passed almost as quickly as it had come.

He slowly opened his eyes, only to find his vision obscured by a great deal of darkness, as if he were somewhere very large, and open, where the darkness swallowed up everything past the few feet of meager light from the small fire at his feet. He was sitting on a rocky surface, leaning against something that felt even colder than the stone. He couldn't see what it was, but the attempt to move confirmed that the manacles on his wrists were painfully tight. His arms were firmly secured behind him, pulled backwards in a twisted embrace of a large, stone obelisk.

"You are awake," the voice announced, thick with a mountain-born accent that sounded like one of the older dialects, long forgotten by the local Avars. "Good, this will make things easier for us."

The figure was further back in the shadowy darkness cast by the blazing bonfires that stretched back along a path behind him all the way to the far wall of the cavern. Tibor could make out little of the man's face in the darkness, although this was soon remedied as unseen torches flickered to life around him with a simple gesture of his host's hand.

In the fresh light, he could make out the familiar features that were a combination of the man he and Dar had encountered earlier – his nose had the hard curve of Arcady Sorkin, but the hairline was sharp and receded, as it had appeared when Voros entered the chamber beneath Trinity Church; Arcady's narrow, piercing eyes looked him over, although the jawline was clearly that of Voros, clenched and twisted, making his mouth into a pensive grin. He looked like both men, yet neither; his long black hair falling in tangled wisps across his shoulders.

Here, he was who he was, and not what he chose to make himself appear to others.

"We want to know why you are here," Voros said plainly, as more of a statement than a question, though his thickly accented words were hard for Tibor to understand at first. In his hands, he fiddled with a ceramic vase, no larger than the length of his forearm, with dirty, faded paint peeling from the sides, sealed with a wooden plug covered in wax. He held it casually in his hands as if weighed nothing – it seemed to occupy his attention more than the young man in chains – he shifted it back and forth, examining it with his dark eyes, looking back & forth between Tibor and the vase.

"Me too!" was all Tibor could reply. Voros did not seem to notice.

"You are not part of our plan," Voros continued, "and we would prefer you not be here at all, but that *ügyeskedő* is not one to ever leave well enough alone – she brought you here against all the rules, and now seeks to use you to upset our ambitions, without ever even asking us what it is we mean to do!" He scowled as if insulted by the thought.

"I really don't give a damn about your plans," Tibor responded, "I would have been fine if you would've just left me alone. But you're the one who kidnapped me, remember?"

Voros walked closer, up to the edge of the water, and looked across at him, smiling and tilting his head ever so slightly. "One and the same, but you still pretend you are not. You would do her bidding and pretend your will is not your own, when her will is yours... and theirs?" He paused, considering something to himself as the flames made the shadows dance as they flickered.

"Why do you still pretend you aren't who you are?" he finally asked.

"Who I am?" Tibor couldn't help but sound confused.

"Yes," Voros answered, his voice almost a whisper. "You know this place. Your desire to return to these lands was unstoppable – you couldn't bear it when you were torn away." He was walking slowly now, around the edge of the narrow channel of water, and Tibor had to turn to follow him, grateful that he turned around before going completely out of sight behind him.

"You went 'home', only to find to that this was ever more a home for you than anywhere else, so you wanted to return... But all is not as you expected..." Voros continued examining the vase, still talking, though it seemed he was talking as much to himself as he was to his captive. "She brought you back and you weren't ready – you didn't come as you were –you came as you are... Interesting. Extremely unusual..."

"Do you even remember what you were doing here before?" He turned to look at Tibor this time, seeking the answer in his eyes more than in any words he might say in response.

Which was just as well because Tibor had nothing to say. He knew that things had been different this time, and it seemed that Voros knew as well. He had dreamed of finding a way back to Vengriya ever since he had woken from his coma. Now that he was here, yes, things were definitely different, and he had been struggling to understand why. He could see Voros watching him, almost as if he could sense his confusion, and was waiting to see if he could sort things out on the spot.

Before he could think of a response, he felt a tremor in the rock beneath him; a moment later he could hear it, growing louder as the shaking increased. Cries went up around the cavern, and it was only then that he realized there were a great many people in the vast chamber. He caught glimpses of men in all manner of armor – leather, chainmail, plate, simple furs – scrambling to steady themselves against the tremors as they looked around in terror, uncertain if the cavern were going to collapse on them.

In the expanded light, he could now see that the cavern was ringed with other obelisks similar to the one he was chained to, and each seemed to flicker and glow as the earth rumbled.

Voros was the only one who appeared unfazed by the rumbling and shaking. As if sensing that this was the right time, as the tremors seemed to peak, he casually raised the clay jug over his head and brought it down hard upon the rocky floor of the cavern, shattering the vase and the waxen seal. Empty of any liquid, Voros bent to pick away the larger pieces of pottery container and rose with a small, rolled scroll in his hand. This, too, was sealed with a large waxen seal, but he was quick to break this with a quick snap and unfurled the old but well-oiled parchment.

Tibor was too far away to see whatever might have been written on it, but he could see the thin smile creep across the old wizard's face. Voros looked up at Tibor, still smiling, and stepped closer again to the edge of the swirling water that separated them.

"It seems we do not need to worry any longer," he said slowly, holding out the parchment as if he were displaying some prized possession, "you and your friends have simply run out of time!"

He released his grip on the paper and let it fall into the water, which quickly swept it up in the current. Tibor could see it swirl around to his left, like a child's paper boat released into a creek, floating above the waves as the oil fought to resist the penetrating power of the water. As it floated around behind and emerged on his right, he could see that whatever had been written on the parchment was now blurred by the water – the old inks momentarily regaining some of their brightness as they flowed into one another and then were washed away by the flow of water, after which the parchment sank beneath the surface and disappeared.

As if on cue, the cavern was filled with the low rumbling sound that signalled the return of the tremors, but with greater intensity. It lasted but for a moment and was punctuated by an explosion of stone off to his right, where one of the obelisks circling the chamber had flared to light and then crumbled into bits.

Then everything was quiet again.

The sound of gravel rubbing underfoot brought his attention around, to see that Voros was now in front of him, having crossed the watery moat in a blink and was staring at him – through him, it seemed. Tibor could not turn away – Voros's eyes became deep pools of blackness, with reflections of flames from the torches swirling deeper into the abyss. He could feel himself being pulled into that void – this was no window to a soul, he thought, or the wizard in front of him had none – nothing but emptiness and dark.

"I don't know why I'm here, but I know why you are," Tibor spurted out desperately. He didn't have any idea of what was going to happen next, but if time was his enemy, then he needed to find more of it... time for help to come; to figure out an escape; for the world to explode; for literally anything to happen that might improve his situation!

Voros cocked his head to the side, waiting for Tibor to continue...

"I know this place," he paused, speaking slower now that he had his attention, "...and what lies beneath. This... is a prison. Not for me – here – but far below. Something ancient, and evil."

"Is this a memory?" Voros asked, curiously, "...or a realization?"

"I know that you brought the plagues to ravage Vengriya; but they were merely a happenstance; a distraction; a side-effect of what you are doing... what you are unlocking..." Tibor continued.

"You seem to know many things," Voros whispered, "but not everything – pieces of the whole; you have words, but no meaning; no purpose. And without purpose, you are not as dangerous to us as we had feared..."

"We think she will be disappointed when she learns the truth," he said, almost sadly, crouching down to kneel on one knee beside him, putting his hand on Tibor's head, touching his hair as if the texture of it was foreign to him. Slowly brushing his fingertips down the side of Tibor's face, he paused to gently pull the skin down below his eye, peering into the whites of the eye, as if he were trying to see what lay behind – looking for whomever was pulling the puppet strings.

There was a moment's pause, then Tibor screamed as he could feel Voros reach into his mind, as easily as someone might reach into a pocket, fumbling to find loose change. The scream was equal parts of pain and defiance against the intruder. But try as he might, Voros was there, sifting through his memories, standing beside him in every important moment in his life, watching, examining, scanning each frame.

Searching… for something.

He didn't know what the mage was looking for, but he cringed as every memory – happy and sad – became corrupted by his presence. Like an old movie being projected on the walls of the cave, his blank eyes stared outwards as his mind relived the moments that were etched most strongly into his memory.

Try as he might, he could not control the path the wizard wandered in his mind. Voros stayed away from his childhood – perhaps it bored him –but he was everywhere else – drinking with his friends, travelling with his family vacations, campfires at the cottage, college parties, parents fighting, a litter of puppies, the tears in his mothers' eyes – hated memories mixed with his happiest; triumphs and failures; he saw things recent and fresh, and things he had hoped were long forgotten; all were unfolded for him to relive, unravelling before the power of the wizard's mind digging within his. Voros was cruel in his workings: hovering over the moments of shame, failure, loss, embarrassment; these he seemed to revel in, even if they were not what he was searching for.

He was helpless to view his memories unfolding like a book within his own mind. They flashed rapidly, pausing occasionally on those scenes that seemed to catch the deranged Angyaloks' dark curiosity.

In one of the oddest moments, he found himself in a comic shop, flipping through boxes of old issues, and watching as a figure entered the shop, approaching him slowly. The shadowy form was framed by the glare of light from the window, obscuring all details of the face. Like watching a TV with bad reception, he could see himself look up from his browsing, pause for a moment of recognition before backing away, breaking into a run as he cleared the door, racing out into the street… then blackness. Nothing.

Until, finally, it stopped.

Tibor had stopped screaming when his breath had expired and had struggled to simply gasp for air throughout, just to keep from passing out – a mercy that Voros denied him. He couldn't tell if it had been seconds, minutes, or hours that he had endured the scourging of his mind, his memories, everything that made him who he was – but however long it had taken, he was exhausted beyond all measure by the experience.

His limp form sagged back against the stone obelisk, relaxing the chains and manacles that had been cutting into the flesh of his wrists as his body had struggled and strained against the intruder. He could barely hear the wizard talking as he moved away. Memories still flashed within his head as he struggled to recover, but each was different now – darker, shadowy – tainted by a presence. Voros was now a permanent part of how he would ever recall his most vivid memories, a shadow in his mind's eye.

He had been struggling to keep from crying, but finally relented, too tired to control his emotions any longer. He burst into uncontrollable tears as he curled up against the rough, cold, stone of the cave, letting his tears flow to mingle with the water of the cavern pools.

"Sad. So sad. Not even a first kiss!" Voros sneered aloud, turning away before pausing and looking back again, deep in in his own thoughts… "And no true memories of this world either. Interesting." Turning again to leave he continued to think aloud. "We are almost certain that this is the work of that she-witch – she gave you something, didn't she? Something to close your mind – yes, that it most certainly it!"

"You do not have anything of the shade about you," he seemed to ponder aloud, tilting his head as he examined his captive. "We thought you were here to disrupt our plans, but now we think not. You haven't come here with purpose – you have come only to escape…"

"You're nuts," was all Tibor could whisper, though Voros didn't seem to be paying attention. "Of course, I came here to escape – you were trying to kill us!"

"This is where you come to run away…" Voros continued as if he hadn't heard the interruption, "…from everything you hate about your life. You were a hero… once… but we put an end to that. We hoped you would stay away, but we knew you were trying to return, so we had to put an end to that. Then, unfortunately for all of us, you still found your way back. But now we see that you are but an empty shell, much as the shade was before we destroyed him. It was a shame that he took his secrets with him to his grave, but we have found a way to achieve our goals without them. And now, without the sword, you have no hope of stopping what has been started."

Tibor rubbed his chin on the collar of his shirt, trying to wipe off the coldness that he felt where Voros had touched him. When he looked up again, Voros was already walking away from him, and the torches that had been lit on the small island were slowly flickering out again.

"You're not going to kill me?" Tibor asked quietly, feeling stupid for even putting the words into the air, that it might remind the wizard of something on his to-do list that had slipped his mind.

"We thought about it once," he replied, "but it is clear to us that you are not the threat you might have been. If anything, you alive will burden your companions, and we will kill them all more easily. Even the poorest fisherman prefers live bait on his hook."

"Your friends will be here soon," he called back over his shoulder as he walked away, "we must prepare their welcome..."

*****Hunting Cybille*****

Indeed, the Baron was correct in his assumptions. The serving girls were incredibly observant – so much so that the Baron made a mental note to find a way to put them to better use in the future – and they quickly narrowed their search to two noblewomen that had disappeared from the night's festivities much earlier than anyone would have deemed proper.

Tar Farkas and Tar Kalmar were the objects of their attention, though it seemed that Tar Kalmar was not in the castle and had not been observed since much earlier the night before (a fact which made her young husband near apoplectic when he learned she was nowhere to be found). Tar Farkas, on the other hand, was roused from her sleep despite the late hour of the morning and was quickly overwhelmed by the gravity of her situation and intimidated into cooperating by those involved. She did not hesitate to agree to show the adventurers where they conducted their worship of the goddess – she cowered and cried when they asked her about her nocturnal activities, all under the watchful gaze of her much older husband, from whom it was apparent all of the privileges of her title were derived.

It was just before noon that they rode out from Diosgyor and up the mountain road, with Jason and Tar Farkas in the lead, and a number of castle guards following behind, all in search of the cult and their kidnapped companion. Torick, Shagron and Omar rode with Dar and Kiara in the center of the column, and while they couldn't help but notice the sullen manner on Ferenc this morning, they did not press him on the reason.

Most had taken the Baron up on his offer of fresh horses for the journey, although Shagron and Jason insisted on keeping theirs – Shagron even apologized to Gypsy for even hearing the suggestion that he might change out his mount. Everyone who was close enough to observe could almost swear that Gypsy responded as if the horse understood every word he said.

Each kept their thoughts to themselves as they rode out, unsure of even why they were so concerned about this stranger, despite Dar's insistence on his importance. They did agree that he was a guest in their lands and deserving of their protection, and that perhaps there was a chance that it was Voros Vazul that was behind his being taken.

When they put the question to Tar Farkas, she admitted to having encountered Tibor on the road the night before and taking him – under direct orders from a strange man who had been sheltering in the caves beyond their hidden temple. They knew little about him except that he had emerged from the darkness one night, almost a year ago, as they were conducting their rituals to Cybille, and offered them his wealth and protection in exchange for their providing him with food, provisions, and the shared security of their secretive location.

Until he gave them the task of meeting Tibor on the road, they had actually had very little interaction with one another. It was clear from Dar's reaction to these tales that she believed the man in the caves to be the man – the Angyalok - they were looking for.

"It had better be!" Omar was quick to offer, "We have been travelling through hell for weeks now, supposedly on the hunt for someone – or something – that we have yet to even lay eyes on, or even be sure that is truly the cause of all the ills that have befallen the whole realm. I, for one, am getting tired of all this pointless riding!" There were many tired looks exchanged with this outburst – several that seemed to agree and some that did not.

"I can understand why Jason and Ferenc are so quiet this day…" Dar responded, bringing a blush to Kiara's face as she quickly turned her head to examine something on the opposite side of her saddle, though not changing pace with the others. "…but this, from you? Are you so disappointed not to have found a guild house worthy of the name in town last night?"

Omar looked at her sharply, though he couldn't hide the surprise in his face.

"What?" Dar continued, "You didn't think we knew you were of the thieves' guild – a 'guild master' even? The Prince practically announced it to everyone when he brought us together!" By the looks being exchanged again, it was apparent that not everyone had picked up on that particular detail.

"You look young, and most people assume that stitchings are done to create wizards, but it wasn't that long ago that our forefathers stitched for skill in almost every trade and craft, from the mystical to the mundane. You must have stumbled onto someone quite skilled in shadow-craft. Oh, don't be surprised that we have been paying so much attention to you. Whatever Louhi did to get you started on the path, she at least directed you towards the mystic arts – that is her way – but you have shown an unhealthy fondness for power, and so it was decided that you needed to be watched – primarily for any sign of instability or insanity as you continued to use the stitching ritual – but these observations are also quite effective at keeping us informed of some of your, shall we say, less 'socially acceptable' habits?"

Dar gave Omar a knowing smile, causing him to glance away ever so slightly.

"I do not apologize for who I am!" he stated in a very forthright tone.

"Or for whom you might become, it seems," Dar replied. "Don't get me wrong though, I am not judging. I am not one to judge right or wrong in anyone – I leave that for Shagron…"

"Don't drag me into this!" he quickly replied, spurring Gypsy a couple steps ahead.

Dar smiled and continued, "…I merely believe that we must all be familiar with one another's skills and capabilities if we are to work well together in any encounter. To know that you have skills as a rogue, and not just as a spell-caster, is something we ought to factor into any plans we devise." She paused before continuing, "…as well as any plans for how to profit from selling afterwards the spoils of our efforts."

This drew a quick turn from Omar to stare at her, but she was adjusting the reins on her mare's bridle and was not paying him any direct attention. Clearly, she knew, he thought, even though she hadn't even been present for the encounter, or his fencing of the recovered goods, she knew. And now he would have to decide what to do about it…

They wound along the path, crossing from the rolling earth of the hills into the hard rock of the Bukk Mountains. Here the Matras range ended and the Bukk began, and the stone was noticeably different – at least to Torick, who had some recent experience in the general area – the hard granite of the Matras gave way to a blacker rock – harder, sharper, and strewn about as if expelled from the depths of the earth in anger and fury. It lacked any of the windswept softness of the Matras Range, and just seemed harsher, harder, and more impassable than a typical mountain. This perhaps was part of the reason why the Imperium failed to breach the range in the past, saving Gomor from their dominion. Ferenc's trail grew cold here, and they began to follow the directions of Tar Farkas much more closely. It was remarkable to Jason how she managed to find an easily walkable path through rocks that appeared impassable – until you got close enough to see the small spaces hidden behind the larger stones, where the ground was level and smooth, and they wound their way over a small rise to then descend into a gap between the rising hills, which slowly widened into a small canyon, with the rock outcroppings rising around them and shielding them from the rising mountain winds.

Dar paused for a moment at they passed through the winding stone path, looking around as if sensing the magicks in the air – something that had been placed there, to cloud their senses and obscure the path from the unknowing. She considered doing something to disrupt the enchantment, then decided against it – perhaps it would be wiser to save her strength and not risk raising the alarm for whoever was maintaining the obfuscation – rejoining the others, she found they had arrived at their destination.

Before them, they could clearly see the worn pavestone floor of the rocky basin that had been cleared centuries before to permit the faithful to gather. A white mist flowed across the floor of the grotto, slowly dispersing on the gentle breeze, after emanating so strongly from the large crevasse in the flat wall of rock that closed off the dead-end canyon. The grotto was empty of all life, except for the last flutters of a crow that had recently dropped near the fissure in the wall and was in the process of succumbing to the noxious vapours.

It flopped about slowly among the scattered corpses of so many other birds that their remains were more numerous than the pavestones, victims of their baser desires to shelter in the warmth of the venting gases. Intermixed among the bodies was the occasional mountain fox or other unfortunate carrion seeker that had followed the scent of decay, seeking an easy meal and instead finding only death.

Tar Farkas halted the party and pointed to the fissure. "There. The Plutonium. *"The Gates of Hell"* - That is the entrance to our temple."

"There? In the cave?" Dar asked her.

"You think us fools?" exclaimed Ferenc. "This is a place of death, not *'fertility'*!"

"Cybille is many things…" Tar Farkas pronounced, "…Mountain Mother, mother of gods, protector of realms, harvest mother, the wilderness… in all these things there is death, but for there to be death, one must first create life, and that is what we celebrate… in peace…" she added for emphasis. "The mother protects her children within… you would be wise to leave them be. They have harmed no one!" Her stern tone began to slip into a plea, though none seemed to be heeding her.

Dismounting and hobbling the horses on the far side of the grotto, as far away from the drifting mists as possible, the group considered their options.

"Tell us what lies within," Shagron demanded of the lady, sternly, but respectfully.

"Or what?" she retorted, "Will you strike a woman? Will you break your vows and besmirch your reputation?"

"His reputation isn't very much these days," Omar added sarcastically, "nor do any of the rest of us care what others may hold in their regard." He fondled the blade of his stiletto and spun it by the tip on his finger. She got the point.

"It is a short passage, opening into a cave. The mist vents out the passage when the fissure is uncovered. Too long to hold your breath as you pass but stay upright and you will be able to breathe… and survive." She glanced over at Shagron, who had made the journey in his plate armor, expecting a good fight. "You will not fit in that…" she noted with a wry smile, "you will likely wedge yourself halfway through and die choking on your own tongue, along with anyone who follows."

"Right then," Jason started, "quick & quiet followed by strong & loud," he suggested, his look darting from Omar first, then to Shagron and Ferenc, "and you three will cover the rear and follow us in," looking lastly at Torick, Dar and Kiara. "I go with Omar and we will seal the fissure to stop the mist and scout the cave for threats. If there are any, you will all join us soon enough to dispatch them. Any objections?"

There were none.

"Good! You there, Captain…" Jason turned to Caspar, "you can take her back to the castle and let the Baron decide what to do with her – or her husband perhaps – for our part, we are done with her. Oh, and mark the trail as you leave, so we can find it again if we need to." Caspar saluted, took Tar Farkas by her wrist and turned back to the horses with the other castle guards that had accompanied them on the ride.

*****The Gates of Hell*****

Omar approached the cave entrance cautiously, pulling a wet cloth up over his mouth and nose as he entered, holding his stiletto in a guarded pose ahead of him. He paused for a moment to listen, quickly shushing the others – which irritated Shagron the most, as he struggled to unbuckle his heavy pauldrons without the aid of a squire, stowing the armor across Gypsy's saddle. When everything was silent, Omar listened and then turned back to the others.

"Music," he stated, "I hear music… Someone is definitely inside."

His knees bent, the low passage was easily passable for someone of his small size – though he quickly had some doubts about someone of Jason's stature following him through, for even though he knew the scout could be quiet, he was afraid to say that Tar Farkas was right – size would definitely work against them here. Taking one last deep breath before committing, Omar did his best to move as quickly as he could without disturbing the low-lying fog for Jason coming behind him. The were a couple of turns in the passage that he had to navigate in the dark, but it wasn't long before he stepped out of the passage into a widened section of the cave.

There was a light within the cave that made it possible to see his surroundings, and he was able to observe the vent immediately before the cave entrance from which the poisoned gasses spewed forth. He dropped low to the ground and crept forward, finding himself on a small ledge that was slightly higher than the rest of the much larger cavern that opened up beyond him. There were a few larger rocks to his right, and he silently made his way to better cover behind these and took in the scene before him.

The music grew louder as he entered the cave, the pulsing of drums and the shimmering chime of tambourines echoing louder and louder, punctuated every so often by the loud, unmistakable clang of a sword striking a shield. Reaching the small outcropping of rocks as he could hear Jason emerging from the tunnel some ten paces behind him, Omar looked out at the expanse of the cavern before him.

The floor sloped away, with the black rock rippling down in a natural step formation. The far end of the chamber was at least three hundred paces from where he was hiding, and his view was aided by the generous placement of torches and braziers around the walls, not to mention the large bonfire that burned in the center. These were not needed to heat the cave as there were several apparently natural vents in the rock of the chamber, from which the superheated steam continuously spewed forth, rising to the ceiling, and escaping through more unseen channels in the rather porous rock. All seemed to contribute to the strong sulphur smell that permeated the humid air of the cave, although none seemed to have the same poisonous effect as the vent right in front of the entrance.

All of this was secondary though to the occupants of the chamber, who were in the midst of the strangest ceremony Omar had ever seen. Truthfully, as his age was not advanced, it would be better to say that the ceremony unfolding before him was stranger than anything he could have ever imagined, yet alone actually witnessed in his young life.

There were women all about the chamber, perhaps twenty in all, each in various stages of undress, wildly dancing and cavorting to the rhythmic beat of the music. The musicians – four in number – were perhaps the only men in the chamber, and perhaps also the most clothed, as they played the same pounding beat that set the tone for all of the activities. Omar then corrected himself as he saw there were a few other men present – further down the sloping floor, towards the far end of the cavern, a more levelled section of the floor provided a small stage, which was surrounded by several the ladies clad in their wispy blue silk robes.

In the center, four naked men, lean and muscular, spun and twirled, holding small, round metal shields and short stabbing swords – this was the clanging that he had detected earlier. They moved in time with the drums, their movements more of a dance than a fight, entertainment rather than sport – acrobatic, with leaps and spins that were purely a means of displaying their well-oiled physiques for the observing crowd.

Jason crept up beside him as he was surveying the full scope of the ceremony unfolding around the chamber, and both of them had their attention focused on what had the appearance of an ordination occurring in the very center of the chamber. Here, a strong but portly fellow had just finished being ceremoniously undressed and was being led forward into a small trench along the floor of the cave. He crawled the last few paces and then lay prone beneath a heavy metal grate. He lay there, motionless, as a procession from the far side of the cave emerged from an opening leading a large but emaciated bull across the chamber.

Suffering from the withering as much as everything else, it was a meager sacrifice that they hoped would be acceptable to the goddess. Ringed with flowers, and its horns painted a bright yellow, matching the bright yellow patterns painted on its hide, the bull followed calmly to the ditch, and onto the metal grate, which creaked and shifted over the prone priest lying underneath it. With unexpected swiftness, the high priest stepped forward and sliced open the throat of the bull, barely a heartbeat after the woman leading the beast had fastened the harness to a post, holding the alarmed animal in place as its precious lifeblood spilled out in a flood of hot, steaming richness, draining through the slits in the metal grate, saturating the acolyte lying below.

The bull tried to pull against the harness, but it was well secured into the black rock, and very quickly it succumbed to the mortal wound on his neck and slumped to the ground, breathing its last upon the prone priest who was clasping his hands in prayer and celebration in the pit below. When the flow of lifeblood had almost stopped, the acolyte was helped from the pit by the high priest, who proudly presented him to the ladies of the cult in observance.

Standing upright and proud, covered from head to toe in the blood of the bull, he was applauded by the crowd, who then moved forward to take turns wiping the blood, still steaming in the cold of the cavern, from his skin.

As he emerged, the high priest proclaimed in a loud voice that echoed in the cavern over the drumming:

"Uplift the tambourines, native to the Phrygian."

"Happy he who, blest man, initiated in the mystic rites, is pure in his life…

who, preserving the righteous Orgia of the great mother Cybille, and brandishing the thyrsos on high, wreathed with ivy, doth worship Dionysus."

"Come, ye Bakkhai, come, ye Bakkhai, bringing down Bromios, god the child of god, out of the Phrygian mountains into the broad highways of the world!"

In short order, jugs of water were brought forth and poured over the newly ordained acolyte, and cloths, held by gentle hands wiped away all traces of the hot, fresh blood. In the process, their gentle ministrations – slowly wiping, caressing, cleansing – produced an effect on the young priest that anyone might expect to see in a virile young man, surrounded by so many adoring women.

The same gentle hands had at the same time been guiding the man to a table, which they now gently eased him back upon as they continued to caress and encourage his arousal. Lying back on the raised stone surface and letting the moment take him, the acolyte was carried away by the waves of pleasure produced by their careful attentions, until he was no longer able to control himself.

Sensing the impending reaction, the attending ladies quickly stepped back, giving Omar and Jason an unobstructed view of the high priest, now standing beside the prone acolyte, placing a golden knife in the man's hand...

"*No, no, no, no, no...*" Jason began to whisper rapidly in anticipation of what was happening.

And, after a few quick, deep, breaths, the acolyte proceeded to swiftly sever his manhood from his body with one swift motion of the gilded blade!

From what followed next, it was difficult to tell if the acolyte had screamed at the climactic moment of his self-mutilation, for the cavern echoed more loudly from the simultaneous cries let out by Jason and Omar, who both practically leapt up from their hidden perch in shock at the proceedings.

Surprising everyone, the musicians ceased their playing and all eyes quickly turned to the two shocked observers, now standing clearly visible to all, entirely unable to mask the expression on their faces that demonstrated their empathy for the newly initiated eunuch and feeling a profound sense of vulnerability despite their many layers of clothing, armor, equipment, and gear.

The moment seemed to hang in the air for an eternity, until the cries of alarm rang out at the sight of the intruders, and hands began reaching for weapons. Omar turned to Jason, who quickly reacted.

"Hold them off!" he ordered the boy, "I'll seal the vent!"

Jason turned and moved quickly back to the steaming vent, taking a deep breath before stepping in close and seizing the capstone with both hands. Putting his full frame into the task, he was surprised to find the stone to be lighter than he expected, nearly flipping it over entirely as he lifted and then reset the stone over the opening, blocking the steady stream of gases. He stumbled back before taking another breath of untainted air, then moved over to the opening as the last wisps were funneling up the passage on the draft, hollering the "all clear" for others to hear, hoping they would follow through quickly.

Behind him, Omar had resumed his hidden position behind the rock outcropping as he quickly considered his options for how to "hold them off", as Jason had asked. Still reeling from the shock of what they had watched, and the panic at being discovered, his first thought was to summon his favourite tool – fire – and engulf the cavern. Yet despite his desperation, he was still a young boy at heart, and these were women – his mother had taught him better than to raise his hand against a woman, regardless of the situation – he struggled to consider what conjurations he had learned that might subdue them peacefully, or at the very least, protect him and Jason until the others arrived.

He could hear the rush of footsteps and screams of the cultists echoing around the cave, and knew he had to do something before the two of them were overrun. Finally focusing on an idea, he reached into his pouch and grabbed a token – to help focus the casting – and stood up from his hiding place to face the rush of cultists and cast his spell… but the cavern was empty!

Well, almost empty – near the far end of the chamber, he could still see the high priest moving away from him, towards several smaller tunnels in the far wall. He was moving slowly, helping the newly initiated eunuch step gingerly over the uneven folds in the black rock of the floor – though cauterized quite effectively, the young priest would not be running anywhere for some time to come.

Everyone else had fled, and in the newly emptied chamber, they now saw more clearly the faint flickering of torchlight disappearing down several of these tunnel entrances that they had not noticed in their first survey of the scene. The panicked screams of the cultists still echoed loudly out of the tunnels, rebounding off the rocks walls and making it difficult to judge just which direction the sounds were coming from.

By the time the rest of the party had emerged from the entrance passage, Jason had rejoined him in scanning the room, where everything was still except for the steam rising from the rocks – and from the still warm blood of the bull.

"So, where is everyone?" Shagron asked quietly, looking over their shoulders.

"They were here a moment ago," Jason assured him. "I'd describe the scene for you, but I think I would need a few drinks first!" to which Omar nodded in agreement.

"Did you see Tibor?" Dar asked. "No," Jason answered.

"They must have him down one of these passages," Dar considered.

"If they brought him here at all," Jason reasoned.

"Tar Farkas said they brought him here…"

"And you trust someone who is part of a secret cult to be telling the truth?"

"No," Torick interrupted, "He is here. I can see it."

"What?" Jason asked, with just the slightest hint of confusion in his voice.

Torick didn't answer him directly, but he looked at Shagron when he spoke next. "I can see that he is in a cave. He is bound, barely conscious…" he trailed off as he locked eyes with Shagron.

Shagron held his gaze for a moment before speaking. "Barely conscious, but alive. Yes, I can sense it, too," he added.

"It's cold, where he is, and not much light, but he is not alone…" Dar spoke in an even tone, stepping closer to Torick and Shagron, as if they were talking of a shared dream. "He is close…"

"How do you all know this?!" Kiara was the first to ask, though the question was written clearly on the faces of all the others.

Dar broke her gaze with Torick and looked at the others.

Shagron seemed to be as mystified as the others, while the expression on Torick's face let her know that he was considering the situation, and quite quickly put it together for himself. He was opening his mouth to say something when Dar spoke first.

"He is linked with us," she began, "by a magic more ancient than stitching. A magic that links realities far more extreme than the planes of power that mages delve into with their summoning. There is too much that cannot be explained here, in this moment, but it enough to say that we…" she looked at Shagron and Torick, "are connected, and when we are close enough, we can sense much of what each other is experiencing."

"He should not be here…" Torick said quietly.

"Why you? You three? And not all of us?" Jason asked over Torick's quiet comments.

Dar raised her hand and shook her head, "There is not time for questions here. We must find him, before Vazul realizes this too, or it will be our undoing. And if we are undone, there will be no one to oppose his plans!"

"So where is he, then?" Ferenc queried her, "Which tunnel do we take?"

Dar looked at him and then back across the cavern – still empty but for the two priests, still naked, hobbling out a tunnel in the furthest corner of the cave. "There…" She pointed after them. "We follow them to their master, and to our friend."

*****Endgame*****

It did not take long to traverse the cavern and follow the short passage taken by the priests. Shagron, holding the rear guard, looked back on several sets of peering eyes, watching and waiting for their chance to escape the cave after the adventurers had passed through. The Cult was no threat to them, he felt certain, but they hid something away from prying eyes – a cover of activity to keep anyone who was curious from venturing beyond the enthralling display of their erotic ceremonies. He sensed no evil in any of them, which made him comfortable with turning his back on them to enter the next passage.

He looked into the darkness, doing his best to fight down the terror that clawed away at his heart and sought to rob him of his courage. He had delved into the depths before. To this day he was still plagued by the nightmares – real and imagined – of what they had found.

It had been a noble quest – they fought against an evil that often hid from the light, but they had not bargained for everything they were going to face, and he emerged with scars on his mind and soul that would never fully heal. He had shared some of this with Ralof earlier, but not with the others in the party.

Now Ralof was gone, and he found himself facing the darkness again.

His breathing was loud now, echoing in the small tunnel. His head ached and he could feel his pulse pounding in his head – in the silence of the tunnel, it became hard to tell if the pounding was in his head, or if it were the footsteps of someone coming up the passage behind him! He spun around – a reflex, his sword at the ready – expecting something to see someone – anyone – charging from the rear! But there was nothing.

His breathing was harder now, fighting for air, boxed in by the stone surrounding him. He put his hand out to the wall of the tunnel and felt the cold hardness of the rock. Immovable. He could reach out with his other hand and touch the other side – it was a small tunnel, and he didn't know where it led...

This was different than when he had escaped Mercurum – Ralof had been with him, constantly chattering; here, he was alone; his friends had gone on ahead –

he was covering the rear; he couldn't see their torches anymore – didn't know if they were still waiting for him. His mind took him back – back to that awful time he had spent in the depths – the constant fighting, ambushes in the dark, afraid to sleep even for a moment, the evil, the death – there was no parade for the victorious heroes when they had emerged, because no one had even known they had ventured in. In truth, none would have missed them if they hadn't returned. They were hunting for glory – and riches. It had started with saving a village from some raiders, then one thing lead to another, and they found themselves on the adventure of a lifetime for no reason other than following a trail of battles – each one grander than the one before, and each one promising greater glory and riches to the victors. He had been one of the victors, but he was still just a man, and every man has limits. He had reached his and vowed never to go into the under-dark again. Glory and riches were one thing, but evil is powerful, and the more you push, the more it pushes back. They had pushed hard for the greatest glory, and now he was never going to be able to escape their pushing back. He saw no need to make matters worse.

He shook his head, trying to clear his mind of such thoughts. *Was he afraid? Was this what fear felt like?*

He had always prided himself on being without fear – he would worry, but not actually fear things – it was his adventurer's heart, he told himself. *An adventurer's heart, bound by a warrior's code. That's what he was.*

He took a deep breath, taking in the cold damp air of the underground. *Despite everything, it was familiar to him.*

Not to be feared, he told himself as he exhaled. *It was what it was.*

He took another deep breath.

And he was who he was.

Exhale.

A rock. An anchor. Fear was not something he could be allowed to entertain, for if he were to hesitate, then what hope would any of the others have – he was the light that fought the darkness.

Another deep breath in.

Then.

Now.

Forever.

It seemed for a moment that he was able to see his path forward a little clearer now, and he began to move again, following the small twists and turns of the path, until he stepped out the other side of the passage, and it was as if someone had turned on a light. He had caught up to the others, who were only a few strides ahead of him now, and they were startled to see that their silhouettes were casting a shadow as Shagron emerged behind them. A glow of white light seemed to radiate from him as he straightened his back after stooping through the tunnel, and slowly flexed his tense, muscled frame.

They turned to look as he moved between them on the path to the head of their small column, looking out into the even grander cavern that spread out before them.

"It seems your faith has not failed you yet, Sir Knight," Dar commented, moving aside slowly to let him take in the landscape that unfolded before them.

Shagron said nothing but nodded to acknowledge her at his side.

"Everything okay?" she asked.

"Just needed a moment to catch my breath," he answered, holding his gaze forward.

If they had been impressed with the size of the first cavern used by the cultists for their ceremonies, then the sight before the party of adventurers now was truly awe-inspiring.

They stood on the precipice of a small cliff, and the floor of the cavern fell away sharply for nearly fifty feet; from there the floor sloped away at a steady angle, until the cave was nearly a hundred feet in height at the center of the roughly circular chamber; like an unfinished bowl on a potter's wheel, spiral markings in the cavern floor radiated outwards from the center.

The cavern itself was several hundred yards across, though they could only glimpse the lowest part of the wall at the far side; they could not see directly across as the ceiling of the cave sank inwards, much like the floor, though not as steeply, and stalactites dangled everywhere, slender and long, like a giant porcupine turned on its back! Water dripped from many of these, gathering in pools in the floor below, each slowly draining towards the center, where an unseen source heated the sulphury-smelling liquid, turning it to steam and sending it on its way again, back up to the ceiling in a never-ending cycle.

Though the glow emanating from the Holy Warrior of Ukko was inspiring, it did little to illuminate the vast cavern before them – instead, light was provided by a multitude of fires and torches that were spread across the rocky terrain; light that told them they were very much not alone here, and from the earlier commotion and fleeing cultists, it was clear their arrival was no longer a surprise.

Scattered between the numerous stalagmites and rocky growths that protruded from the cavern floor, makeshift shelters, tents, and lean-tos dotted the landscape, marking the presence of a mercenary force, recently gathered, well equipped, and now hastily reaching for their weapons and fastening on various pieces of armor as guards signaled the alarm.

Listening to the sounds of activity as the interior of the mountain seemed to come to life, Shagron, Torick and Dar all seemed to point at once to a tall black obelisk that dominated the center of the cave. There, despite the distance, they could see a small figure chained and seated at the foot of the monument, and they knew at once it was Tibor.

"We need to get there..." Dar stated, still pointing as Shagron began to look around the small plateau for some means of descending, "...and we need to go through them..." she swung her arm down, where most of the mercenary force was camped, on the near side of the cave, between them and the obelisk.

"There are stairs, here..." Shagron shouted, to the right of where they had emerged.

"Great!" Jason chirped, "...we can get down, but then what? — we fight our way through a horde of well-armed, well-prepared-and-waiting-for-us mercenaries?" he said sarcastically as he readied his bow at the edge of the outcropping, already picking out targets.

"Not a problem!" Omar interjected, moving up to the edge of the overlook, placing his hand on Torick's back for balance as he leaned out to look down at the drop below the cliff's edge. He stepped back and his hands began to glow red, summoning his fire.

Torick glanced back at Omar, then over at Dar.

Placing her hand gently on Omar's shoulder, Dar spoke quickly. "Okay, before we all run off on our own, perhaps I can suggest a plan?" There was almost an audible sigh of relief from Ferenc and Jason, who had already taken a few nervous steps to their right, putting a little more distance between themselves and Stiletto...

"They knew we were coming, and now they know we're here..." she started, with only the slightest glance at Shagron, "...so there is no element of surprise, and they know what we're here for, and where we have to go to get it, so we have no choice but to be direct about it! Torick & I will stay here and create a diversion, keeping their numbers disorganized. Shagron, Jason, Ferenc and Kiara will descend and make their way to the obelisk."

"What about..." Omar began to say, but she continued, looking at him directly, with her hand still holding his shoulder firmly but gently.

"I need you to lead the way to the center of the cavern, with as much stealth as you can. The others will follow, but you will go faster on your own if you are unseen, and we need your particular skills to release his bonds."

Omar nodded his understanding, though couldn't hide the disappointment that he clearly felt as the heat began to dissipate from his clenched hands.

"Above all, do not confront Voros without me!" she finished, though she was unsure if any were left to hear.

Shagron had already begun to march down the winding path of stairs and sloping trail that led down the back edge of the plateau and around to the front of the cliff face. Omar, seeing the rest of the group moving down the path, looked down the cliff face and decided to step forward off the ledge, much to Dar's surprise.

Dropping quickly at first, Omar began to slide along the loose stone that had been crumbling along the incline of the cliff face, almost as if surfing the now flowing slide of rock and debris as he slid down the steep incline. He deftly stepped from one stone to another, choosing the larger rocks in the slide to ride the rapid descent to the floor of the cavern, beating the rest of the party despite their head start.

'Perfect' he thought, *'we will do much better to stay unnoticed if we can stay ahead of the ridiculous, righteous glow of the holy warrior that was bound to draw everyone's attention.'* Surveying the terrain, with towering stalagmites that resembled a forest of stone, he was pleased to see the abundance of shadows cast by the many torches and bonfires that reflected their flickering light off the slick, glistening stone surfaces. Channeling only the slightest amount of energy to extend the shadows, he darted forward into the maze ahead of his companions.

Surveying the same terrain, Torick and Dar stood looking down from the small plateau, watching the dust quickly settle after Omar's unexpected leap of faith. Quickly moving past their witnessing such an astonishing display of dexterity, Torick began his summoning, channeling raw physical energy from one of the many planes of force that would suit his needs. He had said nothing to Dar yet about what he was planning to do, but he could sense that she knew, and approved. Ever since that day in Aquincum, when she had up and flown away, they seemed to be very well aligned on almost everything.

Dar slowly took a few steps back as he wove his hands in the intricate patterns that shaped and directed the extra-dimensional energy being channeled by the Angyalok mage.

Torick stared straight ahead as he wove his pattern, preparing to unleash his will on the panorama spread out before him. Pulling his mind back, away from focusing on any one rock or stone, the enormous cavern became less of a natural environment in his mind, instead transforming into the malevolent grimace of a giant dragon – the many stalagmites and stalactites becoming rows and rows of gleaming, pointed teeth, ready to crush down mercilessly upon his friends on the cavern floor below.

This is where he released the waves of raw energy, sweeping his arms across the entire scene before him, unleashing a devastating wave that shattered everything in its path as it rushed outwards in a wide arc across the cavern.

****

They had been camping here for only a few days – the summons had come weeks ago, and they had answered, dutifully, sworn to their master. A dozen barbarians from Uzhgorod occupied the ground closest to the small island in the center of the cave. Csikos from the great plains of Nyirseg camped to their left, finding a spot with the fewest stalagmites interrupting the cavern floor, all the while bemoaning that they had to leave their horses behind when they came. The wild men regretted this too, as there was little fresh meat to be found underground. Across the rest of the cavern, it was a scattered display of the assembled mercenaries – guild members from Sopron; men-at-arms defected from Prince Farkas; huntsmen from Temeskoz.

There were men from beyond the lands of Vengriya as well, and though fewer in number, they appeared more seasoned: two Spartan warriors, with their great round shields had been the most recent to arrive, travelling from the South to answer the call; four horse-archers from the East - like the Csikos, bereft of their mounts in the darkness of the cavern - turned their round faces and narrow eyes on the Csikos as if sizing up their competition; and amid all of these were scattered dozens of mercenaries, bounty hunters, warriors, and thieves – warriors all, sought out by Voros and his henchmen to play their part in his plan. Warriors, but not wizards – Voros did not trust wizards, and so he did not seek them out for his plans.

Come they had, to do his bidding for the promise of treasure and rewards beyond their imagining. Making camp between the rocky outcroppings, they had waited – days for some; weeks and months for others – they waited in the cold, damp, darkness of the cave, watching as Voros came and went, casting his magic, and with each casting, it was they who felt the earth begin to shiver and quake beneath them with increasing frequency. Some questioned the soundness of their surroundings, but there was little else for them to do. They sharpened their blades, fletched their arrows, and made sure they were ready. They had not been told what to be ready for, but they knew that a fight was coming, and they had been assembled to protect Voros from any who wanted to interfere with his work.

And so it was that they had all been there to hear the panicked screams of the worshippers of Cybille that morning. They did not need to be told to beat the drums to raise the alarm, to stoke their campfires to make the cave brighter, to be ready for whatever was coming. And they did not need to be told that the people emerging from the tunnel at the edge of the cavern were the reason they were there – it was something that most of them seemed to feel in their bones, as if the arrogant glowing spectacle of the holy warrior wasn't enough to raise their ire and signal that the time had come to fight.

Cries erupted across the hollow stone chamber as they rallied their courage and began to make their way forward to the cliff. They could see the party descending the stairs and were eager to cross blades. They were not concerned about the low profile of the two who remained on the small plateau – they would reach them soon enough and put them all to the sword… then the world came crashing down around them, and all hell broke loose!

****

Shagron and the others were just reaching the foot of the path to the cavern floor and were turning to face the center of the cavern where the small pool of steaming water that was the target of their attentions beckoned. Ferenc and Kiara kept low behind the rocks, returning fire with their bows as several smaller projectiles whistled through the air towards them.

Jason glanced up the rock wall at their backs before they took their first steps into the fray, hoping that their wizards had come up with something that would give them some cover as they advanced. He was rewarded by a thunderous boom as Torick cast his spell, and then the world began to fall down around them. If he had still been looking upwards, he would have seen the rocks exploding across the cavern, freeing the dagger-like stalagmites from the calcified grip of the ceiling, freeing them to drop like a rain of death on the ground below.

Shagron was the first to charge forward as the wave of falling rocks crashed to earth in front of them, believing that it was safe to follow once the stones had fallen. Amidst the thunder of the falling and exploding rocks, screams from the assembled mercenaries cut through the stale, sulphuric air of the cave, as those who could not dodge the collapsing ceiling were either crushed or impaled where they hid. Having left his shield and heavy armor behind, Shagron advanced with both hands on the hilt of his bastard sword, giving him the strength to parry a hammer that swung out at him blindly from behind a pillar of stone. Before he could counter, an arrow pierced the leather hides of his foe's meager armor, leaving him little more to do than to spin away from the parry and let the body fall across the path behind him.

Kiara nocked another arrow as Ferenc put his bow aside in favour of his longsword in such close quarters. Jason's long strides quickly brought him up beside Shagron as they did their best to move quickly but cautiously across the open areas in the terrain. It was becoming increasingly apparent that whatever Torick was doing, the impacts were coming to either side, leaving their path forward open. Jason ducked another wild swing, as their attackers also seemed to recognize that there were some spots now that were safer than others and were now converging on their path. Turning his duck into a roll, he came up swinging behind him, slicing into the unprotected tendons behind his opponent's knees, dropping him with a howl of pain.

They were moving forward effectively as the dust and debris from the shattering rock formations was beginning to rise up in clouds around them, obscuring their vision in the already dimly lit cavern. Kiara found herself taking a knee to focus on a shot when a burst of dust obscured her shot, forcing her to put her bow away and switch weapons. She could hear the clang of steel as Ferenc engaged with her target, although as she drew her blade and began to step forward again, she was surprised to see that he was gone – she could see none of her companions through the billowing dust, nor could she hear them over the cries of the wounded and dying.

An arrow glanced off the curve of her helm, reminding her that while Ferenc may have disappeared in the fog of combat, she remained exposed – several archers had sheltered beneath a natural arch of calcified rock, and were quickly zeroing in on her location. She moved closer to one of the larger rocks nearest her and waited as the dust from the most recent stalagmite crash began to settle before she darted into the opening that remained and chased after Ferenc and Jason.

Ferenc was beginning to break a sweat as he crossed blades with a pale-faced mercenary who looked more like a thief than a true warrior, but he had to admire his skill with a blade. He parried another flurry of attacks from the long-haired albino while trying to wipe the dust from his eyes to see the attacks clearly – the thief was quick! Finally batting aside the lighter blade, he followed through and cleft his blade deep into the pasty white flesh of the thief's shoulder, spraying a bright stream of crimson blood across them both. The dead weight of the lifeless body pulled his blade down, forcing him to place his foot on the bleeding torso and kick the body off his blade! He turned to beckon to Kiara to hurry, only to have the path blocked by yet another rock, collapsing a moment later and crashing down between them. The way back blocked, he yelled for Kiara and began to search for another way around, unsure if she could even hear him over the echoing thunder of the crashing rocks all around the cavern...

Kiara had gone no more than a few steps into the opening between the rocks before she realized that the path was now blocked. She only had a moment to consider her options as an arrow glanced off the crown of her helm and she instinctively rolled forward and followed the trail to the left. The rocky ground sloped downward into a shallow trench, and she stumbled into several inches of stale, murky water that splashed around her feet as she rose from her roll into the cover of the trench.

Wiping a wayward strand of wet hair from her face, she found herself confronted by two csikós, one cracking his whip while the other had drawn a long, curved sabre. The approach was not wide, so the one with the sabre hung back as his friend snapped the whip around her head. She had to be quick to avoid its stinging touch, but she was not overly concerned about it. She thought about tangling the long cord on her blade, but that was clearly what the other swordsman was hoping for, to give him the chance to dart in while she couldn't parry. So instead of her blade she offered up her right arm, letting the lash of the whip coil around her forearm as she held it up on the next strike, and then spun her body around to entangle more of the cord and give her more leverage against the surprised csikós. She was ready to parry the sabre as the other plainsman rushed into the fray and countered with a swift blow to his abdomen that left him clutching his own bowels, trying to keep them from spilling out onto the ground before him.

The one holding that whip had dropped his now useless weapon and was reaching for a blade when she continued to follow through on her arcing attack on his companion, spinning her blade into his forearm as he tried vainly to offer some defense that would spare his life. It didn't work.

She paused for a moment over the two bodies and wondered if all of the mercenaries they had seen gathered in the cavern were this incompetent – if so, it wouldn't take as long as she thought to make short work of them all. She was roused from her thought by the clanging of a weapon against a shield, and she looked up to see a Spartan warrior, his spear held in one hand, and his large round shield, notched on either side to allow the spear to extend from a shield wall, held firmly in his other. He was crouched, in a low stance that she could tell could let him defend or spring forward to strike equally effectively.

In her head, she corrected her earlier assessment, as the Spartan seemed much more competent than the other two combined. She kept her eyes locked on the warrior as she let the lash of the whip drop from around her arm, and slowly drew her second blade, crossing both in front of her as she steadied her breathing and waited for the attack to come.

'What the hell would she do?' Ferenc asked himself, staring at the wall of broken stone that was blocking the path. The cavern was large, but so too, were the rock formations that were dropping from the ceiling like massive hammers – even after they broke, they towered over Ferenc, with no hope of climbing over – especially not with the archers still having their way with anyone who stuck their head out for too long!

'She would keep moving!' he told himself, and then began thinking about how to rejoin her from his side. He turned to move forward again along the path that Jason and Shagron had taken, looking for the next branch or opening where he could double back. The natural features of the cave and the chaos from the falling rocks were quickly creating a maze of stone, surrounded by clouds of steam & sulphur!

Moving quickly, he passed through a cloud of steaming vapour erupting from the floor and blindly ran straight into a bare-chested Norseman, tackling him to the ground. They struggled for a moment before he felt two other pairs of hands grab him by the shoulders and hoist him to his feet. Held by the chain of his mail shirt, he struggled against their grasp as the first warrior regained his feet. Almost without thinking he kicked out at the groin of the barbarian in front of him, and as he doubled over in pain, he placed his other foot on the back of the groaning warrior's head and threw his weight upwards and back, spinning over the two that were holding him by his mail shirt.

The flipping motion twisted him free of their grasp and he landed in a crouch on the ground between them, sword still in his hand. He adjusted his grip and quickly swept the back of the legs of the man on his right, crippling him instantly, then carried his motion across the kneecaps of the other, opening wide cuts in his thighs as the sharpened blade sunk deep into the muscle of the leg, and then rode up the bone as it sought the path of least resistance to expend the energy of the blow.

Their screams of pain lingered as they dropped, unable to fight on but not yet ready to die. Ferenc could see the last barbarian standing across from him, hefting his axe as he took a deep breath, angrily recovering from the kick that some might have considered "unsportsmanlike". Ferenc didn't really care what anyone else thought – in a fight to the death, there was no such thing as "manners" as far as he was concerned. He rose from his low stance and parried the first swing of the axe, spun to his left and parried again, catching the haft of the axe with his blade just under the head of the weapon.

The Norseman released his grip on the axe with one of his hands and tried to punch at him, pulling back the axe and swinging again in a wide circle. Ferenc stepped back to avoid the wild swing and was ready to spin in again behind the sweeping blow before the warrior could recover, thrusting deep into his exposed backside. Unarmored, unprotected, the Norseman eye's widened in surprise as he first felt the piercing pain of the blade in his back, followed by the sight of the gleaming metal suddenly protruding from his chest right beneath his chin, the thin rivulets of his own blood running quickly down the length of the blade like a rich, dark wine being poured across glistening silver. It was the last thing he ever saw.

Ferenc did not stop to admire his handiwork. Pushing the body off his blade with his foot, he looked for a path to the right – what would have been Kiara's left – and continued his way back to her.

Dar calmly watched as the chaos of the combat unfolded across the cavern. She had knelt by the edge, resting on her heels, leaving herself free to observe and react – and to let Torick be the larger target of the two of them, should anyone hostile cast their attentions upwards. There had been perhaps two hundred warriors gathered on the near side of the cavern, intentionally camped between them and their objective. At least half had been either killed or disabled by Torick's channeling, bringing the ceiling of the chamber down upon them. A great deal of dust and debris hid many of those that remained, making it hard to determine how best to safely intervene. Small openings appeared allowing her to fire missiles of blue energy from her hands that quickly dispatched those that she might glimpse in the open, but the noise and confusion made it clear that there remained much to be done.

It soon became clear that the mercenaries' force had been wise enough in their placement to have set a group of archers at a relatively high point on the cavern floor. From Dar's vantage point on the outcropping, she could see several bowmen sheltering under a rock shelf that afforded them some cover from the falling stones, while also allowing them to fire at her companions below. Concentrating for a moment, she decided on an appropriate plan for dealing with them.

Closing her eyes, she focused on the image in her mind's eye, seeing the fog of dust that hung in the air; she saw the wind rising that would gather this dust and debris, gather it and swirl it up to the ceiling of the great cave, forming a cloud-like mass in the darkness, which churned and swirled like an angry storm cloud that one might have seen rolling across the plains on a hot summers' night – the sort of storm that brought no moisture, but would rain down lightning and crashes of thunder, that would make the peasants huddle together in the sturdiest hut in the village for shelter.

She saw this in her mind, and it happened in the cavern.

Many looked about as the wind appeared from nowhere; the dust flew up and away, giving the archers a clear view of their targets, which drew them all out of the cover, eager to make the most of the chance for a clean shot. But in the time it took to notch their arrows to the string, draw back their bows, and aim for their targets, it was time enough for Dar to release her will upon them. In a flash, the pent-up energy of the wind, the heat, and the ever-increasing static charge that she had created in the unnaturally small space for a storm cloud was unleashed, and a forking bolt of energy ripped across the chamber and struck the small group of archers with its full force, exploding upon them and the calcified rock they were hiding under.

Pieces of stone and flesh were scattered across the chamber, and the flash was followed by a near-deafening boom that shook loose what few remaining stalactites still hanging from the ceiling, causing even more pandemonium.

Torick flinched back from his perch on the plateau, struggling to clear the blinding white spots that the arcing flash had burned into his vision. Blinking repeatedly to regain his focus, he looked over at Dar.

"Maybe a little warning next time" he suggested sardonically.

Dar offered a modest smile in return and shrugged her shoulders innocently, before turning her attention back to the ongoing action unfolding below.

Torick did the same, spotting Shagron and Jason almost at their destination; at the same time, he could see more armored mercenaries approaching their position and he decided on a course of action. Removing two of his throwing daggers from his bandolier, he held them out in the palm of each hand. It was much too far to consider throwing, but with a bit of concentration, each blade floated away from his hands and flew with a flash of speed towards their targets.

Such small slender blades were not typically used against such well-armored opponents, but Torick had been relishing the opportunity to try out the edge of his newest blades against a real target, and this seemed like the perfect chance. Channeling energy, he guided the blades directly to their destination, each one striking home with pinpoint accuracy and sinking deep into the plate armor of two of the lead warriors that had been charging towards Shagron. Surprised by the blow, they stopped their forward progress and reached to remove the slender hilts that had kept the daggers from penetrating further. Before either could grab a dagger, Torick dropped both his hands with a swift, sweeping motion, and the blades each sliced downwards through the breastplates of their victims, eviscerating them cleanly as the unnaturally sharp blades moved through the man-made steel like they were slicing through warm butter. They dropped to their knees and fell over, slowly dying as their blood mixed with the streams of water on the cave floor, fumbling to comprehend how they had gone from invulnerable to dead in so swift a moment.

Torick, still watching from his perch, removed two more daggers and repeated the missile attack on two more of the heavily armored mercs that continued to race towards Jason, before feeling confident that those two were doing well enough that he should look to help elsewhere. He surveyed the shadows for a moment until he saw Kiara engaged with the lone Spartan warrior.

She was moving gracefully to avoid his spear while raining strikes on the overly large shield with her blade, slowly whittling away at the edges while the Spartan seemed to be constantly pushing her backwards. She was almost backed up against a small rock ledge so Torick decided she might need some help. One target – one blade. He reached for another dagger, and quickly sent it on its way.

Perhaps his mind was a little distracted, or perhaps he just didn't anticipate their movements well enough, but the blade struck the Spartan's shield instead of the warrior himself, which Torick nevertheless put to good use by guiding the blade to slice the instrument completely in half, much to the shock of both the Spartan and Kiara. Torick lost sight of the blade as it carried through the shield and dropped to the ground, embedding itself somewhere in the rock below the water they were standing in.

The Spartan flung aside the remaining half of the shield as the same time as he thrust forward with his spear, causing Kiara to fall backwards as she ducked to avoid being struck. Torick tensed as he prepared to cast another spell, then suddenly he saw Ferenc appear from nowhere.

Ferenc had been moving quickly around rock falls and jumping over steam vents as he tried to find a way back to Kiara. His speed had surprised several opponents that he had quite literally charged through before turning to dispatch them before their surprise wore off.

Putting his head down and moving quickly through another cloud of steam, he found himself crashing into a wall of stone on the other side, just managing to roll his right shoulder into the hit before he collided, softening the impact a little and saving his skull. Collecting himself, he saw the backside of the banded leather armor of a Spartan in front of him, lunging into an opponent that he could not see. He saw the shield fall away and the soldier lunge forward, and he quickly decided to take advantage of the exposed backside to dispatch the unfortunate warrior before he knew Ferenc was there. Thrusting deep under the ribs and up into his chest, the Spartan dropped, and Ferenc guided his fall to the side. His grin was ear-to-ear as he stood over the fallen Kiara, happy to have found her, and even more to have possibly saved her life – she would absolutely hate that!

Torick relaxed and exhaled a deep breath that he hadn't realized he was holding, releasing the energy he had begun to channel through his hands, and then flexed his fingers. Dar looked over just then, as Torick rolled his read to relax his shoulders. She was just about to remark to herself that he never seemed to lose his composure, but then a concerned look came over his face. He reached for his last dagger and was surprised to find only an empty sheath. He looked at his hands with confusion, as he had counted his blades as he used them, and this was not a simple mistake – one of the blades was missing...

Ferenc was grinning at all the possibilities of that happy thought as he stood over her, and that was the way Kiara would remember the moment. The moment as the tip of a spear exploded out of Ferenc's chest, spraying his warm blood across her as she looked on in horror – the wide grin turning to confusion as he stared at the flared tip of the spear that had suddenly appeared before him, as if from nowhere – and he did not seem to comprehend that he was already dead.

Torick swore aloud and raised his fist in the air, hammering it down into his hand in an uncharacteristic display of anger. Below, a large rock had risen into the air, mimicking his gesture, and then slammed down into the second Spartan warrior that had arrived behind Ferenc. Too late to stop the spear, the second warrior was instantly crushed to bloody pulp.

Kiara reached out to catch Ferenc as he fell forward onto her, and she rolled him into her lap. His eyes had locked on hers the whole time and remained thus as she held him. He was still, not breathing, lifeless as she brushed his hair back from his face. She did not want to look away, feeling as if he might still be there, somewhere, behind the large, dark brown eyes. A rush of emotions was building, ready to spill over, and she was a moment away from a scream when Dar appeared at her side. She looked up through tear-filled eyes as Dar crouched down and placed her hands on Ferenc's chest while looking at Kiara. They were both silent for a moment, understanding the moment for what it was, before the crash and screams of battle around them became louder to their ears once again.

"I will take him to safety," Dar said quietly, "You finish this for him."

Kiara nodded, looking down at Ferenc's body as Dar lifted him from her lap, channeling an unseen energy to float his prone body in the air before her. Kiara picked herself up, then picked up Ferenc's blade and placed it on his chest, folding his lifeless arm over it, to keep it from falling. Grabbing her own blade from where it lay on the ground beside her, she took a deep breath and steeled her resolve.

Dar looked in the direction that the Spartans had come from, towards the center of the cavern where they could hear the sounds of Jason and Shagron still fighting. With her right hand channeling the energy to carry Ferenc, she raised her left, concentrating for a moment until it began to glow a bright orange, then cast forth a stream of fire down the path, illuminating shadows and setting fire to several lurkers who had been hiding further ahead on the trail.

Kiara gave her a nod, took one last look at Ferenc, wiped her eyes on her sleeve and then turned and sprinted down the rocks between the fallen stones, following the path of the flames.

Dar did not wait long to open a small slice of white in the blackness of the shadows, stepping into a hole in space that emerged back on the plateau beside Torick. She placed Ferenc's body down near the tunnel opening and returned to stand beside their Angyalok mage.

"The others have done their part, now it's time for me to do mine!" she spoke aloud, "It's time for me to face Voros."

****Escape *****

Omar approached the island slowly, having reached the center of the cave well ahead of Torick's magic. The mercenaries had left their camps and raced to a small cliff where his friends had emerged, leaving him alone in the center of the cavern, and free to cross the slowly swirling waters and approach the monolith to which Tibor had been chained. Hidden in the shadows, he slipped close and whispered to announce his presence to the prone form.

"Time to go," he said quietly, as he deftly slipped one of Torick's daggers from his tunic and smoothly sliced through the cold iron of each manacle, releasing Tibor from his bonds.

For his part, Tibor tried his best not to jump when the voice beside his ear surprised him with a greeting, and he quickly looked around to see if anyone was watching. Seeing the coast to be clear, he pulled his arms forward and rubbed his aching wrists, trying to restore the circulation and see just how badly the cuffs had rubbed his skin raw.

He looked around the obelisk to see Omar, still sheltered in the shadows, and nodded his thanks.

"Where is Voros?" Omar asked softly.

"I don't know, but it doesn't matter…" Tibor whispered back, "we're too late to stop what he has started, and he's probably already left…"

Omar's gaze drifted up from Tibor's face, focusing on something behind him in the cave.

"Yeah, I wouldn't be so sure about that!" he stated, no longer trying to be quiet. Tibor turned around and saw the figure approaching from the far side of the cavern.

Omar looked around, trying to guess just how much time they might have before Jason, Shagron and the others caught up to them.

"Let's buy ourselves some time, shall we?" he said casually, staying low beside Tibor and retrieving a small vial from his belt. He removed the stopper and tossed the vial over to the watery moat, hearing more than seeing the glass skidding along the rock until it plunked into the water. Waiting only a moment, he closed hos eyes then snapped his fingers, flicking a small stream of fire from his hand to the water's surface, which immediately burst into flame. The flames raced upwards nearly fifteen hands in to the air, and Tibor could feel the rush of heat on his face – a welcome change from the damp cold of the cave.

"We're going to need some help to deal with Voros," Omar explained.

"Can't we just make a run for it?" Tibor asked.

"Uh, '*no*'! We didn't come here to run away…" Omar answered very matter-of-factly, looking Tibor up and down as if reconsidering his opinion of the strange visitor that Dar had spoken so highly of. In truth, he didn't know what to expect, but he certainly had the impression that this was supposed to be someone pivotal in their fight against Voros, and yet here he was wanting only to run away… he was more than a little concerned.

Omar tried to gaze through the flames in Voros' direction, to keep track of just how close he was getting. Eventually the flaming water began to die down, and Tibor could see that all the water in the shallow moat had been consumed, and very little now trickled in from the surrounding cavern, no doubt disrupted by Torick's interventions. They could also see that Voros was now less than fifty yards away from them, standing in a small clearing that was empty of any fallen rocks or debris. He had placed markings on the ground around him, and a row of torches lit the path from where he stood all the way back to what appeared to be another exit from the cavern. Omar was assessing what to do next when he heard the metallic scraping of heavy armor approaching from behind, which he desperately hoped was going to be his friends arriving on the scene.

They both split their attention – not taking their eyes off Voros for longer than they had to – and glanced back to see Jason and Shagron marching forward, surveying the scene, and quickly taking up positions between Omar and Voros. They were joined almost immediately by Kiara, wielding two swords at the ready as she reached the clearing.

Jason nodded as she came up to his right, as Shagron was on his left, and she returned the greeting.

"Ferenc?" he asked.

She shook her head, her eyes fixed on Voros. Jason glanced back at the smoking debris field where the moans and cries of the dead and wounded could still be heard, dropped his head for a moment, then returned his gaze to the rogue Angyalok wizard opposite them.

"Dar and Torick are coming, right?" Omar asked, addressing no one in particular. No one answered immediately, though they all looked around, as if expecting them to magically appear.

Omar looked at Tibor. "Can you do *anything* that would be helpful to us right now?" he asked urgently.

"What?! Me? I…no," he stammered.

"Great!" Omar stated sarcastically. Standing over Tibor, Omar moved to the front of the obelisk, taking up a position between the wizard and Tibor, still not sure what their plan of attack was.

Shagron and Jason both leapt across the small dry ditch that still circled what used to be the island, and began to close with the wizard, moving to opposite sides as they approached, hoping to split his attention. Their chainmail hung about their shoulders like a dead weight, and the fatigue was evident in their eyes if not their arms.

They had been swinging their heavy blades for what felt like hours as they made their way through a gauntlet of opponents unlike any they had even encountered before, displaying an impressive ability to avoid getting seriously injured along the way – there were various nicks and cuts in their armor, and while the arrows might have failed to pierce the chain, they would surely still have left their mark beneath. A small bead of blood ran down Jason's temple, from a wound that lay hidden by his sweat-soaked hair.

Shagron's only noticeable injury was a purpling bruise on the right side of his chin, which did little to impair his grim smile as he approached the wizard. He held his sword in a low guard, taking deep breaths through his mouth as he tried to recover the energy needed for one more fight. But as much as both he and Jason intended to muster all their courage to engage the wizard, in their hearts they knew that it would not be a blade that would lay him low in the end. They were the obvious threat, but the not the serious one. The serious threat had yet to appear, and Voros knew it.

Just a few yards away, they could see the wizard's eyes, darting back & forth, seeing every opponent on the field in front of him, sizing up each one and preparing to defend against each. A dull hue of light that was not from the torches almost seemed to hum about him as he channeled in preparation for what was about to come.

"I don't suppose you would like to surrender yourself to judgement, in the name of Arch-Duke Satopluk…" Shagron began, "…Prince of Nyirseg, rightful ruler of the Seven Tribes of the Avar lands…"

The whirring whistle of an arrow interrupted his parlay, flying directly at where the heart would have been on any mortal mage, only to deflect with a snapping noise that echoed in the now silent chamber, having struck something unseen only inches before it would have struck its target. The wizard's eyes looked now at Kiara, who let fly several more shafts with her bow, which all met with the same effect. Staring back at his glare with a dark resolve in her own eyes, she made a flourish of drawing one more time, now that she clearly had his attention, which allowed Jason and Shagron to close the last few steps and strike.

Their blows landed solidly and cleanly, cleaving through his body and rendering gaping wounds on both sides.

Voros did not cry out as he swayed about, like a marionette being pulled in too many directions. The exposed flesh of his wounds, appearing first as gruesome blows to his body, slowly started mending themselves - the flesh coming back together, leaving no seam, scar or trace. Voros rolled his head to his left, still dazed yet fully in control, and stared first at Shagron. Raising his hand, he released a bolt of green energy that lifted Shagron from his feet and threw him back, burning the flesh beneath his mail.

Turning his attention next to Jason, he raised a glowing fist, channeling yet another spell, only to have Jason strike first, carving his blade through Voros' extended arm, nearly severing the hand at the wrist!

Again, there was no scream of pain or recognition of being hurt at all, though he seemed to be quite distracted by the movement of his fingers, despite the hand now hanging from just a single tendon. With a child-like gaze he daintily lifted his severed hand with the other, holding it over the stump of his wrist and watching as the flesh warped, flowed, and melded itself together again.

Jason himself then hesitated, unsettled by the bizarre scene he was witnessing, unsure if striking another blow would have any true effect. The choice was made for him when he saw the long thin tendrils of red fire extend towards the wizard from Omar's hands, reaching out and grasping the rogue mage and lifting him into the air, where the flames grew in strength and sought to consume everything flammable in their grasp.

At this, they saw the first sign that the wizard might yet feel pain, as he screamed aloud in response to the arcane fire that seared his body. But it did not last.

A gust of power radiated through the chamber as Voros dispersed the flames, though Omar followed up his spell with a rapid-fire burst of flaming knives that struck the wizard in quick succession as he landed again on the ground. The heavy stench of burning flesh filled the air as the sound of his screams rose louder, though it was not simply an indication of pain – the voice grew in tenor and tone until it flew towards Omar as a shout of rage that carried force and energy with it, knocking him back against the stone of the obelisk.

Tibor rushed to his side to prop him up as the roar of power from the wizard subsided. Kiara continued to nock arrows and let them fly, optimistic that one might slip through a distraction in his defenses, while Jason also sought to find a weak spot where he might strike the wizard now that the flames had abated. Helping Omar back to his feet, Tibor could feel the ground begin to tremor and shake once again – this had been happening more frequently since Voros had completed his spell earlier, and he sensed it did not bode well for them to stay underground if this continued.

"This is OUR world," Voros yelled at them defiantly, "you cannot force us from it!"

He turned once again toward Shagron, who had regained his footing and once again was seeking to land a blow with his heavy blade when he was suddenly thrown high into the air, falling back down to the rocky floor of the cavern with a heavy thud that sent his small metal helm rolling across the ground after his body had come to rest – Tibor couldn't see any movement after that.

Tibor was very uncertain of their chances for escaping with their lives at this point, and he felt helpless – more than that, he felt responsible – they had come here for him, and he was proving to be more than useless, if such a thing were possible. He could feel his pulse racing, his heart was pounding, and his head was beginning to swim as he struggled to think of how to help. Seeing Shagron's prone body on the rock after being flung in the air, something within him snapped – he had felt the shock and bewilderment as Shagron was lifted into the air, then the same weightlessness in his stomach as the lift became a fall, then the shock of the sudden stop as he landed. He could feel it in his heart that the holy warrior was not dead – not yet – but realization hit him like a hammer in the same way that the impact had hammered the paladin.

He felt what they felt – Shagron, Torick, Dar – he saw what they saw; he knew when they were close; and when they were close, it was almost as if they were one and the same, sharing every experience, every sight, touch, taste, smell – every experience.

In a single moment, it was if a light had gone on, and he was suddenly able to see clearly, when before he had been stumbling around in darkness.

He remembered the room where he had first awakened – not at home, but here, in Vengriya. Not when Dar had arrived, but earlier, when the young servant girl in Ascanium had been washing and dressing him – she had lifted his head and he could remember her soothing words as he felt the pain of the needle, again & again.

He reached around to the back of his head, up into the hairline, where it was hard to see, and felt the small scar – a single line, one or two inches in length, crossing back & forth six or seven times.

A stitching?

He had been stitched.

A daze of realization clouded his thoughts as he watched Kiara dive into the ditch to avoid a shock blast similar to the one that had scorched Shagron. She managed to avoid any harm to herself, though her bow was not so lucky – the string had snapped, and the wrappings began to smoke, forcing her to abandon it and draw her two blades once again. With her back to the wall of the ditch, she paused to catch her breath before she would need to jump up and race to close the gap for melee combat. She caught Tibor watching her, to which she nodded – grim, resolute – and then vaulted from her cover and raced to the attack.

'Enough!' he told himself, as he clenched his hands, took a deep breath of his own, and pounded his fist against the stone beneath him. He was here for a reason, and he needed to prove his worth – if not now, then when?

Slowly rising to his feet, he straightened his back and began to walk forward into the one-sided combat that was unfolding in front of him.

The others were preoccupied with countering Voros' attacks and attempting to find a weakness, and did not notice Tibor's approach at first, but he watched them – with every parry, swing, deflection, and counter he felt his emotions build; with every spell the wizard landed, with every wound and every cry, he felt his resolve surge.

He had reached the edge of what used to be the moat of the small island, and he leapt up to the top edge, just as Kiara had done. He took a deep breath and was readying himself to call out, when his voice seemed to get stuck in his throat, like when you find yourself in a dream, trying to yell, but nothing comes out. Twice he cried out, and twice his voice failed him.

But the second time, Voros turned to look at him. There had been no sound, but he was aware of him. He had an instant to realize that he hadn't really made much of a plan for what to do next – he had just presumed the power would come to him when he needed it, as it had back at Preston Springs.

But he felt nothing.

And as quickly as the moment had come, it was gone – smashed away by the pummeling force of a hammer blow of energy from the Arch Mage that knocked him backwards, flying back onto the small island, crashing into Omar as he was trying to focus his own channeling, pinning them both against the obelisk.

Tibor moaned as he fought to remain conscious, hearing only Voros' laughter ringing in his ears as he slumped against Omar's motionless body.

Later, he would only vaguely be able to recall Dar's sudden appearance over them, defiantly calling out to the wizard.

"Enough!" she yelled, planting herself firmly on the ground between Voros and Tibor.

"This ends now!"

It had taken Dar and Torick only a moment to make the series of small portal jumps to reach the center of the cavern, having made sure that the rest of the party had made it through the army of mercenaries. Though she had warned them not to engage with Voros until she arrived, she knew they were reckless enough to ignore her advice, but she was not overly concerned – such are the consequences for ignoring the wisdom of one's elders after all.

Torick kneeled down behind her to check on the two slumped bodies beside the obelisk. As he did so, he could see the lines of energy tracing their way through the mineral veins that marked the rich ore in the rocky floor of the cavern – they flowed and pulsed, tracing their way to where Dar stood, and ultimately into whatever he thought she must be channeling.

Dar was lit with energy – a literal lightning rod for arcane power, as she channeled the taltos energy of the world beneath her, melding and merging it with magical energy she was channeling from beyond this plane. The energy arced from her body to her bracers, then to the ground, crackling and hissing anywhere it made contact.

"Voros!" Dar called him out. "Face me, garaboncid!" she shouted.

Voros turned to face Dar, unconcerned about Kiara and Jason now – rightfully so, as they were stepping back, unsure of just what was going to happen next, and not wanting to get caught in the crossfire.

"Very well, Taltos…" Voros replied "Let us finish this. My work here is done, and even now, with all your power, you are still a pup! You cannot stop what is coming, and you know this!"

Widening her stance, Dar braced herself as energy continued flowing to her. As a Taltos, she had expected that the responsibility for confronting and defeating the Garaboncid would fall upon her shoulders – that had always been the way of such things: the Taltos opposed the Garaboncids and maintained the balance of all things in nature.

That was tradition.

When she combined her birthright with the study of channeling, her magic only grew more powerful – far more than any traditional Taltos, but that was good – because Voros Vaszoly was far more than a typical Garaboncid. The Angyalok Arch-Mage was already incredibly long-lived by nature, able to learn much as a weather witch in just a single lifetime, and yet had also joined with others who had come before.

Which was why she knew she was going to stop him.

In truth, though she had helped Prince Svato find these heroes, she had remained quite concerned that the group might not be enough to deal with an Angyalok Arch Mage. The world had fewer and fewer mages in it these days, and she was truly worried that ones like Omar, though stitched, would still not be ready to face such a foe as Voros. But their purpose was never to actually defeat Voros – they were there to do the work of finding him, calling him out, draining his energy; it was up to her to actually face him.

She was a Taltos.

The Taltos.

She had been raised for this from birth – not just for Voros, but to stand against any garaboncids that would trouble the land, and by opposing, end them. Yet even her strength had limits.

She had studied arcane lore to increase her power beyond that of any other Taltos, but then, so had Voros.

So, there were some questions yet in her mind as she readied herself to finish off the matter at hand, hoping that the others had done their parts well enough…

Voros was ready for her when she began to move forward, but she did not move towards him directly. Moving nimbly and gracefully, she leaped most of the way over to Shagron's side, checking first that he was still alive, before pausing a moment to reach down to his side and relieve him of his holy blade.

She hefted the heavy blade in her right hand, feeling the grip and balance of the design, admiring the colours of the steel as the channeled energy gave her the strength needed to wield it with but a single arm. She smiled as she felt the energy rebalance, and the sword now felt as light as a feather to her.

From her crouched position, she leapt to the attack with a burst of speed that seemed to catch everyone off guard. Even Voros looked surprised as her arc took her high into the air, then flashing downwards towards him, the glowing blade crackling with energy as it deflected off his defenses.

Recovering from their shock, Jason quickly rejoined the action, though his blade, too, deflected off a barrier of energy that the arch-mage had created to protect himself. He had to duck ever so slightly to avoid one of Kiara's blades as her blows did the same, sparking as they careened off the barrier in his direction. They had only a moment to consider their next action before the barrier pulsed and knocked them both back, creating more distance between them and Voros. But not Dar.

Holding her ground against the arcane energy he projected, she struck again and again with Shagron's blade, each time seeming to close the distance by a few more inches, pushing back the barrier with a relentless onslaught of fury — a battle of wills as much as a contest of magicks.

Voros was on the defensive now — unhurt, but increasingly worried by the force of the attacks from the young Taltos. Seeing no other openings, Kiara and Jason backed off and circled back to help Shagron, who was slowly recovering and groggily trying to sit up. Dar, meanwhile, seemed to be growing in the fierceness and ferocity of her attacks, and they could begin to see that the arcing flashes of energy around the arch-mage were as much magical attacks emanating from Dar, and not simply the force of the blade she was wielding with such violent intent. Tendrils of energy snaked out and around from Voros, trying to wrap around and catch the nimble taltos as she danced in circles around the struggling wizard, who was having difficulties keeping track of her location amidst the flashes and smoke. Dar parried each of the tendrils, slicing and dispersing his attacks with the energy she channeled through the blade, at times releasing bolts of energy from her hands to continue to test the ever-weakening barrier that Voros maintained.

Below them, Omar had regained his feet and looked over at the hunched form of Torick, who was fervently focused on trying to wake the unconscious Tibor, to see the battle unfolding.

Despite the power of his stitching, the fourteen-year-old boy was still humbled and excited by the action and energy on display in the battle before him. The cries of the wounded warriors that lay scattered across the cavern floor were drowned out by the crackling bursts of energy that roared and echoed like a thunderstorm under the earth! He was so overwhelmed by the battle that he hadn't even noticed that he had drawn the fae slayer-dagger from where he had hidden it beneath his shirt. The blade almost seemed to hum in his hand, as if knowing that there was work to be done — work it was uniquely made for doing!

Almost as if he could sense the humming of the weapon in Omar's hand, Torick slowly raised his head, and turned to see the young Avar apprentice standing behind him, his eyes settling quickly on the now glowing fae blade in the boy's hand.

He acted instinctively, without hesitation.

Omar was snapped back into the moment by a flash in front of him — Torick had spun to his side, and, with a sweep of his arm, Omar was struck by a wave of force that nearly snapped his arm above the wrist, ripping the slayer-blade from his grip and sending it flying into the air across the cavern.

Omar cried out at the unexpected attack, cutting himself short when he locked eyes with Torick, seeing a look of deep anger - mixed with disappointment - that surprised and scared him.

Neither of them said a word.

Omar felt himself shrink under the Angyalok wizard's gaze, hunching his shoulders ever so slightly as he nursed his injured arm, which was enough for Torick to, turn and help Tibor to his feet.

Torick now directed his attention to the mage battle, to see what aid he could offer Da, only to freeze and catch his breath in a moment of shock.

Without planning to do so, his disarming strike on the young Omar had flung the fae blade into the air across the cavern, flying faster than either he or Omar could ever have thrown it.

To his utter amazement, it had flown towards the dueling wizards, and - without focus, aim or true intention - its accidental course took it up and through the outstretched arms of the garaboncid wizard, ever so slightly nicking the small finger of his left hand with the tip of the blade as it passed by.

It was a small cut – not even enough to interrupt whatever spell the wizard was casting – but it was enough for the blade to have fulfilled its only purpose for existing, before it sailed on into the darkness of the cavern.

From the small finger of his left hand, the edge of the smallest cut appeared, enough for scarcely a single drop of blood. But it was enough. The edges of the cut began to blacken, the darkness slowly creeping into the flesh of the wizard's corporeal form, bit by bit consuming first his finger, then his hand, moving up his arm with a fiery pain that infected every cell of his body with the blade's singular, deadly curse.

With a howling scream, of both rage and confusion, Voros tore at his arm, ripping his sleeve away until the nails of his fingers cut into the flesh of his shoulder – willing to tear his arm apart to stop the spread of whatever had infected him.

Despite the reputation of the fae blade, its effects were not instantaneous, and it seemed there was a chance he might yet survive the deadly effect of the otherwise mortal wound, as he desperately tried to claw his arm from his body in a grisly display of self-mutilation.

Yet that was not the only threat to his life in this place.

For Dar, it was the distraction she needed.

It took but one more blow from the Holy Blade for Dar to break Voros' distracted guard, wiping away his wards and leaving him defenseless. Clutching at his now useless, corrupted limb, he looked spent, defenseless, exhausted; his body wracked with pain, he looked no more the fearsome foe that had plotted to kill them all: sweat and blood matted his once flowing hair to his forehead; what was left of his mutilated arm hung limply at his side; fear mixed with desperation in his eyes as he awaited the final blow from the Taltos sorceress, as she floated, rippling with fire & energy before him.

He looked at her, as if he might have some final words to offer, but there was nothing left but the look in his eyes – anger mixed with sadness, and defeat.

Dar did not hesitate – she spun the blade in a sweeping arc, gathering her focus into a single, final stroke.

The channeling sent a warm rush through her entire body, surging like a wave, then bursting out through the blade as she released everything into the weary form of the Angyalok wizard. The blast of magical energy rendered him swiftly and cleanly, releasing all his channeled energy into the air of the cavern with a massive, brilliant flash of light.

The wave of euphoric energy was quickly followed by a wave of exhaustion that hit Dar like a hammer when she was finished. She relaxed and let it wash over her as the energy left her body, her arms hung limp at her sides, and the heavy sword hilt slid out of her hand and fell to the ground with a heavy thud.

With the energy gone, she felt her desperation depart as well, leaving her wanting nothing more than to just lie down where she was and rest on the cold stone floor of the cavern.

Tibor watched the energy of the battle subside – not just as the crackling forces of the channeling faded into the darkness, but the strength now seemed to escape from the warriors of their company: shoulders slumped; weapons once held strongly became immense weights, lowered from their ready stances; swords and bows became crutches and staffs on which to lean.

They slowly rejoined one another near what had been the small island in the center of the cave, and exchanged looks, reassuring one another that the deed was, in fact, done. Tibor felt apart from their circle, and so it was he who first noticed the slight movement in the prone form of the defeated Angyalok wizard, lying on the ground a few feet away.

He stumbled over to the burned, bloodied body of the arch-mage, and knelt beside him as he could see the shudders of pain work their way through his failing form. The wizard rolled his head to one side to look at Tibor, and he had to stop himself from pulling away at the sight and smell of the horrible burns that the channeled magic had inflicted on their enemy.

"What did you do to me?" Tibor demanded of the dying wizard, still overwhelmed by the shadows that haunted his mind.

"*What did you do to our world?*" Voros replied, his voice rasping as he fought to draw air into his seared lungs.

The answer did nothing for Tibor.

"You've lost!" he added sharply, as if the words could inflict one more wound on the dying mage.

"*Lost? Ha!*" Voros answered, spitting blood with his words, "*We have done all that we were charged to do, our duty is fulfilled.*"

"*This is what we do — we sacrifice ourselves to protect our people… our land… We are the Protector, and we have done what we had to do.*"

"*Now we can rest a moment, until we are needed again…*" he paused, struggling to find the breath to speak.

There was a moment of silence before a small smile crept into his expression.

"*Can you feel it?*" the dying wizard asked him, as he looked sideways, beyond them both, to a small pool of water that yet remained in the rocky floor of the cavern. Almost imperceptibly, the smooth surface of the water was disturbed by ripples. Then once again.

"*She is coming…*" Voros rasped, as a cracking and crumbling noise began to be heard coming from the edges of the cavern, as small stones shifted and fell with the growing tremors.

"*She is coming to reclaim this land for us…*"

Tibor could almost swear the ground beneath them had begun to move, to lift, as they were speaking.

"*…and you cannot stop her now!*"

"Dar!"

Not far from the fallen wizard, Jason lent an arm to Dar and helped her back to the stone circle, carefully stepping over the shattered fragments of the last obelisk. But for the moans of some of the wounded mercenaries, the cave was silent, A silence broken first by an observation from Omar.

"Is it just me, or did this seem a lot easier than I expected?"

"Easy?" Kiara practically shrieked back to him in reply. "You think Ferenc dying was easy?!"

"No, I didn't…" Omar began, but stopped, realizing there was nothing more he could say that would soften the rage in her glare. He hung his head until he felt a mailed hand on his shoulder.

"Easy lad, I know what you meant…" Shagron offered as he took his rest on a stone beside him, taking back his blade when Dar offered the hilt to him. Sheathing it carefully he spoke again.

"I also thought the wizard would be harder to stop. With all due respect to the young ranger" he nodded to Kiara, and back to the further reaches of the cavern where Ferenc still lay, "I truly did not expect so many of us to still be standing in the end."

Kiara shook her head, her eyes brimming with tears, and turned back to retrace their path to the mouth of the cave, where Dar had taken Ferenc's body.

Omar was listening, still trying to give Kiara his best look of sympathy, when he felt an unusual tugging at his chest. He raised his hand to fumble at his tunic, trying to identify the source of whatever was suddenly moving beneath his vest, only to narrowly avoid having his fingers removed as the razor-sharp knife he had 'borrowed' from Torick earlier sliced its way out of where he had tucked it away for safekeeping and flew into the air. Following its course, he could see the blade come to a stop just above Torick's outstretched hand, followed shortly by the other blades he had cast earlier in the combat, all returning to his summons, and stacking neatly in his hand as he finished his spell.

"It was fortunate" Torick stated flatly, "…that we had a fae blade in the company, to catch the wizard unawares, and give us the opening we needed."

"These, on the other hand, are quite unique blades…" he said, locking eyes with Omar in a very serious stare, "not the sort of thing one should ever leave lying about…" Torick's expression was grim, and his eyes narrowed as he regarded the young Avar mage, recalling the scene earlier when he had seen him standing above him with the fae blade drawn.

Omar quickly avoided his gaze, unwilling to apologize about taking the throwing knife, and unsure how to explain what his intentions may have ever been for the fae blade. His attention was soon turned to the growing noise of rocks falling and breaking in the cavern around them.

What started slowly as a distant cracking noise became a loud, thunderous roar, as the floor of the entire cavern began to give way, crumbling and falling into a hollow, black void that lay hidden beneath their feet.

"Dar!" Tibor shouted to his friends, "I think we need to go! Now!"

Alerted, the rest of the group began to scramble, making a mad dash across the floor of the cavern – cursing as they weaved between the fallen stones that had just moments earlier been so key to their victory over Voros' mercenaries – seeking the safety of the passageway that had brought them here.

Torick and Dar channeled to open the small dimensional gates that they themselves could pass through to hasten their exit but could not offer such to the rest of the company, who were forced to race to their escape on foot.

Battle-weary but now reenergized by adrenalin, they vaulted rocks and wove their way through the debris as the floor of the cavern slowly began to crumble and fall away. In the center of the cave the pillar where Tibor had been chained was the first to fall, as cracks spread like a spider's web from the center and ate away at the floor with increasing speed. Screams of panic echoed in the chaos as the wounded from the earlier battle were consumed by the crumbling cavern.

Exhausted and breathless, the company staggered onto the rocky outcropping by the mouth of the tunnel entrance before the last of the rocky floor gave way to blackness. They joined Torick and Dar who were waiting anxiously, only then pausing to look back at what was happening behind them.

Tibor could not see into the pitch blackness, nor could he see what had become of the cavern floor, as the void was deeper than their meager light could penetrate. But everyone could hear the rumbling that continued after the last stones had fallen – a rumbling that soon became a different sort of rhythm.

A rhythm of in, then out.

A deep drawing in, then a release.

Breathing.

The trembling in the earth began to grow stronger again as the breathing rhythm increased in pace and vigour, like someone – or something – awakening from a long sleep.

"What is that?" Jason asked, by default looking at the mages and taltos in the group.

"The cracking of bones and joints, unmoved in centuries…" Dar answered, "…flexing and stretching, popping and loosening, beginning to move and remember their strength, not unlike a sleeping bear awakening after a long winter."

"But this is not a bear," she continued. "This is something larger. Much larger. And beneath the cavern is not a den, but a prison." She looked over at Tibor. "You found this, in the old tomes. The ones we thought were myths and not history."

"What are you saying?" Kiara began hesitantly, "What myths?"

It felt as if the entire mountain was shaking around them now, and they were grateful that Torick had already shaken down anything that might have wanted to fall on them by now. The tremors no longer paused but shook everything in a continuous quake.

"What myth?" Dar repeated Kiara's question. "*The* myth."

"Voros Vazul was a garaboncid – a weather witch." Dar explained. "But he didn't just cast his own spells to create the great plagues. We were fools not to see it. He was breaking the great seals – the obelisks you see all around the cavern – these are the locks on a prison. Each lock was powerful, and when each lock was broken, it released a warning to let people know the lock had been opened – that the prison was one step closer to being open!"

"That sounds like a pretty harsh warning, don't you think?" Jason added.

"They were made to be something that couldn't be ignored," Dar continued to explain. "Unfortunately, they weren't ignored – they were forgotten! As each seal was broken, each magical lock undone, the warning signs grew, but the people forgot what they were being warned about, and so nothing was done until it was too late."

"Now…" she finished, "…Sarkany's prison has been undone, the gate has been opened, and now he is coming!"

"Wait – what?" they shouted at her, incredulous. "That's insane! Sarkany?!"

"That's just a legend! Stories!" Omar shouted over the rumbling, recalling the stories his own mother had told him not all that long ago. The voice in his head answered before anyone else could.

'It's true…'

"Voros Vaszoly's plan…" Dar shared, "…was to release Sarkany upon the world. His sole purpose is to rid the world of the Avar race. Sarkany is back, Matras Vadas is a myth, and Isten Kardja is lost to us!"

"Shit!" Shagron was on his feet, leaning on his sword, looking out over the darkness of the cavern, where they could no longer see farther than the faint light of his aura would illuminate. There, in the deepest blackness of the void, they could sense the movement –it was right there, almost close enough to touch, but just out of sight. Rising up from below the cavern, stretching, then rubbing against the rock of the ceiling, and showering down a rain of stones and dust around the edges of the cavern, as the debris cascaded down the sides of the massive form that they knew was there but could not see. Except for Shagron.

Shagron closed his eyes, and reached out, with his heart as much as with his mind, drawing upon his faith to help him see the evil that is in men's hearts, and to know the just from the wicked. With creatures it was sometimes harder, for nature is not inherently evil – it is predatory and cold, driven by necessity, but not entirely without compassion either.

Here though, this… this thing that Voros had released from captivity, it was not of nature. It was of heaven & earth; and created with a purpose – a solitary purpose – to cleanse the unworthy from the world. It was darkness, and because of that, Shagron could see it; feel it. The smoky blackness of the evil was so intense that it gave form and texture to the shape in his mind's eye.

He could see the scales – layer upon layer, rippling with the flexing of the great muscles beneath the skin; he saw the massive hide coiling upon itself again and again as it raised itself up from the darkness of depths, pressing up against the dome of rock that was the ceiling – the mountain of stone that had been placed over its tomb as a marker for all to know and beware.

Then he saw as it released the pent-up energy in its coils and thrust upwards with a monstrous roar, shattering the mountain top above them, and blasting the rocks, trees, ice and debris into the air for miles. It was like a volcano had exploded upon the land, and the shaking was felt as far away as Ascanium to the East, and beyond the borders of Gomor in the West.

It was still light outside as the mountain exploded, allowing a few rays of the late afternoon light to filter back into the remains of the grand cavern, which now resembled little more than a hollowed-out crater – still large in size, but empty now of all meaning and purpose.

Shielding their eyes from the falling sand & dust that hung in the air, trying not to choke on their breath, they were able to glimpse the massive form of the great wyrm as it crawled out of the crater and down the side of the mountain. The earth shook with every step it took as it moved off into the distance, the tremors only ending when it had passed out of sight completely.

Though few of them could claim to have seen the entire beast, what they saw would have made it larger than the great palace in Ascanium.

There was a moment of silence and awe as they contemplated what had just happened. Everyone seemed to need a moment to themselves to internalize the scale and proportion of what they had seen. Several of them reflected on the tales they had heard as children – that Sarkany would come and punish them for their pride; Sarkany would steal away children who misbehaved, or didn't eat their dinner; every child imagined their worst fears when they conjured up their imagination for what Sarkany might look like – a creature with seven heads; a long body and a snake-like tail; it was supposed to have walked upright, like a man, and challenged the hubris of the hero; it taught humility to the bold and prideful, and could not be killed – only imprisoned – for as long as there was ego, Sarkany would feed.

But this felt worse than what any of them had ever imagined as children. As adults, they had forgotten the old nursery tales, and focused on more temporal things; but this, today – this was a monster. A monster that was as large as a mountain, that would crush you without even knowing you were there.

It was a surreal moment, broken only by the scattered sound of falling rocks, as debris slowly sifted down from the massive crater in the side of the mountain.

Jason stepped over to where Kiara had lain Ferenc's body, near the entrance of the passage where they had first emerged into the cavern. He knelt beside his friend, examining the wound, and then slowly wiping the blood-smeared hair from Ferenc's face – he cupped his hand against the still-warm cheek. Kiara stood behind him, watching over his shoulder.

"He saved my life," she told him, "we were separated by the rocks, and he came back to find me."

Jason did not respond or look at her, instead his eyes went to Shagron.

"You're the holy one – is there nothing that that can be done?" he asked, his voice steady, but desperate.

Shagron shook his head slowly. "If Ralof were here – if he were yet in Ukko's good graces – perhaps the All Father might make an exception… but he has died the ultimate death: a warrior who dies in combat can ask for no better. He will be drin–"

"Oh, shove it!" Kiara let out harshly, her eyes full but not yet shedding a tear. "We ask for our own sakes as much as for his, and I'm sure he would prefer ale with his friends, *here,* over anything else, as I'm sure you would… if all your friends weren't dead already!"

Shagron didn't respond to the spite in her words, though he did stop talking and began to slowly pick up his gear to prepare for the walk out to the horses – if they were still there. Kiara continued to glare, not at anyone in particular, and everyone was happy to avoid her gaze for the moment. Finishing whatever silent prayers he knew, Jason folded Ferenc's arm across his chest, and as unceremonious as it had to be, he lifted Ferenc by the waist and hefted him over his shoulder, ready to walk back out the same way they had come in. Kiara lit a torch and led the way for him.

Dar got ready to follow Shagron, believing she was the last to leave, when she noticed that Tibor was still standing at the edge of the plateau, quietly looking down into the endless blackness of the pit.

"Coming?" she called to him.

He turned and looked at her, though his mind seemed elsewhere, distracted.

"Something on your mind?" she asked.

He nodded, "Yeah." He was looking past her as he talked, as if he were focusing on something miles away.

"That... that thing is massive..." he said.

"Yes."

"I was useless here..." he continued, "...too afraid to even try to help, and god knows I don't have any idea how I would've helped anyway, but..."

"What do you mean?" she asked quietly, "No one was expecting anything of you today..."

"Yes, you were!" he said, interrupting, "You came to find me because you thought I could help. You brought me here because you thought I could help! You expected me to do something that would matter in this fight, and I was completely useless!" His voice was rising as he spoke, which caused the others to pause at the mouth of the passage.

"You aren't useless here," Dar told him, "you just haven't found your way yet. You are connected to this world..."

"...as an escape!" he finished the thought for her. "Voros told me as much!"

"What would Voros know of such things?" she retorted.

"He knows... he knows... he knows that I came here to hide." He looked directly at Dar now. "I came here to hide from him when he was chasing us. I came here before when I wanted to hide from everything else in life that hurt! When things get bad, I run away. That's what I do! I play games while the world falls apart around me, and I am happy when an imaginary character gets a chest of gold – it's not real but it makes me forget everything bad all around me! And then finally something snapped, and I ended up here, just to get away from everything else wrong in my life!"

"How do you–" she began, but Tibor cut her off,

"*How* doesn't really seem to matter for anything, does it? All that matters it that it happened. For the life of me, I can't remember what I was doing when I was here before, but this is where I hid when I had my accident, and then I brought us here to get away from Voros in the Sanctuary...!"

"*You* brought us?" she asked incredulously, "That was *me*, not *you* that did that!"

He stared at her coldly, "You. Me. What's the difference?"

Dar was silent as she stared at him.

"You, Shagron, Torick – I can feel it – there's a connection there that I can't explain, that I don't understand, but it's real, and..." He put his hands through his hair, squinting his eyes as if he were fighting a monstrous headache. "You gave me something to numb me to it, but even Voros knew it was there – he was looking for it, but it was gone. That's why he chose to use me as bait rather than kill me – he knew I wasn't a threat to him!"

"And now this," he added, "the biggest frigging monster I have ever seen, and we're supposed to what? Fight it? Kill it? How?!"

Dar held her tongue, letting him speak. The more he talked, the calmer he became, his anxiety venting into the void of the cavern.

The rest of the group were waiting silently as well, not entirely sure they knew what the two were talking about...

"Tibor..." she finally started speaking, slowly and calmly, making sure she had his attention, "You need to go."

"Go?" he asked, "Where? Where do you run from something like that?" She could her the mix of pain and confusion in his voice.

"Run? No. Not run..." she answered, "You've done enough running. You need to stop running!"

"But where? Where do I need to go that matters for any of this?" He turned his back on the void of the cavern and looked into the blue-green of her eyes, as if to find the answer there.

"Home," she said simply.

One word, spoken with such a sense of sadness and burden of responsibility that it pained her to say it. Dar stood with Tibor, holding his hands gently. She looked him up & down, straightening out the torn rags that were all that remained of his gambeson and undershirt. The bruises and cuts from the chains were all quite visible, even in the dim light, and she seemed sad for his injuries.

She straightened up to meet his gaze, and with a soft smile, she raised her hands and cradled his face. He was so tired, and right now, he felt like everything was washing away, freeing him to do nothing more than gaze back into her deep blue-green eyes. It was a calming moment, interrupted only slightly by a single word from somewhere distant...

"Dar?!"

Shagron called out from the small plateau where they had first entered the cavern. He hadn't shouted, but the concern in his tone was clear – Tibor felt he should be paying more attention to something, but the warm feeling that flowed over him in this moment was such a welcome comfort, replacing the pain of his injuries, that he decided not to resist it.

All else seemed faded and unimportant. Veiled from sight.

Omar and the others exchanged looks as they watched Dar and Tibor float out from the edge of the small plateau, hovering above the blackness of the abyss from which the dragon had just emerged.

Tibor was completely focused on Dar, forgetting even what they had just been talking about, on the verge of letting exhaustion carry him to sleep.

As if sensing this, Dar tightened her grasp on his face, snapping his attention back into focus, back into the moment.

"You need to go…" she said softly, "…" She seemed as if she was going to say something more, but the words escaped her. Instead, she released her hands from his face, freeing him from her grasp and letting him drift gently backwards. It only took a moment before gravity resumed its jealous hold on his form, pulling him down into a silent freefall into the abyss.

He fell through the open air, and then below where the floor of the cavern used to be and quickly disappeared into the depths of the dark, all the while holding his gaze on her deep, mesmerizing eyes, until she, the light, and everything else, disappeared from his sight.

Everyone was silent.

Omar and Kiara rushed forward to the edge to look down, but there was nothing to be seen but darkness.

Darkness and silence.

End of Book 1
of
The Sword of God Saga

For more information about the author, the world of Vengriya, Isten Kardja, and upcoming books in '*The Sword of God Saga*' check out:
www.isten-kardja.com

Manufactured by Amazon.ca
Bolton, ON

33298089R00259